WALTER BESANT.

THE

WORLD WENT VERY WELL THEN

𝔄 𝔑𝔬𝔳𝔢𝔩

By WALTER BESANT

AUTHOR OF

"ALL SORTS AND CONDITIONS OF MEN" "ALL IN A GARDEN FAIR"
"THE CHILDREN OF GIBEON" "HERR PAULUS"
"FIFTY YEARS AGO" ETC.

ILLUSTRATED

NEW YORK

HARPER & BROTHERS, FRANKLIN SQUARE

CONTENTS.

ILLUSTRATIONS.

THE WORLD WENT VERY WELL THEN.

CHAPTER I.

HOW JACK HEARD TALK OF LANDS BEYOND THE SEA.

IN a small back parlor, behind an apothecary's shop, were sitting two boys and a girl. The boys were aged respectively twelve years and ten; the elder of them was a tall and strongly built lad, with curling hair of a dark brown, and eyes of much the same color; the younger, fair-haired, and of slighter proportions. The girl was nine; but she looked more, being tall for her age. Her hair was so dark that it looked almost black. It hung loose, in long curls or ripples, not being coarse and thick, as happens generally with hair that is quite black, but fine in texture and lustrous to look upon. Her eyes, too, were black and large. The elder boy and the girl sat side by side in the window-seat, while the other boy sat at the table, having a pencil in his hand and a piece of paper before him, on which he was drawing idly whatever came into his head. All three were silent, save that the elder boy from time to time whispered the girl, or pinched her ear, or pulled her hair, when she would shake her head and smile, and point to the great chair beside the fire, as much as to say, " If it were not for that chair, Jack, and the person in it, I would box thy ears."

It was not a cold day. The sun shone through the lattice window, and fell upon the heads of the two who sat together, and motes innumerable danced merrily in the light; yet there was a coal fire burning in the grate. On one hòb simmered a saucepan, with some broth in it or compound of simples (while the children sat waiting, the apothecary's assistant stepped in noiselessly, lifted the lid, took out a spoonful, sighed, tasted it, shook his head for the nastiness of it, and went back into the

1

shop). On the other hob stood a kettle, singing comfortably—
kept there always, day and night, but not for making tea, I
promise you. As for the room itself, it was exactly like a
ship's cabin, being narrow and low, and fitted with shelves
and drawers. On one side was a pallet, something like a
bunk in an officer's cabin, with a flock mattress upon it, and
a pair of blankets rolled up snug. Here the apothecary slept
when the weather was cold, that is to say, nearly all the year
round. Herbs and drugs tied in bundles hung from the rafters,
as onions hang in a farmhouse; the window was a lattice,
with small diamond panes set in lead; above the mantelshelf
hung a silver watch; on the shelf itself stood a pair of brass
candlesticks, the model of a ship full rigged—her name written
in red ink on a wooden stand, " *The King Solomon*, of Bristol "
—a pair of ship's pistols, a tobacco jar, and two or three long
pipes. The apothecary's great wig, which he wore every evening at the club, hung from a peg on the wall behind the elbow
chair; and in the corner of the room opposite the chair there
was a very fearful and terrible thing until you grew accustomed
to it, when you ceased to fear it. This was nothing less than
a stick painted red and black, with bright-colored feathers tied
round it, and surmounted by a grinning human skull. It was a
magic stick, called, we were told, the Ekpenyong, or skull-stick,
by the Mandingo sorcerers—a thing only to be handled by an
Obeah man, the possession of which is supposed by negroes
either to confer or to proclaim wonderful powers, and cut from
a juju or holy tree. Beside it lay two musical instruments,
also from Africa—one a hollow block of wood covered with a
sheepskin, and the other a kind of rude guitar. This stick it
was which caused the apothecary to be greatly respected by
the admiral's negroes, as you will presently hear. He who
has such a stick can catch the shadow, as they say, that is, the
soul, of a man; and set Obi upon him, that is to say, bring suffering, sorrow, and shame upon him. So that the possessor of
a skull-stick is a person greatly to be feared and envied.

There was an open cupboard beside the fire, in which were
household stores, such as bacon, cheese, butter, bread, strings
of onions, a two-gallon jar or firkin of rum, plates and knives,
for the room was a kitchen as well as an eating-room and a
sleeping-room. Once a week or so, if business was slack and

"In the small back parlor behind the apothecary's shop."

there was nothing else to do, the assistant might, if he thought
of it, come with a broom and sweep the dust out into the street.
But I do not remember that the room was ever washed. And
what with the tobacco, the stores in the cupboard, the rum, the
drugs hanging from the rafters, and the contents of the shelves,
the place had, to a sailor, exactly the smell of the cockpit or
orlop deck after a long voyage; for in that part of the ship
are kept the purser's stores, the bo's'n's stores, the spirit-room,
the surgeon's storeroom, the midshipmen's berths and their
mess. For this reason, perhaps, its owner, who had been a
sailor, would never open the window, and always, on returning
home, sniffed the air of the room with a peculiar satisfaction.

The great chair—which might have served for the chair of
a hall porter, having a broad low seat and a high back with
arms—was stuffed or padded with three or four pillows, and
in the midst of the pillows lay an old man sleeping. This was
Mr. Brinjes, the famous Apothecary of Deptford. He was
small of stature and thin: his face (over one eye was a black
patch) was creased and lined like a russet apple, which shrinks
before it rots; his chin was hollow; his head, covered with a
padded silk nightcap, was sunk deep in the pillows like a child's;
he lay upon his side; his feet, stretched out, were propped on a
footstool; one hand was under his cheek, and the other hung
over the arm of the chair (you might have noticed that the
skin of his hand was wrinkled and loose, as if the bones belonged to an occupant smaller than was at first intended). As
he lay asleep there he looked like one in extreme old age, such
as may be seen in country villages, where they take a pride in
showing the visitor, in proof of the healthiness of the country
air, some old gaffer of a hundred years and more sitting before
a fire.

Through the open door could be seen the shop. It was small,
like the parlor behind it. The rafters were hung with dried
herbs; the shelves were full of bottles. There was a chair for
the reception of those patients who could not stand; there was
a counter, with scales great and small; a pestle and mortar; a
box containing surgical instruments—the pincers for pulling
out teeth, the cup, the basin, the blister, and the other horrid
tools of the surgeon's craft. The assistant stood at the counter, rolling pills and mixing medicines—a sallow, pasty-faced

youth with a pair of swivel eyes, which moved with independent action; a young man who walked about without noise,
and worked all day without stopping, yet looked discontented,
perhaps because he was compelled to taste the medicines, and
his stomach kicked thereat. The door was always open, because the window gave little light, partly because it was never
cleaned, partly because there was a shelf with bottles before it,
and partly because the glass was full of bull's-eyes, which give
strength, no doubt, yet keep the room obscure. At the end
of the counter was the stool on which Mr. Brinjes sat every
morning, in his gown and nightcap, from eight o'clock until
half-past twelve, receiving patients. Before him, on the counter, was a great book, containing, I now suppose, a Repertory
or Collection of Instructions concerning Symptoms of Diseases
and Methods of Treatment; but the common sort always supposed that it was a book of Spells, and to be the means by
which Mr. Brinjes was enabled to communicate with a certain
Potentate, who helped him and did his bidding, at what price
and for what reward these people freely whispered to each
other. On Sunday morning (this must have been a bitter bo-
lus to the Evil One) Mr. Brinjes and his assistant let blood
gratis to whoever wished for that wholesome refreshment;
and every morning he pulled out teeth at a shilling or half a
crown (according to the means of the customer), his assistant
holding the patient in his chair, and receiving those kicks and
cuffs which in the extremity of his agony the sufferer too often
deals out.

In such a town as Deptford it is natural that the common
people should resort to the herb-woman for the cure of their
ailments. It was not until she had failed that they came to Mr.
Brinjes, and then with doubt whether he would choose to treat
them. As for his power to cure, if he pleased, there was no
doubt about that. It was whispered that he knew of charms by
which he could constrain a person, even in the misery of toothache, to fall sound asleep, and continue asleep while Mr. Brinjes
would take out a tooth, without causing him to awaken, or to
feel any pain whatever; but these things we may not believe,
however well authenticated, unless we would seriously accuse
him of magic. As for fevers, rheumatisms, difficulty of breathing, coughs, scurvy, and the other afflictions by which we are

reminded that this is but a transitory world, it was believed by
the better sort of Deptford that there was no physician in London itself more skilful than Mr. Brinjes, and that by certain
preparations, the secret of which he alone knew, and had learned
in his voyages in many foreign parts, especially on the West
Coast of Africa, where the negroes possess many strange secrets
of nature, he had acquired a singular mastery over every kind
of disease. He has been known, as I myself who write this
history can testify (it was in the case of Admiral Sayer's great
toe), to relieve a man in one hour of the gout, though he had
been roaring for a fortnight with his foot tied up in flannel.
It was also whispered of him that by magic or witchcraft Mr.
Brinjes could bring diseases upon those who offended him, and
that he could avert all the misfortunes to which mankind are
liable in shipwreck, drowning, wounds, and death. But it is
idle to repeat the things which were said of him. Certain it is
that he possessed wonderful secrets for the cure of disease, however he came by them. Warts he removed by looking at them,
and by a prophecy that they would be gone in so many days; a
sprained ankle he would set at ease by simply rubbing the part
with his open hand; sciatica, lumbago, pleurisy, and other such
disorders he healed in the same way, foretelling on each occasion how long it would be before the malady would cease.
Those who were so treated declared that the apothecary's hand
became like a red-hot iron in the rubbing. Rheumatism, it
was certain, he cured by making the patient carry a potato in
his .pocket; though what he did, if he did anything, to the
potato first, in order to endow it with this virtue, is not known.
As for earache, faceache, toothache, tic, and such disorders, it
was believed that he could order their removal at will. Further,
it was said of him that he could, also at will, command these
diseases to seize upon a man and torture him. How he did
this, no one can explain; but the testimony of many still living
proves that he did it. I pass over the report that in calling these
pains to seize upon a man, his one eye glowed like a red-hot
coal and sent forth flashes of fire. Such rumors show only
how much he was feared and respected by the people. They
came to him also for amulets and charms, which he did not
always refuse to give, for protection of those who carried them
from drowning, hanging, burning, the shot of cannon, and the

stroke of steel. It is true that his amulets were simple things;
we cannot understand how the tooth of a snake, even with the
poison in it, can avail against drowning if one who cannot swim
should tumble into deep water, nor how the head of a frog
wrapped in silk, can, without any other magic, protect a man
against the gallows. But there are many other things which
everybody believes quite as difficult to explain; as, for instance,
why the gall of the barbel causeth blindness; why cock ale
cureth consumption; why an onion hung round the neck of a
beast, and the next day boiled and buried, cureth distemper in
cattle; or why the finger cut from the hand of a hanged man
taketh away a wen. Yet these are in the nature of amulets as
much as any of those prepared by Mr. Brinjes. At this time
he had been in the town some fifteen years, having appeared
one day about the year 1735. Nobody knew who he was or
whence he came; his parentage, his Christian name, his birth-
place, were all unknown. He never spoke of any relations,
and at his first coming he seemed to be as old as now, so that
some, when they saw the sign of the Silver Mortar put up, and
the gallipots ranged in the shop, laughed to think of so old and
decrepit a man beginning trade as an apothecary.

Whatever his age, he was not decrepit, but strong and hale,
though shrunken in figure, with a wrinkled skin and a face covered with lines and crow's-feet. He suffered from no ailments,
was always brisk and active, and had, in his talk and understanding, no apparent touch of age. Further, it soon became known
that here was a man who could effect marvellous cures, so that
the people began to flock to him, not only from Deptford and
the river-side, where he first courted custom, but also from
Greenwich, on the one hand, and Redriffe, Bermondsey, and
Southwark, on the other.

He received these people every day—from eight in the morning until half past twelve—dressed in an old brown coat, gone
into holes at the elbows, or even without any coat at all; on
his head, an old scratch wig; and on his feet, slippers tied
with tape. But slovenly as was his dress, and unworthy the
dignity of a physician, he was sharp and quick with the patients,
telling them plainly, while he gave them medicine, whether
they would recover or when they would die, and whether he
could help them or not. At the stroke of half-past twelve he

got off his stool and retired to his parlor, where, with his own hand, he every day fried or griddled a great piece of beefsteak, with a mess of onions, carrots, and other vegetables, and presently devoured it, with a tankard of black beer, choosing to do everything with his own hand, even to the filling of his kettle and the washing of his dishes, rather than have a woman-servant in the place. This done, he made up the fire, put away his plates, settled himself among his pillows, and fell fast asleep. Thus he continued for two or three hours, no one daring to disturb him or to make the least noise. When, on this day, he began to move, stretching out first one leg, and then the other, turning over on his back, and fidgeting with his hands, the elder boy nodded to the younger, who reached a bundle of papers from the topmost shelf, and laid them on the table as if in readiness. This done, they waited.

The old man yawned, sighed, and opened his remaining eye —'twas a pale blue eye of amazing keenness and brightness. Then he sat up suddenly with a start, and looked about him with a quick suspicious glance, as if he had been sleeping in some place where there were wild animals to fear or savage men. You could then perceive that his features were sharp, and apparently not much altered by his years, his chin being long and pointed, his lips firm, and his nose straight, as if he were a masterful man who would have his way. As for his remaining eye (no one ever learned where the sight of the other had been lost), though it was so bright, it had a quick and watchful expression, such as may be perceived in the eyes of those creatures who both hunt and are hunted. You will not see this look in the eyes of Dido, the lioness of the Tower, because the lion hunts but is never hunted. Being reassured as to tigers or fierce Indians, Mr. Brinjes rose from the chair, and as if not yet wholly awake, yet already conscious, he took a glass and half filled it with rum, then, with the utmost care and nicety (your drinkers of rum punch care very little how much rum is in the glass, but are greatly afraid of putting in too much of the other components), added sugar, lemon, and water. This done, he stirred the contents, rolled it about in the glass, and drank half of it.

"I have again returned," he said, "to the world of life. To all of us who are old, when we close our eyes in sleep we know

not whether we shall not keep them closed in death, which sometimes thus surprises those who have lived long. But I have returned—aha!—and with reasonable prospect of another evening of tobacco and punch." Here he sipped his liquor. "I
take this glass of punch, boys," he explained, "for the good
of the stomach, and the prevention of ill humors and vapors.
Otherwise these might rise to the brain, which is a part of
man's mechanism more delicate than any other, and as easily
put off the balance as the mainspring of a watch." Here he
drank again, but slowly, and by sips, as becomes one who loves
his drink. "I am now old; when a man is old he is fortunate if he can breathe free, sleep sound, walk upright, eat his
dinner, and still drink his punch. Some men there are, not so
old as myself—no, not by ten years—who fetch their breath
with difficulty, whereas I breathe freely; others are troubled
and cannot sleep for racking pains, whereas I have none; and
others cannot eat strong meats, and would die—poor devils!—
of a bowl of punch. Better be dead than live like that; better
lie buried with a mile of blue water over your head, and the
whales flopping around your grave on the sea-weed. There
can be no more comfortable and quiet lying than the bottom
of the sea." He shook his head solemnly. "When a man
cannot any longer fight and make love, there is but one thing
left to rejoice his heart." He finished the glass. "And when
he cannot drink, let him die."

He sat down again in his great chair; but he sat upright,
looking about him, now thoroughly awake and alert.

"In sleep," he said, "it is as if one were already dead; awake,
it is as if one could not die. Ha! Death is impossible. The
blood it runs as strong, the pulse it beats as steady, as when I
was a boy of thirty. Why, I am young still! I am full of
life! Give me fifty years more—only a poor, short fifty years
—what is it when the time has gone?—and I will make, look
you, such a medicine as shall keep a man alive forever! It will
be done some day, alas! when I am gone. It will be too late
for me, and I must die. But not yet—not yet. Oh! we are
born too soon—a hundred years and more too soon. When
a man is old he is apt to feel the near presence of Death.
Not, mind you, when he is asleep, or when he is awake, but
when he is between the two. Then he sees the dart aimed at

his heart, and the scythe ready to cut him down, and the bony
fingers clutching at his throat.　It is as if life were slipping
from him, just as the pirate's plank slips under the weight of
the prisoner who has to walk upon it."

"When a man's time comes," said Jack, with wisdom borrowed from his friends at Trinity Hospital—"when a man's
time comes, down he goes."

"Ay.　It's easy talking when you are young, and your time
hasn't come by many a day; the words drop out glib, and
seem to mean nothing.　Wait, my lad—wait till you have had
your day.　To every man his day.　First the fat time, then
the lean time; or else it's first the lean time, then the fat time.
For most, old age is the lean time.　But the world is full of
justice, and there is always a fat time in every man's life.
When there's peace upon the seas, the merchantman sails free
and happy, buying skins and ivory, spices and precious woods,
for glass beads and cotton.　So trade prospers.　And then the
king's sailors and marines and the privateers must needs turn
smugglers, and so find their way to the gallows.　Then cometh
war again, and the honest fellows have another turn with fighting and taking of prizes and cutting out of convoys.　Yes,
boys, the world is full of justice, did we but rightly consider;
and every one doth get his chance.　As for you, Bess, my girl,
it shall be a brave lover, in the days when thou shalt be a lovely girl and a goddess.　As for you, boys—well—and presently
you will become old men like unto me."　He sighed heavily.
"And then"—he took the saucepan from the hob, stirred it
about, and·smelled the stuff that was simmering in it—"I doubt
if this mixture——　Children, we are all born a hundred years
too soon—a hundred years at least.　Yet if I had but fifty
years before me, I think I could find the secret to stay old age
and put off natural decay.　The Coromantyns are said to have
the secret, but they keep it to themselves; and I have questioned Philadelphy, who is a Mandingo, in vain.　Well"—
again he sighed, as he put back his saucepan—"I have slept,
and I am alive again, with another evening before me, and more
punch.　Let us be thankful.　Jack, unroll the charts, and let
me look upon the world again."

The charts, which the younger boy had already laid upon
the table, were stained and thumb-marked parchments, origi-

1*

nally drawn by some Spanish hand, for the names were all in Spanish; but they had been much altered and corrected by a later hand—perhaps that of Mr. Brinjes himself. They showed the Atlantic and the Indian oceans, together with a map of the Eastern Islands and the unknown Magellanica, or Terra Australis. The last-named was traversed by several lines in blue ink, showing the routes of voyagers both early and recent, each with a name written above it, as Magellan, 1520; Francis D'Ovalle, 1582; Mendana, 1595; Drake, 1577; Candish, 1586; Oliver Noort, 1599; Le Maire, 1615; Tasman, 1642; John Cook, 1683; Woodes Rodgers, 1708; Clipperton, 1719; Shelvocke, at the same time. There was another route laid down across the ocean, much more devious than any of the others, and without name, and marked in red ink.

When these maps were spread out upon the table, Mr. Brinjes rose and stood gazing upon them, as if, by the mere contemplation of the coast lines, he was enabled actually to see the places which he had visited or heard of. There was no place in the whole world that is visited by ships (because I do not pretend that Mr. Brinjes knew the interior of the great continents) whereof he could not speak as from personal knowledge, describing its appearance, the character of the people, the soundings, and the nature of the port or roadstead.

But mostly Mr. Brinjes loved to talk of pirates, rovers, or adventurers, whether of Queen Elizabeth's reign, when they had a golden time indeed, or of our own time, which has seen many of these gentry; though now, instead of receiving knighthood, as was formerly the custom, they are generally taken ashore and hoisted on a gibbet. Thus Mr. Brinjes would lay his forefinger on the island of Madagascar, and tell us of Captain Avery and his settlement on the north of this great island, where every one of his men became like a little sultan or king, each with a troop of slaves, and being no better than pagans, every man with a seraglio of black wives. For aught anybody knows to the contrary, they or their sons are living on the island in splendor to this day, though their famous captain hath long since been dead. Or he would point out the island of Providence, in the Bahamas, where there was formerly a rendezvous, which continued for many years, of those who combined together to prey upon the Spanish commerce. "And think not,

boys," said Mr. Brinjes, solemnly, " that to sail in search of the
great plate ships can be called piracy, for pirates are the common enemies of all flags, and must be hanged when they are
taken prisoners; whereas he who takes or sinks a Spanish vessel performs a meritorious action, and one that he will remember with gratitude upon his death-bed, since they are a nation
more bloodthirsty, cruel, and avaricious than any other, and
papists to boot. It is true that there were some of those who
sailed from Providence that took other ships, of whom Major
Bonnet was one. Boys, I knew the major well. He was a
gentleman of good family from Barbadoes, and I cannot but
think that he was unlawfully hanged, the evidence being sub-
orned. A man of kindly and pleasing manners, who loved the
bowl and a song, and was greatly loved by all his crew and
those who knew him. But he is gone now, and those like unto
him as well, so that the Spaniard sails the Atlantic in peace,
though we have robbed him of some of his dominions. Alas!
what things the Spanish Main hath witnessed! what deeds of
daring, and what sufferings!"

Then he pushed this chart aside, and considered that which
showed the West Coast of Africa, a part of the world which he
regarded with a particular admiration, though I have always
understood that it is full of fevers and diseases of a deadly
kind. He knew, indeed, all the harbors, creeks, river mouths,
and other places from Old Calabar to the Gambia, where such
notorious desperadoes as Captain Thatch, otherwise called
Blackbeard, or as Captain Bartholomew Roberts, made their
rendezvous, where they refitted, and whence they sailed to
plunder the merchantmen of all countries. These men Mr.
Brinjes knew well, and spoke of them as if they had been
friends of his own, and especially the latter. I know not in
what manner he acquired this knowledge of a man who was
certainly a most profligate villain. He it was whose squadron
of three ships was destroyed by Captain Sir Chaloner Ogle, of
the *Swallow*, in the year 1722, the pirate himself being killed
in the first broadside, and fifty-two of his men afterwards hung
in chains along the coast near Cape Coast Castle.

"Boys," said Mr. Brinjes, "those who know not the West
Coast of Africa know not what it is to live. What? Here,
there are magistrates and laws; there, every man does what he

pleases. Here, the rich take all; there, all is divided. Here, men go to law; there, men fight it out. What do they know here of the fierce passions which burn in men's hearts under the African sun? There is summer all the year round; there are fruits which you can never taste; there are—but you would not understand. How long ago since I have seen those green shores and wooded hills, and watched the black girls lying in the sun, and took my punch with the merry blades who now are dead and gone? Strange that the world should be so full of fine places, and we should be content to live in this land of fog and cold!"

Then he pushed this chart away also, and took another, that of the great Pacific Ocean, marked, as I have said, with half a dozen routes, and especially by a broad red line, without a name or date. When Mr. Brinjes laid his finger on this route, he became serious and thoughtful.

"It is forty years"—he began—"forty years since I sailed upon these seas. Of all the crew, doth any survive, save me alone? Forty years! The men were not so fierce as those on the West Coast—the air is milder—they would rest and sleep in the shade rather than fight. Forty years ago!"

The boys were silent, till he should choose to tell us more.

"On board that ship I was rated as surgeon, and at first had plenty to do sewing up wounds and healing broken heads; for though there was a rule against fighting, it was a reckless company of rum-drinking, quarrelsome, fighting devils as ever trod the deck. We had music on board: two horns, till one fell overboard, two violins, and a Welsh harp. In the evening, when there was no fighting, there was music and dancing. 'Twas a happy barky. It was a merchantman, and we shipped our crew and fitted out at Kingston first and Providence next."

" Where the pirates used to assemble?" said Jack.

" True. The crew were mostly rovers. What then? If you venture into the Pacific you must needs carry a fighting crew. We had plenty of arms and ammunition, and not a man on board but had been in a dozen actions by sea and land. But only a merchantman."

Jack shook his head, as if there were doubts in his mind. Then he laughed.

Mr. Brinjes laid his finger on the red line where it began at Providence Island.

"Forty years ago. It was a voyage among seas where there's never a chart; among reefs and rocks not laid down, and along shores no sailors knew. The end of the voyage was disastrous, but the beginning promised well, for the men were full of heart, if ever men were, and the prize we were after was worth taking."

"Prize?" said Jack. "For a merchantman?"

"Merchantman she was, this side Cape Horn. I only meant this side. When you double the cape, that is another matter. A man in those seas sails as happy under the Jolly Roger as under the Union-Jack. A merchantman she was, and built at Bristol, christened the *King Solomon*, four hundred tons; and when we sailed she carried twenty-two long nine-pounders and two three-pounders, with a crew of one hundred and seventy men, besides a dozen or so of negro grummets. Don't you forget, my lad, there's only two flags in those seas—the Spaniard and the Jolly Roger. Take your choice, therefore." He paused to let that choice be taken. "We sailed through Magellan's Straits, taking six weeks over the job, what with contrary winds and storms. When we got out of that place— which, I take it, is the worst navigation in the world—we steered nearly due north for Juan Fernandez, where the Spaniards go from the South American ports to fish. Here it is on the chart." His finger was following the red track. "A mighty pretty place it is. This is where Woodes Rodgers set ashore one of his men and left him alone. After watering, we sailed away, still north, to the Galapagos, where the pirates rendezvous."

"They are pirates then, after all?" Jack interrupted.

"The Spaniards call them such, whereas if they do fly the black flag, it is only to strike more terror into the enemy, and make them quicker to cry for quarter. Pirates, were we? Well, pirates or not, there was no man on board that craft but was an honest Englishman by birth. At Galapagos Islands we laid up to scrape and tallow the vessel, and to cure the scurvy, which had already broken out, with the limes and oranges and bananas which grow wild there, as well as the tobacco plant. The pigs run wild there, too; and if the wells only ran rum as well as water, one might as well be in heaven at once; and there would be no need for the sailor to put to sea any more, nor any wisdom in leaving those islands." He sighed, thinking of pleasant days in the Galapagos. "But we were not cruising in these seas for pleasure, and we had our work to do. Wherefore we made haste and got to sea again. What were we cruising for? Why, my lads, in hopes of coming across the great Spanish galleon, which goes twice every year from Manilla to Acapulco and back laden with treasure, so that every man on board, could we take that ship, would be made for life.

"When we left the Galapagos every man's heart was light, and there was nothing on board but drinking, singing, and gambling, with a fair wind, and the ship taut and trim, and within a few days of the Spaniard's course. He sails these seas as if they were his own, with never a thought of trouble or meeting an enemy. We had fair weather for ten days, making, at a guess, a hundred and eighty knots a day on a nor'west course; so that, after a week or so, we were in the latitude of Acapulco, and, according to my observations, two hundred miles west of that port, that is to say, almost in the track of the galleons, which sail, as is well known, in an even course about lat. 13 N. And for why? If you set sail from Manilla—here," he pointed out that distant island on the chart, "through the Strait of Mindovo, and past Cape Espiritu Santo, you have got between the Ladrones and Acapulco, which is close upon two thousand knots, nothing but blue water. If any other nation besides the Spanish held these seas, they would have been everywhere navigated long ago. But these lubbers care for nothing but to keep out of danger, wherefore they sail where there are no islands. Sometimes, by reason of contrary winds, and the compass, which veers about in these waters as if the devil had it, these ships are blown north and south. I have conversed with Spanish sailors who had been thus driven north, and they reported open seas, though the charts and maps do still lay down a continent between Asia and America.

"It is a most terrible voyage, full of dangers, on account of the tempests which blow there, and because the crews have to live so long on salted provisions and bad water, whereby many grievous diseases are engendered, of which I learned something. There is, for instance, that disease which the Spaniards call the ' Lobillo,' which doth commonly fall upon men who have been living at sea for many weeks upon this diet. I do not know the remedies, if any there be, for this affliction, whereby the body swells up like a bladder which is blown out, and the patient falls to prattling and babbling until he dies. There is also what they call the Dutch Disease, which attacks the gums, and is, I take it, nothing but scurvy, and can only be cured by being set ashore. Then there is an intolerable itching of the whole body, caused by the saltness of the beef and of the air. For this there is no remedy but patience and limes, when these can be procured. There are insects also, which the Spaniards call ' Gorgojos,' which are said to be bred in the biscuit, and creep into the body, under the skin, whence they are difficult to dislodge, and do itch intolerably day and night, so that some have been known to go mad with the discomfort of it, and have leaped overboard.

" When, therefore, we were in the latitude where we might expect any day to see a sail—every sail being a Spanish ship and every Spanish ship a rich galleon—a reward was offered to him who would first spy a sail. But here we were unlucky, for a hurricane fell upon us, drove us off our course, and for four days we scudded, looking for nothing else but destruction, being too low in the waist and too high in the stern for such weather. However, by the Lord's help, the storm at length abated, but not before we were driven a long way north of our course, and in sight of the great island named California." He covered it with his thumb. " Nobody hath yet circumnavigated this island ; but it is reported mountainous and sterile. Yet—Lord! what a place for rovers when they get the sense to make here a settlement for the annoyance of the Spaniard ! Madagascar itself was not more plainly marked out by Providence for the use of rovers. I am old now, or else would I plant a colony myself, with a fleet of half a dozen frigates and a few fast-sailing sloops, and so destroy the Spanish trade of the Pacific. No European sail, I take it, hath gone farther north."

Indeed, the coast line at this point was dotted to show that it was conjectural ; it ran straight across the Pacific, in the line of latitude 35 N., to join the coast of China.

" The storm then abating, we repaired damages, and set sail

again, designing to shape our course southward, with the view of getting once more into the enemy's course. That night, I remember, the light of Saint Elmo showed upon the foretop, at which we greatly rejoiced, as a certain sign and promise of fair weather, and every man saluted it mannerly, as they used in the Mediterranean. On the sixth day after the storm we sighted an island not laid down on any chart; but we touched not at it. Three days later, the sea having been as smooth as the pool of the Thames, we made land again. This time it was the island of Donna Maria Laxara, so called after a Spanish lady, who here leaped overboard and drowned herself for love. But mark the ways of Providence! If it had not been for that tempest, which drove us off our course, what happened afterwards never would have happened."

" What did happen ?"

" A strange thing. The strangest thing that ever you heard of. If you want to be rich, Jack, my lad, I will some day teach you how; and that in the easiest way you can imagine. If I live—alas !"

" What way ? Tell me now."

But Mr. Brinjes would tell no more. He continued gazing at the chart, and following an imaginary course with his forefinger, as if he loved the recollection of that voyage, even though the end of it had been disastrous. Then he pushed it from him with a sigh.

" Forty years ago, it was, boys. Forty years ago."

It was in this way, among others, that Jack acquired the knowledge of geography and the thirst which continually grew greater for voyaging among the strange and unknown parts of the habitable world. In the end, as you shall hear, no one went farther afield or had more adventures.

CHAPTER II.

HOW JACK CAME TO DEPTFORD.

Of these two boys, one—namely, Jack Easterbrook—was not a native born of Deptford, but of Gosport. And since it is his history that has to be related, it is well that the manner of his coming and the nature of his early life should be first set forth.

On a certain warm summer afternoon in the year of grace seventeen hundred and forty-four, when I, who write this history, was but a child of seven, and Castilla six (we are now nearing threescore years, and on the downward slope of life), there sat beneath the shade of a great walnut-tree, on a smooth bowling-green, two gentlemen and a lady, the former on a rustic bench of twisted and misshappen branches or roots, and the latter in an elbow-chair. The lady, who had a small lace cap on her head, and wore a laced apron, held a book in her hands; but the hands and book lay in her lap, and her eyes were closed. The two gentlemen were taking an afternoon pipe of tobacco. One of them—this was Rear Admiral Sayer—was at this time some fifty-five years of age. He wore a blue coat with gold buttons, but it was without the famous white facings which his majesty King George the Second afterwards commanded for the uniform of his naval officers; his right leg had been lost in action, and was replaced by a wooden leg now stuck out straight before him as he sat on the bench. He had also lost his left arm, and one sleeve of his coat was empty. He wore a full wig of George the First's time; his face was full, his cheeks red, and his eyebrows thick and fierce, yet his eyes were kindly. There was a scar across his forehead, which a Moorish scimitar had laid bare.

His companion wore the wig and cassock of a clergyman; he was, in fact, the Vicar of St. Paul's, Deptford. At the back of the bowling-green stood the house—of modern erection—with a pediment of stone, and pilasters, and a stone porch, very fine; on either side of the house was the garden, filled with fruit-trees and beds for vegetables. The garden was surrounded by a brick wall, older than the house, covered with lichen, stone-crop, wall-pellitory, yellow wallflowers, and long grasses. The house and garden were protected by great iron gates, within which marched, all day long, an old negro in the admiral's livery, and wearing a cockade, armed with a cutlass. A small carronade stood beside the gates, for the purpose of announcing sunrise and sunset; and there was a mast, with standing gear and yards complete, at the head of which floated the Union-Jack. Two children were playing with the bowls on the grass; and in a

chair, so placed that the hot sunshine could fall with the greatest effect upon her face, there sat a negress, already old, a red
cotton handkerchief twisted round her head, and in her lap
some knitting. But Philadelphy, like her mistress, was sound
asleep.

It was a sleepy afternoon. The drones and the bumblebees
—"dumbledores" we called them—buzzed lazily about the
flowers; the doves cooed sleepily from the dove-cot; there was
a hen not far off which expressed her satisfaction with the
weather and her brood by a continual and comfortable "took—
took—took;" the great dog lay asleep at the admiral's foot, the
cat was asleep beside it; from the trees there came, now and
then, the contented note of a blackbird; and the flag at the
mast, which was rigged within the iron gates, hung in folds,
flapping lazily in the light air. The two children played for
the most part in silence, or else in whispers, so as not to awaken
Philadelphy. The two gentlemen smoked their tobacco in silence—it was not a day for talking; besides, they saw each
other nearly every day, and therefore each knew the other's sentiments, and there was no room for discussion.

Suddenly there were heard footsteps outside, and just as one
awakes out of a dream, so all started and became instantly
wide-awake. Madam took up her book, the admiral straightened his back, the vicar knocked the ashes out of his pipe, and
the children ran to the gates, which Cudjo, the negro, threw
wide open, a grin of welcome on his lips. Then there appeared
a boy, dressed in a blue coat not made for him, and too long in
the sleeves, worn and shabby, dusty with travel, with brass buttons; his knitted stockings were torn, showing his bare legs;
he wore a common speckled shirt like the watermen's children;
on his head was a little three-cornered hat, cocked in nautical
fashion. He strutted proudly across the grass, regardless of
his rags, with as much importance as if he had been a full-
blown midshipman. For my own part, I have never lost to
this day the sense of his superiority to myself and the rest
of mankind. Castilla makes the same confession. Like myself, she owns that, child as she then was, she felt her inferiority
to a boy so masterful. He was at this time, and always, a singularly handsome boy, tall and big for his age, his head thrown
back, his brown eyes full of fire, and his hand at all times ready

to become a fist. His hair was long, and lay in curls, and untied, upon his shoulders. After him walked the negro who had
brought him from Gosport, and now carried on his shoulder a
box containing all the boy's worldly goods. They consisted of
a toy ship, carved for him by some sailor at Gosport, a pistol
which had been his father's, his mother's Bible, a Church prayer-
book, and a knife. This was all the inheritance of the poor
boy. As the servant bore this precious box through the gates,
he knocked the corner against the rails.

"Steady," said the boy, turning sharply round, "steady with
the kit, ye lubber !"

The first lieutenant himself could not have admonished a man
more haughtily. Then he halted, and took a leisurely observation of the scene. Presently he espied the admiral, and recognizing in his appearance and dress something nautical—it would
have been difficult to mistake the admiral for anything but a
sailor—Jack stepped across the lawn, lugged off his hat with a
duck and a bend, and said : "Come aboard, sir. With submission and dutiful respect, admiral."

The admiral laid down his pipe, and leaned forward, hand
on knee, his wooden leg sticking out before him.

"So," he said. "This looks like the son of my old friend.
What is thy name, child ?"

"Jack Easterbrook, sir ?"

"The son of my old shipmate ?"

"The same, sir."

"Parson," said the admiral, "forty-five years ago I was just
such a little shaver as this, and so was his father. Hang me if
the boy isn't a sailor already ! Thy father, boy, was carried
off by a sunstroke while his ship was lying in Kingston Harbor."

"Yes, sir."

"In command of his majesty's frigate *Racehorse*, forty-four."

"The same, sir."

"And thy mother, poor soul ! is dead and gone too ?"

"Yes, sir," said the boy, looking for a moment as if he would
cry. But it passed. The admiral took his stick and rose from
his chair.

"Let us," he said, gravely, "overhaul the boy a bit. Thy
father, Jack, was the best officer in his majesty's service—the

very best officer, whether for navigation or for fighting—which is the reason why they kept him back, and promoted the reptiles who crawl up the back stairs and make interest with a great man's lackey. He now lies buried in Jamaica, more's the pity. Look me in the face, sirrah—so. A tall and proper lad — a brave and gallant lad. What shall we make of him ?"

Jack's face became a lively crimson at this question. We were now all gathered round him—Castilla looking shyly and with admiring eyes ; and I, for my own part, thinking that here was the finest and bravest boy I had ever set eyes on.

" Well, now," said the admiral, holding the boy's chin in his hand and looking at him steadily, " I warrant, Parson, this boy will be all for book-learning, and we must make him a scholar —eh ? Then, some day, he shall rise to be a reverend doctor of divinity, a dean, or even a bishop in lawn sleeves. What sayest thou, Jack ?" Here the admiral took his hand from the boy's chin, shut one eye, and looked mighty cunning.

Jack shook his head dolefully, and then laughed, looking up as if he knew very well that this was a joke.

" Well, well, there are other things. We can make thee a compounder of boluses, and so thou shalt ride in a coach and wear a great wig, and call thyself physician. 'Tis a fine trade, and a fat, when fevers are abroad."

But Jack again shook his head and laughed. This was a really fine joke, one that can be carried on a long time.

" He will not be a physician. The boy is hard to please. Well, he can, if he likes, become a lawyer, and wear a black gown, and argue a poor fellow to the gallows. Of such they make lord chancellors. At sea their name is shark."

" No, sir," said Jack, with decision, because every joke hath its due limits. " No, sir, I thank you. With submission, sir, I cannot be a lawyer."

" Here is a boy for you. One would think he was too good for this world. Perhaps he would like to wear his majesty's scarlet, and follow the drum and fife, and fight the king's enemies on land. It is as great an honor to bear the king's commission by land as by sea. It is a good service too, when wars are going, though in times of peace there is too much disbanding by half. But a lad might do worse. Think of it Jack !"

"Jack stepped across the lawn, lugged off his hat with a duck and a bend, and said, 'Come aboard, sir.'"

"Oh, sir!" said Jack, coloring again, "I would not be a soldier."

"Then, Jack, Jack, do thy looks belie thee? What? Wouldst not surely choose to be a sneakin', snivelling quill-driver in a merchant's office?"

"No, sir; I would rather starve! Sir," said Jack, his eyes flashing, "I would be a sailor, if only before the mast!"

"Why, there!" cried the admiral, laying his hand on the boy's head. "What else could the boy be? He is salt all through. Hark ye, my lad: do thy duty and thou shalt be a sailor, as thy father was before thee. Ay, and shalt stand in good time upon thy own quarter-deck and carry thy ship into action as bravely as thy father, or even good old Benbow himself."

Thus came Jack to Deptford, being then nine years of age.

Some things there are—I mean not travellers' tales of one-legged men, and such as have their heads between their shoulders, and griffins and such monsters, but things which happen among ourselves and in our midst—which are so strange that the narration of them must be supported by whatever character for truth, honesty, and soberness of mind may be possessed by the narrator and those who pretend to have been eye-witnesses. As regards the history which follows, it is proper to explain that there is, besides myself, only one other person who knows all the particulars. Mr. Brinjes, it is true, knew them; but he has gone away long since, and must now, I think, certainly be dead. The admiral, before his death, was told the truth, which greatly comforted him in his last moments; and I thought it right to tell all I knew to my father, who was much moved by the strangeness of the circumstances, and quoted certain passages from Holy Writ as regards the practice of witchcraft and magic. Perhaps the man Aaron Fletcher knew something of the truth, but in the end he was convicted as a notorious smuggler, and sentenced to transportation to his majesty's plantations, where he died of a calenture, being unable to endure the excessive and scorching heat of the sun, and his spirit broken by the overseer's whip. Everybody, it is true, knows how Captain Easterbrook brought his ship home, and what followed. This is a matter of notoriety. There is not a

man, woman, or child but can tell you the astonishing and wonderful story, the like of which has never been in the history of the
British navy.   They have even made a ballad of it, very moving, which is sung in the sailors' mug-houses, not only in Deptford itself, but in Portsmouth, Woolwich, Sheerness, Chatham,
and Plymouth.   But to know one fact is not to know the whole
history.

As for me, who design to write the truth concerning this
strange history, it is well that you who read it should know
that I take myself to be a person of reputable life and of sober
judgment, and one who has the fear of God in his mind, and
would not willingly give circulation to lying fables.   My father,
the Rev. Luke Anguish, Artium Magister, formerly of St. John's
College, Cambridge, of which society he was a fellow, was the
first vicar of St. Paul's Church, Deptford; the new church, that
is, in the upper part of the town, which was completed in the
year 1736.   By calling, I am a painter in oil-colors; not, I dare
say, a Sir Joshua Reynolds or a Gainsborough, yet of no mean
repute as a painter of ships.   It were unworthy of me to say
more than that my pictures have met with approbation from
persons of rank, and that I have been honored by the highest
patronage, even by members of the House of Lords, not to speak
of the lord mayor and aldermen.   As for the contention of
Castilla that her husband is the finest painter of ships ever
known, that may be the partiality of a jealous and tender spouse.
I am contented to leave the judgment of my work to those who
shall follow after me.   I do not paint ships upon the ocean, because I have never yet gazed upon the ocean, and know not,
except from pictures, how the sea should be painted, or a ship
rolling upon the sea.   My subjects are ships in harbor, ships
lying off Deptford Creek, ships in dock, ships in building, ships
in ordinary, ships ashore, ships in the Pool, ships sailing up and
down the river, and especially with the sun in the west shining
on the sails, and painting all the cordage as of gold, just as happened when Jack brought home his prize; also ships lying in
an autumnal fog, and great barges sunk down to an inch of free-
board with their cargoes of hay.   Nothing finer can be painted,
to my mind, than the picture of such a barge lying on a still
and misty day, with the sun overhead like a plate of copper,
the brown sails half lowered, and the ropes hanging loose.

I suppose that the best place in the world for a boy who is about to become a sailor, as well as for one who loves to paint ships, must be Deptford, which seems to many so mean and despicable a town. Mean and despicable to Jack and to myself it would never be, because here our boyhood was spent, and here we played with Castilla; here we first learned to sit by the river-side and watch the craft go up and down, with those at anchor and those in dock. At Deptford, where the water is never rough enough to capsize a tilt-boat, we are at the very gates of London; we can actually see the pool: we are, in a word, on the Thames.

The Thames is not, I believe, the largest river in the world; the great Oronoco is broader, and, I dare say, longer; the Nile is certainly a greater stream. Yet, there is no other river which is so majestic by reason of its shipping and its trade. For thither come ships, laden with palm-oil and ivory, from the Guinea Coast; from Norway and Riga, with wood and tallow; from Holland, with stuffs and spices and provisions of all kinds; from the West Indies, with rum and sugar; from the East Indies, with rice; from China, with tea and silk; from Arabia, with coffee; from Newcastle, with coal. There is no kind of merchandise produced in the world which is not carried up the Thames to the port of London. And there is no kind of ship or boat built to swim in the sea, except, I suppose, the Chinese junk, the Morisco galley, or the piratical craft of the Eastern Seas, which does not lie at anchor in the Thames, somewhere between Greenwich Reach and London Bridge. East-Indiamen, brigs, brigantines, schooners, yachts, sloops, galliots, tenders, colliers, hoys, barges, smacks, herring-busses, or hog-boats—all are here. And not only these, which are peaceful ships, only armed with carronades and muskets for defence against pirates, but also his majesty's men-of-war, frigates, sloops of war, cutters, fire-ships, and every kind of vessel employed to beat off the enemies of the country, who would prey upon our commerce and destroy our merchantmen. On that very day when Jack came was there not, lying off Deptford Creek, the *Redoubtable*, having received her stores, provisions, and ammunition, and now waiting her captain and her crew?—and I warrant the press-gang were busy at Wapping and at Ratcliffe. Beside her lay the sloop-of-war *Venus*, the *Pink*, and *Lively*, and off

the dock mouth was the *Hector*, lying in ordinary, a broad canvas tilt or awning rigged up from stem to stern. So that those
who look up and down the river from Deptford Stairs see not
only the outward and visible proofs of England's trade, but also
those of England's greatness. Or, again—which may be useful
to the painter—one may see not only at Deptford and at Redriff, but above the river, at Wapping, Shadwell, and Blackwall,
every kind of sailor ; they are mostly alike in manners and in
morals—and one hopes that to sailors much is pardoned, and
that from them little is expected—but they differ in their
speech and in their dress. There is the phlegmatic Hollander,
never without his pipe ; the mild Norwegian ; the fiery Spaniard,
ready with his dagger ; the fierce Italian, equally ready with
his knife ; the treacherous Greek ; and the Frenchman. But
the last we generally see—since it is our lot to be often at war
with his nation—as a prisoner, when he comes to us half starved,
ragged, and in very evil plight. Yet give these poor French
prisoners only warmth, light, and food, and they will turn out
to be most light-hearted and merry blades, always cheerful and
ready to talk, sing, and dance, and always making ingenious
things with a knife and a piece of wood. Perhaps if we knew
this people better, and they knew us better, we should be less
ready to go to war with each other.

Those who live in such a town as Deptford, and continually
witness this procession of ships, cannot choose but be sensible
of the greatness of the country, and must perforce talk continually with each other of foreign ports and places beyond the
ocean. Also because they witness the coming and going of the
king's ships (some of them pretty well battered on their return,
I promise you) ; and because they hear, all day long, and never
ending, save on Sunday, the sound of hammer and of saw, the
whistling of the bo's'ns and foremen, the rolling of casks, the
ringing of bells, and all the noise which accompanies the building and the fitting of ships ; and smell perpetually the tar and
the pitch (which some love better than the smell of roses and
of violets)—they cannot refrain from talking continually of
actions at sea, feats of bravery, and the like. All the townspeople talk of these things, and of little else. And, besides,
in these years there was the more reason for this kind of conversation because we were always at war with France and Spain,

fighting, among other things, to drive the French out of America, and so to enable the ungrateful colonies to make us, shortly afterwards, follow the lead of the French. Every day there came fresh news of actions, skirmishes, captures, wrecks, burnings. The Channel and the Bay of Biscay swarmed with French privateers as thick as wasps in an orchard. There was not a lugger on the coast of Normandy but stole out of a night to pick up some English craft; every fleet of merchantmen sailed under convoy, and every sailor looked for death or a French prison unless he would fight it out unto the end.

The people of London are strangely incurious—many there are who know nothing about the very monuments standing in their midst—and so that they can read every day the news from France and Spain, they care little about their own country. Therefore Deptford, which lies at their very gates, is as little known to them as if it were in Wales. Some, it is true, come every year on St. Luke's Day to join the rabble at Horn Fair, landing at Rotherhithe, and walking to Charlton with the procession of mad wags who carry horns on their heads to that scene of debauchery and riot; and once a year, on Trinity Monday, the elders of the Trinity House assemble at the Great Hall behind St. Nicolas's, and after business go to church, and after church, dinner at the Gun Tavern on the Green. And the ships of the royal navy come and go at the royal yard almost daily. Otherwise Deptford hath no visitors. I do not say that it is a beautiful city, though, as for streets, we have the Green and Church Street; and as for monuments, until late years there were the great House and gardens of Saye's Court, now lying desolate and miserable, partly enclosed in the King's Yard and partly given over to rank weeds and puddles. Here it was that the great Peter, Czar of Muscovy, once lived. There are also the two churches of St. Nicolas and St. Paul, both stately buildings, and temples fit for worship, the latter especially, which is like its sister churches, built about the same time, of Limehouse, St. George's, Ratcliffe, Hoxton, Bethnal Green, Hackney, St. Martin's-in-the-Fields, Camden Town, and others—majestic with its vast round portico of stone and its commanding terrace. Then there are the two hospitals or almshouses, both named after the Holy Trinity, for decayed mariners and their widows. To my own mind these monuments of benevolence, which stand so

2

thickly all round London, are fairer than the most magnificent king's palace of which we can read. Let the great bashaw have as many gilded palaces as he pleases for himself and his seraglio; let our palaces be those which are worthy of a free people, namely, homes and places of refuge for the aged and deserving poor, and those who are quite spent and now past work.

I suppose there are few places richer and more fortunate than Deptford and its neighbor, Greenwich, in these foundations. At the latter place there is the great and noble Naval Hospital, now inhabited by nearly two thousand honest veterans; they will never, be sure, be turned out of this, their stately home, until England hath lost her pride in her sailors. There is Morden College, for decayed merchants; there is Norfolk, also called Trinity, College, for the poor of Greenwich, and of Dersingham, in Norfolk; and there is Queen Elizabeth's Hospital, for poor women. So, at Deptford, we have those two noble foundations, both named after the Holy Trinity, one behind St. Nicolas's and the other behind St. Paul's, the latter especially being a goodly structure, with a fair quadrangular court, a commodious hall, and gardens fitted for quiet meditation and for rest in the sunshine during the latest trembling years of life. I do not think that even Morden College itself, with its canal in front and its stately alleys of trees, or Norfolk College, with its convenient stone terrace overlooking the river and its spacious garden, is more beautiful than the Hospital of the Holy Trinity beside St. Paul's Church, Deptford, especially if one considers the stormy, anxious, and harassed lives to which it offers rest and repose. They have been lives spent on the sea; not in the pursuit of honor won at the cannon's mouth and by boarding-pike in fighting the king's enemies, but in the gathering of wealth for others to enjoy, none of their gains coming to themselves. The merchant captain brings home his cargo safe after perils many and hardships great; but the cargo is not for him. His owners, or those who have chartered the ship, receive the freight; it is bought with their money and sold for their profit. For the captain and the crew there is their bare wage; and when they can work no longer, perhaps, if they are fortunate, a room in a hospital or almshouse, with the weekly dole of loaves and shillings.

The tract of land (it is not great) lying at the back of Trinity

Almshouses and the Stowage, contained by the last bend of the creek before it runs into the river, is rented by two or three market-gardeners, and laid out by them for the production of fruit and vegetables.

As these gardens lay retired and behind the houses, no one ever came to them except the gardeners themselves, who are quiet, peaceful folk. About the orchards here, and the beds of asparagus, pease, endive, skirrett, and the rest of the vegetables grown for the London market, lies ever an abiding sense of peace; and this although one cannot but hear the continual hammering of the dock-yard, the firing of salutes, and the yohoing and roaring of voices which all day long come up from the ships upon the river. I know not how we came to know these gardens, or to find them out. I used to wander in them with Castilla, when we were little children, with Philadelphy for nurse; we took Jack Easterbrook to show him the place as soon as he came to us; we thought, I believe—as children love to think of anything—that the gardens were our own, though, of course, we were only there on sufferance, and because the gardeners knew we should neither destroy nor steal.

Perhaps the chief reason why we sought the place (because we had gardens of our own at home) was that, just beyond the last bend of the creek, there stood, on the very edge of the steep bank—here twenty feet above low-water mark—an old summer-house, built of wood. It was octagonal in shape, having a pointed roof of shingle, with a gilded weathercock upon it. Three sides contained windows, all looking upon the river; another side consisted of a door; and a bench ran round the room, except on the side of the door. It had once been painted green, but the paint was now for the most part fallen off; the shingle roof was leaky, and let in the rain; the weathercock was rusty, and stuck at due east; the planks of the wall had started; the door hardly hung upon its hinges; the glass of the windows was broken; and the whole structure was so crazy that I wonder it kept together, and did not either tumble to pieces or slip down the steep bank into the ooze of the creek. In this summer-house the great czar Peter, when he was learning how to build ships in Deptford Yard, would, it was said, sometimes come to sit with his princes or heyducs, on a summer evening, to drink brandy, to look at the ships, and to med-

itate how best to convert his enslaved Muscovites into the likeness of free and honest English sailors. We had small respect
for the memory of the czar, but as for the old summer-house,
it was all our own, because no one used it except ourselves.
For us it was a fortress or castle where we could play at being
besieged, the ships in the river representing the enemy's fleet.
Jack would sally forth and perform prodigies of valor in bringing in provisions for the garrison. Or it was our ship, in which
we sustained imaginary broadsides, and encountered shipwreck,
and were cast away, Jack being captain and Castilla the passenger, while I was alternately bo's'n, first lieutenant, or cook,
according to the exigencies of the situation. But very soon
Jack grew too big for these games, and left us to ourselves.
Then we fell to more quiet sport. It was pleasant to watch
the ships go up and down the river, and fine to see how the
tide rushed up the creek below us, making whirlpools and ed-
dies, and setting upright the boats lying on their sides in the
mud, and trying to tear down the bank on which stood our
rickety palace. We seemed to know every craft, from the
great East-Indiaman to the Margate hoys or the Gravesend
tilt-boats, by face, so to speak, just as we knew the faces of the
naval officers who walked about the town. And, thanks to
Jack, we knew the history of every ship of the king's navy
which came to Deptford, and all the engagements and actions
in which she had ever taken part.

Across the creek, and as far as the woods and slopes of
Greenwich, there are more gardens, so that at springtime it
was a beautiful thing to sit in the summer-house and look forth
upon a great forest—it seemed nothing less to our young eyes
—covered with sweet blossoms and tender green leaves, which
formed a strange and beautiful setting for the ships in the river. I have painted this picture several times, and always with
a new pleasure, so sweet and charming it is. When I began first
to draw, it was in this place; but it was when Jack had ceased
to play with us, because he would only have laughed at me. I
drew the ships with trembling pencil, Castilla standing over me
the while. The dear girl could never hold a pencil in her hand;
but she could tell me if my drawings were like. Now, to draw
ships that are like real ships is the most important of all. The
time soon came when I was never without a pencil in my hand

and paper to draw upon. I drew everything, just as some boys
will read everything. I drew the ships and the boats, the creek
and the bridge, the sailors, the skeletons of half-built ships in
the great sheds, and the girl who stood beside me.

The picture of a lad who draws while a girl stands beside
him—that might stand for the picture of my life. It is a life
which has been, I thank God, free from anxiety, trouble, or calamity. Once I painted such a picture (having Castilla and
myself in my mind). I drew a youth of eighteen seated before a window, just such a window as that of the old summer-
house. The window showed a merchantman, or part of a merchantman, slowly making her way up the river with wind and
tide. Her foremast and mainmast were gone, and in their places
two jurymasts rigged with a stay-sail; her bowsprit was gone,
and her figure-head carried away and lost; her bulwarks were
broken down. Yet she was safe, and her crew and cargo were
safe, and the evening sun was upon her, so that she showed
glorious in spite of her battered condition, and seemed like
some poor human soul which, after many troubles, gets at last
into the haven where she may lie at rest forever. The boy in
my picture was gazing upon his sketch as if comparing it with
the original. Beside him stood a girl of the same age—be sure
that she was a very beautiful girl, gentle and composed, full
of holy thoughts—who looked down upon the lad. Thus it is
always. The man considers his work, and the woman considers the man, loving his work because she loves the worker, yet
not, like the man, carried away by admiration for the work, as
knowing that all man's work is perishable and transitory, and
that the breath of fame is fleeting. The picture of the girl is
the true portrait of Castilla as she appeared at the age of eighteen, taken from the many drawings which I made of her at
that time, her hair a light brown, falling in waves artlessly upon
her shoulders, and her eyes a clear deep blue, to present which
upon the canvas would want a Reynolds or a Raphael. Alas!
if Sir Joshua had painted this picture, then, indeed, would you
have caught in those eyes the light of virtue and goodness, and
you would have seen about that brow a divine halo, which I
have always seen there, but have not the art to represent. This
it was which the ancients meant when they figured their god-
desses wrapped about with a cloud.

And beside our quiet lives there ran the tumultuous course of a life whose parallel I know not anywhere.

We did not, it may be supposed, stay always in the old summer-house. As we grew older we roamed about the country, Jack sometimes condescending to lead the way (though he would rather have spent his whole time in the yard among the ships). There is a pleasant country lying south and east of Deptford. You may, for instance, cross the bridge over the creek, past the toll-gate, and so by Limekiln Lane and London Street, a pleasant road among the orchards, you will reach the town of Greenwich, with its great hospital; and if you please to leave this unvisited, you may turn to the right, and so up the hill by Brazenface Avenue, and into the Wilderness. Beyond the Wilderness is Blackheath, a wild and desolate spot, with never a house upon it, covered with furze-bushes. Gypsies camp here, and it is said that footpads and highwaymen lurk among the caves; but we never met any. One can come home, by way of Watersplash, along the stream, which is here no longer Deptford Creek, but the Ravensbourne—a pretty brook of pure water, with deep holes under trees, and babbling shallows, running between high banks, where the primroses in March and April lie in thousands. The holes are full of jack, which we sometimes caught with float and hook; and here in spring we went birdnesting, and in summer we picked the wild roses, and in autumn gathered nuts, sloes, and blackberries. Farther afield there is Woolwich Common; or Eltham, with the ruins of King John's palace, the walls of which still stand, and the moat may still be seen, now dry; and the king's banqueting-hall, which is used for a barn, stands stately with its Gothic windows. And if one follows up the windings of the Ravensbourne there are presently the swelling uplands of Penge, with their hanging woods; and Norwood, Westwood Common, Sydenham Wells, and many other rural places, pleasant for those who love the haunts of singing birds and wild-flowers and the babble of brooks and remoteness from the walks of men.

But for such a boy as Jack, what are all the charms of Nature compared with the ships, and the docks, and the river? You can get orchards everywhere, but not a seaport and a dock-yard. You can find rustics, and you may meditate in woods all over the country, but you cannot talk everywhere, as you can at Deptford and Greenwich, with sailors, old and young, of the merchant service and the king's navy. The sailors are rough of speech and rude of manners; they live in mean houses; but in every house there is something strange and wonderful brought from foreign parts. The very landsmen, and those who work at mechanical trades, are half sailors, though they do not wear the sailors' petticoats; for they are shipwrights, boat-builders, fitters of state-cabins, carvers who decorate figure-heads and ships' sterns, or are employed in the victualing yard or in the carpenters' shop, or they are ships' painters, rope-makers, or are employed to scrape clean and calk ships' bottoms; so that the whole town makes its living by the sea. No one speaks or thinks of anything but the sea and the things which are concerned with the sea. What, for instance, did the people of Deptford know about the conduct of the allies and the king's land forces during the late war? Yet they knew of every naval action that was fought, and the name of every ship engaged; and there were men of Deptford, both pressed and volunteers, with every fleet and squadron. The streets were always full of sailors; the officers of the ships in commission and fitting out were always passing in and out of the dock-yard gates, and in sunny weather the benches by the stairs, at the upper and lower water gates, were crowded with the old fellows watching the craft go up and down, and listening to the ribald jests of the watermen, and ready to talk all day long with a certain lad of bright eyes and brave face, who was never tired of listening to them.

What with the old men of Trinity and the pensioners of Greenwich, the boy heard stories enough of the sea and the ships and those who sail therein. Some of the men were so old that they could remember Admiral Benbow and his cowardly captains. There was not a single action fought in the first half of this century but was represented among the Greenwich pensioners, some of whom were in it, and had lost an arm, a leg, an eye, or anything else that can be shot away and leave the trunk still living. I can still see Jack standing before some old veteran with a hook for a hand, his eye kindling, his cheek aflame, his fists clinched, his lips parted, because in imagination he saw the deck knee-deep in blood, the boarders leaping upon the enemy like tigers upon their prey, the ship capsized or sinking, the French flag struck, and because he heard the roaring of the great guns, the rattle of the muskets, the clash of cutlasses, and the groans of the wounded.

There are many other things at sea besides fighting, chasing, and boarding. Jack learned the daily life, for example, from these old fellows, with the duties and the discipline. He heard about foreign ports and strange lands ; certainly one would never be tired of visiting wild and unknown countries, where there may remain yet to be discovered strange races of men, with fruits and flowers as yet unseen and undreamed. But there are also, alas ! storms and hurricanes, wrecks in mid-ocean, with, as the almsmen could tell us, boats laden to the gunwale with sailors who have escaped the sinking ship only to be tossed helpless on the sea with never a drop of water to drink or a mouthful of biscuit to eat. Or there are those who are cast away upon some desolate rock or unknown island, where they live on sea-birds, fish, mussels, and the like, till they die or are taken off. And some are thrown upon cold and inhospitable coasts, such as that of Labrador, where the cruel cold causes their hands and feet, their noses and ears, to fall off—there was one poor wretch in the hospital thus mutilated—and where the North American Indians (the most savage and the most ruthless race in the world) take them prisoners, and torture them before slow fires. Or there are treacherous pirates, who steal aboard, murder the crews, and pillage the ship. Or there are Moors, who make slaves of honest English sailors, and constrain them to row in their galleys, bare-backed, with the master or bo's'n walking above them on a kind of bridge, armed with a whip to scourge the bare backs of those who seem to shirk their work. Or there are French prisons, where the captives are starved on thin soup and bread for all their diet. Or there is the accursed Inquisition, into whose clutches many sailors have been known to fall, and for their endurance in the Protestant faith have suffered the torture of the rack, and even martyrdom at the stake. And, again, there are such perils as falling overboard, fire at sea, scurvy, yellow jack, and mutiny. And there is the evil—intolerable it would be to landsmen—of the captain's tyranny, or, which often happens, the malice, envy, or jealousy of a first lieutenant, with endless floggings and rope's-endings all day long. And, again, there is the danger that, after show-ing the greatest zeal, bravery, and activity in service, a man may be passed over by the favoritism which prevails in high quarters and the want of friends to help him. Is it not a dreadful and a shameful thing that there should be men grown old as lieutenants—nay, even as midshipmen—who have fought in a hundred battles, and spent their lives upon salt-water, only to feel a new mortification every voyage in serving under men young enough to be their own sons?

As for myself, the talk of these old men filled me with a kind of contempt for the seaman's lot. One cannot choose but admire the intrepidity, worthy of a stoical philosopher, with which these men face, every day, possible death; yea, and exhibit the most wonderful constancy under pain, and the strangest insensibility to danger. This, I say, commands our admiration. Yet the lot of the meanest landsman seems to me easier than that of a sailor, and I would rather be a hedger and a ditcher upon a farm than even a commissioned officer aboard the finest ship that ever floated. But we landsmen know not the strength of that longing for the sea which pos-sesses some lads, and drags them as by chains or ropes to the nearest port (thus was Jack drawn irresistibly by the hand of fate), and so aboard; and once on the ship's books, there is no other way possible, and the lad becomes for life a sailor, to spend his days rolling about on a wet and slippery deck, yet happier than if he were ashore; like unto those rovers of old, the north-country men, who could stay long in no place, but roved from port to port, landing here and there, and devour-ing the substance of the people, even to the southern coasts of Italy and the islands of Greece.

CHAPTER III.

HOW JACK LEARNED OF THE PENMAN.

HERE were materials enough to fire the imagination and awaken the ardor of a boy about to become a sailor. But these were not all. For at home—the admiral's house having become this orphan's home—there was talk all day long of

2*

fighting and foreign seas, and things nautical. Jack's patron, or guardian, had been engaged in many of the actions fought during the eleven years' war between the years 1702 and 1713. He was on board the *Resolution*, which carried Lord Peterborough when she was intercepted by a French squadron, and was forced to run ashore in order to save her from falling into the hands of the enemy; he was on Sir George Byng's ship, the *Royal Anne*, in Sir Cloudesley Shovel's fleet, when that hero perished off the Scilly Isles; he was a lieutenant on board the *Assurance* in that gallant action with the French commander Du Guai Trouin, of the *Achille*. In this battle he lost his arm; his leg he lost in the capture of a Moorish corsair during the reduction of Morocco, in the year 1734. After this he retired, receiving the rank of rear-admiral, and settled at Deptford, then about forty-two years of age. He presently discovered that it is not good for man to live alone, and therefore took a wife, who in due time bore him a child, Castilla. His daughter, who, if anybody, ought to know, says that her father possessed in an eminent degree, and daily in his lifetime exhibited, most, if not all, of the virtues which should adorn the Christian who is also an officer of high rank in his majesty's navy. The Christian virtues, it is sure, vary according to a man's station in life. We do not expect certain things from princes which are indispensable to those of lowly and humble lot; from an admiral of the fleet we do not look for meekness, patience, humility, or resignation; a choleric disposition is allowed to him; the habit of applying sacred names to things profane is excused in him; and if he who has commanded a man-of-war is not to have his own way in everything, who should? As for obedience to the commandments, it may be shown that the admiral followed them all. Thus, for honoring his parents, he did more—he was proud of them, because they came of a good stock—and honored himself on their account; he killed nobody save in battle, though he drubbed and belabored his servants every day; he robbed nobody, except in an honorable way, as in taking a prize; he was envious of nothing but the Frenchman's ships; he freely forgave everybody, even those who transgressed his orders on board ship and sinned against his patience, as soon as he had soundly flogged them. To bear malice when a man had paid for his

fault with three dozen was not in the admiral's nature. And
that he was of a truly good heart and a benevolent disposition
was clearly shown by his treatment of Jack Easterbrook.

There were also many others, formerly of the naval service,
who were contented to spend the evening of their days in this
town of Deptford, which is not on the sea, yet lives by the
sea. Among them was that famous traveller George Shelvocke
the younger, who accompanied his father in the circumnavi-
gation of the globe in the year 1720, and was never tired of
relating the perils, sufferings, and adventures of that voyage,
and the wonders of the South Seas : an account of the voyage
hath been published for the curious. There were also Captain Mayne, who commanded the *Worcester* in Admiral Vernon's expedition ; Captain Petherick, resident commissioner
of the yard, who had a goodly collection of books of voyages,
which he suffered Jack to borrow and to read ; Mr. Peter
Mostyn, formerly cocket-writer in his majesty's custom-house,
and an ingenious, well-informed gentleman ; Lieutenant Hepworth, late of General Powlett's marines ; and Mr. Underhill,
retired purser of the king's navy.

To be a purser is to hold a thankless office : it is he who is
blamed for every barrel of damaged pork, and for every box
of weevily biscuit ; he can please none, wherefore it is best
for him not to try. As for the pleasures of a purser's life, I
know not what they are. He must face the dangers of the
deep with the rest ; he must endure tempest and shipwreck ;
cannon-ball and grape-shot spare the purser no more than the
first lieutenant, if he be on deck ; and when the ship is cast
away the purser drowns with the captain. Yet for all these
perils he gets neither promotion nor honor. Would any man
boast of having been purser, and therefore kept below in the
cockpit with the surgeons and the wounded men, during the
most gallant action ever fought ? Yet there is one consolation
for the purser. He can, and does continually, by his accounts,
his purchases, his bribes and percentages, suck so much profit
out of every voyage that he is presently able to leave the service and purchase a cottage, where, with a patch of garden to
cultivate, perhaps a wife and children to cheer him, a few companions, a pipe of tobacco and a glass of punch, he may forget
the darkness of the orlop-deck, the stink of his storerooms,

the great tallow-candle in the glass lantern, by the light of which he had to keep his accounts and inspect his stores ; the rolling of the ship, the thunder of the cannon in a battle, the cries of the wounded, the crash and wreck of the great ship on a rock, or the alarm of fire ; yea, and even the daily purgatory caused by the tricks of the midshipmen and the gibes of the gunroom.

These gentlemen met nearly every night at the " Sir John Falstaff," by the Upper-Water-Gate, for punch and conversation ; they also came often to the admiral's house, and were, one and all, kind to the lad who was thus brought among them, and freely talked with him ; so that, being of an inquiring mind, and thus running about in the dock-yard, and talking with old officers, common sailors, and pensioners, and with the help of the apothecary, who from the first loved the boy, I think there was no part of the world, as there was no action of recent times, with which Jack was not as well acquainted as if he had been there. At the beginning he was placed under my father, who made him begin the study of the Latin language, which he could not stomach, and would never willingly look into any books except those which are concerned with the sea, such as Captain Park's " Defensive Wars by Sea," a very instructive work ; " The Practical Sea-Gunner's Companion," and even the " Rigging Tables," over which he would pore contentedly for hours. He was also fond of reading voyages, and especially those volumes of Harris's and Purchas's collections—the first of the former, and the first and fourth of the latter—which are concerned with the South Seas, towards which his imagination was greatly drawn by his conversation with Mr. Brinjes and Mr. Shelvocke. That he was always fighting other boys, especially the rough river-side lads, and was seldom without some external sign of combat, such as a black eye, cut lip, and swollen nose, certainly did not lessen him in his patron's regard, because, when all is told, the most valuable quality in a sailor is the love of fighting.

So strong and courageous was he, so ready to fight, and so uncommonly backward in owning himself beaten, that none of his age and stature dared to contend with him—save at stone-throwing and at a distance—except one, of whom mention is here made ; not because a boy's fights are matters of serious history, but because the fighting between these two, thus begun, was continued after both became men, and with consequences most important. This boy was the son of a boatbuilder in the town; his name was Aaron Fletcher. In strength, age, and stature, nearly the same as Jack; in bravery and spirit, equal to him. Yet whenever they fought—which was often—Aaron was defeated, because he lacked the dexterity and quickness of eye which beat down mere strength and render courage useless. Yet Aaron would not own to inferiority; and whenever the boys met, they began to snarl at each other like a pair of terriers, and the first stone was thrown, the first taunt uttered, the first blow delivered, and then at it again, like French and English.

Further, that he neglected his Latin, went to sleep in church, put powder in the negroes' tobacco, tied ropes across the road to throw down belated wayfarers, and played a thousand pranks daily may be admitted. These things only cost him a flogging when he was found out, and endeared him more and more to his guardian.

When Jack was eleven years of age, the admiral, regardless of my father's protestations of the perils encountered by those who are ignorant of the classics, placed him wholly in the charge of Mr. Westmoreland, who, although only a penman by trade, had acquired so great a proficiency in arithmetic, the rudiments of navigation, the taking of observations, and the working of logarithms that he had no equal in the town, and was perfectly able to instruct a young gentleman before he went on board. In all these branches the boy showed and displayed an uncommon zeal and quickness. But, I verily believe, if he had thought that the study of Hebrew or Chaldæan would have helped him forward in his profession, he would have entreated my father to teach him.

Mr. Westmoreland, his master, was a mild and gentle creature who loved nothing but the study of mathematics and the art of fine writing, so that though he wrote letters for any who came to him, and copied deeds for the attorney, and wrote out his sermon large and fair for the Vicar of St. Paul's, he always turned from these labors with joy to his books and his calculations. He was in appearance short and bent, with rounded shoulders, and with a hump (which made the boys call him

"My Lord"). His voice was high and squeaky. He wore round horn spectacles; when these were off, you perceived that his eyes were soft and affectionate. His forehead was high and square, and he wore a plain scratch-wig. He was a patient teacher, and bore an excellent character for uprightness and piety, though he was despised by the rougher sort, because, although he was now no more than forty, or thereabouts, he could not fight, or even defend himself.

He lived next door to the apothecary, in that row of houses on the north side of the Trinity Almshouses where reside the better sort of tradesmen, such as the sexton of St. Nicolas; Mr. Skipworth, the principal barber and wig-maker, who shaved all the gentry in the place, and kept four assistants continually employed in dressing and flouring their wigs for them; the master measurer's assistant, and the master shipwright's assistant. But these honest folk did not call Mr. Brinjes their equal. He, for his part, took his pipe nightly at the "Sir John Falstaff" with the gentlemen, while they used the "Plume of Feathers."

Under Mr. Westmoreland's instruction, Jack learned all that the ingenious penman had to teach him, except his fine handwriting and the beautiful flourishes with which a dexterous pen can adorn a page; and by the time he was twelve years of age he understood the use of the compass, the sextant, the ship's charts, all the various parts of a ship and her rigging, and a great deal of geography and naval history.

As for the parts of a ship, he learned them chiefly in the yard, where he would wander among the sheds and watch the building of the ships, the repair of those in the dry-dock, and the fitting out of those in the wet-dock, the bending of the great beams by steam, which is made to play upon them until they become soft, the making of rope, the cutting and shaping of pulleys and blocks, the forging of anchors, and every part of the business belonging to the construction of ships. Then, again, he learned the names and purposes of all the ropes, running and standing gear, sails, flags, signals, sailing rules, and rules for action, and his natural curiosity made him inquire into and acquaint himself with the way in which everything is made, and may be repaired or replaced. He learned all these things from natural eagerness and interest in every-

thing concerning a ship; but in the end this knowledge stood
him in good stead, because there is no detail in the conduct
and construction of a ship which ought to be below the notice
of the officers, a fact which many commanders forget, leaving
the navigation of the ship to the master, her seaworthiness to
the carpenter, and the health of the crew to the purser. Surely
if, as hath been advanced by some, every boy is born with a
clear vocation for some trade or profession, just as Paul, though
an apostle, was also a tent-maker, and Luke, at first a physician, and Peter a fisherman (afterwards of men), then, most
certainly, Jack, by right divine and special calling of Providence, was a sailor.

While he sat every morning at work with his mild instructor,
Mr. Westmoreland, there was always present a little girl, three
years younger than himself, a child with black hair, rosy cheeks,
and big black eyes. When it was winter weather this child
sat in a little chair beside the fire; when it was warm and
sunny, she sat in the open doorway. She was a grave child,
who seldom played with other children; she had no dolls or
toys; she took great pleasure in household things, and from
a very early age was her father's housekeeper; when she grew
older she became his ruler as well, ordering things as seemed
to her best. And though her father was so fond of books and
learning, this girl would never so much as learn to read. One
does not, to be sure, expect girls in her station to acquire the
arts of reading and writing, if only because they have no books,
and never have occasion to write. These arts would be as
useless to them as the knowledge of riding, or dancing the
minuet. But it was strange that Bess should be so different
in disposition as well as in appearance to her father; and
stranger still, that so rickety a man should be the father of so
strong and stout a girl. As for her mother, no one knew
whither she had gone, or what had become of her; it was said
by those who remembered her that she was as comely as her
daughter, but a termagant and a shrew in temper, who led her
mild husband a terrible life, even sometimes taking the broom-
stick to him, and beating him over the head with it, poor man!
or laying about her with the frying-pan, as ungoverned women
use towards those husbands who, like Mr. Westmoreland, are
afraid, or too weak of arm, to keep them in submission by the

same methods. She left her husband (he bore the loss with Christian submission) a year or two after marriage, and was reported to have been afterwards seen at Ranelagh among the ladies and gentlemen there, dressed in a hoop, all in silk and satin, patches and paint, and fan in hand, very fine, and carrying a domino, just for all the world as if a penman's wife could become a gentlewoman.

From the very first a singular friendship existed between Jack and this girl. He brought her apples, comfits, and cakes, which Philadelphy, Castilla's black nurse, made for him; he played with her, and made her laugh; then he teased her, and made her cry; then he coaxed her into good temper again. She was a child who fell into the most violent storms of passion, which none but Jack could subdue; he took a pleasure both in exciting her wrath and appeasing it. On the other hand, he never tried to enrage or to tease Castilla, perhaps because she was possessed of such extraordinary calmness and sweetness that it was impossible to provoke her, and it was waste of time, even for a boy who loves teasing, to practise upon one who regards it not. Bess, for her part, was one of those who would rather be teased into anger than neglected. It was pretty to see how she would sit when he was at his lessons with her father, watching him silently, and how she would follow him, when he suffered her, submissive and obedient; though there was nobody else in the world, not even her father, to whom this wilful girl would submit. There are some men to whom women willingly and joyfully submit themselves, and become their slaves with a kind of pride; but there are others to whom no woman will submit. Of the latter kind was Mr. Westmoreland, Bess's father, who was born to be ruled by his wife. Of the former, Jack was one; when he was only a boy the sailors' wives and daughters in the street would call after him for a pretty lad, and bid him come and be kissed; and when he was a man grown the maids would look at him as he passed along the street, and would follow him with longing eyes. But if a woman becomes the slave of a man, she will have him to be her slave in return; for where there is great love, there is also great jealousy; and also where there is great love, there is also the possibility of great wrath and great revenge—as you will presently discover.

In one word, long before he went on board as a volunteer, young Jack Easterbrook was eager to feel the deck rolling under his feet, and to hear the first shot of his first action; he was also well advanced in all the knowledge of ropes and rigging that the gunner has to teach the youngsters aboard. It is further to be noted that, at this early age, and before he went to sea, the boy had already acquired the settled conviction that all things which the round world contains, and the kindly earth produces, belong especially to the sailor by right divine, and were intended by Providence for his solace when ashore; that to provide for him, and for his comfort, landsmen toil perpetually; that while he is fighting our battles for us, we are gratefully devising, contriving, making, compounding, and inventing all kinds of things for his enjoyment when he comes back to us; such, for instance, as strong wine and old rum, music and fiddles, songs and dances, tobacco and snug taverns; he is to have the best of all; for him the most beautiful women reserve their favors, and desire to win his affections before those of any landsman whatever. Young and old, man, woman, boy, and girl, we all loved the boy. There was not in Deptford, or in Greenwich, a more gallant lad, one more brave and resolute, nor one more handsome. For all his fortune he had but his resolution and his sword. And he went forth to conquer the world with so brave a heart and a carriage so sprightly that the men laughed only for the pleasure of looking upon him, and the women cried. I am sure that the true soldier of fortune hath always made the women cry.

At the age of eleven, also, the admiral, by permission of the captain, was enabled to place the name of the boy on the books of the *Lenox* as a volunteer, although he did not send him yet to sea, considerately holding that this age is too tender for the rough usage of boys aboard ship, though many boys are sent away so early. But by entering him on the ship's company he secured that his rating as midshipman should begin at thirteen and his commission as lieutenant be obtained at nineteen. So that, although the boy was still working with Mr. Westmoreland, he was supposed to be cruising with Captain Holmes aboard the *Lenox*.

CHAPTER IV.

HOW JACK FIRST WENT TO SEA.

In the autumn of the year 1747—the last but one of the war then raging—the admiral judged that the time was now arrived when the boy should join his ship. "For," he said, "the lad is already nearly thirteen, and tall for his age; and he knows more than most youngsters have learned after twelve months at sea. He grows masterful, too, and will be all the better for the rope's-end which the gunner hath in store for him, and for the mast-head, where he will spend many pleasant hours. And as for the captain—Dick Holmes is not one who will skulk, or suffer his crew to skulk. What better can happen for a boy than to sail with a fighting captain?"

"'Tis a brave lad, admiral," said my father—'twas at the club or nightly assemblage at the Sir John Falstaff. "By such stuff as this let us pray that England's fleets will always be manned. They have never heard of Selden's *Mare Clausum*, and know not his argument, which is, to my mind, conclusive. Nevertheless, they go forth to support those arguments by a kind of blind instinct, which I take to be in itself a clear proof of his sound reasoning."

"I have never met any Mary Clausum," said the admiral, "to my knowledge. Polly Collins there was in my time, at Point—a black-eyed jade. But Jack is, as yet, full young to think of any Polly of them all."

"Nay, 'tis the title of a learned work. I meant only that if England is to be queen of the seas, which France and Spain still dispute with us, and are likely to dispute for a long while, it is well that we have such boys, and plenty of them. There can never be too many Britons born in the world."

"True, doctor; especially if we go on expending them in this fashion."

"We send forth this tender child, sir," continued the Vicar

of St. Paul's, "to a hard and rough life. He may be wrecked; he may be killed in action; he may lose his limbs; there are a thousand perils in his way. Yet we do not pity him, because, if his life must needs be short, it will be honorable. And he is in the hands of Providence."

"That is true, doctor. Though as to danger, hang me if I think he is worse off aboard ship than he would be ashore, what with sharks and lawyers, rogues and murderers, robbers and cheats, to say nothing of the women. And on board ship they cannot get at a man. And as for hardships — why, every youngster looks forward to being an admiral at least, and to lead his squadron into a victorious engagement — and sometimes he does it, too."

"As for me, admiral," said Mr. Brinjes, "I shall bid good-bye to the lad with a vast deal of pleasure. He will go never a day too soon. Keep a lad too long and he gets stale. As for dangers, I think you are right. But there are dangers afloat which the landsman does not know, and more dangers than the enemy's shot or a gale of wind. A boy may have a bully for first lieutenant, or a tyrant for captain." Here his only eye flashed fire, from which one may conjecture that he had himself experienced this accident, and still cherished the memory; "or a skinflint and a cheese-scraper for a purser—"

"Nay, nay," said Mr. Underhill, "the purser is forever in fault."

"Or a lickspittle for a master; there are rogues and scoundrels afloat as well as ashore. Mark you, if it is bad for the midshipmen, 'tis worse for the crew; in such ships are floggings daily, and mutinous words whispered 'tween-deck, with rope's-ending and continual flogging, no matter how smart a man may be; and yet they wonder why men rise sometimes and murder their officers and carry off the ship under the black flag. Pirates? Why, even if they knew that the gibbet was already built whereon they were to hang in chains till they dropped to pieces, do you think they would not have their revenge, and then a free and a merry life, if only for a short year or two before they die?" and with that Mr. Brinjes looked about him so fiercely that for a while no one spoke.

"These words are better said ashore than afloat," said the admiral, presently. "I've tied up a man and given him six dozen—ay, or hanged him for mutiny—for less than that, Mr. Brinjes."

"Very like, very like," returned Mr. Brinjes, recovering his good temper. "I will remember it, admiral, if ever I ship with you. As for the boy, now—this boy of ours—he will do well, and will turn out a credit to us all, admiral. I have never known a more resolute lad, or one better fitted for the work before him. I have taught him, for my own part, how the land lays as regards the wickedness of men, both ashore and afloat. He is prepared for a good deal; and so far, I think, never was a lad sent abroad better prepared. He knows as much, doctor, not to speak boastfully, as a Roman Catholic confessor. Now when a boy is fully acquainted with devilry, he need fear no devils, male or female."

The ship on whose books he was borne—namely, the *Lenox*, Captain Richard Holmes—was now refitting at Sheerness, being under orders to join the West Indian squadron of seven ships under Rear-Admiral Knowles, at Port Royal, Jamaica. A beautiful ship she was, nearly new, a third-rate, of seventy guns, though at this time she carried no more than fifty-six, and a complement of six hundred men. You shall hear presently with what singular good-fortune the boy began his course. This good-fortune continued with him unbroken until the event which I have to relate, so that, in thinking of Jack, I am reminded of that Lydian king who was told by the philosopher to count no man happy until the end. Always, in every ship, he gained the good opinion of the superior officers; always the actions in which he fought were victorious; promotion and distinction, prize-money, and escape from shot and cutlass wound —what more could a sailor desire? To be sure, there was one voyage which proved disastrous. Even here he escaped drowning when so many perished. Besides, this was in time of peace.

It is generally believed that boys are shipped off to sea because they are too loutish and stupid for the arts by which landsmen rise. But we do not hear that such lads rise to distinction by reason of loutishness. This is not the way with those who live in a dock-yard town. There the flower of the youth flock to the service, and there is no lack of volunteers, even for ordinary seamen, in time of war. There are skulkers, it is true, but they are more common at Wapping than at Deptford. As for officers, happy that boy who wears the king's uniform; envied is he among his companions. You may judge he wants but little admonition to encourage him in zeal.

"Boy," said the admiral, catechising the lad before he joined his ship, "what is thy first duty?"

"Respect for superiors, sir," said Jack.

"Right; and the next? No argument on board. And when fighting begins, don't gape about the ship to duck for any cannon-shot that flies overhead, but stand steady at quarters, eyes open, and hands ready. What? Many a chance comes of showing your mettle when least expected, as when a boarding attack is repelled, or the word is given to leap on board and at 'em. Be ever ready, yet not too forward, lest it seem a reflection upon thy betters. Wait till thy time comes. When it does come—but, by the Lord, Jack, I have no fear of thee!"

Other directions the admiral gave the boy, which may be here omitted, the more particularly as they referred to the conduct which a boy should observe in port and on shore; and the admiral's warnings were plain and clear, and such as may be read in the Book of Proverbs. My father also admonished the boy, particularly on the wickedness of profane swearing. Of this he was likely to hear only too much, and, indeed, his captain was reported to be one who enforced his orders with a great deal of hard swearing. My father also addressed a few words to this young sailor on the evils of immoderate drinking, too common on land, though restricted by wholesome discipline at sea. And he instructed the boy how he should govern himself, keep his temper in control, guard his tongue, fight his shipmates no more than was necessary for self-respect and honor; and how, when the time should come when he himself was to be put in authority, he should be merciful in punishment, and err on the side of leniency, remembering that though a man's back must suffer for his sins, he should not be torn to pieces and cruelly lacerated—as is the practice on board some ships—save for the most heinous offences against order, morality, and discipline. "The ancient Romans," added my father, "could, if they chose, flog a slave to death. Yet it was counted infamous to use this power. The captain of a king's ship has this power also, seeing that he may, if he so please, order a man as many as five hundred lashes—a truly dreadful punishment, under which the strongest man may succumb. Reserve this power when thou hast it, Jack. Three dozen, or even one, in the case of young sailors, may be as efficacious as six dozen; a wholesome discipline is better served by moderation than by cruelty."

I know not how far my father's admonitions produced good fruit. In after-time, Jack was ready enough to rap out a profane word. On the other hand, he was beloved by the men on account of his punishments, which were as certain after offences as the stroke of the ship's bell, but never cruel. It were to be wished some captains on land as well as at sea would remember that three dozen may be sometimes as good as six dozen. It was but yesterday that a poor fellow, a grenadier, under sentence to be shot for desertion, had his punishment commuted, as they called it, to five hundred lashes. He appealed, and the previous sentence was confirmed; therefore he went boldly to his death, thinking it better to be shot than to be tortured by the lash until he died.

Then we all engaged upon Jack's sea-chest; and I suppose no bride ever contemplated her new furniture and house linen with more pride and satisfaction than Jack bestowed upon his chest. It was strong and stoutly made, with a till and two trays. It contained his uniform coat, his watch coat, a glazed hat for night watch in bad weather, two hats each with a gold loop and a cockade, his stockings, shirts (they were of the finest kind, fit for a young gentleman, with lace ruffles), his boots, handkerchiefs, crimson sash, and his hanger. Besides these things there were his log-books, ruled and prepared for him by Mr. Westmoreland; pens cut for him by the same hand; a quadrant, with a day and a night glass; the "Elements of Navigation," the "Sailor's Vade-Mecum," the "Sea-Gunner's Companion," and a book on the "Method of Computing Observations," so that he was amply provided with his favorite reading. To these were added, by my father, a copy of the Holy Bible, with the Book of Common Prayer. These things, with a pocket compass and a tin pannikin or two, a book of songs, and a few other trifles, made up Jack's outfit.

When all was ready and the time of departure was come, the admiral put into his hand a purse full of guineas, and told him that until such time as he should be rated midshipman, an allowance of thirty guineas a year should be given to him. This is a liberal addition to a boy's pay, and I doubt whether any other youngster on board the *Lenox* possessed so splendid an addition to his two pounds a month.

On the morning of his departure our young hero appeared dressed for the first time in his blue uniform coat, with the gold loop in his hat, and his hanger at his side, trying to look as if he had worn it for years, and was unconcerned about his personal appearance. He was going down to Sheerness in a tilt-boat, accompanied by two of the admiral's negroes, to get his sea-chest aboard, and provided with a letter for the captain. We all went down to the Stairs with him—the admiral, my father, Castilla, and myself, with Philadelphy. We found, also waiting on the Stairs, Mr. Westmoreland and Bess, Mr. Brinjes, and the boy Aaron Fletcher.

"Farewell, Master Jack," said Mr. Westmoreland, in his cracked and squeaky voice—"farewell; I shall never have so good a pupil again. Forget not the rules for the right placing of the decimal point, and do not neglect practice in the tables of logarithms."

"Good-bye," said Jack, shaking his hand. "I will remember. Good-bye, Bess." He laid his arm round the girl's neck —she was now ten years of age, and as tall as Castilla, though a year younger—and kissed her on both cheeks. "Good-bye, my girl; give me another." He kissed her again. Bess said nothing; but the tears rolled down her cheeks, and her father drew her away to make room for his betters.

Then Jack saw Aaron, and he laughed aloud.

"Ho! ho! Aaron Fletcher. There isn't time for a fight this morning, Aaron," he said; "give us your hand."

Aaron took the proffered hand, but doubtfully.

"I thought I'd come to see thee start, Master Jack," he said; "and I wanted to say—"

"Well?" asked Jack, for the lad hesitated.

"To say when you come back—if it's next year or next ten years—I'll fight you again, for all your gold loop."

"So you shall, Aaron; so you shall," said Jack, with another laugh. "That's a bargain."

"And so, with a kiss to Castilla and a shake of the hand to me, and after receiving the blessing of the admiral, who needed not to spoil its solemnity by a profane oath, he leaped into the boat, took the strings, and ordered the men to give way. But he looked back once, and waved his hand, crying out, " Good-bye, Bess." So his last thought was of the penman's girl.

" When he comes home, Aaron," said Bess, wiping her tears, " Jack shall beat you into a jelly."

" I'll break every bone in his body for him," said Aaron. " Oh, I wish he would come back to-morrow ! And you may be there to see, if you like."

" I shall tell him the first thing when he comes back. What ? You dare ask him to fight ? You ? I wonder, for my part, that a midshipman should dirty his fist upon your face.

The admiral looked after the receding boat, his red face full of affection and emotion. Beside him stood my father, in wig and cassock, as becomes a doctor of divinity. Mr. Brinjes, in his brown morning coat and scratch wig, looked a strange companion to them. But the watermen on the Stairs stood aside even more respectfully for him than for the admiral. He might, indeed, knock them over the head with his gold-headed stick, but he could not, like Mr. Brinjes, scatter rheumatic pains and toothache among them.

And here a singular thing happened. There is no man more free from superstitious terrors, I think, than myself. Yet I cannot but remember that while Castilla cried, and I myself should have liked nothing better than to cry, but for the unmanliness of the thing, the old witch-woman—she was nothing less—this Mandingo prophetess, whose powers were as real as those believed to belong to Mr. Brinjes—began to shiver and to shake, and her teeth to chatter. To be sure, it was a morning in December, but mild for the time of year, and the sun shining. No doubt some cold breath struck her face, and made her shiver. But to Philadelphy everything unexpected was full of prophetic warning, could she read it aright.

" What does it mean ?" she murmured. " What in the world can it mean ? I dun know what this shiver means ; Mas'r Jack come home again, I think, and play mischief with some of us. There's trouble sure for somebody ; trouble and crying. Dun you be afraid, Miss Castil ; ole Philadelphy know plenty words to keep off the devil."

She meant that she had plenty of incantations or charms by

" ' Good-bye, Bess.'   He laid his arm round the girl's neck, and kissed
her on both cheeks."

which to avert and ward off evil. I am sure there was never a witch-woman or Obeah man on the African coast or in Jamaica had more spells and secrets of magic and unholy craft than this old negress.

CHAPTER V.

MIDSHIPMAN JACK.

THUS was Jack fairly launched and started upon his profession. As regards a boy's first days at sea, they are reported by all to be the most miserable in his whole life. For the quarters of the youngsters, volunteers and midshipmen, on a ship of the line are beneath the lower gun-deck, on what they call the cockpit or the orlop. This is a dark and gloomy place, below the level of the water; no daylight can ever come to it, and there can be little access of pure air. Here the purser has his stores, the surgeon keeps his drugs, the bo's'n and carpenter their ropes and spare gear, so that the place smells continually of tallow, beef, pork, tar, and bilge-water. It swarms with rats and cockroaches; in time of battle the wounded are brought here, near the after-hatchway, as to the safest part of the vessel. Here the youngsters hang their hammocks and stow their chests. As for their mess, it is with the surgeon's mate, the master's mate, the purser's mate, and the captain's clerk. To boys brought up delicately the food is coarse; new-comers have to run the gauntlet of rough jokes and the horse-play which, among these lads, passes for wit; it is that kind of wit to which the only answer is force of fist. The young sea-lion's play is always like a fight, and generally ends in one. Therefore if a boy on board a ship love not fighting he had better tie a kedge-anchor round his neck and drop overboard. But if, like Jack, he loves and is always ready for a fight, and will engage with the first who offers, however big and strong he may be, then the society of the midshipmen's mess may become delightful to that boy, for the wish of his heart will be gratified. I believe this was Jack's case; he hath told me how, for a week or two, he fought every day; and how, at the termination of each encounter, he found reason to thank Aaron Fletcher for his tough-

3

ness and obstinacy, which had taught him useful lessons.   Further, there are tricks to be endured, such as stealing of a boy's breeches when he is dressing, so that he is late on deck, and is consequently mastheaded ; or the greasing of his head with tallow while he is asleep ; with many other nauseous jokes, all of which have to be borne with good-humor until an opportunity occurs of revenge ; or the little tyranny of one who, because he is a head taller, thinks he can do as he pleases ; one such did Jack fight every day—getting, to be sure, the worst of it—until the big fellow had no more stomach for the fight, and left his adversary in peace.   As for the gloom of his quarters, and their narrowness and discomfort, why, Jack had seen them often enough, and knew what to expect, and cared not two pins for them.   As for sea-sickness, Jack never felt it. The rough sea-fare he liked ; and as for the daily duty and the sharp discipline, these were part of the profession, and designed for the safety and government of some hundred lives and the accomplishment of the ship's purpose.   If a sailor would be happy, he must, I take it, acquire, as soon as possible, the feeling of association.   Everything has to be shared ; if he take on board with him and nourish the desire, common to all landsmen, of getting as much comfort for himself as he can seize, he will never be easy.   Comfort, I suppose, and ease of body, are served out on board a man-o'-war in rations and pannikins, like the rum.

Jack's good-luck began, as I have mentioned, with his first voyage ; that is to say, whatever good-fortune can come to one so young fell to him, as you shall see.

The *Lenox* sailed on December 5, 1747, and meeting with none of the enemy on her voyage, joined Admiral Knowles at Port Royal, in Jamaica, on February 8—a short passage, the ship being a fast sailer, and ably handled.

As this war took place when I was a child, coming happily to an end when I was but twelve years of age, I know little about it, save that my early recollections are all of activity in the yard, the going and coming of ships, the building and launching of ships, the hurry and the business of war.   There were some very fine engagements at sea, of which I know only one or two ; those, namely, in which Jack was engaged ; and there were some memorable actions fought on land, of which that of Dettingen was one. There are in every century so many wars; there are in every war so many actions, every one of which, in the eyes of those who have fought on the victorious side, and especially in the eyes of the admiral or general, is so memorable that it will remain forever in the history of the world as a feat of arms never to be forgotten. This vanity is like that of the poet, who thinks that for an ode to " Fame," or to " Victory," published in the *European* or the *Lady's Magazine*, he is covered with glory and crowned with an everlasting wreath of bays. One immortal victory is succeeded by another; one general causes his predecessor to be forgotten; one poem is followed by another; then both are suffered to repose between the leather binding of the volumes which contain them. It is only the work of the painter which lives on the walls for all men to admire in all ages to come.

I say, then, that whatever imperishable glory surrounds the names of those who conducted for the allies this war, I know of none except that which belongs to one squadron in the last year of the war. An account of it may be read in Mr. John Hill's *History of the British Navy*, itself compiled from the papers of the late Honorable Captain George Berkeley, R.N., which stops short at this chapter, the book having been published at the beginning of the next war. What I know of it is taken from the description of these affairs given me by Jack himself.

The *Lenox*, then, arrived at Port Royal on February 8, 1748. The captain was heartily welcomed by Admiral Knowles, who was on the point of sailing on an expedition from which the best was hoped. By the greatest exertions, the ship was provisioned in readiness to join, and the squadron—Governor Trelawny accompanying the admiral—left Port Royal on the 13th, with design to attack Santiago, or Saint Jago, the most important town and port of Cuba, next to Havana. The squadron was strengthened by a detachment of two hundred and forty men of the governor's regiment. The fleet was met with contrary winds, which were so long and persistent that the admiral resolved upon changing the plan of the expedition. It was therefore decided to make an attack upon Port Louis, on the south side of Hispaniola. Thither, therefore, the wind being favorable, they sailed, and arrived in good order. On the 8th of March, the ships being then almost within pistol-shot of the walls, the attack was commenced; the cannonade lasted three hours, at the end of which time the enemy's guns were silenced, and the governor proposed to capitulate. He sent an officer off with propositions, which the admiral refused, and sent back his own, giving an hour for consideration. Before the end of that time they were accepted, and the place was taken. "I believed," said Jack, telling me of this, his first action, "that every cannon-shot that struck the ship or flew through the rigging was going to knock my head off, not thinking that, by the time I heard the noise of it, the danger was over. Yet I was resolved to stand at my quarters, and do my duty as well as I could; but for the life of me I could not help ducking my head, till the gunner spied me, and found time to fetch me a clout on the head, saying, 'You fool, that cannon-ball was half a mile beyond the ship before you ducked. Hold up your head, and remember that, when it is knocked off, you will have no time to duck out of its way.' So, with that, I plucked up, and was comforted to see the men at the guns, none of them killed, and none of them ducking. So I was highly ashamed of myself, till they told me afterwards that, at the first engagement, most everybody ducks. As for the captain, he was on the quarter-deck, and scorned to show the least fear; and the men at their quarters only laughed, even when a shot struck the ship and fragments of the timbers went flying about. But it was fine to see how, one by one, we silenced the guns. Only I should like to see fighting at close quarters. This pounding with the big guns at long range is not to my taste."

There was some work for the boats as well, for the enemy set fire to one of their ships, and endeavored to send her alongside the admiral's ship; but boats were sent off, which towed her clear, and took possession of two more designed for the same purpose, though the enemy's musketry fired smartly on them all the time. Our loss in the whole action was only ten men killed, among whom were Captan Renton, of the *Stafford*, and Captain Cust, a volunteer, with sixty wounded. The loss of the enemy was a hundred and twenty-eight killed. The fort contained seventy-eight cannon and a vast quantity of ammunition and stores, the whole of which was taken possession of, and the fort blown up.

I dare say it was a small business, but it seemed a great one to the boy, who thus took part in an action for the first time.

This affair concluded, the admiral proceeded to put into execution his design upon St. Jago.

The attack, however, failed, because they found a chain across, with two large ships and two small ones, filled with combustibles, and ready to be set on fire at the first attempt to break the chain. This was mortifying, and added nothing to the admiral's reputation. But six months later it was Jack's good-fortune to take part in a spirited action with the Spanish squadron between Havana and Tortugas. It was in October, and, I believe, after the peace had been signed; but this they knew not. The Spanish fleet consisted of the same number of ships as our own, but larger, and with double the number of men. There was a court-martial afterwards, and the admiral was reprimanded for not shifting his flag when his own ship was disabled. Therefore the action is not one of those in which the country can take the most pride. But this had nothing to do with a young midshipman, and no one ever denied that the *Lenox*, for her part, was admirably fought and handled, seeing that when the *Cornwall*, the admiral's ship, was disabled, the *Lenox* had to sustain the fire of the whole of the squadron until the arrival of the *Canterbury* and the *Warwick*. At sundown the Spaniard began to retreat, but not before their great ship, the *Conquestador*, was taken. Admiral Knowles has been further reproached with not prosecuting the pursuit with greater vigor. However that may be, he fell in, two days afterwards, with the Spanish admiral's ship, the *Africa*, and blew her up. Whatever might have been our success, it cannot, therefore, be denied that we took two out of seven ships, and compelled the rest to run away. As for Jack, he had learned now to receive the enemy's broadsides without ducking. "But what amazed me most," he told us, " was that there was no shouting or crying among the men. They were all as cool as if they were firing a salute at Spithead. When a man was wounded and fell he was carried below, so there was not much of the groaning and shrieking that landsmen talk about. Why, those fellows of ours will have a leg sawn off and never groan. Whereas, if a man is killed, you can't expect him to groan afterwards. To be sure, I've never seen a fight with a boarding party. And I say, Luke, the first time you see a man killed, when he falls down in a heap on the deck, and his face turns quite white, and his arms and legs lying out any way, as if he didn't care what was going to happen, it makes you feel sick and dizzy. But the men only laugh, because every one takes his turn, and you can't escape the bullet that is bound to kill you. If it wasn't for knowing that nobody would be able to feel happy and work with a will while the shots are flying about. Luke, there's another thing " —here his voice dropped to a whisper—" there's a thing I never knew before nor suspected. There's cowardly captains, even in the king's navy; captains who won't crowd on the canvas in pursuit, and drop out of action, pretending to be disabled. They never told me that; not even Mr. Brinjes told me. And half-hearted captains. Why, if all they say is true, we should have been inside St. Jago, instead of sheering off after a broadside or two. But there's more brave captains than the other sort, and so you'll see when next we have a brush."

For the *Lenox*, with Admiral Knowles's squadron, had now returned, and the ship was paid off, and Jack had made his way home again, when you may be sure we killed the fatted calf and gave him welcome. He was gone on that voyage for the best part of two years, and was now fifteen years of age, and looked eighteen, being so big and strong. The sun and the wind had painted his cheeks a lively color, his hands were brown, his speech was rough, and his bearing was manly. Wonderful it was to see the confidence and the manliness of one so young, to say nothing of the pride he took in the exploits of his ship. These, we presently discovered, lost nothing in the telling. He brought home a most beautiful necklace of red coral, which had been found in the fort of Port Louis, belonging, no doubt, to one of the mulatto or half-caste women, who were both the slaves and the mistresses of the Spaniards in those parts. He showed it to me one day, and I expected he would give it to Castilla. Fortunately I told her nothing about it, and presently I saw it round the neck of Bess Westmoreland. It is so common at Deptford to see girls of her class decorated with gold chains, coral necklaces, jewelled brooches, and all kinds of finery (for a few days only, because they speedily send the things to London to be sold), that no one asked who had given the child an ornament so unsuitable to her position. As for

Castilla and myself, if Jack before he went away was going to be a hero, he was now actually become one; we were fully persuaded that when, at Port Louis, the boats towed off the fire-ship with the musket-balls spattering in the water, it must have been Jack who sat in the stern; and when the *Conquestador* surrendered it must have been in terror at the sight of this youthful conqueror, terrible with his sword in his hand; and when the *Africa* blew up, it was because the Spanish admiral perceived that he could not hope to contend any longer with this young sea-lion; and, considering the admiral's want of spirit, it was nothing but the presence of Jack that saved the fleet from disaster. I began to draw pictures, representing episodes in the three actions in which our hero had taken part, such as Jack repelling boarders, laying about him with such an intrepid air as commanded terror and admiration in all who beheld it. Behind him stood the British tars, ready to back him up with cutlass, pistol, and pike. Or another, in which I displayed the two ships at close quarters, with grappling-irons, and Jack leaping singly upon the enemy's deck, a pike in one hand and a cutlass in the other; and there was Jack laying the gun that was to hit the enemy between wind and water, and so sink her; he performed the operation with thoughtful face, the captain standing by, wrapped in admiration. They were wonderful pictures. Jack laughed at them, but did not deny that perhaps there might be truth in the subjects. I gave them to Castilla, who put them away. She hath since assured me that she hath kept them out of regard for the hand which drew them. That is doubtless true, since she says so. But I think there must have been, at the same time, some admiration for the hero of those designs.

I do not describe the joy with which the admiral received the boy, nor the pleasure with which he listened to his account of the actions he had witnessed. As for the manner in which Jack sought out Mr. Brinjes, everybody knows the contempt with which the combatant branch regards the civil branch, though the surgeon's mate, by order of the navy office, is considered a gentleman, and messes with the midshipmen, so that there was condescension in a midshipman visiting an apothecary. Yet, as Mr. Brinjes was an old friend, Jack could not but treat him with kindness, mingled with superiority. More-

over, he had by this time himself visited the places of which
Mr. Brinjes loved most to speak.   He had seen the negroes of
Port Royal and Spanish Town, and those of Bridgetown, Barbadoes ; and of St. Kitt's ; though as yet he had never seen the
Guinea coast.   One is not afloat for nearly two years without
learning and hearing things.   So that for every tale which Mr.
Brinjes had to tell Jack had now half a dozen.   And I remarked
that, like the apothecary, Jack loved to figure as the hero in his
own stories.   This is a temptation to which men are all liable,
and especially sailors ; because, I suppose, they are looked upon
by the world as certain to have had adventures ; and there is
no man in Greenwich Hospital who has never been wrecked,
or cast away, or been attacked by savages and by sharks, or
had a brush with pirates.

As regards the quality of these stories and the art of making
and telling them, if there is any art in so simple a thing as the
telling of a sailor's yarn, it must be owned that the apothecary
showed himself the superior.   For it is required of such a tale
that there must be fighting in it, with much bloodshed, narrow
escapes, starving in boats, pirates, and desert islands.   All of
these were supplied by Mr. Brinjes, whereas poor Jack had as
yet nothing but his three battles.   Bess, you may be sure,
came to sit with us in the room behind the shop, and to hear
Jack talk.   She sat in the window-seat, her hands folded in her
lap, gazing at her hero all the time, and speaking not a word
save when Mr. Brinjes or I ventured to interrupt the flow of
Jack's manly conversation.

Two days after Jack returned the promised fight with Aaron
Fletcher came off in my presence and that of Bess, who, I believe, was the chief instigator of the combat, having a vehement desire to see Aaron punished for certain disrespectful
words spoken in Jack's absence.

He was a little older than his adversary, and now bigger of
frame, and as hard as was to be expected of a young man who
spent his days and nights chiefly in a fishing-smack—he called
it a fishing-smack—between Ramsgate, or Leigh, in Essex, and
the coast of Holland or France.

They fought in the gardens behind the Stowage.   It is beneath the dignity of history to describe an encounter with fists
between two boys.   Sufficient it is to say that Jack took off

his coat laughing, and the other scowling; that they fought for
an hour, with some vicissitudes; Aaron, so to speak, carrying
heavier metal, but Jack handling his guns with more dexterity;
that Bess stood by, clapping her hands when Jack's fist went
home, and taunting Aaron when he fell, which made both combatants the fiercer; that, finally, Aaron was disabled, and had
to retire from the conflict by the dislocation of a finger, which
gave Jack the victory.   But both were so mauled and bruised,
their faces so covered with blood and swollen, that the battle
must have ended in neither being able to see.

"I'll fight you again—and again after that," said Aaron,
mopping his face, with savage looks.

What did they fight for?   Well, one was a gentleman and
the other a mechanic; one was a midshipman in the king's service, and the other was a smuggler.   Surely these things were
enough.   If you want more, remember that, even at sixteen, a
youngster may fall in love and be jealous.   Aaron was already
in love with the black eyes of Bess, who was now nearly twelve,
but like a Spanish girl in this respect, that at twelve she might
have passed for fifteen at least.   And Bess, who would have
none of him, thought of nobody but our handsome Jack.

CHAPTER VI.

THE "COUNTESS OF DORSET."

WITH the return of the fleets and the signing of the Peace
of Aix-la-Chapelle came a great reduction of the naval estimates, which, in the year 1750, provided for no more than ten
thousand men instead of fifty thousand.   This step, although
it returned thousands of men to the merchant service, the coast
service, the colliers, the fishing trade, and the river, sent back
more than were wanted, so there was great distress with men
out of work all round the coast, and a large increase of smuggling.   Many regiments of marines were disbanded at the same
time; and so men who, having been long engaged in active
service, had lost the arts of peace and forgotten their former
trades, were thrown upon the country seeking employment, and,
for the most part, finding none.   Again, from the dock-yards
    3*

were dismissed an immense number of artificers, such as skilled shipwrights, carpenters, figure-head carvers, painters, decorators, and the like, besides a host of unskilled laborers, who had been receiving good wages, and now found themselves without work, and for the most part without money. Add to this that the trade of those who get their living out of the ships and the sailors and by navy contracts was suddenly shrunk into nothing, like a bladder which is pricked, and you will understand why, though the country breathed and the merchants of London and Bristol rejoiced, the seaports and dock-yard towns groaned and lamented. As for the shipwrights, there is always employment for some in one or other of the private building-yards, such as Pett's or Taylor's, or in the repairing-docks, as the Acorn and the Lavender; but what are these, even when working their utmost, compared with the king's yards and their continual demand in time of war? It is true that a large number of disbanded soldiers, marines, and artificers received grants of land in Nova Scotia, and were transported thither. But there are not many in proportion to the whole number who can suddenly become farmers, and who fear not the cold of that inhospitable place. As for the unfortunate sailors, there were, to be sure, always new hands wanted for the merchant-ships; but a man cannot look to get a berth as soon as he desires, and other work they can do none. No one ever heard of a sailor following the plough, or becoming a shoemaker, or working in a carpenter's shop. It seems as if keeping the watch, bending the sails, and working the guns make a man unfit for other kinds of work. The disbanded soldier may turn his hand to anything, but not the sailor. So that when his pay and prize-money are all spent —which never takes the honest fellow long, so ready is the assistance of his friends—he has nothing to do but to lean against the posts or to stand about the river-side, waiting for a chance. Often for a lodging he is reduced to sleeping on the bulks in the open street, and for his food to take whatever may be given him by the charity of his fellows. And at last, where this fails, if he cannot ship even on a hoy or a hay-barge, what wonder if he takes to running a fishing-smack over to France for brandy? And then one hears of a desperate affray with the king's officers on the Sussex coast; and these are the times when the roads become infested with footpads—men driven desperate by pov-

" Bess stood by, clapping her hands when Jack's fist went home."

erty, who might have remained honest fellows had they been
kept to their colors or to their ships; and in the houses of
Deptford, where there had been plenty, and the laughter of little children, were now crying women and hungry babes, with
the dreadful temptations of poverty and hunger. I am sure
there is no more terrible temptation than this; let us never
cease, rich and poor together, to pray in the words commanded,
"Give us this day our daily bread."

There are some who think that the custom of disbanding the
troops and paying off the men is an evil one, because, they
argue, first, if you would secure peace, be prepared for war, as
is shown in lively fashion by the fable of Æsop; and if you
are always ready to fight, the enemy will be less ready to give
provocation; and next, a better plan, if the forces must be reduced, would be to diminish them gradually, by suffering those
to go who wished, and enlisting no more, so that speedily and
without injustice an establishment on a peace footing could be
secured. But in the navy office prudent counsels have never
yet prevailed (I say this not of my own wisdom, but from general consent of those who have had opportunity of studying
things naval), and I suppose will not, until some great calamity
befall our country, and make us call for neither Whig nor Tory,
but for those who desire the greatness and the prosperity of
these islands.

Sad indeed was the case of the younger officers—the midshipmen like Jack — who had little interest, and now feared
that they might never become lieutenants. The more choking
it was because everybody had been looking for a long war,
with plenty of prize-money and quick promotion. And now,
in the estimation of many, not only was peace signed, but it
was assured, and would be lasting; because, these sagacious
politicians of the coffee-house asked, why should France wish
to make war again, having received not only so severe a lesson,
but also terms of peace far more honorable than she could have
expected? The events of the next few years have shown very
plainly how anxious France has been to keep her word and to
maintain peace. Perhaps, now that we have at last happily
turned her out of Canada and the East Indies, and reduced her
power in the West Indies, her turbulence may abate for a time.
But one knows not; we are nearing the end of the eighteenth

century, and we cannot tell what may happen before that end arrives. However, the merchant adventurer naturally desires peace, and therefore is ready to prophesy that peace will be lasting, because we are always glad to believe what we desire. I have heard that the activity of the French yards was never relaxed during these years of peace; certainly they never commenced any war with more magnificent fleets than those which they sent to sea a few years later, in the year 1756.

As for Jack, after being ashore for two or three months, and finding no prospect of employment, he began to hang his head and to be despondent, longing to be afloat again, and seeing no chance. In truth, there was little in a landsman's life that he cared for, being, at this period, not much better than a sea-cub, a species of animal little loved by any except those who know that he will grow into a lion. That is to say, he took no joy in reading, unless it was the description of a sea action—always, to my thinking, tedious to read. Jack, who did not think so, used to illustrate the history with the aid of walnuts placed in position, and showing, to his imagination, better than any drawing, how the fight was conducted. The gentle arts of poetry, music, painting, and dancing had no charms for him. He liked not the society of ladies, old or young, nor the polite conversation which pleases them; and as yet he had not felt the passion of love. I believe he was set against the sex by Mr. Brinjes, who loved no woman except such as had a black and shining skin, and lived somewhere about Old Calabar. As for Bess, she was the most congenial companion to him at this time, because she never tired of listening to his talk about the sea, and what he was going to do. But as for love, he had none for her at this time. Of this I am assured.

Everybody has heard of the *Countess of Dorset;* how she set sail in order to navigate the great Pacific Ocean, and never returned; and how for many years nothing was known of her fate any more than is known of the fate of Sir Cloudesley Shovel. It is matter for regret that the single officer who was saved out of that wreck and survived the incredible sufferings which followed should not have been able to narrate in lively and moving fashion the particulars of this grievous disaster. Surely a history as instructive as that of Commodore Anson might be made of this voyage. But now, I suppose, it will never be written.

Soon after the peace, the *Countess of Dorset*, which was lying up in ordinary, was fitted out in Deptford Yard. She carried an armament of forty-four guns, and was a frigate well reported as a sailer and for behaving well in heavy weather; ships being, as is well known, capricious in this respect; so that you may construct two vessels of exactly the same measurements, on the same lines, and yet, while one is easily handled and is obedient to her helm, the other shall be lubberly and difficult to steer; and one shall sail fast and the other slow: so that when any vessel is launched it is impossible to tell beforehand what she will be like, and one cannot judge by the behavior of a sister ship. As for her destination, it was as yet unknown; but some thought she was to form part of the Jamaica fleet.

One afternoon, however, the admiral called Jack, and held a serious conversation with him.

"Thou art now, my lad," he said, "truly becalmed and in the Doldrums; or, worse still, in a leeward tide, and drifting on the rocks. In a word, if a berth be not found before long, thou mayst give up all further hopes of the king's navy. I am sorry for thee, lad. There is John Company, to be sure; they have a hundred vessels, they say; but their commanders are fond of their ease; and, besides, without interest in the India House, how can one hope for promotion? It would grieve me to see thee mate of a merchantman. Yet, what help?"

"I can ship as an able seaman, sir, as soon as I am old enough."

"Ay! ay! But we must hope for something better. Listen, my boy. I have this morning conversed with the commissioner of the yard, Captain Petherick, who has imparted to me a secret. The *Countess of Dorset* is bound for a cruise in the Southern Seas. I have, therefore, sent an application in thy name to the navy office. Because, Jack, though it is not the service I could have wished for thee, yet, seeing that there is little chance of anything better, we must e'en make the best of it, and if we get thee billeted on her as midshipman, we shall be fortunate. The voyage will be long and tedious. There will be no fighting, unless, which I doubt, the captain judges it well to seek out and capture the Manila galleon. They say there are islands out there filled with black pirates and cannibals, but I never heard of any honor to be obtained in fighting these poor devils. When you have gotten across the Pacific Ocean, there may be engagements with Chinese and Malay fellows. They have stink-pots and poisoned arrows. You will have to fight them at close quarters with pike and cutlass and boiling pitch, as well as with guns. But where is the glory of such an action compared with an engagement, yard-arm to yard-arm, with a Frenchman or a Spaniard of equal weight?"

"I should like to go, sir," said Jack.

"The Lord knows," continued the admiral, "when you would come back again. And meantime, while you and your company were cruising in unknown waters, another war might break out, and you would lose your chance, which, indeed, would be the devil."

"But if no war break out, then my chance may be lost the other way."

"It would so, Jack. Perhaps we might get thee a berth— but of midshipmen there are plenty, and of ships in commission there are few. Yet the commissioner tells me they have secret intelligence that the French are busy in Toulon and Rochelle. What doth this mean if peace is to continue? And complaints have been received from New England of infractions by the French. Is this a sign of peace? However, we know not. The king grows old; the young prince is reported to be of a pacific disposition—but talking is vain."

The admiral's application proved successful. Jack was appointed to the *Countess of Dorset*.

When Mr. Brinjes heard of this appointment and the sailing orders of the ship, he showed a strange emotion.

"What?" he asked. "Thou too art going to the South Seas, Jack? Why, it may be that the ship—but I know not— 'tis unlikely, or—which I doubt. Thou art young yet, Jack; but if I tell thee my secret, though without imparting, yet, the latitude and longitude, while in those seas, thinking of what I shall tell thee, and mindful of the future, thou mayst take observations, and when the ship comes home we will talk further of the matter. For look ye, my boy, I am sure that I shall not die before I have seen again that place—but wait until I have told thee. What? You think I am but a poor apothecary admitted to sit among gentlemen because I can cure their gout for them, and feared by the common sort because I can bring rheumatism upon them? You shall see. You think I have nothing but the few guineas in my till. Why, then, listen, and keep the secret for me; though, if all the world knew, no one would be one whit the for'arder. Yet keep the secret; and now, boy, reach me down the chart."

CHAPTER VII.

MR. BRINJES CONCLUDES THE STORY OF HIS VOYAGE.

THOSE who will read this history through, and then consider the various parts of it, will not fail to be amazed with the manner in which Jack was prepared for the fulfilment of his fate and for the close of his life (if that hath yet happened) by a crowd of circumstances which seem to have indicated it and led him irresistibly. For, first, it was permitted to him—a rare thing—to make the acquaintance of two who had voyaged upon the South Seas—I mean as officers, and of the better sort; for of those who had set foot on Juan Fernandez, fought the Creolian Spaniards at Payta, Guayaquil, and Panama, and insulted their settlements in the Philippine Islands, there were many in Greenwich Hospital, and the Trinity Almshouses, of Deptford. Of these two, one, the apothecary, would relate his adventures in a moving manner, so as to make a boy's cheek burn and his pulses beat. The other, it is true, was a phlegmatic man, but there were parts even of his narrative—as, for example, when the castaways built a crazy boat, thirty feet long, and put to sea only forty strong, yet resolved to attack the first Spanish vessel they sighted, though they had but three cutlasses and half a dozen muskets and a small cannon, for which there was no stand, so that it had to be fired from the deck; and for all their provision nothing but stinking conger-eel, dried in the sun, and one cask of water, fitted with a musket barrel, by which each man drank in turn—I say that there were parts of his narrative which would fire the boy, and make his eyes bright. For the hearing of such sufferings only stimulates a boy who is intended by nature for a sailor. Next, there were the books

lent to him by Captain Petherick, all of voyages, especially in
Oceanus, Australis, and Magellanica. And, thirdly, he was,
while yet a boy, to sail across the great Pacific Ocean, which is
said to fill those who have once voyaged on its waters with a
strange love and desire to return thither, if only to meet with
shipwreck and starvation. What follows, however, was the
story which Mr. Brinjes now completed—a strange story, truly.

"I told you," he began, "that we were driven off our course
north of the latitude in which we hoped to sight the great Manilla ship. She carried I know not how many cannon, and I
know not how many hundreds of men. But we were a hundred
and twenty strong, all well-armed, resolute men, and they were
Creolian Spaniards, a cowardly crew, who, when they have fired
their small-arms, can do no more, and when the English lads
board the craft, fall to bawling for quarter, and strike their flag.
There is but one rule in these waters; it is to attack the Spanish flag whenever you find it, and to look for no resistance once
you come to close quarters, unless the officers, which sometimes
happens, are French; then they will fight. Now mark what
happened to us. The same tempest which drove us so far
north caught the Manilla ship as well, of which we were in
search, and drove her also out of her course, treating her even
more roughly than ourselves. We sighted her one morning at
daybreak. There could be no doubt about her; there are not
many ships of her build in the North Pacific. As soon as we
were near enough to make her out, all hands were called to
quarters, and we prepared for action with joyful hearts, loading
the guns and small-arms, and sharpening cutlasses and pikes.
As we drew nearer, and the daylight stronger, the sea being
now quite smooth, save for a gentle swell, we perceived a
strange thing, namely, that her mainmast and her foremast were
gone by the board, only her mizzen standing; her bows and
bulwarks were stove in, and her rudder was lost. She was drifting about upon the water, helpless as a log. She had no sails
set; most of her rigging was cut away. We fired a shot by
way of signal, but received no reply; then we drew nearer. Not
a man could be seen. Were they all hiding down below, or
were they hatching some treachery? We ranged presently
alongside, cautiously standing to our guns, and expecting nothing less than a broadside. But the guns, on the upper deck

at least, were not manned, nor was there a soul to be seen, or
the least sign of life. However, our boarding party leaped
aboard with a shout, expecting some trick of the enemy. Boys,
there was not a man left in all that great ship. How they got
off—by what boats or on what raft—I know not, nor did I ever
learn. She was deserted; she was floating about those lonely
seas, a great treasure-ship, with all her treasure still on board.
Why, she was not ours by right of conquest; she was ours by
the law of the sea, because she was a derelict. We were pirates,
if you please, or rovers, or adventurers. Whatever we were,
that ship was our own because we picked her up."

"What!" cried Jack. "No fighting?"

"None, my lad. On that voyage there was no fighting with
the Spaniards from beginning to end. As for this great inheritance, into which we came without a question or a blow, 'twas
all left undisturbed on board with the precious cargo of which
it formed a part. Strange it was to walk 'tween decks and see
them filled with the bales of silks, the spices, the rich stuffs,
that the galleon was carrying to Acapulco. There was also a
beautiful collection of small-arms, and swords with jewelled
hilts, pistols with carved stocks, brass carronades, and such
carved work in wood, for the staterooms and the captain's cabin, as one could sell in London for its weight in silver at least.
There was also a great quantity of wine, which was seasonable,
for our spirits were well-nigh drunk out, and there was no prob-
ability of our getting more. We took all the wine and the arms,
and as much of the silks and embroidered stuff as every man
pleased; so that we went about as fine as so many princes, with
purple and crimson sashes. The spices we mostly left on the
ship; but the powder we took out of her, and all her provisions.
And then we found the treasure. It was packed in small iron-
bound chests, in gold pieces of eight and other coins, worth, as
near as I could calculate, judging from the weight, about two
hundred and fifty thousand pounds of our money. Think of
two hundred and fifty thousand pounds, to be divided among a
crew of simple rovers! When we first found this treasure, and
understood how much it was worth—namely, allowing eight
shares for the captain and eighteen for the officers, nearly two
thousand pounds apiece for every man—we were amazed at our
wonderful fortune, and looked at each other like stuck pigs.

However, we got the boxes on board, and laid them safe in the
captain's cabin, and set fire to the galleon, which blazed furiously, and presently blew up, and so an end of her. And as for
us, we sailed away, and began to feast and to drink, and to make
merry. And for the first few hours I think there was never
so happy a crew in the world."

"Well," said Jack, "if prize-money were all they wanted.
But to have no fighting with the Spaniards—why, one would
as lief take the money out of a till."

"There was a great deal of fighting. I said only that there
was no fighting with the Spaniard."

"What other fight was there, then?"

"That evening we made a great feast on deck, all the ship's
company sitting down together to as noble a salmagundy,
onions being still plentiful, as one would wish to see. And
with the salmagundy—which is sailor's food, truly, yet I want
no other as long as I live, unless it be lobscouse and sea-pie—
we drank the finest wine, designed for his excellency the gov-
ernor-general of the Manillas, that was ever drawn from cask.
Such wine one may never hope to taste again. What? Topers
who drink strong black port and Jamaica rum (which yet I
love), what know they of the soft and luscious drink these
papistical Spaniards enjoy daily, sitting in their cool and shady
houses, while the negroes and the Indians work for them in the
sun? But when the drink got into us, the quarrelling began.
When rovers quarrel, they fight. The men were light-headed,
to begin with, thinking of their great windfall; and the Spanish wine is heady when you have taken much more than a
quart or two, and they very soon began to quarrel over the division of the money. For some wanted to tear up the articles,
whereby the captain took eight shares and the officers eighteen,
and all to share and share alike. And then swords were drawn
and pistols cocked; and those of us who had kept reasonably
sober went hastily below. Among these were the first and
second mates, and the bo's'n, and myself. But the captain was
mad with drink. We kept below, while the trampling and the
fighting went on all night long, for they stopped only to drink,
and then fought again like so many devils, not caring with
whom they fought, still less for what cause. The men were
resolute fellows, but they never showed half so much courage

" They stopped only to drink, and then fought again like so many devils."

against the enemy as they did against each other; and those who had been in the morning the heartiest friends and brothers were at night murdering each other with the utmost ferocity.

"They stopped at last; not because they were appeased, but because they were tired; and all slept on deck, some lying across the dead and wounded. It was a strange sight when we ventured on deck, the work of fighting being over, and saw them in the moonlight all lying about among the cannon, mostly in the waist, dead and living together, the blood still running out of the scuppers. The man at the helm was killed, and lying over his wheel. There was no watch; there were no lights; all sails were set, and the ship was swiftly sailing over the smooth waters with no one to look out, no lights in the bows, and no one to care whether we struck on a rock or not. There were thirty wounded men, whom we carried below and dressed their wounds; but fifteen of them died, their blood being heated by the wine and the salt provisions.

"At sunrise most of the men woke up and shook off their drunkenness, and ashamed they were to find the captain and twenty men killed by the night's quarrel. First they sat and looked at each other, sorry and angry. Then they took consolation, thinking there were still enough men to navigate the ship, and fight her, if necessary; and then some one whispered that there were fewer by twenty to share the treasure.

"So we threw the bodies overboard without any funeral service, and the men resolved to quarrel no more, and all shook hands together.

"I suppose the thought of the money filled all the men's minds, because in the afternoon, when the drinking began again, the quarrelling began. The captain being dead, they could no longer quarrel over his eight shares; but the officers were left, and they began about their shares. Now I am sorry to say that both mates, instead of running down below again with the bo's'n and me, stayed on deck and took part in the quarrel. That was a worse night than the other, because it began earlier. Ten more were killed that night, and a great many wounded. What was worse, the morning brought no cessation, but they fought all day long, and for three days and three nights, drinking all the time like devils, as if they desired that as many should be killed as possible, and as few left to divide the treasure.   In the end, when they desisted, we were reduced to sixty men, most of whom had wounds of some kind, and some died afterwards of fever, so that we numbered no more than fifty. I suppose that such a thing hath never before happened, that a ship for four days and four nights should sail any course she pleased, being without a steersman or a captain or a watch, having all sails set, and yawing about as she pleased, just as the breeze changed, and so sailing all the time before the wind.   It was surely a miracle that we were not all cast away and destroyed.   At last, however, the men grew tired and sobered, frightened by the deaths of so many, and now awakened to the new danger that if we met the Spaniard we might not be able to fight him nor to protect our huge treasure.

" So we held a serious council.   First, we were now all rich men, and it behooved us to think of getting home safely with our money, and to run no risks more than we could help, and not to go in search of other ships, but to keep out of the enemy's way.

" Did one ever hear before of an English crew keeping out of the Spaniard's way ?   But the treasure made cowards of us all.   Every man valued his own skin because he was now the owner of so much wealth.   Why, what had been before the fighting a share worth two thousand, was now worth four at least.   Not a man among us but was worth four thousand pounds and more.   Even if we had sighted another galleon, I doubt whether we should have ventured to attack her.   And the men grew moody and scowling, every one sitting apart, counting his gains and wishing his shipmates dead, so that his own share should be greater.   Never was a ship's crew fuller of murderous thoughts and evil jealousies.   Even the wounded men dying of fever could not die quietly, but must shriek and cry out for life, because they were now all made men."

" Better have tossed the treasure overboard," said Jack.

" As for our course, we had now sailed a good bit to the south, but we knew not and we never knew where we were. Look at the chart.   Here is the island of Donna Maria Laxara. We were driven north from that island, and we presently sailed south, no man regarding the navigation.   The latitude I was able to calculate ; but as for the longitude, that was lost, and

we knew not how to recover it, there being no one on board
except myself who could so much as read.

"After our council, however, we appointed watches, and attended somewhat to the sailing, keeping her course south, in
hopes of fetching Juan Fernandez or Masa Fuera. But, lord!
we were hundreds of miles to the west, though we knew it not;
and as for Juan Fernandez, we should none of us ever see that
island again. So we sailed day after day, but slowly, because
the winds were light. The sun now grew hot; we were within the
tropics. The men had somewhat recovered their spirits, and
bragged what they would do when we got home, and how they
would fling the money about. Some were for Kingston, but
some for Portsmouth; and I have always felt compassion for
the girls of Point that they never had the spending of this great
haul. For my own part, I always knew that something was
going to happen, for surely such a crew of murderers would
never be suffered to get safely to port with so much wealth.

"The first thing that happened was that we were becalmed.
I know not where, but I think somewhere hereabouts." Mr.
Brinjes pointed to a spot near the middle of the Pacific, far
from any other track. "We were becalmed so long that we
drank out all the Spaniard's wine, and now had nothing to
drink except water, and that so long in the casks that it was, so
to speak, rusty. Also, we soon found that we had not a great
quantity of provisions left; and the scurvy showed itself with
the Lobillo, of which we lost two or three men. And now, if
there was no more fighting, there was no more singing and
making merry. The men amused themselves with gambling:
some of them played away all their shares, but presently won
them back, and then lost them again; or they passed the days,
which were tedious, in fishing for sharks—the sea was full of
them; sometimes they killed them for food, but one soon gets
tired of eating shark; sometimes they played with them, for
they would catch two, and put out the eyes of one, and tie their
tails together, and so drop them into the sea, when it was pretty
to see them pull different ways, and fight and bite at each
other, just like Christians. Or they would catch one and tie a
plank to his tail, so that he could not dive under water or swim
away without dragging the plank with him, and so went mad,
and lashed the water in his rage. And strange things hap-

pened. One day, while we were still becalmed, the needle began to turn all ways, as if the witches had got hold of it—the
Jamaica Obeah men know that secret—and another day the sky
turned violet-color with green clouds, very terrifying, and in the
night the sea was a blaze of light, so that we were all alarmed,
and one young fellow went mad, and cried out that the Day of
Judgment was come, and called upon the sea to hide him from
the face of an offended God, and so jumped overboard and was
drowned. I think we must have been becalmed for six weeks.
At last, however, a breeze sprung up from the nor'west, and so
we continued our course, if that can be called a course which
was sailing blindly, on an unknown sea.

"Jack," Mr. Brinjes cried, "it will be thy lot—wherefore I
tell thee this history—to cruise upon these waters. Not upon
the course which the Spaniards take, but west and south of
their route. There wilt thou meet, as we did, with strange and
beautiful islands filled with kindly people, who paddle in canoes
and swim like fishes, and hold all things in common, and live
naked. In those latitudes it is always summer all the year
round, with warm, balmy air; and nobody heeds the time, and
there are always rich fruits to eat and delightful fish to catch.
They have no religion, and therefore are not afraid; they have
no knowledge of the ten commandments, and therefore know
not the nature of sin, and have no conscience to trouble them;
they have learned nothing of any future world, and therefore
are not anxious; they have no property, and therefore know
not envy; they have no diseases, except the incurable disease
of age; although their lives are happy, they fear not death,
upon which they never think; they neither murder nor rob.
What is our modern civilization, what is the politeness of the
age, compared with such happiness as theirs? What is there
a man can hope for better than warmth and plenty, the love of
women and the friendship of men, with constant health, sunshine, and joy. Do they murder each other? Do they fight
duels with each other? Do they gamble away their fortunes?
Do they steal and rob? Do they entice away another's wife?
Are they clapped into prison for debt, and kept there until they
die? Are they hanged for forging, coining, and shoplifting?
Are they flogged at the cart-wheel for anything they do? Are
they made to work all day so that another man may grow rich?

Are they teased with wars? Must they be starved so that
priests may get fat? Do they go in misery and anxiety all
their days for fear of the Bottomless Pit?" Mr. Brinjes enu-
merated many other things, which are not the blessings of civilization, yet exist among us, and not among these savages.
"Why, for the mere joy of living among this people, and
breathing their soft air, our men forgot even their great treasure and their jealousies, and became, as it were, foolish; they
quarrelled no longer; they rejoiced to go ashore and court the
friendship of these soft savages, and to give them beads, knives,
fish-hooks, or any little thing, in return for which the people
gave them everything they had; for a string of beads or a
piece of bright-colored silk they would bring out all they possessed; for a bottle of rum they would, I verily believe, have
sold their island. Ah!" Mr. Brinjes heaved a deep sigh.
"I have known true happiness on the African coast; but there
the air is hotter, and men's passions are fiercer—well, I love the
fierce passion and the temperament which breaks suddenly into
flame; but I have never seen or heard, anywhere, of any place
where the folk are so gentle as in these seas, and life is so
easy and so sweet. Heaven keep them long from the accursed
Spaniard!

"And as for wonders, I have seen strange things, indeed,
which men would not believe. Boys, I do not lie: I have seen
bats as big as rabbits, and terrible great serpents which hang
from the trees head downward, and have power by their
breath — I know not how — by their breath alone, to draw
wild beasts—nay, and man as well—towards them, and so to
break their bones and devour them; calamaries, or squids,
are there with arms ninety feet long—many have seen them,
and avow the truth — which can clutch a whole ship and
drag it under water; there are springs of water which have
virtue to turn fish into stones; there are flying cats and women-
fish—yea, fish with heads and breasts like unto women, and
tails like the mermaids'; there are shell-fish big enough, each
one, to dine a boat's crew, and yet leave meat to spare; there
are birds' nests so big that six men cannot fathom one; there
are beautiful lizards, of all colors, as big as calves. Am I lying
to you? No, boys. There was an island where we gathered a
pannier of earth for the cook's galley, to lay under his fire.

Would you believe that six months afterwards we found a bar
of gold beneath it, melted out of this little bucketful of earth?
But we could never find that island again.   As for the people,
the men mostly go naked, or nearly naked, and the women have
a kind of petticoat, made sometimes of feathers and sometimes of
skins, and they have hair so long that it trails upon the ground;
their language is a jargon that no one can understand; and if
they worship anything, which I doubt, they worship wooden
images.   Tasman found some of these islands, but he has never
been where I have been.   No living man—the rest being dead—
has been where I have been.   Tell me not of Captain Shelvocke!   He only followed the Spaniard's track.

"We cruised about contentedly, leading a life like that of
King Solomon himself, among these islands—how long, I know
not, for we stayed sometimes for whole months off one island.
Perhaps it was fifty years, but I think it was no more than two
or three.   There was no more talk of the treasure.   Some of
our crew died; some refused to leave the islands, even for their
share of the treasure, and preferred a black wife and a life of
ease under a warm sun, with palm-wine and pandang (which is
their kind of food), to any more dangers upon the water.   So
at length, out of our company of a hundred and twenty, there
were but five-and-twenty left among whom to divide the great
sum of money.   This would give ten thousand pieces each.
But by this time, the ship—poor thing—was fallen into disrepair, and most of our stores were now expended, so that
what with rotten cordage, which would hardly hold a sail, and
a leak which she had sprung somewhere, which gained daily,
and planks now so soft that you could put a knife into them
as into a rotten apple, and her bottom covered with green weeds,
like a ditch beside a hedge-row at home, I, for one, doubted
whether she would hold together at all if bad weather came.
But in these islands we never found any bad weather.

" By this time all our clothes were worn out.   Stockings and
shoes we had none, but no one wanted them.   For coat and
shirt and all, we had the bales of silk which we found on the
galleon; and let me tell you that, in a warm climate, there is no
wear like silk, being both soft and cool.   We had suffered our
beards to grow; we had left off carrying arms, and nobody
quarrelled or fought.   Our provisions were long since gone,

but we had palm-wine, such as the islanders make, and pandang, and we were dexterous at fishing. If we left one island and sailed to another, it was only for the sake of change, for sailors are always a restless folk; and we thought of nothing but to continue the joyful, easy, and happy life that we were leading.

"It was I, there being no officers left, who broke up this contentment, and called the men together to speak seriously. I pointed out to them very earnestly that we must resolve, and that immediately, whether we would settle upon some friendly island and break up the old ship, or whether we would without more delay attempt the voyage home. I told them that we were all rich men, and could take our ease for life, if only we succeeded in getting home; but that we had a leaky and crazy ship, with rotten cordage, worm-eaten planks, and foul bottom, and that we must first put her in some kind of repair before we could think of getting round Cape Horn, and if we did not speedily attempt these repairs the poor old barky would founder beneath us. The men lazily replied that they cared nothing whether the ship fell to pieces or no, and were content to live forever upon one of these islands among the blacks, of whose soft manner of life they were enamoured, and wanted no more fighting or tempests. Such softness stealeth over the souls of all who dwell in these latitudes. This is the reason why the Creolian Spaniard—he of Mexico, Cuba, or Acapulco— is so poor a creature as compared with the Englishman, for the heat and softness of the air have sapped his courage and made him a coward. One or two among us, however, having still something left of courage, and some recollection of home, persuaded them to consent that we should, when we could find a convenient place, endeavor to heel the ship over and scrape her, stop the leak, if we could, and make her ship-shape for rougher weather.

"A few days afterwards we came to a small archipelago, or collection of small islands. They were not the coral islands, which lie low, and are surrounded by a reef of coral, but were all like hill-tops, rising sheer and steep out of the water, green and wooded to the top, and apparently uninhabited. In one of these we found a curious natural dock or basin, deep and narrow, for all the world like the Greenland Dock at Redriffe, and as suitable for our purpose as if we had made it ourselves.

4

Here we resolved to make our dock-yard, and to begin by heel-
ing over the ship to get at her bottom.   Wherefore, in case of
accident, it was first agreed that we should put the treasure
ashore in the only boat we possessed, the great storm having
stove in the others.   We lowered the boxes, and put in the
boat five men, of whom I was one, with intent to row ashore,
lay the gold in some safe place, and then return to tow the
ship into this creek, or rocky natural dock.   So we put off,
thinking no danger, and rowed to land.

"Now mark what happened.   The ship was lying, when we
left her, in smooth water, all sails furled.   There was no wind,
not a breath of air; if we had dropped our kedge, which we
could not, because there was no bottom, the ship would have
ridden anchor apeak.   The time of day was afternoon, when
air and water are at their stillest; and she was in a kind of
channel or narrow sea, with these islands all around, which I
should say were quite desolate and uninhabited, yet full of
trees and fruits, with plenty of fresh water.   We had no more
than the length of a furlong to row, the water being deep and
the shore of our island shelving steep down into the sea.   We
landed, hauled up the boat for fear of accident, and began to
carry ashore the boxes, in order to lay them together under the
trees.   You think, perhaps, that a treasure of two hundred and
fifty thousand pieces of eight is a mighty great matter.   So it
is, yet they may all be stowed in a few small boxes.   We laid
them down, then, and left them (no one being on the island
except ourselves) at the foot of a palm.

"And there, my lads," Mr. Brinjes added, slowly—"there
they are to this day.   For sure and certain I am that no ship
hath been among these islands since.   And I know that I
could find the place again."

"Why did you leave the treasure there?"

"You shall hear.   When we got down to the shore again, a
strange thing — nay, a miracle — had happened.   The ship,
which we left, as I said, only a furlong from the land, was now
—as near as we could guess—two miles.   She had none of her
canvas spread; there was no breeze to speak of, and yet she
was slipping through the water away from us at six knots an
hour, as near as we could guess.   Wonderful it was to see a
ship, without wind or sails, moving so fast.   Whether it was

witchcraft — which I sometimes think — or a strong current,
which may have been the cause, I cannot tell; but our ship
had slipped away, and left us behind. We rowed after her;
but a little boat, with one pair of oars, cannot overtake a vessel
going six knots an hour, with two miles and more to overtake.
Then we thought to make the crew put the ship about, if they
could. We shouted and made signals; but, so far as we could
discern, no one on board noticed. Perhaps the men were all
bewitched, as, I think, must have happened; perhaps they were
drinking or sleeping, because in those days they generally spent
the time in sleep whenever they were not drinking or fishing.
She seemed to move faster and faster, and the evening was
coming on. The sun got low; we had only time to row ashore
before the darkness was upon us; and the last we saw of the
poor old ship was the sight of her spars, with the sinking sun
behind them, and the red sky above, and the water spread out
before us like a sheet of copper.

" What became of that ship and her company I know not.
But I doubt not that the craft is broken up, and the crew are
all dead long ago. For either she struck a reef and was
wrecked, and the crew drowned, having no boat, or—which
may very well have happened—the leak grew upon her, and
she made so much water that she foundered; or they may have
made a raft, and landed on some island, where they lived, and,
in due course, died of too much palm-wine. And this was the
best that could happen to them.

" As for us five men who were left upon the island, we hoped
at first that the ship would come back for us, but she did not;
then we made up our minds to stay there, and we built a kind
of house, and made ourselves easy, and fished, and made pandang. No man need starve upon these islands. But after a
while we grew tired of the life, and so resolved to attempt escape. So we buried the treasure at the foot of the palm where
we had first laid it, and on the trunk we cut a mark; then we
rigged a sail of palm-leaves, calked the boat with cocoa fibre,
took some water and such provisions as we could lay up in
store, and so left our island, and sailed eastward. We were
still among islands, and we sailed among them for many weeks
—I know not how long. For still, when we were out of sight
of one island, we would sight another and yet another, but not

all friendly, nor all so soft and affectionate as those we had left behind us. So we crept on, from shore to shore and from cape to cape, until at last we reached the open sea, and no land in sight at all, and presently no provisions."

"And what happened then?"

"My lad," said Mr. Brinjes, "it is a terrible thing to be at sea with no provisions either to eat 'or to drink. Those who have water may go on for a long time, though I have been told that the body presently swells up and grows restless, and one must move about, which in a small boat is difficult. But to have neither food nor water! Then the men's eyes grow fierce and eager; horrible gnawing pains tear them to pieces. All day long they gaze upon the water for a sail, though they know, as we knew, that there can be no sail in those parts. At night they sleep not, but groan, and wish it were day. Then the pains increase, and one would willingly die but for the agony of death; and then the men cease looking upon the ocean, but look in each other's faces, none daring to say what is in every man's mind."

Here he was silent for a while.

"All this time we had a steady, gentle breeze, so that we sailed easily over smooth water; and all the time we were followed by a shark, which never left us, and was a certain prognostication of death, which we knew and understood. My lads, when that boat was picked up—which was by a Spanish brig sailing for the port of Acapulco—there was but one man left. All the rest had parted their cable, and the shark had eaten them—that is, some parts of them. The survivor hath never told any one how he kept himself alive. Perhaps he was able to catch a few fish; perhaps he caught a wild bird; perhaps it rained, and he caught the water as it fell. If ever you do pray for yourself, Jack—but it is best to take your own luck, and to pray for others—pray that you be never condemned to sail in an open boat without provisions." I have read in some book of shipwrecks that sailors have been known, in the extremity of their hunger, to kill each other for food. Did Mr. Brinjes and his boat's crew resort to this dreadful method?

"As for the treasure," he concluded, solemnly, "I have bequeathed it, Jack, to thee and to Bess Westmoreland here in equal parts. We will sail together some day and dig it up. I am old, but I shall not die until I have seen those seas again. We will go together, Jack, and thou shalt be rich. But even now thou art going thither, happy lad! When thy ship comes home, we will get a brig somehow, and sail away together— Captain Easterbrook in command—and steer for those islands. I know not their longitude, but as to latitude I am very sure they are about the parallel of 20 S. Oh, I shall find that archipelago. I cannot die until I have breathed those airs again and found the treasure. Jack, thou art heir to a greater estate than any man in England can boast. There is no earl or duke who shall hold up his head beside thee. Thou shalt be a prince, and Bess shall be a princess."

He rolled up his chart, and returned to his chair and his pillows, sinking into them with the exhausted air which made one perceive that he was already arrived at extreme old age.

"Forty years ago!" he groaned. "Where are they gone, those forty years which have taken away my strength? They made me a slave in Acapulco, a slave to a Creolian Spanish devil, who daily flogged and kicked me. Jack"—he sat upright, and his eye flashed fire—"when we have recovered the treasure we will burn the town of Acapulco, and roast alive every Spaniard in it. Oh, that I could have then got back to the island! But that I could not; and very soon I perceived that I must somehow escape, unless I was to be a slave for life, worse than a negro slave, and made to change my religion or burn. This, though I had lived among the islands like a pagan, I was unwilling to do. I therefore ran away, and committed myself to the Indians, by whom I was taken across the Isthmus of Panama, where I lived in the woods among my friends the savages for two years and more before I could find an English ship among those which came trading for mahogany to the coast of Yucatan which would take me off. So that of all that long journey I brought back to Jamaica with me but one thing —my blue-stone for the cure of snake-bites." He pulled it out of his pocket. "When you are bitten by any of the reptiles and insects of the forest, even by the most venomous, you may apply this stone (I have tried it on myself after a deadly snake-bite), which sticks on the place, and doth not fall off till it hath sucked up all the poison, when it drops of its own weight, and must be put into milk before you can use it again. Forty years ago! When I was young and could enjoy! Life mocks us, Jack. Sometimes I think that we are the sport and the laughter of the gods; but we know nothing. It flies before you have more than tasted of its joys. Give me fifty years more—only fifty years—and set me on the African coast among the Coromantyns, and I will find the secret which their wise women know. It is in the African forests that the herb grows which can cure all disease, even the disease of old age. With my treasure I could buy it, or find it, or compel them to yield it up. Happy boy! happy boy! Go breathe those airs of heaven, and gaze upon those purple islands. If thou lightest upon an archipelago somewhere in latitude 20 degrees south, where the islands are like hill-tops covered with wood, search for one which has on its north side a creek like a natural dock, then look for a palm-tree marked with a cross, and dig beneath it for a treasure. But if thou dost not find that island, then when thy ship comes home we will go together and seek for it, and find the treasure—thine inheritance!"

CHAPTER VIII.

THE "COUNTESS OF DORSET" SAILS.

"I always knew," said Jack, "that Mr. Brinjes had been a pirate. I believe he was surgeon to Bartholomew Roberts, who was killed by Captain Sir Ogle Chaloner in the *Swallow.* Wherefore he ought, if he had his deserts, to be now hanging in chains with his brother pirates on the Cape Coast. Fifty of them there are dangling in a row. Now we know that he is a cannibal as well, because it is certain he must have eaten up the other four men in the boat. I wonder how the last two determined the matter? And we know that he is the possessor of a great fortune buried under a palm-tree, on an undiscovered island in the South Seas. It is as useful to him as a bag of diamonds in the moon."

"But he says that he shall sail with you in search of it."

"Likely, likely," said Jack. "Who knows what may happen? He is, I take it, now a hundred years old. He keeps

himself alive by his craft. If he was going to die, I suppose
he would begin to repent. As for his treasure, what do I care
for his pieces of eight, unless it were to buy a frigate and man
her with a gallant crew, and go fighting the Spaniards and the
French?"

They were prophetic words, but this we knew not. Yet you
shall hear.

Then the *Countess of Dorset* sailed away, with Jack as one
of her midshipmen, upon her long and perilous voyage. She
was under orders to sail by way of the Cape of Good Hope,
and to survey the coast of that vast unknown continent or island
called in part New Holland and in another New Guinea. This
accomplished, as far as might be possible, her captain was instructed to cross the ocean and explore that other great island
called New Zealand. She was to search after and report upon
places which might be of advantage to the British flag. After
this she was to continue her voyage of discovery even into the
antarctic fields of ice; to penetrate as near to the south pole as
was possible, and she was to return by doubling Cape Horn.
So that, had she come home in safety, her crew would have
circumnavigated the globe.

It would seem, I venture to think, consistent with the dignity
as well as with the interest of a great maritime people, such as
the English, were such voyages as this always afoot, so that
when one exploring ship returned another might be despatched;
undertaken not only for the discovery of unknown continents
and islands, but also for the enlargement of commerce and the
enriching of this realm. In the old days the world was nothing but the Mediterranean with the lands lying around that
great sea. Man has extended it east and west, north and south,
so that we can now boast that we know all the islands of the
Atlantic and the Indian Ocean—navigators say that in those
seas there remains no more to be found—with the countries of
Asia (even China and Japan have been described and exactly
mapped by the Roman Catholic missionaries). We know the
eastern coast of North and South America from Labrador to
Cape Horn, and we are able to lay down the harbors and river
mouths of Africa, though of its interior little has yet been
visited.

There will perhaps come a time, if the English take the matter in hand without fear of Spain, when the whole world shall be fully explored, so that there will be nothing left to discover, neither strange races nor strange creatures nor wonderful plants. My father, who had in his library a copy of the great " Mappa Mundi," or Atlas, of the late learned Mr. Senex, would often converse seriously on the possibility of finding in some hitherto unexplored part of the world the long-lost Ten Tribes, still, he would fondly imagine, practising the Levitical law in its Mosaic integrity, without adding to it or subtracting from it, and in ignorance of the glosses introduced by Rabbinical and Talmudic doctors. He looked to find this people in vast numbers (in conformity with prophecy) somewhere between the springs of Tigris and Euphrates, or perhaps more to the north, and even on the slopes and among the valleys of the mountains called Caucasus; but he would confess, without crediting the idle legend of the Sambatyon River, which seems a monstrous story, they may have wandered farther afield, and perhaps are now on some remote island of the Black Sea, the Red Sea, or even the Indian Ocean. " The recovery of these tribes," he said, " would be a great consolation to pious persons, and would doubtless prove a mighty weapon in the hands of the faithful; or, apart from the Israelites—though this people must be ever foremost in our thoughts—it may very well be that there exist, in some remote countries which have had no intercourse with the outer world for many centuries, some people who were once a branch of the Roman empire, and have never heard of its decline and fall, who know nothing of Christ or Mohammed, or of the Hindoo superstitions, but still worship after the manner of the Greeks and Romans. 'Twould be strange indeed to witness the rites of Jove and Venus; those of the great Sun god; of Ceres, the goddess of fertility; of Bacchus, the god of joy and wine; and of Pan, of whose death these people perhaps know not. Or it would be strange to see them flocking to consult the oracles. And one would willingly, if it were allowed to a Christian, be initiated into the mysteries of Eleusis, long since lost, though some have pretended that they are concealed in the Sixth Book of Virgil's Æneid, and some still look for them in Apuleius's Golden Ass. Again, there must be somewhere on earth the Wandering Jew, named Cartaphilus, Ahasuerus, or, according to others, Isaac Laquedem, who is credibly reported to have been last seen, and that not so very long ago, in Paris. To sit down and talk with him, if his memory is still good, would be like finding a Fifth Gospel. Or there may be in the interior of that great southern continent which they call New Holland great and powerful nations, with another civilization than our own, and arts of which we know nothing. We have, it is true, invented gunpowder, the use of which, to rude people, appears a kind of magic, and we have contrived by our wit many ingenious mechanical devices. But there are surely many other secrets which man can compel nature to surrender; and there may be tribes which possess these secrets—as, for example, if one may so speak without blasphemy, the command and control of lightning, which now strikes here and there at random, as we say, if anything in this world is suffered to be at random; and the mastery over the other elements of the earth—the wind, the storm, the ice, the snow—which now only obey the word and will of the Lord. Or there may have been discovered in those countries—who knows?—a universal medicine for all diseases; for since death is the necessary result of decay or disease, when it is not accident, there may be races who have discovered some herb or simple by virtue of which natural decay may be prevented, and so man may continue to live as long as he please—which for the devout Christian, who looks forward to his eternal rest, would not be long. Or there may even be found offshoots or colonies of such ancient races as the Phœnicians, of which stock came the Carthaginians; and so we may perhaps at length learn by what accident this branch of the Semitic race—a most civilized and cultivated branch—hath left no literature at all, either of poetry or history; or of the Ethiopians, called by Homer, for some reason unknown to us, blameless. They were expelled from Egypt by the people whose descendants are now called Copts. Without doubt they were an interesting people, and remarkable for their primitive virtue, which may have survived. I would look for them on the western shores of the Red Sea. Or somewhere in the world, perhaps in the Pacific Isles, or in the unknown heart of Africa, or the great continent of the southern seas, there may be races of giants, dwarfs, and Amazons; for there must certainly be some foundation for the stories of such people. There is also the far-famed kingdom

4*

of Prester John, which some will have to be the Empire of
Abyssinia, whose king and people are known to form a branch
of the Christian Church. They boast themselves to be descended from King Solomon and the Queen of Sheba, which
may possibly be the case, although Holy Writ affords no warrant for the belief. One would be pleased to learn also if the
many strange stories narrated by the Venetian traveller Marco
Polo be true, or whether he hath repeated things which were
merely related to him, as is done by Herodotus. And again,
there is the journey of Mandeville, in which are described men
with but one leg, and hippotains, or creatures half horse, half
man, so that there may be truth in the legends of Centaurs,
though some have thought them to have been merely a people
loving horses, and addicted to riding.

"Then to descend to creatures : there are existing somewhere, perhaps, whether in the hot and burning forests of
South America, through which the great river Oronoco flows,
or in the African deserts, creatures like the winged dragons
of which so many stories have been told, with salamanders and
other monsters ; and in the sea, hideous monsters with bodies
many fathoms long, the vast mass floating like an island on
the ocean ; and great calamaries, of which sailors have reported
some with long arms capable of seizing and dragging down to
the bottom of the sea, ship, cargo, crew, and all."

Thus my father would discourse at length ; but Jack hath
assured us that in this terrible voyage of his they encountered
nothing bigger than a whale, or more terrible than a shark ;
nor any winged dragon, or serpent more dreadful than the
kinds already known ; while as for the "Ten Tribes," or for
any men who know more than the Europeans, or have acquired
a form of civilization worthy our attention, he does not believe
that there are any such.

We looked not for any news of the *Countess of Dorset* for
three years at least, because on the voyage on which she was
bound there are no friendly ports where a vessel may receive
or send home despatches, though, doubtless, many where fruit
and water may be obtained. We did not expect, therefore,
to hear any tidings of her until she should return. It was not
until fully three years had passed away that we first began to
ask ourselves when the ship might be expected to return.

But no news came of the ship, and no letters from those aboard her. The fourth year passed, and still there came no news ; and so the fifth, and still no news.

Then those who remembered Jack Easterbrook, and loved him, began to misdoubt that something had happened to the ship ; and when the sixth year had almost gone without a word, there were few who kept up heart, or had any hope in them. As for the admiral, he mourned for Jack as for his own son, believing that he must have been cast away with all the ship's company. " For," he said, " had they not all miserably perished, some intelligence would ere now have reached us. At the navy office they have written off the ship as wrecked, and the officers and crew as dead men, and the clerks have told the women who came to ask after their husbands that they may e'en look after fresh husbands ; though this proves nothing. And though ships have been known to be delayed and forced back by continual and contrary winds, or caught by storms and losing their masts, yet did I never hear of a ship overdue for three years, and then arriving safe. Long ago the underwriters, had she been a merchant vessel, would have paid off the insurances. No, gentlemen, there is no hope. Our boy is drowned !"

" We were wrecked upon the island of Juan Fernandez," said Mr. Shelvocke, " where we lived in great misery, on the entrails of seals and such like for many months ; and should still be living there but for the armorer and carpenter, who built for us a craft thirty feet long, in which we embarked, having no other provision than conger-eel, cut into strips, each strip dipped into the sea, and dried in the sun. A more loathsome food 'twere difficult to find. Yet we escaped, taking the Spanish ship the *Santo Jesu*, and so came safe home again."

" Then," said the admiral, to whom this story was not new, " the boy may still live, or, at best, he may linger on some island among the savages, living on shell-fish and the like, and so is as good as dead, since we shall never see him more. Poor lad ! poor lad ! a braver boy never stepped."

" With submission, admiral," said Mr. Brinjes. " That something must have befallen the ship I do not doubt. It is a sea full of coral reefs, sunken rocks, strange currents, and in the northern and southern parts there are, it is certain, sudden storms. We cannot guess what has happened ; still, I am sure that the boy will come back to us. Ask your old negress, admiral, who is a witch ; ask Philadelphy if that boy's eyes when he sailed away were the eyes of one who is going to his death. She can read the eyes of men—ay, and has often read for me, sitting in my shop, in the eyes of those going forth to sea whether they will come back or no—and never once has she proved wrong. Now, admiral, I have examined the chart over and over again, but can get no comfort from it, nor any clew to what may have happened. An ocean where there are no ports, and where there is but one vessel sailing across it, like the South Pacific, where the *Countess of Dorset* sailed upon—those waters can give no help. But that boy, admiral, has not been drowned. And he will return to us. His fortune is long and stormy, as Philadelphy, at my request, hath proved in many ways—by the bowl, by the cards, by the mirror, and by the glass ball. I have also had his nativity calculated, and I learn the same story. And by what small arts and knowledge I possess, I have learned that his life will not be cut off untimely. What, gentlemen ? Do the stars lie ? Is there no truth in the magic of the Mandingo woman ?"

It is a consolation to know that a happy end to anxiety is certain, even by witchcraft. Yet Jack did not return, and no news concerning his ship.

Many of the crew were Deptford men ; volunteers after the peace. Their wives, or widows, on the advice of the clerks in the navy office—who were now without hope concerning the ship—married again. This, however, is common among seafaring folk, and the worst that happens, should the husband come home again, is generally no more than a fight and a cracked skull, with forgiveness over a bowl. Nay, there have been cases known in which the true husband has contentedly renounced his wife, and either married another woman or gone away to sea again ; perhaps to seek out a new wife in some other port.

These six years, as you may suppose, were not spent at home without changes. The elders seem to stand still and suffer no change during six years, unless it is that their locks, if they had any to show, would grow gray ; but in these days of wigs and shaven cheeks there is nothing (happily) to mark the approach of age, save the trembling limb and the crow's-feet, which cannot be concealed. As for me, I was fourteen or thereabouts when the *Countess of Dorset* sailed away, and therefore, after six years, I was twenty, and a man grown, though not to the robust stature promised by Jack when he left us. Castilla was now past eighteen, and, in my eyes, more beautiful, as they say, than the flowers in May. Nothing surprised me more when Jack returned (for I promise you that the black witch was right, and Jack did return) than his coldness towards this nymph. If a fine complexion, eyes of heavenly blue, melting lips, rosy cheeks, and smiling mouth, with light hair curling naturally about her forehead, and a figure slight and tall : in short, if Hebe herself—who was the goddess of youthful and virginal beauty, as Venus is the goddess of that riper beauty which is no longer ignorant of love—was lovely, then was Castilla at that time, and as sweet, gracious, and obliging as ever was Hebe, the cup-bearer to the gods. Why, when Jack came home, I looked to see him fall at her feet at the mere contemplation of so much beauty. But no ; he was stark insensible. Castilla moved him not ; and this for a reason that you shall shortly learn.

It was during this six years—to speak for a moment of myself—that I passed through the greatest trouble of my life, and touched the highest happiness that I could hope or pray for. My father had, as he thought, set me apart for God's sacred ministry, as Samuel was set apart, from childhood. He had taught me from the first to consider this the holiest vocation for man, as, doubtless, it must be confessed by all ; and he had taught me as much Latin and Greek, with the composition of Latin verses, as I was permitted by my natural parts, which are not great, to acquire. And while he perceived very well that it was not in my power to become a great scholar like himself, he comforted and encouraged me by the consideration that piety and virtue are within the power of every Christian man, together with the other qualities which adorn the sacred profession of priest or minister.

When I grew to the age of sixteen or thereabouts, the time at which a boy generally begins to bethink himself of the future, I found, first, that I could not look forward to the cassock without a feeling of repugnance ; and, secondly, that there

was no other manner of work in which I took any interest,
save one, which for a while was not to be thought of. Indeed, I did not myself consider it possible, though I knew very
well that there were some—nay, a good number—who live
creditably by exercising the art of painting, which was the
only thing I loved.

By this time I was arrived, by continual daily practice, and
by some natural aptitude, at a certain proficiency, so that my
drawings of ships and boats and the like were, if one may say
so, creditable and fit to be shown to any judge of such matters. ʹ But when I ventured to hint, in my father's hearing,
that a life spent in this occupation, which he considered friv-
olous, might be full of delight to one who loved drawing, the
thing was received with so much displeasure that I dared not
for some time to open the subject again, but went on, under
his directions, making bad Latin verses and reading Cicero and
Virgil.

I then began to consider my destined profession with such
a distaste as amounted to abhorrence, insomuch that had I
persisted in taking those vows which my father intended and
designed for me, I should have committed a most deadly sin,
if not the sin which is unpardonable. And yet I ventured not
to open my conscience to my father, fearing his displeasure,
and knowing very well how much he had set his heart upon
my following in his footsteps. I was at length encouraged to
do so, however, partly because it smote my soul with contri-
tion to go on pretending acquiescence in my father's wishes,
and partly by a thing which made my project appear more
likely of success, or, at least, less likely to end in disastrous
failure.

There was a certain John Brooking, of Deptford, now very
well known to painters, and to such fame as belongs to modern painters. He was about ten years older than myself, and
at first was but a shipwright's assistant in the yard, but had
no heart for his work, and wasted his time in drawing the work-
shops, the docks, the timbers, bulkheads, anchors, everything
that there is to be drawn in the yard, even giving up to his art
the whole of his Sundays. He was a good-natured, harmless
kind of man, who cared little for himself, and had no ambition except to paint all day, to earn enough for his daily wants,

and to spend the evenings drinking with his friends. He
presently left the yard and went away to London, designing
to sell his drawings. But before he went he gave me great
help in teaching me, so far as he himself knew them, the elements of perspective, with certain simple rules of geometry
and the arrangement of lights, and showed me how to lay on
water-colors, and how to get the proper tints, and how to produce the effects I desired. I know not how he lived for a while,
but one day I met him in the streets of Deptford, and he told
me with glee that he had found a man, a dealer in pictures,
in Leicester Fields, who would buy his drawings of ships, as
many as he chose to paint, at a guinea apiece (N.B.—He afterwards found that this honest dealer sold the same pictures
for ten guineas apiece), and that therefore he was now a made
man, and had nothing to do but to go on with the work he
loved, and paint every day ; which he did, until he died of a
consumption, brought on, I suspect, by much strong drink.
However, I went to London, and visited him one day at his
lodging. He had a single room at the top of a house in a court
close to the Fields, where his friend the dealer had his shop ;
it was a good-sized room, with a large window looking north,
which is the best direction for light. This was his painting-
room, and his living-room, bedroom, and kitchen—all in one.
Never was a room so littered and untidy and dirty. But John
Brooking cared nothing for dirt. He worked there all day
long, so long as the light lasted, or he made sketches and studies by the river-side, which he afterwards made into finished
pictures in this simple studio, where he stood at his easel, never
tired, a knitted nightcap on his head, and in his shirt sleeves,
and a tobacco-pipe, broken short off, between his lips ; for he
loved tobacco as much as any old gypsy woman.

Well, his success, such as it was (but indeed I thought of
nothing then except how just to live by my work, so only that
I could do the work I desired to do), inflamed me, and I resolved to tell all to my father ; which, to make a long story
short, I did, though with many misgivings.

He is dead now ; and, I doubt not, hath gone to the rest
provided for the faithful. It is a place where my love and
gratitude may not reach him. I have never passed so unhappy a time as that when it seemed as if I must continue my

preparation for the university, in order to perjure my soul by declaring falsely that I was singled out by Heaven to follow the holy calling of a minister; and I have never felt so truly happy as on that day when my father, with tears in his eyes, bade me vex my soul no longer, for it should be with me as I wished.

So I left Deptford, and went to London, to become a pupil of the celebrated Mr. Hayman; and I hope that I have since done justice to the instructions of that great painter. But I came home often, partly to sketch among the ships, and partly to see Castilla.

Enough of my affairs, which concern this story but little.

CHAPTER IX.

AARON FLETCHER.

THE sixth year came—nay, it had run half its course and more—yet no news of the *Countess of Dorset*. And there was no longer any doubt that the ship was cast away, and all the crew long since dead. As for Jack, who had been our hope and our pride, of whom we had said that a youth so brave and so masterful must needs rise to greatness, and bring credit upon himself and those who had been his friends, none now ever spoke a word; or if they did, it was but to say that the loss of the boy had brought age upon the admiral, and that 'twas a great pity a youth of such goodly promise should thus untimely perish. The stars had lied; witchcraft and magic had proved of no avail.

Jack was dead. In the club at the " Sir John Falstaff " his ship was never talked of, nor was there any further speculation as to her course, for the admiral's sake, even by Mr. Brinjes. And by all the world the boy was well-nigh forgotten. When the greatest of living men, he whose name is most in men's mouths, dies, the daily life of the world is no whit changed; and his place, even in his own work, whatever that may be, is speedily filled up. What, then, can one expect in the case of a boy?

But in Mr. Brinjes's parlor, where now Bess Westmoreland sat every afternoon, for company, and to cheer the old man's

*" He stood at his easel, a knitted nightcap on his head, and in his
shirt sleeves."*

heart, Jack was not forgotten. These two talked about him still. More than this—superstitiously trusting to the negress's magical practices—they confidently expected that he would return again. Well, in the event the forecast proved true; but if we are to trust to such an oracle, where is religion? If an ignorant negro woman is permitted to find out by her witchcraft the secrets of the future, and to foretell them, what shall become of religion? Then farewell faith; farewell prayer; farewell trust in divine Providence; farewell learning, since ignorance succeeds where wisdom fails.

In six years Bess had, like Castilla, grown from a child to a woman. She was now in her seventeenth year, not yet filled out to the fulness of her figure, but already tall and shapely. If she had been dressed in rags she would have commanded attention; but she was careful of her dress, and went always becomingly attired, though not above her station (the coral beads that we know of were placed away in some drawer or box out of sight). She was so tall that she topped her father (but he was round-shouldered) by a head and neck, and there was no girl in all the town within her height by an inch and more; she bore herself like a lance, so straight and upright was she. Her nose and chin looked as if they had been carved by a skilful sculptor out of marble, so clear and delicate were they; her eyes were black, as was her hair; but rosy red her lips, and pearly white her teeth. Like many black-haired women, her cheek was full, but somewhat pale in color, and her throat was white, not with such a whiteness as lent another charm to the complexion of Castilla, which, although of a sweet and delicate white, yet glowed with a rosy warmth. The whiteness of Bess was a colder or deeper white—a white that does not reflect the light, such as some Italian painters have delighted to portray; her hands were small, and her forehead low, as the Greeks loved it; as for her eyes, they were soft and deep, save when she was roused, and then, indeed, they flashed fire and flame. As became her station, she wore no hoop, and dressed her hair in a simple knot; but she walked as if her limbs were of springing steel, and I am sure no princess in a hoop and patches could have walked more like a goddess; her arms, when she was at work, were the whitest ever seen, and the best shaped.

I have never disguised, and shall never disguise, my belief, though Castilla will not agree with me—that is, she assents, but without warmth—that Bess was the most beautiful girl then living; and this I can the more fairly say, because I was never in love with her, any more than a painter is in love with his model. As for love between Bess Westmoreland and myself, that was always impossible. Yet for suitors she never lacked any, though she sent all away, not with discourtesy, or with mockery, or with mirth, as some girls will—as if it is a fine thing to dash the hopes of an honest lad, and as if lovers can be had for the trouble of picking them up—but with firmness and with dignity, being too proud to encourage them, or to suffer them to believe that she wanted their wooing. Some of them were substantial and reputable men, whom the daughter of a mere penman might have been proud to marry. Why, if he had died, what would she have done for her daily bread? To my own knowledge one of her wooers was gunner's mate in the king's navy, another was a master wheelwright in the king's yard, a third was foreman in the Greenland dock, and I dare say there were more of equally respectable place. It became a proverb that there was no man good enough for Bess Westmoreland; and the other girls, who might otherwise have been envious of her charms, regarded her with open admiration, because she was not only much more beautiful than themselves, yet wished to carry away none of their sweethearts.

One lover alone, out of all, stuck by her, and refused to take her "No" for an answer. This was Aaron Fletcher, now grown into a young giant, who carried on his father's business of boat-builder, yet was of roving disposition, and kept his smack at Gravesend or at Leigh, in which he went fishing. Those, however, who spoke of those fishing voyages were apt to laugh, and to ask why that fishing-boat never came back by daylight.

"I have told you," said Bess—"I have told you a hundred times, Aaron, that I will not listen to you. Wherefore go away in peace, and trouble me no longer. Why, there are dozens of other girls in Deptford, and plenty better-looking than me, would take you, and that joyfully."

"There are not plenty for me," he replied. "I want but one. And, Bess, I shall never give up asking. There's nobody in the world loves you better, or would do more for thee.

Why am I not good enough? There's money in the stocking,
Bess, now father is dead—ay! and more than you think—and
more to come. There's as good business doing in my yard as
in any boat-builder's on the river, not to speak of the smack,
which does a tidy stroke, take year and year about. I am not a
drunkard, though once a week or so I may take my glass with
the rest. I am strong, and I am young. I wouldn't strike a
woman nor treat her cruel. I'd be true and faithful. Come,
Bess, what is the matter with me, that thou canst not say
'Yea?'"

Well would it have been for her, and for another, too, if she
could have said "Yea," and taken him. Why did she not?
He was tall and strong, and handsome of his kind; he was not
esteemed to be ill-tempered; he was not at that time a drink-
er, save of a cheerful glass; he had a good character, save
for the reputation of these fishing voyages of his, which did
him no hurt with any one. Did not the admiral himself put
Aaron's Nantz upon his own table? He would have made
Bess a good husband, if any could, because such a woman, if
she is to be happy, must needs have a strong man for a husband, and one who will rule her and make her respect him.
Well indeed it would have been for her if she had taken this
brave fellow; but she could not.

"Bess," he said, "you can't be thinking still upon that midshipman? Why, he was but a boy, and you were a child.
He's cast away and dead long ago; and if he was not, he
wouldn't remember you."

But she made no reply.

"'Tisn't for love of him, Bess, is it? Why, I fought him
half a dozen times; and if he were to come back, I would
fight him again."

She laughed scornfully. "'Tis true, Aaron, the last fight I
saw; and where were you at the end of it? Rubbing your
head, and looking ruefully at your broken finger. And where
was Jack? Walking away with a laugh. But don't talk to
me about Jack. Perhaps he is dead. Living or dead, I don't
suppose he would remember or care for a poor girl like me.
But I can't marry you, Aaron."

"You shall," he continued, with an oath. "You shall. I
will make you promise to marry me."

This was a prophecy not made by an oracle. Yet, strange to say, it came true—in a sense. To be sure, it was not the sense that Aaron intended. It has been observed that such prophecies, together with all the prophecies of witches and magicians, when they do come true, never happen in the way hoped for when the prophecy is uttered. Certainly, as you shall see, Aaron's prophecy did turn out true, but the result was not what he had expected and desired. In the same way Mr. Brinjes's prediction about the South Sea also proved true, yet not in the sense desired and expected by him. As you shall also discover.

" Very well," said Bess, " I will promise to marry you, Aaron —when I love you. Can a girl say fairer ? Go away now, Aaron ; go away and find some other woman who wants to go marrying, and take pity on her, if you can. But as for me, I will marry no man."

However, he renewed his importunity, offering her presents, which she refused, such as parcels of lace, flasks of Nantz for her father, rolls of silk, and so forth, all got, I doubt not, in the way of his fishing, and always declaring, in his masterful way, that sooner or later she should promise to marry him.

CHAPTER X.

HOW JACK CAME HOME AGAIN.

AND now I have to tell how Jack was joyfully restored to us. It was in sorry plight, and after many disasters and sore privations, which killed his companions, but left him—to look upon—none the worse, when he came back to good food and decent clothes again. I think that no one had ever a more wonderful story to tell, and yet there was never a worse hand at telling his adventures. Lucky it was for Ulysses, and for Æneas, that they found poets to sing their sufferings and their wanderings, for, I dare say, the former, at least, would have made a poor hand at telling them himself. A greater than Ulysses was here ; and no one, until now, has ever told, save imperfectly, the story of his voyage. It will never be narrated

as it ought to be, movingly, and to the life; and the sailing of
the *Countess of Dorset* among the Pacific Islands, and the discoveries which she made, and the dreadful calamities which be-
fell the ship and the crew, will no more be remembered than
if she had been some poor and insignificant collier, cast away,
with her crew of half a dozen men and a boy, on the Goodwin
Sands.

It is also a strange circumstance that his life should have
been saved by the man who, man and boy, was his steady and
constant enemy. Nay, as you will see in the sequel, his life
was once more saved by the same hand—a thing which clearly
shows the hand of Providence, if it were only designed in
mercy as a rebuke to the man who desired and even endeavored
to compass the death of his enemy and rival. Yet I never
heard tell that Aaron Fletcher repented of the hatred which he
always bore to Jack.

One night in the month of September, and the year seventeen hundred and fifty-six—a dark and cloudy night, the stars
hidden and no moon, a light breeze flying, but only in puffs,
and hardly enough to fill the canvas, and a soft and soaking
rain falling—a small vessel, rigged with foresail, spritsail, mainsail, and topsail, was slowly making her way across the German
Ocean. Her name was the *Willing Mind*, of Sheerness; she
was manned by a crew of five, two more than are generally
taken on board a fishing-craft of her dimensions. Of these
men the skipper sat in the stern, the ropes in his hand, two
were lying asleep beside the skipper, covered with a tarpaulin,
and two were in the bows keeping watch. She carried no light,
but she was sailing well north of the track of outward-bound
vessels, and was by this time too close to the Essex coast to
fear being run down by colliers. Perhaps the watch was on
the lookout for lights on the coast, or for a king's revenue-cut-
ter, of which there are many along the east coast, and they
greatly molest this kind of craft, overhauling them suspiciously, and searching for brandy and the like, impressing the honest fishermen on board, and sometimes even imprisoning them,
haling them before a magistrate, and bringing them to trial;
and even, if they show much resistance, hanging them; and
by their very appearance always obliging the crew to throw
overboard, if they have time, the whole of their cargo. It gen-

erally consists of a strange kind of fish, in the shape of kegs, runlets, and jars, with bungs and corks in their mouths. Perhaps the *Willing Mind* showed no light because the skipper and his crew dreaded being captured by a French privateer; for we were again at war with France, and the Channel was crowded with these hornets, though, as a rule, they hardly ventured north of the Goodwin Sands, or off the Nore.

The boat slipped through the water slowly and silently, save for a gentle ripple in the bows. There was little way on her, but she kept moving.

" I take it," said the skipper, grumbling, " that it is already past midnight; we ought to have made Shoeburyness by now. In three hours it will be daylight, and perhaps the dogs upon us—and with such a cargo !"

" The breeze will freshen with the dawn, master," said one of the men in the bow.

" And then it may be too late. And we haven't had such a cargo for a twelvemonth. What is that off the starboard bow ?"

" It looks like a buoy. But it can't be a buoy !" It was a black object, indistinct as yet, but they were nearing it. Presently a hoarse cry of " Sail ahoy !" came across the water. It was repeated twice.

" It is a boat, with four men in her," said the watch, making her out. " A little dingy she is. Now what the plague is she doing out here ?"

" Sail ahoy !" came across the water again. And now they could distinguish the figures of three or four men standing up in the boat.

The skipper cursed and swore, and put up his helm.

" Sail ahoy ! for Jesus' sake ! We are sinking !" cried the men.

The skipper cursed and swore again, louder and deeper; but he altered his course, and bore down upon the boat.

There were five men in her, but one of them lay in the stern with his head upon his arms, motionless. The boat had neither oars, mast, nor sails; she was half full of water, and the men were baling her with their hats.

" For God's sake, take us aboard !" they cried. " It is as much as we can do to keep afloat, and we are starving !"

" Who are you?" asked the skipper.

" We have broke from a French prison," they told him;
" and four days out, and nothing to eat."

Still the skipper hesitated.

" Cap'en," said one of the men, " we can guess pretty easy
who you are and what is your business. That is nothing to
us. Take us on board. You sha'n't regret it. Only take us
on board and give us something to eat, and set us ashore on
English soil; and if you were laden with all the brandy there
is in the world, you should never be sorry for coming to our
help."

The skipper cursed them again for interrupting his run.
But it would have been the most shocking inhumanity to refuse; therefore, with a bad grace, and sulkily, he ordered them
to get on board as quickly as they could. This they did; but
they had to help the man in the stern, because he had got an
open wound in his head and had lost much blood, besides being nearly starved. So they lifted him in and laid him on a
tarpaulin, and cast off their crazy little boat, and the smack
went on her course again.

Then the skipper, who was not wanting in generosity, though
he cursed them for stopping him, pulled out of the locker such
provisions as might be expected in such a craft—consisting
only of bread, mouldy Dutch cheese, and some onions. But,
Lord! if these had been the greatest dainties ever set before
an alderman, the men could not have devoured the food more
greedily; even the wounded man lifting his head and eating
ravenously. When there was nothing at all left to be eaten, the
skipper passed round a bottle of brandy and a pannikin, which
were received with heartfelt gratitude too deep for power of
speech. For cold and starving men, bread and cheese and
onions make a banquet; but brandy in addition—oh! 'twas
too much!

When they had eaten up everything, therefore, and drunk as
much brandy as their rescuer would give them, they began, as
sailors will, through a spokesman, to relate their story. Everybody knows that at the outbreak of the war the French fleet
put so many privateers to sea, and we had so few, that there
was nothing but the capture of English merchantmen going
up and down the Channel, and the French prisons were soon

choked with poor devils laid up by the heels, and waiting for
a general exchange, or for the close of the war, to be released.
Three of the men had been taken by a privateer out of a West-
Indiaman, and conveyed with others up the country to a place
called St. Omer, which is a fortified town some twenty miles
from Dunquerque, and about the same distance from Calais,
and were then clapped into prison in the citadel, or the barracks, or the town jail, I know not which. Wherever it was,
they found there, among the other prisoners, the man who lay
wounded on the tarpaulin, not able to sit up, and saying nothing. And he it was, they said, who had devised the plan of
their escape. There were a dozen more who were in the plot,
and should have made the attempt, but at the last moment they
lost heart, as always happens in an adventure so desperate, and
remained behind. As things turned out, it was lucky that
there were no more of them, because there was certainly no
room for any more in their rickety little boat.

I do not rightly understand how the escape was effected, because in the subject of fortifications I am ignorant, though Jack
hath often endeavored to explain to me the nature of scarp,
counterscarp, bastion, and so forth. However, they surmounted
all these difficulties, and in the dead of night they found themselves on the right side of the ramparts—that is, on the outside
—and with open country all round them. Then, steering by
the stars, they made due north. Before they got half-way on
their journey they were surprised by dawn, and forced to seek
a hiding-place, which they found in a wood or coppice beside
a river, where the shelter was good, though the lying was wet
and swampy. Here they stayed all day, with nothing to eat except a few berries, then happily ripe. At nightfall they started
again, and, as they judged, soon after midnight found themselves on a sandy coast somewhere between Calais and Dunquerque, near a place called Gravelines. But there was no boat
on this open and deserted coast, and they wandered up and
down for a long time seeking for one, and fearing lest they
might again have to seek a night's shelter. When, at last,
they found one, it was hauled up high and dry on the sand.
This would have mattered little ; but, unluckily, her owner, or
a man who behaved like her owner, was sleeping on the sand
beside her. There was no choice, but they must needs have

her, and while they dragged her down to the sea, the Frenchman woke up, and perceiving that he was being robbed of his
boat, he lugged out a knife and made at them, and before he
could be fairly knocked on the head, gave their leader a desperate cut across the face, from which he lost a great deal of
blood and was much weakened. They got him safely into the
boat, however, though he was fainting from the wound, and so
put to sea, and hoped to be able to row across the Channel, if
they should have the good luck to 'scape the privateers, and
make the port of Dover in eight or ten hours; or perhaps they
might be picked up by some English ship, if they were lucky.
They had neither mast nor sail in the boat, and there were no
provisions in it of any kind. Also, as they quickly discovered,
she very soon sprang aleak, and had to be baled out continually.
They rowed on, however, taking turns, for three or four hours.
Then a most unfortunate thing happened. For while two of
them were rowing lustily, in their eagerness to lose no time,
and to get across and land on English soil again, and the oars
being not only small, but old and rotten, they both snapped
short off close to the rowlock at the same time. This accident
dashed all their hopes, for though they tore up two of the
boat's planks, thinking to row with them, it was slow work;
then they tried to make a sail with a shirt and one of these
planks, there being a light breeze from the sou'west, and they
got, as they supposed, into the current. They were carried
certainly, as they discovered at daybreak, out of sight of the
French coast, but also, which was another misfortune, outside
the track of ships, and so, though they saw many sail in the
distance, they passed none near enough to be picked up, and
in this miserable condition tossed and drifted for four days
and four nights, and were now well-nigh spent, and the leak in
the boat growing every moment worse, so that she threatened
to fill with water and to sink under them unless they baled continually.

"It's easy guessing," they repeated, after they had told their
story, "what you've got on board: that's no concern of ours.
Only you put us ashore. Without making bold to inquire further, tell us where we are, and how far from shore."

"As to where we are," said the skipper, "the night is dark,
and I don't rightly know. But to the best of my guessing we
5

are not far from Shoeburyness, which should lay right ahead ;
but the shore is low, and difficult to make out."

" Mate," said the spokesman, " land us as far from any port
as you can.   I guess the press is hot up the river."

The skipper said that there was a very hot press ; that, as to
himself, he was going to land at Shoeburyness, where he could
put them ashore and they could then shift for themselves, and
make their way inland, if so be they had friends anywhere.

" As for this poor fellow," said the man, pointing to the one
who was lying down, " he says he's an officer, though he doesn't
look like one in those rags of his.   So he's got nothing to fear
from a press.   Don't put him ashore, skipper.   Take him to
some place where he will get his wound dressed.   If what he
says is true, he will be able to pay you for the service."

" I will take him," said the skipper, " to Gravesend.   That is
all I can do for him.   After that he must shift for himself."

Shortly after this, and before daybreak, they made the land
between the village of Southend and Shoeburyness.   Here they
landed the four men, who, with many vows of gratitude, expressed in sailor-like fashion — namely, with appeals to the
Divine Power to blast them and sink them if they ever forgot
this service — quickly vanished inland.   It matters nothing
what became of these poor fellows ; but intelligence came from
Maldon shortly afterwards that a gang of four men, dressed like
sailors, had been apprehended stealing a sheep.   They made a
desperate fight, and one of the *posse comitatus* was dangerously
wounded.   In the end they were overpowered, and taken to
Chelmsford Jail, where in due course they were all hanged.
If these were the men landed from the *Willing Mind,* the poor
wretches had better have remained in their prison at St. Omer,
where, at least, they were living a life of innocency, although
half starved with their meagre soup and sour bread.   But perhaps the men who were hanged were another gang.

Now, as regards the cargo of the *Willing Mind*—I mean
that load of fish, all with corks and bungs in their mouths—it
would be a shame for me to disclose where it was landed, and
by whom it was received, though one may know very well.   I
am not a spy and an informer ; the revenue officers may find
out for themselves the secrets of the trade which they have to
stop, if they can.   I say not whether it is such a trade as a

person of tender conscience may undertake, but, at least, this much may be said for it—that those who practise it know beforehand the risks they run, and the punishment which awaits them if they are captured.

Enough to say that the landing was successful, and that about noon that day the *Willing Mind*, now in ballast, was running up the Thames with full sail, wind and tide favorable, bound for Gravesend; and the wounded man was so far recovered that he was now sitting up and looking about him. He was a wild creature to look at, being, to begin with, horribly thin, as if he had had no food for months; he had suffered his beard to grow, and it now covered his whole face, so that he looked like a Turk, with his hair long and uncombed; his head was bound up with a dirty and bloody clout, which hid one eye; there was blood upon his cheek. Presently, while he looked about him with lack-lustre gaze, the pain of his wound being great, his eye fell upon the skipper, and he started and became suddenly alive and alert.

"Aaron Fletcher, by the Lord!" he cried.

"That is my name," replied the skipper. "I am not ashamed of it. But I don't know you, mate."

"You have forgotten me, Aaron. If you had known me, you would have been all the more anxious to save my life. Of that I am well assured. We should have foundered in five minutes. As for me, I cared nothing whether we sank or swam. All is one to a starving man. Give me another tot of brandy, Aaron. Don't you recognize me now?"

"Man, I never clapped eyes on you before to my knowledge. But since you know my name, and therefore, likely, where I live, so that you might do mischief, let me tell you"—here he insisted or emphasized the assurance by a dozen or two of round oaths, such as he and his kind have always ready to hand for all purposes—"that if you are going to turn informer, after all you have seen, it would be better for you if we had thrown you overboard at once with a shot to your heels. One or other of us, my lad, will have your blood."

The other men of the crew murmured approval of this sentiment with additions of their own invention, about cutting the weasand, breaking bones and limbs, gouging out eyes, and so forth.

"The same old Aaron," said the man. "Why, you have not changed, save that you are stouter and bigger. The same sweet and unsuspicious temper. I wonder if there is another such treat in store for us both as we had when last we met?"

"Who the devil are you?" asked Aaron, staring, partly because the man knew him, and because so ragged a fellow should talk with such boldness. But as yet quite unsuspecting.

"That, my friend, if you cannot guess, I shall not tell you. As for your kegs, fear not. I care nothing where they were bestowed, nor to whom they were consigned, nor where they came from. So far as I am concerned, you are safe. Besides, you have saved my life. This cut in the head, d'ye see, cost me so much blood that I do not think I could have endured another night of starvation. Why, man, I have had to live for weeks with nothing but a taste now and again, when the chance came, of putrid seal or rotten fish! I'm downright tired of starving."

"Who are you, then?" Aaron looked at him hard, but could make nothing of him.

Yet it was strange that he did not begin to suspect. This, I take it, was because, like everybody else, he had quite made up his mind that Jack was long since dead, and so he was gone clean out of his mind. This is so when a man is dead. His face goes out of our mind because we never think to meet him again.

"Well," he said, at length, "it don't signify a button who you are. You've got nothing against me, even should you lay information. But you're down on your luck, whoever you be. And you've the cut of a sailor about you. Wherefore, mate, take my advice and keep well inshore, for the press is hot all the way from Margate to Chelsea, and, wounded or not, they'll have you if they can, and three dozen or more for skulking, if you are not fit for duty in four-and-twenty hours."

"Thank you, Aaron," the man replied, and so lay down again and went to sleep. But Aaron kept looking at him, uneasy, yet not able to remember him.

So they made their way to Gravesend, and arrived off that port in the afternoon.

"I thank you, Aaron," said the passenger, waking up and getting to his feet. "The food and the brandy and the sleep

have set me up again. I believe I shall be able to walk the
rest of the journey. One more favor, Aaron. After saving
my life it is a small thing for you to do. I am without a single
penny. Lend me a shilling, which I will bring myself to the
boathouse and repay you when you come home. You don't
know me, Aaron! Why, man, how goes the boat-building?"

Aaron produced the money, still staring with all his eyes, as
the children say.

"A shilling, Aaron, is not much. If it was six years ago, I
should say we would fight for it." So he dashed back the hair
that hung about his face, and looked Aaron full in the face with
a laugh.

"Good Lord!" cried Aaron. "It's Jack Easterbrook!"

"Mr. Easterbrook, ye dog. I am in rags, but I am a king's
officer still, and you are nothing but a common smuggler."

"It's Mr. Jack Easterbrook," Aaron repeated. "He's come
back again!"

"As for this shilling, Aaron, shall we fight for it now?"

"But— Oh Lord! How in the world did you get in such
rags as this? And where's the *Countess of Dorset?*"

"As for the rags, where I got them was in the Isle of Chiloe,
off the Patagonian coast, and if I had not got them I should
have come home as naked as Adam in his innocency. And as
for the *Countess of Dorset*, her timbers are where I got my rags,
on the coast of South America, and her crew are mostly beside
her timbers, such parts of them, that is, as the crabs have not
been able to devour."

"O Lord!" Aaron gazed as if at a ghost, and could say no
more.

"Do they think me dead, Aaron?"

"All of them—except, I'm told, Mr. Brinjes."

"Oh! And the admiral?"

"It isn't for the likes of me to know what his honor thinks,
sir," said Aaron. "But he's been going heavy for a good time
past, and they do say as how he frets more than a bit about
your drowning."

Jack was silent for a bit.

"And Bess Westmoreland?" he asked.

"What has she got to think about you for? You are a gentleman, though in rags at this present moment. As for Bess,

she is but the daughter of a penman. She belongs to the likes
of us, not to gentleman officers."

"She must be grown a big girl now. Well, Aaron, and Mr.
Brinjes ?"

"He's a devil. He's worse than ever. He gave Lance Pegg,
of Anchor Alley, the rheumatics last week, and threatens her
with worse for rope's-endin' that girl of hers. He's a devil!
and never a day older since your honor went away."

"So, Aaron, you have saved my life, though you did not intend it. Yet I take it kindly. I do not think you would have
suffered your old townsman and your old crony, whom you used
to fight whenever you met him, to drown, if you had known
who was in the boat."

"I would not, sir," said Aaron, stoutly. "Yet, to tell the
truth, I'd as lief you were at the bottom of the sea, in Davy's
locker, where we all thought you were, and where you ought
to be by rights, your ship and the crew all being there except
you."

"Give me thy hand, Aaron."

So they shook hands.

"As for the shilling, sir," said Aaron, "let me make it a
guinea ; and if your honor will let me pay for a decent suit of
clothes, or shoes, at least—"

"Nay, Aaron. As you found me, so shall they find me.
The shilling will be enough to pay for all I want ; and I have
gone so long barefooted that my feet are as hard as leather,
and feel not the road. As for the shilling, we will, perhaps,
fight for it. But not yet. You would not, I am sure, being an
honorable man, wish me to fight until I have recovered my
strength. Farewell, Aaron."

So he stepped ashore, and with such lightness of step as reminded Aaron of the old days when Jack stepped down the
street in his midshipman's uniform, free and careless. He was
light of step because of the joy of returning home, yet he was
still somewhat dizzy and weak. However, he had a shilling to
pay for supper, and he had but twenty miles to walk, or thereabouts—a short distance for those who are strong and well, but
a long journey to be done on foot by a man with an open wound
on his forehead, and half starved to boot, so that it is not surprising that he did not reach Deptford till noon next day.

The next day was Sunday.

At half-past twelve the Vicar of St. Paul's finished a most learned discourse upon certain philosophical systems of the Phœnicians, the Chaldæans, the Greeks, and the Egyptians, deducing Christian truths, by the method known as analogy, from each. Castilla, I remember, sat with folded hands, and eyes fixed upon the preacher, as if she understood every word. And the admiral slept. The poorer part of the congregation behaved after their kind; that is to say, the men slept, the women sat perfectly still, and the boys fidgeted. When one became too noisy, he was taken out by the beadle and caned in the churchyard among the tombs, the other boys all listening, and counting the strokes, as if the number administered was in itself a fine lesson. (The same thing may be observed both in the army and navy.) When I read that the Papists attach a particular merit to mere attendance or presence during the performance of their mass, I cannot but think that the same indulgence might be extended to our poor ignorant rustics and servants for their patient attendance at the sermons of which they understand nothing.

When the morning service was ended, the vicar came down from the pulpit and walked into the vestry, preceded by the beadle carrying his stick of office, and followed by the clerk. Then the people all stood up in respect to the quality, who led the way out of the church. First there walked down the aisle the admiral, his wig that morning combed, curled, and powdered, and with him his lady in hoop and satin, and his daughter Castilla in hoop and sarsnet, very beautiful to behold. After them came Mr. Pett, the shipbuilder, with his wife and family; Mr. Underhill, the retired purser, who was a bachelor; Mr. Mostyn, the Cocket-writer of the Customs; Mr. Shelvocke with his family, and others who lived in the genteel houses beside the bridge; and with them I walked down the aisle, though only a painter, and an apprentice at that. When we had passed down the aisle, and conversed for a few minutes, standing on the great stone terrace which makes St. Paul's Church so stately, we separated, some taking the pathway through the churchyard to the right into Church Lane, and others to the left into Bridge Street. I walked beside Castilla, who carried her Book of Common Prayer and was silent, doubtless meditating on the

spiritual truths of the vicar's sermon. Behind us came three
out of the admiral's four negroes, and Philadelphy, splendid in
her red silk handkerchief and a blue speckled frock. And
after us came the common sort, flocking out together, the
boys, for their part, glad that the sermon was finished, and
all of them longing for the Sunday's beef and pudding. The
poor do certainly exercise the virtue of patience more than the
rich, especially at a sermon, of which, when a learned divine like
my father preaches it, they can understand not one word. So
that one may forgive them for the unrestrained joy which, on
every Sunday, the faces in the side aisles manifest at the conclusion of the discourse, not only of the boys and girls, but of
the grown-up people as well. Among those who followed after
the better sort were Mr. Westmoreland, the penman, and his
daughter—he bent and feeble, round-shouldered and meek, leaning on his stick, and by his side Bess, tall and upright as a
lance, dressed somewhat finer than those of her condition are
wont to go, and holding her head in the air as if she were a
queen. Strange that her father should be so meek and humble, and that no learning of the catechism could teach Bess
meekness or humility. There is, I now understand, a certain
quality in beauty which prevents its owner from lowliness,
however humble be her station. The young fellows looked
after Bess as she came forth from the church ; but she regarded them with proud eyes, and passed on disdainful, as if she
were too high and good for any of them. Therefore they followed after the other girls, who were as willing as Bess was
proud, and perhaps, in these honest fellows' eyes, not much
less beautiful.

Just opposite the churchyard gate, close to the principal entrance of Trinity Hospital, we observed, as we passed into
Church Lane and turned to the right, a fellow leaning against
the posts. He was tall and big-limbed, but thin and wasted, as
if he had been suffering from some disease or dreadful privations. One could very well see that he was a sailor, though in
his dress, such as it was, there was little to show it. He wore
a common sailor's petticoat or slops ; he had a ragged waistcoat, buttoned up to the neck, because he had neither shirt nor
cravat ; he was bareheaded and barefooted ; his hair was long
and matted ; round his forehead was tied a dirty clout or hand-

kerchief, red with streaks of blood, so that he seemed to have but one eye.

As we came out of the churchyard I caught sight of him, and thought naturally how he would look if he were drawn just so in those rags, and put into a picture, making one of a group. And I saw, but suspected nothing—how could we be all so foolish and blind as not to see, with half an eye, who it was?— how he started when we came forth from the churchyard, and made as if he would move towards us, perhaps to beg, but checked himself, and waited where he was.

But the admiral stopped, and surveyed him leisurely from head to foot. Then he lugged out his purse and found a shilling, which he bestowed upon the man.

"My lad," he said, "thou art a sailor, and thou hast fallen among thieves, belike. I will not ask where thy wound was gotten, nor in what company; nor how thou art in such ragged plight. Take this money. Go into dock and refit. When this is spent, come to me for another. And when all is well again, volunteer and serve the king, and so keep out of mischief."

He shook his gold stick with admonition, and stumped away. But the man took the coin and held it in his hand, without saying a word of thanks, I still watching him in my foolish way, because so picturesque a rogue had I never seen, most of our ragged vagabonds spoiling their beauty, so to speak, by going in an old wig torn in half, burned, uncombed, and dirty, that hath, perhaps, been used by a shoeblack to rub the shoes in his trade. There is no picturesqueness possible in an old wig. Yet I was not so stupid but I saw in the man's eye a look which was both wistful and sorrowful, though I did not then interpret it in that manner.

So the admiral went on, followed by his good lady, who held her skirts in her hand, and stared at the man in her turn, as ladies sometimes look at such poor wretches—namely, as if they were of a different clay, and had another kind of Adam for their father. But one must not expect a gentlewoman such as the admiral's lady (she was by birth distantly connected with the Right Honorable the Earl of Bute, and a Scotswoman) to understand how, beneath the most rugged exterior, there may be found admirable qualities of courage and fidelity. So she

5*

gazed upon him, turned her head, and went her way after the admiral. After her came Castilla. " Poor man !" she said, in her sweet way, " I would I had some money to give thee; but I have none. Truly thou art to be pitied. I wish thee better fortune and a ship."

She had been taught by her father, and fully believed it, that the only place where these rough tarpaulins were happy and out of mischief was on board ship. Seeing that they are so often drunk and fighting and in trouble on shore, perhaps she was right. But then ashore there is no bo's'n, and there is no cat-o'-nine-tails, save for pickpockets. So she looked at him compassionately, and he moved his lips as if he would have spoken, but did not. And so she passed on her way.

Then came I myself. I said nothing, but he looked at me with a kind of sorrowful wonder. I remembered directly afterwards what that eye of his said as plain as it could speak; but at the moment I was deaf to its voice, and blind and stupid, thinking only of a bundle of rags on a tall figure, and how the man and the rags would look in a picture. After ourselves came the negroes and Philadelphy. The men rolled their eyes at this poor fellow with the contempt that a fat and well-fed negro always feels, forgetful of his skin, for a starving white man, and if their master had been out of hearing they would have laughed aloud, and even rolled on the ground, in the enjoyment of his suffering. Nothing makes a negro laugh more joyfully than to see somebody hurt. That is, perhaps, why some of their kings celebrate their most joyful festivals with horrid murders and rivers of blood. Philadelphy followed her young mistress, and had no eyes for any one else, being, though a witch and a sorceress, and an Obeah woman, faithful to Miss Castilla.

When we had passed, the vicar came out of the vestry, and so into Church Lane.

" Why, my friend," he said, stopping to contemplate the scarecrow, " where hast thou gotten these rags and this wound ?"

" I have escaped, sir, from a French prison, and have received a hurt on the forehead."

Something in his manner touched the vicar.

" Are you a common sailor ?" he asked.

" Do I look like aught else, sir? Heard one ever of an officer in such rags as mine?"

" Yet you speak like an educated man. And your voice seems familiar to me. Follow me to the vicarage, my poor man, where you shall have a plate of victuals and a tankard of ale, and we will see what can be done to replace some of these rags, which are not proper for a Christian man and an honest man to wear."

" How doth your reverence know that I am an honest man?"

" Nay, that I know not, and there are many rogues abroad. But it is not for me—God forbid!—to attempt to separate the sheep from the goats. Therefore, sheep or goat, follow me and be welcome, in the name of our Saviour."

The vicar left him, and he turned and would have followed, but for one thing.

We who were a few yards in advance, unthinking and unsuspecting, heard a cry which stopped the very beating of our hearts.

The cry was from Bess Westmoreland.

She too saw the ragged sailor when she passed through the churchyard gate. But she did not, like the rest of us, pass on and think no more. She suddenly broke from her father, pushed the crowd away to right and left, and fell on her knees upon the muddy ground, catching the man by both hands, like a mad thing, and crying:

" Oh, Jack! Jack! Jack! He is home again! Jack Easterbrook has come home again!"

Then, as we crowded round, we saw the tears run down his face. It was the first time and the last that ever any man saw Jack weep; yet he had plenty to cry for, both before this and after. He caught the girl by both hands, and bent over her, saying, as we all heard:

" Oh, Bess, Bess, none of them remembered me—not even Luke; none of them thought of me! But you remembered me, Bess! Oh, Bess! you remembered me!"

CHAPTER XI.

THE VOYAGE OF THE " COUNTESS OF DORSET."

THEN we all crowded round him, shaking his hand and rejoicing; and the admiral first swore at Jack for playing a trick
upon us (but, alas! it proved to be no trick), and then at
himself for his stupidity, and then could say nothing for the
tears which drowned his voice and ran down his cheeks. And
Jack declared first that he would never part with the admiral's
shilling, and next that he would not put off his rags until he
had first eaten the vicar's plate of victuals and drank his tankard.
This he did: and the vicar said grace solemnly, with thanks for
the safe return of the long-lost sailor; and we all flocked round
him to see him eat and drink. A pretty sight it was, for he
had not tasted honest roast beef for six long years. Then,
though it was Sunday, nothing would do but they must ring
the church bells, as if they would bring down the tower about
their heads. And Mr. Brinjes came running in shirt sleeves,
waistcoat, and nightcap, just as he left his shop, the lancet still
in his hand with which he had been bleeding people all the
morning.

Thus we carried home our poor ragged prodigal. After the
first confusion was over, I looked for Bess, but she had slipped
away, unheeded.

Then came the barber, and cut off his frightful beard,
trimmed and powdered his hair, and tied it behind with black
ribbon, so that he looked now like a Christian. More suitable
clothes were found for him, and as for his wound, Mr. Brinjes
dressed it for him, and covered it with plaster, telling him that
it was an ugly gash, but in a few days would be healed, save
for the scar across his forehead, a thing which no sailor heeds;
and then he stood before us, a proper and handsome fellow indeed. He had left us a lad, and he came back to us a man,
over six feet in height, and with broad shoulders and stout legs

"He caught the girl by both hands, and bent over her."

to match. His cheeks, 'tis true, were somewhat hollow and pale, because he had been on short commons for four years, as you will presently learn.

Now you will believe that we were eager to know what had befallen him; but we could at first get little talk with him, for all that afternoon there came to the house people of every kind, anxious to see and converse with this young hero, who had, it was reported in the town, escaped from the French after six years of captivity. The Church service in both churches was, that afternoon, read to empty pews, because all the worshippers were in the admiral's garden. Among them came the widows of those Deptford men who had sailed with Jack in the *Countess of Dorset*; many of them had long before this married again, and all were anxious to hear of their late husbands, inquiring particularly into the circumstances of their death, and appearing to find consolation in considering the dreadful nature of their sufferings. There came all Jack's former friends, who had not forgotten him, such as almsmen from Trinity Hospital, and pensioners from Greenwich; old sailors from Deptford and Rotherhithe, and even shipwrights and dock-yard carpenters. Mr. Westmoreland came, but without his daughter; and even, though this seems incredible, some of the Thames watermen, who had the grace to remember Jack Easterbrook. All the afternoon Cudjoe and Snowball, who ought to have been at church, trudged about with foaming tankards and mugs, giving everybody who desired an honest glass to drink the lieutenant's health (he was still only a midshipman, but they gave him promotion). And there were a thousand questions asked one after the other, so that long before the evening, when we were to have an account of the voyage, we knew pretty well what had happened. And, though it was Sunday, there was brewed a great bowl of punch for the evening; and in the end the admiral was carried to bed, and many of the guests retired with a rolling gait and thick voice; while as for me, the next morning showed, by trembling fingers and headache, besides the memory of uncertain steps, that I, too, had rejoiced among the rest beyond the limits of soberness. Among the company were, first, my father, the Vicar of St. Paul's; then Captain Petherick, the commissioner of the king's yard; Mr. Stephen Pett, who hath a ship-building yard of his own, where many fair vessels have been built; Mr. Mostyn, cocket writer in his majesty's custom-house; Lieutenant Hepworth, formerly of General Powlett's regiment of marines; Mr. Underhill; Mr. Shelvocke (the younger), who had himself been round the world in the year 1720, as everybody knows who has read the account of his father's voyage, and the malicious book concerning the same voyage written by Mr. Betagh, his captain of marines. There was also Mr. Brinjes. And I, for one, presently observed with pride that we had here assembled together in one room—a thing which could hardly be compassed in any other town, except Portsmouth, Plymouth, and Chatham—three men who had at three separate times sailed upon the great unknown Pacific; and of these two had actually circumnavigated the globe.

I have observed, having been born and brought up among men who delight in telling and hearing stories of battle, escapes, shipwrecks, and the like, that the hero of a hundred adventures is seldom as ready to tell them as he who hath in all his life experienced but one; and that, often enough, not of his own seeking, but against his own desire, and even entered upon in bodily fear. Yet Virgil makes Æneas relate his wanderings movingly and in the finest verse; and Shakespeare tells how Othello would, in the hearing of Desdemona, fight his battles over again. As for Jack, he had encountered so many perils, and met with so many adventures, and those of so extraordinary a kind, that one would not expect the hundredth part of them to be told in one evening. There were enough to fill a dozen books of travel, such as are generally written, most of them with no adventures more terrible than the upsetting of a coach or the appearance of a footpad; nay, I have never seen any books which contained such wonders as Jack had witnessed, if we except the voyages of Captain Clipperton, Captain Shelvocke, and Commodore Anson; and none of these commanders ever sailed among the islands which the *Countess of Dorset* visited. Yet he was not able, at first, to tell us much about them; and it was only by continual questioning and persuading him to talk, with the map lying open before him, that we could get him to unburden his mind of some of the things he had seen and undergone. Some men—of whom Jack was one—are so constituted that they do not seem to understand what people want to know, or what they should tell them. Our hero was not reticent, I am sure, from any fear of appearing boastful, because sailors love, above all things, to speak of their own adventures; but because, first, he felt, on this the first day of his return, new and strange to us, after six years of absence; and next, he was never good at narrating, save stories of fight; and further, it is not easy for any one to gather up immediately, and at short notice, all the recollections of the past six years. When a man has been two years with savages, or two years in a Spanish or French prison, he is apt to forget some of the things which happened before, even though they passed among the unknown islands of the Pacific Ocean.

"As for her course, now," he began, doubtfully. He had before him the map of the world, on Mercator's projection, by John Senex. It was my father's copy, and although the map is not on so large a scale as a ship's chart, yet it was big enough to serve. Deptford is too insignificant to be marked, and Jack's finger, when he would indicate the ship's starting-point, covered the whole of Kent, Middlesex, Essex, and Surrey. "As for her course, now," he repeated, looking at the map doubtfully, considering how best to begin. Perhaps he had forgotten how to use a map, since he had not seen one for four years. Castilla was standing on one side, looking over his shoulder, I at the other side. The admiral sat opposite, his red face filled with benevolence and affection. Surely there never was a kindlier face in the world. Behind him and beside the fireplace was his lady, not carried away so greatly by the general emotion, partly because she never entertained the same love for Jack that filled her husband's breast, and partly because, like most women, she was not in the least degree interested in foreign lands and savage races, and partly because she knew not the bottom of a map from the top. The gentlemen sat round the table as they chose, and at the sideboard the two negroes had charge of the smoking bowl. I love negroes for one thing: that is, for their fellow-feeling when any occasion for rejoicing and feasting arises. They would like the whole of their lives to be spent in feasting, drinking, and laughing. For instance, I do not suppose that these two rascals had given one single thought to Jack during the whole of his six years' absence, yet here they were, their mouths broad-grinning, their faces shining, their eyes twinkling and dancing, moving nimbly about with the glasses, taking care, with the greatest zeal, that the admiral's was kept always full, and that none of the gentlemen should be allowed so much as to glance inquiringly in the direction of the bowl. Had it been the return of their own son they could not have shown a livelier joy. N.B.—Later in the evening, when the admiral was in bed and the guests gone, they finished the bowl themselves; and had it not been for Jack, who in the morning was so good as to pump upon them, they certainly would have incurred the wrath of the admiral, for they were, even at eight o'clock in the morning, and after a night's sleep, still more than half seas over.

"Oh, Jack," said Castilla, "to think that you should remember her course after all these years!"

"Easy a bit, my lad," said the admiral. "Take another glass before we begin. Gentlemen, fill up. Fill up the gentlemen's glasses, ye black rogues! This is a joyful evening—an evening out of ten thousand. And to think that none of us knew him except Bess, the penman's girl! Castilla, my dear where were your eyes?"

"Indeed, sir, I was thinking of the vicar's discourse, else I am sure I should have known Jack."

"And where were yours, Luke? and where were mine?—to treat him like a ragamuffin tarpaulin! Well, well! Fill up Mr. Jack's glass, Snowball. Drink, my lad; Castilla loves a sailor who can take his whack. Drink her health as I drink thine, dear lad."

Castilla laughed. She loved soberness and temperance; but Jack did not come home every day.

"As for her course, now," said the admiral.

"We sailed from Deptford—"

"You did, my boy, and I well remember the day, six years ago, when the *Countess of Dorset* dipped her ensign and fired her salute. The boy tells me, gentlemen, that for four years he has never tasted punch—poor lad! nor quaffed a tankard of ale—think of it! nor sat down to a comfortable pipe of tobacco; nor known the comforts of a hammock in a seaworthy and weather-tight vessel. For four years! Your reverence, it is Sunday evening; but with respect to the cloth "—the admiral turned his face, rosy and beaming as the setting sun, to my father—" when the prodigal son came home, did his father

THE WORLD WENT VERY WELL THEN.

ask the chaplain, who, I suppose was a Levite, whether it was the Sabbath Day before he ordered the fatted calf to be killed and roasted ?"

"We do not learn that he did so," replied my father. "Though, doubtless—"

"Then, sir, suffer us to believe, for our satisfaction at the present juncture, that the event, like another one of later occurrence, happened on the Sabbath Day. Then have we authority of Holy Writ for making merry on the Sabbath Day."

At this display of wit they all laughed, without rebuke from the vicar.

"Go on, Jack; go on, my lad. I must still be talking, when it is Jack we want to hear. Your health, my lad, your health. I never thought to see thy honest phiz again. Thy hand again, Jack. This is a joyful evening, gentlemen. Damme, I say again, a joyful evening." Yet the tears stood in his eyes.

We were all moved, and the admiral more than any. But Mr. Brinjes sat in his place, his one eye, like a ball of fire, fixed on Jack. I knew that he was recalling his own voyage in the southern seas, and thinking of his treasure. It was as if some scent or fragrance of the islands which he loved to talk about was clinging to Jack.

Then our returned prodigal went on with his narrative, and if the interruptions of the admiral are not set down, with his ejaculations and oaths, it is because, were everything to be told, no history would ever come to an end. Wherefore they are omitted ; nor have I tried to set down all that Jack said, nor a tenth part, on this evening, because half the time he was answering questions from Mr. Shelvocke, who must needs show his knowledge of those seas, and from Mr. Brinjes, who had also sailed upon them, and from Captain Pethcrick, who was a great lover of geography. I have also ventured to omit that part of his narrative which related to the behavior of the crew, the sailing qualities of the ship, and those matters generally which concern sailors and which would only be understood by them. "We sailed, as you remember, admiral, carrying with us twenty-five guns, with a crew of one hundred and twenty men all told, and provisions for twenty-four months. Gentlemen, with submission, I venture to remark that no navy provision exists which will last twenty-four months, for the biscuit becomes weevilly, and the pork and beef rancid; and as to the cheese and the salt butter— But there !"

"He is right," said Mr. Underhill.

"We were fortunate, however, and fell in, before we suffered much from this cause, with provisions of another kind. The last land that we saw was the Start, and the next was Cape Finisterre. We then stood away for the Island of Teneriffe, where we designed to take in wine, rum, and brandy, the captain being of opinion that to keep a merry heart in the crew—which is above all things desirable on a long voyage—a double ration is often necessary; wherefore we laid in at the town of Santa Cruz a great store of malmsey, canary, and verdina, which is a greenish-colored wine and strong bodied, but keeps well in hot climates.

"After leaving Teneriffe we were becalmed for three weeks; during which, I remember, we caught two very fine sharks, off which the men regaled. Then we touched at St. Helena. After this we were driven off our course by the trade-wind, and sighted Tristan d'Acunha; we put in at the Cape, and after leaving Algoa Bay we steered nor'-nor'east, passing the southern point of Madagascar, where we expected to meet with pirates."

"I fear they are all dead," said Mr. Brinjes. "Their settlement was on the northeast coast, which is not so full of fever as the southwest. Dead now they must be, every man. And I doubt if their children, darkies all, would have the spirit to carry on the business."

"Our course was now to the coast of New Holland, the object of the voyage being, as the captain told us, to discover new lands, and, if possible, countries where British settlements might rival those of Spain in the Manillas and the Ladrones."

"You did not visit the Manillas, then?" said Mr. Shelvocke. "There is nothing in those seas which can surpass the Manillas in beauty and fertility."

"The pope," said my father, "pretended, in his pride, to confer upon the Spaniards all the lands beyond the Atlantic, including, I suppose, Magellanica, or the Pacific Ocean, which was not then discovered."

"We had bad weather crossing this great ocean, whereon we sailed for two months, or thereabout, with never a sight of

land. Then we began to find seaweed, with cuttle-bones and
bonitos, and after two or three days we sighted land; but,
finding nothing except rocks and foul ground, we stood off
again."

His finger was now on the coast of the great unknown southern island called New Holland. "On the third or fourth day
we found an opening in the land, and anchored in two fathoms and a half of water. We called the place Shark's Bay,
and we stayed here a week. The shore is shelving to the sea,
and we saw there a kind of animal like the West Indian mac-
caroon, save that it has long hind-legs, on which it jumps;
and I think it was there that we found an ugly kind of guana,
which stinks. The natives were naked black men, some of
them painted with a kind of pigment, and their hair frizzled.
They seem to live on shell-fish, and carry lances with heads of
flint."

"I had hoped," said my father, "to hear of some polite and
civilized nation, with arts and sciences, and traditions of the
patriarchal religion, and of gentle manners."

"Their manners," Jack continued, "are beastly, and their
ways are treacherous; and as for religion, we saw no sign of
any. How can savages have any religion who live on mussels?
I have lived on them myself, and felt no promptings of religion all the time, but only discontent and swearing. Well, gentlemen, we continued our voyage, and I dare say we carried
the coast-line a good bit farther than this map shows; but my
memory serves me not on this point, and my own as well as the
ship's log was lost when the ship was cast away."

"Our course," said Mr. Shelvocke, "was north of these latitudes. Wherefore I have never visited the shores of New
Holland. This I regret the less, having seen the Manillas."

"When we reached the most southerly point, which, I dare
say, may be somewhere near to the place on the map, the captain called together his lieutenants, the master and the captain
of marines, and over a cheerful glass opened his mind to them,
as we presently heard in the gunroom. He said that his orders were general, and that it was reported by those who had
sailed on those seas, particularly by those who thought it no
sin to hoist the Jolly Roger—"

"It is not," said Mr. Brinjes, stoutly, "provided that it is in Spanish waters only. I have myself sailed under the cross-bones and skull. Sin? Why, it is a commendable action to maul and harass the Spaniards."

"The captain said that it was reported," Jack continued, "that there are islands in those seas of incredible wealth, compared with which Mr. Shelvocke's Manillas are poor; but that the Spaniards either endeavor to keep the secret of these islands to themselves, or they have not the curiosity to seek them out. His design was, therefore, to seek for these islands, even though we might have to fight the Spaniards should we meet them; and if any place should be found to possess the wealth they are supposed to contain, then, Spaniard or no Spaniard, to plant the flag of Great Britain upon them; and, if Heaven should prosper our enterprise, presently to return by the Straits of Magellan.

"So we steered a course northeast by north, across an open sea, with fair winds, sighting no land at all until we were in latitude twenty degrees south, or thereabout, when we came to a great island; if, indeed, it be not a part of the great Southern continent. Gentlemen"—Jack broke off here—"I cannot tell you all, nor a tenth part, of what we saw in those seas. There are thousands of islands, all much finer than you can imagine."

"They are—they are," said Mr. Brinjes. "I have seen them myself."

"Our own course," said Mr. Shelvocke, jealously, "was in the northern latitude, the islands of which are incomparable."

"And of what kind are the people?"

"For the most part we found them gentle and generous. No travellers have ever visited these islands that we could learn; they know nothing of the Spaniards; they are black, and go naked, and they can all swim like fishes."

"They can," said Mr. Brinjes, "especially the young women."

"Of what kind is their religion?" asked the vicar.

"I think, sir, that they have none"—Mr. Brinjes shook his head—"at least we saw no signs of any; though, of course, we could not talk to them in their own language. The islands are so close together that it is impossible to sail more than a day or two without coming in sight of a new archipelago; some there are which we judged as big as Ireland, perhaps, and others not more than half an acre; some there are which are only coral reefs lying in a circle round smooth water, no bigger than some of the West Indian keys, and some there are which are covered with great mountains and volcanoes."

"It is true—it is quite true," said Mr. Brinjes.

"And as for the riches of them?" asked one of the company.

"I know not if there be any. We made such signs as we thought would make them understand that we wanted gold and precious stones; but they produced none, and we believed that they have no knowledge of gold, even if there be gold in their mountains. Of pearls there must needs be plenty, seeing that there are oysters in abundance. But we saw none."

"No gold and no jewels!" said my father. "Happy islanders!"

"And they seem to have all things in common."

"Wherefore the main temptations to sin," said my father, "are removed. Where there is no private property there can be no robbery, no envying, no jealousies, no overreaching. Oh, thrice-happy people, if they knew their own happiness!"

"If we had not lost the log," Jack continued, "we should have covered these seas with islands never before seen, even by Dampier, Magellan, Drake, or Rogers. Now, no one knows where they are, and I alone, of all living men, unless it be Mr. Brinjes, have seen them. As for our gallant company"—here he paused and looked around him solemnly. I have noticed many sailors do the same thing; it is as if they were counting those present, to be sure that they, too, are not shipwrecked men—"they are all dead by now, I doubt not. Unless some escaped of whom I know nothing, who may be living yet among the Indians."

"Fill his glass," said the admiral. "Gentlemen, let us drink to the memory of these poor fellows, cast away, and now dead."

"There is no such sailing," Jack continued, "anywhere in the world—"

"There is not," Mr. Brinjes interrupted.

"—save for the constant temptation for the men to desert, and live in indolence among those people. Better would it have been, save for one who now sits here among you all, had the whole ship's company gone ashore and stayed there, to live in the warm air and sunshine of that climate."

"Better to die a Christian than live a heathen," said the vicar.

"Well, we had the Church Service read every Sunday morning," said Jack, "which was no doubt a comfortable thing for the poor fellows to think upon when the rocks were cracking their skulls like egg-shells. But as for the sailing, so long as we were among the islands, it was like cruising upon a pond, with fresh fruit, and fish of all kinds, and wild birds in plenty to be shot. Sir"—he addressed the vicar—"this place is surely the Garden of Eden, though there is in Scripture no mention made of any seas. Of this the captain, who was a sober and religious man, was well assured."

"The site of the garden," said my father, "hath been placed in Mesopotamia, between the Tigris and Euphrates, or in Arabia Felix, or at the foot of the Caucasus, or near Damascus, but never, that I know of, in Magellanica or Oceanus Australis. And I know not how it could be there, unless the Euphrates and the Nile have greatly changed their course."

"It cannot be anything else but the Garden of Eden," said Jack; "though, perhaps, in the Deluge much of it was swallowed up, and only the tops of the mountains left above water."

"Should we ever," said the vicar, "find that garden, which doubtless exists somewhere upon the earth—nay, some have pretended to have seen it—we shall also find the gate, and at the gate the angel with a flaming sword turning in every direction to keep the way of the Tree of Life. But it may very well be that, when the curse of labor was imposed upon man for the sin of Adam—in consequence of which some parts of the world were afflicted with aridity and sand, other parts were covered with ice and snow, others, again, became marshes, and others became hard and unprofitable for the toilers—that some parts were left by merciful design in their virginal and pristine beauty, just as they left the hand of the Creator at the dawn of the first Sabbath, being reserved for this generation to discover, so that faith might be strengthened, and true religion revived in the world, by so striking a proof of the divine narrative. But let us go on, for the hour groweth late."

"Alas! gentlemen, there is very little more to tell, and the rest of the history of the ill-fated *Countess of Dorset* is all misfortune. We came at length to an end of these islands, which we parted with to our great regret; and so, with open sea, steering now east or southeast, with design to make Juan Fernandez or the Island of Masafuera, when we were within thirty or forty leagues, according to our reckoning, of these islands, there fell upon us a dreadful gale, or succession of gales, which lasted a week or more, so far as I remember, the ship driving before the wind under bare poles. Then we lost our foremast, and presently both mainmast and mizzenmast went by the board; and for great waves and the force of the wind I never experienced the like. We rigged a jury-mast with difficulty, and a foresail to steady her head. By this time our bulwarks were broken and our boats stove in, so that there was very little hope left us, except that the gale might abate, in which case we might keep her afloat—for now she had sprung aleak, and the men were kept day and night to the pump—until we could make some kind of raft. As for our guns, we heaved them overboard, with everything else that would lighten the ship. Gentlemen, the gale did not abate; on the contrary, it blew harder, if that were possible; and I think everybody on board had given up hope. As for the men, some of them did their duty to the last; but some of them became mutinous, and wanted to get to the spirit store, and go down happy. Which is, I take it, a fool's way of dying."

"It is," said the vicar.

"I have seen them die that way," said Mr. Brinjes. "Some men have even walked the plank, after drinking a pint or so of rum, dancing and laughing, and with the end of a song on their lips. But, no doubt, 'tis better to go down sober. Besides, there is always some hope for a sober man, but none for a drunken one."

"I do not know, gentlemen, how long this lasted. We unshipped our rudder, I remember, which finished our misfortunes, for now the ship lay like a log in the trough of the waves, which rolled her about as they pleased. And how many were washed overboard I know not; nor how many were left in the ship when, at last, she struck the rocks and was beaten to pieces. I would rather face a dozen broadsides than wait again, for a week or more, with death almost certain at the end of it. To judge from the haggard faces of those who waited with me, and to remember my own mind—why, we die a hundred deaths

in the mere apprehension and waiting for it.   Most of us died
in earnest before long.   For one morning, when the daylight
came, we saw before us a most dreadful sight, namely, the coast
of Patagonia, which is the most inhospitable, I suppose, in the ·
world, and the most terrible, by reason of its rocks and preci-
pices.   We were driving right upon the coast.   Then, indeed,
we gave ourselves up for lost.   When we struck, the sea lifted
her and beat her against the rocks, breaking and grinding her
timbers as if she had been nothing bigger than a Portsmouth
wherry ; and the waves broke over her at the same time, washing the men from the places where they were clinging.   As for
me, I was carried off, and what happened to me afterwards I
know not, save that I lost consciousness, and when I recovered
I found myself lying on a ledge of rock ; but how I got there,
whether carried thither by some great wave or upon some piece
of wreck, I know not.   The first thing I did was to make sure
that I had no bones broken.   I was not, indeed, hurt in any
way, save that from head to foot I was covered with bruises,
which were of small account.   And then I turned to look at
the wreck.   We were surely landed in the worst place in the
world ; it was a narrow creek, or bay, between high cliffs, into
which the sea rushed with violence inexpressible.   Already the
ship was broken up, save for the afterpart, where there were
still clinging two or three poor wretches ; below my feet, in the
boiling water, grinding against each other, were pieces of wreck,
and, most terrible to see, there were mangled bodies of our poor
fellows, dashed against the rocks and among the broken timbers.   It is wonderful to think that any of us escaped.

"At first I thought that I was alone, the only man saved.
But there were others, and I found that most of them, like
myself, could not tell how they had got ashore, and why they
were not, like their shipmates, dashed to pieces.   There were
fourteen of us in number, and no more came ashore ; wherefore, seeing the violence of the waves and the impossibility of
swimming in such a sea, we concluded that the rest were all
drowned.   When the wind abated, which was the next day, we
managed to get up to the rocks some of the timber and wreck
washed ashore, and made some kind of shelter ; but we could
not light a fire, and it was now the winter season in these latitudes, and cold.   There were one or two casks of provisions

which reached the shore unbroken and not touched by the sea ;
we lived upon them while they lasted, our drink being rain-
water, of which there was plenty. When this supply ceased
we had nothing to subsist upon at all but shell-fish, of which
there were at first great quantities, but we presently exhausted
them, and then we had to leave our hut, such as it was, and to
move on along the coast in order to find more. We were all
the time as men in a dream, not knowing where we were nor
what to do ; all day we gazed stupidly at each other, and all
night we crouched together for warmth. But when the time came
that we must leave our rocks we began to take counsel. My
companions were common sailors, rude and ignorant fellows ;
and as for me, I knew nothing except that I was certain that
we must be somewhere upon the western shore of South America ; that part of it which is called Patagonia. Now if we
marched south we should in time come to the Straits of Magellan, through which there might pass some ship ; but how long
we should wait, or how great the distance might be, we knew
nothing. And every day's march would bring us into colder
and more desolate regions. On the other hand, if we marched
north we might, in the long run, reach the Spanish settlements,
which are reported to stretch southward very far. But, again,
should we reach them, it was most likely that they would murder us, or hand us over to the Inquisition to be burned alive
for heretics. However, we decided in the end to march north,
which we did, leaving behind four of our number who had died,
partly of cold and partly of flux, brought on by the shell-fish
diet, which afflicted us in various ways. As for myself, it covered my whole body with an intolerable itching, which flew
from one part to another, so that I got no rest day or night."

"It is a prurigo," said Mr. Brinjes. "There is no cure for
it but a change of diet."

"We were by this time in as miserable a plight as ever be-
fell shipwrecked sailors, for the weather was continually wet
and cold ; as for our clothes, they were rags, wet through day
and night ; we were pinched with hunger ; we had not a shoe
to our feet ; there was not a single tool or weapon, not even a
knife among us. A man, gentlemen, without tools, is in sorry
case. So we began our way along the coast, which we durst
not leave, partly for fear of wild beasts and natives, and partly

6

because while we kept near the sea we should not starve. We wandered in this way, seeking such shelter as we could find, and always wet, cold, and half starved for a month or two—I know not how long. But one day we fell in with a tribe of Indians. By this time, I remember, there were only eight of us left. These men came to meet us, brandishing spears and threatening to kill us; while we, for our part, had nothing to do except to make signs showing how helpless and harmless we were. So they took us with them; and I think I never spent a happier evening than the first, when we lay upon the ground about a great fire, with broiled fish to eat and seal-skin to cover us. We had not been warm or dry for a matter of three months. As for living with them, we soon got tired of that life, except two of our company, who took Indian wives, and resolved to continue among them. For, like us, they lived by the sea-shore, having no knowledge of any agriculture, and devoured fish and mussels, oysters, and so forth, all of which were collected for them by their wives. I have never seen any more dexterous than these poor women in diving and catching fish, which they would drive, by frightening, into some small creek or inlet of the sea, where they could not escape, and were easily captured. They also collected and ate certain berries, which were nauseous at first, but which we presently grew to consider as useful against the disorders caused by a fish diet. But as for the dirt and the vermin, and the savage nature of the life we led, I cannot so much as speak of these things. Sometimes when, by reason of storm and gales, fish was scarce, we were driven to live on the flesh of seals, and that putrid and stinking. And because we depended so much upon the mussels and oysters, we were obliged continually to shift our quarters, and slowly drew more and more northward, until at last we arrived at the most southerly of the Spanish settlements, which consisted of nothing else than a kind of convent and a church with four priests. For my own part, I approached the place with terror, thinking that the stake would be set up and the flames would be consuming us as soon as the priests should understand that we were Englishmen and Protestants. Well, gentlemen, they never so much as asked us of what religion we were. But these good priests—your reverence will forgive me—"

" There are charitable hearts in every country and in every religion," said the vicar.   " Why not in Magellanica ?"

" They gave us clothes to put on ; they washed and dressed our wounds, because by this time we were covered all over with sores and bad places.   They gave us good food, and wine to drink, and they heard our story—one of them could speak English—with tears and pity.   They told us that we must be sent to the nearest Spanish port as prisoners, but bade us be of good courage, because we should be treated well."

" In those remote parts," said the vicar, " the pope and the Inquisition being so far off, there is room for the growth of human feelings, even with priests."

" After six months living among them—a better and a more charitable brotherhood I never hope to meet—there came an opportunity of conveying us to the Island of Chiloe, where there is a Spanish governor.   Now I reckon that the ship was cast away two years and a half after we sailed, it being then midwinter, which, on the coast of Patagonia, is in the month of July ; and I think that we lived with the Indians for the space of two years ; it was time enough to wear out all that were left of our rags, so that we went into the convent with nothing but seal-skin over our shoulders, tied round the waist with a thong of seal-skin leather.   We stayed at Chiloe, where we were treated more hardly than with the priests, yet not cruelly, for three or four months, when the governor was able to send us on to the port of Callao."

" He is now," said the admiral, " prisoner of the Spanish, and within reach of the Bloody Inquisition.   Snowball, fill up Mr. Easterbrook's glass.   Keep it full, ye lubber ! at such a time he needs all the punch he can swallow."

" Out of the whole ship's company there remained now but six.   They put us in prison, but they gave us wine and food, chiefly beans, bread, and onions, as good as they had themselves, and sometimes chocolate.   Presently there came a priest, and began to talk about our heretical condition, and the dangers we ran should we continue in obstinacy.   This made us mighty uneasy, as you may imagine, because the Inquisition—the Holy Inquisition, as they call it—is established at Lima, whither, the padre informed us, we should shortly be taken.   It seemed likely that we had only escaped drowning to suffer the rack and the stake. I hope, gentlemen, that I should have done my duty even to the end, had there been no escape. Meantime I cast about how to get out of their clutches. We had a good deal of liberty within the prison, and many visitors came there bringing cigarettos, which are rolls of paper containing tobacco, to the prisoners, who were mostly half-caste, in prison for stabbing, or sailors for mutiny, the authorities caring little how the prisoners pass the time so long as they are kept in limbo. In this way I made the acquaintance of an honest Frenchman, captain of a trading brig, who, I found, hated the priests and all their works, and took pity on me, seeing that I must either become a convert or be burned. He therefore brought me a disguise, and conveyed me safely out of prison on board his own ship, where I remained stowed away in the hold until he sailed out of harbor. As for the other men, three of them recanted their errors, as they called it, and walked in the procession at an *auto-da-fé* at Lima, where the other poor fellows, who stuck by their guns, were burned alive."

" 'Tis a damnable nation," said Mr. Brinjes.

" Say rather," said the vicar, " that it is a nation under the curse of a gloomy superstition, which prompts them to commit these cruelties."

" As for me, I worked before the mast, and found the French sailors, when I could talk their lingo, an honest set of fellows. But when we got to Brest, we learned that war had broken out; and so I was a prisoner again, and marched as a common sailor, with others in the same plight, from one place to another, till we came to St. Omer."

CHAPTER XII.

HOW JACK THANKED BESS.

EARLY in the evening, when the common sort had all gone away, well filled with the admiral's best October, and before the gentlemen arrived, Jack left us, and stole quite unnoticed from the house. As he left us, so he returned, no one having observed that he had been absent for a moment. Yet we were all of us talking and thinking of no one else, and believed that

he was still among us. So, in a play at the theatre, when the
mind is fully charged and occupied with the hero, so that one
can think of nothing but his adventures, we do not perceive
that he is no longer on the stage before our eyes; and when
he presently returns, we do not remember that he has ever
been out of our sight, and all that has passed seems to have
been done in his presence.

But why Jack left us, and whither he went, I have since
been told, and that, as one may say, on credible authority—
namely, by the only person who knows.

In short, he left us to go in search of Bess, his heart being
already inflamed by the thought of her beauty, and fired with
gratitude because, of all his old friends, she alone recognized him.
Ulysses was recognized by none but his dog. Why, Jack
would have been less· than human, a mere senseless log, had
he not been moved by this circumstance. And so far from
senseless, his was a heart as easily inflamed as touchwood.

Bess was sitting on the floor before the fire, her father being
somewhere abroad, I suppose, in conversation with his friends
and cronies, the sexton and the barber. It was Sunday evening, therefore she had no knitting or work of other kind in her
hands. She could not read, and therefore she had not taken
one of her father's books ; and she was alone, therefore she
was not talking. Outside, the night had already fallen, but
she was not one of those who waste good money by burning
candle and fire at the same time, unless for the sake of work.
The red firelight played upon her cheeks, and made them glow,
and upon her eyes, and made them red balls, and upon the
walls of the room, which were covered with specimens of the
penman's art, pasted on the wainscot, and on the sideboard,
where stood the candlesticks of brass, and the snuffers polished
and bright, with the house pewter, which shone like silver, so
good a housewife was this girl. Her hands lay folded in her
lap, and she was leaning forward as if reading faces in the red
coals, as children sometimes love to play. I think she saw
one face only, and that a strange, wild face, with matted hair
and long beard, and a bloody clout across the forehead. As
to her thoughts—who can read the thoughts that crowd into
the head of a young girl ? I would not dare to say that up to
that time Bess was in love with her old playfellow; yet it is

certain, because Mr. Brinjes spoke so much of him, that he often occupied her mind.   Nor was it, I venture to say, all on Jack's account that she would listen to none of Aaron Fletcher's advances.   Yet she must have been hard-hearted indeed had this home-coming failed to move her soul.   I have sometimes thought that if at this time Jack had made no advances to her, she must presently have taken Aaron and thought no more of her old playfellow, save as of a gallant gentleman belonging to a class above her.   No man can speak positively of a woman's mind ; but I am assured that it is seldom in the nature of a woman to love any man—though she may greatly admire him—until he hath first shown and proved by words and looks that he thinks of her and loves her.   Therefore, if Jack had made no advances—however, it is idle to talk of advances ; such a man as Jack doth not make advances, they are for cooler and more cautious men ; he lands, charges, and carries by storm the fortress which expected to be besieged by well-known rules.

Now, as she sat there watching the coals glowing in the fire, Bess suddenly started, and her heart ceased to beat, for at the door she heard a step.   She remembered that step after six long years, and the latch was lifted, and Jack himself came in—a thing she had not so much as ventured to hope, though she expected that he might in a day or two call to see her father, if he should still remember his former instructor.

She sprang to her feet, half afraid, yet rejoicing.

" Bess !" he cried, hoarsely.   " You had not forgotten me ?"

He was dressed now, shaven, and washed ; a tall and handsome man, though pale and somewhat hollow in the cheek.

" Bess !" he repeated, holding out both hands, " have you nothing to say to me ?"

" Oh, Jack ?" she whispered, timidly.   But now she was trembling, and really afraid of him, because there was a look in his eyes which frightened her : a strange look it is, which painters, for the most part, have failed to catch ; it is one which makes the eyes soft and glowing ; it is the look of love and longing.   Bess had never seen that look, and it frightened her.

" Jack," she said, " shall I go and look for father ?"

" Oh !" he answered, " you knew me, Bess !"   His voice was husky.   " All the rest had forgotten me ; but you knew me. Look for your father? Not yet, Bess! not yet! Oh, Bess!" He said no more, but caught her hands, drew her towards him, and kissed her a thousand times.

Then, in a moment, all her love went out to him. She gave him all her heart. Thenceforward she was no longer afraid of him; yet she was his servant and his slave, though he called her mistress.

"My dear," he said, presently, "let me look at my sweetheart. Nay, the firelight will do to light those eyes; no need of a candle. Oh, the sweet face! And what a tall girl she is! Is it the firelight on her cheeks, or is she blushing because her lover hath kissed her? And, oh, the rosy lips! Kiss me, Bess. Kiss me, and tell me that you love me. My dear, I had forgotten no one at home—no one; but until you caught my hands to-day, I did not know how much I loved you. And now, tell me, pretty, hast thou sometimes thought of Jack?"

"Oh, yes," she told him. "I have never forgotten—never; and I knew you were not drowned, whatever they said, and Mr. Brinjes always declared that some day you would come home again. Often and often I have gone to Philadelphy and inquired of her concerning a young sailor—meaning you, Jack —but I did not tell her who it was, and always her reply was that he was safe, and would come home again, though to be sure, she said, there were dangers in the way. She is a proper witch, and knows. But, oh! Jack, go away; this is foolishness; you must not kiss me any more, because you are a gentleman, and I am only a simple girl, and the daughter of a plain man. You must not talk of love to me; you must not think of me, Jack. I know you would not laugh at me, and mock me; but you must not think of me, Jack. Why, there are fine ladies in plenty who would die for love of you!"

"And could you die for love of me, Bess? Oh! how could I live so long without thee?"

"Oh, Jack!" she murmured, laying her head upon his shoulder, "I would rather die of love for you than live for the love of some one else; and, oh! if you left off loving me I should sit down and pray to die at once."

He kissed her again—I know not how many times he kissed her—telling her, which was quite true, because his thoughts ran not that way, that he cared not a fig for all the fine ladies in London town, with their nimby-namby, piminy ways, and their hoops and paint; but he loved an honest girl with roses of her own in her cheeks, who would love him in return. And so their pretty love talk went on, with thee and thou, and kisses sweet as honey to this girl, who knew not how or why she should conceal her joy and her love.

"I never knew," Bess told me afterwards, "no, I never knew what happiness could be until I sat that evening with my sweetheart's arms round my waist, and my face upon his shoulder, so that he could kiss me as often as he pleased, and whisper that he loved me. Oh, why—why should he love me? he so handsome and so splendid, and I so simple a maid. What are a girl's good looks compared with a man's? And how should he be able to love one who is not a gentlewoman—he who might, had he chosen, have married a countess?"

When he left her, which was all too soon, because the admiral would be expecting him, the girl fell upon her knees and prayed. This was a thing (she confessed it to me herself) which she had never done before in her life, except in church, and according to the Forms contained in the "Book of Common Prayer." If one may venture so to speak of a book which hath engaged the thoughts and labors of learned and pious men since the foundation of the Church—I mean the "Book of Common Prayer"—there is one unfortunate omission in its forms: it provides, that is to say, for all the other great events in life, namely, birth, baptism, marriage, the arrival of children, sickness, and death, but there is no form of prayer for the betrothal of a man and a maid. Yet there are many appropriate lessons that might be taken for it from the Old and New Testament; and there are many grateful and joyful Psalms; and there are lovesick verses; better, surely, were never written; especially in the Song of Solomon; and, without doubt, if ever there were occasion for prayer and praise, it is when a pair of lovers promise in private what they will presently promise in the sight of the congregation. Bess, poor child, knew no prayer fit for the occasion; but she knelt upon the floor, and with tears she thanked God for the safe return of her lover, and implored him to extend his continual protection over him.

When Mr. Westmoreland came home at half-past eight, he

was astonished to find that his daughter had forgotten to put out the bread and cheese and beer. Heard one ever of housewife forgetting to lay the supper? And though he talked about nothing but Jack Easterbrook—his unexampled sufferings and his wonderful and providential preservation—this strange daughter of his was so cold and unfeeling about her old playfellow that she hardly said a word, but made haste to go to bed, where she was removed from her father's chatter, and could lie contentedly awake all night long, her foolish heart beating with the joy of this great happiness.

CHAPTER XIII.

JACK ASHORE.

THE next day, accompanied by the admiral and Captain Petherick, Jack went to the navy office in Seething Lane to report himself.

And here began trouble he did not expect. For, seeing that they had long since written off the ship as cast away, and her company as dead, at first it appeared as if Jack had lost his seniority for certain, even if he had not been removed from the king's service. The latter view was stoutly maintained by the clerks, who argued that if a man has been written off as dead, he must be dead, or else—a thing impossible and absurd, if not treasonable—the navy office must be charged with error; so that, if he should afterwards be so rash as to return, he must either be considered out of the service, or must begin again at the bottom of the ladder; otherwise their books would have to be rewritten; very likely the estimates must be amended, and perhaps even a new audit undertaken. There was much correspondence on this subject carried on between the various departments; and, for aught I know, it may still be going on. While it was still in agitation, they began to send him about, like a ball at the game of cricket, from one office to another. First, they sent him to the surveyor's department, which required him to make a return of the ship's stores and their expenditure up to the conclusion of the voyage; and asked him also to produce the purser's, bo's'n's, and carpenter's ac-

6*

counts, the muster-book, and the log-book, these books being always, by regulation, required of the captain on his return. The clerks in the navy office, who receive fifty pounds a year, and live at ten, or even twenty times that rate in war time, thus showing how an honest man may prosper merely by the handling of ship's books and the passing the captain's papers, gave this young officer, from whose handling no profit could be obtained for themselves, as much trouble as Jacks-in-office possibly can ; and, being themselves bound and tied by all kinds of rules, they were able to hamper grievously any officer who doth not first grease their palms.

Next, when Jack expected to receive the six years' pay, which was certainly due to him, there was trouble with the comptroller's department, which contended that, as he had not served for more than two years, he was entitled to no more than so much pay, and that only when it could be proved that he had served to the satisfaction of the captain, who, we know, was dead and gone ; and that, as regards the four years of wandering and captivity, they must not count as service at all.

Thirdly, when Jack asked permission to pass his examination in seamanship for lieutenant's rank, it was objected by the clerks of the secretary's department, first, that he had not, in accordance with the regulations, put in his log-books or journals ; secondly, that he could not show the certificate of the captain ; and thirdly, that he had not served for the six years required by the rules of the service. At all these vexatious delays Jack lost his temper, and would, in the navy office itself, give the clerks, in good fo'k's'le English, his opinion as to their motives and their honesty, which, of course, exasperated those gentlemen, and made them stand out still more stiffly for the letter of the law.

Now, while these things were under consideration, the commissioners themselves, being informed of what had happened, sent for Jack, and examined him personally concerning the ship's course, the discoveries she had made, the natural riches of the islands among which he had sailed, and the possibility of establishing settlements and posts upon them which might prove effective in restraining the insolence of the Spanish, and in preventing the establishment of the French power in those regions. Finally, they instructed him to draw up, without further delay, a report upon the voyage, as full as his memory would allow, for the information of the commissioners and the government, containing all that he could remember of the course, and what he had observed concerning those islands, and especially on the force of the Spaniards on the South American shores; and, which was no doubt gall and worm-wood to the clerks, my lords the commissioners were gracious-ly pleased to order that the rules of the service should in this case be suspended, and that, in consideration of Mr. Easter-brook's previous good character, and undoubted sufferings after the wreck of his ship—for which he could not be held in any way accountable—his seniority should be restored to him, his years of wandering and captivity should be all counted as years of service, and that he should therefore receive full pay for the whole six years of service as midshipman on board a first-rate—namely, at two pounds five shillings a month, which made the handsome sum of one hundred and sixty-two pounds; and, lastly, that he should be permitted, on passing his examina-tion, to assume the rank and uniform of lieutenant, with the assurance of a commission to a ship as soon as it was possible to find one for him. This promise was given him so gravely, and by so great a personage, that Jack placed the most certain trust in it.

It was easier for Jack to pass his examination in seamanship and navigation, and to put on his new uniform, than to write the report asked of him; for he had never the pen of a ready writer, nor had he the least knowledge of the art of composition; he had forgotten how to spell even simple words, having been deprived of books for four years; and he had almost forgot-ten how to write. He, therefore, by the admiral's advice, sought the help of my father, who questioned him minutely on every point; and then, with the assistance of the charts, drew up with his own hand the required report; though, with pardonable license, it purported to be written by none other than Mr. Easterbrook. It contained all the information which the author could elicit by careful and repeated examination, and, if published, would have proved a work of the greatest curiosity and instruction, embellished with the charm of learned and scholarly style which was so much admired in my father's sermons, enriched with reflections and meditations proper for

the various scenes and adventures through which the (supposed)
writer passed, and made useful for meditation by Scriptural
references. The report was accompanied by a chart showing
part of the western coast of New Holland, with that portion
of the Pacific Ocean lying south of the equator over which the
Countess of Dorset had sailed. This part of the sea was depicted, by the hand which drew the chart, as covered with islands, on both sides of the ship's way, lying as thick as daisies
on a grass border. Mr. Westmoreland it was who drew the
chart; but he was advised and assisted by Jack himself, and
by Mr. Brinjes. He painted the water blue, and the islands
and coasts red. Another hand—I say not whose—decorated
those parts of the ocean where no ship hath yet sailed, and
nothing is yet known, with spouting whales, dolphins at play,
sea-lions sporting on rocks, and canoes filled with black men.
The same hand designed and painted in the northern part of
the ocean, off the island of California, the lively representation
of an engagement between the great seven-decked Spanish galleon from Manilla, and a small English vessel, the former striking her colors, and the latter flying the flag of her country,
and not the Jolly Roger, as Mr. Brinjes desired. In the left-
hand corner Mr. Westmoreland drew the mariner's compass,
below which he wrote a respectful dedication to my Lords the
Commissioners, signed with the name of John Easterbrook,
midshipman on board the *Countess of Dorset*. The whole was
finished and adorned with many flourishes, and in the penman's
finest style. He was so proud of his work that, I believe, he
expected nothing less than a public commendation of it in the
London Gazette, with a handsome reward in money.

Strange to say, this report, which we hoped would have been
published by order of the admiralty, was received in silence,
and was never afterwards noticed at all. I know not what became of it, for Jack obtained no acknowledgment of it, nor was
any praise or reward, that I ever heard of, given to the penman, and I suspect that the report has never been read at all,
but still lies on the shelves of the navy office. But, in truth,
the wreck of the *Countess of Dorset* made little stir at the time,
because this intelligence arrived when the public mind was
greatly agitated by the depredations of the French privateers,
which were now sweeping the Channel and picking up our mer-

chantmen, and with the efforts made by the government to
protect our coasts and the seas, so that the loss of this ship
more than three years before, even in so lamentable a manner,
affected people little. All this done, however, Jack returned
to Deptford, taking up his quarters with the admiral, and in
very good spirits, being well assured that before long he would
have his commission, and that there was going to be a long and
spirited war, the French having begun with great vigor, and
being already flushed with success, so that they would take a
great deal of beating. He had also jingling in his pocket—
no sweeter music, while it lasts—the whole of his pay for six
years. With this money he was enabled to purchase a new
outfit for himself, having landed, as we have seen, with nothing in the world—no, not even as much as a shirt. However,
he very soon procured a sea-chest, and filled it once more with
instruments, books, and a new kit, including his lieutenant's
uniform, in which it must be confessed he looked as gallant
and handsome an officer as ever put on the blue and white, with
none of the effeminacy and affected daintiness which too often
spoil the young soldier as well as the London beau. Rather
did Jack incline to the opposite vice, being, as his best friends
must admit, quite deficient in the graces, ignorant of polite
manners and conversation, unused to the society of ladies, and,
among men, knowing but little of what some have called the
coffee-house manner—that, I mean, which one learns by intercourse with strangers and general company, in which it is
necessary to concede as well as to demand, to yield as well as
to maintain. Yet no swaggerer, or offender against the peace
of quiet men, though he certainly walked with his head in the
air, as if the whole world belonged to him, and, as if it was
his right, took the wall of every one, unless an old man, a crip-
ple, or a woman, and that with so resolute an air that even the
bully-captains of the street—who are always ready to shoulder
and elbow peaceful men into the gutter, and, on a mild remonstrance, to clap hand to sword-hilt, and swear blood and murder—these worthies, I say, stepped meekly, and without a word,
into the mud when they beheld this young sea-lion marching
towards them, over six feet in height, with shoulders and legs
like a porter's for breadth and strength, splendid in his blue
coat with gold-laced hat, his crimson sash, his white silk stock-

ings, and white breeches. One thing I commended in him,
that he wore his own hair, having it powdered decently, and
tied in a bag with a black ribbon, a fashion which especially
becomes a sailor, first, because a wig at sea, where everything
should be taut and trim, must be troublesome ; and, secondly,
because if it be blown overboard, what is a man to do for
another ?

Fortunately for the street captains, Jack went seldom to London, where the noise of the carts and the crowd in the streets
offended him. He loved not to be jostled. And the amusements of the town pleased him not. Once we went together
to see the play at Drury Lane ; the piece was a comedy, very
ingenious and witty, representing modern manners, or that part
of modern manners which belongs to the nobility, where, I suppose, there is always intrigue, and the conversation always
sparkles with epigram ; the meaner kind know not this kind
of life. It is pleasant to look on, and the house laughed and
applauded. But Jack sat glum, and presently grew impatient
and went out, and would have no more of it.

"Why," he said, "call this a play of modern life ? If a
man were to say to me one half of what these people continually say to each other—one calling the other, though in fine
words, ass, rogue, liar, or clown—I would have cleared the
whole stage long ago. Where is the English spirit gone ? Let
us get away."

I asked him whether he did not think the theatre made a
fine sight, with the beautiful dresses of the ladies. But even
this did not please him.

"Dresses ?" he said. "Why, they are designed for no other
purpose than to make the poor souls hideous. Hoops, powder
and paint, hair dressed up ; I should like, my lad, to show you
beside them a bevy of South Sea Island girls, barefooted, with
a simple petticoat tied round them, and their long hair flying
loose. Then would you understand how a woman should look.
I know a girl"—he checked himself—"well, put her, dressed
as she is, in a box at the theatre, and she would be like the
full moon among the twinkling stars."

I might have replied (which is, I suppose, the truth) that
women have no thought of form, and cannot understand that
curve which Hogarth has drawn. Therefore they understand

not why men love a woman's figure, and regard fashion as nothing more than an exhibition of costly and beautiful stuffs, silk, lace, and embroidery, to set off which the figure serves as a frame or machine on which they may be hung. Otherwise women would strive for a fashion at once becoming and fitted to the figure, which they would then never alter, as the Greeks retained always the same simple mode.

With these views as to ladies' dress, it is easy to understand that Jack found very little pleasure in visiting Ranelagh or Vauxhall, though the freedom of Bagnigge Wells was more to his taste. Nor did he delight in the coffee-houses. I took him to the Smyrna, where the politicians resort, and to the Rainbow, where the wits and templars are found; to the White Lion, in Wych Street, where they have concerts and women who sing. But he found the conversation insipid and the manners affected.

There was only one place of public resort which he heartily approved. It was the famous mug-house in Long Lane, whither one evening we went, Mr. Brooking, the painter, taking us thither. It is frequented by many brethren of the brush, who for some reason are always more inclined to mirth and gayety than the sober merchant. In this room there are fiddles and a harp; the room is divided into small tables which drink to each other; a president calls for a song, and one song is followed by another till midnight, the company drinking to each other from table to table, some taking strong beer, some flip, some rumbo, and some punch. Jack admired greatly the freedom of conversation, which had nothing of the coffee-house stiffness; the heartiness with which one table would drink a bout with another; the tobacco and the singing, for which this mug-house was then famous, and all with so many jokes and so much laughter that it was a pleasure to think there was so much happiness left in the world.

But most of his time Jack spent at Deptford, his mornings in the yard among the ships, and his evenings at the Sir John Falstaff with the admiral, or in the officers' room at the Gun Tavern, whither the lieutenants and the midshipmen resorted for tobacco and punch.

There remained the afternoon, which, had he chosen, he might have spent with the admiral's lady and Castilla.

"Our conversation," said that sweet girl, "hath no attraction for Jack. He loves sailors better than ladies, and tobacco better than tea; and he would rather hear the fiddle than the harpsichord, and the bawling by a brother-officer of a sea-song than a simple ditty from me."

I suppose that Castilla was naturally a little hurt that Jack showed no admiration for those accomplishments of which she was justly proud. No one played more sweetly or sang more prettily the songs which she knew than Castilla. Every girl likes a little attention; but this young sea-bear gave Castilla none. Every girl likes to think that her conversation is pleasing to the men; Jack showed no pleasure at all in Castilla's talk. He was thinking, though this we knew not yet, of another girl, whose charms bewitched him and made him insensible to any other woman.

At this period of his life it is certain that Jack loved not the conversation of ladies, finding it perhaps insipid after the fo'ks'le talk he had lately experienced in the French prison and his savage life among the Indians. "If a man," he said, "must needs associate with women at all, give me a woman who is not squeamish over a damn or two, and lets a man tell his story through his own way, without holding up her hands to her face and crying fie upon him for naughty words; and one who can mix him a glass of punch—ay, and help him to drink it—and won't begin to cough directly his pipe of tobacco is lit. As for your cards, and your music, and your drinking of tea, it is all very well for landsmen. I dare say you like handling about the cups for madame, and passing the cream and sugar to the young misses."

"You can take your tea as the admiral takes his, Jack, with a dram of *rosa solis* after it."

"What is it at best but a medicine? Why not ask people to come and drink physic together? Why not ask Mr. Brinjes to prescribe, as he does, his tea of betony, speedwell, sage, or camomile? Or, if you must drink messes, there is chocolate, as the Spaniards have it. But as for tea, with the strumming of a harpsichord, and playing at cards for counters, and ladies talking fiddle-faddle, and Castilla asking you if you like this, or you would rather choose the other, I confess, my lad, I cannot endure it."

"Castilla, Jack?   Surely she is to your taste?"

"Why, as for that, she is a delicate slip of a girl; she has soft cheeks, it is true, and brown hair.   Give me a tall, strong woman, who knows her own mind and what she likes, and likes it in earnest.   Give me a woman with a spice of the devil."

"Well, Jack," I said, surprised that he was not already in love with Castilla, "there are plenty of women in Deptford who are all devil, if they can tempt you."

He had got already, though I knew it not, a woman who possessed her full share of the element he so much desired.

In the afternoons, therefore, he did not court the society of Castilla, but he went back to his old custom, and sat for the most part in the apothecary's parlor; not so much for the pleasure which he took in the conversation of that worthy and experienced gentleman, as that in this way he could enjoy the company of another person, who generally came in *accidentally* about the same time, but through the garden gate and the back door, while the lieutenant marched in boldly, for all the world to see, through the shop.   As Mr. Brinjes slept for the greater part of the afternoon, these two could say what they pleased to each other without fear of being overheard.   And nobody so much as suspected that they were in this room except the assistant, who stood all day at the counter rolling boluses, pounding drugs, and mixing nauseous draughts.   One might have chosen a sweeter-smelling place for love-making, but then it had the look of a cabin, and something of its smell, and Jack found no fault with it.

"We talked," Bess told me, in the time when her only pleasure was to think and talk about Jack, and when there was no one but myself with whom she could speak about him—"we talked all the afternoon in whispers, so as not to wake up Mr. Brinjes, who slept among his pillows.   We sat in the window-seat, my head on his breast, and his fingers played with my hair, and sometimes he kissed me.   Jack told me all he was going to do; he was to get his commission, and go fighting; he would go for choice where there were the hardest knocks; they would make a vast deal of prize-money; and he would get promoted, and made captain, with twelve pounds a month, and then, when he came home, he would marry me."

"And did Mr. Brinjes," I asked, "never wake up and interrupt this pastime?"

She laughed. "Why, when he woke up, he would say: 'Kiss her again, Jack. She is the best girl in Deptford. I have saved her for thee. Kiss her again.' He has always been kind to me, and would never believe that Jack was drowned, and would still be talking of him, which was the reason why I knew him again when he came back. And then Mr. Brinjes would sit up and talk about his treasure, and how he shall some day fit out a ship, and we are all to go sailing after the treasure, which is to be my marriage-portion, when it is recovered, so that Jack will marry, after all, the greatest heiress in England."

These things I heard, I say, after Jack went to sea again, and while Bess, like so many women, sat at home waiting and praying for her lover's safe return. All that time no one knew, or so much as suspected, what was going on. Otherwise, I fear, hard things would have been said of poor Bess by those of her own sex. Men, in such matters, judge each other more leniently and with less suspicion.

If, now, Jack had not been first recognized by Bess; if he had not gone to see her the first day of his arrival; if—but what doth it profit to say that if such and such things had not happened other things would have turned out differently? It is vain and foolish talk. Our lives are not governed by blind chance; and we must not doubt that, for some wise end which we know not and are not expected to know, or even to guess, all that happens to us is ordered and settled for us beforehand.

CHAPTER XIV.

THE MEDDLESOME ASSISTANT.

THE first trouble came to the lovers through the meddlesomeness and malignity of the apothecary's assistant. Had Jack known what this man did, I think he would have made him swallow the contents of every bottle in the shop. But he never knew it; nor had he the least reason to suspect the assistant. James Hadlow (which was his name) was a man of small stature and insignificant aspect, made ridiculous by his leathern apron,

which covered the front of him from chin to toes, and was too
long, having been made for a taller man, his predecessor. His
eyes, as has been already stated, were, as to their movements,
independent of each other. He seldom spoke, and went about
his business steadily and quietly; a man apparently without
passions, who had no more compassion for a sick man than for
a log of wood; a man who never loved a woman or had a friend,
and who, when he was afterwards knocked on the head in a
waterman's house of call while dressing wounds caught in a
drunken broil, left no one to lament his loss. Neither man nor
woman in Deptford ever regarded him at all, any more than
one regards the fellow who brings the wine at a tavern. Yet,
which is a thing we should never forget, there is no man so meek
that he cannot feel the passion of resentment, and none so weak
that he cannot do his enemy a mischief. Now, for something
that was said or done, or perhaps omitted—I know not what—
this man conceived a malignant desire for revenge. I know not
which of the three had offended him—perhaps Jack, who was
masterful, and despised little and humble men; perhaps Mr.
Brinjes himself, who was hard towards his servants; perhaps
Bess. But, indeed, if a creeping thing stings one, do we stop
to inquire why it hath done us this mischief?

Everybody in the town knew that Aaron Fletcher wanted to
marry Bess, and that in her pride she would have nothing to
say to him, and had refused him a dozen times. It was also
known that Aaron went about saying that he would crack the
crown of any man who ventured to make love to his girl—calling her openly his girl—even if he were a commissioned officer
of the king. When so tall and stout a fellow promises this,
young men, even brave men, are apt to consider whether another woman may not be found as beautiful. Therefore, for
some time, those who would willingly have courted Bess kept
away from her, and, in the long-run, I am sure that Aaron
would have triumphed, being constant in his affections as he
was strong and brave. Unhappily for him, Jack Easterbrook
returned. First of all, when Aaron came up from Gravesend, a
few days later, and became a peaceful boat-builder again in
place of a smuggler, he began to watch and to spy upon the
movements of Bess, employing a girl whose father worked for
him at his boat-building, and lived in a house nearly opposite

to that of Mr. Westmoreland. She reported that Bess stayed at home all day long, and though Lieutenant Easterbrook had been to the house, it was only to see her father, who came to the door and spoke with him there, and Bess never met him. So that, although Aaron heard the story of her recognizing him in his rags, he thought little of that, and made up his mind that the lieutenant had quite forgotten the girl, and cared no more about her, even if he had ever thought of her; and when Jack, by the grace of my lords the commissioners, appeared in his new uniform, he seemed to be so much raised above Bess in rank that it was impossible he should any longer think of her. Moreover, Aaron discovered that the lieutenant's mornings were spent in the yard, his afternoons with Mr. Brinjes, and his evenings at the tavern; so that, except for the fact that there was no woman at all in the daily history of the lieutenant—a suspicious circumstance where a sailor is concerned—he felt satisfied. This officer would go away again soon; meantime he thought no more about Bess. When the lieutenant was gone, his own chance would come. For my own part, I sincerely wish that things had been exactly as Aaron wished them to be —namely, that Jack had quite forgotten the girl, and that he had fallen in love with Castilla or some one else, and that Bess, weary of much importunity or softened in heart, had accepted the hand of this great burly fellow, who loved her so constantly. Whereas— But you shall see.

It happened, however, one evening about eight o'clock, when Jack had been at home some three weeks, that Aaron, sitting alone in his house, which stood on one side of his boat-building yard, overlooking the river between the Upper and the Lower Water Gate, heard footsteps in his yard without. He rose, and, opening the door, called to know who was there at that time, and bade the visitor come to the house without more ado.

His visitor proved to be the man Hadlow.

"What the devil do you want?" asked Aaron. Mr. Brinjes himself was a man to be treated with the greatest respect, but his assistant, who was not credited with any magical powers, and could certainly not command rheumatics, or give any more pain than is caused by the drawing of a tooth, was regarded with the contempt which attaches to the trade of mixing nauseous medicines. "What do you want here at this time? I have not

sent for any of your bottles, and I don't want any of your
leeches."

"I humbly ask your pardon, Mr. Fletcher. I have brought
no bottles and no leeches."

"Then what are you come for?"

"I humbly ask your pardon again, Mr. Fletcher, seeing that
I am but a poor well-wisher and admirer—"

Here Aaron discharged a volley of curses at the man, which
made his knees to tremble.

"I have come, Mr. Fletcher, desiring to do my duty, though
but a poor apothecary's assistant, who may one day become an
apothecary myself ; when, sir, if a tooth wants to be drawn, or
a fever to be reduced, or a rheumatism—"

Here Mr. Fletcher gave renewed proof of impatience.

"Then, sir, I have come to tell you a thing which you ought
to know."

"Say it out, then, man."

"First, I am afraid of angering you."

Mr. Fletcher turned and went back into his room, whence he
emerged bearing a thick rope's-end about two and a half feet
long. This, in the hands of so big and powerful a man as
Aaron Fletcher, is a fearful weapon. He used it for the cor-
rection of his 'prentices, and it was very well known that there
was nowhere a workshop where the 'prentices were better behaved or more industrious. Such was the wholesome terror
caused by the brandishing of a rope's-end in the hands of this
giant.

"Hark ye, mate," he said, balancing this instrument, so that
the assistant turned pale with terror, and his eyes rolled about
all ways at once, "you have angered me already, and if you
anger me more, you shall taste the rope's-end. Wherefore lose
no more time."

"It is about Bess Westmoreland. Oh, Mr. Fletcher?"—for
the boat-builder raised his arm—"patience ! Hear me out !"
The arm went down. "It is about Bess Westmoreland. Everybody knows that you have "—here the arm went up again.
"And it is about Lieutenant Easterbrook. Bess and the lieutenant— Oh, sir, have patience till you hear what I have to
tell you !"

"My patience will not last much longer. Death and the

devil, man! what do you mean by talking about Bess Westmoreland and Lieutenant Easterbrook? He has seen her but
once since his return."

"By your leave, sir, he sees her every day."

Aaron threw the rope's-end from him with an oath. Then
he caught the man by the coat collar, and dragged him into
the room.

"Come in here," he said. "By the Lord, if you are fooling
me I will murder you!"

"If that is all," the man replied, "I have no fear. I am
not fooling you, Mr. Fletcher; I am telling you the sober
truth."

"Man, I know how the lieutenant spends his time. He is all
the morning in the yard, looking at the ships and talking to the
officers. In the afternoon he sits with Mr. Brinjes, and in the
evening he drinks at the tavern. As for the girl, she never sees
him."

"You are wrong, sir. But, oh, Mr. Fletcher, don't tell any
one I told you! The lieutenant is the strongest man in the
town—next to you, sir—next to you—and the master can do
dreadful things if he chooses; and Bess herself in a rage—have
you ever seen Bess in a rage? Oh, sir, first promise me not to
tell who gave you the intelligence."

"Do you want a bribe?"

"No, I want no bribe. I hate 'em—I hate 'em. And the
one I hate most is the lieutenant, because if I was nothing better than the dust beneath his feet he couldn't treat me with
more contempt."

"Go on, man. Tell me what you have to say, and begone."

"He goes every afternoon to Mr. Brinjes."

"I know that."

"You think he goes to talk to the old man, I suppose? He
does not, then. My master sleeps all the afternoon. If he didn't
sleep, he would die. He says so. The lieutenant goes there
to make love to Bess."

Aaron turned pale.

"She comes in every day by the garden gate and the back
door, so that no one should suspect. And no one knows except
me. But I know; I have looked through the keyhole. Besides,
I hear them talking. Every day she comes, every day they sit

together, he with his arm round her waist, or round her neck
playing with her hair, and she with her head upon his shoulder
—kissing each other and making love, while the master is sound
asleep by the fire."

"Go on."

"When the master wakes up he laughs, and he says, 'Kiss
her again, Jack.' Then he laughs again, and he wishes he was
young again."

"Is that all?"

"That is all. For the Lord's sake, Mr. Fletcher, don't let
any one know who told you. Mr. Brinjes would kill me, I
think. And mind you, Mr. Fletcher, whatever you do, remember that the master is able to kill you, and will, too, if you harm
the lieutenant. He knows how to kill people by slow torture.
There's a man in the town now, covered with boils and blains
from head to foot, says it's the apothecary hath bewitched him.
Don't offend Mr. Brinjes, sir."

"My lad," said Aaron, grimly, "I doubt whether I ought not
to take the rope's-end to your back for interfering with me
and my concerns. Now if you so much as dare to talk to any
man in this place about what you have seen and told me—whatever happens afterwards—remember, whatever happens afterwards—it is not a rope's-end that I shall take to you, but a
cudgel; and I shall not beat you black and blue, but I shall
break every bone in your measly skin. Get out, ye miserable,
sneakin', creepin' devil!"

That was all the thanks that the poor wretch Hadlow ever
got for the mischief he had made; but the thought that he had
made mischief consoled him. Something was now going to
happen. So he went his way, contented with his evening's work.

Then Aaron sat down, and began to think what he should
best do. He had been full of Christian charity towards the
man who was not, after all, as he feared, his rival; there would
be no more talk of quarrelling and fighting between them; the
shilling need not be fought for; the lieutenant belonged to a
different rank; in course of time Bess would tire of her resistance, and would yield. Now all was altered again. His old
rival was still a rival, and there must be fighting.

Presently he rose, and walked up the street to the penman's
house.

Mr. Westmoreland was at the tavern with his friends the assistant shipwright, the sexton, and the barber. Bess was sitting alone, with a candle and her work.

"Bess," said Aaron, "I want to have a serious talk with you; may I come in?"

"No, Aaron. Stand in the doorway, and talk there. I am not going to let anybody say that I let you into the house when father was out of it; but if you want to talk foolishness, you can go away at once. It is high time to have done with foolishness."

Aaron obeyed—that is to say, he remained standing at the open door, and he said what he had to say.

"It is for your own good, Bess; though you won't believe that anything I say is for your own good."

"What is it, then?"

"It is this. Every afternoon you go to Mr. Brinjes's parlor to meet Lieutenant Easterbrook. You go out by your garden gate, so that no one may see or suspect, and the lieutenant goes in by the shop. In the parlor, while the old man is asleep, you kiss each other and make love."

She sprang to her feet.

"Aaron, you are a spy."

"I have been told this, but I did not spy it out for myself. Very well, then, spy or not, think Bess. The lieutenant has never yet got appointed to a ship; perhaps he never will. He has got no money; he cannot marry you if he would. If he were to marry you, the admiral would never forgive him; if he doesn't marry you, why—there—Bess."

"Is that all you have to say?" she asked, trying not to lose her temper, because she had the sense to perceive that it would not please her lover if she quarrelled about him with this man. "Is that all, Aaron?"

"Why, I might say it a thousand times over, but it wouldn't amount to much more than this. He can't marry you if he wants to; and if he doesn't want to, a girl of your spirit ought to be too proud to listen to his talk."

"Aaron, you shall pay for this," cried Bess, with flaming eyes.

"You a lady, Bess? You to marry a king's officer? Know your own station, my girl. You are the daughter of the penman, and you can neither read nor write. But there's a chance yet: send him packing first, and then you shall see."

" Aaron, you shall pay," she repeated; "you shall pay."

" I say, Bess, I will give you another chance. Before your name gets dragged in the mud and you become the town talk, send him packing, and you shall have me if you please. Bess, I love you better than the lieutenant, for all he wears silk stockings. I love you in spite of yourself, Bess. You've been a fool, but you've been carried away by your woman's vanity, and there's not much harm done yet. Give him up, Bess, and you shall find me loving and true."

In his emotion his voice grew hoarse and thick. But he meant what he said, and it would have been better if Bess had taken him at his word on the spot. But she did not. She was carried away by her wrath, but yet so governed that she knew what she was saying.

" It is six years," she said, " since I looked on while you fought him and were beaten. I liked nothing better than to see you defeated and Jack victorious. Because, even then, you pretended to have some claim upon me, though I was but a little girl. Now, Aaron, I should like nothing better than to see Jack beat and bang you again until you cried for mercy." Her eyes were flashing and her cheek red, and she stamped her foot upon the ground. " Oh, I should like nothing better!"

" Should you, Bess—should you?" he replied, strangely, not in a rage at all, but with a great resolution.

" To see you lying at his feet. You, his rival!—you! Why, you may be bigger—so is a collier bigger than a little sloop. That is a great matter, truly? You his rival! To think that any woman whom he has once kissed should ever be able so much as to look at you—oh, Aaron! But you don't know; you are too common and ignorant to know the difference there is between you."

" You would like to see him beat and bang me, would you, Bess? Why, then, it is as easy as breaking eggs. You shall have the chance. All you have to do is to tell your fine lover that, as regards that shilling—he will know what shilling I mean —I am waiting and ready to have that repaid, or to take it out in another way—he will know the way I mean. And then, my girl, if you like to be present, you can. But I promise you the

7

beating and the banging will be all the other way, and your fine
lover, gentleman and king's officer though he is, shall be on his
knees before he finds time to swing his staff. You tell him
that about the shilling. If you will not, I will send a message
by another."

"I will tell him. Now go away, Aaron, lest you say something which would anger me still more."

So he went away. But Bess told her lover, who laughed,
and said that Aaron was a greedy fellow whom there was no
satisfying, but he should do his best to let him have a good
shilling's worth, and full value for his money.

CHAPTER XV.

HORN FAIR.

This conversation happened in the second week of October.
The opportunity of repaying the shilling occurred on the 18th
of that month, which is St. Luke's Day, and consequently the
first day of Horn Fair.

All the world has heard of this fair. It is not so famous a
fair as that of St. Bartholomew's, the humors of which have
been set forth by the great Ben Jonson himself. It has never,
like that fair, been honored by the presence of the Prince of
Wales; nor has so ingenious a gentleman as Mr. Harry Field-
ing ever written plays to be acted at Horn Fair, as he hath done
for Bartholomew. Nor is it as good for trade as the ancient
Stourbridge Fair. Yet for noise, ribaldry, riot, and drunkenness it may be compared with any fair held in the three king-
doms, even with the old May Fair, now suppressed, which they
say was the abode of all the devils while it lasted. As for
trade, there is never anything sold there—neither horses, nor
cattle, nor cloth, nor any pretence made of selling anything,
except horns and things made of horn, with booths for children's toys, penny whistles, and the like, gingerbread, cockles,
oysters, and so forth, together with strong drink, and that the
worst that can be procured of every kind.

It is frequented by a motley crew, consisting of a noisy London rabble: rope-makers from St. George's, Ratcliffe Highway,

sail-makers from Limehouse, shipwrights from Rotherhithe, sailors from Wapping, all the City 'prentices who can get holiday, the shabby gentry of the King's Bench rules, together with a sprinkling of beaux and gallants who come here to riot. Hither flock also a great concourse of men and women from the country, who come in their smock-frocks and new white caps to drink, dance, look on and gape, bawl, laugh, and play upon each other those rough jokes which commonly lead to a fight. There is not, in fact, anywhere in the world a fair which hath a more evil reputation than Horn Fair. Yet I dare affirm that you shall not find a single London citizen who hath not paid one visit at least to Horn Fair; while there are many London dames—ay, of the finest—who have been tempted by the curiosity of their sex, and in order to see the humors of famous Horn Fair, have dared the dangers of a rabble seeking enjoyment after their kind, and in the manner which best pleases their brutish nature.

Yet it was in such a place as this, and among such people, that the lieutenant was called upon by Aaron to redeem his promise and to fight him for the shilling; and although he might very well have refused to answer the challenge in such a place, Jack thought it incumbent upon his honor to fight, even though it should be like a Roman gladiator in the arena. Had he been invited to take a glass in a booth at the fair, or to eat hot cockles with bumpkins, he would have treated the proposition with scorn; but because he was asked to fight, his honor, forsooth! was concerned, and he must needs go—so sacred a thing is the law of honor concerning the duello. No doubt in this case his delicate sense of honor and his inclination jumped, as they say, and he was by no means displeased to try his courage, strength, and skill against so doughty a champion as Aaron Fletcher. Yet I do not think there was another officer in the king's navy who would have done what he did.

All sorts of ridiculous stories are told of Horn Fair and its origin, with a foolish legend about King John, which I pass over as unworthy of credence, because every painter who hath studied Italian and ecclesiastical art, and the symbolical figures with which saints are represented, knows very well that Luke the Evangelist was always figured in the pictures having with him the horned head of an ox, for which reason, and no other,

the Charlton Fair was called Horn Fair, being held on St. Luke's
Day. It is a pity that the mob cannot be taught this—though,
for my own part, I know not why an ox should go with the head
of St. Luke—and so be persuaded to carry their horns soberly
in memory of the saint who wrote the third gospel.

The visitors, if the day is fine, begin to come down the river
as early as eight in the morning, and for the most part they remain where they land, at Cuckold's Point, Redriff, eating and
drinking, until the procession is formed, which starts at eleven
or thereabouts, and by that time there is a vast crowd indeed
gathered together about the Stairs, and the river is covered with
boats carrying visitors from London Bridge, or even from Chelsea. As for the quarrels of watermen and the splashing of the
passengers and the exchange of scurrilous jokes, abuse, and foul
language, it passes belief. However, the passengers mostly get
safe to the Stairs at last, and, after a quarrel with the watermen
over the fare, they are permitted to land. Those who join in
the procession array themselves in strange garments : some are
dressed like wolves, some like bears, some like lions, some
again like wild savages, and some like Frenchmen, Spaniards,
Russians, or the lusty Turk, and some wear fearful masks ; but
all are alike in this respect, that they wear horns tied upon their
heads in various fashions. The women among them, however,
who ought rather to be at home, do not wear horns upon their
heads, but masks and dominoes. Those who can afford it have
ribbons round their hats, the streaming of which in the breeze
greatly gratifies them ; some carry flags and banners, all together shout and bellow continually, and the procession is followed by all the boys, to judge from their number, who can be
found between Westminster on the west and Woolwich on the
east.

This magnificent procession, which is almost as good as the
Lord Mayor's Show, leaves Rotherhithe, headed by drum and
fife, at eleven in the forenoon, and marches through Deptford,
across the bridge by way of the London road, through Greenwich to Charlton Common.

Jack stood with me at the gate of the admiral's house, looking on as these Tom Fools passed, playing their antics as they
went along. It seemed to me strange that a man of his rank
should take any pleasure in witnessing the humors of the mob ;

but I thought as a fool, because there is something in every sailor, whether he be an officer or not, which makes him delight in singing and dancing, and causes his ears to prick up at the sound of a fiddle or a fife. Besides, as regards this sailor, it was six years and more since he had seen any merry-making at all, unless, which I know not, the half-starved Indians who entertained him had any songs and dances of their own.

"I must go to the fair this afternoon, Luke," he said. "Will you come with me, lad?"

"What will you do at the fair, Jack? It is a rude, rough place, not fit for a gentleman."

"Do you remember the last time we went? It is seven years ago. Ever since I came home I have felt constrained to visit again the places where we used to play. There is the crazy old summer-house in the gardens. I have been there again. The place is not yet fallen into the creek, though it is more crazy than ever."

"And Mr. Brinjes's parlor? Have you been there?"

"I have been there," he replied, with hesitation, "once or twice—to look at his charts. His treasure is on an island in the North Pacific, whither our ship did not sail. Yes, I have been there—to see his charts, in the evening. In the afternoon he sleeps, and must not be disturbed."

"And now you must needs visit Horn Fair again. Well, Jack, I am a man of peace, and, very like, there may be a fight. So take with you a stout cudgel."

"There is another reason also for my going," he said. "It is because Aaron Fletcher will play all comers at quarter-staff."

"Why, Jack, surely you would not play with Aaron before all this mob of rustics and common men?"

"I must, brave boy. For, look you, Aaron saved my life. There is no question about that. The boat must have gone down in half an hour, and I with it, if he had not lugged me out. Therefore if he asks me to do so small a thing as to fight him, the least I can do is to gratify him, and to fight him at such place and in such manner as he may appoint. I promised him this, and now he sends me word to remind me of my promise."

"But the man is a giant, Jack."

"He is a strapping fellow. But if he is six foot four, I am

six foot one and a half.   His reach is longer than mine, it is
true.   But do not be afraid.   I have got back my strength, and
I think I shall give a good account of him.   However, my word
is passed to fight him when he wishes ; and whatever happens
I must go.   He thinks to defeat me before all his friends.   He
is a braggart fellow, and we shall see, my lad."

We walked over to Charlton after dinner ; Jack in his lieutenant's uniform, with new laced ruffles and laced shirt and
cravat, very noble.   He carried his sword, but, following my
advice, he provided himself as well with a stout cudgel, in
which, I confess, I placed more confidence than in his sword.
For why ?   A man thinks twice about using a sword upon a
mob as he would upon an enemy, but an oaken cudgel does not
generally kill, though it may stun.   Therefore he lays about
him lustily if he have a cudgel, and spares not.

There was no hurry about the quarter-staff play, which would
not begin until three o'clock, and we strolled about the fair
among the crowd, looking at the shows, of which there were
many more than I expected to find.   But Horn Fair is happily
placed in the almanac, so that the people who live by shows,
rope-dancing, and the like, can go from Stepney Fair to Charlton, and so from Charlton to Croydon Fair.   There was, to begin with, a most amazing noise, with beating of drums, blowing
of trumpets, banging of cymbals, ringing of bells, dashing of
great hammers upon the boards, whistling, marrow-bones and
cleavers, each one thinking that the more noise he made the
more attractive would be his show.   The booths were filled
with common things, but these gilded, tied with bright ribbons
and gay-colored paper, so as to look valuable, and with wheed-
ling girls, in tawdry finery, to sell them.   And here I found
that my companion speedily forgot the dignity of an officer and
became like a boy, buying things he did not want because some
black-eyed gypsy girl pressed them into his hand with a "Sure,
your honor will never regret the trifle for a fairing for your
honor's sweetheart.   A proud and happy girl she is this day,
to have her captain home again."   And so on, he laughing and
pulling out a handful of silver and letting her take as much as
she pleased, whether for shoes, pattens, leather breeches, gingerbread, cheap books, or toys in horn, whatever she pleased to
sell him.   Jack bought enough of everything to stock a found-

ling hospital, but mostly left his purchases on the stalls where he found them, or gave them to the first pretty girl he met in the crowd. There certainly is something in the air of the sea which keeps in a man for a long time the eagerness of a boy. A London-bred young man of three-and-twenty, which was Jack's age, is already long past the enjoyment of things so simple as the amusements of a fair: he despises the shows, gauds, and antics which make the rustics and the mechanics gape and laugh. As for Jack, he must needs go everywhere and see everything, and this year there were a wonderful number of shows.

There was, for instance, the young woman of nineteen, already seven feet ten inches high, and said to be still growing, so that her well-wishers confidently expected that when she should attain her twenty-fifth year she would reach the stature of nine feet, or, perhaps, ten. We also saw the bearded woman. This *lusus naturæ*, or sport of nature, presented for our admiration a large full beard, a foot long and more, growing upon the whole of her face, cheeks, chin, and lip, so that her mouth was quite hidden by it. She was by this time, unfortunately, fully fifty years of age, and her beard well grizzled, so that we had no opportunity of knowing how a woman in her youth and beauty would look with such an ornament to her face. It would then, I suppose, be soft and silky, and brown in color. But perhaps she would look not otherwise than a comely young man. This woman was a great strong creature, who might have felled an ox with her fist; she had a deep voice and a merry laugh, and made no opposition when Jack offered her a cheerful glass. We saw the Irish giant, also, who was a mighty tall fellow, but weak in the knees; and the strong woman who tossed about the heavy weights as if they had been made of pasteboard, and lifted great stones with her hair. And, since where there are giants there must also be dwarfs, we saw the Italian Fairy, a girl of sixteen, no taller than eighteen inches, and said to be a princess in her own country. It has been remarked by the curious that whereas giants have always something in their carriage and demeanor as if they were ashamed of themselves, so dwarfs, on the other hand, are the most vainglorious and self-conceited persons imaginable. This little creature, for instance, dressed in a flowered petticoat and a frock of sarsnet, walked about her stage, carried herself and spoke with all the airs of a court lady or a fine city madam, though where she learned these arts I know not. As for other shows, there was a menagerie wherein were exhibited a cassowary, a civet cat, a leopard, and a double cow—a cow, that is, with one head and two fore-legs, but four hind-legs. There was a theatre, where they performed the *Siege of Troy* in a very bold and moving manner, and with much shouting and clashing of swords, though the performance was hurried, on account of the impatience of those without. There were lotteries in plenty, where one raffled for spoons of silver and rings of gold; but as for us, though we essayed our fortune everywhere, we got nothing. There was a fire-eater, who vomited flames and put red-hot coals into his mouth; there was excellent dancing on the slack-rope, which is always to me the most wonderful thing in the world to witness; there was a woman who danced with four naked swords in her hands, tossing and catching them, presenting them to her breast, and all with so much fire and fury that it seemed as if she were resolved and determined to kill herself. Jack rewarded her after the dance with a crown and a kiss, both of which she received with modesty and gratitude. There was also a ladder-dance, in which a young man got upon a ladder and made it walk about, and climbed up to the top of it and over it, and sat upon the topmost rung, and yet never let it fall—a very dexterous fellow.

"Why," said Jack, presently, "what have you and I learned, Luke, that can compare with the things which these people can do? Grant that I know the name and place of every bit of gear in a ship, and that you can paint a boat to the life, what is that compared with dancing on the slack-rope or balancing a ladder as this fellow does it?"

At the time I confess I was, like Jack, somewhat carried away by the sight of so much dexterity, and began to think that perhaps showmen, mountebanks, and jugglers have more reason for pride than any other class of mankind. Afterwards I reflected that the wisdom of our ancestors has always held in contempt the occupations of buffoon and juggler, so that, though we may acknowledge and even praise their dexterity, we are not called upon to envy or admire them.

Outside the booths, and apart from the theatres and shows,

there was a stage, on which, at first sight, one only discerned a
fiddler, a fifer, a drummer, and a fellow dressed in yellow and
black, with a long tin trumpet. This was the stage of the great
High German Doctor; his name I have forgotten, but it was a
very high and noble-sounding one. There were tables on the
stage, and beside the musicians were the doctor's zanies, who
tumbled and postured, and danced the tight-rope, and his shell-
grinders and compounders, every one of whom, in turn, ha-
rangued and bamboozled the mob. As for the doctor himself,
he was not at first on the stage at all; but presently the man
with the tin trumpet blew a horrid blast, and bawled out,
'Room for the doctor, gentlemen! Room for the doctor!" and
the people parted right and left, while, mounted on a black
steed, that learned person rode very slowly towards the stage.
The saddle was covered with red velvet; it was provided with
a kind of lectern, on which was a big folio volume, which the
doctor was reading, paying no heed to the crowd, as if no moment could be spared from study. A fellow dressed in crimson led the horse. The doctor was a tall and stout man, with
an extraordinary dignity of carriage and solemn countenance,
dressed in a gown of black velvet and crimson velvet cap, like
unto the cap of a Cambridge *medicinæ doctor*. Then the man
with the tin trumpet hung out a placard upon the stage, on
which was the great man's style and titles, and these he bellowed forth for the information of those who could not read.
We learned, partly from the placard and partly from this fellow, that the great man was physician to the Sophy of Persia
and to the Great Mogul, tooth-drawer to the King of Morocco,
and corn-cutter to the Emperor of Trebizonde, the Grand Turk,
and Prester John; that he was the seventh son of a seventh
son; that it was seven days before he sucked, seven months
before he cried, and seven years before he uttered a single
word, so long was this wonderful genius in preparing for his
duties. As for his medical studies, we were told that they had
occupied his attention for five times seven years, in the cities
of London, Leyden, Ispahan, Trebizonde, and Constantinople,
and that he was at that moment twelve times seven years of
age, without a gray hair or a missing tooth, and with children
not yet three years old, so efficacious were his own medicines,
as proved upon himself; while his servants never knew an ill-

7*

ness nor even an ailment (the drummer, I observed, had his
face tied up for a toothache). When this fellow had done
the music began, and the zanies tumbled over each other,
and turned somersaults, while the mixers of the medicines
bawled out jokes and made pretence to swallow their pills.
Finally the doctor himself stood before us, and made his ora-
tion.

" Gentlemen all," he said, " I congratulate you on your good-
fortune in coming to Horn Fair this day, for it is my birthday ; and on this anniversary I give away my priceless medicines for no greater charge than will pay for the bottles and
boxes in which they are bestowed. On all other days they are
sold for their weight in gold. I have here "—he held up a
plaster—" the Cataplasma Diabolicum, or Vulnerary Decoction
of Monkshood, which heals all wounds in twenty-four hours if
applied alone ; if taken with the Electuary Pacific—show the
Electuary, varlets !—it heals in a couple of hours. I have the
Detersive, Renefying, and Defecating Ophthalmic, which will
cure cataracts and blindness, and will cast off scales as big as
barnacles in less than a minute. I have for earache, toothache,
faceache, and tic a truly wonderful vegetable, an infusion of
peony, black hellebore, London-pride, and lily-root. Here is
a bottle of Orvietans, for the expulsion of poison, price one
shilling only. Here is the Balsamum Arthriticum ; here the
Elixir Cephalicum, Asthmaticum, Nephriticum, et Catharticum.
Gentlemen, there is no disease under the sun "—here the trum-
peter blew the tin trumpet—" but I can cure it. Rheumatics "—
bang went the drum—" Asthma "—bang went the drum between every word—" Gout—Sciatica—Lumbago—Pleurisy—
Melancholy ; in a word, there is nothing that I cannot cure at
a quarter the cost of your town doctors. No more disease,
gentlemen, no more pain ; step up and try the Cataplasma Diabolicum, the Electuary Pacific, the Detersive Ophthalmic, and
the Vegetable Infusion. Step up and buy the medicines that
will make and keep you in hearty good health, so that you shall
live to a hundred and fifty—ay, even, with care, to two hundred
and fifty—knowing neither age, sickness, nor decay."

The people laughed incredulously, and yet believed every
word, which I suppose will always be the case with the mob,
and began to push and shove each other in their eagerness to

"Room for the doctor, gentlemen! Room for the doctor!"

buy the wonderful medicines.   For his part, Jack listened open-mouthed.

"Why," he said, "what fools we are, Luke, to let this for-eign fellow go, who hath so many secrets!   Why do not we keep him and get his secrets out of him, and so let there be no more sick-lists to be kept?"

Then he would have gone on the stage and bought every-thing the doctor had to sell, but I dissuaded him, pointing out that the fellow was only an impudent impostor.

And before every show were ballad-singers bawling their songs.   Their principal business at fairs is not, I am told, to sell their ballads so much as to attract a crowd and engage their attention while the scoundrel pickpockets go about their business unwatched (one was caught in the fair while we were there, and, for want of a pump, was put head first into a tub of cold water, and kept there till he was wellnigh drowned); and everywhere there were men who grinned and postured, girls who danced, boys who walked on stilts, gypsies who told fort-unes, women bawling brandy-balls and hot furmety; there was the hobby-horse man, with his trumpet and his "Troop, every one, one, one!" and a hundred more, too numerous to mention. And for food, they had booths where they sold hot roast pork, with bread and onions and black porter—a banquet to which the gentry at the fair, whose stomachs are not queasy, did infi-nite justice.

We saw so many shows and booths, and Jack appeared so contented and happy in looking at them, that I confess I was in hopes he would forget his promise to fight Aaron, the pros-pect of which, in this fair, crowded with the rudest and rough-est men, pleased me less every moment.   But, if you please, his honor was concerned. Therefore, when the hour approached, he remembered it—to be sure, one might be expected to re-member a promise to meet and to fight so big a man as Aaron Fletcher—and he cast about in order to find the amphitheatre or booth where the duello was to be held.   We presently found it, on the skirts of the fair, and a little retired from the noise. It proved to be nothing more than a square enclosure of canvas, fastened to upright poles, with no roof.   Those who came to see the sport paid an admission fee of one penny.   Within the booth there were rough benches set along the sides, and in the

middle a broad stage two feet high. There was music playing
as we went in, and on the stage a little girl of ten dancing very
prettily and merrily. The place was filled; I knew many of
the faces: those, namely, of the Deptford men, come to stand
by their champion. It appeared as if they knew what was going to take place, for at the sight of the lieutenant there were
passed around looks and nods and every indication of heartfelt
joy. Drawers ran about with tankards and mugs of ale, and
most of the men were accommodated with pipes of tobacco.
There were also some women present, and of what kind may
be easily imagined. Sufficient to say that they were fit companions of the men. The people did not greatly care for the
dance, which was too simple and innocent for them. When
the little girl finished and jumped down from the stage there
came forward a scaramouch dressed in the Italian fashion, who
played a hundred tricks, posturing and twirling his legs about
as if they had been without bones or joints. But the people
were impatient, and bawled for him to have done. Wherefore
he too retired, and then they roared for Aaron Fletcher, the
Deptford men being foremost in their desire for his appearance.
He leaped upon the stage, therefore, quarter-staff in hand,
stripped to his shirt, and twirling his weapon over his head as
if it had been a little walking-cane. Then the place became
hushed, as happens when there is going to be a fight of any
kind, because fighting goes to the heart of every man, and
makes him serious and anxious at the beginning, but full of
fury as the fight goes on. Aaron was a terrible great fellow
to look at, thus stripped of his coat and standing on the stage
before us all.

"I challenge the best man among ye," he said, looking at the
lieutenant, "gentleman or clown, king's officer or able seaman,
for a guinea or a groat, as ye please."

Then he twirled his staff again, and walked round the stage,
like a game-cock before the battle.

"Shall I give him a chance with the meaner kind first, to
show his mettle and to breathe him?" said Jack. "'Twould
be charitable."

There sprang upon the stage from the crowd a stout and
lusty youth, not so tall as Aaron, but of good length of limb
and resolute face. 'Twas the champion of Eltham, as we

learned from the crowd. He was clad in a smock-frock, which he laid aside.

"I will play a bout for a crown," he said, lugging out the money, while his friends shouted.

Then they began; but, Lord! the countryman was no match for the Deptford player, and the shouting of our townsmen was loud to see the play that Aaron made, and the dexterity with which his staff, as quick as lightning, played on his adversary's head and ribs, his legs and arms. So that very soon, throwing down his staff, the fellow leaped from the stage, and would have no more.

"It was pretty," said Jack. "The rustic hath had his lesson."

Then another; this time one who had played and won at Bartholomew Fair, and now advanced with confidence, trusting to his activity and the rapidity of his attack, which were, indeed, astonishing. But, alas! his leaps and bounds were of little avail against the long reach and the heavy hand of the giant, and he fell to rise no more.

Then the mob roared and shouted again.

"This fellow is soon satisfied," said Jack. "It is my turn now."

He laughed, and took off coat, waistcoat, and hat, giving them to me for safety. Thus reduced to his shirt, he stepped forward and mounted the stage, the crowd being overjoyed and beyond themselves in the anticipation of a fight between their champion and a gentleman in laced ruffles, white-silk stockings, and powdered hair. Certainly nothing so good as this had ever before been seen at the fair.

Then I became aware of a strange thing. There stood within the door—not sitting down, but standing—just within the folds of the canvas, no other than Bess Westmoreland and her father. Who would have thought to see the penman at Horn Fair? Nothing could be more out of place than this pair among the waterside men and the ruffians in the booth. Bess stood upright, holding her father's hand, not for her own protection, but to assure him of his safety, while he, stooping and round-shouldered, looked about him, as if fearing violence of some kind. I now perceived that Bess was come for no other purpose than to see this fight; to be sure, it was arranged beforehand, and there was no reason why she should not hear of it from Aaron; but I had not thought Bess would have come to such a place to see such a sight. I declare I had not the least suspicion of the truth, so carefully had the lovers kept their secret. Bess took no notice at all of the rabble, her eyes fixed upon the stage as if the people were not even present; no great lady waiting at the door of the theatre for her chair could look more proudly upon the common herd—the linkboys, chairmen, and lookers-on—as if they were beneath her notice. Her lips were set, and her brow contracted, and her cheek was pale; but I knew not the cause, unless it were from terror at the approaching battle. Yet why did she come to see it?

She came, as I learned soon afterwards, confident in her lover's triumph, and anxious to increase the discomfiture of his adversary and her rejected suitor. Since that day I have ceased to wonder why the Roman ladies and matrons took pleasure in witnessing the fights of gladiators, and why, in the days of tournaments, gentle ladies went to see their lovers tilt. The joy of battle, I am sure, is as great in the heart of woman as in that of man. Certainly no one in the crowd watched the combat with more eagerness and interest than did Bess, whose eyes flashed, lips parted, and bosom heaved with the passion of the fight. As for her father, in the hush before the battle began I heard him exclaim, " It is the lieutenant and Aaron! Oh, dear, dear! they will do each other some grievous harm. Bess, ask them to desist. Is it for this you brought me here, wilful girl? Grievous bodily hurt they will do to each other."

No one paid any heed to that poor man. Even the drawers ceased to run about with tankards, and no man called for drink.

Jack took the quarter-staff, which had already been used twice ineffectually, poised it in his hands, and turned a smiling face to his adversary.

" I have kept my promise, Aaron," he said; but this the mob did not hear. " We will fight for that shilling. Bess is in the doorway, looking on. It seems as if we were fighting for more than a shilling, does it not?"

Aaron made no reply in words, but he laughed aloud. Perhaps he remembered how, seven years before, when last he fought with Jack, Bess was looking on at his defeat. This time he was confident in his strength. She was come again, looking to see him worsted. She should be disappointed.

There was no lack of courage about the man. Courage he had, and plenty. He was a good three inches taller than his adversary, which at quarter-staff gives a great advantage; he was quick of eye and of fence; he was heavier and stronger; and his first two combats had scarcely breathed him. On the other hand, he was opposed to a man who for six years and more had led the hardest life possible, with no indulgences— wine, beer, tobacco, indolence, or anything to soften his muscles or dim the eye. Now Aaron, as everybody knew, was fond of a glass, and though no sot, once a week or so was drunk. And he had already begun to put on flesh. As they stood face to face one might have gone a hundred miles and never seen so fine a couple.

And then, at tap of drum, the fight began, and for a while everybody was mute.

Jack, I perceived, was resolved at first to stand on the defensive, for two reasons. First, because his enemy showed wrath in his scowling eyes, and therefore would, perhaps, spend his breath and strength in furious onslaught. Next, because, as he told me afterwards, it was not until he held the weapon in his hands that he remembered he had not played for four years and more. One would think he might have remembered so important a fact before. It is an admirable custom in some ships for the crew, both officers and men, to amuse themselves daily at quarter-staff, single stick, and boxing; but Jack had been out of a ship for four years. Still, if his hand was a little out, his eye was true. Aaron's game was twofold. First, he would beat down and overpower his man by superior strength and advantage in reach; and, secondly, by feints and leaps, shifting his ground, and changing the length of his weapon, by coming to close quarters and then retreating, to cheat his adversary's eye and disconcert him even for a single moment, when he would deal him a decisive stroke. This was a very good design, and hath often served. But Jack was not to be so caught. No man at quarter-staff, however strong, can beat down an adversary who has learned the art of parry, which is more than half the battle; no man, however quick and active, can disconcert an enemy who knows how to follow his eyes steadily. Jack, therefore, lost no ground, and was never touched; so that, though he delivered no stroke, the ease with which he met Aaron's blows presently caused the spectators to roar with admiration. In all kinds of fighting there are two first principles, or rules, to be carefully learned. The first of these is never to lose sight of your enemy's eye, and the next is never to lose your temper. A third is to know how to strike when the occasion comes. If a man at this rough game chance to lose his temper he loses the game. This is what Aaron did. It maddened him that he could not strike his enemy, and it maddened him still more to hear the roars of the people at the dexterity which defeated him. Moreover, he knew that Bess was looking on; therefore he became more furious, and delivered his blows more rapidly, but with less precision. "Don't fight wild, Aaron," shouted his friends, but too late; while the fellows in the booth began to jeer and laugh at him, asking why he did not strike his man, with a "Now, Aaron! now's your turn! Hit him on the head. There's a brave stroke missed," and so on, foreseeing that if the lieutenant could only keep cool and wait for his chance the victory would be his.

Jack told me afterwards that while they played the old skill came back to him, and his confidence, so that he could afford to play with his man and bide his time, receiving all the blows, whether at full length, half length, or close quarters, with patience and good temper.

This strange duel, in which one man struck and the other only parried, lasted long; insomuch that the spectators left off shouting, and looked on with open mouths. It lasted so long that Aaron was now raging and foaming, breathing heavily, and plunging as he struck with the staff. As for me, I wondered why Jack did not strike. He had his reason; he wished to strike but once, and therefore he waited. At last the chance came. Aaron left his head exposed, and then, with a thud which might have been heard outside the booth, the lieutenant's staff resounded on the side of his enemy's head, and Aaron fell prone upon the stage—senseless.

It is said that when a gentleman fights a common fellow the mob is always pleased that the gentleman shall be victorious. I know not if this be true, but I know that the fellows in the booth rose as one man, even the Deptford men, and cheered the victor to the sky.

Jack stepped from the stage, a little heated by the fight, and put on his coat, waistcoat, and hat.

"Aaron is a very pretty player," he said, "but he should not have challenged me until he was in better condition. There were half a dozen poor fellows aboard the *Countess of Dorset* who would have beaten him. Here, my lads"—he now became again an officer—"Aaron is a Deptford man, like me. Take care of him, and spend this guinea in drinking the king's health."

So the fellows tossed their greasy caps in the air, and the tapsters tied their apron-strings tighter, and began to run about with tankards and mugs while the guinea was drinking out, and Jack strode down the booth, the men making a lane for him, and crying, "Huzza! for the noble captain!" Meanwhile no one took any notice of the fallen champion, who presently recovered some of his senses, and sat up, staring about him with distracted eyes.

"Why, Mr. Westmoreland," said Jack, at the door, as if he had not seen him before, "you at Horn Fair? I might as soon have expected to see you at Vauxhall."

"Nay, sir, your honor knows I value not such merriment. But Bess would bring me here. 'Tis a wilful girl. Nothing would serve her but she must see the humors of the fair. Girls still crave for mirth."

"You ought to be at home among your books, Mr. Westmoreland. Go home. Luke will walk with you, and I will take care of Bess—good care, good care—and bring her safe home after she has seen the fair. Come, Bess, will you see the wild beasts or the slack-rope dancers? Take him home, Luke; take him home."

So saying, he seized Bess by the hand and drew her away, leaving the old man, her father, with me. I observed that though Bess cried "Oh!" and "Pray, lieutenant," and "Don't, lieutenant," and "Fie, lieutenant," she laughed, and took his hand without any reluctance, but rather a visible satisfaction, because she had certainly got the properest man in all the fair.

"The lieutenant," said Mr. Westmoreland, "is strong enough to protect any girl; though, as for Bess, Mr. Luke, she is strong enough to protect herself. Nevertheless"—he broke off and sighed—"nevertheless, a motherless girl is a great charge for a peaceful man, especially when she is strong and determined, like my Bess. What am I to do, sir? I cannot whip and flog her; I cannot lay my commands upon her if she doth not choose to obey me. I cannot make her marry if she still says nay. And the men, they are afraid of her pride and wilfulness. Such a headstrong girl will never make an obedient wife."

"It is a situation, Mr. Westmoreland," I said, "full of danger."

"What is worse, Mr. Luke," he went on—"what is worse is that she scorns the man Aaron Fletcher himself—a substantial man, though they do·say he knows the coast of France. Yet he would cheerfully take the risk of her masterful temper and her wilful ways if she would but say yea."

"Why, Mr. Westmoreland, as for that, I am sure there are plenty of men ready to be fired by such charms as your daughter Bess possesses."

He shook his head.

"Charms? I know not what they are. Black hair and black eyes may please some, but I know not whom. Let us go from this wicked and riotous place, Mr. Luke. Peaceful men have no place here. The lieutenant will bring her home; though, more likely than not, they will quarrel on the way, both of them being masterful, and Bess will have to find her way back without him. Yet she ought to be proud of the honor he hath done her, and perhaps she will be meek for once, and behave pretty."

So we turned and made our way out of the throng, and so home.

"I am sorry," said Mr. Westmoreland, presently—"I am very sorry that Mr. Easterbrook hath fought and vanquished Aaron Fletcher. I would rather have seen Aaron the conqueror."

"Why?"

"Because Aaron is a cruel and a vindictive man. He was bragging among his friends of the sport they would witness at the fair, and he has been humiliated. Now he will have his revenge, if he can, for the disgrace put upon him in the presence of his friends; and Bess hath been at the fair with the

lieutenant, and I know not what will happen. He is a revengeful man, Mr. Luke ; and, unhappily, he is in love with Bess, and
wants to marry her—a thing that, with my experience, I cannot
understand. Well, it is a terrible thing, a terrible thing, for a
peaceful man like me to have such a daughter. A humble man
should pray for ugly daughters, who are also meek and obedient. They may wait for their beauty till they get to heaven.
I want nothing but peace, Mr. Luke, so that I may continue my
studies in algebra and logarithms, for which end, and no other,
unless it be the furtherance of goodly writing, I was sent into
this troubled world."

The next day I learned from Jack that he had taken Bess to
every show at the fair; that he had given her as noble a supper
as the place afforded ; that he had fought and overthrown three
fellows who waylaid them on the road home, and would have
robbed him of his money as well as his fair charge ; and that
he safely convoyed her, about midnight, to her father's door.
The admiral heard of the evening's adventure, and laughed,
saying that Bess was a lucky girl to get such a proper fellow
to show her the fair. But I do not think that either Jack or
the admiral related the story of the fight and the subsequent
doings to madame and Castilla.

CHAPTER XVI.

IN THE SUMMER-HOUSE.

I AM a dull person in suspecting or guessing at passages of
love. Yet I had seen Bess dragging her father to Horn Fair
in order to witness the fight, and I marked the flash of triumph
in her eyes when Aaron fell, and the unconcealed pleasure with
which she accompanied the victor.

On Sunday morning, a day or two after the fair, another
thing happened which ought to have made me suspect. It was
in church. Soon after the service of Morning Prayer began I
observed an unwonted agitation among the feminine part of the
congregation, and presently discovered that the eyes of all were,
with one consent, directed upon a certain seat in the north
aisle, occupied by Bess Westmoreland and her father. The

reason of this phenomenon was that Bess had come to church attired in a very fine new frock made of nothing less than sarsnet,
with a flowered petticoat, a lawn kerchief about her neck, and
a hat trimmed with silk ribbons, so that among the women
around her in their scarlet flannel, and the girls in their plain
camblet, linsey-woolsey, and russet, she looked like a rose among
the weeds of the hedge. Few of the gentlewomen in the
church were more finely dressed. As to them, their eyes plainly said, if eyes can speak, "Saw one ever such presumption?"
And as for the baser sort, they first gazed with admiration and
envy unspeakable, and then sniffed and tossed their heads, as if
nothing would have induced them to put on such fine things ;
and then they looked at each other, each with the same question
trembling on her tongue, each one longing to ask aloud, "Who
gave her the things?" For there is some strange quality in the
female conscience (I mean only in a seaport town) which en-
ables every girl to accept joyfully and gratefully whatever a man
may give her, and at the same time to flout and scorn all other
girls for doing the same thing ; so that what is a virtue in herself must be a clear sign of immodesty or forwardness in another.

One would not deny that the girl was worthy of blame ; for
though there are no longer sumptuary laws, yet every woman
knows how far she may in decency, and with due regard to
her station, carry her love of finery. Bess, however, wore these
things not of her own will, but by desire (say, rather, command)
of a certain person. There is, again, nothing strange in a Deptford girl suddenly appearing in the colors of a rainbow, especially after a ship has been paid off, though very soon the silks and
satins go to the Jews who buy second-hand clothes, together
with the trinkets and the ribbons ; and madame returns to her
russet frock, her blue apron, and speckled handkerchief. But
this, which is of daily occurrence among the common sailors'
wives, one would not expect of a respectable girl, such as Bess.
It is quite certain, and one must not excuse her conduct, that
she should not have ventured to church thus attired. Yet I, for
one, was ready to forgive her, first because she looked so mar-
vellously beautiful in these fine feathers, and next because she
bravely bore the artillery of these eyes, and held herself tall
and upright, looking straight before her, as if no one was gaz-

ing at her, and as if she wore what belonged to her. Women are your true levellers: they have no respect for rank: even a peer is but a man to them, and a countess is but a woman. They are ready to measure their own beauty beside that of any lady in the land; there is no girl, however lowly, who would refuse, for conscience' sake, the honorable attentions of a gentleman; and the silly creatures, I am told, whisper continually to each other tales of humble girls raised to the condition of princesses.

There was another person in the church besides myself who seemed as if leniency and readiness to forgive this presumption possessed his heart as well. This was the lieutenant, who, from his place in the admiral's pew (the corner nearest the reading-desk, with his back to the altar), regarded the girl steadfastly during the whole service, insomuch that I feared lest madame or Castilla herself should observe it, and be offended at so indecent a proof of admiration in divine service. But Castilla did not discover it, partly because she hath never been able to understand how a gentleman can regard a common girl with admiration (she still considers that Jack's passion for Bess was caused by the sorcery and craft of Mr. Brinjes), and, therefore, was not likely to suspect such a thing; and partly because Castilla's eyes in church were always fixed upon her book, as she followed the words of the service, or they were humbly dropped upon her lap during the sermon, as if she closely followed the argument, and was being convinced by my father's reasoning. Now, as hath been already explained, the vicar's sermons were written for the perusal of scholars rather than for the understanding of the unlearned.

The service over, we walked out in due order, and so by the gate into Church Lane, as we had done on that day, three weeks before, when our prodigal came home to us in rags. And then, after a little talk, we separated, Jack going with the admiral's party, and I returning to the vicarage for dinner.

After dinner, the afternoon being warm and sunny, I took my hat and walked leisurely towards those gardens of which I have already spoken, where were the orchards of plum, pear, apple, and cherry, and where the old summer-house overlooked the creek. It would be, I thought, pleasant in the gardens with no one but myself, and I could walk about among the trees, watching the gray lichen on the bark and the sober tints of the autumnal leaves, and perhaps find, in the view of the Greenwich Reach, something new to observe and note. One whose profession is to paint ships of all kinds can never grow weary of watching them, whether at anchor or in motion ; just as one who paints figures loves to be forever contemplating the human figure, whether in action or repose.

The air was still and soft, the day warm, although it was already the twentieth day of October. The fruit was all picked now, and the leaves beginning to dry at their stalks, because the leaves of apple, plum, and cherry do not turn brown, but drop off while they are yet green ; yet the green is quite another hue than that presented in spring and summer, and I wonder that no painter has painted the greens of autumn, as well as the yellow, red, and brown. I have myself attempted a sketch in April, showing parts of that long stretch of garden all the way from these gardens to Greenwich Hospital, which at that season look like a vast cloud of white and pink blossom resting on the green branches which here and there peep out.

This afternoon the tide was high. There was moored close to the mouth of the creek, and on the opposite bank, a barge, which, with its brown sail lowered, its thick mast, and its hanging ropes, formed so pretty a set-off to the trees of the orchard beyond that I stood awhile to gaze upon it. I have drawn many barges, below the bridge at Wapping Stairs, and in Chelsea Reach, and in other places, but I never drew any prettier picture than that of the barge in the creek at high tide, the woods behind it ; only, as artists can, I made a change. For I presently sketched the barge, and waited until the following spring, when I painted a background of apple and cherry orchards in blossom.

Well, when I had looked at my barge and made a note of it, and of one or two other things, being in a leisurely mood, and quite certain that I was alone in the garden, I lifted the latch of the summer-house door and walked in.

I declare that I suspected nothing. If I had known who were in the place I should have beat a drum, or blown a trumpet, or fired a cannon, to announce my approach, sooner than steal thus unawares upon them. But I did nothing, and pushed the door open without ceremony. Heavens ! There was Bess Westmoreland, her head upon Jack's shoulder, while his hand clasped her waist and his lips kissed her cheek! Who would have suspected this? I was so surprised that I stood speechless, I dare say with mouth wide open, as one sees on the stage, where gestures of all kinds are exaggerated. Yet not so amazed but I saw what a pretty picture they made, he in his blue coat and crimson sash, and his hat with the king's cockade; she in the pretty frock for which the women were now railing at her behind her back. A young man and a beautiful girl embracing cannot but make a pretty picture. As for this, I made a sketch in oils six months later. Bess stood to me for her portrait very willingly when I promised that the picture should be given to her sweetheart when he should return. As for the lieutenant, I got a fellow, for a shilling or two, to stand in the attitude I wanted, while the face I drew from memory, with the assistance of Bess. I painted them in the summer-house, and through the window you can see a ship slowly going down the river. For a reason, which you will presently learn, I never gave that picture to Jack; and, for my own reason, I have not sold it, but keep it hung up at home in my studio, though Castilla loves it not, and will never, if she can help it, look upon it—perhaps because the picture renders scant justice to the beauty of Bess, whose flushed cheeks, parted lips, and heaving bosom I endeavored, but perhaps with insufficient success, to portray upon the canvas. Nor, I am aware, is justice done to the passion expressed in the lover's eyes, in his bending head, nay, even in the arms with which he held the nymph to his heart.

"Zounds!" cried Jack, as Bess screamed and started, and pushed him back, and sunk upon the bench, her face in her hands. "Zounds and fury!" He stepped forward, his fists clinched, fire and distraction in his eyes. He was so carried away with his wrath that he did not at first even recognize me, and made as if he would draw his sword and make an end of me.

"Why, Jack," I cried, "I knew not thou wert here! How should I know?"

Upon this he let fly a round dozen or so of sailors' oaths, such as may be heard in Flagon Row or Anchorsmith Alley, sound and weighty oaths, every one more profane than its predecessor. The language of the fo'k'sle is, we know, readily and greedily acquired by every officer, and is too often adopted as his own to the end of his days.

"I knew not, Jack, indeed," I repeated, "that any one was here. What? Should I spy on your actions? As for what I have seen—"

"Let me go, Jack!" cried Bess; "oh, let me go! He will tell my father, who will send me away for a servant. And perhaps he will tell Aaron, who would murder you, if he could, without being hanged! Oh, Jack! what shall I do?"

"I shall tell no one, Bess," I said. "Why, it is no business of mine to go repeating what I have seen accidentally. Am I the town barber?"

Jack looked doubtfully; then he laughed.

"Cheer up, Bess," he said; "no harm is done. Luke will never betray an old friend. He came here to draw the ships, which is all he thinks about. He will go away, and he will forget all about it."

"Nay," I said, "I shall not forget. But I shall hold my tongue."

"I won't trust no one—only you, Jack," said the girl.

"Hark ye, Luke—" Jack drew her closer to himself, and laid his arm round her neck—"hark ye, lad. Thou hast discovered what was not meant for thee—nor for any one—to know. That signifies nothing for a lad of honor. But for Bess's sake, swear it. Take an oath on it."

"I swear, Bess," I declared to her, "that I will speak no single word of what I have seen and learned. If there were a Bible here, I would kiss the book to please you. You may trust me, Bess."

"You may, indeed, Bess," said Jack. "Hands upon it lad."

So we shook hands, and in all that followed afterwards I told nobody what had happened; and the thing was so managed that it was never suspected by any one except Aaron. It seems wonderful that no one in Deptford found it out, because it is a place where one half the women are continually employed in watching and spying upon the other half, and find their chief happiness in detecting things which it was desired to keep secret, forgetting that others are employed in exactly the same inquiry after their secrets. Just so one hath observed a row of monkeys in cages, each thieving from one neighbor's dish while the other steals from his.

"Trust all or none, Luke," said Jack. "Thou shalt know all, and be a witness between us. Listen. I have told Bess that I love her, and that when I come home again I will marry her. If I had not fallen in love with so much beauty and loveliness, I should have been a most insensate wretch, unworthy to be called a man. Was there ever a more charming nymph?" He kissed her again, while her great eyes swam with the pleasure of so much praise. "Thou shalt paint her for me, Luke. And as for Bess, she says that she loves me. I believe she lies, because how such a girl, so soft and tender, can love a rough sea-bear like me, who knows none of the ways to please a woman, passes understanding. But she says she does, and I will question her further upon this point when thy great ugly phiz is no more blocking up the gangway. And she will not believe that I am in earnest, Luke. That is my trouble with her. She will have that I shall go away and forget her, as many sailors do."

"So he will," said Bess. "They all go away and forget the girls who loved them. And then I shall break my heart and die; if I don't, I shall hang myself."

"So, Luke, listen and be a witness. What do I care who her father is? Such a girl deserves to be the daughter of a commodore. Talk not to me of gentlewomen born. Where is there any woman, gentle or simple, with such eyes as Bess, such lips as Bess, such hair as Bess?" I declare he kept kissing her at each sentence, she making no manner of resistance. "So I will swear to her, in thy presence, Luke, to make it more solemn, and to make her believe my word. I, Jack Easterbrook "—he took her hand at this point, as if he were actually marrying her in church, and by the minister or priest—"I, Jack Easterbrook, do solemnly promise and vow that I will never make love to any other woman and never marry any other woman than Bess Westmoreland, and that I will never think of any other woman at home or in foreign parts. First, I must get commissioned; and then, when the war is over, I will come back and marry my Bess. Kiss me again, girl. This is my solemn promise and oath, in which I will not fail, SO HELP ME GOD!"

I have often since that day wondered at the amazing force of the passion which could make so young a man call down upon himself the awful vengeance of offending Omnipotence if he broke a vow of constancy towards a girl he had seen but twice

8

or thrice ; for I count as nothing the time when she was a child, and he came to her father for lessons.

As he spoke the last words his eyes grew dim with tenderness, and he stooped and kissed the girl on her forehead, as if to seal and consecrate the vow. As for her, she was transfigured. I could not believe that love could so powerfully change a woman's face. She had reason for triumph; but it was not triumph in her eyes ; rather was it a kind of humble pride—a wondering joy that so gallant a man should love her, with a doubt whether it was not, after all, a passing fancy, and a fear that she should not fix his affections.

"Oh!" she sighed—"oh, Jack!" and could find no more words.

"Bess," I said, "vows ought not to be all on one side. If Jack promises so much, what hast thou to promise in thy turn ?"

"Tell me what to say. Oh! I am only a poor girl. What can I promise him ? I am so ignorant that I do not know what to promise. Jack, do you want me to say that I will be faithful ? No—you cannot. Why, is there any man in the world to compare with you ? If a woman cannot be true and constant to you, she cannot be true to any man. As for the rest of them, I value not one of them a brass farthing. Oh!" she laughed and clasped her hands. "Why, I am content to be his slave, Luke—yes, his slave, to toil and work for him all day long —his slave—his servant—" She fell on her knees before him. "Oh, Jack, command me what you please! I want nothing more than to obey your orders."

Wonderful it was how love made this ignorant and wilful girl at once eloquent and humble. Jack lifted her up, and held her by both hands.

"You are a king's officer, Jack," she went on, speaking rapidly. "I must try so that you shall not be ashamed of your wife. I am but the daughter of a penman, I know. He writes letters for sailors, and teaches mathematics to midshipmen and young sailor officers, if there are any. But I have time to learn, and I will find out how to bear myself like a gentlewoman, and to talk like one, and to dress myself as a gentleman's wife ought to dress herself. I will make my father teach me to read and to write, and as for manners—I will go to Mr. Brinjes. He will do anything in the world for you, Jack, and for the woman of your choice."

One could not choose but laugh at thinking of Mr. Brinjes as a teacher of polite manners and conversation. He had learned the most approved fashion, no doubt, among the Mandingoes and the Coromantyns. Yet the earnest and serious manner in which the girl spoke made the matter moving. However, enough was said, and I offered to go, but she caught me by the hand.

"Stay, Luke," she whispered. "Jack, some of you break your vows; but you will not, Jack—you will not? As for me, I need not promise, for I cannot choose but be true to mine."

She laid her head upon his breast, and I left them, shutting the door, and going very softly.

"In the evening I saw Jack again.

"Luke," he said, "I am the happiest man in the world, because I have got the best girl in the world. What do I care that her father is but a penman? What does it signify that she cannot read or write? Reading does no good to any girl that ever I heard of, but fill her head with fond desires. But one thing sticks: when I am away who will keep the men from her? There is Aaron Fletcher—him I knocked on the head; I wish I had beaten out his brains for him. They tell me he is mad for love of her, though she would never say a word to him. I doubt I may have to fight him again before I go. To be sure, Mr. Brinjes promises to protect her; but he is old and feeble."

"Why," I said, "he will protect her by the fear with which he is regarded. One must needs respect a man who can scatter rheumatics among those who offend him."

However, I presently promised him that in his absence I would sometimes visit the girl, and comfort her, and keep up her heart; although if it came to a fight with Aaron, he was able to work me to an anvil, as they say, with fist or cudgel.

Then I begged him to consider seriously what he was about to do. First, that he was a gentleman by birth and rank, who might look to marry a gentlewoman; next, that he had no fortune, and as yet no prize-money, and only a lieutenant's half-pay; and lastly, that if he married he was likely to lose the admiral's favor.

"Truly," he replied, "I have considered all these things."
I don't believe that he had considered one of them before that
moment. "And I am resolved that there is no other happiness
but in marrying Bess. As for duty, it points the same way, because I am promised to her. When duty and inclination point
the same way, my lad, what room is there left for doubt? Answer me that. Why, if I lived a thousand years, I should never
love any other woman as I love my Bess. What puzzles me,"
he went on, "is why the landsmen haven't fallen in love with
her long ago. None of your mincing, mealy-mouthed fine
ladies, all patches and powder, made up so that you know not
what they are like with hoop and petticoat, but an honest lass,
true and loyal—you can see what she is like, for she wears
neither hoop nor powder—and she tells no lies, and you know
her mind directly she speaks. That is the girl for me, Luke.
Hang me if I understand why she wasn't long ago the girl for
you."

"Fortunately for me," I said, "your inclinations and mine
are not set on the same woman."

"Why, if I had been in your place, Luke, I would have carried off the girl, if I could have got her in no other way. If
she were to change her mind now, and to refuse me, I would
carry her off, whether she liked it or not. There would be a
prize to tow into port, and all for myself, Luke—all for myself!"

CHAPTER XVII.

IN BUTCHER ROW.

"AARON," Mr. Westmoreland said, "is a cruel and revengeful man."

Afterwards I remembered these words. For my own part I
did not understand this judgment, though I had known Aaron
all my life, first as a great hulking boy, and then as the strongest and biggest man in Deptford. On what grounds did Mr.
Westmoreland consider him cruel and revengeful? The judg-
ments of weak and timid men, like those of women, are shrewd
and often true. Yet Aaron had done nothing of which the

world knew on account of which he could be called cruel and revengeful. Masterful and headstrong he was, and the world accounted him a brave man, but not revengeful. The present moment, however, was likely to bring out whatever evil passions lay in his soul, for he had been publicly humiliated and brought to shame by the man who had taken from him the woman he loved; and when he met his friends in the street they seemed to be laughing in their sleeves at him. Therefore Aaron conceived an act of revenge which was as audacious as it was villainous. If he was revengeful, it must be admitted that he was also bold.

He first showed his teeth on the Monday morning after the fight at Horn Fair. Bess was engaged in making a beefsteak pudding for dinner, her sleeves rolled up, singing over her work. Her father sat at his desk before the window bent over his work, with round spectacles on nose, undisturbed by his daughter's singing. A sudden diminution of the light caused both to look up. Aaron Fletcher's great body was blocking up the doorway.

"Bess," he said, roughly, "come out to me."

"Good-morning, Aaron," said Mr. Westmoreland. "The weather still holds up, and keeps fine for the season."

"Come out, Bess," he repeated, taking no notice of her father.

"What do you want to say to me, Aaron? If it is the old thing—"

"No, it is not the old thing. Come out, I say."

She obeyed, rolling her apron over her bare arms, and came out into the street, her father looking after her, apprehensive of mischief.

"Well, Aaron?"

He looked upon her with love in his eyes, had she been able to perceive it, and to be moved by such a gaze. But she had no pity for him, and no feeling.

"It is not the old story, Bess," he said. "As for that, I've had my answer. What I came to say was this. I asked a simple question—twenty times I asked that question. 'Twas not only by reason of thy good looks, Bess—though they go for something—'twas because, of all the Deptford girls, there was none so quiet and so steady. Well, the time has come when no honest man will ask thee that question again."

"Have a care, Aaron," she replied, with flaming cheek, because she knew what he meant very well. "Have a care, Aaron. You'd best."

"Bess, it is because I love thee still that I came to say this. No one else will say it, though they may all think it. You were with him at the fair all the evening. It was not till nigh upon midnight that he brought thee home. Is that an hour for a respectable girl? You meet him secretly at the apothecary's every day. Therefore I say again—Bess—beware."

"Oh! If I were to tell him," she began; "if I were only to tell him what you have dared to say !"

"Nay—tell him all. I care not a brass button. Tell him I said he is fooling thee. I will tell him that to his face. What care I for any lieutenant of them all? He to marry? Why, he has got nothing. He is fooling thee. Mischief will come of it, Bess. Thou art too low for him, and yet too high."

"Thank you for your pains," she replied. "As for me, I can take care of myself even if all the world should take to spying through keyholes. As for trusting myself with the lieutenant, I think I am safer with him than with a smuggler—yes, a mere tarpaulin smuggler. You can go, Aaron. 'Tis a fine morning for a run down the river, and I dare say a sail across the Channel will do you good, and cure the headache from last Friday's cudgelling. But take care, Aaron. Some day, perhaps, we may see thee, if thou art not prudent, dangling in chains over there "—she pointed to the Isle of Dogs, where there were then hanging on the gibbets three poor wretches— " or walking after a cart-tail with the whip across your shoulders; or, maybe, marched aboard ship in handcuffs for the plantations. Get thee gone, meddler !"

"I have said what I came to say. As for thy fine lover, Bess, he crows now, but it will be my turn next, and that when he little looks for it. He has not yet done with me."

She laughed scornfully, and returned to her pudding, tossing her head, and murmuring with wrath that bubbled and boiled over into broken words, insomuch that her father trembled.

As for Aaron, he stood still for a moment, looking wistfully after the girl. I think he bore no malice on account of the joy with which she witnessed his downfall; nay, I verily be-

lieve that this morning he meant the best for her, and only
mistrusted the lieutenant. Then he turned and walked slowly
towards the town.

Everybody knows that there are streets in Deptford where
honest and sober people would not willingly be seen. They
are the resort of the vile creatures which infest every seaport
town, and rob the sailor of his money. Barnes Alley, French
Fields, and the Stowage are full of these people, the best of
whom are oyster-wenches, ballad-singers, and traders in smuggled goods. The houses are chiefly of wood, black with dirt;
every other door hangs out the checkers as a sign of what is
sold within. Here and there may be seen the lattice of the
baker or the pole of the barber. The men in these streets
wear for the most part fur caps, with gray woollen stockings
and speckled breeches. Their shoes are tied with scarlet tape,
and they are never without a cudgel. The women have flat
caps, blue aprons, and draggled petticoats. The talk of the
people corresponds to their appearance. One of these streets
is called Butcher's Row. In the midst of it, on the north side,
stands a house superior to the rest, having an upper story and
a sign carved in wood over the door—that of the " Hope and
Anchor." There is a broad staircase within, also rich with
wood-carving, and a room wainscoted with dark oak, where
those sit who drink something better than the common two-
penny.

Every tavern hath its own class of frequenters; those who
use the Hope and Anchor are the men whom custom-house
officers, the clerks of the navy offices, and police magistrates
agree in regarding with suspicion. They are, for instance,
men who have dealings with smugglers, yet never venture
their skins across the Channel; men who traffic in sailors'
tickets, and defraud their wives of their pay; men who sell
ship-stores of all kinds, and are modestly reluctant to show
where they got them; men who buy up, before the navy office
is ready to pay, sailors' prize-money; those who live by finding recruits for the East India Company's service, and keep
crimps'-houses, where, according to some, murder is as common as drunkenness and theft.

Into that house, therefore, Aaron walked, and, without any
questions, for he knew the place, made his way into the parlor,

where was sitting a man who, to judge by his friendly greeting, expected him.   He was seated beside the fireplace, where,
though it was a sunny day and warm for the season, a great
coal-fire was burning.   He was provided with a tankard of
small ale and a pipe of tobacco, though it was still the forenoon, when industrious men have not begun to think of tobacco.   In appearance he was about fifty years of age ; his cheeks
were purple and his eyes were fiery ; his neck was swollen ; as
for his nose, it was battered in the bridge, so that the original
shape of it could no longer be guessed.   And there was a deep
red scar across his cheek, which might be a glorious proof of
valor in some great action, and might also be a mark by which
to remember some midnight brawl.   He wore a scratch-wig and
a brown coat with metal buttons, worsted stockings, and a muf-
fler about his neck.

This man was a familiar figure in Deptford, whither he came
by boat once a month or so for the transaction of business.
The nature of his business was not known for certain, and
there were different reports.   It was whispered by some that
he stood in with Aaron Fletcher, receiving and selling for him
those cargoes of his which he brought across the Channel and
landed on the coast of Essex ; by others it was said that he
ventured on his own account ; and again, it was whispered by
some that he was a government spy, who ought to have his
ears sliced ; and by others that he procured information for the
navy office when there was going to be a press, and therefore,
if justice was done, should be carbonadoed.   All this might
have been true.   What every one could observe with his own
eyes was, that he bought, and paid a good price for, all those
things which sailors bring with them from foreign ports, such
as embroidered cloths, brass pots, figures in china, silver orna-
ments and idols, or even living creatures, as hyenas, wolves,
monkeys, parrots, mangooses, lemurs, and the like.   He was
liberal with his money, and generous in the matter of drink ;
yet he was not regarded with friendly eyes, perhaps on account
of that suspicion regarding the navy office and the press.   As
for his name, it was Jonathan Rayment.

He nodded his head when Aaron appeared at the door, and,
lifting his tankard, drank to him in silence.

" How goes business ?" asked Aaron.

"Business," Mr. Rayment replied, mournfully, "was never worse. Honest merchants are undone. My next ship sails in a week, and as yet I have but a poor half dozen in the place."

"That is bad."

"And a sorry lot they are. One is a young parson who hath spent his all, and, in despair, took one night to the road, and now thinks the hue-and-cry is out after him. Another is a 'prentice who hath robbed his master's till, and will be hanged if he is caught, and yet snivels all day because he fears the Great Mogul's black Spahis almost more than he fears the gallows. One hath deserted twenty-one times from the army, twice from the navy, and once from the marines, but a dissolute fellow, and rotten with disease and drink; the wind whistles through his bones. Yet he would rather cross the seas and fight for the Honorable Company than be taken and receive the five hundred lashes which are waiting for him. He might as well die that way as by disease, for he will certainly drop to pieces before he reaches Calcutta. Another is a lawyer's clerk, who, I believe, hath forged his master's name—a rogue who will fight, though small of stature. Another is a footpad, for whose apprehension ten guineas reward is offered, and so mean and chicken-hearted a rogue that I must e'en give up the fellow and content myself with the reward. Sure I am that the first smell of powder will kill him. A sorry lot, indeed. Well, if the war continues, I am ruined. For every lusty fellow can now find employment, either in a regiment or on board a ship, and there will soon be no debtors or footpads. Alas! Aaron, I remember, not so long ago, when the peace was proclaimed, and the regiments disbanded, and the ships paid off. Then we had for nothing our choice of the best. Rogues are cheap when 'tis their only choice between the gallows and the Company."

The meaning of all this was that the respectable Mr. Rayment was nothing more nor less than a crimp by trade; one, that is, who seeks out and deludes, inveigles, or persuades recruits for the service of the East India Company, whether for their land or sea service, keeping them snug in the house till the ship sails. As regards their navy, the Company hath, I have been told, a fleet of a hundred ships afloat, to man which is difficult, and requires the service of many such men as Mr. Rayment, whose methods are, as is well known, to decoy or persuade

8*

young men, and especially young men who are friendless or in trouble through some folly or crime, into their houses, and there keep them, whether they will or no, by violence, if necessary, but more often by keeping them drunk, so that they know not what they have undertaken, or what papers they have signed, until the time comes when they can be put aboard.   As for the service of the Company, the young gentlemen who are sent out by the Honorable Council to Calcutta or Madras as writers or clerks do frequently, as everybody knows, arrive at great riches, and come home nabobs.   But I never yet heard that any of the poor fellows who have been decoyed into the crimps' houses and shipped on board an East-Indiaman for foreign service in the Company have ever returned at all, rich or poor.

Between Aaron and this man there was some understanding or partnership, but of what nature or to what extent I have not learned.   Rayment had a shop in Leman Street (quite apart from the houses in which he kept his recruits), where he sold many things besides the curiosities which he bought of the sailors in Wapping and Poplar as well as at Deptford.   Perhaps he disposed of Aaron's cargoes for him after a run.   Perhaps he arranged, with Aaron's help, for the passage of those gentlemen, whether Jacobites or Frenchmen, who are anxious to get backward and forward between England and France without the observation or the knowledge of the government of either country.   There is abundant occupation for such gentry as Mr. Rayment, whose end is often what rogues call a dance in the air.   And just as Aaron had his boat-building yard, which is a most innocent and harmless business, so Mr. Rayment had his innocent shop in Leman Street, and was to outward seeming an honest citizen, who went forth from his shop to church on Sunday morning dressed in black cloth, white-silk stockings, and japanned shoes, with a newly curled and powdered wig, like the best of them, and was permitted to exchange the time of day and the compliments of the season with gentlemen of reputation and known piety.   Thus many villains walk unsuspected among honest men.

"Well," said Aaron, "I dare say you will not starve.   What do you say, now, to a tall recruit ?"

" What do you want for him, Aaron ?"

" You shall have him for nothing."

Mr. Rayment looked suspicious, as one that feareth the gifts of his friends, and shook his head.

"For nothing, Aaron? What do you want me to do for you, then?"

"Nothing. I will give you a tall and lusty recruit. That is plain, is it not?"

"The door is shut, Aaron. Tell me what you mean."

"Give me the men to take him, and he is yours."

"To take him?" Mr. Rayment whispered. "Is he not a willing recruit, then? I love a fellow who is in trouble, and desires to be put into a place of safety."

"I don't know about his willingness," said Aaron, grimly.

"If he is not willing, is he a fellow to be persuaded easily? As far as a skinful of punch is concerned, I care not about the expense, so long as I get a lusty fellow."

"He is in no trouble, and he is not willing. It will take half a dozen men to carry him along, and a week's starvation to make him even pretend to be willing."

"'Tis dangerous, Aaron. I like not this kidnapping work. We crimps have got a bad name, though every one knows my own honesty. Yet we must not openly rival the press."

"Why, you have done it hundreds of times."

"Ay, for the picking up of a starving rustic, or a drunken sailor, or a disbanded soldier, and swearing, when they are sober again, that they have enlisted; that is neither here nor there. And it is for the good of the poor fellows. Their pay is regular, and the climate considered by some to be wholesome. It is playing the part of Providence to help the poor men with the service of the East India Company."

"No doubt," said Aaron.

"Give me your recruit who comes red-handed, the runners after him, and asks for nothing but to be shipped safe out of the country as soon as possible. I care not how many rogueries he hath committed. Give me your lusty villain who hath stolen his master's horse, or the gallant who hath squandered all his stock. These give no trouble. But with pressed and kidnapped men it is different."

"I doubt if you could persuade this fellow," said Aaron; "not if you made him drink a cask of brandy."

"We have had misfortunes, too," Mr. Rayment continued.

"Only last May there was brought to my house as sweet a country lad as you would desire to see. He was in trouble about a girl, and desired to serve the king. Well, in the morning, when he got sober and learned that he was enlisted in the service of the Company, he behaved shamefully. Nothing would do but he must go free or fight for it. So my honest fellows tried persuasion, and in the end there were collar-bones and ribs broken, and that country lad was carried out and laid upon Whitechapel Mount, stripped, and as dead as any gentleman can wish to be. Think of the loss it was to me."

"Well," said Aaron, "your fellows must not persuade my man that way."

"What does it mean, Aaron."

"It is a private matter. You need not have anything to do with it. Send me half a dozen stout fellows, and you shall know nothing at all about it, except that another recruit was enlisted, who stayed at the house till the ship sailed, and was taken on board drunk and speechless. You will have nothing to do with it but to lend me your men and your house."

"I don't like it, Aaron. It may turn out bad. Has the man friends ?"

"He has. Yet this his friends will never suspect."

"I don't like the job, Aaron. Kidnapping should only be practised on strangers and rustics. Is he a tradesman ?"

"No. It is a private grudge, Jonathan. I will make it worth your while. I must have this man put out of the way. He is a lieutenant in the king's navy."

Mr. Rayment jumped from his chair.

"A king's lieutenant ! Aaron, would you hang us all ?"

"Sit down, you fool. It is a safe job. Besides, you shall have nothing to do with it. Sit down, and listen."

CHAPTER XVIII.

A DARK NIGHT'S JOB.

THE evenings towards the end of October set in early; and when there is no moon the nights are as dark as in midwinter. It is therefore a favorable season for the footpads who molest the roads outside great towns, the thieves who prowl the streets, and the highwaymen who stop the coaches.   At Deptford there are neither footpads nor street prowlers, though robbers enough, Lord knows; but they rob, for the most part, on a different plan, and within the houses.   In times of peace, when a sailor cannot readily find a ship, or a disbanded marine cannot find work, there have been known cases of robbery about Deptford and Greenwich.   But in such a year as 1756, when the sailors were all too few for the king's ships, and they were continually enrolling new regiments of marines, no one in these towns gave a thought to the dangers of footpads, and a child might have carried by day or by night a bag full of guineas from the dock-yard gate to the bridge without fear of molestation.   Least of all would such a man as Jack Easterbrook trouble his head about robbers.

He left the Gun Tavern, where he had spent the evening with the lieutenants and midshipmen who used the house, at a quarter before ten or thereabouts, carrying no other weapon than his hanger, and began leisurely to walk home down Church Lane.   The upper part of this road, when you have passed the church and the Trinity Almshouses, is darker than the lower part, by reason of great trees and a high hedge on either hand. Light or dark, 'twas all the same to Jack, who marched along the middle of the road, head in air, his thoughts turned on Bess, as they commonly were at this time, or else wondering how long before he should receive his promised commission. Soon it certainly would be, even though, through favoritism and lack of interest, he should, for the present, be passed over, because officers and men were growing scarce, and my lords the commissioners wanted all they could get.   And once afloat again, with, if kind Heaven willed, a fighting captain, there would be prizes and prize-money, and perhaps swift promotion. And then home again, to the arms of his dear girl.   This, I take it, is the dream of every sailor; whereas, for many, instead of returning to the arms of a fond mistress, they are lowered, with a cannonshot at their heels, into the cold ocean, or come home lopped of half their limbs, only to find their inconstant mistress in another's arms.

Now, as he was thus striding along, swinging his arms as he went, he became suddenly aware of shuffling footsteps and whispers, which betokened the presence of men lurking behind the trees; but before he had time to ask himself what this might mean a fellow rushed out from the darkness, armed with a pistol in one hand, which he pointed at Jack's head, and a lantern in the other, which he turned, unsteadily, in the manner of one who is afraid, upon his face, crying, "Your money or your life!"

Jack was so astonished that for a moment he made no reply. Then he sprang upon the fellow, and caught him by the throat. "My money or my life! Impudent dog, I will squeeze thine own life out!" And so shook him in his grasp—thumb on breathing-pipe—as a terrier shakes a rat, so that the man dropped pistol and lantern, and would have experienced the fate of the rat in another minute but for the help of his friends. As it was, he would have cried for mercy, but he could neither cry out nor breathe, so tight were the fingers at his throat. Indeed, when he was rescued, half a minute later, his face was already purple, his eyes starting from his head like a shrimp's, and his tongue swollen, so that he was fain to sit upon the ground awhile, and for ten minutes or so he knew not whether he were really dead and in the next world, and therefore about to reap the reward of his many villainies, or whether he were still living and ready, for his greater damnation, to swell that long list.

When the light of the lantern fell upon Jack's face there followed a sharp, short whistle, and upon that signal half a dozen lusty fellows sprang upon him at the same moment from both sides of the road. He had no time to draw his sword or to make any resistance of any kind, for one of them fetched him from behind, while the others threatened him in front, so foul a stroke with an oaken cudgel that he fell like a log and without a word senseless upon the ground, dragging with him the man whom he held by the throat.

Then the men all crowded over him ready with their cudgels, and as courageous as you please, their man being down. But it is of no use to cudgel a senseless man.

They were joined by another man—it was Aaron—a tall fellow, truly. He seemed like a giant among these ruffians, who, after the kind of riverside villains, were short of stature, though stout. This man stood over the fallen lieutenant, and looked upon the prostrate body with eyes of satisfaction.

"Jack sprang upon the fellow, and caught him by the throat."

"He fell at once," said Aaron, as if dissatisfied. "I looked for more fighting. I thought there would be much more fighting. I hoped to see him do his best before he was overpowered. Show a light here." One of them—not the first villain, who was now sitting on the ground slowly getting his breath, and still wondering whether he were dead or not—held the lantern before Jack's face. The eyes were closed, and his cheek white.

"Master," said the man, "I doubt the gentleman is killed outright. This is a bad job for all of us."

"Killed! Saw ever one a man killed by a stroke of a cudgel? I wish he was killed. I wish he was dead and buried. Yet he shall never say that I caused him to be killed. Such a man as this does not die of a cracked skull. Show the light again."

This time he looked more carefully. The lieutenant was in a dead swoon, just as Aaron himself had fallen into at Horn Fair, but it was a far shrewder knock and a deeper faint. Aaron raised an eyelid, but there was no sign of life or any shrinking from the light. And now he saw that blood was flowing from the wound.

"He will lie quiet for a while yet. Well, men, here is your new recruit."

The men looked at each other, and murmured that with king's officers—for now they saw the uniform by the light of the lantern—they would not meddle.

"Not meddle, ye villains?" cried Aaron; "why, you have meddled with him already, and have well-nigh murdered him, and will very likely hang, every mother's son, for this night's job. Wherefore take him up and carry him away; 'tis your only chance to save your own necks. Get him across the river with all despatch, and snug in-doors."

The men hesitated. One of them murmured, with an oath, that they would not hang alone.

"When he comes to his senses," Aaron continued, taking no notice of this threat, "tell him that at the least movement you will brain him. But you are not to brain him, remember, or your master will lose the very best recruit he ever had, and will cause you all to swing. What? There is enough against you for every man to swing." This assurance was made more emphatic by the language which this sort most readily understood. Still the men hesitated. The king's uniform frightened them. They had often enough kidnapped a poor drunken sailor, but never before a lieutenant. Then Aaron swore at them, and stamped his foot upon the ground.

"Quick, I say. What? You dare to argue? Take him up. So. Cover him with a jacket to hide his white stockings and breeches, though the night is dark. That will do—now—with a will."

They took him up, the whole six sullenly lending a hand, and carried him as men carry a drunken man.

"Carry him to the Stairs, and row him across the river as quickly as you may. Bestow him in the upper room at the back, where you keep the chains and the bars for your unruly recruits. Watch him by day and night. He will try to escape, that is certain; as soon as he recovers consciousness he will try to escape. Let him understand that he will be knocked on the head if he makes the attempt. And remember he is a match for any three of ye—ay, the whole six, I verily believe —for he is as strong as Samson. If he succeeds in escaping he will have you all in Newgate. He will drag the house down, if he can, in order to escape. You are in great danger, my friends, whatever happens. Yet I would not have him murdered. If he is not put on board alive there will be a warrant out against you for highway robbery and violence, and hanged you will be, every man. Therefore, I say, take care of him." Thus he spoke; now showing that he wished the man dead, and then warning them not to kill him. "It is but three or four days' nursing, with chains and a watch set day and night, and then you shall hocus his drink and put him on board, and shove the drunken beast down the companion to the lower deck with the recruits, and the bo's'n's rope's-end first, in case he complains; and the triangles next, in case he is stubborn and mutinous. I should like to see him tied up for three dozen. Now, march."

The men replied nothing, but slung their burden and prepared to obey.

"March, I say; and look ye, the press was last night out on Tower Hill, and the night before they were busy at Redriff, where there was fighting and warm work, so that the men's spirit is up, and they will brook no resistance. Perhaps—I know not—they are out to-night at Deptford. If the press should take you, carrying a king's officer, unconscious and with an open wound in his head, my mates—why—you are dead men —and already little better."

The men needed no more, but marched off at the double, as they say, the thought of the press lending wings to their heels.

"To knock down," said Aaron, when they were gone, "and to kidnap a lieutenant in the king's navy, and to ship him, drugged and drunk, on board an East-Indiaman for a recruit, is, I should say, high-treason at the least. But none of the fellows know me, and who is to prove that I gave the orders? If the lieutenant is dead already, they will throw his body into the river. If he is not dead, most of these poor fellows will surely hang, for one or other of them is certain to turn king's evidence. Yet if he tries to escape, they will kill him, being used to murder, and thinking little of it. If they knew it, this is their best chance. If they do not kill him—what then? He goes aboard. And then. I know not. He will be put on board in rags. No one will believe him if he calls himself an officer. I doubt if the lieutenant will come back again to Deptford. Whether he comes back or not, they cannot charge the thing to me."

Certainly there never yet was conceived a more diabolical plot, or one of greater impudence, than to waylay and kidnap an officer bearing his majesty's commission, to keep him close prisoner in a crimp's house, chained and half starved, watched day and night, and then, as was intended, to thrust him down into the hold of an East-Indiaman, seemingly stupid with drink (but in reality bereft of his senses by some noxious drug), and to pretend that he was a volunteer recruit. It is very well known, and matter of common notoriety, that many men have been thus kidnapped and kept prisoners, and then shipped under this pretence. They are carried below, apparently drunk, and laid among the other recruits, for the most part a most desperate, villainous company. Here they lie, and when they partly recover they are already out to sea, in the gloomy 'tween-decks, most likely speechless with seasickness, among strange and horrible companions, and no one on board who will so much as listen to their story. Here was revenge indeed, if only it could be carried out! And what was to prevent? I have never heard that a king's officer hath been thus treated, which makes it the more wonderful for Aaron to have devised so bold a scheme. Yet not so bold as it seems, because if Jack could thus be carried on board, in rags, unwashed, unshaven, his hair about his ears, who would believe his affirmation that he was a commissioned officer? Why, if such a ragamuffin told this tale to the petty officers he would be rope's-ended, and if to the first lieutenant or to the captain himself, he would most likely be tied up and accommodated with three dozen, and perhaps six dozen, for insubordination; for the officers of the company are said to be as ready as those of the king's service—who, Heaven knows, are never too lenient—in dealing with refractory recruits. Yet sooner or later, one would think, the thing would be discovered, though not on board the ship. Then the lieutenant would return home and prefer his complaint, and punishment would follow. But Aaron, only an ignorant fellow, thought of nothing but revenge. There are some men to whom the most terrible punishment in the future seems as nothing compared with the gratification of present revenge.

The gang of rogues had not gone farther towards the town than St. Paul's Church, marching quickly along the middle of the road, ready at the least alarm of the press to drop their burden and to run in all directions, when they encounter another party, consisting of three negroes—one carrying a lantern—and a gentleman with a wooden leg. The negroes were, like these villains, armed with cudgels, but they also carried cutlasses.

"Halt!" cried the gentleman, who was none other than the admiral. "Turn the lantern on these men, Cudjo."

The negro valiantly advanced and showed a light upon the party. They wore sailors' clothes, namely, slops or petticoats, short jackets, and hats turned up straight on all three sides; and their hair was long, and hung about their necks. It was, indeed, their business on the Tower Hill, and in the neighborhood of Ratcliffe, Shadwell, and Wapping, to pretend to be honest sailors, and therefore to wear their dress.

"Why," said the admiral, "they are sailors! Whither bound, my lads, and what are you carrying?"

"By your leave, your honor," said one of them, "we are carrying a comrade who is too drunk to walk, and we are fearful
of leaving him in the hedge-side by reason of the press."

"Ay—ay—the press. Well—my lads, I would that the
press could take you all, and confound you for a poor, lousy,
chicken-hearted crew. I wish I knew where the press is this
night, that I might set them on to you. I wish my negroes
were six instead of three. Go your ways. March, Cudjo."

The men made no reply, but hurried away as quickly as they
could. The admiral looked after them awhile.

"I doubt," he said, "that all was not right. They looked a
plaguy cut-throat set of rascals. Perhaps 'twas not a drunken
comrade after all."

Then he continued his way home in the usual marching
order, but slowly, because a wooden-legged man who has
twinges of gout in his remaining toes does not walk fast.
Presently the man who held the lantern spied something in
the road which glittered. He picked it up. 'Twas a gold-
laced hat, with the king's cockade.

"Men," said the admiral, "this is the hat of an officer.
What does this mean? Look about you, every one."

The road was quite dark, owing to the trees and the cloudy
night. Presently, however, the men found a pistol in the road,
and beside it the traces of scuffling feet and torn lace, and,
worse still, plain marks of blood upon the road."

"Here," said the admiral, "hath been wild work. Torn ruffles—a gold-laced hat—a pistol—and a gang of bloodthirsty
cut-throats carrying a body with them. A drunken comrade,
forsooth! And afraid of the press; would to God the press
might take them red-handed! Whom have they murdered?
For murder, surely, it is, and nothing less. Men"—he turned
to his negroes—"I am wooden-legged, and cannot run. Wherefore do you leave me here, and with what speed you may hasten
after that company, and call upon them to surrender, and if they
will not, raise the town upon them. Draw cutlasses—shoulder
cutlasses—quick march—double. Run, ye black devils, as if
your horny grandfather himself were after you!"

If the admiral had ordered his negroes to jump from London
Bridge or the Monument, they would have done it, I am quite
certain, so great was the terror with which they regarded him.

Therefore, at the word, they drew their weapons, and set off running with the greatest resolution, and at a pretty brisk pace, showing all the outward signs of zeal and of courage.

Alas! negroes are in essentials all alike. No man ever yet found courage in the black African, any more than industry, unless the white man was behind him with Father Stick for patience, or honesty, or encouragement.

The night was dark. Nothing more daunts a negro than darkness, because to him the night is peopled—especially when there is no white man present—with all kinds of fearful and terrible creatures; therefore, in their running, they presently began to feel the gloomy influence of the hour, and their speed slackened gradually. Next, they were no longer young; and it would be foolish to expect of those whose wool is gray the courage which they never possessed when it was still black. Thirdly, the admiral was out of sight and out of hearing. And, again, if the enemy refused to surrender, whom were they to alarm? What were they to say? What road were they to take? Lastly — a consideration which weighed with them above all others—what if they were, unhappily, to overtake the men? They were but three to six—and three feeble old blacks to six lusty young whites! Then might occur difficulties unforeseen by the admiral, who naturally thought that his own crew must always gain the victory.

These doubts and difficulties suggested themselves to the brave fellows at one and the same moment, namely, the first moment when they thought their footsteps out of the admiral's hearing. They halted and looked at each other.

"Breddren," said Snowball, "let us stop and deliberation ourselves. Where am de enemy? Fled—flown—yah! De poo' coward!—run clean out of our sight!—'fraid to face brave black man!"

"S'pose," said Cudjo, "we wait just quarter ob an hour; then go back and tell his honor—men clean gone; run away before us, for fear ob us?"

This was agreed to. Nothing more was said, but all three sat on a door-step, and waited until they thought the quarter of an hour seemed to be passed, and they thought they might safely return.

Even if they had followed the party across to the Stairs, supposing they knew which direction to take, they would scarcely have overtaken them, so expeditious were the men in getting to the river and in pushing off, the bank being at this time quite deserted.

Therefore, when they thought a reasonable time had elapsed, the valiant negroes returned slowly, but still brandishing their cutlasses. Arrived within five minutes of the house, they broke into a quick trot, so that they reached the doors in a panting and breathless condition, as happens to those who very earnestly and zealously carry out instructions.

They reported that at the bottom of Church Lane they came upon the enemy, and called upon him to surrender at discretion or take the terrible consequences. The enemy chose the latter. and retreated rapidly. In other words, they all vanished, but whether down Butcher Row or in the direction of Rogue Lane, which leads into the open fields, south of Rotherhithe, they could not tell, and in the darkness and uncertainty they thought it best to return for further orders.

"Why," said the admiral, "'tis a dark night truly. And if they have sailed out of sight, and we have lost them, there is no more to be said," and so put away the torn ruffles, the laced hat, and the pistol, in case they might be wanted for evidence of robbery and violence, if not of murder, and ordered the men an extra ration of rum, and so to bed. Fortunately he had no suspicion that the hat and ruffles belonged to Jack Easterbrook, otherwise his night's rest would have been disturbed. As for the pistol, however, that he discovered, on examination, had not been discharged.

<hr>

CHAPTER XIX.

IN THE CRIMP'S HOUSE.

MR. JONATHAN RAYMENT was not only a crimp (though at his shop in Leman Street they knew not this, and in his houses they knew not his name), but he was a crimp in a large way of business, as they say of honest trades, being the possessor of half a dozen houses in different parts of London, all kept for no other purpose than the receiving of recruits for the service of the East India Company. There is no concealment about this business; everybody knows that they are crimps' houses. One of them was in the high street, Wapping; one in Chancery Lane; a third in Butcher Row, at the back of St. Clement's Church; and another in Tothill Fields. He employed a good many men to decoy and entrap his prey. Some among them went dressed soberly, like substantial citizens, or in scarlet, like half-pay captains, and frequented the gambling-houses, where they made the acquaintance of those who were driven to despair by losing all; some haunted the coffee-houses, taverns, theatres, and mug-houses. Here they picked up young countrymen who had run through their money, 'prentices who had robbed their masters, and even young gentlemen of quality who had wasted their substance in riotous living, and now saw nothing before them but a debtor's prison. Others, again, worked chiefly in the neighborhood of Wapping and the town, being always on the lookout for rustics and laboring men out of work, disbanded soldiers, paid-off sailors, men discharged for misconduct, and rogues in hiding. These they either bought or entrapped, and sometimes when they could not persuade they hesitated not to kidnap. It was from this gang that the six fellows came who assaulted Jack.

When they got to the river-side, still running at the double, being horribly afraid of the press, and knowing not whether they might not encounter the gang face to face, they made all haste to deposit their charge in the boat and rowed off. Presently the cold air playing on Jack's bare head began to revive him, and he half opened his eyes and began to collect his senses. Fortunately the men paid no attention to him, or it might have been all over with him. At first he understood nothing except that he was in a boat, but on what water he knew not. Next he understood that the men were rowing upstream. And so, little by little, some knowledge of what had happened came to him, and he wondered whither they were taking him, and why he was thus treated. He understood, that is to say, that he had been attacked, and perhaps robbed, and that he had been in a swoon. More he knew not. "No voyage," he told me afterwards, "ever seemed longer to me than this three quarters of a mile from Deptford to King Edward's Stairs. And I knew not whether to rejoice or to tremble when the men shipped oars and the boat's bow struck the stairs." The event was doubtful, and only one thing certain, namely, that he was in hands which meant no good to him; that he had been knocked silly for a time, and was still incapable of making resistance; that it was growing late, and good people were abed; and that he had been conveyed to the other side of the river, where honest people are scarce. For all these reasons he resolved upon continuing senseless as long as possible. If, he thought, it had been intended to kill him, why had they not done so right out? Why had they not tumbled him into the river? Why had they taken all the trouble of carrying him to the river-side and so across the water if they were going to kill him? And if not, what were they going to do with him?

King Edward's Stairs, whither they brought him, are the next but one, going down the river, to Execution Dock. These stairs are at no time in the day so well frequented as Wapping Old Stairs and Wapping New Stairs, higher up, or Shadwell Stairs, lower down. After dark they are for the most part deserted, or simply used by the river pirates and night plunderers for the landing of the booty they have gotten from ships and barges. On this night there were no watermen on the stairs, and only, at the head, clustered together for warmth under a pent-house, which would keep off rain, if not wind and cold, half a dozen of the miserable boys who pick up their living in the mud of the river, and are called mud-larks or rat-catchers. When they grow up they may perhaps become lumpers or scuffle-hunters, if they are lucky, and so get a chance of dying in their beds; but for the most part they are destined to become what are called light-horsemen (that is, robbers of ships lying in the river) and plunderers working for the receivers of Wapping and Shadwell, and pretty certain to be either knocked on the head in some brawl or hanged for robbery.

The boys looked up on hearing the steps, but seeing a dead body (as it seemed) being carried by half a dozen men, they prudently observed silence and lay snug, lest they themselves might be put into the condition of being unable to give evidence. The men carried their burden up the steps, cursing and grumbling at the weight—a body measuring six feet one is not a light weight even for six men to carry. Then they turned the lantern once more upon his face.

"He is stark dead," said one. "Let us empty his pockets and chuck him into the river."

"No, no," said another. "Bring him along. He is not dead."

So they lifted him up and carried him along the streets, where by this time the taverns were closed and the people all gone to their beds. Jack knew very well that they must be somewhere among those streets of sailors' houses and sailors' shops which lie between the river-side and the market-gardens of Shadwell and Wapping. But still he understood not what was intended by carrying him here.

Presently they halted at a house; it was in the high street, Wapping. By this time Jack had cautiously opened his eyes. He saw that he was in the hands of a company of six. What had these fellows to do with him? Why did they take all this trouble?

Then the door was opened, and they carried him into the house and up the stairs into a room at the back. Here they flung him down upon the floor, and that so roughly that his wound was opened, and he swooned away once more.

When he recovered he found that they were dragging his clothes from him.

"Now," said one of them, "throw a blanket over him, Parson. Lay them things ready for him to put on; they're the clothes of the poor devil who died here last week. If he wants to escape he will have either to run naked or put on those duds, instead of his fine uniform, which will change him so as his own mother won't know him again. Perhaps she won't get the chance of setting eyes upon her boy for many a year to come. Now, then, smart's the word, ye lubbers; we've got our man snug and safe, and now we'll have some supper, and watch turn about."

Jack was now wide awake, but his head was still heavy. Things looked black. He was in a house at Wapping, and he was stripped naked; he had an open and bleeding wound in the head; a bundle of rags was lying beside him in place of his own clothes; he was guarded by half a dozen ruffians, as ugly and villainous-looking a crew as one may desire. In looking at them, being, perhaps, a little light-headed with his wound, he began to think about Mr. Brinjes's piratical crew, and how they fought and killed each other. Perhaps these gentlemen might begin to fight after they had taken their supper. Perhaps they would all kill each other. Meanwhile he lay perfectly still, with one eye half open.

Then the man they called " Parson " came up-stairs, bringing food and drink, which he set upon the table, and they took their supper, for the most part in silence, or, if there was any talk, it was disguised and rendered unintelligible by the oaths and cursing which wrapped it up. The fellows, in fact, were uneasy; they had faithfully carried out their orders, but they knew not what might happen in consequence to themselves. It is the punishment of such men as these that they must needs do what their master bids them, as much as if they were bound hand and foot to the devil, because they are one and all in his power, and he might cause every man to be hanged if he chose. The " Parson " had now lit the fire, which was blazing cheerfully, and there was a candle on the table. The room was small, and the windows were barred ; the air was heavy and stinking. As for the " Parson," Jack observed that he was a young man, whose face bore the marks of deep dejection, but not of the brutal habits which were stamped upon the faces of his associates. And he was dressed in a cassock. What was a clergyman doing in such a house ?

When the men had eaten their supper they began to pass round the pannikin. They passed it so quickly that Jack hoped they would speedily get drunk, so that the fighting might begin. They did get drunk, but they did not fight. One after the other they fell asleep, until two only were left awake. These were to take the first watch, and had therefore been obliged to spare the pannikin. The Parson quietly laid the four who were asleep upon the floor, their feet to the fire. Then he took the candle and looked at Jack.

" Our new recruit," he said, speaking with the voice of a scholar, and not in the coarse and rude speech of his companions—" our new recruit appears to be overcome with fatigue. Zeal for the service hath, doubtless, laid him low."

He laid aside the hair and looked at the wound. " It is more than fatigue," he said. " I perceive that he hath received a

9

hurt. It is not uncommon with those who come to this house."

"He fell down," one of the men replied ; "and he fell down so gallows hard that he knocked his head upon a stone, and hasn't opened his eyes nor his mouth since."

"Gentlemen, the man hath an ugly wound. 'Twere a pity—his honor would take it ill—if anything happened to this man, a tall and proper fellow, for want of a little care. By your permission I will bring cold water and dress his wound."

They made no objection, and the Parson presently returned with a clout and cold water, with which he washed the blood, and applied plaster to the wound. As for the bleeding, it was caused by the cutting of the ear rather than the blow on the skull. This done, he laid a blanket over Jack's bare limbs.

"He will now," said the Parson, "when he recovers, lie easier. It is long since you brought in so brave a recruit. Call me, gentlemen, when he recovers ; the pulse is quick and strong ; he will not long be senseless. I am but in the next room. Shall I bring you some more rum, gentlemen ?"

"You may, Parson. The jug is out. Fill it up. We have four hours' watch before us. And more tobacco."

The fire was now burning low. Through the bars of the windows Jack could see the stars, and presently a clock hard by struck twelve. He was a recruit, he now understood. In other words, he had been kidnapped, and was in the house of a crimp. Everybody has heard of such places, but they do not generally kidnap officers of the king's navy. However, it seemed as if they were not going to murder him, which was a comfort. No man, not even the bravest, likes to be knocked on the head in a house of crimps while helpless and faint.

The men who were on watch filled and lit their pipes, and began to talk in low voices.

"I'm queerly sleepy, mate," said one. "How hard they breathe, don't they ?"

"There were no orders about his purse," said the other. "Five guineas and a crown. That's a guinea and a shilling apiece. Little enough, too, for our trouble. What about the clothes ?"

"There's no orders about the clothes. Let us have them too."

"No. Let us burn the clothes. Guineas can't tell no tales; but a king's uniform can. Best burn 'em."

"Mate," said the other, "I don't like the job. It's no laughing matter, I doubt. Let us cut his throat at once while the others are asleep. We can slash his face, and lay him naked in the fields, so as no one won't know him again."

"Same as we did that other fellow who tried to get away. We took him to Whitechapel Mount, though."

"We've knocked many on the head before."

"But never a king's officer. This one won't order up no man again for six dozen, will he?"

"Perhaps he is dead already."

The speaker rose and took the candle. Then he stooped beside the motionless figure and slowly passed the candle across the eyes. If you do this before a man who is sound asleep he will become restless and uneasy, if he is not actually awake; if you do it to a waking man, it is difficult indeed for him not to open his eyes or wink them. But Jack made no sign.

"He is still senseless," said the man. "I wonder if he is really dead?" He felt his heart. "No; his heart is beating."

"Mate?" asked the other. Jack understood, though his eyes were closed, that there was a gesture as of a knife across the throat.

"'Twould make all sure," he said; "dead men tell no tales. Suppose we were to ship him, what is to prevent their finding out that they've a king's officer on board? Suppose we finish him off now, who will be able to split on us? Let us take and do it — you and me — while he's unconscious. What is it? One slice of the knife, and we've done with him in a neat and workmanlike manner."

"Hold hard a bit, mate. What about the tall fellow on the other side? You heard what he said. Besides, the Parson knows. We can't cut the Parson's throat as well. But it's the tall fellow I fear, not the Parson."

"If it comes to hanging," said the other, swearing horribly, "damme if I swing alone!"

"You'll have me kicking alongside of you, mate, and the rest of us. We shall all swing in a row."

"Ay, and he shall kick with us. Oh, I know who he is."

"Who is he?"

"That's my secret.   I know him, and that is enough."

"Tell me, my hearty."

"His name is Fletcher—Aaron Fletcher. He's a boat-builder by trade, but he's got a boat of his own, which he keeps sometimes at Gravesend, and sometimes up the Medway, and sometimes she lays off Leigh, in Essex, where I've unladen many a cargo for him. If so be we are brought into trouble by this night's job, pass the word for a warrant to arrest Aaron Fletcher. Don't you forget the name—Aaron Fletcher, of Deptford, him as give the orders, and stood behind the tree, ready to whistle when the lantern showed we'd got him."

"I won't forget, mate.   Let us leave the job till to-morrow. If it's to be a throat job, take in the rest: make 'em all have a hand in it—Parson and all.   Every man shall have his hand in it.   What! are we two to be hanged and the rest get off?"

They went back to their pipes and their rum.

"The ship sails next Saturday at noon," said one.   "We've got but five recruits, counting the Parson, and I doubt if the captain will let him go.   Because why? 'Tis useful and handy to have a man in the place like the Parson, who won't get drunk, and does the housework beautiful, and doesn't look outside the doors for fear of being taken.   There's the 'prentice and the footpad and the fellow who sits and snivels all day long.   What with the war and the new ships and the new regiments, the Company's service will go to the dogs; and what is to become of us?   It is a poor show after the stout fellows we used to hale on board, all so drunk that they couldn't stand."

"The captain says business must get better, and he can't have a set o' lazy rogues eating their heads off.   Why did the captain send us to Deptford? He must be in it as well."

"If he is, who's to prove it? He didn't give no orders. Pass the pannikin."

Their pipes being now out they began to drink faster, Jack looking on, half tempted to pretend recovery and to ask for a tot of the drink.   Fortunately he refrained; for in a short time he perceived that their heads began to drop and their eyes to swim.   "Never," thought Jack, "have I seen men get drunk in this fashion before."   Then they caught at the table to prevent falling, and poured more rum from the jug into the pannikin and drank it, but with unsteady hand. Then their heads nodded heavily at each other, with wild eyes, as if they would fain keep sober; and then one of them fell from his chair upon the floor, and, with a drunken curse upon his lips, fell instantly fast asleep. "The rum must have the devil in it," Jack said to himself.

There was now only one man left of the whole six. It was the man who was so anxious to finish off the job in workmanlike fashion. He looked round him stupidly. His five comrades were lying on the floor, breathing heavily. His eyes fell upon the corner where Jack lay. He rose up and opened the sailors' knife which hung round his neck.

"I'll cut his throat," he said, with drunken cunning, "while the others are asleep. In the morning I shall say they did it, and I looked on, but couldn't prevent, so drunk they were, and me the only sober one. The captain he won't let 'em all be hanged, poor devils! when I tell him how they got drunk, and would do it, whatever I could say." Here he rolled, and nearly fell. He reached for the jug, and drank from it. Then his legs gave way beneath him, and he fell upon his back. He tried to get up, still holding his knife in his hand, and meditating the murder. But he fell back, his head pillowed upon a sleeping brother's leg. "I'll cut his throat," he said, "first thing in the morning, before the others wake. If Aaron— Aaron—comes to ask—I'll cut his throat too—and the Parson's too—and the captain's. I'll cut all their throats."

He said no more, and then there was nothing heard but the heavy breathing and snoring of the whole six. And Jack heard the clock of St. John's strike two. He was not killed yet, and the murderers were dead drunk. If only he could find the strength to get up, and to put on the rags which lay beside him in place of his own clothes!

CHAPTER XX.

OF JACK'S ESCAPE.

THIS resolution of the doubt whether he was to be immediately slaughtered or not naturally gave the lieutenant considerable satisfaction. The villain who was chiefly set upon his murder was fast asleep, breathing heavily, the knife still in his hand with which he had intended to carry out his diabolical design had not the rum overmastered him.

He tried to sit up. Alas! his head was like a heavy lump of lead which he could not lift. That he was stripped naked would have mattered little ; he had a blanket, and the fellows had not taken off his shoes, so that, had he got out into the street, he would have appeared bareheaded, wrapped round the body with a rug, like a savage, yet, as to his feet, dressed in white silk stockings and silver-buckled shoes. Sailors have been turned out into the street in even worse plight than this, and certainly one would rather escape naked than not at all.

So he lay, listening and watching, for two hours and more. Then the candle, which had been flickering in the socket, went out suddenly, and there was no light except a dim red glow from the dying embers in the fireplace, and the house seemed perfectly quiet.

"This," said Jack, listening, "looks more hopeful. If only I could sit up."

He confessed afterwards, and was not ashamed to confess, that he was greatly moved with fear during this uncertainty of his fate, and that no action at sea could compare for dreadfulness with this helpless lying in a corner, expecting at any moment to be slaughtered like a poor silly sheep. "For," he said, "if a man cannot fight he must needs be a coward. There is no help for him. I shall never laugh at cowards more. I had no strength left in me to make the least resistance—no, not so much as a girl. And I looked every moment to hear one of those villains stir and wake up."

They did not stir or make the least sign of waking, but Jack heard footsteps on the stairs. "Here comes another murderer," he thought; "it is now all over with me, and I shall see my Bess no more. Poor girl! Will she murder Aaron in revenge? Or will she never find out, and marry him? Oh, for ten minutes of my old strength and a cudgel!"

The extremity of his agitation gave him power to lift his head and to sit upright, leaning against the wall, and looking for nothing less than immediate death.

The footsteps were those of the man in the cassock whom they called the Parson. He carried in his hand a candle, with which he surveyed the room and the sleeping men. Then he turned to the prisoner.

"So," he said, "you have come to your senses, and can sit up. Do you think you can stand and walk?"

"If you mean to murder me," said Jack, "do it at once, without more jaw—of which we have had enough."

"I have no such thought, sir. Murder you? Heaven forbid! Why should I murder you?"

"Then hush, or you will wake these fellows."

"Wake them?" The Parson kicked the man who lay nearest him. "Wake them? If the house was in flames they would not wake up till they were half burned. In this place, sir, we know our business, and how to doctor the drink so as to produce as sound a sleep as is thought necessary. For instance, you may sing or dance, or do anything you please, but you shall not wake up these fellows. I have done the job for them, and they are safe for six hours and more to come."

"What do you want with me, then?" asked Jack. "You are one of them, and yet—"

"I am in this house for my sins and for my punishment, not for my pleasure. Ask me no more. As for what I want with you, I am come to set you free."

"To set me free? Is it possible?"

"Sir," said this strange creature, "you are astonished to find any conscience at all in such a place, which is, indeed, truly the habitation of devils. Yet I would not have your murder added to my guilt; and, upon my word, sir, when these villains come to their senses, I believe there is no chance for you whatever. For, sir, consider. The kidnapping of a king's officer, and the shipping of him on board an East-Indiaman, is a thing which cannot fail to be discovered, and it is certainly a hanging matter. I know not what madness possessed them to attempt it. Therefore they are mighty uneasy, and though they have put off the matter for the night, because you were senseless, and no man likes to kill another in his sleep, yet to-morrow morning, when they come to themselves and consider the danger they are in, they will, I am certain, resolve to de-spatch you in order to make all sure, and then, after slashing your face, they will lay you in some open and exposed spot, as Whitechapel Mount or the Market Gardens, or very likely, if it seems easier done, they will tie a stone to your feet and drop you into the river. Because, sir, the body once out of the way, and not to be recognized, who is to prove the murder, unless one of the villains turns informer?"

To this Jack could make no reply, but still he marvelled greatly that such a man should be in such a place.

"Certain I am," the Parson continued, "that never man had a more narrow escape than you. And had you been conscious, or showed any signs of life, they would have brained you. Therefore I kept coming and going, because, though the house reeks with murder, I think that they would not go so far as to murder you before my eyes. But come, sir, it is close upon early morning, and already nearly three of the clock. Rise, if you can, and dress yourself in these rags that are left out for you. Indeed, sir, I cannot restore to you your clothes, which are down-stairs, because I wish it to appear that you have es-caped by your own wit and daring. Quick, then, and put on these things."

Then, as Jack was unable of himself to stand, this Samari-tan, for he was nothing short, brought him a chair, and helped him to raise himself into it, and clothed him as if he were a child. The things which he had to put on were so old and ragged that they would scarce hold together, and they were so dirty that no ragamuffin of the street would have picked them out of the gutter; no scarecrow in the fields ever had such clothes. They consisted of nothing more than a pair of cor-duroy breeches and a dirty old knitted waistcoat, both in tat-ters and full of holes. Nevertheless, when Jack had them on, his courage came back to him. A man feels stronger when he

has put on his clothes. Also, perhaps, he was already somewhat recovered of the blow.

"I feel," he said, "as if I could now make some fight."

"It needs not," the Parson replied. "Talk not of fighting,
but lean on me, and we will try to get down the stairs. Remember, it is your only chance to get out of the place before
these fellows awake. I have something that may revive you.
Try now if you can stand."

He could, though with great difficulty. Surely never was
there stranger figure than Jack at this moment. The ragged
waistcoat was too tight to button round his chest; the cordu-
roy breeches were too short for so tall a man, and showed his
bare knees; the white silk stockings and the silver buckles ill
assorted with a dress so sordid; and, to crown all, one side of
his head, where the Parson had partly washed it, showed his
natural hair, with streaks of blood upon the neck; but the
other side was powdered and tied back with black ribbon.
But Jack thought little of his appearance.

"Good," said the Parson. "Now lean your hand upon my
shoulder, and we will go slowly."

"I wish I was strong enough first to handcuff and make fast
these rogues," said Jack.

"Come, sir, your life is at stake, and mine too—if that mattered. Think not upon revenge."

"Aaron," said Jack, "my turn will come. As for revenge,
I say not. I would not kill him; but tit for tat is fair. Easy,
Aaron—easy. You would make me prisoner, and ship me
for a recruit! Very well, Aaron, very well. I shall get my
turn soon! Come, Parson, if that is what you wish to be
called."

So this strange parson supported him slowly and gently down
the stairs and into the kitchen, where he found a chair for him,
and set upon the table cold meat and bread, and poured from
a jar a glass of rum.

"This," he said, "is not drugged. You can drink it without fear. Yet be moderate, for you are still weak. So; now
eat a little, but not much, and then you shall go away in safety.
But forget not to thank God, who hath delivered you from
death and from a den where murders and villainies call aloud
for the vengeance which will certainly fall upon it."

9*

Who, thought Jack, would expect an exhortation to religion in a crimp's house?

As he ate and drank his strength came back to him, although he still remained dizzy, and somewhat uncertain of step.

"Man," he said, when he had taken his supper, "who and what are you, and why do you live here among these people?"

"I came here because I am a villain, like my masters; and I stay here because, like them also, I have no other way of escaping the gallows. Is that reason enough?"

"They call you Parson; you wear a cassock; you talk like a scholar. What hath brought a scholar to such a place?"

"They may call me bishop, if they please. I am the servant of these men. They say unto me, 'Go,' and I go; or, 'Come,' and I obey. If there be any greater degradation for a scholar than to live as cook and servant to fetch and carry drink for a crew of cut-throat crimps, I would fain know what it is. Methinks I would offer to exchange."

"Why," said Jack, "for the matter of an exchange, you might ship as purser's mate, and see how you like that; but hang me if I understand how a clergyman should get to such a place."

Jack now considered his rescuer more carefully. He was a young man not more than five or six and twenty; his cassock was not old, but it was battered and stained with grease; his shoes had no buckles, but were tied with string and were down at heel; his wig was not one which consorted with his sacred calling, being nothing better than an old 'prentice's bob minor, short in the neck, in order to show the buckle of the stock, and as old as any of the worn-out scratches, jemmies, and bob majors which the people fish for at a penny a dip in Petticoat Lane, and even a boy who blacks boots might scorn for the purposes of his trade; but his face was delicate and handsome—a face very far from the dissolute looks of the fellows up-stairs.

"Look ye, brother," said Jack, "you have saved my life. What can I do for thee?"

"Nothing," the Parson replied. "I am a lost rogue, though not, I hope, beyond the reach of pardon, and you can do nothing, I thank you."

"Thou hast saved my life. Damme, rogue or not, take my

hand. Nay," for the other hesitated, "I will have it. Give
me thy hand. Now, then, we are brothers. What hast thou
done?"

"It is true," he said, "that I am an ordained clergyman of
the Church of England. Unworthy that I am, I may call myself a clerk in holy orders."

"I am in a very pretty rig for an officer in the king's service;
but hang me if you are not in worse for a parson."

"Sir," the poor man began, with hanging head, "I lost my
curacy by the death of my rector, and I could get no other, nor
any preferment at all, not even the smallest, having no interest
and being unknown to any bishop or private patron. Then I
quickly spent my little stock—not, I can truthfully avow, in extravagance, or waste, or vicious courses; and I presently found
that I had nothing left but one poor shilling. This I was
unwilling to spend, and I walked about the streets picking up
crusts or turnips that had been dropped into the gutter, until I
became well-nigh desperate. Sir, you see before you a common
footpad. Dressed as I was in the cassock of my profession, I
ventured to stop a gentleman in the street, and to demand his
money or his life."

"Did he give you his money?"

"No. He turned out to be a man of courage—a thing which
I had not looked for. Therefore he drew his sword, and I fled,
he running after me, crying 'Stop thief! stop thief!' I escaped,
and got home unperceived, as I thought, to my lodging. Never
again shall I hear that cry without a knife piercing my heart.
The next day I went to the nearest coffee-house, meditating
death by my own hands. It is a terrible thing to be a suicide,
but worse is it to live among these rogues. I fell in with the
captain, as they call him, the owner of this house and another
like it in Chancery Lane. He, perceiving my trouble, accosted
me, and presently brought me here and gave me strong drink,
under which I told him all."

"But why do you stop here against your will?"

"Because, alas! the hue-and-cry is out after me. In some
way—I know not how—the gentleman I thought to rob found
means to know my name. If I venture forth I shall be arrested,
and presently hanged. For that I must not complain, because
the punishment might be taken mercifully in atonement for my

offence. But there are others—" here he choked, and the tears came into his eyes.

He drew a paper from his pocket and gave it to Jack. It was a piece of a *Gazette*:

" Last evening we hear that a robbery was attempted about ten o'clock in Chancery Lane by a man dressed as a clergyman, who stopped a gentleman and demanded his money or his life, but being confronted by a drawn sword, ran away. The villain succeeded in escaping, but will be discovered, the gentleman being confident that he knows who he is, and can swear to him."

" How long ago was this ?"

" It is now six months. I have entreated the captain to ship me with the rest, but he will not, saying that he hath never had in the house a servant who would neither steal nor drink."

" Six months ! Why, man, a hue-and-cry that is six months old ! Courage ! Tell me thy name."

The poor man made a clean breast of all, telling him his name, and trusting him, in short, with his neck. But no one could converse with Jack or look into his face without trusting him. As for his name, it must not be set down. For the man who had thus sunk to the lowest ignominy was presently enabled to return to his own station and his sacred profession, no one knowing aught of what had happened. Not only did he resume his ministry, but he obtained a curacy, and in time received preferment, being now the incumbent of a London church, and greatly beloved for his devotion, eloquence, and learning, so that it is thought by many that if promotion goes by merit he may soon become a bishop. And since no one knows, except myself, this episode of his early manhood, let the thing remain forever a secret.

" And now," said the clergyman, " the time is getting on. Go while the way is clear. Go, sir. And forget this vile house and the unhappy men that are in it."

" As for forgetting the house," said Jack, " you shall see how I will forget the house."

" You must go away dressed as you are, because I would not be suspected. Wherefore I shall leave the door unlocked and unbarred. Here is a cudgel for you, but you will not need it. All the rogues of Wapping—whose name is Legion—are asleep at this hour. Go, then, and remember that never, even in battle, will you be nearer unto death than you have been this night."

He opened the door, which was carefully locked and bolted, and set the prisoner free.

It was now past three o'clock in the morning, and still quite dark. The cold air made Jack shiver in his rags, but it revived and refreshed him. He looked up and down the street. There were no passengers at that hour save the market-gardeners' carts, which were already lumbering along, filled with vegetables, to the markets of the Fleet and Covent Garden; the rest of the world was still sleeping. Then he surveyed the house carefully.

"'Forget this house,' quoth his reverence? I shall first forget Aaron Fletcher."

It was too dark to observe particularly any distinguishing marks. There was no sign hung out. The ground-floor was lower than the street, and the upper story, which projected two feet and more, and looked as if it were going to fall at any moment, had thick bars outside the windows. "I shall know the house again," said Jack, "by the bars. And now, gentlemen, sleep on and dream—I wish you pleasant dreams—until I come back, which will be, I take it, before you have yet awakened."

CHAPTER XXI.

A RUDE AWAKENING.

ABOUT six o'clock in the morning, when, at this time of year, it is already daylight, there marched down the high street of Wapping a company seen there often enough in the evening, when they are expected and men are prepared for them, but seldom so early. Who, indeed, expects a press-gang at daybreak? The party consisted of a dozen sailors, armed each with a short cudgel, and a lieutenant in command, with a drawn cutlass. With the officer walked a tall man, young, bareheaded, and strangely attired in a ragged knitted waistcoat, tattered breeches tied up with a string and loose at the knees, and yet with white silk stockings, shoes with silver buckles, and, on one side only, powdered hair. The streets at this time are already full of those who are hastening to the day's work; most of the houses are open, and the maids are at the doors twirling their mops, or at the windows throwing open the shutters; or, in the more genteel houses, they are plastering the door-steps with yellow ochre.

'Twas indeed the press-gang, more dreaded than revenue officers or Bow Street runners, and its appearance at this early hour caused everywhere the liveliest curiosity and the greatest consternation. Those who met them either stopped still to look after them, their faces full of apprehension, or they ran into open houses, or they fled without a word, or they turned into a side street or court, for fear of being taken for sailors. Many of those who fled were landsmen and honest mechanics, because, when the press is hot, it does not always respect landsmen, although the law is peremptory against taking any but sailors. This company, however, paid no heed to any, whether they ran or whether they stood, marching along without attempting to seize them, though some of the men were Thames watermen, and others were lightermen, and some dockmen, and others mere river pirates and plunderers, or, as they call them, receivers, copemen, rat-catchers, coopers, mud-larks, light horsemen, and lumpers, all of whom have been held to be sailors within the meaning of the act.

Presently the man in rags, who seemed to be leading the party, stopped and looked about him.

"Ay," he said, "I believe this to be the house. Now, my lads, steady all; for we have 'em, neat and tidy, just as if they were so many rats caught in a bag."

As soon as the people in the street understood—this took them no long time—that the press (out, no doubt, on some special and unusual business of the greatest importance) was actually going to visit the crimp's house, probably in search of the malingerers, deserters, or cowardly skulkers often lying there, in hope to be snug and out of the way, there was a lively curiosity. For skulkers these people entertain a mingled curiosity and contempt—the former on account of their cunning at disguise and hiding, and the latter because, the sea being their trade, they will not bravely follow it. The workman, no longer fearful of his own safety, stopped to look on, his tools in his bag, careless if he should be late at his shop; the waterman,

who, at first sight of the party, trembled for himself, stopped
on his way to the Stairs where he plied, though he might thereby
lose an early fare, and stood curious to see what might happen,
blowing into his fingers to keep them warm; the maids came
out from the house doors and stood around, mop in hand, expressing at first their opinions of the press, without any fear of
the lieutenant, or respect to authority—there are certainly no
such enemies of good government as the women. But when
these honest girls found that the press was not come to carry
off their lovers, but in order to visit the house about which
there was so much mystery, and concerning which there were
told so many stories, they stopped their abuse, and waited to
see what would come of it. Within those barred windows
strange things were carried on. Terrible stories are told of
crimps' houses. Fearful sounds had been heard proceeding
from this house; shrieks and cries for mercy, and the trampling of feet. Sometimes there was singing, with laughter, and
the noise of men making merry over drink; sometimes there
were loud quarrels, with the noise of fighting. Those who entered this house were generally carried in; those who came out
were generally carried out. It was said that sometimes those
who were carried out were not drunk, but dead; and that they
were not put into the boat to be shipped on board an East-
Indiaman, but to be dropped into the river at mid-stream, with a
stone tied to their feet. Therefore the crowd, which increased
every moment, looked on with satisfaction. They might now be
enabled to see for themselves what manner of house this was.

"I think, sir," said Jack to the lieutenant in command, "that
if you would leave two men at the door, we can with the remainder very easily dispose of the rogues in the house, whether
they are awake or asleep."

The house was not astir yet; the door was not yet opened;
the shutters of the ground-floor windows were not yet thrown
back. It looked, in the broad daylight, a dirty, disgraceful
den; the doors and shutters black with dirt and want of paint;
the windows of the upper stories seemed as if they had never
been cleaned since they had first been put up, and some of the
panes of glass were broken.

"If they are awake, they will fight," said Jack. "But they
have no pistols, so far as I could see."

The door yielded to a push. The parson had, therefore, left the door as if Jack had escaped by unlocking and unbarring it.

Jack led the way up-stairs, and threw open the door of the room in which he had so nearly met a horrid and violent death. Behold! All the men were lying just as they had fallen, some on their faces, some on their backs, their mouths open, and breathing heavily. The fire was out, and the air of the place was horribly close and ill-smelling.

"Here they are," said Jack, as the lieutenant followed him. "Saw one ever lustier rogues? Here is a haul for you."

"They are dressed like sailors," said the lieutenant, looking at them with curiosity and misgiving. "But I doubt it. I have never known crimps' men to be sailors. Mostly this sort are river-side rogues, and to take them on board would only be to put into the fo'k's'le so many past-masters in all villainy."

"That is true," Jack replied, "and I doubt they will want continual smartening from the bo's'n; and such mutinous dogs that they will at first spend half their time in the triangles. Yet if you refuse them I must needs have them hanged; and this I am not, I confess, willing to do, because there is one other who must then hang with them. And I would not, if I could avoid it, compass his death."

"Then I will press them," said the lieutenant, making up his mind. "Ready with the handcuffs! Stand by! Handcuff every man!"

The sailors pulled them up one after the other, waking them with kicks and cuffs, and made each man safe. Thus, shaken violently out of their sleep, they stood gazing stupidly at each other, still only half awake, and not knowing what had befallen them, or where they were, or anything at all.

"Bring them down-stairs, and into the open," the lieutenant commanded. "Rouse up every one of them with the pump. Now for the rest of the house."

"I believe there are no other sailors here," said Jack; "only two or three poor devils in hiding till they can be shipped for the East Indies."

The men went through the house, and presently returned, bringing four or five prisoners—namely, the recruits of the company. A most valuable addition they would have made to the service, truly, for a more scarecrow, terrified crew could not be found anywhere. As for the 'prentice, a white-faced, puny wretch, who had robbed his master's till, at the sight of the officer with a drawn sword, and the men, their faces fierce and unrelenting, standing round, he immediately imagined that they were all come for his own arrest, and that this was the first step towards Newgate and the gallows. Wherefore he fell upon his knees, blubbering.

"Alas!" he cried. "I am a miserable sinner. I confess all. I have robbed my master. Oh! let me have mercy. Let me live, and I will pay all back. Only let me live!" And so on, as if the noose was already ready for him, and the rope hitched to the gallows.

The next was a sturdier rogue. He would have been hanged for coining false money had he been caught. But he understood that a company of sailors is not sent forth to arrest men charged with civil offences. Therefore, and in order to save his neck, he very readily volunteered, and, being a brisk, smart lad, though a rogue from childhood, and a thief, forger, coiner, and pickpocket, I dare say he turned out as good a sailor as can be expected of a landsman; and if he could not go aloft to bend or reef a sail, he could help to man a gun and carry a pike. The third man was the deserter, who represented himself as a man milliner, and was suffered to go free, because milliners are of little use on a man-o'-war; the next was a bankrupt, once a substantial tradesman, who had ruined himself with drink and vicious courses, and came voluntarily to the crimp's to be enlisted in the Company's service, in order to escape his creditors. But his face was so puffed and purple with drink, his limbs so trembled beneath him, that I doubt whether he would have lasted the voyage. There was another, whose wife was a termagant, and extravagant to boot, and he was flying from her and from her debts. He, too, offered to volunteer, saying that he would rather dwell with the devil than with his wife; but the lieutenant would not have him. And another there was who was a broken gamester, a gentleman by birth, and a physician from Glasgow University, a native of Jamaica, where he had at first a good fortune, but was now fallen from his former condition, without friends, estate, or money, and held no other hope except to take service with the Company. There were one or two others, but all of them, except the false coiner, the lieutenant, without inquiring further into their characters or their histories, ordered to go about their business; but as for the 'prentice, who still blubbered that he was a repentant sinner, and asked permission only to live, he fetched him a box o' the ears and a kick, and bade him go his way and be hanged.

This poor wretch, who had been torn partly with terror at the thought of going to the Indies to fight, being a desperate coward, and partly with remorse, made haste to obey the lieutenant, and departed; and what became of him, whether he went to his master and confessed and obtained pardon, or whether he was thrown into Newgate and hanged, or whether he fell into worse courses, I know not—"The way of transgressors," saith Holy Writ, "is hard."

There remained the Parson, who said nothing, but waited patiently for his fate.

"As for this man," said Jack, laying his hand upon his shoulder, "he is my prisoner. Leave him to me."

This, then, was Jack's revenge. He might have seen the men swing—and they deserved nothing short of hanging—but it pleased him better to think of these fat, tender-skinned, delicate, overfed, and drunken rogues, as cowardly as they were pampered, howling under the lash, and mutinously grumbling under the discipline of a king's ship. They were mere landsmen, who had never been to sea at all, even if they had ever been on board a ship (if they had, it was only to look for something to steal). But they had lived on the river-side all their lives, and knew the talk of sailors; and they equipped themselves—a part of their trade—in slops and round jackets, the better to decoy their victims.

The men were still so stupid with the drug they had taken that they understood nothing of what was done until they had first had their heads held under the pump for a quarter of an hour. Then they began to remember what had happened; and, seeing their late prisoner with the party of captors, they cast rueful looks at one another, and, like the poor 'prentice, looked for nothing short of Newgate, and for the fatal cart and the ride to Tyburn—which, indeed, for this and many other crimes, they richly deserved.

It would have gone hard with Aaron had this been the destination intended for them by their victim. Nothing is more

distasteful to a rogue than to hang alone, when his brother
rogues have escaped. It offends his sense of justice. Perhaps,
however, the going out of the world in so violent a manner, in
company with an old friend, is felt to be less cold and com-
fortless than to go alone. But Aaron, as well as these men,
was reserved for another fate.

This business despatched, and the men, now fully awake,
drawn up two and two in readiness to march, Jack addressed
them with great courtesy, though the sailors of the press
grinned and put tongue in cheek.

"Gentlemen," he said, "last night your honors were good
enough to offer me the hospitality of your house; you also de-
bated very seriously whether you should not murder me; that
you did not do so is the cause why your honors are now handcuffed. You will go with these honest sailors, and you will
thank me henceforth every day of your lives for my goodness
in getting you impressed. Such brave lads as you will rejoice
to run up aloft in a gale of wind; and the enemy's shot you
will value no more than a waterman's jest. You are so smart
that the bo's'n's supple-jack will never curl about your shoulders, nor his rope's-end make your fat legs jump. As to drink,
I fear there has been more punch served out in this house than
is good for your health; that is better ordered aboard. And
it will do your honors good to see each other made fast to the
triangles while the cat-o'-nine-tails sweetly tickles his fat back.
Perhaps you fresh-water sailors know not the tickling of the
cat. Gentlemen, you have a truly happy life before you. I
wish your honors farewell."

It was the first speech Jack ever made. If it was not eloquent, it was to the point and intelligible.

I do not think that the fellows understood one word of what
he said, being fully possessed with the belief that they were
going to Newgate and afterwards to be hanged. And when
they presently found themselves taken on board the tender and
shoved below-deck, and understood that they were pressed for
sailors, at first they grinned with joy. One who is threatened
with death counts escape on any conditions, even the hardest,
a thing to be welcomed with joy unspeakable. But when they
discovered, after a few days' experience on board, what was
meant by service at sea—a life of little ease, hard work, and

short time for sleep, and rough food, with the kicks and contempt which all true man-o'-war's-men show for lubbers, a limited ration of rum, and the necessity of immediate obedience—some of them fell into despair, and would skulk below till they were driven upward by the bo's'n's supple-jack and the gunner's rattan, and these laid on in no stinted or niggard spirit. Some became mutinous and insubordinate; none of them knew anything of a seaman's duties, in spite of their sailor's dress, and were useless save for the simplest work. Therefore it naturally came to pass that before long, one after another, they were tied up and soundly trounced, whereupon, their backs being soft and tender and unused to the lash, and their dispositions cowardly, and being ignorant of discipline and respect to their officers, when prayers for pity failed, they fell to cursing the captain and the lieutenants, the bo's'n, and the ship's crew, shrieking and screaming like mad women. So that they stayed where they were for another six dozen, and this admonition and instruction were repeated until they were finally made to understand that a man-o'-war is not a crimp's house, nor a tavern at Wapping, where every man can call for what he chooses, sleep as long as he pleases, and take his pleasure; but a place where work has to be done, orders must be obeyed, and punishment in default is as certain as the striking of eight bells. Whether any of them ever returned I know not, but the house was broken up and their old occupation was destroyed, though no doubt other crimps' houses were soon established in their place.

When the press-gang were gone there remained Jack, still in his rags, and the unlucky recruits.

"As for you fellows," he said, "my advice is, sheer off. This house is closed. There is no shelter for you here. Go and hide elsewhere."

"Where shall we go?" asked the poor gamester. "Here at least we got meat and drink. Whither shall we go?"

They obeyed, however, and went out together, parting at the door and skulking away in different directions, perhaps to be picked up by another crimp.

"Brother," said Jack to the parson, "come with me. First let me put on my own clothes, and then we will find a lodging for thee. Thou hast saved my life. Therefore, so long as I have a guinea left, thou shalt have the half."

At first the poor man refused. He burst into tears, declaring that kindness was thrown away upon a wretch so disgraced and degraded as himself; that it would be better for him to stay where he was, and to receive with resignation the evils which he had brought upon his own head. "What," he asked, "can be done for a man for whose apprehension a reward is offered and the hue-and-cry is out?"

"Hark ye, brother," Jack repeated, "thou hast saved my life. If thou wilt not come with me willingly, hang me but I will drag thee along! What! wouldst remain alone in this den? Come, I say, and be treated for thine own good. What! There was no robbery, after all. As for the hue-and-cry, leave that to me. I will tackle the hue-and-cry, which I value not an inch of rogues' yarn."

I do not know what he understood by the hue-and-cry, or how he was going to tackle it; but, being always a masterful man, who would ever have his own way, he overcame the parson's scruples, and presently had him away and safely bestowed in a tavern at Aldgate, where he engaged a room for him, and sent for a tailor, making the parson put off his tattered cassock and his old wig, and sit in a nightcap and shirt-sleeves until he was provided with clothes suitable to his profession, and a wig such as proclaimed it. Then Jack bade him rest quiet a day or two, and be careful how he stirred abroad, while he himself made inquiries into his case, and this matter of the hue-and-cry.

Now mark, if you please, the villainy of the man Jonathan Rayment. There never had been any reward offered for the arrest of this poor man at all; there was no hue-and-cry after him; the gentleman whom, in the madness of his despair, he had thought to rob, had not followed and tracked him; nothing was known about him at all; and his friends were wondering where he was, and why he sent no letters to them. The story of the hue-and-cry and the reward was invented by Mr. Rayment, who was, I believe, eldest son to the Father of Lies, in order to keep the unhappy man in his power, so that he could use him as the servant (or slave) of the house as long as he pleased; or, if he thought it would be more profitable, could ship him as a recruit at any time. And while he was persuading this contrite sinner that the whole town rang with his wickedness, no one in the world knew anything about it, and there was no reason why he should not go openly to the St. Paul's coffee-house and sit among his fellow-divines. Briefly, Jack shared, half and half, all the money he had with this poor man, who presently obtained a lectureship, and afterwards a City church, and is now, as I have already stated, a most worthy, pious, devout, learned preacher, benevolent, eloquent, and orthodox, justly beloved by all his congregation, and, I dare affirm, none the worse because in his youth he experienced the temptation of poverty, was even suffered to fall into sin, felt the pangs of remorse and shame, and endured the torments of companionship with the most devilish kind of men that dwell among us in this our town of London.

So they, too, went away, Jack being restored to his own garments, though his purse, containing four or five guineas, was not in his pocket. And now the house was empty. The crowd had broken up and gone away, but the neighbors still gathered about, talking over the strange business of the morning. Presently they began to look in at the open door. There were no sounds or sign of occupation. Then they opened the doors of the rooms, and looked curiously about them. The lower rooms were furnished with benches and tables, the wainscot walls gaping where the wood had shrunk, and the floors made brown with soot and small-beer to hide the dirt. There was a kitchen, with a pot and frying-pan and some pewter dishes, tin pannikins and some remains of food, and, which was much more to the purpose, there was a small cask of rum, three fourths full. The neighbors made haste to taste the rum provided, being curious to discover whether it was a stronger and more generous liquor than that to which they were themselves accustomed. In a few minutes the rumor of this cask spread to right and left along the street, and everybody hastened to taste the rum, and continued to taste it until there was no more left. It was strong enough and generous enough to send them away with staggering legs and fuddled brains. Up-stairs there were bedrooms with flock mattresses laid upon the floor, and in one room there were rings and staples and chains fixed in the wall for safely securing mutinous recruits. But all the rooms were foul and filthy.

When the neighbors went out the boys came in and took

possession joyfully, with no one to check or hinder their mischief. Never before had boys such a chance. When they left the house there was not a whole pane of glass left in the windows, nor a bench, chair, or table that was not broken, nor any single thing left that could be carried away.

Next day the " captain "—that is, the worthy dealer in curiosities, of Leman Street, Mr. Jonathan Rayment—himself walked over to Wapping, in order to inquire into the health and welfare of his recruits and their numbers; he was also anxious to know what had happened in the adventure with the king's officer.

You may understand his surprise and dismay when he found everybody gone and everything broken. They had even torn away the wooden balusters and ripped up the wooden steps. Nothing was left at all—not even those poor, helpless creatures, the 'prentice and the parson. Where could they be ?

He did not dare to ask. Something terrible had happened. As for himself, he hurried home to hide himself in his shop until the danger was over. A curse upon Aaron Fletcher, and on his own foolishness in suffering his men to meddle with Aaron's private quarrels ! And a good business now broken up and destroyed; for how could the house be carried on without his men ?

He looked to hear an account of his men in the *Gazette;* how they were brought before the lord mayor and charged with highway robbery, and even sent to Newgate for trial. Strange ! There was nothing. Nor did this worthy tradesman ever learn what had happened, for Aaron could tell him nothing, except that the lieutenant had escaped; and he never dared venture to ask in Wapping. But he lost his servants and his recruits, and for a long time the business of crimping in those parts languished.

One thing remains to be told about this eventful day. In the evening, work being over, Aaron Fletcher was sitting alone, his pipe in his mouth, in the cottage where he lived, at the gates of his boat-building yard. He was in good spirits, because the lieutenant was reported missing. Perhaps he was dead. It would be the best thing in the world if he was dead. What then ? No one could say that he had any hand in it.

"Aaron!" cried a voice he knew—"Aaron Fletcher, open the door!"

He dropped his pipe and turned pale, and his teeth chattered. It was the lieutenant's voice, and he thought it sounded hollow. He was dead, then, and this was his ghost come to plague him. Aaron was a man of courage, but he was not prepared to tackle a ghost.

"Aaron," the voice repeated, "open the door, or I will break it in, ye murderous villain. Open the door, I say!"

Aaron obeyed, his cheeks ashy white, and his heart in his boots.

It was no ghost, however, but the lieutenant in the flesh, tall and gallant, and apparently none the worse for the night's adventure, who walked in, followed by Mr. Brinjes. He was arrayed in his great wig and velvet coat, in honor of the club, whither he was going. This splendor added weight to the words which followed.

"Aaron," said the lieutenant, "or Cain the murderer, if you like the name better, there was, last night, a purse in my pocket, containing, as near as I can remember, the sum of five guineas and a crown. Your friends have taken it from me. Give me back those five guineas and that crown."

"What friends? I know nothing about any friends or any five guineas. What mean you? I know nothing about the matter. It was not I that knocked you on the head, lieutenant."

"Why—see—you are self-convicted and condemned. Who spoke of knocking on the head? How should you know what was done unless you were one of them? Five guineas, Aaron, and a crown, or"—here he swore a great oath—"you go before the magistrate to-morrow with your friends the crimp's men, and answer to the charge of highway robbery, and thence to Newgate. And so, in due time, to Tyburn in a comfortable cart. Five guineas, Aaron."

He held out his hand inexorably, while Aaron trembled. This man was worse than any ghost.

"Pay the money, Aaron," said Mr. Brinjes, "and thank your good-fortune that you have so far got off so cheap. So far, Aaron. Not that we have done with you. Look for misfortune, friend Aaron." He said this so solemnly that it sounded like a prophecy. "Men who get crimps to rob for them and kidnap for them cannot hope to prosper. Therefore expect misfortune. You have many irons in the fire; you can be attacked on many sides; you build boats; you run across to the French coast; you sell your smuggled lace and brandy. Misfortunes of all kinds may happen to such as you. But you must pay this money, or else you will swing; you will swing, friend Aaron; and when you have paid it do not think to escape more trouble. I say not that it will be rheumatism, or sciatica, or lumbago, all of which lay a man on his back and twist his limbs and pinch and torture him. Perhaps— But look out for trouble."

Aaron lugged out his purse and counted five guineas, which he handed over to Jack without a word.

"What?" cried Mr. Brinjes, his eye like a red-hot coal, "the lieutenant forgives you, and you think you are going to escape scot-free! Not so, Aaron, not so; there are many punishments for such as you. I know not yet but you must swing for this, in spite of this forgiveness. Many punishments there are. I know not, yet, what yours shall be. Come, lieutenant, leave him to dream of Newgate."

CHAPTER XXII.

THE PRIVATEERS.

THE time allowed to a sailor in which to make love is short, being no more than the interval between two voyages. (He generally makes up for brevity by the display of an ardor unknown to landsmen.) And now the hour approached when Jack must tear himself from the arms of his mistress, and go forth again to face the rude blast, the angry ocean, and the roaring of the enemy's guns. Regardless of his former sufferings, he desired nothing better than to put to sea once more; and he was not one to go away crying because there would be no more kisses for a spell.

Among the king's ships laid up in ordinary at Deptford during the seven years' peace was a certain twenty-eight-gun frigate called the *Tartar*. I know not what had been her record

10

up to this period; but that matters nothing, because it will be allowed that she is now very well known to all French sailors, and regarded by them with a very peculiar terror. She was built on lines somewhat out of the common, being sharper in the bows and narrower in the beam than most ships. She rode deep, but she was so fast a sailer that nothing could escape her when she crowded on all her canvas and gave chase; a beautiful ship she was, to my eyes, even while laid up in ordinary, with the topmasts taken out of her, and her upper deck covered with tarpaulin, like a long tent.

"But," said Jack, "you should see such a ship sailing. What do you landsmen know of a ship, when you have never seen one running free before the wind, every inch of canvas set—studdin'-sails, stay-sails, flying jib, sky-scrapers, and all? You draw ships, Luke; but you have never even seen a ship at sea."

That was true; but, on the other hand, I never attempted to draw a ship sailing on the ocean, nor have I ever painted waves or the open sea.

"Wait till you have seen the *Tartar* in a brisk nor'wester, her masts bending, she riding free, answering the least touch of her helm like a live thing—for that matter, a ship at sea *is* a live thing, as every sailor knows, and has her tempers."

Jack became enamoured, so to speak, of this vessel from the first day when he revisited the yard and saw the carpenters and painters at work upon her, and desired nothing so much as to be commissioned to her; for it was quite certain that she would be manned and despatched as soon as they could fit her out. (At this time they were working extra hours, and from daybreak to sunset, the men drawing increased pay, and all as happy as if the war were going to last forever.

"She is," he said, "a swift and useful vessel, and wants nothing but a fighting captain, who will not wait for the enemy, but will sail in search of him and make him fight. I would she had such a captain, and I was on board with him!"

He presently got his desire, as you will hear, and the ship got such a captain as he wished for her.

Meanwhile the days passed by, and still his appointment was delayed, so that, in spite of his amour, he began to fret and to grow impatient. The great man on whose word he relied had made him a clear and direct promise, from which there could be, one would think, no departing. "Trust me, lieutenant," he said; "I assure you that you shall be appointed to a ship with as little delay as possible." Yet appointments were made daily, and his own name passed by. What should we think, I humbly ask, of a plain merchant in the City who should thus disregard a straightforward pledge? Yet what would ruin the credit of a merchant is not to be blamed in a great man. By the advice of the admiral Jack once attended the levee of his noble patron; but, being unaccustomed to courtiers' ways, ignorant of the creeping art, and unused to push himself to the front, he got no chance of a word, or any recognition, though he says his patron most certainly saw him standing in the crowd; and so came away in disgust, railing at those who rise by cringing, and swearing at the insolence of lackeys. He then made a personal application at the navy office, where the clerks treated him with so much rudeness and contempt that it was a wonder he did not lose his temper and chastise some of them. So that his affairs looked in evil plight, and it seemed as if he might be kept waiting for a long time, indeed, and perhaps never get an appointment or promotion. For though the peace estimates had reduced the navy from the footing of fifty thousand officers and men to that of ten thousand—so that when the war broke out again the admiralty were wanting officers as well as men—yet, as always happens, the applicants for berths were more numerous than the berths to be given away; and the favoritism which is everywhere, unhappily, in vogue at the admiralty, hath always reigned supreme.

"Of one thing," he declared, "I am resolved. If I do not get my appointment before many months I will seek the command of a privateer, or at least the berth of lieutenant on board of one. There is, I know, no discipline aboard a privateer; the men are never flogged, and are generally a company of mutinous dogs, only kept in order by a captain who can knock them down. But they are sturdy rascals, and will fight. I hear they are fitting out a whole squadron of privateers at Bristol; and there is a craft building at Taylor's yard, in Redriff— I saw her yesterday—which is never intended to carry coals between Newcastle and London, or sugar between Kingston and Bristol. She means letters-of-marque, my lad. Perhaps I could get the command of her. I am young, but I am a king's officer; and if you come to navigation—well, one must not boast. I will not stay at home doing nothing—what! when there is fighting? No. I must go too, and take my luck. If they will not have me either in the king's service, or on board a privateer, or in the Company's navy, why, my lad, there is nothing left but to volunteer and go before the mast. They would not refuse me there, I warrant, and many a poor fellow has done as much already."

It is true that, on the reduction of the naval force, there were many unfortunate young men, chiefly among the midshipmen, who saw no hope of employment, being without interest, and therefore were obliged to give up the king's service, and either to get berths on merchantmen or to take commissions in the Company's service; or even, as certainly happened to some, to volunteer for service before the mast. Some became smugglers, some (but these were chiefly officers from the disbanded regiments) became town bullies and led-captains, some strolling actors, and some highwaymen. The fate of these poor fellows was much in the mouths of the young officers waiting, like Jack, for a ship, who met and talked daily at the Gun Tavern.

Fortunately our lieutenant was not called to embark on board a privateer, for he found a friend who proved able and willing to assist him. This was the resident commissioner of the yard, Captain Petherick, who took up Jack's case for him, and that so effectually, though I know not in what way, that he presently procured for him the appointment promised him, and which most he desired, namely, that of third lieutenant to the frigate *Tartar*, to which Captain Lockhart was now appointed. And he was a fighting captain indeed, if ever there was one.

I am sure that on the day which brought him his commission there was no happier man in Deptford than Lieutenant Easterbrook. He had now been in the service for nearly ten years, and for seven of them had been, through no fault of his own, debarred from every opportunity of distinction. Behold him, therefore, at last, with his foot well on the ladder, albeit very near the lowest rung, holding his majesty's commission as Lieutenant to H. M. frigate *Tartar*. On that day it happened that the bells were ringing and the guns firing, to commemorate I know not what event. To Jack and to his friends it seemed as if the bells were ringing and the cannon were fired in his honor, and to celebrate his appointment.

"As for her orders," said Jack, "I care little whither we are sent, because it is certain that there will be hot work to do wherever we go. The French, they say, are strong in North American waters, and they are reported to be fitting out a great fleet at Toulon; they are also reported to be collecting troops at Boulogne and at Havre for embarkation, no doubt for the invasion of the English coast, if they pluck up spirit enough. Well, Bess, we shall be among them, never fear."

There was, as many will remember, a great scare at this time that the French were preparing to invade us, and there were some who talked mournfully of another battle of Hastings, and of King Louis coming over to be crowned at Westminster Abbey. The smugglers (who in times of peace are hanged, but in times of war are courted) reported great preparations along the French coast, though not, so far as could be learned, comparable with the gathering of men and material they made in the year 1745, when they were preparing to back up the Pretender. Nevertheless the danger was thought to be so pressing that everything else must be neglected while the government provided for the home defence; and the *Tartar* (though this we knew not yet) was destined to join the Channel Fleet. Meantime, as is mere matter of history, the French very leisurely put to sea from Toulon, with the finest fleet, I think, that the world had ever seen, and had plenty of time to take Minorca. Then followed the unlucky Admiral Byng's famous engagement with the Marquis de la Gallissonnière, which, though we call it an inconclusive action, the French have construed into a most glorious victory. Never can one forget the rage of the people and the cry for revenge that rose up from every coffee-house, from every tavern, from the Royal Exchange, filled with great merchants, and the mug-house, filled with porters, and wherever men do assemble together. A bad beginning of the war it was; and all that year, except for the execution of the admiral, we had nothing to cheer us. Even this, though a sop for the rage of the nation, was a poor consolation, because no sooner was it done than men began to ask themselves whether, after all, the admiral had not done his duty. There were floods of epigrams and verses written, both upon Byng and De la Gallis-

sonnière, if they may be considered a consolation.   In time of
defeat and disgrace the soul is soothed, at least, when something
biting has been said upon the cause or author of the shame.
This is an art greatly practised by the French, who have always found in its exercise a peculiar satisfaction for their many
disgraces both by sea and land, and for the loss of all their lib-
erties.   And for the sake of a good epigram they are said to go
cheerfully even to the Bastile.

At this time, besides the preparations for invasion, which
were perhaps exaggerated, the Channel swarmed with French
privateers, and these full of courage and spirit.   At the first
outset, and until we had taught them a lesson or two, they were
bold enough to attack anything, without considering disparity
of numbers, that flew the English flag.   Had the French king's
navy been handled with as much resolution as these privateers,
commanded and manned often by simple fishermen, the result
of the war might have been very different.   They put to sea in
vessels of all kinds; nothing came amiss for a craft of war with
letters-of-marque when these rogues first went a-privateering;
nothing in their earliest flush of success seemed too small or too
badly armed for a venture against the richly laden, slow-sailing
English merchantmen, which, taken by surprise, offered at the
beginning of the war, it must be confessed, but a cowardly resistance.   Again, nothing was too big to be fully manned and
equipped.   Every craft that lay in the ports, from Dunquerque
to Bordeaux, became a privateer, from a simple fishing-smack,
a fast-sailing schooner, an unarmed sloop carrying two or four
six-pound carronades and thirty or forty men, to a tall frigate
of thirty guns, well-gunned, and manned by three hundred
sturdy devils, emboldened by the chance of plunder, and eager
to attack everything, from an East-Indiaman to a potato-coaster.
Very good service was done during the course of this war by
our own privateers, of whom there were presently a great many,
though it must be owned that the French beat us both for the
number of their piratical craft and their success.   Certainly
they had a better chance, since for every French merchantman
there are fifty English.   We were always capturing their privateers, but their number never seemed to lessen, however many
lay in our prisons.   Why, in one year—I think it was the year
1761—we took no fewer than one hundred and seventeen pri-

vateers, manned by five thousand sailors; yet in the same year, in spite of their conquests, we lost over eight hundred merchantmen, taken from us by these hornets swarming under our very noses.

"Kiss me, Bess," said Jack; "we will sail on Sunday, or Monday at latest. Kiss me again, my girl. Our orders have come. We join the Channel Fleet, where there will be rubs for some, as is quite certain."

"Among the privateers, Jack?" Bess was as brave a girl as any, yet she shuddered, thinking of this dangerous service, in which one has not to take part in a great battle once in the cruise, and so home again to brag about the broadsides and the grape-shot, but to fight daily, perhaps, and always with a desperate crew, whose only chance is victory or escape. "Well" —for his eyes clouded at the first appearance of fear in her face—"if thou art happy, Jack, then will I try to be happy too. Alas! why cannot women go into battle with their lovers? I could fire a pistol, and I think I could thrust a pike with any who threatened thee, Jack. But we must still sit at home and wait."

"Now you talk nonsense, Bess. Do you think I could fight with thee at my side? Why, I should tremble the whole time lest a splinter should tear thy tender limbs. Nay, my dear; sit at home and wait, for there is nothing else to do. And sometimes think of thy lover. Let me read the future in thine eyes." She turned them to him obediently, and as if the future really could be read in those great black eyes. "I see, my dear, a sailor coming home again, safe and sound, prize-money in his pocket, promotion awaiting him. His girl waits for him at home. He rushes into her arms and kisses her—thus, my dear, and thus, a thousand times. Then he buys her a house as fine as the admiral's, and furnishes it for her with his prize-money; and there is a garden for salads and for fruit. She shall eat off china—no more pewter then. She will have the finest pew in church and the most loving husband at home, and—what? I see a dozen boys and girls; and every boy in his majesty's service, and every girl married to a sailor. There shall be no woman in the world handsomer or happier. Give me a kiss again, my dear."

CHAPTER XXIII.

A SAILOR'S CHARM.

That evening Bess did a thing which is forbidden by the Church; in what part of the Prayer-book I do not know, but I have always understood that it is prohibited as a grievous sin. She went to seek the advice of a witch.

The sailors and their wives sometimes importuned Mr. Brinjes to bestow upon them, or to sell them if he would, some kind of charm or amulet, either to maintain constancy in separation (this charm, though largely in request, is, if all reports are true, of small efficacy), to prevent drowning, against incurring the wrath of the captain, and punishment by the cat-o'-nine-tails, against being killed or wounded in action, and against hanging —which may happen to any, though there are fewer sailors hanged than landsmen. Sometimes, if he was in good temper, or if the applicant was a young woman of pleasing appearance, Mr. Brinjes would consent, and send her away happy, with something in a bag which he called a charm. Whether he himself believed in his charms I know not, but there are still living some who declare that they have escaped hurt or drowning wholly through the efficacy of the apothecary's charm. Yet if a man hath this power, why should he not be so patriotic and benevolent as to extend it over the whole of his majesty's navies, so that not a sailor among them all should ever be shot, drowned, flogged, or cast away? It is like the arrogance of the Papist priests, who profess to be able to forgive sins. Why not, then, forgive at once, both great and small, mortal and venial, all that the world, living or dead, hath committed, and so make mankind whole? Whatever his belief concerning his own powers, Mr. Brinjes without doubt entertained a high respect for those of Castilla's black nurse Philadelphy—a true witch if ever there was one.

"I know not," my father once said on this subject, "whether the practice of magic hath in it anything real, or whether the whole is imposture and superstitious credulity. The Bible doth not teach us clearly one way or the other. Yet, by implication, we may understand that the arts of sorcery were in old times practised successfully, otherwise there would not have been promulgated commandments so express against those who work hidden arts, practise divination, inquire of a familiar spirit, consult the dead, or fabricate charms. And certainly it hath been the belief in all ages, and among every race of whom we have knowledge, that power may be magically obtained by men whereby they may compel the help of demons and spirits, and in some way foretell the future. Nebuchadnezzar divined with arrows; the false prophets deceived the people with amulets; the Bene Kedem, the Chaldæans, the Philistines, and the Chosen People, in their backsliding, worked hidden arts'; Pharaoh's magicians turned their rods into serpents; Rachel carried away his Teraphim from her father, Laban. What forbids us to believe that sorcery may still be living in our midst, though lurking in dark corners for fear of the law and of the righteous wrath of pious men ?"

The old negro woman knew, of a certainty, many secrets, whether they were those of the black-art or no. Mr. Brinjes would talk to her in her own Mandingo language, which he had acquired while on the west coast of Africa. She it was who assisted him in the compounding of those broths which used to simmer on his hob, to be tasted by the shuddering assistant. By these and other secrets of which he was always in search, and forced the woman to reveal by terror of his magic stick with the skull, he hoped to cure disease, to arrest decay, and to prolong life. I suppose that it was by conversation with him that Bess was led to consider Philadelphy as much wiser in witchcraft than Mr. Brinjes. Therefore she resolved to consult her, and went to her that very evening with all the money she had in the world, namely, a crown-piece and a groat.

The negroes of the admiral's household occupied quarters of their own, built for them without the house, in West Indian fashion, containing a common kitchen and sleeping-rooms. Here Bess found three of the men, one of them being on guard, with the old woman. They were squatted on the floor, in the kitchen, round a dish containing their supper—a mess of cuscoosoo, which is made of flour roasted by some art in small

10*

grains, and served with salt fish, onions, red pepper, and butter
—a strong-tasting food, but not displeasing to the palate nor
unwholesome. Every race has its own dish. The Spaniards
have their olla podrida, the Hindoos their rice, the Chinese
their birds'-nest soup and dried sea-slugs, and the Mandingos
their cuscoosoo. There was no other light in the room than
the glow of a great coal fire, which these negroes love to have
burning all the year round, and in the winter never willingly
leave. As for candles, why should negro servants have luxu-
ries which poor white folk cannot afford to buy? Candles are
for those who wish to read, play music, cards, and practise the
polite accomplishments; not for those who sit about the fire for
warmth.

"Hi!" said Philadelphy, looking up curiously. "'Tis Bess,
the penman's girl."

"I want to speak with you, Philadelphy," said Bess.

The old woman nodded, and the men rose, took up the dish
of cuscoosoo, and retired, as if they were accustomed to these
consultations, and knew that their absence was expected. A
witch must, in fact, be quite alone with those who inquire of
her.

When they were gone the old woman crept closer to the fire,
the light of which seemed to sink into her skin, and there to
become absorbed (the blackness of Philadelphy's cheeks not being shiny, as is that of some negresses, but dull), while her eyes
shone by the firelight like two balls of fire.

"What is it, dearie?" she asked. "Is thy lover inconstant?"

"How do you know I have a lover?"

"It is written on thy face and in thy eyes, dearie."

"I have come for a charm," she replied, blushing to think
that she carried her secret written on her face so that all could
read.

"Hush! The admiral he say, 'No charms here, Philadelphy.' Whisper. What kind of charm? Is it a charm to make
thy sweetheart love thee?"

"He loves me already." Bess hesitated a little. Then she
added, "He is a sailor. I want a charm for a sailor."

"I sell very fine charm—proper gri-gri charm. Eh! When
Massa Brinjes wants pow'ful charm for gout and toothache he

sends for Philadelphy, and puts his skull-stick on the table.
Then I give him what he wants. I got charm for 'most everything. Massa Brinjes very good Obeah doctor; he learn in
Mandingo country when he live among the rovers. Hi! Fine
times the rovers had before they were all hanged up. Hi!
But he don't know so much as ole Philadelphy. When he
want to learn, mus' come to de ole woman. Hi!" As she
spoke, her eyes rolling about so that the whites, in the firelight, were glowing red, she held out her hand for the money,
but went on talking and asking questions without waiting for
a reply. "Mus' come to de ole woman. Everybody comes to
de ole woman. Some day I die—what you do then? Hi!
What kind of charm you want? I sell very fine charm. Will
you buy charm for true love? Once your man get that charm
upon him he can't even look at another woman. That charm
make all other women ole and ugly. Hi! Tell me, dearie, will
you have that charm? I sell charm again' drowning. No man
drown with my charm on him. Will you buy that charm? I
sell charm again' shot and sword. No man ever killed who
carry my charm. I sell charm to bring him home again. Hi!
You like your sweetheart come home again? How much money
you got for de ole woman, dearie?"

"I've got a crown and a groat. Is that enough?"

"Give it to me!" She clutched the money greedily. "S'pose
you rich lady, too little. S'pose you poor girl, 'nuff for kind
ole Philadelphy."

"Will the money buy all the charms?"

"Buy all?" The old witch laughed scornfully. "She think
she a queen, this girl, for sure. Buy all? Dearie, if your crown
and your groat was a bag of gold guineas you couldn't buy
but only one charm."

"Then, if I can only have one, which shall it be?"

"Take the love charm, dearie. That the best for eb'ry
girl."

"No," said Bess, proudly, "I will not buy a love charm. If
my sweetheart cannot remain constant without a charm to
keep him I want no more of him. Well—then—he might be
drowned. But he has passed through so many dangers already
that I do not think he will ever be drowned. He might be killed
in action. Let him come home safe and sound, whether he loves

me or not.   Yes, I will have the charm against killing and
wounding."

"Most girls," said the old woman, "rather see their sweethearts die than be false."

"I will have the charm against shot and cutlass," said Bess.

"Very well.   I make fine gri-gri — pow'ful charm.   Hi!
charm to turn aside every bullet.   You wait."

Then the old woman rose slowly, being, in spite of her magic
powers, unable to charm away her own rheumatism, and fumbled in her pocket, a vast sack hanging beneath her dress, which
contained as many things, and as various, as a housewife's cupboard.   From the rubbish lying in its vast recesses she produced a small leather bag, apparently empty, tied with a long
string, which, after securing the bag with half a dozen knots,
was long enough to be slipped round the neck.   To untie these
knots and to open the bag was to destroy the whole charm.
More than this, it was to invite the very danger which was
sought to be averted.   Two or three years afterwards I was
present when the bag was opened.   It contained nothing more
than a small piece of parchment, inscribed with certain characters, which I believe to have been Arabic, and very likely a
verse of the false prophet Mohammed's book, the Koran; there
was the head of a frog, dried; the leg-bone of some animal,
which may have been a cat or a rabbit; the claw of some wild
creature; a nutmeg and a piece of clay.   This was a famous
collection of weapons to interpose between a man's body and a
cannon-shot!

"Take the bag in your hand," said the old woman.   "Now
go down on your knees and shut your eyes, and take care not
to open them, whatever you hear or feel, while you say the
words after me:

> "'Shot and bullet pass him by;
> Pike and cutlass strike in vain;
> Keep him safe, though all may die;
> Bring my sweetheart home again.'"

Bess did as she was commanded, holding the bag in her
hand, and keeping her eyes tightly closed, while she repeated
these words on her knees.   She declared afterwards that, while
she said the words, there was a rushing and whirling of the air
about her ears and a cold breath upon her face, and, which was

strange, though she held the bag tightly by the neck, she felt
that things were being dropped inside it.

"Now, honey," said the old woman, "gri-gri done made.
You open eyes, and stand up."

So Bess obeyed, looking about her fearfully. But there was
nothing to see, and the old woman was now crouching beside
the fire again. But the bag, which had been empty when she
took it in her hand, was now filled with something.

"Give your lover," said Philadelphy, "this bag. Hang it
round his neck. And say the words again, with your eyes shut
and his as well. Let him never take it off or look inside it, or
tell anybody of it. Hi! you very fine girl, for sure; yet sometimes men go away and forget. Hi! Den you fly roun' like a
wildcat in a trap. Well, dearie, come to me s'pose he does go
untrue. I make beautiful figure for girls when sweethearts
prove false; put him 'fo' the fire, an' stick pins into him. Den
he all over pain." Bess told me that she thought of Aaron,
and of a way to punish him; but, fortunately, she had no
more money, else I fear that Aaron would have passed a bad
winter.

When she had the charm the old woman offered to tell her
for nothing, by several methods, the fortune of her lover. All
her methods led to surprising results, as you shall hear; and
then Bess went away, carrying with her the precious bag. The
next thing was to persuade Jack into putting it on. Now every sailor is full of superstition; and the bravest man afloat is
not above carrying a charm if one is given to him. But, of
course, he would not have it known.

"Jack," said Bess, "don't be angry with me for what I have
done."

"What have you done, child?"

"I've been—I've been—Jack—to a witch. Oh! a real witch!
But she does not know your name or anything about you.
And I've got a charm for you! Here it is." She lugged the
precious thing out of her bosom. "No, Jack; don't touch it
yet. You must never try to open it, or to find out the secret
of what is inside, or else the charm will be broken. And, Jack
—promise me—promise me— If you will wear this round
your neck, close to your skin, you shall never be hit by shot
nor shell."

Jack laughed; but he took the little black bag out of her hand and looked at it doubtfully.

"Why," he said, "as for such a trumpery thing as this, is it worth the trouble of hanging it about one's neck?"

"I might have had a charm to keep you safe from drowning, Jack; but I thought that you have had so many dangers already that there can be no more for you. And I might have had one to keep you true to me; but, oh! Jack, what good would it do to me if you are true only to be killed? Besides, if you cannot keep true to me without a charm you cannot love me as you say you do—yes, Jack I know you do. I scorn witchery to keep my lover true."

"A lock of thy hair, Bess, is all I ask. I will tie that round my wrist. 'Twill be quite enough to keep me true, and to save me from drowning, and to turn aside the bullets."

There is, indeed, a common superstition among sailors that a lock of their mistress's hair tied round the wrist will carry them safely through the action.

"You shall have a lock of my hair as well, Jack. Oh! you should have it all if I thought it would keep you safe. Only let me hang this round your neck. There; now I take off the cravat and unbutton the shirt, and drop it in—so. Shut your eyes, and keep them shut, while I say,

> "'Shot and bullet pass him by;
> Pike and cutlass strike in vain;
> Keep him safe, though all may die;
> Bring my lover home again.'"

No phenomena attended this incantation.

"And now, Jack," Bess said, "you can open your eyes again. Cannon-shot shall not harm thee; bullet shall turn aside; sword and pike shall not be able to do my dearie hurt.

"'Tis woman's foolishness, Bess. Yet have I heard strange stories about these old negresses. They are sold to the devil, I believe. The charm can do no harm, if it do no good. One would not go into action with an advantage over one's ship-mates. Yet it is well to be on the safe side; no man knows what power these old women may have acquired; and every man has his true-love knot for a charm. Well, Bess, to please thee, my dear, I will wear it."

"Then, Jack, I can let thee go with a lighter heart. When

the wind blows I shall tremble, but not when I hear of sea-fights and the roaring of cannon."

"Some men carry a Testament," said Jack. "Many a bullet has been stopped by a Testament, which is natural, as against the devil and all his works, of which the Frenchman and the Spaniard are the chief. Some of them carry a caul to escape drowning. But they commonly get shot; though why a caul should attract the bullets, or whether it is better to be shot or drowned, I know not. But give me a true-love knot, my girl, to keep me safe, with a lock of thy black hair to tie about my arm, and a kiss of thy dear lips for charm to keep me true. And tell no one about this charm of the black witch."

She let down her long and beautiful hair, which fell below her waist, and cut off a lock three feet long. Then Jack bared his arm; why, the lovesick lad had tattooed it all over with the name of Bess. There was Bess between an anchor and a crown, Bess between two swords, Bess under a Union-Jack—well, there could be no denying, for the rest of his life, his vows of love for Bess. She laughed to see these signs of passion, and tied her lock of hair round and round his arm, securing the two ends tightly with green silk. With this, which is every woman's amulet, and the old witch's charm, surely her Jack would be safe.

In everything that followed Jack continued to wear this charm about his neck both by day and night. It is, we know, most certain that this superstition concerning amulets is vain and mischievous. How can a witch by any devilry preserve a man from lead and steel? How can a leopard's claw and a verse from a so-called sacred book stand between a man and the death that is ordered for him? To think this is surely grievous sin and folly. Besides, it is strictly forbidden to have any doings with witches; and what was forbidden to the people of old cannot be lawful among ourselves. Yet one cannot but remark, as a singular coincidence, that in all his fighting Jack had never a wound nor a scratch. Perhaps, however, his escape had nothing to do with the gri-gri.

"When I had gotten the charm," the girl went on, "I asked Philadelphy to tell my sweetheart's fortune. So she said she would read me his fortune for nothing, and she drew the cards from her pocket, and spread them out upon the table, and began to arrange them. Then she pushed all together and began again. Then she told me she would go no further until I told her who was my sweetheart, because she saw an officer with a sword."

"Go on," said Jack.

"Oh! It is wonderful! I told her he was a sailor; but as for his name, that mattered nothing. So she began again, and told me. The fortune began so well that it was marvellous; and then she stopped and mumbled something, and said that there was a coil which she did not understand, but she thought she saw—she said she thought she saw—the devil, Jack; and herself as well. And she could not read the fortune, because she could not understand any more of it. But it was the most surprising fortune in the world, whether good or bad. Then she asked me to look in her eyes, and she would read my own fortune there. Can you read my fortune there, Jack?"

"I see two lieutenants of his majesty's navy in those eyes, Bess. Is that fortune enough for you? One in each eye. Is not that enough for a girl?"

"They are but one, my dear," she said.

"And what was the fortune that she told you, Bess?"

"She said, 'Come what may come, thou shalt marry thy lover.' So I am satisfied. Come what may come. What care I what may come?—oh! what can come that will harm me?—so that I keep the man I love? What more can I desire? What more can I ask? I am so poor that I can lose nothing. Fortune cannot hurt me. And, come what may come, I shall keep the man I love. You will come back to me, Jack, and I shall have—oh! I shall have—my heart's desire."

It was on Saturday morning that the ship dropped down the river with wind and tide, her company and armament complete, new rigged, new painted, fresh and sweet as a lady just from her dressing-room, while the cannon roared the parting salute. I remember that it was a misty morning in December, a light southwest breeze, and the sun like a great red copper pan or round shield in the sky. And as the ship slowly slipped down Greenwich Reach the shrouds and the sails shone like gold, and were magnified by the mist.

The admiral stood on the quay with Castilla, and with them Mr. Brinjes.

"Go thy way," said the old sailor. "Go thy way and do thy duty. Castilla, my dear, there is only one good thing for a man—'tis to sail away from the land of thieves and land-sharks, out into blue water to fight the French."

"And what is good for a woman, sir ?"

"Why, my child, to marry the man who goes to sea. Farewell, Jack. Maybe we shall never see thee more. Let us go home, Castilla."

I went on board an hour before they sailed. Jack could do no more than whisper a word as he held me by the hand. Oh, heavens! my heart leaps up within me, even now, as I remember those eyes of his so full of love and tenderness. "Take care of her, Luke "—this was what he said—" take care of her until I come home to marry her. My pretty Bess! 'Tis a loving heart, Luke. She is thy charge, lad. Good-bye, dear lad, good-bye!"

I knew that she must be sitting in the old summer-house, waiting to see the ship go by, and there, indeed, I found her. Jack parted with her early in the morning. I knew not what passed between them; but it was surely very moving, because no pair loved each other more deeply than these two.

"He is gone," she said. "It is all over. But he loves me. Oh! I am sure he loves me. Yet something will happen. Philadelphy saw the devil and herself. Between the two something is sure to happen. Oh! we shall never be so happy again together—never again."

"Why," I told her, "people always think that the future can never be like the past. There are plenty of happy days before you, Bess. Jack will come home again some time, maybe a first lieutenant—who knows ?—or a captain in command. Then we shall have peace, I suppose, once more, and Jack will remain ashore, and you will be his wife."

"Yes. What did Philadelphy say ? Come what may come, thou shalt marry thy lover. Oh, I am not afraid. I saw him on the quarter-deck as the ship sailed past. Oh! he is the bravest and the handsomest man in all the king's service ; and who am I that he should love me ? Luke, you know how ladies talk, and what they say. Teach me that way. Oh! Luke, teach me, so that he shall never be ashamed of his sweetheart.

My Jack! my sailor Jack! Steel nor lead shall not harm him;
but the ship may wreck or sink. Oh! my heart! my heart!
When shall I see thy dear face again?"

CHAPTER XXIV.

AFTER JACK'S DEPARTURE.

When Jack was gone I suppose that Deptford remained just
as full of noise and business as before. As much hammering
went on in the yard; there was as much piping and shouting
on the river; there was as much drinking and brawling in the
town. But to some of us the place seemed to have become
suddenly and strangely quiet. Our lieutenant had been ashore
three or four months in all, yet he filled the town with his
presence—a thing which only strong and masterful men can do.
Most of us, when we go, are not missed at all, and our places
are quickly filled up, whether we sail away to sea upon a cruise
or are carried to the grave.

Whoever is absent, the events of the days continue to follow
each other and to occupy the minds of those who wait at home.
'Twas a stirring time, and though others, and worse, have followed, and we are even now in a great war, the issue of which
no man can predict, it seems to me that those years were more
full of interest than any which have followed. Why, one remembers even the things that are most readily forgotten;
how, for instance, the *Speedwell* yacht moved against wind and
tide, and beat four miles an hour; how four tradesmen of the
City were in a pleasure-boat off Margate when they were picked
up by a French privateer and ransomed for three hundred and
twenty pounds; how the wounded soldiers were brought home
and carried through the town in wagons; how the recruits
quartered in the Savoy mutinied, and were quickly shot down;
how Mary Walker, of Rotherhithe, was barbarously murdered,
and her niece hanged for the crime (though there were many
who wept for the poor girl, and believed her protestations of
innocence, which she continued, with cries and tears, to the
very end); how seventy men of the *Namur* walked all the way
from Portsmouth to the admiralty to complain of their rations,

and fifteen were hanged for punishment; and how—a thing which pleased me much—there was a great sale of pictures, at which a Claude Lorraine fetched as much as a hundred guineas, a Correggio £40, a Rubens £79, and a Raphael over £700. But these are now old stories, though then they made talk for the world.

Bess, keeping mostly at home, applied herself diligently to acquire the arts of reading and writing, so that her lover might never be accused of marrying an illiterate woman. These arts, mastered even in childhood with great difficulty and painful labor, are far more difficult to acquire after one has arrived at maturity. By great patience, however, Bess so far succeeded that, after two years' application, she was able to make her way slowly through a page of large and clear print, leaving out the hard words. This achievement satisfied her, because she was not in the least degree curious concerning the contents of books, and did not desire information on any subject whatever. She also learned to write her own name, her father teaching her; 'twas, I remember, in a fine flowing hand, with flourishes after the penman's style; but she could write nothing else, nor could she ever read the written character. To one who considers the ignorance of such a girl as Bess, who neither reads nor writes, doth not hear the talk of exchanges and coffee-rooms, and has never been to school, her mind must seem a state of darkness indeed. The whole of the world's history, except that portion of it which is connected with our Redeemer, is entirely unknown to her. Geography, present politics, the exact sciences, the fine arts, poetry, and letters—all these things are words, and nothing more, to her. Such was this girl's ignorance, and such was her apathy as regards knowledge, that she desired to learn nothing except what would please her sweetheart. With this end in view she used to lay out the charts on the apothecary's table, and would make Mr. Brinjes tell her about all the ports at which Jack had touched, and the seas over which he had sailed. " I love Jack," was all the burden of her song. He was never out of her mind; the world might go to wrack, and she would care nothing if only her lover remained in safety and was brought back to her arms.

She begged me to tell her what other things, if any, a gentle-woman generally learns, so that she might teach herself these

things as well. Willingly would I have done this, but on inquiry I could not discover anything—I mean any serious study
—which was necessary or possible for her to undertake. I
knew but one gentlewoman with whom to compare Bess. This
was Castilla. Certainly Castilla had commenced the study of
the French language ; but I know not how far she advanced, and
I have not learned that she was ever able to read a book in that
tongue. Then, in the matter of arts and sciences, Castilla was
certainly as ignorant as Bess. And when I came to consider
the subject, I could not discover that she was any fonder than
Bess of reading, or more desirous to extend her knowledge by
means of books. There are, it is true, certain accomplishments
in which a young gentlewoman is instructed. Castilla had
learned to dance, and in the assembly there were none who performed a minuet with more grace, though some, perhaps, with
more stateliness, because she was short of stature. In a coun-
try-dance she had no equal. But Bess, for her part, who had
never been taught by any dancing-master, could dance a jig, a
hay, or a hornpipe, rolling like a sailor, snapping her fingers, and
singing the while, so as to do your eyes good only to see the
unstudied grace and spirit of her movements. Then Castilla
had been taught the harpsichord, and could play at least three,
if not four, tunes. But Bess had never even seen a harpsichord, and as she did not possess one she could not be taught
to play upon it. Then there is singing. Nothing is more
pleasant to the ear than the singing of a beautiful woman.
Castilla had a low voice, but it was sweet and musical; she
had been taught to sing by the same master who had taught
her the harpsichord, and she could sing several songs. To
please my father she used to sing "Drink to me only with
thine eyes ;" to please the admiral she sang "To all you ladies
now on land ;" to please me she sang "Sweet, if you love me,
let me go ;" and all so charmingly, never dropping a note, making no mistakes in word or tune, and with such grace of voice
and pretty gentle ways that it ravished those who heard her.
But as for Bess, she had a full rich voice, and she sang out
loud, so that she might have been heard half-way across the
river. She knew fifty songs, and was always learning new ones.
She would listen to the ballad-singer in the street, and to the
sailors bawling in the taverns, and would then go away and

practise the song by herself till she was perfect. She sang
them all to please Jack; but after he was gone she sang
no more—sitting mum, like a moulting canary-bird. It was
pretty to listen while she sang, sitting with one hand upon
Jack's shoulder, and the other clasped in his lovesick fingers:

> "The landlord he looks very big,
>   With his high cocked hat and his powdered wig;
> Methinks he looks both fair and fat,
> But he may thank you and me for that.
>   For oh! good ale, thou art my darling,
>   And my joy both night and morning."

Or, sometimes, " Why, soldiers, why should we be melancholy,
boys?" or, " Come all ye sailors bold, lend me an ear." Another was a plaintive ditty, the choice of which we may believe to
have been inspired in some prophetic mood:

> "Early one morning, just as the sun was rising,
>   I heard a maid sing in the valley below:
> 'Oh! don't deceive me. Oh! never leave me.
>   How could you use a poor maiden so?'"

As regards housewifery, Castilla could make conserves, cakes,
puddings, and fruit-pies, and she could distil strong waters for
the stillroom. Bess, for her part, could make bread, pies of all
kinds, including sea-pie, onion-pie, salmagundy, and lobscouse;
she could cook a savory dish of liver and bacon, of beefsteak
and onions, of ducks stuffed; she could make tansy puddings,
and many other pleasant things for dinner. She could also
brew beer, and had many secrets in flavoring it with hops, ivy-
berries, yew-berries, and other things. As for needle-work,
Castilla could, it is true, embroider flowered aprons, and do
Turkey work, and tent stitch, work handkerchiefs in catgut,
and such pretty things. But Bess could knit stockings for
her father or herself; she made her own frocks and trimmed
her own straw hats. As to playing cards, Castilla knew a great
many games, such as Quadrille, Whist, Ombre, Pope Joan, and
Speculation; but Bess, for her part, could play All-fours, Put,
Snip-snap-snorum, Laugh-and-lie-down, and Cribbage. Then,
but this signified little, Castilla collected shells, which were
brought to the house by sailors, and made grottoes; she could
also cut out figures, and even landscapes, in black paper; she
could make screens by sticking pictures on paper; and she

knew several pretty girls' games, such as Draw-gloves, and Questions, and Command. Bess knew none of these little accomplishments; and as for games, she loved best the boys' sports, such as Tag and Thrush-a-thrush, which she used to play with Jack and me when we were young. The chief difference, so far as I could understand, in the education of the two girls was that one could carry a fan, manage a hoop, and behave after the manner of gentlewomen, which the other could not do. And I could not recommend Bess either to put on a hoop, or to buy a fan, or to powder and paint, or to lay on patches, by all of which things she would have made herself ridiculous.

There are some things, however, which cannot be learned. Such are sweetness of disposition, that finer kind of modesty which belongs to gentle breeding, grace of carriage, respect to elders, and the equal distribution of favors and smiles, so as not to show too openly the secret preferences of the heart. In all these things Bess was naturally inferior to Castilla, and these, unfortunately, I could not teach her, nor could Mr. Brinjes.

I could therefore advise her nothing but to study at every opportunity, and especially in church, the carriage and demeanor of the quality and the fashion of their dress, which I recommended her to adopt at such a distance as her means and station would allow.

You may be sure that there were many at Deptford who waited anxiously for news of the *Tartar*—most of the crew belonging to the town, and none of them being pressed men, but all volunteers, who took the king's bounty. But for three or four months we heard nothing. Then news came to the dock-yard, and was taken to the club in the evening by the resident commissioner.

"Admiral," he said, "and gentlemen all, I bring you good news. 'Tis of the *Tartar*."

"Good news?" cried the admiral. "Then the boy is well. Bring more punch, ye black devil!"

"The *Tartar* has put into Spithead with a thumping prize. Twelve men killed, and the master and mate. Twenty wounded; but only the second lieutenant among the officers, and he slightly."

"This is brave hearing, gentlemen," said the admiral.

"The prize is a privateer from Rochelle, twenty guns and one hundred and seventy men. She made, it is reported, a gallant resistance. No doubt we shall have further particulars by private despatches."

In two days there came by the post two letters, both from Jack. One of these was for the admiral, which I do not transcribe, although I was privileged to read it; and another for me. I knew very well that the letter was not for me, but for another. Wherefore I made an excuse for not opening it before the company, and carried it off to Mr. Brinjes, where I found Bess sitting, as was her wont in the afternoon.

"I have heard," she said, "that there has been fighting on board the *Tartar*. The people in the town are talking about it."

"Jack is safe, and the *Tartar* has taken a prize, Bess; and here is a letter."

So I tore it open in her presence. It was exactly as I thought. That is to say, there were a few words directing me to give the enclosed packet to his dear girl, the mistress of his heart; and she very joyfully received it, snatching it out of my hands with a strange jealousy, as if she grudged that anybody should have in his hands, even for a minute, what belonged to her and was a gift from her lover. It was the same with everything, down to the smallest ribbon which Jack gave her—she could not bear that another should so much as touch it, even a man. As for a woman being allowed to look at her lover's gifts—well, it was a jealous creature, but she loved him.

First, like a mad thing, she fell to kissing the letter. "Oh!" she cried, holding it with both hands, but kindly permitting me to scent its fragrance, which was, to say the truth, like a mixture of bilge-water, lamp-oil, cheese, rum, and gunpowder— "oh, it actually smells of the ship!" In fact, the letter, no doubt from having been written on paper long kept below with the purser's stores, smelt of that part of the ship where the stores are kept. "It is just like violets," she added; but the smell of Jack's ship was better to her than that of any violets. And so she kissed it again.

"Shall we read it?" I said. "The letter, I suppose, was meant to be read as well as to be kissed."

She gave it to me reluctantly.   I do not think she wanted to know the contents.   Enough that Jack had written her a letter. What greater proof of love could be given to any girl?

"Do you think he *wanted* it to be read?" she asked. "Wouldn't he be contented if he knew that I had it safe and was keeping it next to my heart, against his coming home?"

"You are a fool, Bess," said Mr. Brinjes; "let Luke read it. Why, the letter will tell us all about the fighting.   Why else should he take the trouble to write a letter at all.   Do you think a man likes writing letters?   As for me, I never received a letter in my life, and I never wrote one."

She gave up the letter with a sigh.   If she had been able to read it herself, no one else would have seen it.

"Jack having taken so much trouble," Mr. Brinjes continued, "'twould be disrespectful not to read it.   What he writes to you, my girl, he writes for me as well."

"'Mistress of my heart,'" I began, reading the letter.   "Is that meant for you, Mr. Brinjes?"

"Except a word or two just to show that he hasn't forgotton you, Bess, of course.   Why, as for that, such words mean nothing except that the boy is in love.   I've known a man so bewitched with love as to call a half-naked black wench his goddess and his nymph.   Yet it seemed to please the girl.   Go on, Luke."

"'Mistress of my heart'"—while I read, Bess sat in the window-seat, her hands clasped, her eyes soft and melting, her breath caught short and quick, and continually interrupting with ejaculations—such as, "Oh, Jack!" and "Oh, my brave boy!"—wrung from her heart by the joy of loving and being loved.   But these I omit.

"Mistress of my heart and queen of my soul!   My dearest Bess,—Since I sailed from Deptford I have thought of you every day and every night. If I were by your side I should give you a thousand hugs and kisses.   There never was a more lovely maid than my Bess.   My dear, we have had our first tussle, and warm work it was; but the enemy is now snug and comfortable under hatches, where he will remain until we come to anchor in the Solent, and carry him up Porchester Creek to rest awhile.   I think he has got a headache, Bess, after the noise of the guns, and perhaps the small shot have given him a toothache, and the cannon-balls have very likely made his legs rheumatic.   We had a fine time the last bout ashore, hadn't we, Bess?   I sha'n't forget the room behind the shop, nor the summer-house where Luke caught us kissing, and you blushed crimson. Well, I dare say I shall get ashore again some time, though not, I hope, like our poor carpenter's mate, who has had both legs amputated, and will now forever go on stumps. If your Jack came home on stumps, would you send him about his business, Bess? We fell in with the enemy—"

"Here the letter begins," said Mr. Brinjes. "What went before was like the froth on a pot of stingo."

"We fell in with the enemy on the morning of the 18th, this being February the 20th. We should have missed her altogether, but, by the blessing of Providence, the fog cleared away and showed us the ship, half a mile or thereabouts off the weather bow. 'Twas in full Channel. She hoisted the French flag, and we returned the compliment—such was our politeness—with a cannot-shot, pitched a yard or two wide of her. The enemy scorned to show her heels (wherefore I honor her, and give her what is due); perhaps because she carried heavier weight of metal and a larger complement than the *Tartar*. As for the engagement which followed, it lasted for an hour or thereabouts; and then, on our coming to close quarters and preparing to board, Monsieur hauled down his colors, finding he had no stomach for pikes and cutlasses. Which was his stratagem; and mark the treachery of this bloody villain. For while we prepared leisurely and unsuspecting to take possession, he bore up suddenly and boarded us. Fortunately, he had to deal with a well-disciplined crew; but the fighting was hand to hand for a while before they gave up the job, and tried to back again to their own deck. There were fifty of them in the boarding party, and not one got back, nor never a prisoner made, such was the rage of our men. So we gave them no more chance for treachery, but boarded in our turn; and hand to hand it was again, till all that was left of them were driven under hatches, where they now remain. There were a hundred and seventy of them when the action began, and we've thrown eighty bodies overboard. Consequently, there are ninety prisoners. Our master, who is as tough a sea-dog as lives, calculates that at this rate—namely, and that is to say, every ship in the king's service taking one French ship a week, killing or disabling half the crew, and taking prisoner the other half—we shall in less than a twelvemonth leave his French majesty never a sailor or a ship to his back, and so he must surrender at discretion. But I doubt, for my own part, whether we shall have such good luck as this; and it may be a year and a half or even two years before we are able to make an account of all the French fleets. We have lost twelve, killed and wounded; the second lieutenant has parted with half an ear, sliced off by a French cutlass, and the master's mate is killed, his brains being blown out by a pistol fired in his face. But we have revenged him, my dear Bess. When the fight was over I drank your health in the wardroom in a tot of rum, being, thank God, without a scratch."

Here was a gap, as if the letter had been interrupted at this point and resumed later on.

11

"We are now, my dearest Bess, anchored at Spithead, and about to transfer our prisoners up the harbor to Porchester Castle, where they are to lay by until the war is ended or they are exchanged. 'Twill be a change for them and a rest, and no doubt they will be glad to be out of danger. 'Tis a convenient place for a prison, having two great towers, besides a smaller one, with a high wall all round and a ditch. And if the prisoners do escape, they will find the country-side rejoiced of the opportunity to murder them, being a savage people, and much incensed with all French privateers. So, my sweetheart, no more at present from thy faithful   JACK.

"Postcriptum.—Thy true love-knot is round my arm, and I wish my arm was round thy neck. I forgot to say that the prize is the *Mont Rozier*, of La Rochelle; she is, we hope, to be purchased for the king's navy—a handy, useful ship, well found. Her captain was killed in the second part of the action. Otherwise, I think he would have been hanged for treachery. I love thee, Bess—I love thee!"

There was a beautiful letter for any girl to receive—full of love and kisses, and of gallant fighting! When I had read it through, she sat awhile perfectly still, the tears running down her cheeks. Then she made me read it again, more slowly, and bade me mark with pencil the passages which most she fancied. She could not read the writing, but she could rest her eyes on those places and remember them. She was quick at catching up and remembering things, and when she had heard the letter read a third time, she knew it all by heart, and never forgot it.

This was the only letter which Jack ever wrote to his mistress. Other letters he wrote to the admiral, telling him of the wonderful exploits of the *Tartar*, and of his share in the actions, but never a word more to Bess. The days passed on, and the girl sat, for the most part in silence, waiting. So sat Penelope expectant of her lord. Still she spoke of him; still she carried his letter in her bosom, wrapped in silk, and would take it out and gaze upon it, the tears rolling down her cheek. If she hoped for another letter, if she felt herself neglected, if she doubted his fidelity, I know not, for she said nothing.

In that interval she grew more beautiful. Her face, thus set upon the contemplation of one thing, became pensive and her eyes grave. She smiled seldom, and the loud laugh which Jack loved, but which reminded others too much of her former associates, was no more heard. By constant endeavor, by imitation, by refraining from her old companions, and by keeping guard over her speech, she softened, not only her manner, but

also her appearance. Poor Bess! What would she say and
suffer if she should learn that her Jack had ceased to love
her? Yet what other interpretation could be put upon his
long silence? It was at Christmas, 1756, when the *Tartar*
sailed. It was in August, 1760, that Jack returned, and all
that time only this one letter, though there had been many
written to the admiral.

"He will find," said Bess, "when he comes home, that I can
read very well. And I know the charts of the seas where he
sailed. If only he still will think me beautiful."

"Why, Bess," I told her, "as to beauty, there is no doubt
about it. So if that is all there is to fear, have no pain on
that score." There was, however, a great deal more to fear;
but this one dared not so much as to hint in her presence.

"There is a storm brewing," said Mr. Brinjes; "I feel it in
the air. I know not what he may think when he comes home:
she is a handsome creature, and he may be for beginning all
over again. Yet my mind misgives me. Why is there no letter, nor never a word to you, unless he has forgotten her? As
for falling in love with another woman, that is hardly likely,
seeing the busy life the poor lad hath led. But he hath forgotten her, Luke. Most women look for nothing else than to
be forgotten when their husbands and lovers go to sea; they
forget and are forgotten. Well, why not? Better so; then
they suffer the less when one of the men is knocked o' the
head and another goes off with some one else when his ship is
next paid off. But Bess is different, and we have encouraged
her; there will never be any other man in the world for her,
except Jack. So, my lad, look out, I say, for squalls."

Of course we heard news of the *Tartar*. Did she not fill
half the *Gazette?* There never was so fortunate a ship, nor one
more gallantly commanded. One cannot enumerate or remember half the prizes that she made in her first year's cruise in the
Channel. A month after taking the *Mont Rozier* she encountered the *Maria Victoria*, twenty-four guns and two hundred
and twenty-six men; and after a sharp engagement compelled
her to strike. The ship was taken over into the king's navy,
under the name of the *Tartar's Prize*. Then, in April, Captain
Lockhart fought the privateer *Duc d'Aiguillon*, of twenty-six
guns and two hundred and fifty-four men. The French did

not surrender till they had lost upward of fifty killed and wounded. In May the privateer *Penelope*, of eighteen guns and one hundred and eighty-one men, was taken; and in October the *Comtesse de Gramont*, eighteen guns and one hundred and fifty-five men. She also was purchased into the navy. But the crown of the *Tartar's* exploits this year was the chase and capture of the *Melampe*, of Bayonne, one of the finest privateers ever sent out from port. She was mounted with thirty-six guns, and had a crew of three hundred and thirty men. The *Tartar* chased her for thirty hours, and fought her for three hours before she struck. She also was added to the king's navy as a thirty-six gun frigate; and a very useful vessel she proved.

Such achievements as these greatly disheartened the French, and raised our own spirits. They did not, it is true, quite reach the ambitious aims of the master of the *Tartar;* yet they called forth the gratitude of the nation. Therefore, at the end of the year, the merchants of London and Bristol combined to present Captain Lockhart with pieces of plate; the first lieutenant of the *Tartar* was transferred to the command of the *Tartar's* prize the *Melampe*, which was renamed the *Sapphire;* Jack was transferred to this ship, with the first lieutenant; and the master of the *Tartar* was promoted to be lieutenant. As for the prize-money due to the officers and men, that amounted to a very pretty sum; but I do not know how much fell to Jack as his share.

CHAPTER XXV.

LIEUTENANT AARON FLETCHER.

WE, who are always slower than the French—"but," said Jack, "we hold on the tighter"—now began to send out privateers on our own account, though for the most part neither so numerous nor so well found as the French. The men were not wanting, nor the spirit, but the prizes were not so many, and the prospect of gain not so attractive to our English seacoast men as to the French. Mention has been made of a ship building in Mr. Taylor's yard at Rotherhithe; Jack was right

when he pronounced her fit for something better than a lubberly sugar-ship. She was, in fact, the venture of a company
of London merchants, and she was intended from the first for
letters-of-marque. A dangerous venture; but there was revenge in it, as well as the hope of profit; and, besides, two or
three successful cruises will sometimes cover the whole cost of
ship and crew, even if on the next voyage the ship is wrecked
or taken. As for a crew, there is not much difficulty in getting volunteers for a privateer, where there is no flogging, and
for the most part no discipline, and an officer has very little
more authority than he can command with fist and rope's-end.
The prospect of taking some rich merchantman from Marti-
nique, laden with a great cargo of spices and sugar, is attractive, to say nothing of the fighting, the chance of which, happily, ever inflames a Briton's heart. No such desperate actions
are recorded during this war as those in which our privateers
were engaged. The best privateersmen are said to be not the
regular seamen, to whom an action comes as part of the day's
work, but those amphibious creatures found all round our
coast, and especially about the Channel, who pretend to be engaged in the most innocent and harmless pursuits, and may be
found following the plough or driving the quill, or with an
apron in a barber's shop flouring a wig, or even behind a gro-
cer's counter weighing out pounds of sugar. Yet this is but a
show and pretence, and their real trade takes them to and fro
across the Channel, to the great detriment of his majesty's revenue. Privateering to such as these is a kind of smuggling,
but a finer kind, which one follows without the necessity of
sometimes fighting the king's officers, and sometimes murdering an informer. Moreover, a fat merchantman is a far richer
prize to bring home than a boat-load of kegs. Therefore, when
the *Porcupine* (so they called her) was launched and fitted and
armed with eighteen nine-pounders and two six-pounders for
her quarter-deck, there was no difficulty in finding a crew
of picked men as good as any on board a king's ship, though
lacking in discipline—a hundred and twenty in all. The crew
of the *Porcupine*, indeed, showed the stuff of which they were
made before the ship sailed. It was in September of the year
1757, when the hottest press ever known in the Thames was
undertaken, and not only were the lanes and alleys of Deptford,

Wapping, and Ratcliff scoured for skulking watermen and sea-men—the river being wholly deserted for fear of the press-gang—but also the colliers and ships in the Pool were boarded and their men taken, leaving no more than two able seamen for every hundred tons, according to William the Third's Act. The gang boarded the *Porcupine*, but the men seized their arms and threatened to fight for their liberty, whereat the lieutenant in command withdrew his men and sheered off, judging it pru-dent not to engage his company of a dozen or twenty with six-score resolute fellows.

Meantime Mr. Brinjes's prediction of misfortune as regards Aaron Fletcher came true—one knows not whether he did any-thing by his own black arts to bring about the calamities which fell upon him at this time. For, first of all, his boat, as fast a sailer as might be found for crossing the Channel, was picked up by a French privateer, who cared nothing for her being en-gaged in smuggling or in conveying information or spies back-ward and forward from France to England or from England to France. All is fish that comes to the Frenchman's net. There-fore the *Willing Mind* was taken in tow, and presently sold at auction in Boulogne Harbor; and so Aaron lost not only his boat, but also his crew of three men, who were like rats for wariness, and could speak both French and English.

Thus went the greater part of his business; and he hung his head, going in great heaviness, and in his cups cursing the apothecary, whose blood he threatened to spill, for causing his boat to be taken. But worse followed. His boat-building yard had become slack of work, and most of his hands were discharged. This was caused by his own neglect, and might have been repaired by steady attention to business. Unhap-pily, one night the yard took fire, and everything was burned except the little cottage within the gates, where Aaron lived alone. And then, indeed, he raged like a lion, swearing that he would kill, maim, and torture that devil of an apothecary who thus pursued him. But Mr. Brinjes was no whit ter-rified.

Despite these things, we were all surprised to hear that Aaron was going on board the *Porcupine* privateer; and still more as-tonished when we learned that he was appointed third lieuten-ant, his proper place being before the mast, or, at best, bo's'n's mate, or gunner's mate, for he was quite an illiterate fellow, who had learned nothing of taking an observation, except how to make it noon, and knew nothing, save by rule of thumb, of navigation. However, he knew the coast of France as well as any Frenchman, which was, I suppose, the reason why he was appointed an officer; and, besides, he had acquired (and truly deserved) in Deptford, Greenwich, and Rotherhithe the reputation of being a brave, reckless dog, who would fight like a bulldog. For such work as was wanted of him, no doubt he was as good as any man who had passed his examination in Seething Lane.

Then Aaron got himself a coat of blue, like that worn by the king's officers (but without the white facings), edged with gold —very fine. This he put on, with white stockings, white breeches, and a crimson sash, with a hanger—for all the world as if he were lieutenant of the royal navy—and a hat trimmed with gold-lace. Thus attired he strutted up the street, the boys shouting after him, till he came to Mr. Westmoreland's shop, where Bess sat at the door, her work in her hand. "Well, Bess," he said, "nothing was good enough for thee but an officer and a gentleman. I am an officer now, and if any man dares to say I am not a gentleman, I will fight him with any weapon he pleases. Since one officer has gone away, Bess, take on with another. Don't think I bear a grudge. Nay, I love thee still, lass, in spite of thy damned unfriendly ways."

"You an officer, Aaron?" Women like fine feathers for themselves, but they are never dazzled with fine feathers in others. "You an officer?" She surveyed him calmly from head to foot. "White stockings do not make a gentleman. Your clothes are grand, to be sure. Pity you have not a better shirt to match so fine a coat." Aaron's linen, in truth, had neither lace nor ruffles, and his cravat was but a speckled kerchief. "Go, change thy linen, Aaron, before pretending to be a gentleman. Well," she continued, perceiving that he was, as she desired him to be, abashed by the discovery of this deficiency, "as for thy dress, 'twill serve for a privateer. Go fight the French, Aaron, and bring home plenty of prize-money. But think not thyself a gentleman."

So she went in-doors and left him. I know not whether he bought himself a shirt to match the coat, but I am sure that on board the white stockings and the white breeches were safely stowed away, and a homelier garb assumed.

Aaron's sea-going lasted no great while. The captain of the *Porcupine* was a certain Stephen Murdon, who had commanded an armed merchantman in the China trade, in which he had seen fighting with the pirates, Chinese and Malay, which infest the narrow seas. He was a very brisk, courageous fellow, skilful in handling his ship; and she being a fast sailer he was generally able to choose or to decline an engagement, as suited him best. For instance, he would not engage a French privateer if he could avoid so doing, on the principle that it is foolish for dog to bite dog, and because it is the business of the king's ships to clear the Channel of privateers; but with a merchantman, however strong, he was like a bloodhound for the chase, and a bull-dog for fighting. I do not know how much prize-money he would have made for himself, but his owners were at first very much pleased with their venture, and promised themselves great returns. Unfortunately a circumstance happened which brought the *Porcupine's* cruise to an untimely end. There were many complaints from Holland against the English privateers, who mistook Dutch for French colors, and treated them accordingly. Captain Murdon was one of those who were suspicious of Dutch colors. Unfortunately he one day overhauled a Dutch vessel conveying to Amsterdam no less a personage than the Spanish ambassador; and, on the pretence that she was sailing under false colors, plundered the ship, taking out of her, as the complaint of the captain set forth, a purse containing seventeen guineas, twenty deal boxes containing valuable stuffs, and three bales of cambric, the whole valued at two hundred guineas. Nor was this all, for this audacious Captain Murdon helped himself as well to his excellency's chests and cases containing jewels and treasures.

There was a great outcry about this affair, and Captain Murdon (who was very well known to have done it, but it was pretended there was no evidence) hastened to hand over the *Porcupine* to her owners, paid off his crew, and recommended his officers to lie snug for a while. I know not who had the booty, but the officers and crew had none. As for himself, he was provided with a ship in the East India trade, so as to get more speedily out of the country. The government offered twenty

pounds reward for the discovery of the ship which had thus
insulted a friendly power; but no one took the offer seriously,
and war immediately afterwards breaking out with Spain, no
further trouble was taken in the matter.   But thus Aaron's
chances of prize-money were lost, and he himself returned to
Deptford little richer than when he went away.   Captain Murdon offered him, it is true, a berth on board his new ship; but
Aaron had no desire to go fighting Chinese pirates, and therefore stayed at home.   Then he began to pretend that he was
putting up his building-sheds again; but, as you shall see, he
had no luck: his fortune had deserted him.

CHAPTER XXVI.

HOW MR. BRINJES EXERCISED HIS POWERS.

It was on Saturday, the last day of June, in the year of
grace 1760 (our lieutenant having then been away at sea two
years and a half), and on the stroke of seven, that Mr. Brinjes
sallied forth from his shop.   He was dressed—being now on
his way to the club at the Sir John Falstaff—in his black velvet
coat with lace ruffles; he carried his laced hat under his arm,
and had upon his head his vast wig, whose threatening foretop,
majestic with depending knots, before and behind the shoulders, proclaimed his calling.   In his hand he bore his gold-
headed stick (not the famous skull-stick); his stockings, which
in the morning were of gray woollen, knitted by the hands of
Bess, were now of white silk; and his shoes were adorned with
silver buckles.   He was no longer apothecary to the scum of
Deptford: he was in appearance a grave and learned physician.
Yet if one looked more closely, it might be discerned that
the wig was ill dressed; the ruffles at his wrist torn; that one
or two of the silver buttons had fallen from his coat sleeves;
that his stockings were splashed a little, and there was a rent
in one; and that his shoes were only smeared, not brightened.
These, however, were defects which Mr. Brinjes did not heed.
It was enough for him to possess and to wear a coat and a wig
which became the company which met at the Sir John Falstaff.
    He stood awhile looking up and down the street, first cast-
    11*

ing his eye upward to note the weather—a thing which no one
who has been a sailor neglects, whether he goes upon deck or
leaves the house. The sky was clear, the wind southerly, and
the now declining sun shone upon the houses, so that, though
mean and low, they glowed in splendor, and the apothecary's
silver pestle showed as if it were of pure, solid silver, and the
penman's golden quill as if it were indeed of burnished gold,
and the barber's brass vessels across the way, catching the sun
by reflection, shone as if they too were of gold ; while the diamond panes of the upper lattice windows were all on fire, and
one's eyes could not brook to gaze upon them ; the red tiles of
the gables, though they were overgrown with moss, seemed as
if they had newly left the potter's hands ; and the timber-work
of the house fronts was like unto black marble or porphyry.
No painting was ever more splendid than those mean houses
under the summer evening's sunlight. At the barber's door
there arose a curious cloud, which produced an effect as of a
white mist rising from the ground. It was, however, nothing
but one of the 'prentices flouring the vicar's wig for Sunday.
Lower down the street there was leaning against a post the tall
form of Aaron Fletcher. He had nothing now in his appearance of the gallant privateer, being dressed as becomes a tradesman, in a fur cap, gray stockings, round shoes, and a drugget
waistcoat ; yet there was in him something that looked like a
sailor : however you disguise him, the sailor always betrays
himself. His hands were in his waistcoat pockets, and his
eyes were fixed upon the Golden Quill, because he hungered
still for a sight of the girl who lived beneath that sign. In
spite of his strength and his courage, one word from Bess
would have made this giant as weak as a reed. But as for her,
she would no more so much as speak friendly with him, being
angered at his importunity.

Bess sat in the open doorway, partly screened from the glare
of the evening, and partly sitting in the open sunshine, because
she was not one of those who fear to hurt their complexions.
She was working at something which lay in her lap, and sat
with her back turned to Aaron, as if she knew that he was
there, and would not so much as look at him. Through
the door one might see her father at his work, spectacles on
nose.

Mr. Brinjes looked at her, still standing before his own door. Then she raised her head, hearing his footstep, and laughed. She always laughed at sight of Mr. Brinjes in the evening, because, in his great wig and velvet coat, on his way to the club, he was so different from Mr. Brinjes in his scratch or his night-cap, sitting in his parlor or his shop.

"Saucy baggage!" said the apothecary. "Stand up, and let me see how tall thou art."

She obeyed, and stood up, overtopping Mr. Brinjes by more than the foretop of his wig; she was, in fact, five feet eight inches in height, as I know, because I measured her about this time. It is a great stature for a woman. She was now past her twenty-first year, and therefore full grown, and no longer so slim and slender in figure as when Jack sailed away at Christmas, in the year seventeen hundred and fifty-six. She was now a woman fully formed; her waist not slender, as fine ladies fondly love to have it, but like the ancient statues for amplitude, her shoulders large and square rather than sloping, her neck full and yet long, her skin of the whitest, her hair and eyes of the blackest; as for the eyes, they were large and full, and slow rather than quick of movement—a thing which betokens an amorous or passionate disposition; her face, as one sees in the faces of certain Italian painters, with an ample cheek, full and rosy lips, with a straight nose and low forehead. About her head she had tied a kerchief. For my own part, I have always maintained that Bess was the most beautiful woman I had ever looked upon in Deptford or anywhere else, though one may admit, what Castilla insists, that, however beautiful a girl may be, she belongs to her own class. Truly, all poor Bess's troubles came to her because she loved a gentleman.

Mr. Brinjes surveyed her critically. Then he sighed, and said, "Thou art, I swear, Bess, fit for the gods themselves. Well, child?" and then he sighed again.

"Is there news?" she asked.

"I hear of none," he replied, gravely. "Bess, the time goes on. Is it well to waste thy youth on a man who comes not back? There are other men—"

"Talk not to me," she cried, impatiently—"talk not to me of other men. There is no other man in the world for me but Jack. As for other men, I scorn 'em."

She drew from her bosom half a sixpence, tied to a piece of black ribbon. This she kissed and put back again.

"It is long since we had news of him," Mr. Brinjes went on, doubtfully, and dropping his voice, because Mr. Westmoreland sat within, poring over his books.

"He loves me," she replied, in a whisper. And the thought caused her cheek to glow, and her eyes became humid. "He told me he should always love me. Why, a man cannot be continually writing letters. He wrote to me once, which is enough—to tell me again that he loves me. And I think of him all day long."

"Well said, girl! That is only what is due to so gallant a lover."

"I belong to him—I am all his. Why else should I desire to live? Why do I go to church, if not to pray for him!"

"Good girl! Good girl! Would that all women had such constant hearts! I have known many women, whether at home, or at Kingston, or on the Guinea Coast. Some I have known jealous; some full of tricks and tempers; but never a one among them all to be constant. Good girl, Bess!"

"Sometimes I think—oh!—suppose he should never come back at all! or suppose I should learn that another woman had entrapped him with her horrid arts!"

Mr. Brinjes smiled, as one who knows the world. "Sailors do sometimes fall into traps," he said. "They are everywhere laid for sailors. Perhaps in another port—nay, in half a dozen ports, he may have found—nay, child, be not uneasy. Why" —here he swore as roundly as if he had been an admiral at least—"a thousand girls shall be forgotten when once he sees thy handsome face again. What though his thoughts may have gone a-roving—though I say not that they have—they will come home. The lieutenant will be true. Gad! There cannot be a single Jack of all the Jacks afloat who would not joyfully come back to such a sweetheart."

"Oh, yes!" She made as if she would draw something else from her bosom, but refrained. "I have his letter, his dear letter. Jack is true. He swore that no one should ever come between him and me."

"There is another thing, child. He left thee, Bess, a slip of a girl seventeen years old, with little but great black locks

" Mr. Brinjes surveyed her critically. Then he sighed and said, ' Thou art, I swear, Bess, fit for the gods themselves !' "

and roguish tricks. When he comes back he will find another Bess."

"Oh!" she cried, in alarm. "But he will expect the same."

"And such a Bess—such a beautiful Bess—fit for a prince's love."

"I want no prince but Jack," said Bess, her eyes soft and humid and her lips parted.

"He will be satisfied. Rosy lips and black eyes, shapely head and apple cheek, dimpled chin and smiling mouth, and such a throat! I have seen such, Bess, in the girls of the Guinea Coast when they are young; just such a throat as thine —as slender and as round, though shiny black. For my own part, I love the color."

"Happy boy! happy girl!" he cried, after sighing heavily. "I would I were young again, to fight this lover for his mistress. Tedious it is to look on at the game which one would still be playing."

"There is one thing which troubles me," she said. "It is the importunity of Aaron, who will never take nay for his answer. He comes every evening—nay, sometimes in the morning—telling me the lieutenant has forgotten me, and offering to take his place. And he will still be saying things of Jack (who cudgelled him so famously). If I were a man I would beat him till he roared for mercy." Her eyes now flashed fire, I warrant you, sleepy and calm as they had looked before. "But I can do nothing, and Luke is too small and weak to fight so great a man. He stands there now—look at him!"

"Patience, my girl—patience. I will tackle this lovesick shepherd."

More he would have said, but Mr. Westmoreland himself came to the door, his quill behind his ear, with round spectacles on his nose, blinking in the sunshine like an owl or a bat, as if the light was too much for him. He was dressed in a rusty-brown coat, worn so long that the sleeves had exactly assumed the shape of his arms; the cuff of the right arm was shiny, where it had rubbed against the table; and the back was shiny, where it had rubbed against his chair. On his head was a nightcap of worsted. Strange it was that so feeble a creature should be father of such a tall, strong, and lovely girl. Yet these contrasts are not unknown.

"A fine evening, Mr. Brinjes," he quavered, in his squeaky voice; "a fine evening, truly."

"Truly, Mr. Westmoreland."

"Is there news of the lieutenant?"

"I have none, sir."

"Pray Heaven he be not killed or cast away. Many brave youths are nowadays killed or cast away at sea. You remember Jack Easterbrook, Bess?" She looked at Mr. Brinjes and smiled. "I have never had a scholar (to call a scholar) like unto him. Dolts and blockheads are they all, compared with him. Never such a lad—never such a lad for quickness and for parts."

Mr. Brinjes nodded, and went on his way. Mr. Westmoreland spread his hands out in the sunshine as one who stands before a warm fire, and he pushed back his nightcap as if to warm his skull. But his daughter sat still, the knitting-needles idle in her lap, and her eyes fixed as one who hath a vision, and her lips parted as in a dream of happiness. Poor child! it was her last.

Mr. Brinjes walked slowly down the street until he came to Aaron Fletcher. Then he stopped, and surveyed the man from head to foot.

"Aaron," he said, "have a care—have a care. Thou hast been warned already. A certain girl, who shall be nameless, is food for thy betters, master boat-builder — food for thy betters."

Aaron muttered something.

"Why, it is but two years and a half agone, if thou wilt remember, good Aaron, that a certain thing happened. Wherefore I warned thee that trouble would follow. Has it followed? Where is the *Willing Mind?* Captured by the French. Where is the prize-money thou wast to get from the privateer? Her cruise was cut short. Where is thy building-yard? It is burned down. Where is thy business? It is gone. Thus would-be murderers are rightly punished. Wherefore, good Aaron, again I say, have a care."

Aaron made no reply, but shuffled his feet.

"And what do we here?" Mr. Brinjes asked, sternly. "Do we wait about the street in hopes of catching a look—a covetous and a wanton look — upon a face that belongs to another

man? Aaron Fletcher, Aaron Fletcher, I have warned thee
before."

"With submission, sir," said the young man, "the street is
free to all. As for my betters, a boat-builder is as good as a
penman, I take it."

"Go home, boy; go home. Leave Bess alone, or it will be
worse for thee."

"I take my answer from none but Bess."

"She hath given thee an answer."

Here the young man plucked up courage, and fell to railing
and cursing at Mr. Brinjes himself—a thing which no one else
in the whole town would have dared to do—not only for losing
him his boat and building-yard by wicked machinations and
magic, but also for standing, he said, between him and the girl
he loved, and keeping her mind filled with nonsense about a
king's officer, who had gone away and forgotten her, whereas, if
it had not been for this meddlesome old apothecary—the devil
fly away with him, and all like unto him!—the girl would have
been his own long ago, and he would have made her happy.

"Here is fine talk!" said Mr. Brinjes, at length, and after
hearing him without the least signs of anger. "Here is a
proper gamecock! Aaron, thou must have a lesson. So!
That hollow tooth of thine, my lad—the one at the back, the
last but one in the left-hand lower jaw!" The fellow started
and turned pale. "Go home now quickly." Here Mr. Brinjes
shook the gold head of his walking-stick threateningly, while
his one eye flamed up like a train of powder. "Go home; on
thy way the tooth will begin to shoot and prick as with fiery
needles. Go, therefore, to bed immediately. It will next feel
as if a red-hot iron were clapped to it and held there, and thy
cheek will swell like a hasty-pudding. The pain will last all
night. In the morning come to me, and perhaps, if I am merciful, and thou showest signs of grace and repentance, I will
pull out the tooth. Thou canst meditate all night long on the
incomparable graces of the girl who can never be thy sweetheart."

The young man received this command with awe-struck eyes
and pale cheek. Then he obeyed, going away with hanging
head and dangling hands—a gamecock with the spirit knocked
out of him.

Strange that a doctor should be able to cause as well as cure
disease! As Aaron Fletcher drew near to his workshop he
felt the first sharp pang and pricking of toothache. When he
reached his bed the misery was intolerable. All night long he
rolled upon his pallet, groaning. In the morning he repaired
to Mr. Brinjes, dumfounded, his face tied up, seeking for nothing but relief.

"Aha!" said Mr. Brinjes. "Here is our lad of spirit—here
is our lover! Love hath its thorns, Aaron, as well as its roses.
Sit down—sit down. The basin, James—and cold water. It
is a grinder, and will take a strong pull. Hold back his head,
James—and his mouth wide open. So—with a will, my lad.
It is done. Go no more to the neighborhood of Bess Westmoreland, my lad. 'Tis a brave tooth, and might have lasted a lifetime. The neighborhood of Bess Westmoreland is
draughty, full of toothaches and rheumatisms. I think I saw
another hollow grinder on the other side. Take great care,
Aaron. Avoid Church Lane, especially in the evening. Go
thy way now, and be thankful that things are no worse."

CHAPTER XXVII.

IN COMMAND.

WHEN Mr. Brinjes had disposed of this importunate swain,
he went on his way, and presently entered the Blue Parlor,
where some of the gentlemen were already assembled, waiting
for the arrival of their president or chairman, the admiral, who
was not long in coming, with his escort of negroes.

When he had taken his seat, his pipe filled, his gold-headed
stick within reach, he rapped upon the table once.

"Gentlemen," he said, "good-evening, one and all."

Then he rapped upon the table twice.

Immediately the landlord appeared at the door, bearing in his
hand a great steaming bowl of punch, which he placed before
the president. One of the negroes filled a brimming glass and
gave it to his master. Then he filled for the others, and passed
the glasses round; and the admiral, standing up, shouted,
"Gentlemen, his majesty's health, and confusion to his enemies!"

This done, he sat down, and prepared to spend a cheerful evening.

By this time it was eight o'clock, though not yet sunset, though the western sky was red and the sun low in the west. With much whistling of pipes and ringing of bells the day's work at the yard hard by was brought to a close. Whereupon a sudden stillness fell upon the air, broken only by the hoarse cries and calls from the ships in mid-river now working slowly up-stream, with flow of tide and a light breeze from the south or southeast.

"Gentlemen," said the admiral, with importance, "I have this day received despatches from Jack Easterbrook, my ward, which I have brought with me to gladden your hearts, as they have gladdened mine." He tugged a packet out of his pocket, and laid it on the table before him. "He writes," continued the admiral, "from his ship, the *Sapphire* frigate, Captain John Strachan, and, to begin with, the letter is dated November, but appears to have been written from time to time as occasion offered. At that time he was with Admiral Sir Edward Hawke, whose health, gentlemen, we will drink."

They did so. The admiral proceeded, with the deliberation which belongs to one-armed men, to open the letter, and after calling for a candle, to read it.

" ' *November* 22, 1759.'—The boy writes, gentlemen, as I said before, from aboard the frigate *Sapphire*, Captain Strachan, then forming part of Commodore Duff's squadron, and of Sir Edward Hawke's fleet, blockading the port of Brest. It is his account of the action, whereof intelligence reached the admiralty six months ago. Humph! At the beginning the boy presents his duty and respect, which is as it should be. He is well, and without a scratch. But the news is six months old, and of the stalest. Yet it is welcome. Now listen.

" ' I wrote to you last when we were driven by stress of weather to raise the blockade of Brest, and put in at Torbay.' —He did, gentlemen, and you heard his letter read—' I hope my letter came to hand.'—It did.—' By stress of weather to raise the blockade of Brest.'—This letter-reading is tedious work ?' " The admiral took another drink of punch, and proceeded, folding the letter so as to catch the light, and reading very slowly. " ' When the gale abated we put to sea again, but found that the Frenchman had slipped his cables and was off. 'Twas a fisherman of Beer, a little village on the Devonshire coast, who saw the French fleet under full sail, and brought the news. We found out afterwards there were twenty sail of the line and five frigates that sailed out of Brest, being bound, as was conjectured, for Quiberon Bay. But this we could not rightly tell. However, we crowded sail and after them, the wind blowing fresh, the water lumpy, and the weather thick, so that we made a poor reckoning, and the fleet was much scattered. However, on the sixth day, being the morning of the 20th, the signal was hoisted of the enemy's fleet, and the admiral gave his signal to close up for action. Well, there they were in full sight, but apparently with mighty little stomach for the fight; and instead of shortening sail and accommodating us like gentlemen, they scudded before us. However, towards eight bells, when the men had taken their dinners and their rum, and were in good fighting trim, and ready to meet the devil himself on his three-decker'—'tis a deuce of a boy, gentlemen—' the *Warspite* and the *Devastation* had the good-luck to come up first with the French rear, and the action began. Very soon we all drew up, and pounded away. As for the *Sapphire*, we, with the *Resolution*, 74, were speedily engaged with the *Formidable*, 80, Rear-Admiral Verger; and a very brisk engagement it was, the Frenchman being full of spirit. But he had the sense to strike after three hours of it, and after losing two hundred men killed and wounded. There was a very good account made of the other ships, though not without misfortunes on our part. The *Thésée*, 74, thinking to fight her lower-deck guns, shipped a heavy sea, and foundered, with all her crew. She would have made a splendid prize indeed, and a magnificent addition to his majesty's fleet. But it was not to be.'—The decrees of Providence, gentlemen," said the admiral, " are not to be questioned or examined. But it passes human understanding to see the sense of sinking the *Thésée* instead of letting her become a prize and an ornament to King George's navy, and useful for the cause of justice." Then he continued reading : " ' The French ship *Superbe*, 70, also capsized '—dear, dear, gentlemen ! another loss to us—' and went down, I think from the same cause. So here were two good ships thrown away, as one may say, by lubberly handling. We had bad luck

with two more noble ships: one of them, *Héros*, as beautiful a
74 as you ever clapped eyes on, struck; but the waves were,
unluckily, running too high for a boat to be lowered, and in
the night she ran aground. So did the *Soleil-Royal*, 80; and
next day we had to set fire to them, though it was enough to
bring tears to the most hard-hearted for thinking how they
would have looked sailing up the Solent, the union-jack at the
stern, above the great white royal. Our misfortunes did not
end here; for H. M. S. *Resolution* unfortunately went ashore
too, and now lays a total wreck, and all her crew drowned. The
Essex also went ashore and is lost, but her crew saved. As for
us, it was stand by, load, and fire for nearly three hours, but
only two officers killed and three wounded, with twenty men
killed and thirty wounded. I think the Mounseers, who were
safe within the bar of the river, will stay there so long as we
are in sight. For though they pounded us, we've mauled
them, as I hope you will allow. 'Tis thought that we may be
despatched in search of Thurot's squadron. So no more at
present, from your obedient and humble JOHN EASTERBROOK.'
Well, gentlemen, this is my letter, and what do you think of
it ?"

"Always without a scratch," said Mr. Brinjes. "Well, the
lad is as lucky as he is brave. Every bullet has its billet. Pray
that the bullet is not yet cast which will find its billet in Jack!
Admiral, let us drink the health of this gallant lad."

And then they fell to talking of Jack's future, and how they
should all live to see him an admiral and a knight, and in command of a fleet, and achieving some splendid victory over the
French. But Mr. Brinjes checked them, because, he said, that
to anticipate great fortune is, as the negroes of the Gold Coast
know full well, to draw down great disaster. But still they
talked of the brave boy who had grown up among them, and
was now doing his duty like a man.

Now, in the midst of this discourse, the landlord ran into the
room, crying, "Admiral and gentlemen, here comes a French
prize up the river ?" And all, leaving their pipes and punch,
hurried forth into the garden.

There is no more gallant sight than the arrival of a prize, especially when, as then happened, she comes up the river at the
sunset of a glorious summer day, when the yellow light falls

upon her sails and colors every rope of her rigging, and when, as then happened, she bears about her all the marks of a long and terrible battle—her bulwarks broken away, her mainmast gone, great rents and holes in her side, her sails shattered, and even the beautiful carved group which once served for a figure-head, such as the French love, broken and mutilated.

"A French prize, truly, gentlemen," said the admiral. "There is a French cut about her lines—and look! there is the white flag with the union-jack above."

She came up Greenwich Reach, her sails bent, slowly, as if she was ashamed of being seen a prisoner in an English port. At her stern floated the flag of the French navy, the great white flag with the royal arms in gold. But above this flag there floated the union-jack. And every gentleman in the company tossed his hat and shouted at the sight.

"Landlord," said the admiral, "fetch me your glass, and quick. The evening falls apace."

The landlord brought a sea telescope.

"She's a 58-gun ship, gentlemen. There has been warm work. Mainmast gone; to'gallant mizzen carried away; bows smashed; rigging cut to pieces. Seems hardly worth the trouble of bringing up the Channel. But"—here he wiped the glass with his coat sleeve, and applied it more curiously— "who is that upon the quarter-deck? Gentlemen—gentlemen all—it is—it is—it is none other than Jack Easterbrook himself in command! Damn that boy for luck! Cudjo, ye lubber, bring me my stick: Gentlemen, we will all hasten to the yard, and board the ship as soon as she drops her bower. Landlord, more punch! Jack's home again, and in command of a prize! And, landlord, if I find my negroes sober when I come back, gad! I'll break every bone in your body!"

In this triumphant way did Jack come home, in charge of a splendid frigate, the *Calypso*, taken after as obstinate an action as one may desire or expect, by the *Sapphire*, in the chops of the Channel, and sent to Deptford under command of Lieutenant John Easterbrook, to be repaired and added to his majesty's navy.

CHAPTER XXVIII.

HOW BESS LISTENED FOR HIS STEP.

IT was not until nearly midnight that Mr. Brinjes came home
—a late hour even in London, where they turn night into day ;
but at Deptford there is not so much as a single drinking-house
open at that hour, and every one, rogues and honest men, the
virtuous and the abandoned, are all alike in bed and asleep.
The moon was full, and the street was as light as day. Over
the penman's shop the lattice window was partly open.

"It is Bess's room," said Mr. Brinjes. "She is asleep, and
dreaming of her lieutenant. And he hath forgotten her. 'Tis
pity she had not listened to Aaron's voice. He hath surely
forgotten her, seeing that he hath well-nigh forgotten me, and
asked no questions at all concerning her. Sleep on, Bess ; sleep
on, my girl. To-morrow thou wilt not sleep at all ; and the
next day, or the next, will come the whirlwind ! Perhaps the
sight of thy charms—but I know not—I know not. Our honest lad is changed."

He opened the door of his shop, and went into his own
den.

At nine of the clock or thereabouts, when the early chins had
been shaved, and the wigs dressed and sent round to the gentlemen, Mr. Peter Skipworth, the barber, found time to run
across the street to his gossip and neighbor, the penman.

"Great news, Mr. Westmoreland !" he cried. "Great news
for Deptford !"

"Why ?" asked the penman. "Is another czar coming
here ?"

"No, no. But the lieutenant has come home."

"Lieutenant Easterbrook ?"

"What other ? He came up the river last night, in command
—think of that ! the lieutenant in command !—of a prize sent
here to be repaired and added to his majesty's navy. The admiral ordered his negroes to get drunk, so great was the wor-

thy gentleman's joy; and now they lie like hogs at the Sir
John Falstaff, and cannot yet be awakened, though 'tis nigh
twelve hours since they rolled over."

" Lieutenant Easterbrook, who once was Jack, whom I taught
the elements of navigation — he hath returned ?" Mr. Westmoreland was slow of catching news, being always wrapped in
the study of mathematics.

Bess stopped her work at the first mention of his name, and
listened, her heart beating, and her cheek now flushed, now
pale. Oh! he was come home again !

" We have not yet seen him," the barber continued, " though
I expect he will come to have his hair dressed and his chin
shaven. None other hand but mine shall touch them, I promise
you. The landlord of the Sir John Falstaff says that a more
gallant gentleman he hath never set eyes upon."

" Ha !" said Mr. Westmoreland. " That the lieutenant is safe
and sound, I rejoice. But the brave boy who was so good at
his figures, he, neighbor, will no more return to us. He is gone,
and will never come back again. Where is he now—that boy ?
Where are now all the boys who have since grown into men ?
What has become of them ? I doubt he will forget his humble
friends and well-wishers." The barber ran back to his own
shop. " Dost remember the lieutenant, Bess ?"

But Bess made no reply. He was come back—her splendid
lover! How could she answer her father's prattle, or think
about anything but Jack and love ? Already she felt his arms
about her neck, and his kisses on her cheek; and she was suffused with blushes and the glow of happiness.

She would not, she thought, betray her eagerness and her
joy. Therefore she went about her household work as usual,
yet with a beating of her heart and expectancy, as if he might
send the apothecary's assistant for her at any moment. When
all was done, and the whole house as neat and clean as any
lady's tea-table, Bess went up-stairs to her bedroom, and began
to prepare for her sweetheart, her heart filled with gladness and
pride that he was come home again in a manner so glorious;
and with terror, also, lest she might have lost some of her
charms. She looked in her glass. Nay, she was more beautiful, she saw plainly, than when he left her nigh upon three
years ago : her eyes were brighter, her figure fuller, her lips

ruddier, her skin whiter, her cheeks rosier. If Jack loved her for her beauty, he must needs, she knew, and smiled at the pleasing thought, love her now much more. Then she drew his letter from her bosom, where it lay wrapped in its silken bag, and read it all over again, knowing the words by heart. "There is not," it said, "in all the world a more beautiful girl than my Bess, nor a fonder lover than her Jack."

She put on her finest and best—with the coral beads which Jack had given her to hang round her neck, and the ribbons— also his gift—would he remember them as well? She dressed her hair in the way he used to love, and then, when all was ready, she stole down the stairs, and so out by the back way to the apothecary's parlor, that bower of love, though it was not also a bower of roses and fragrant flowers.

The room was empty. In the shop sat Mr. Brinjes, in his place, the great book before him; the assistant, James Hadlow, stood at the counter rolling and mixing, and the shop was filled with women who had brought sick children.

"Mr. Brinjes," cried Bess.

"Ay, ay, my girl," he replied.

"He has come home!" she cried, heedless now of the women and their gossip.

"Very like—very like—so they tell me."

"So they tell me!" she echoed, laughing. "As if it mattered nothing. Yet he will but shake hands with the admiral and come here. 'So they tell me,' he says."

"I come, Bess," he replied, looking at her sadly; "I come in a few minutes. Now, you women who have had your answer and your physic, take your brats away. This morning I am benevolently disposed, and will cure them all. Go away, therefore, and prate no more. I come in a few minutes, Bess."

So she waited, glowing with the anticipation of her lover's welcome, her eyes soft and humid, her bosom heaving; and what with the tumult of her soul and her finery—for, as I have said, she had put on her coral and her ribbons—and all his gifts, looking truly a most beautiful creature. At half-past twelve Mr. Brinjes closed his great book, descended from his stool, and came into the parlor.

"I have seen him, Bess," he said. "I saw him last night."

"Oh! you have seen him, and you did not wake me up to

tell me. You have spoken to him. What did he say? How
doth he look? What did he ask about me? What messages
did he send? And is he wounded? Is he safe and well?
Oh! but he will be here directly. Even now his step may be
in the street. Listen!—no—not yet—he will come to tell me!
Why, you tell me nothing. Once you said that my Jack might
forget me. I will not tell him that, Mr. Brinjes, because he is
masterful, and I would not anger him against you. Why, you
tell me nothing. I have put on all the things he gave me.
Am I looking well? Do you think he will find me changed?"

"For your questions, Bess, he looks strong and well, though
somewhat changed in manner, and colder than of old; and to
some of us he might have shown more civility. For me, I complain not, though he gave me but a cold hand; but Mr. Shelvocke may justly complain, and Mr. Underhill—though one,
truly, was but a supercargo, and the other but the purser."

"Jack can never forget his old friends," said Bess, "any
more than he can forget his old love. But he is now in command of a prize."

"Bess, my girl," said Mr. Brinjes, very earnestly, "don't build
hopes on the promise of a sailor. My dear, I know the breed,
all my life, being now past fourscore and ten. I have lived
among sailors. I tell thee, child, I know them. With them,
it is out of sight out of mind. When a man goes fighting,
hath he room in his mind for a woman? And the more a
woman loves a sailor, the less he loves her. If he hath forgotten thee, my dear, let him go without a tear or a sigh, for
there are plenty other men in Deptford who would gladly possess thy charms."

"Stop!" she cried, flying out, suddenly. "Why, you are
talking like a mad thing! You don't know my Jack. How
should you know him? How should you know any men except the pirates, your old friends, and the rough tarpaulins who
come here to be healed? Who are you, a little common apothecary, to talk of men like the lieutenant? How are you to know
the ways of the king's officers? Why, if you have been to sea
in a king's ship, 'twas only to mess with the midshipmen and
the purser's mate."

"Well, Bess, well," he replied, not angry, but bearing the
attack with meekness. "That shall be as you please. If your

man is constant, he will seek thee here, in the old place. If he is not, we will, I say, be reasonable, and expect no better than others receive."

"Oh! If you were a young man—a man like Aaron," cried Bess, "Jack should beat you to a jelly for this."

"Ay, ay—very like, very like. You shall beat me if you like, my girl. Bess," said Mr. Brinjes, looking her earnestly in the face, "if it would give you any pleasure, and bring your lover back, you should beat me yourself till you could lay on no longer."

"My lover will come back to me," she replied. "He will be here this morning or this afternoon. Of course he will come as soon as he can."

"Perhaps. But he is changed. He sat among the gentlemen of the club last night, but it was to please the admiral, not himself. He wanted none of our company. I sat beside him, but he asked me no question at all. What!—should I not know the lover's eyes? Bess, he hath forgotten thee."

"You are a liar!" she replied, springing to her feet as if she would take him at his word and lay on till she could lay on no longer. "You say this because you are old and ill-tempered, and envious of younger people's happiness. Who are you that Jack should remember you? Who but a common sailors' apothecary—and he a lieutenant in command?"

"Ay, ay, my girl; pay it out. I am a sailors' apothecary. I am old and envious. Pay it out. I value not thy words— no, not even a rope's yarn—because, Bess, I love thee, my dear, and I would not see thee unhappy about any man. What is a man worth beside a lovely woman? If I were a woman, would I throw my love away upon a single man? Two years and more hast thou wasted upon this fine lover, who, when he comes back, hath never a word to ask—not even, 'How fares my Bess?'"

"Why," said Bess, "how could he ask concerning me before those gentlemen? Say no more, Mr. Brinjes, for I would not be angered and show a red cheek when he comes. You know that I am easily put out. Besides, you are only laughing at me, and I am a fool to fly out. Jack will come to me as soon as he can leave his ship. Very likely he will not get away until the evening."

12

So she sat down on the window-seat, and recovered her spirits, feeling no doubt at all, nor any misgivings, and began talking merrily of what she would say when he came, and what he would say to her, and how they would brew him a glass of punch such as he loved, before they suffered him to say a word of his own adventures, and how she would fill for him a pipe of tobacco, thinking—poor wretch!—that her lover was unchanged not only in his affections, but also in his manners.

Then Mr. Brinjes made his dinner; that is to say, he fried his beefsteak and onions, and presently ate them up, with a tankard of black beer. After dinner he took a glass of punch, filled and smoked a pipe of tobacco, and then, rolling himself in his pillows, fell fast asleep, as was his wont.

Bess meantime, her wrath subdued, sat in the window-seat, waiting. But the step she looked for came not.

So passed the afternoon.

Towards three o'clock Mr. Westmoreland, who had been so much occupied with his work that he forgot his dinner, began to feel certain pangs in the internal regions, which he at first attributed to colic, and blamed himself for greediness at meals; but as the pain increased and became intolerable, he pushed away his papers and sat up, suddenly remembering that he had not had any dinner at all, and that these were pangs of hunger. Three o'clock, and no dinner! Where in the world was Bess?

He was accustomed, however, to small consideration from women, and proceeded to rummage in the cupboard, where he found some cold provisions, off which he made a very good dinner. Then, as the day was fine and the sun shining, he stood in the doorway enjoying the warmth.

As he stood there he saw, marching up the street, no other than the lieutenant himself, whom he recognized, though he was greatly changed, having now not only filled out in figure and become a man, who when last seen was a stripling, but having acquired the dignity of the quarter-deck and the assurance which comes of exercising authority.

However changed, Jack did not forget his old friend.

"What!" he said, "Mr. Westmoreland! Thou art well, I hope, my friend?"

"I am better than I deserve to be, sir, and glad to see your honor safe home again."

" Why, Mr. Westmoreland, the bullet that has my heart for
its billet hath not yet found me, though it may be already cast
for aught I know. Thou art still busied with logarithms ?"

" By the blessing of Heaven, sir," said Mr. Westmoreland,
" I have had much to do, both in the advancement of fine penmanship and the calculation of the logarithmic tables."

Jack nodded and passed on ; but he remembered something
and laughed. Then he hesitated, and looked back into the
penman's room.

" You had a daughter, Mr. Westmoreland—Bess, her name
was, and a comely girl. I hope she is well. But I see her not
in the shop. No doubt she is married long ago, and the mother
of thumping twins."

He laughed and nodded and went on his way.

" My daughter, your honor—" Mr. Westmoreland began ; but
the lieutenant was already out of hearing.

" Now," said the penman, " saw one ever a better heart ? He
not only remembers me, which is natural, seeing that I was his
instructor, but he remembers my girl as well. Where is Bess ?
She will laugh when I tell her. Mother of twins ! Ho ! ho !
' Thumping twins !' he said. Bess will laugh."

About four in the afternoon Mr. Brinjes woke up, and slowly recovered consciousness, until he felt strong enough to take
his afternoon punch ; after which he sat up and became brisk
again, looking about the room, and remembering all that had
been said.

" Bess," he cried, " hath your lover come ?"

She shook her head.

" Courage, my girl, courage. Perhaps when he sees thy
comely face again he will remember. What ! To be loved
by such a girl would fire an Esquimau or a Laplander. Take
courage, therefore. There is no more beautiful woman in Deptford, Bess. Take courage."

" I am waiting for my sweetheart," she replied, coldly.
" Why should I take courage ? He hath been delayed by his
affairs. He will come presently."

" Bess," Mr. Brinjes whispered, " there is a way to bring him
back."

" To bring him back ? This old man will drive me
mad !"

"There is a way, Bess. The old negro woman gave thee a charm to keep him safe from shot and steel. She will give thee one, if I compel her, to bring him to thy knees. Nay, she will not at thy bidding. And for why? Because she wants Miss Castilla to marry the lieutenant. Yet if I compel her, she will make thee such a charm. Then he must needs come straight to thee, his heart mad with love, though a hundred fine ladies tried to drag him back."

"I know not what you mean."

Mr. Brinjes took up his famous magic stick, the stick with the skull upon it. "It is by virtue of this stick, which gives its possessor, she believes, greater Obeah wisdom than she hath herself attained unto. Wherefore if I order her to do a thing, she cannot choose but obey, else I might put Obi upon her. She hath given me the secrets of all her drugs, by means of which, if I live long enough, I may find out the greatest secret of all, and be like unto the immortal angels. She shall obey me in this as well, Bess. Say but the word, and she shall bring him back, though Castilla die for love of the handsome lieutenant."

"No, no," said Bess. "He has not forgotten me."

"Child, I *know* that he has. Why, when he went away, if he thought of you, his eyes softened. He could not look upon me without remembering his days spent in this room. Yet his eyes softened not. Believe me, he will come here no more. It is strange. I know not what will happen. Sure I am that I shall sail once more upon the southern seas, with Jack upon the quarter-deck. A dozen times or more have I inquired of Philadelphy, and still she sees a ship with Jack—and me—and you, Bess—you. Why, I am ninety years of age and more, girl. Shall I get that charm for thee! If I could get it no other way, I would even bribe her with this stick, when all my Obi leaves me, and I shall cause and cure diseases no better than the quacks of Horn Fair and of Bartholomew."

But Bess shook her head.

"I will have no charm," she said. "If Jack will forget me, let him forget me. But he has got my name tattooed upon his arm, and he has got my lock tied round his wrist. If these will not charm him back, nothing else shall."

So she fell into silence. But at seven in the evening, when

Mr. Brinjes put on his wig and coat for the club, she arose and went home.

"Why," said her father, "where hast been all day, girl? There was no dinner. Well, it matters not," because her face warned him not to rebuke her, "it matters not, and, indeed, I found enough cold bits in the cupboard. But, Bess, thou hast missed a sight."

"What sight?"

"The sight of a gallant gentleman. I have seen the lieutenant. He passed by this way to the admiral's. 'Tis a brave officer now; no taller, perhaps, than when he left us last; but then he was a stripling, and now he is well filled out, and set up as brave and comely as one would wish to set eyes upon."

"And he came to the shop to see me, then?"

"You, Bess? Why should he wish to see you? No, no. A gentleman like that cannot be expected to remember a mere girl. But he had not forgotten me, for when I saw him, and took off my cap to him, he stopped and kindly asked me how I fared. His honor is not one who forgets his humble friends."

"Did he ask after me?"

"He did, I warrant. He said, 'You had a daughter, Mr. Westmoreland.' So he looked into the room as if he would give you too a greeting; but no one was there. So he said, 'But she is married long ago, I dare swear, and hath thumping twins by this time.' 'Thumping twins,' he said, Bess. His honor was always a merry lad. He remembered me directly; and he hath not even forgotten thee, Bess. Do not think it."

He had not, indeed. But his remembrance was worse than his forgetfulness. Better to have been forgotten than to be thus remembered.

Then her father left her to take his pipe and have his evening talk with his cronies; and Bess was left alone in the house. Just so, nearly three years before, she had been left sitting by the fire, when her lover came to her and embraced her, with words which he had now forgotten but she remembered still! Oh, if he should now, as then, lift the latch, and find her there alone, and she could fall upon his breast and tell him all the things in her heart!

She listened for his footstep. Other steps passed by the house, but not the step she looked for; and then her father came home, cheerful and full of talk about the gallant deeds of the lieutenant, and she must needs give him his supper, and listen and make reply.

The apothecary was right when he said, "Sleep on, Bess, sleep on. Thou wilt sleep but little to-morrow night."

CHAPTER XXIX.

"HE HATH SUFFERED A SEA-CHANGE."

Our lieutenant was engaged all the morning with the port admiral and with the navy office, but in the after-part of the day the admiral made a great feast for him, as he had done on his last return, to which I was bidden with the rest. But the change which I perceived in him greatly surprised me, and indeed all of us. For the young sea-cub, rude in speech and careless of behavior, was quite gone. Behold in his place a gentleman of polite manners, and as careful of his speech as if he had been all his life in St. James's Street. This was indeed astonishing.

There are, it is certain, too many captains in the king's ships who have never known better company than they find in a Portsmouth tavern, so that the ridicule which has been lavished upon naval captains is not undeserved; there are also ships which are no better, as a school of manners for the young officers, than Portsea Hard, so that the lieutenants and midshipmen in such vessels hear nothing but rough language with profane swearing, and even at the captain's table, which is copied in the wardroom and the gunroom, find the manners of a Newcastle collier. There are also captains who should never have left the polite part of town, because they pine continually for the pleasures of the theatre and Ranelagh, the clubs of St. James's Street, Covent Garden suppers, and gambling-houses; who reek of bergamot, and appear daily on the quarter-deck dressed as if for the park, and in their hair not a curl out of place, or a single touch of pomatum and powder abated. These men are not those who crowd all sail in pursuit of the enemy, and hasten to lay yardarm to yardarm. The sailors call them Jacky Fal-las, and respect nothing in them but their authority over the cat-o'-nine-tails. Other captains again there are (under one of them it was Jack's good-fortune to serve) who possess such manners, and in their cabins exhibit and expect such conversation and behavior, as one finds in the most polite assembly, yet are no whit behind the most old-fashioned sea-dog in courage. What could we expect of Jack when he came home to us, after four years spent in wandering among savages, and in a French prison among common sailors, but that he should be rude and rough? What else could we expect, after sailing under a commanding officer of good birth and breeding, than that he should return with polished manners and softened language?

This fact explained part of the change which had taken place in him. But it did not explain all, for Jack, who had formerly avoided the society of ladies, now astonished us by his demeanor towards madam and Castilla, especially the latter, whose conversation he courted, addressing himself to her continually, so that she was fain to blush under his manifest and undisguised admiration.

This would not have been wonderful in any other man, because eyes of heavenly blue, light brown curls, delicate features, a lovely shape, and the sweetest complexion in the world might well call forth admiration. But Castilla could boast the same charms, though not so ripe, three years before, when they moved him not a whit. Rather he regarded them with the contempt of one who has only eyes for the darker charms. Alas! the same look was gathering in his eyes—the look of tenderness and of a hungry yearning—while he gazed upon Castilla which had wont to be kindled by the black eyes of our poor Bess.

"Now," cried the admiral, when madam retired with Castilla, "'fore Gad! we'll make a night of it. Clean glasses, ye black devils, and brisk about! Jack, I hope the liquor is to your liking. I love the Mediterranean, for my own part, because the wine is cheap and strong and plenty. Drink about, gentlemen, and when you are tired of the port, we will have in the punch. Gentlemen, let us drink the health of the lieutenant!"

So the bottle began to fly, and the company presently grew merry, and all began to talk together, every man speaking of the glorious actions in which he had taken part, and, as is natural when the heart is uplifted with generous wine, every man thinking that the victory was won by his own valor. Thus the admiral related how he had planted the British flag on the island of Tobago; and before he had finished the narrative Mr. Shelvocke interrupted in order to tell the company that it was he alone who had with his own hand sacked and burned the town of Payta, and it was he who boarded the Spanish ships on their escape from Juan Fernandez; next, the good old admiral struck in again to explain who it was that had made Sir Cloudesley Shovel's victories possible. Captain Mayne, at the same moment, remembered that the powerful assistance he had lent to Admiral Vernon at Portobello had never been properly set forth by historians, and so on. But our hero, who had seen already more engagements than any man present, though he was not yet twenty-four, spoke little, and I observed, which was indeed remarkable in a naval officer, and would be, in this drinking age, remarkable in any man, that he did not drink deep. Presently, when the others were flushed in the cheeks, and some of them thick of speech— the first signs of drunkenness—Jack rose, saying, "By your leave, admiral, I will join the ladies."

"What?" said the admiral. "Desert the company? Exchange the bottle for a parcel of women? For shame, Jack, for shame! The punch is coming, dear lad: sit down—sit down."

But Jack persisted, and I rose too.

"Go, then!" the admiral roared, with a great oath. "Go, then, for a brace of gulpins!"

The ladies, who expected nothing but an evening to themselves, as is generally their lot when the men are drinking together, were greatly astonished at our appearance.

"Indeed, Jack," said Castilla, "Luke, we know, does not disdain a dish of tea with us. But you—oh! I fear you will find our beverage as insipid as our conversation."

Formerly Jack would have replied to this sally that, d'ye see, Luke was a grass-comber and a land-swab, but that for himself there was no tea aboard ship, and a glass of punch or a bowl of flip was worth all the tea ever brought from China— or words to that effect. Now, however, he laughed, and said, "Nay, Castilla, was I ever so rude as to find your conversation insipid? As for your tea, it will certainly, since you make it, be more delicious than all the admiral's port."

At this she blushed again, and presently made the tea and gave him a cup with her own hands, hoping it was sweetened to his liking; and he drank it as if he were accustomed to taking it every day, though I know not when he had taken tea last. He would not, however, drink a second cup, which shows that he did not greatly admire its taste. Now at the Rainbow, in Fleet Street, I have seen gentlemen who will take their six or seven cups of tea one after the other at a sitting. And the same thing may be seen with ladies when the hissing urn has been brought in and the tea goes round.

Then Castilla asked him a hundred questions about his cruise and his battles, which Jack answered modestly and briefly, while still in his eyes I marked that look of admiration—I knew it well—growing deeper and more hungry, and Castilla, observing it too, continually blushed and stammered, and yet went on prattling, as if his looks fascinated her, as they say that in some countries a snake will so charm a bird that it will sit, still singing, until he darts upon it and swallows it up.

After this he asked her to sing. Her voice was gentle and sweet, but of small power, and in the old days it had no charms for him compared with the strong, full voice which was at his service in the apothecary's parlor. But she complied, and sang all the songs she knew in succession.

Jack listened, enthralled. " 'Tis well," he said, with a deep sigh, "that we have no Castilla on board."

"Why, Jack?"

"Because life would be so sweet that the men would not fight, for fear of being killed."

"Thank you, Jack," she said. "I never expected so fine a compliment on my poor singing."

"There never were any sirens on board ship," I said, clumsily. "They are always on land, and sing to lure poor sailors to destruction."

"Fie for shame, Luke!" cried Castilla. "That was not prettily said. Am I trying to lure Jack to his destruction, pray?"

We all laughed; and yet, when one comes to think of that

12*

evening, I perceive that this innocent creature was actually and unconsciously playing the part of the ancient siren, because she certainly lured the lieutenant to the fate that awaited him.

Then Jack offered to sing, somewhat to my dismay, because I remembered certain songs which he had formerly bawled at the Gun Tavern and in the apothecary's parlor. However, he now sang, his voice being modulated and greatly softened, an old sea-song, with a burden of " As we ride on the tide when the stormy winds do blow," very movingly, so that the tears stood in Castilla's eyes.

We heard, in the next room, the voices of the admiral and his guests growing louder and faster, and conjectured that the evening would be a short one. This speedily proved true, and the negroes wheeled every man home to his own house, except the admiral, whom they carried up-stairs. As for us, madam went to sleep in a chair, and we sat down to a game of Ombre, Jack showing himself as pleased with the simple game we played as he had been with the tea and the singing. At the same time his eyes wandered from his cards to Castilla's face, and he played his cards badly, losing every game.

" I cannot remember, Jack," said Castilla, when we finished, " that you were fond of cards when last you were at home, unless it were All-fours."

" He also played," I said, " Cribbage, Put, Laugh-and-lie-down, and Snip-snap-snorum "—all of these being games over which, when played with Bess, he had shown great interest.

" Nay," he replied, earnestly, " I entreat you, Castilla, to forget wholly what manner of man that was who came home to you in rags. Think that he had been for two years among the midshipmen, and then for three years among the savages and the Spaniards, and then was thrown into a French prison to mess with common sailors. If you do not forget that rude savage, forgive him, and understand that he has gone, and will no more be seen. As for the things he did, I look upon them with wonder. Why, if I remember aright, Luke, that sea-swab did not disdain to fight a smuggler fellow at Horn Fair before all his friends."

" He did not, Jack," I said. " But we loved the sea-swab."

" We should have loved him better, Luke," said Castilla, gently, " if he had given more of his company to ourselves and less to the apothecary. I know how his afternoons were spent, sir;" she nodded and laughed, and he changed color and started; but of course Castilla knew nothing about Bess.

"He is gone," Jack repeated, "and I hope that a better man has taken his place. As for your society, Castilla, he must be an insensate wretch indeed who would not find himself happy when you are present."

"Thank you, Jack;" she made him a courtesy and smiled, yet blushed a little. "I perceive that another man indeed has taken his place. Poor honest Jack! He spoke his mind, and loved not girls. Yet we loved him—perhaps;" she looked up at him, but dropped her eyes beneath his ardent gaze. "Perhaps, before long—"

"Perhaps, Castilla," said Jack, earnestly, "you may be able to love the new man better than the old."

"It is late," she said, blushing again. "Good-night, Jack." She gave him her hand, which he held for a moment, looking down upon the pretty, slender creature with eyes full of love. And then she left us, and went to bed.

I declare solemnly that I had loved Castilla ever since I could talk; yet in one evening this sailor made fiercer and more determined love to her than I in all those years. Indeed, as she hath since confessed to me, she knew not, and did not even so much as suspect, that I loved her.

"Come into the open, dear lad," said Jack, presently, after a profound sigh. "Let us go into the garden and talk."

In the garden, what with the twilight of the season and the full moon, it was as bright as day, though eleven o'clock was striking by St. Nicholas's Church clock. We walked upon the trim bowling-green, and talked.

"There is her bedroom," said Jack, looking at the light in Castilla's chamber. "See! she has put out the candle. She is lying down to sleep. What—oh, lad!—what can a creature like that, so delicate and so fragile, think of such rough, coarse animals as ourselves? Do you think that she can ever forget or forgive the rude things I have said to her? Do you think she remembers them, and would pay them back?"

"Jack, Castilla has nothing to remember or to forgive. Do you think she harbors resentment for the little rubs of her childhood?"

"She is all goodness, Luke; of that I am convinced. She is as good as she is truly beautiful; of that I need not to be told. As for her beauty, there is nothing in the world more lovely than the English blue eye and fair hair. It is by special Providence, I suppose, and to reward us for hating the pope and the French, that they are made as good as they are beautiful."

"Did you always prefer fair hair to dark, Jack?" I asked, in wonder that a man should have so changed, and should have forgotten so much.

"As for what I used to say and think, dear lad, let that never be mentioned between us. Why, it shames me to think of what an unmannerly cur I must have seemed to all in those days. Talk not of them, Luke, my lad."

Poor Bess! She was included among the things belonging to those days. I dared not question him further.

"It is our unhappiness," he went on, "that though we would willingly remain on shore, honor and our own interest call us to go to sea again. Therefore I know not how far a man who is at present only a lieutenant might hope to win so fair a prize as Castilla. To be sure, she is a sailor's daughter, and knows what she would expect as a sailor's wife. Yet to leave her alone, and without protection! She would have you, to be sure, for her protector while I am gone."

Heavens! It was not yet three years since he had solemnly committed another woman to my care. Had he quite forgotten that?

"In a word, Jack," I said, with bitterness in my heart, "you have seen Castilla, since your return, but three or four hours, and you are already in love with her."

"That is true," he replied. "I am in love with her. Why," he laughed, "you are thinking, I dare swear, of three years ago, when you caught me in a certain summer-house, kissing another girl."

I acknowledged that I remembered the fact. "Is she," I asked, "quite forgotten? Yet you swore that you loved her, and vowed constancy."

"Well, my lad, every sailor is allowed to be in love as often as he comes ashore, for that matter. And as for the girl— what was her name?—I believe I did make love to her for a while. And now I hear that she is married, and already the mother of twins."

"Who told you that?"

"Her father, the penman."

"But it is not true, Jack. How could he have told you such a thing? Bess hath never forgotten you."

"True or not true, I care not a rope's-end. I am in love with Castilla. Already, you say? Why, a man who did not fall in love with this sweet creature at the very first sight of her would not be half a man. I expect to fight my way through a hundred suitors to get her hand. The admiral loves me, and I think he would willingly make me his son-in-law. But I must go to sea once more before I can offer to marry her. Therefore, for her sake, I shall go to London and turn courtier. I shall attend the nobleman who once promised me an appointment. He hath now, doubtless, forgotten both the making and the breaking of that promise. That matters nothing. I shall pay my court to him. I shall practise those arts by which men creep into snug places : it needs but a supple back and an oily tongue. Come to see me in a week or two, and I will wager that I shall be his lordship's obedient servant, and that he will presently give me a command, if only of a pink ; and that Castilla shall be promised to me."

All these things came to pass, indeed. Yet the result was not, as you shall learn, what he looked for.

CHAPTER XXX.

ALAS! POOR BESS!

Alas! poor Bess!

You have heard how she spent the first day, and with what a heavy heart she went to bed. In the morning she plucked up heart a little. As for what the lieutenant said to her father, what matter if he did say that she was already married? It was his joke—Jack would ever have his joke. He had been busy all day. The evening he must needs spend with the admiral, his patron and benefactor. But he would not—he could not — fail to see her the second day. So again she dressed in her best, and repaired early to her place in the apothecary's parlor, where she took her seat and waited. But she laughed no longer, nor did she prattle. Jack came not; he was in London, taking a lodging in Ryder Street, and buying brave things in which to wait upon his lordship. And the third day she went again—but now with white cheeks and heavy eyes, and she rocked herself to and fro, replying nothing, whatever Mr. Brinjes might say to her.

In the afternoon of that day I went in search of her, being anxious, and dreading mischief.

"I know not," said Mr. Westmoreland, getting off the stool— "I know not, indeed, Mr. Luke, what hath happened to the girl, nor where she is, unless she is in Mr. Brinjes's parlor, where most of her days are spent. These three days she hath forgotten to give me any meals, and hath left me alone all day; while in the evening, when I come home, she either sits mum or she goes up-stairs. Nothing disturbs the mind in the midst of logarithms more than a doubt whether there will be any dinner to eat or any supper. At this time of the year I commonly look for soft cheese and a cucumber. But now I have to get what I can. I know not what ails her. If I did know, I question whether I could find any remedy, seeing that she is so headstrong. Sometimes I doubt whether there is some love trouble on her mind. Yet I know not with whom. It cannot be with Aaron Fletcher, because she has refused the young·man several times. Besides, his affairs are said to be well-nigh desperate, his boat being lost, his yard burned down, his boat-building business thrown away; yet if it is not Aaron, who can it be? Because, sir, though my daughter hath her faults, and those many, being as to temper equalled only by her mother, now in Abraham's bosom, or—or perhaps elsewhere," he added, being a truthful man, "yet she is not one who courts the company of men, nor listens willingly to the voice of love."

Mr. Brinjes, though it was in the afternoon, was talking with his assistant in his shop.

"You will find her," he said, "within. I have left her for five minutes, for it teases me to see her thus despairing. The worst has yet to come, because she is not a girl to sit down peaceably under this contempt. Well, for that matter, every

sailor is inconstant, if you please ; and the women know it and
expect it. But Bess is no common Poll o' the Point, who
looks for nothing else than to be forgotten. Nor did she first
seek him out. Yet I knew what would happen, because such
love as his was too hot to last—else would it burn him up.
There was a Bristol man in Captain Roberts's company was consumed for love of a young Coromantyn girl, wasting away and crying out that he was on fire, yet never happy unless she was at his
side. It is a natural witchery which a few women possess, by
which they make men love them, and draw the very soul out
of the man they love. Bess hath this power: she can make any
man love her, and when she loves a man she can bewitch him
so that he shall never be happy but at her feet. Why, Jack
hath forgotten her. Yet it is most true that if he but come
back to her for a single day, he would fall at her feet again."

"Nay," I said, " he is already in love with another woman."

"Miss Castilla, the admiral's daughter. It is a passing fancy,
because she is a pretty creature, small and slender. But to
compare her with Bess !—to think that a man can love her
as he can love Bess ! There ! you know nothing of love. Go
in there, and I will follow. I have known," he continued,
being garrulous, as old men often are—" I have known such
cases as this of Bess, the jealous woman who hath been forgotten—ay, I have known them by the hundred. Sometimes
they take it with a sudden rage ; sometimes they cry out for
a knife, and would kill their faithless lover first and themselves
next ; sometimes they throw themselves into the water ; sometimes they murder the other woman ; sometimes they laugh,
and lay for a chance of revenge. One woman I knew who
concealed her wrath for twenty years, but revenged herself in
the end. Sometimes they make up their minds that it matters
little. This case is peculiar ; for the patient is not in a rage—
as yet ; nor has she called for a knife—as yet ; nor has she
promised to hang herself—as yet ; but she sits and waits ; and
all the time the humors are mounting to the brain ; so that we
are only at the beginning of the disorder, and my forecast as
to this disease is, my lad, that we shall have trouble. What ?
Is a fine high-spirited girl to be shoved aside into the gutter
without a word said or any cause pretended ? Not so, sir ; not
so. There will be trouble."

I passed into the parlor with trepidation. Bess lifted her head. Her face was pale and haggard; wildness was in her eyes.

"Where is he?" she cried. "You call yourself my friend, yet you come without him. Where is he?"

"I do not know, Bess, where he is, unless that he is somewhere in London."

"I believe it is you who have kept him from me—yet you call yourself my friend. You have set him against me. Though what you have found to say I know not. I have not so much as looked at another man since he went away, and I have kept his secret for him, so that no one suspects. How dare you put yourself between my sweetheart and me?"

"Indeed, Bess," I told her, "I have said nothing against you. I have not put myself between Jack and you. I have said nothing."

Then she began to rail at me for my silence. Why had I not spoken of her? Why had I not reminded him of his faith and promised constancy? "And where is he," she repeated, "that he does not come to me? Is he afraid of me? Doth he try to hide himself out of my way?"

I told her that he was in lodgings in town, and that his time was taken up with his affairs. And then, because she began to upbraid me again, I thought it was better to tell her the truth, and therefore said plainly that the lieutenant loved her no longer; that he had indeed given me to understand, without the possibility of a mistake, that the past was clean forgotten and gone out of his mind.

I was sorry—truly I was sorry—for the poor creature; for every word I said was nothing less than a dagger into her heart. A man must have been as hard-hearted as a Romish inquisitor not to have felt sorry for her. She heard me with parted lips and panting breath. Is there, I wonder, a more dreadful task than to be the messenger to tell a fond woman that the man she loves now loathes her?

Seeing that she received my information with no more outward symptom of wrath, I began to point out, to the best of my ability, that Lieutenant Easterbrook, when he fell in love with her, was still less than twenty years of age, who had been for six years separated from his countrywomen, and had for-

gotten what an English woman should be; that he might have
fallen in love with one of his own rank but for his long
wanderings among savages and his imprisonment with common
sailors, which had left him rough and rude in manners; that
things were now quite changed, because he was not only an
officer of some rank, but was now a gallant gentleman, keeping
company of the best, and might, if he desired, marry an heiress;
that his long silence ought to have prepared her for the change
in his disposition; and that, seeing nobody except Mr. Brinjes
and myself knew of what had happened, a wise and prudent
girl would show her pride and take her revenge by showing
that she cared nothing for his neglect.   In fact, I said on this
occasion all that was proper to be said.   Mr. Brinjes sat silent
in his chair, but kept his eye upon Bess, as if expecting that
something would happen.

Then, long before I had finished all I had to say, Bess suddenly sprang to her feet with a cry, and burst forth into wild
and ungoverned wrath.   I have seen fishwives fighting at
Billingsgate, a ring of men and women round them, and a truly
dreadful thing it is to see women stripped for battle and using
their fists like men; never before, or since, have I seen a young
and beautiful girl thus give way to passion uncontrolled.   At
first she could find no words to express her wrath; she clutched
at her heart; she tore down her hair; she gasped for breath;
she swung her arms abroad; she swayed her body backward
and forward.   I looked to see Mr. Brinjes go seek his lancet,
and give her relief by breathing a vein.   But he did not.   He
sat looking on coldly and anxiously, as if he were watching the
progress of a fever.   Presently she found words.

I will not write down what she said, because, as regards
myself and Mr. Brinjes, her reproaches were wholly undeserved, and indeed we had been throughout her best friends.
Besides, the ravings of a *femina furens*, or a woman mad with
jealousy and disappointed love, ought not to be set down any
more than those of a man in delirium.   When she came to
speak of her faithless lover she choked, and presently stopped
and was silent.   But, poor soul! all the while she looked from
one to the other of us as if to find hope in our faces, but saw
none.   Finally she shrieked aloud, as if she could no longer
bear this agony, and hurled herself headlong upon the floor,

and so lay, her head upon her hands, her whole body convulsed.

"Let be, let be," said Mr. Brinjes; "after this she will be
better. The storm was bound to burst. Better that it should
rage in this room than that she should go to a certain house
we know of—" he jerked his finger in the direction of the
admiral's. Say nothing to her; if you speak you will make
her worse. Presently she will come round. What? Nature
can go no further, unless she would wear herself to pieces.
And they never go so far as that, whatever their wrath, because the pain of the body becomes intolerable."

He spoke as if she could not hear or was insensible, which
I take to have been the case, for in five minutes or so she sat
up, taking no notice of what had been said, and became partly
rational, and said, calmly, sitting on the floor, that she should
go away and kill Jack first, and herself afterwards; and she
declared that if he dared to address any other woman, she
would tear her limb from limb; so that I trembled for Castilla.
But Mr. Brinjes looked on without surprise or terror, murmuring: "Let be, let be; it will do her good. And I have seen
them worse."

And, indeed, presently she arose from the floor and tied
up her beautiful hair, which had fallen about her shoulders,
and smoothed her disordered frock, and sat down again in
the window-seat, clasping her knees with her hands, moaning
and weeping, and rocking herself to and fro. And at this
symptom of progress or development of the "case," the
apothecary nodded and winked at me, as much as to say that
the disease was taking a favorable turn.

He knew the symptoms, this learned physician, who had
studied woman's nature where it is the most ungovernable and
the most exposed to observation, among the negresses, and, I
suppose, applied to more civilized women the rules he had
learned among these artless pagans; for in fact she speedily
ceased either to weep or to moan, but sat upright, drew a long
breath, and spoke quite gently and prettily, like a little child
who has been naughty, and now promises to be good again.

"I am sorry," she said, "that I have given so much trouble;
I will never do it again. Mr. Brinjes, you have not had your
nap, nor your afternoon punch, through my fault. I will mix

you a glass, and then you shall go to sleep." She did so, and arranged his pillows for him, and in a few minutes afterwards the old man was sound asleep. Then Bess turned to me. "Forgive me, Luke," she said, giving me her hand. "You are my best friend; except this poor old man, you are my only friend. You have never been weary of teaching me how a gentlewoman should behave, so that I should be worthy of a gentleman: and now it has ended in this. He has forgotten me, who have never forgotten him—no, not for a moment, since the day when first he told me—oh, the happy day! He came into the room where I was sitting before the fire, and took me in his arms—oh, in his arms! Could I ever forget him? No, no; not for a moment."

"My poor Bess!" I said, "what can I say—what do—for you in this dreadful trouble?"

The tears stood in her eyes, but she wept no longer.

"I know," she said, after a while, "what I will do. Here is his letter to me." She drew it from her bosom. It went to my heart to see the prettily worked silken bag she had made for it with her own hands. "First, you shall take it to him, Luke, and give it to him yourself. Will you do so much for me? It is not a great thing to ask you, is it? Give it to him, and tell him that he must read it, and then bring it back to me. And, Luke, dear Luke, you have always been kind to me, always my friend, though you know nothing about love, do you? Else you would understand that a woman would rather die than lose her lover. Give him the letter. When he reads it he will remember, and then—then, Luke— You will tell him—oh! tell him"—she laid her hands upon my arm, and gazed upon me with imploring eyes—"tell him, dear friend, that I am more beautiful than ever—Mr. Brinjes says I am—and that I have tried to teach myself the ways of a gentlewoman for his sake; and that I can read and write a little, so that he shall not be ashamed of me; and that I associate no more with the other girls, and have been true to him ever since he went away. Tell him all, Luke, and everything else that you can think of that is kind and friendly, and that will make him want to see me again. Oh, if he were here in this room with me for one hour he would love me again!"

"I will take the letter, Bess," I told her, moved to tears;

"and I will give it to him myself, and tell him all that you wish, and more—more, my poor Bess!"

"When will you give it to him?"

"To-morrow. Will that do?"

So with that promise she appeared to be more contented, and went away, though with hanging head—the poor, fond, loving girl!

"You may give the lieutenant that letter," said the apothecary, "and you may tell him what you please. But, if I know Jack Easterbrook, you might as well try to knock him down with a feather. As for making her his wife, it is out of the question; and to become his mistress without being his wife, Bess would not consent, nor, I think, would Jack ask her. Because, d'ye see, he no longer cares a rope's-yarn about her. Yet if he would come here for a single hour— Bess knows her power : trust a woman who has that power. But I think he will not come. And so there will be trouble—I know not yet of what kind ; there will be trouble."

CHAPTER XXXI.

AN AMBASSADOR OF LOVE.

I READILY accepted the mission ; but, like many other ambassadors, I hesitated when the time came to discharge my trust. For Jack was like those Oriental bashaws who cut off the heads of messengers that bring uncomfortable tidings. First I thought it would be best to give the letter to him at Deptford, so that, if he was moved by pity or by love, he might go straight to the poor girl and offer her consolation. But I had promised to give it the very next day. Therefore I picked up courage and made my way to his lodgings, the letter in my pocket, knowing full well that he would take my interference ill, being too masterful to brook counsel, advice, or admonition from any one, unless it came as an order from a superior officer.

It was about ten o'clock in the morning when I reached his lodging in Ryder Street. He was sitting wrapped in a sheet,

while the barber was finishing his hair with the powder puff.
On the table stood his morning chocolate and cream.

"Ho!" he cried. "Here is the Prince of Painters. Art
come to paint me a portrait, Luke?" (N.B.—I did paint his
portrait, and have it still, a speaking likeness, and a better
piece of work I never did.) "Wait a moment, my hearty, till
this lubber hath finished the top-dressing."

Presently the man finished, and removed the sheet, showing
beneath it a full-dress lieutenant's uniform—to my mind the
blue of the navy is far more becoming to a handsome man
than the scarlet of the army. Just as he rose from the barber's
hands, the man still standing before him, the implements of
the trade in his hand, and I beside him, I heard a rustling of
petticoats outside, and the door was opened by a lady. She
was wrapped from head to foot in a hood, and wore a domino.

"Madam!" said Jack, bowing low.

The lady removed her domino and laughed, and threw off
her hood. Truly a most beautiful creature she was, and most
richly dressed. 'Twas the merriest, most roguish face that one
ever saw, with dancing eyes and laughing lips. I ought to
have known the face, because I had seen it several times; but
I did not, because an actress dressed for a queen or a sultana
seems to change her face as well as her frock. She was, indeed, an actress—very well known indeed to the world, as you
would acknowledge did I write down her name, which I shall
not do for many reasons.

"I have found my hero, then," said the lady, "in his own
—cabin—or is it on his own quarter-deck? Are the decks
cleared for action? Are you ready, sir, to engage the enemy?"

"Alas, madam," said Jack, "I haul down my colors and give
up my sword."

He fell upon one knee, and kissed the hand which the
lady graciously extended to him. Now observe that she took
no kind of notice of the barber or of myself, whom she mistook, doubtless, for an assistant, or some other kind of tradesman. I mean that in what followed my presence was not the
slightest restraint upon her.

"I am a rash creature," she said, "to imperil my reputation
by visiting a lieutenant of the king's navy alone in the morning. Suppose I had been observed?"

"Madam"—Jack made her so fine a bow that I could not help thinking of the Jack who had come home in rags three years before—"could I desire a more delightful task than the defence of your reputation."

"I thank you, lieutenant. But I have a readier defence in my hood and domino. A woman's reputation is quite safe, I assure you, so long as she is not seen. It is in this respect unlike so many gentlemen's honor, which is only safe so long as they are seen. I came not, however, for compliments. First of all, I came to say that I shall be alone this afternoon. You can visit me if you please. Next, my lord is coming to supper with me after the theatre. He will presently call here himself, or send a letter, and will invite you to come with him. To oblige me, lieutenant, you will come."

"Madam," said Jack, with a smiling face, "you were born, sure, to make me the happiest of men."

"The happiest of men!" she repeated, merrily laughing. "Oh! what creatures we women should esteem ourselves, since, with such little trouble, we can make men happy! And how miserable are we that it takes so much more to make us happy! Heigho! You are made happy with a smile, or a kind word, or a hand to kiss, or permission to take supper with us—while we— Oh! we know how little these things are worth. Therefore— No, sir, you have kissed my hand already." At this point the barber, who had been gathering up his tools, retired from the room. I retreated to the window, and gazed upon the street, as if I were anxious not to listen. She, however, took no notice of my presence. "Come this afternoon, then, and this evening; after you have seen me from the front, you can join my lord. But that is not all I had to say, oh, happiest of men!" She laughed again. "This will make you indeed a happy man, if the roar of the cannons and the groans of wounded men are sweeter than the smiles of women."

"Indeed, madam, I cannot understand—"

"What I have now to tell will, I dare say, make a round dozen of women miserable, for my hero is a handsome hero. But not me, sir. Oh, pray, do not think that! An actress, everybody knows, hath no heart. She is but a toy, to be laughed at and played with until the men find another which is newer, and hath less of the gilt rubbed off. Yet I shall be sorry, Jack—do your friends call you Jack?—though it is but the day before yesterday that I made your acquaintance, sir."

"Still, madam," he persisted, "I know not—"

"This is a very fine coat, Jack," she went on, laying her hand, covered with a white glove, upon his sleeve. "I love the color. 'Tis a new coat, too, so that 'twill be a pity to buy another. Perhaps, however, this may be made to do, and methinks it will be greatly improved if we put a little lace upon the lapels and cuffs, and change the button for one with a crown instead of an anchor."

"Madam!" He started and changed countenance, because these additions mark the rank of captain. "Madam! Is it possible?"

"Why, Jack, when a handsome lad does a woman so great a service, and for all his reward wants nothing but to be sent away from her sight, I doubt whether she is not a fool for her pains if she help him—yet—" Here she sighed. "His majesty's frigate *Calypso*, the *Sapphire's* prize, is to be refitted without delay and commissioned. Go, take possession of your own quarter-deck, Captain Easterbrook. Perhaps the next lady whose jewels you save from robbers may make you an admiral." With this she courtesied so as to sweep the ground, as they are wont to do upon the stage.

"Oh, madam!" he cried, "how can I show my gratitude?"

"You will not set sail for a week or two yet, I suppose. Come to me as often as you please. To my brave defender I am always at home."

She held out her hand, but Jack did not, as I expected, stoop to kiss it. On the contrary, he disregarded it altogether, and caught her in his arms, kissing her lips and cheeks. I looked to see her resent this familiarity with the greatest show of displeasure, for here was no simple girl of the lower sort, like poor Bess, but a very grand lady indeed, who, for all she was an actress, had all the noblemen of London at her feet. But, to my astonishment, she only laughed, and gently pushed him from her.

"Jack," she said, "thou hast truly a conquering way. Let me go, sir!"

She laughed again, in her merry, saucy way; put on her

domino, pulled the hood over her head, and suffered Jack to
conduct her to her chair, which waited without.

"Hang it, Luke!" cried Jack, when he came back. "I forgot that thou wast here; and I dare swear madam never saw
thee. Must I never kiss a pretty woman but this virtuous fellow must still be looking on, with open mouth?"

"Shall I tell Castilla, Jack?"—thinking of what might have
happened had Bess been there.

"Why, in a kiss there is no harm, surely; therefore there is
no need to tell Castilla. If this news be true—and it must be
true— Luke, thou art a Puritan. As for a simple kiss which
is snatched, they like it, man. Every woman, except Castilla,
who is a miracle of goodness, likes such kisses."

"Who is the lady, Jack?"

"Why, she is a great actress; and the other night, by a
lucky chance—I was going home at midnight—I heard a woman's scream and a trampling of feet. 'Twas but an attack upon
a lady's chair by footpads, whom it was nothing to drive off
without more trouble than to draw and to slash one of them
across the face. Then I saw her safe to her lodgings. 'Tis a
grateful creature."

"She seems grateful," I said. "Do actresses often appoint
commanders to his majesty's ships?"

"No, Luke; no, my lad, they do not. These appointments
are given according to merit, seniority, courage, seamanship,
and patriotism. That is very well understood, and it is the
reason why everybody is so contented who wears the king's
uniform. But suppose that one of my lords the commissioners
should take a particular interest in a certain lady, and suppose
this lady should have eyes to see all these virtues combined in
one man, and suppose she should be able further so to persuade
his lordship, who, we will again suppose, knows already something of this man. Confess, then, that it would be a lucky
thing for this man were this lady to single him out for the
favor of recommendation."

"Truly, it would be lucky for him."

"Captain of the *Calypso*," he exclaimed. "Why, have I
done badly to command a frigate at twenty-four? What care
I who appoints me, so that I get my chance? Will the world
know? Have I done anything dishonorable? My lord hath

already promised me promotion. I looked to be first lieutenant, perhaps—and now— Luke, my lad, I am so happy that I
could e'en go back to Deptford and fight Aaron Fletcher again,
as I did three years ago at Horn Fair."

"Yes, Jack; I could wish in my heart that you would fight
him again, if it were about the same woman."

"Come, lad," he said, "ease thy mind, which is full of something. Let me hear it."

"Put out of your mind," I said, "Castilla and this actress
and all women, except one. I have been asked by one whom
you should remember to bring to you a certain letter, and to
beg, first, that you will read it, and next, that you will, with
your own hand, restore it to the owner."

With this I took the letter from my pocket and gave it to
him in its silk bag.

"Why," he said, breaking into a laugh, as if the matter were
not serious at all, "this is my own letter. I wrote it, I remember, one afternoon, off Cape Finisterre—I remember the day
very well. Did the girl—Bess Westmoreland was her name—
give it to thee, Luke? Oh! I remember—I was in love with
her. A devilish fine girl she was, with eyes like sloes."

He read the letter through. "To think that I wrote that
letter, and that she believed it! 'Most beautiful woman in the
world.' . . . 'Fondest lover!' Oho! I wonder how many such
letters are written aboard ship the first week after sailing? As
for this—why, Luke, you had better give it back to the girl, if
she wishes to keep it. Tell her to show it to her friends as
the work of a fool. Perhaps her new lover or her husband
might like to have the letter. But, indeed, I think she had
better burn the thing, in case of accidents. Husbands do not
like generally to read such letters."

"She has had no other lovers, Jack, on your account."

"Pretty fool! Bid her waste good time no longer."

"She will suffer no man to speak to her, saying that she belongs to you alone, and thinking you would come home to marry
her."

"I suppose," said Jack, his face darkening, "that the meddlesome old apothecary is at the bottom of this foolishness."

"And myself too. Why, Jack, you solemnly placed her in
my charge. You begged me to take care of her. You tattooed
13

her name upon your arm. Look at your arm. What could we
think? She has learned things for your sake, Jack—such as
gentle manners, and to restrain her tongue, and to govern herself—generally, that is," because I remembered the scene of
yesterday. "You would not know her again."

"Well, Luke, she has therefore been so far kept out of mischief, which is good for every girl. And this is a wicked
world, and seaports are full of traps for girls. Tell her, however, that now she had better lose no time in looking for a
husband in her own station. The fellow Aaron Fletcher would
perhaps make a good husband, provided he kept decently sober."

"Do not blame Mr. Brinjes. He hath warned her continually that sailors go away and break their promises. But will
you see her, Jack?"

"No. What the devil would be the use of my seeing her."

I told him how she had put on her best, and had gone to
wait for him at the apothecary's, and there waited for three
long days. But he was not softened a whit.

"It is their foolish way," he said. "We say fond things,
and promise whatever will please them, and they believe it all.
Why they believe the nonsense, the Lord knows. As for the
men who say it, and make the promises, they believe it too, I
dare say, at the time. 'Tis pretty, too, to see them purr and
coo, whatever extravagances you tell them. I remember, now—"
But here he stopped short in his recollections.

"Jack," I said, "will you pull up your sleeve, and show me
your arm?"

He laughed, and obeyed. It was his left arm, and, as we
know, it was tattooed all over with the once-loved name of
Bess.

"'Tis like the arm of any fo'k's'le tar," he said. "What
was I, in those days, better? Yet, lad, the name hath no longer
any meaning to my eyes."

"Meaning or not," I insisted, "will you give her the letter
with your own hand? Jack, only let her tell you what is in
her mind. That is a small thing to do."

"It would be more cruel than to refuse to see her at all.
Trust me, if this girl gives trouble, I shall know how to deal
with her. If you have any regard for her, bid her spoil her

market no longer, and put maggots out of her head. She
would marry me, would she? Kind soul, I thank her for it
with all my heart. She would marry me, would she? I will
tell thee a thing, my lad, which thou wilt never find out for
thyself with all thy paint-brushes—there is no woman in the
world more hateful to a man than a woman he hath once loved
and now loves no longer. It is like coming back to a half-finished banquet when the dishes are cold and the wine is stale.
Yet the foolish women believe that once in love, always in
love. Better she should learn the truth at once, and so an end." .

He gave me back the letter, and would say no more upon
the subject. But he said I must make a picture of him before
he went away, and he would be painted in the new uniform,
which he would order immediately; and I must go instantly
and tell Castilla of his good-fortune. Thus was I made a go-
between, first to one and then to the other.

"And now, Luke, my fortune is made, if I am only moder-
ately lucky. He who is captain at twenty-four may well be
rear-admiral at thirty, and command a fleet at thirty-five; at
forty he is certainly a knight, and perhaps a viscount; and at
seventy he lies in Westminster Abbey. What could I hope
for better," he asked, glowing with the joy and elation of his
appointment, "than to command a frigate, easy to handle,
swift to sail? Why, it will be the *Tartar* over again, in the
captain's cabin instead of the wardroom. That was warm
work; but I hope to show warmer work still. God knows,
Luke," he said, earnestly, "I say it not in boastfulness, I can
handle a ship as well as the best man afloat, and I can take her
into action, I promise you, as bravely."

So he talked, thinking no more at the time of the actress, or
of Castilla, or of Bess, for the thought of any ship was enough
to turn his mind from a woman, though he so easily fell in love
with a pretty girl. And while he was thus talking of his promotion, and the things he hoped to do with his vessel, there
drove to the house a chariot, with footmen and gold panels,
very splendid, and two gentlemen got down. They came to
visit Jack. One of them was a man no longer young, yet erect
and tall, with aquiline nose and proud eyes. He wore a satin
coat, with a sash, and a star blazing with diamonds. The other
was in the uniform of the army.

Jack sprang to his feet, and bowed to the ground. "My lord," he said, "this is an extraordinary honor. Indeed, I could never have expected it."

"I have come, young gentleman," said his lordship, speaking slowly and with the dignity which became his rank, "to tender you my thanks for the service which you performed the night before last to a certain lady."

"My services, my lord, were trifling, though, fortunately, opportune."

"Had it not been for your assistance the lady would have lost the jewels which she had worn at the theatre. What other loss or insult she escaped, I know not. I learn that, at her request, you have already paid a visit upon her."

"At her request, my lord, I had the honor, yesterday afternoon."

"Believe me, sir, that in return for such a service there is nothing that I can refuse you." Jack bowed again very low. "And since nothing will please you so much as to go back as quickly as possible to the fighting—"

"Nothing so much, my lord."

"Then you must go. Your name, I find, is already favorably known. I have therefore the pleasure of promoting for the sake of merit alone, which is not always possible for a commissioner. You are promoted, sir, to the command of the *Calypso*, the *Sapphire's* prize."

"My lord," said Jack, again bowing low, "I have no words, indeed, to express my gratitude for this great, this unexpected, and undeserved favor." Looking on from the corner of the room, beside the window, I confess I could not help thinking that it would be best for madam to say nothing about that salute upon her lips.

"Then," said his lordship, "no more need be said." He rose, and added, smiling: "Since you will have to go back in a few days to salt junk and pea-soup, captain, make the most of your time ashore. There will be a supper after the play this evening. I will, if you please to honor me with your company, carry you thither in my coach."

"I am honored to be one of your lordship's guests," said Jack.

"A rolling deck, a wet cabin, the smell of tar everywhere,

great sea-boots, the waves flying over the ship, the enemy pitching cannon-balls on board : this is what you like, Captain Easterbrook. Well, sir, you will have plenty of it, for there will be a long war, if all I hear is true. I shall see you, then, this evening. Come, colonel."

CHAPTER XXXII.

HOW THE APOTHECARY DID HIS BEST.

" Tell her plainly," said Mr. Brinjes, "what he said, and how he looked while he said it. Spare her in nothing; so will she the more quickly come to a right mind. What? Didst ever see a surgeon take off a man's leg? Doth he chop here a cantle, and there a snippet, for fear of causing pain? Not he? He ties his bandages and takes his saw, and in five minutes off goes the leg; and though the man may bellow, yet his life is saved."

There was little hope in her face when I went in to her; the trouble of it made my heart bleed. To think that a woman should still so much love a man who had thrown her away with as little thought as one throws away the rind of an apple! I thought she would have hated him. But no; at a word she would have risen to follow and obey him like a slave.

" Bess," I said, " be brave."

" Where is he ?"

" He is in London, at his lodgings."

" Did you give him the letter ?"

" I did. He sent it back to you. Here it is. Courage, Bess. No man is worth so much crying over. It is as I told you before. He loves you no longer. When he thinks of the past, he wonders at himself. When he remembers how much he was once in love, he laughs."

" Doth he laugh ? Oh, Luke, can he laugh ?" It was wonderful to her that the thing which destroyed all her happiness could be to him only the cause of laughter.

" Bess, my dear, I am grieved to the soul that I must tell you this. Alas, he laughs. He can never love you any more. Forget him, therefore. Put him out of your thoughts."

"He laughs at the girl to whom he wrote this letter—oh! this dear letter. Why doth he laugh? I cannot laugh, because I love him."

She rose, and sighed heavily. "Well," she said, "there needs no more, Luke. I have lost my sweetheart. That matters nothing, does it? Thousands of poor women lose their sweethearts every year, in action and in shipwreck. No one pays heed to the women. What matters one more woman? Oh! I would to God that he was lying dead at the bottom of the sea; and I—and I—and I—" She rushed from the room with distraction in her looks.

There was great rejoicing at the admiral's, whither I carried the glad news of Jack's promotion. Castilla attributed it entirely to the extraordinary discernment of his lordship, who deserved, she thought, the highest credit for discovering Jack's real ability and courage, so that he should be promoted, over hundreds of heads, to the command of a frigate, before he was four-and-twenty years of age. Truly it makes one no happier to be wiser, and Castilla knew nothing about the great lady of Drury Lane. Heaven forbid that she should learn anything about that ravished kiss!

The day was marked at the club in the usual manner, viz., by an extra bowl of punch; and I sat beside the admiral and told the company how his lordship, in a splendid satin coat, with a red sash and a diamond star, had condescended in person to inform this fortunate young commander of his promotion. But you may be sure that I told nothing about the actress, even to the admiral, who marvelled greatly at the boy's success, and wondered, being wise by experience, by whose private interest he had been promoted.

But the woman who ought most to have rejoiced was wandering all night long, in wind and rain, over the desolate moor called Blackheath, raging and despairing, because the man who once loved her so tenderly had now forgotten her, and laughed to think that he could ever have thought he loved her. In the morning she came back, mud-stained and draggled, hollow-eyed and wan of cheek, to the parlor behind the apothecary's shop; and here presently she fell asleep, being wholly spent with suffering and fatigue.

Now when Mr. Brinjes came from his shop, and saw her thus

asleep and so pale of cheek, he was moved with compassion, and resolved, though he had not visited London for twenty years, that he would himself try to move the hard heart of her lover.   Accordingly he put off his workday clothes, and reached down his great wig and the coat in which he sat at the club (both of which belonged to the early years of George I.), and so, fully persuaded that he was dressed quite in the modern fashion of a court-physician, he took oars for Hungerford Stairs, whence he walked to Ryder Street.

On the way the boys shouted at him, for he cut the queerest figure, his velvet coat being so old that it had turned green in places, his lace in rags, his old-fashioned wig unkempt and shabby.   But he walked briskly, careless of the boys, and carried his gold-headed stick with an air of majesty.

"Jack," he said, dropping into a chair, "thou art now, I hear, a captain.   Give me a glass of brandy—'tis a long journey from Deptford—and I will drink to thy good luck.   So— this is a pretty, commodious lodging, Jack.   I passed some fine women on the way from Hungerford Stairs.   Have a care, my boy.   Do not suffer any of the fine birds to bring their fine feathers here; else it may cost thee dear.   Be content with some honest wench who will love thee and not try to rob and plunder all the prize-money."

"Well, Mr. Brinjes"—Jack was not, I think, best pleased to see the old man at his lodgings, and more than suspected the errand on which he came—"can I be of any service to my old friend?"

"That depends, Jack—that depends.   The greatest service you could do for me would be not to forget old friends."

"Indeed, I have forgotten no old friends."

"Or old sweethearts."

"Why, as for old sweethearts, my old friend, they may go on so long as to become stale.   This you have often assured me as a matter of your own experience."

"It is quite true," replied the rover, who had not looked to have his own maxims thrown in his face—"it is quite true, I say, that woman is by nature a jealous creature; the nearer to nature you get, the more jealous you will find her.   Something of the tigress in every one.   Wherefore Bess, who is as passionate as a negro woman, is more jealous, I dare say, than a

London fine lady, who hath not the heart to be greatly jealous. Also a woman can never be made to understand such a simple thing as that she ought to be contented with the half share of a man, or the quarter share, or even a short six months of his life ashore. Nor doth she ever perceive when the time arrives that she should cheerfully make way for another. Yet—poor Bess! I am sorry for the wench."

"In South America," said Jack, talking in the same strain, "where they smoke the cigarro, one that hath been half smoked and thrown away is nauseous if it be taken up and lighted again."

"It is so," said Mr. Brinjes. "Every one who hath been in Guayaquil, which is nigh unto South America, knows that it is so."

"Wherefore—" said Jack, but left the conclusions to be drawn by the philosopher.

"The thing is so," Mr. Brinjes repeated. "Jack, when thy first letter came, I knew that the fit was too hot to last. And when no more came, I understood very well what had happened. For my own part, I never loved any woman more than four-and-twenty hours after leaving port. Why, I have seen sailors marrying the day before they sailed, and yet coming on board unconcerned. This forgetfulness is a special gift of Providence, intended for sailors alone. But as for Bess, while you thought no more upon her, she had that letter wrapped in a silken bag and hung about her neck; and every day she kissed and hugged it, thinking, poor fond soul!—women are fools, yet we needs must feel pity for them—that the writer, like herself, would never change. She began to learn things for her lover's sake; she learned to read and write; she watched the ladies in church to see how they dress and how they carry themselves; she made Luke teach her some of their finickin', delicate ways, which don't go down with a sea-pie and black beer, such as you used to love in the days before your breeches were white and your stockings of silk, and while your buttons carried a simple anchor. Moreover, Bess would no longer consort with her old friends, and suffer none of the men so much as to have speech with her. And she made Luke tell her what words and sayings of hers would offend the ears of gentlewomen. In short, there she is, my lad, a woman ready for you; as to manners, so far as I understand the matter, as fine as a countess; as to good

looks, not a countess of them all can touch her; as to figure
—Lord! a finer figure was never made; as to temper, a noble
temper, my lad, quick and ready to flame up. What! One
that will keep her husband alive, I warrant, and stirring. Why,
Jack, we talked of a half-burned cigarro. This one is not yet
even lighted. Try it again, dear lad. 'Tis made, I swear, from
the finest leaf of Virginia. In South America they have none
such. As for truth and constancy, I will answer for them with
my life; and for affection—why, 'tis nothing less than a madness she hath for thee. Come, what want you with fine ladies?
They will but play with you when you are ashore, and forget
you when you are at sea, while, as for Bess, Bess will keep
your house while you are away, and when you come home she
shall be the tenderest wife in the world, and like a faithful
slave for service. What! You would say that by birth she is
below the rank of a commander? Jack, hark ye!"—here he
whispered, as if imparting a great secret—"a beautiful woman
hath no rank. There must be rank for men, otherwise there
would be no discipline on board the ship. Rank was invented
for that purpose; and the pretence is necessary for order's
sake, whether we call each other duke, earl, and noble lord, or
captain, lieutenant, and master. Yet it is, even with men, nothing but pretence at bottom. But for women there is no rank
at all, whatever they may themselves pretend; which is proved,
Jack, by the fact that great men do constantly fall in love with
women of the meanest origin, as witness Charles II. and Nelly
Gwynne. You may put Bess upon a throne, and, my word,
there is not a queen among them all would outshine her black
eyes and beauteous face. Whereas you will never see a woman
of gentle birth fall in love with a clown. Rank is for the ugly
women to console themselves withal, by walking in front of
each other. Give me another tot of brandy, Jack; and think
of her again, I say. Why, I can never get out of my mind that
we shall all three—you and Bess and I—we shall all three sail
together across the broad Pacific to pick up my treasure, and
to burn the town of Guayaquil, where they made me a slave.
I cannot die until that town is burned."

"I know nothing," said Jack, "about your dreams. But,
for the rest, you are too late, Mr. Brinjes. I have forgotten
the girl. All the past foolishness is over and finished."

13*

"Yes," said Mr. Brinjes, looking at him as a physician when he feels the pulse, "yes"—he spoke slowly and sadly—"I now perceive plainly that it is all over. The symptoms are clear. Your eyes warm no more at the thought of the girl. Her chance is gone. The poor child hath had her time. Well, I shall go home again. Pray Heaven my assistant hath not already poisoned a customer or two. Jack, keep out of her way. There will be trouble yet."

"Why, Mr. Brinjes," he laughed, "you do not think that I am afraid of a woman?"

"Nay, I said not that. But—well, we shall have trouble yet. And for these Southern Seas, sure I am that I shall see them again before I die."

So the apothecary went away, having done what he could, and having failed.

"We sailors," said Jack to me, presently, "are great fools in our love for taverns and drinking-bouts and low company, so that those are right who represent us as so many dull dogs who have no manners, and can do nothing ashore but drink about. Why, when I came home three years ago, the Gun Tavern was the height of civilization, the apothecary's dirty parlor was the abode of politeness, and poor Bess was the finest lady in the land.

"We are mostly such mere tarpaulins," he continued, after a space, "that landsmen do well to despise us, though we fight their battles for them, and care not how we are treated, nor how many hundreds they pass over when they make appointments. Then we fall to cursing the service, instead of our own common habits. There was on board the *Tartar* one of the lieutenants (he is now dead) who was a gentleman—I mean by taste and education as well as by birth—who sometimes talked with me, saying that 'twas a pity a lad of my appearance and figure (which he flattered) should not study polite manners for the sake of my own advancement, because, with a little trouble, I might certainly attract attention in high places, and so receive promotion. In this he was partly right, though I now find that great men think they can pay for the service of flattery in promises, as a merchant pays for goods with a piece of paper. But there is a difference, because, if the merchant do not redeem his promise when the day comes, he is dishonored;

whereas if a nobleman doth not redeem his promise, no one
throws the fact in his teeth. And if I had not been so lucky
as to rescue a certain friend of my lord, I doubt whether I
should have got any appointment, to say nothing of promotion.

"But, lad, consider. Here I live among the best; I am
received at a great man's table; I sit in the coffee-house among
the wits or the fops, as I please; I go to the theatre, to Ranelagh, and to Vauxhall; there is the gaming-table, if I choose
to risk a few pieces; if I am ever disposed for a quiet evening,
there is the society of Castilla, the sweetest girl in the world;
if for a sprightly party, there are the suppers of my friend—
my patron, if you please—and this actress. Think you that
after these things I can go back to Mr. Brinjes's stinking parlor and the penman's daughter? She may be as beautiful as
he says—I care not. She is certain to have coarse hands, rude
speech, and plain manners. You might as soon expect me to
go back to the cockpit, and to mess again with the midshipmen, the volunteers, and the surgeon's mates."

CHAPTER XXXIII.

AN INTERESTING CASE.

WHAT would be done next I knew not, yet feared something
desperate, the case lying, on the one hand, between a woman
driven well-nigh mad with love and disappointment, and, on the
other, a man of great determination, inflexible to tears and en-
treaties, and, besides, one who now regarded this poor girl, as
he himself confessed, with as much loathing as he had once
felt love. I have read in some book of travels that there are
certain hot fountains in Iceland which burst forth from time to
time with incredible force, and either scald to death those upon
whom they chance to play, or, by the ground sinking beneath
their footsteps, do suddenly engulf them. We were now—that
is, Mr. Brinjes and myself, who alone knew what was threatening—like unto those who walk upon ground where these fountains break out; for we knew not what ruin might fall upon
us at any moment, caused by the hand of a desperate woman.

No one knows the trouble the poor girl gave us at this time, with her changing moods, her fits, and her despair. For sometimes she would sit for many hours swinging her body backward and forward, tearing a ribbon or a handkerchief with her teeth; sometimes she would sit quite still, her eyes fixed and glowering; then she would suddenly spring to her feet, and cry aloud that she could bear it no longer; sometimes she would threaten death and murder to her false lover, and to any woman who should dare to take him from her; sometimes she would rush from the room and wander away, till she was forced to come back for weariness; and sometimes she would become gentle again, acknowledge her wilfulness, and beg forgiveness for her bad temper and her wild words. But these occasions were rare. She spent the whole day in Mr. Brinjes's house—that is, when she was not in one of her restless moods, wandering over Blackheath, or farther afield, in the woods and fields of Eltham or Norwood. More than once she spent the whole night out, returning in the morning spent with fatigue, her fury only appeased for a time by the weakness of her body. As for her father, she neglected him altogether, so that the poor man was now obliged to provide his own meals, sweep and keep clean his room, and make his own bed. "Yet," he said, "I dare not say a word in remonstrance or rebuke, so terrible is her temper, in which she now seems to surpass her mother, though I confess she doth not beat me over the head with the frying-pan, as my wife was wont to do. Mr. Brinjes, before whom I have laid the case, advises patience. Well, Mr. Luke, I am a patient man. Of that I am very sure. I have been patient all my life—when I was a boy, and the stronger boys hectored it over me; and when I was a 'prentice, and my master half starved me; when I was a married man, and my wife scratched, beat, and cuffed me daily; and now when my daughter is grown up. It is not recorded of the Patriarch Job that his wives and daughters were thus ungoverned."

Sometimes she would speak of her wrongs, and mostly she was grieved because Jack laughed at her.

"If he were dead," she cried, "I could weep for him all the days of my life, thinking he loved me to the end. Oh! I am a fool to care for such a man or to cry over him. He laughs at me. I am a fool. He laughs at me. Why did I not forget him the moment his ship was out of sight, and take another sweetheart ?"

" Pity," said Mr. Brinjes, shaking his head—" a thousand pities you did not."

" Hold your tongue !" she turned on him fiercely. " How dare you speak ? You were all in league to mock at me. Why, 'twas thus you beguiled the poor black negro girls, you and your pirate crew. And then you laughed at them."

" Faith," said Mr. Brinjes, " if a man deserts a black girl she generally murders him for it."

She looked at him strangely, and rushed away, saying nothing.

" I am sorry," said Mr. Brinjes, " that I told her about the negress's revenge, for she is now capable of everything; and perhaps she will go away and put a knife into his heart." This he said calmly, as if murder was too common a thing to surprise him. " There was once a girl—'twas at Providence—whose lover, a smart fellow too, and one of our crew, deceived her. What did she do ? Pretended to forgive him, passed the thing over, treated it as a joke, and played the loving sweetheart to the life, laughing and singing while she served up the poisoned meat that was to kill him. She put in it the herb stramonium, which there grows wild; and the women know its properties very well. She laughed the louder afterwards, while he twisted and rolled on the ground and bellowed in his agony. The men burned her alive for it, because this was an example that might affect them all; but she cared nothing for the torture, for she had her revenge; and whatever was done to her afterwards, nothing would hurt her, so long as she could think of that. Look you, Bess is such another as that negro girl. She is as passionate, and she is as jealous. There has been murder in her mind ever since Jack came home. I have read the thought in her eyes, and now I have put it into words for her. Trouble will come."

It was not this crime that I feared, because our women know not, happily, the use of poisons; and the worst among them shrink from taking life. But I feared that she might rashly and in despair kill herself, or commit some act of violence towards Castilla if she suspected that Jack was paying her attentions, or that she might lose her reason altogether. And indeed in those days I'm sure she was partly mad.

You shall learn what she did.

First, she would hear from her former lover's own lips the sentence of her dismissal. She would read her fate in his eyes. Therefore, one morning, without informing any one of her intention, she took boat and was carried up the river, and so made her way to his lodging in Ryder Street. No neglect of dress could hide the girl's wonderful beauty, but it was unfortunate, the captain being now daily in the society of ladies who omit no point in their attire which may help to enhance their charms, that she came to him in a common stuff frock, that in which she was accustomed to do the housework, and a plain straw hat, so that she looked exactly what she was, the daughter of some tradesman of humble station. This, I say, was unlucky for her. Another unlucky thing was that the captain was not alone in his lodging; and it shamed him that a girl so common in her dress and appearance should thus present herself and call him Jack, and remind him of his broken vows. You will expect, when you hear that Bess found a lady in the room, a scene of mad and violent jealousy. But nothing of the kind happened. And yet the situation was one which might very well have caused a jealous woman to fly out, for the lady, who was none other than the Drury Lane actress, was sitting in a chair, and Jack was standing over her. She was looking up at him, with her merry, laughing eyes, her hair curled over her forehead, and her face as if it were always and naturally bright and joyous (this thing one constantly sees in women who play upon the stage, though I know not why they should be happier than other folk). Her hood, in which she had been wrapped, and her domino lay upon the table, and she was dressed most daintily in some flowered silk, with laced petticoat and kid gloves. Now, like a true woman, Bess no sooner saw this finely dressed lady than she began to think with shame of her own common frock, her hair so rough, and her coarse hands, and to wish that she had put on her best before she left home. I know not what they were talking about, but though the lady was merry, Jack was serious; to be sure, he never passed jests with women, and was not even as a boy over-fond of laughing with girls; perhaps—some philosopher hath remarked—women like best the men who treat them seriously, and as if every interview with them gave birth to what the French call a grand passion.

At sight, however, of Bess, as she stood in the open doorway, Jack started and stepped forward as if to protect his visitor, with a round quarter-deck oath.

"Oh, my poor ears!" cried the actress; "are we on board
ship already?"

Then she marked the face of the woman at the open door,
and there was something in her eyes and attitude which made
her silent. There is a kind of despair which makes itself felt
even by the lightest. This woman she saw had a pale face and
large black eyes, which were fixed steadfastly and piteously
upon the captain.

"Why do you come here?" asked Jack.

"I came to see you. Oh, Jack!" she gasped, and caught at
her heart.

"I have sent you an answer already."

"I have come to hear your answer from your own lips," she
replied, with trembling voice.

"Come, Bess," he said, coldly, but not unkindly, "you are
a foolish girl; the past is gone. We cannot bring back again
what has been. Forget it—and me. And go away. This is
no place for you."

"Forget it? You think I can forget? Have you forgotten,
Jack; tell me, have you forgotten?" she clasped her hands, and
threw them out in a gesture of pain and trouble. "Oh! have
you forgotten—you?"

"I have quite forgotten," he replied. "Everything has clean
gone out of my mind;" but of course his very words betrayed
his memory. "Of course I remember who you are. Your
father taught me arithmetic and writing. You are Bess Westmoreland. We used to play together when we were children.
Then I went away to sea, and I remember nothing more."

"Nothing more," she murmured. "Oh! he remembers nothing more. Oh! is it possible? Can he forget?"

The actress looked on with grave attention. She could read
the story without being told. Partly she was studying a delin-
eation of the passion of disappointed love, rendered better than
anything she had ever seen upon the stage; partly she was filled
with pity. An ordinary gentlewoman would have felt, as Castilla feels, that such a girl has no business to suppose that a
gentleman can love her, the thing being, in her opinion, con-

trary to nature. But the actress knew better. Besides, she
understood that beauty is not altogether a matter of dress. A
woman who is always dressing up in different fashions knows
that very well.

"If you wish," Jack went on, "I will tell you something
more that I remember. But you had better not ask me to tell
you that. Best to go away now, and before harder things are
said."

"There can be no harder things said. Tell me what you
please."

"I remember a young girl and a boy. The boy had been
six years at sea and among savages, and knew not one woman
from another. So he thought he was in love with the girl, who
was no proper match for him. And when he had been at sea
again for six weeks, of course he had clean forgotten her."

"And now you have returned, Jack"—she dragged off her
hat, and her beautiful black hair fell in long curls upon her
shoulders—"look upon me. Am I less beautiful than I was?
You, woman"—she turned fiercely upon the actress—"tell me,
you, are you in love with him? No: I see it in your eyes; you
do not love him. Then you will speak the truth, and perhaps
you will pity me. Tell me, then, am I beautiful?"

"You are a very beautiful girl indeed," said the Queen of
Drury Lane. "Upon the boards you would be a dangerous
rival. Your hair and eyes are splendid; your shape is faultless.
Unfortunately, you have not learned to dress."

"You hear, Jack, what this lady, who is not in love with you,
says of me. I have learned things, too, since you went away.
I am no longer so plain and rustic, and— Oh, Jack!" She
threw herself at his feet, regardless of the other woman. She
must have known that it was a useless humiliation, yet perhaps
she was resolved to drink the cup to the dregs. "Jack, look
upon my name printed upon thy arm; think of my hair tied
about thy wrist; think of all thy promises. Jack, think of
everything. Oh, Jack, be not so cruel!"

Alas! his face was hard and cruel. As she held up her arms
in this humility, he made as if he would push her from him,
and in his eyes, once so soft to her and full of love, she read
now scorn and loathing.

"Go!" he said. "You have had my answer."

Then she rose meekly, and drew from her pocket certain presents he had given her—a necklace of red coral, a packet of ribbons, a roll of lace, the gloves, a broken sixpence—and laid them on the table.

"You shall have again," she said, "all that you have ever given me, except one thing. I keep your letter and your promise. That I will never give you back so long as I live. I know not yet what I shall do. I know not—" She grew giddy, and looked as if she would fall, but presently recovered, and without another word she left the room.

"Are there many such girls in love with you, Captain Easterbrook?" asked the actress. There were tears in her eyes, but she put up her handkerchief. "Are there many such in the world, I wonder? They come not to this end of town. Do you write the names of all the women you love upon your arms? Then they will be a pretty sight for a jealous wife, Jack, when you marry."

"Let her go." He swept the poor trifles, mementoes of bygone love, upon the floor. "Let us talk of something else."

"She is a very beautiful woman," the actress continued, disregarding his words. "There is no woman now upon the boards who would better become the part of a queen, and most certainly none who could better act the part she has just played. 'Twas a moving situation, captain, though it moved you not. I wonder how many women's hearts thou hast broken, Jack?"

"Why, if we come to questions, I wonder how many men would like to make love to you, fair lady?"

"Captain Easterbrook, it cannot escape your penetration that there is not a pretty woman in the world to whom all men would not willingly make love, if they could. As for constancy, they laugh at it, and promises they despise; they trample upon the hearts of the foolish women who love them, and they consider jealousy in a woman a thing past comprehension." She laughed, but her eyes were not so merry as when Bess opened the door. "Well, I am resolved not to have my heart broken, because I have but one, and if it chance to be broken, I doubt if I could piece it together again. Therefore, my gallant captain, my brave Jack, I doubt whether it were wise of me to come here any more. You may, if you please, come to my suppers, to meet my lord and his friends. Look not so glum, captain. Well, perhaps I may see thee once more before thy ship sails. If I do, promise to pretend a little love for this unhappy lovesick nymph. She is a sea-nymph, I take it—one of those whom the poets call naiads. Comfort her poor heart a little, and perhaps when thou art gone she may very likely console herself. Alas! always one loves and one is loved."

" I loved her once. Can she expect—"

" Women are such fond creatures, Captain Easterbrook, that they are not even contented to be a toy for a month or two. As for me, I make men my toys, and as for my heart, it is still mine own. Adieu, thou conqueror of women's hearts and compeller of women's tears. But, Jack "—she laid her hand upon his arm—" look that this poor distracted creature doth not do a mischief to thee or to some one. There was madness in her eyes. I now know how the passion of jealousy should be rendered. It is to stand so, and to look so, and thus to use the hands." She lost her own face, and became Bess, so clever was she at impersonation, and in dumb-show went through the pantomime of a scorned and jealous woman. Then she put on her domino, took her hood, and ran down-stairs.

CHAPTER XXXIV.

HOW CASTILLA WAS BETROTHED.

I do not think there is anything in this history more distasteful to Castilla than a certain episode in it, which one cannot choose but narrate. To omit the incident would be the concealment of a thing which clearly shows the disposition of our hero at this juncture of his affairs, when all seemed prosperous with him, but when his fate was already sealed, and destruction about to fall upon him.

Castilla reproaches me with concealing from the admiral and her mother first the previous engagement with Bess, and next the acquaintance of the captain with the actress of whom mention has been made, and declares that if the admiral had known it he would have forbidden the house to so gay a Lothario. Castilla's general opinion as to her father's character is doubtless correct; but as to her father's conduct, under certain circumstances, I prefer my own judgment. Certain I am that if the admiral (now in Abraham's bosom) had known both these facts—indeed, I am sure that he knew a good deal of the first— he would not on that account have shut Jack out of the house, nor would he have forbidden him to pay his addresses to Castilla.

"As for me," she still says, indignant, even after so many years, "had I suspected the things which you very well knew at the time, sir, I should have spurned his proposals. I have now forgiven him, because, poor boy, he was punished for his weakness in the matter of that witch and her adviser, the apothecary, whom I believe to have been sold to the devil. I forgive him freely, and you know, Luke, that I have long since forgiven you for your part in the deception. But there are things which can never be forgotten, though they be forgiven."

As for my own conduct in the business, I know not why I should have told the admiral, or Castilla either, that a celebrated actress and toast had been rescued from footpads by Jack Easterbrook; that he supped at her house in company with other gentlemen; and that she visited him twice, to my knowledge, in his own lodging, the first time in order to communicate to him the news of his promotion, and the second time—I know not why. I was not a spy upon Jack, and on reflection I think that if the thing had to be done again I should behave exactly in the same manner.

Nor do I know why I should have warned Castilla about the old love affair. It was over and finished. Surely a woman would not be jealous because a lad of nineteen had made an imprudent promise, which he afterwards broke, or because he then fell in love with, and afterwards ceased to love, a certain girl, whether below or above his own rank in life. To be sure, I was certain that some trouble would happen, though of what nature I knew not.

Suffice it to say, therefore, that I heard no more about the actress, but that Jack came often, in those weeks between his appointment and his sailing orders, to the admiral's, and that he made no secret to me of his passion for Castilla. Also he took the ladies to various fashionable places of resort which they had never before seen, because there was no one to take them. Thus, we went one evening to Ranelagh, where there was a very pretty concert in the round room, with dancing afterwards, and a great crowd of ladies beautifully dressed, though none prettier than Castilla, to my simple taste. And on another evening we went to Drury Lane, where the actress, Jack's friend, was playing the principal part; and a more merry, light-hearted creature one never beheld upon the stage. I observed that Jack showed no sign of any acquaintance with her, but discussed her performance as a stranger might be expected to do, calling her pretty well as to looks, but then she was painted up; while as for beauty, give him blue eyes and light hair, at which Castilla blushed. And so home by moonlight, when the watermen are mostly gone to bed, and the river is comparatively quiet. Castilla sat beside Jack in the boat, and I believe he held her hand.

And on the day after the play the admiral was asked, and gave his consent to his daughter's engagement with Jack. He gave it with a livelier satisfaction, he said, than he had felt in any previous event of his life. "Castilla," he said, "this is the greatest day of thy life. For thou art promised to the most gallant officer in the king's navy. I say, to the bravest and the comeliest lad, and to the best heart, though he shirks the bottle and leaves me to finish it. If thou art not proud of him, thou art no daughter of mine."

"Indeed, sir," said Castilla, "I am very proud of him."

Jack threw his arms round her, and kissed her on both cheeks, and on the forehead, and on her lips.

I say no more. Castilla declares now that she never really loved him, though she confesses that she was carried away by so much passion and by her admiration of his bravery. Yet I know not. He was a masterful man, who compelled women to love him, and as the actress said, he had a conquering way with him. I think that if events had turned out otherwise, Castilla would have become a loving as well as an obedient wife. But let that pass. They were engaged, and the club at the Sir John Falstaff had a roaring night, in which Mr. Brinjes heartily joined, because at his age 'twould have been a sin to suffer the fear of approaching disaster to stand between himself and a night of punch and singing and the telling of sea stories.

CHAPTER XXXV.

HOW PHILADELPHY KEPT THE SECRET.

WHEN one reflects upon this time, and upon the conduct of Jack Easterbrook, it seems as if at each successive step the unfortunate man advanced one step nearer to his own destruction. Surely, knowing the grief, the resentment, and the indignation which filled the heart of the woman he had cast aside with no more consideration than if she had been a hedge-row weed, he might well have reflected before sending her intelligence which was certain to drive her into despair. But such as he do never reflect.

Therefore, on the very day when he was affianced to Castilla, he took the surest steps to make Bess acquainted with this certain proof of his desertion; for he led aside the old negro nurse, Philadelphy, and told her that he had a most important thing to communicate, and one which very much concerned her own happiness, and a thing which everybody would be anxious to know; but that it was a profound secret, and must be told to no one, and especially was not to be communicated to any person outside madam's household.

" I know," he said, " that you desire nothing in the world so much as the happiness of your young mistress."

That she assured him, truthfully, was the case.

" So that I am certain you will rejoice when I tell you the secret. Now, Philadelphy, what should you say if Miss Castilla had a lover ?"

" 'Pends on de young gen'leman, sah."

" So it does. You are always wise, Philadelphy. What should you say, then, if she was going to be married ?"

" 'Pends on de young gen'leman, sah."

" You are indeed a wonderful woman, Philadelphy. What should you think, then, if I were going to be that happiest of mortals, Miss Castilla's husband ?"

The old woman looked at him admiringly. Then she began to laugh. Negroes are easily tickled with laughter; they laugh if any one is hurt; they laugh if misfortunes fall upon their friends; and when they are pleased they laugh; Philadelphy therefore laughed for satisfaction and joy, not, as Sarai of old laughed, in derision.

"Is dat de troof, Massa Jack?"

"It is the truth, Philadelphy."

"Ho! ho!" she laughed again. "Berry fine lover for Miss Castil. Berry fine young man for my young mistress."

"It is a secret, Philadelphy," he told her again. "No one knows it except madam, and the admiral, and Castilla, and me. You have been told first of all. That is a great honor for you. But it is a secret as yet. I am to go on board in a few days, and the Lord knows when I shall return. So while I am away do you take care of her, and put in, every now and again, a word for me—you understand?"

She understood very well, and without the aid of the two guineas which he slipped into her hand, that she was to sing the praises of a certain young gentleman. She folded the money in a corner of her handkerchief, and nodded and laughed again. As a secret messenger, or go-between, I think Philadelphy would have had no equal. Her taste, as well as her genius, lay in this art; but unfortunately it was not called into practice, because Castilla had but two lovers, one of whom she lost in the manner you are going to hear, and the other she married without any necessity for a go-between at all.

"You understand," Jack repeated, "that it is a secret. You are not, therefore, on any account to tie up your head in your red turban and to carry the news into the town. You must not think of telling the old fellows at the Trinity Hospital. You must not go to Mr. Skipworth, the barber, with it; and if you tell Mr. Westmoreland, the penman, or his daughter Bess, you will make me angry. I quite depend upon your secrecy, Philadelphy."

The old woman nodded and laughed, and laughed again, promising that nothing should drag the secret from her. But when the captain left her, she hastened to tie her red handkerchief round her head, which was her way of preparing to sally forth from the house, and then she began to mutter with her lips. Next she sat down and laughed again. While she was laughing, two of her fellow black servants came upon her; and being of a quick and sympathetic mind, they sat down and laughed with her, all three rolling about, digging their hands into their sides, and laughing in each other's faces, while the tears ran down their cheeks. When they were quite tired of this exercise, they left off, and the two old men went away about their own business without so much as asking why she had set them off into this mirthful fit; and the old woman, setting her turban right, walked off slowly in the direction of the town.

She did, in fact, as Jack fully expected she would do, everything that she had been carefully told not to do. First, she looked into the gateway of Trinity Hospital. On the sunny side there walked half a dozen of the old men warming themselves. She exchanged a few words with them, admonishing them to keep the secret; then went on her way. Now there are no more ingrained gossips than these old almsmen, who have nothing to do all day long except to tell each other stories, for the most part old and well worn, and to retail news. Therefore, as soon as Philadelphy had gone, these veterans, one after the other, left the hospital and made their way, some to the Stairs, and some to the taverns in the town, and some to the dock-yard, spreading the news, for there was no officer in the king's navy better known than Captain Easterbrook, whom all regarded as a Deptford man, and greatly respected for his courage and his gallant bearing. Moreover, he had among them all the reputation of being a lucky officer. He had gone through so much danger, and hitherto had so miraculously escaped from every kind of peril, that he must needs be a lucky officer to sail with. And now he was going to take command on board as fine a frigate, the French-built *Calypso*, as there was afloat, and not a sailor but would have liked well to sail with him.

When she left the hospital, Philadelphy looked into the kitchen of St. Paul's Vicarage, just to whisper the news to the maids. Thence she went on her way to the barber's, and, calling Mr. Skipworth to the door, she imparted the news to him, with many injunctions to profound secrecy, which he faithfully and joyfully promised, and kept his promise in the way common among barbers, namely, that he passed on the news in strict confidence and a whisper to every customer in turn who came to be shaved.

Philadelphy next crossed the street and looked in at the penman's. Mr. Westmoreland was in the shop, writing a letter for one girl to her sweetheart, somewhere at sea, while another waited her turn. In the corner of the room, beside the fire, sat Bess, her hands folded in her lap, doing nothing, and paying no heed to what went on. The girls disputed what should be said; the scribe listened, and from time to time put down a sentence, catching at their meaning rather than taking down their words.

" Say I keep true and constant," said one, " though all the men in Deptford are asking me to give him up. Tell him that. Tell him I expect as much from him when he comes home— else, he shall see. And if he dare so much as to look at—"

" I wouldn't tell him that," said the other girl. " Tell him that nobody in the town cares a button for him, or even thinks about him, but yourself. He'll think all the more of you for that. Don't never let him think you care a rope's-end whether he goes after the other women or not."

Mr. Westmoreland went on writing while they talked. He civilized, so to speak, their letters for the ladies, taking out the threats, the ejaculations, the accusations, the protestations, and the profane words, whereby he certainly did much to strengthen and to sanctify the bond of affection between the sailor and his mistress, since a lover could not but be moved at receiving a letter so movingly and so religiously expressed. It must surely be a great thing for a man to think of his sweetheart as a quiet, sweet-tempered, and well-conducted woman (as always appeared from these letters), capable of expressing the finest sentiments in the choicest language, and full of gentle piety. Pity it was that when the men came home their mistresses should always fail to talk and to behave up to the standard of their letters!

Without troubling herself about the girls, Philadelphy took a chair beside Bess, and began to whisper. Now, so carefully had Bess kept her secret that no one in the place knew a word about it except Aaron Fletcher, and for reasons of his own he spoke of it to none. Least of all did this old negro woman suspect it. She whispered what she had to say, and then, with a hundred nods and winks, used as signs of mystery and secrecy, she got up and went away.

Bess sat still awhile. The two girls finished their business with her father, and went away. Mr. Westmoreland looked timidly at his daughter.

"Bess, my dear," he said.

She shook her head impatiently.

"Is there any chance that you will come round soon, my dear? I wouldn't hurry any woman's temper on my account, though I may say that it is a month and more since I have had any dinner."

"If I had a knife in my hand this moment," she cried, springing to her feet and tossing her arms in the air—"if I had a knife, I would drive it into my heart—or into his!"

Her father made haste with trembling knees to return to his writing.

That there are times when the Evil One is permitted to have power over us we are well assured, not only from Holy Writ, but from the teaching of learned doctors. I say not that we are to be excused from the consequence of sins committed during such times, because it is on account of our sins that they are permitted. This poor girl, I am very certain, was possessed by the demons of jealousy, rage, and despair. Else the great wickedness into which she now fell would never have been possible to her. Heaven forbid that I should attempt to excuse her! But this day she was mad. On this day, as you will presently confess, she must have been mad.

She continued to sit in the same place, hands clinched, with set eyes gazing straight before her, and cheeks white. From time to time her father looked furtively round. But seeing no change, he went on with his work. Presently he became afraid to sit alone with her. He thought she was mad; he feared that she might get up suddenly and stab herself to death, or perhaps stab him in the back. He was never a brave or a strong man, and, besides, he had already suffered so much from feminine wrath that he considered a raging woman worse than a tigress, and would cheerfully have fought a lion in the arena rather than face his own wife in one of her angry moods. But he had never before seen Bess so bad as this. It wanted a good hour of his usual time of leaving off work, but he got

14

down from his stool, changed his coat hurriedly, and went out to his tavern.

If he went there an hour before his usual time, it was fully an hour after his usual time that he returned. Bess was still in her chair, but she no longer sat upright, scowling and fierce. Her head was buried in her hands, and she was weeping.

Mr. Westmoreland was afraid to speak to her. He crept silently up-stairs, and went to bed supperless.

For in truth something very strange had happened between the time when the penman laid down his work and the time when he came home. The Jaws of Death and the Gates of Hell had been opened.

CHAPTER XXXVI.

HOW BESS WENT OUT OF HER WITS.

IMMEDIATELY after her father had left the house—perhaps he waited until the penman's departure—a man came to the door and stood without. For a few moments he watched and listened. Then he pushed the door open and looked in. The room was dark, and he could see nothing.

"Bess," he cried—it was Aaron Fletcher—"Bess, I know you are here, and it is no use hiding. Come out this instant and talk with me, or I will come in."

There was no answer, and he stepped into the room.

"You can go out again, Aaron," said Bess. "I have nothing to say to you."

"I will go out when I have said what I came to say, and not before," he replied. "If you will listen, Bess, I have a good deal to say."

"Say, then, what you have to say, and be gone." He hardly knew her voice, which was hard. "Of course I know very well what you have come to say. When you have said it once, you can go. If you dare to say it twice, I think I shall have to kill you. But before you take the trouble to say it, or anything else, I tell you that it is no use. There is no man in the world for me now. Don't think of trying."

"Bess"—the man understood what she meant—"d'ye think

that I would come to crow over your trouble? Why— But
you don't understand; you never did understand. A man as
loves you true can't choose but be sorry for your trouble. I
love you that true that I should even like to see you married
to him, if he would have you. But he won't—he won't. Don't
go to think now, Bess, that I'm glad; though I always knew
what would happen, and I hoped that you would perhaps throw
him over and take a better man, and then we might have seen
him crying and lamenting instead of you. Pluck up spirit,
Bess. Curse him. With his head in the air, and his step as
if he was on his quarter-deck, and us men were all his crew,
and you women were all for his own pleasure! Curse him, I
say, for a villain! He went through the town just now dressed
as if he was a nobleman at least, with the people crying after
him for luck, and the fools of women calling blessings on his
head for a handsome man, if ever there was one. Curse him!
Bess, why don't you curse the man who has played you false?
Hast never a tongue in thy head?"

It was too dark to discern her face; otherwise Aaron might
have been well pleased with the jealous madness which filled
her eyes.

Then he cursed the captain again, and with stronger words,
but she answered nothing.

"I knew what he would do. I always knew it. I hate him,
Bess. I have always hated him as much as you hate him now;
or almost as much, because you must hate him, after all he has
done, so that there is no evil you would not rejoice to see falling upon him."

He paused for some effect to be produced by his words, just
as an angler throws his line and stops to watch his float. But
Bess made no sign.

"Who is he?" Aaron went on. "Who is he that he should
have all the good luck and I should have the bad? Why, when
he came to the town he was in rags. I saw him come. He
was a boy in rags. And now he is a captain, with a gold-laced
hat; and I— Well, Bess, I am a bankrupt. That is what I
have come to. And it is through him! Yes, through him and
through that one-eyed devil, who is Old Nick himself, or sold
to him, I am a bankrupt—I am broke! First, through him, I
lost my boat, the *Willing Mind*, took by a privateer; and then,

through him, I lost the prize-money I looked to make; and then, through him, my building-yard was burned. And now I have spent all my money, Bess, and am broke. And all through him! I will be even with him, some day, if I swing for it."

" Say what you have to say, Aaron, and go away."

" I came to say, then, Bess "—he lowered his voice—" will you have revenge ?"

" What revenge ?"

" I tried to take it for myself three years ago. Did he never tell you who got him knocked o' the head and carried off to the crimps ? 'Twas the sweetest moment of my life when he lay senseless at my feet. I done it, Bess. 'Twas none but me. He got off that time. He won't this."

" Revenge ? Do you think I will let you take revenge for me ?"

" Bess — think! He hath deserted you, and broken his promise. And me he has brought to beggary, with the help of his friend the devil with one eye."

" I will have no revenge taken for me, I say. Go, Aaron. If that is all you have to say, go, and leave me alone. Revenge will not bring back his heart to me. He loathes me now as much as once he loved me. I saw it in his eyes. Will revenge change his eyes ? There is nothing for me but to bear it till I die."

Aaron sat down on the table. The tempter to evil was not to be sent away by a single word.

" What !" he asked. " A woman of spirit, and do nothing, though her sweetheart proves false to her, and mocks and laughs at her! Have they told you how he laughs everywhere about you ?" (This was a lie; Jack never spoke about her among his friends.) " Why, the gentlemen all do it; they make bets with each other about such girls as you; and then they go away and tell each other, and laugh about her. Oh, you forgive him! 'Tis sweet Christian conduct. I suppose I should forgive him as well for the loss of the *Willing Mind* and the burning of my boat-yard ?" He stopped to see if his words had produced any effect upon her, but she gave no sign. " You will dance at his wedding, I dare say. He is going to marry the daughter of the admiral—him with the wooden leg."

"He is not married yet."

"He is going to be married," said Aaron—but this was also a lie—"by special license, and without banns, to-morrow; for his ship is under orders, and the captain will set sail in a few days. He wants to be married before he goes. 'Tis a pretty little lady, and he will make her happy. They say he is head and ears in love with her, and nothing too good for her. I dare say he was always a fond lover. You found him a fond lover, didn't you, Bess, in the old days?"

"Are you sure?" she asked. "Oh! the old woman did not tell me this. Are you quite sure? To-morrow? He will marry her to-morrow? So soon! Oh! is there no hope left at all?"

"The negro woman went about the town to-day telling everybody. You can ask her if it is true. What do I know? The captain was not likely to tell me, was he? Well, Bess, it must be a pleasant thing for you to be thinking that his arms are now round her neck, which used to be round yours. He is kissing her red and white cheek now, just as he used to kiss yours, in the old days when he used to make a fool of you. And to-morrow he will be happy with his bride. That is something to make you feel forgiving and well-wishing, isn't it?"

"Oh! I shall go mad!" she cried. "I cannot bear it; I shall go mad."

"To be sure, there are differences. She is a gentlewoman, and you are only a tradesman's daughter. She is soft, and has pretty manners, I dare say, though her father is an old salt. Whatever you are, Bess, no one ever called you soft. She is fair, and you are dark. She loves him, I dare say, better than you ever could. She can wear a hoop, and carry a fan, and paint her face; and as for you, Bess— Why, what is the matter?"

"I will kill him first!" she cried, wildly. "Aaron, I will kill him with my own hand!"

"Nay, Bess, why with your own hand, when there is mine ready for your service? And as for that, you are in such a rage that you would surely bungle it; ten chances to one you would botch and bungle it. Now I am calm. If I take it in hand, I shall make as pretty a job of it as any one can desire. Besides, Bess, if any one is to swing for putting such a villain

out of the way, it shall be me, not you, my girl. For love of
you, and hate of him, I should be content to swing. But maybe— Why, Bess—"

"Aaron" (she laid her hand upon his shoulder, catching her
breath short), "oh! I would rather see him dead and in his
grave than let him marry her."

"He must be dead to-night, then, or he will marry her to-
morrow. Hark ye, Bess: the time has gone for crying. We
must do it at once—this very night. To-morrow he will be
married. The next day, or the day after, he takes the command of his ship. This very evening he hath gone to the club
with the admiral. He will but drink a single glass of punch
with the gentlemen, who will wish him joy, and will then return to his new mistress, with whom he thinks to spend the
evening, kissing and making love. Do you mark my words ?"

"Yes—yes—I am listening."

"In half an hour or so he will be returning by this road.
Suppose, Bess, he should meet us on the way—the woman he
has deserted, and the man he has ruined ?"

"Let us go," she cried; "let us go at once. He shall never
marry her. Let us go! Why, Aaron, are you for hanging
back ?"

"There is time enough—no hurry. See, my girl, I have
brought with me—'tis all I have left of my privateering—a
pair of ship's pistols." He lugged them out of his pockets,
and laid one on each leg, still sitting on the table. "They are
loaded; I loaded them half an hour ago—a brace of bullets in
each, and the flints are new. No hurry, Bess. Let us consider." She was already more than half mad, but he thought
to madden her still more. "Let us consider. All the world
knows thy history, Bess." This too was a lie, because no one
knew it. "When you go forth again the women will point
and say after you, 'There goes the girl who thought to marry
the handsome captain! There goes Bess, who thought to be
the wife of Captain Easterbrook! Pride goes before a fall.
Now she will have to marry some honest tarpaulin, like the
rest, if any be found to have her.' 'Tis a hard fate, Bess.
Whereas—"

"Aaron, let us go. Quick! quick! Give me the pistols."

"Nay, nay. You to have the pistols!" he replied, in no

hurry, and still trying to madden her. "Whereas, if we take care that he shall marry no one, they cannot cry out after you, and he shall not have another wife."

"I would rather he were dead," she said. "Aaron, let me kill him with my own hand!"

"Will you come for me?"—he put up his pistols—"or will you stay with me? 'Tis but five minutes' walk to the dark place in the road where we stopped him once before. But come with me. If you stay here, you will know nothing till I come back, when the job is done. If you come with me, you shall see it done. Why, your revenge will be doubled if you stand by and see it done. And when he falls, Bess, cry out quick that it was thy doing. So in his last moments he shall feel that thou hast revenged thyself."

"Come—quick—before I repent. Let us kill him quickly. Oh, Aaron, I am all on fire. I burn. Come."

Aaron nodded his head, and leisurely rose, satisfied at length with the spirit of murder which he had called up. It made her pant and gasp and tear at his arm to drag him along.

"One word first," he said. "I am not going to do all this for nothing. When the job is done, Bess, you will marry me."

"Yes. You may.marry me, or you may murder me. I care nothing which. Oh, he shall never marry her—never! Come, Aaron, come. We shall be too late."

I say that she was mad. It could not be in any other mood but madness that Bess would become a murderess. Truly Aaron was a crafty and cunning man, thus to turn her thoughts to revenge, and to make a murder done for private wrongs— but did Jack set fire to his boat-yard, or take the *Willing Mind?*—seem as if it were a righteous act of retribution for her sake. Why could he not murder his enemy without dragging Bess into the crime with him? I know not; but I suppose that he thought to bind her to him by the guilty secret which the two would have between them, as if the knowledge would not keep them apart: for, with such a secret, the whole breadth of the world should not be wide enough to keep the two asunder. But it is impossible so much as to guess at the secrets of Aaron's mind at such a moment. One thing is certain, that, like Bess, he was driven well-nigh desperate by his misfortunes, which, however, he was not justified in laying on the captain. Perhaps he had no thought at the time, except revenge, and no other desire than to gratify Bess—whom still, I believe, he loved, after his manner—and himself in the same manner and at a single blow.

"Come," he said.

Then he directed her to go on in advance, so that if any one should pass her on the road they might not connect him with her as a companion, and ordered her to wait for him in that place where the grass strip broadened into a little road-side green planted full of trees. Here she was to await him.

'Twas the same place where, three years before, Aaron had made his first attempt, the failure of which might have deterred him, one would think. But it did not. Here he presently joined the girl.

"No one is abroad," he said. "I have passed none upon the road. That is well. Heart up, Bess. In a few minutes thou shalt be happy, if revenge can make thee happy. He will kiss his fine mistress no more."

"Happy! There is no more happiness for me. Oh, Aaron, quick!—do what thou hast to do quick, lest I repent and stop thee. Oh, Jack—my Jack!—must I murder thee?"

"Keep dark," said Aaron. "Why, you are losing heart already. I am sorry you came with me. Keep dark, I say, and look not forth until the shot is fired. As for me, I scorn to hide. I am here to kill him if I can, or let him, if he can, kill me. He has a sword, and I have my pistols. Let him fight it out. It is a fair battle between us. But keep back, Bess, and keep dark. I think I can hear his footstep."

When, three years before, Jack Easterbrook had walked along the same road at the same time, his head was full of love for the very woman who now stood in the shade of the trees waiting to see him done to death. From the madness of jealous women, good Lord, deliver the men! And from the inconstancy of perjured lovers, good Lord, deliver the women!

As she stood and listened, the sound of his footstep—she could not be mistaken in the step—fell upon Bess's ear, and immediately the captain himself was to be plainly seen in the twilight walking briskly along the road. As for Aaron, in spite of his brave words, he kept in the shade of the trees, feeling, doubtless, as is the way with murderers, more confidence while in hiding than in the open.

Before she heard his footstep, the poor girl, the prey of all the evil passions, stood breathing quickly, her hands clinched, burning with rage, and mad for revenge. Yet mark what happened. At the very first footfall, at the first sound of the step which still she loved, the whole of her madness fell from her as a woman's cloak may fall from her shoulders; her heart stood still, her knees trembled, and her love went out again to him. Also she saw—now was not this a thought sent to her direct from Heaven's throne of Mercy in order to save a poor sinner from a dreadful crime?—she saw, I say, in imagination, her lover lying dead upon the ground, his pale face turned up to the stars, never to come back to life again, and she herself standing over him—who had murdered him. Already she felt upon her forehead the seal of murder as it was placed upon the front of Cain. Already she felt the terrible remorse of murder. Near every crime can be atoned for, except murder. You may rob a man; you may slander him; things stolen may be replaced; things said may be withdrawn; but his life you cannot restore to a man. Therefore there is no crime so dreadful as murder, and no remorse so fearful as that of a murderer, even when his conscience is as hardened as that of Aaron Fletcher himself. "Oh!" Bess told me afterwards, though the poor girl knew not how to put all these her thoughts into words, but could only speak of them brokenly, "I thought that if he were to die, I must die too, and that with no hope of forgiveness, so that I should never sit beside him in heaven, and never ask his mercy. And I saw that if he would leave me, he must; and oh! how could I be so wicked? How could I? No; it was not Aaron's fault; 'twas my own mad, jealous heart."

There wanted but a moment when Aaron would have stepped out and discharged his pistols. There was no relenting in him; he had no qualms of conscience and no forebodings of remorse. He had lost everything—his sweetheart, his boat, his business, his fortune—by this man, he thought; 'twas little revenge indeed in return for so much injury, to kill him. Perhaps afterwards, with the gibbet in sight and the irons on his legs, he might have felt remorse. But one doubts, seeing how hard-

14*

ened are most of the villains who go forth to Tyburn to the
fatal tree, and how little true repentance the ordinary doth witness.

He was waiting, then, the pistol cocked.   His enemy was almost within his reach, when Bess rushed out from her hiding-
place, crying, "Jack! Jack! Save yourself! Save yourself!"

He stopped and drew his sword.

"Fly," she cried.   "Aaron is among the trees with his pistols.   We came to murder thee.   Oh! fly for thy life.   Let
him kill me instead.   He shall shoot at thee through my
body."

She stood before him, her arms out as if to stop the pistol
bullet.

"Stand aside, Bess," said Jack.   "Now, Aaron, ye cowardly,
skulking dog, come out!   Show yourself, man!   Bring out
your pistols, I say!   Come, ye sneaking, murdering villain!"

Aaron might have shot him on the spot where he stood,
breast bared, so to speak, for the pistol.   But he did not, because so great is the power of authority over such men as
Aaron, when one speaks who is in the habit of command, that
he obeyed and came forth meekly, his pistols in his hand, like
a dog who comes at call to be whipped.

"Lay down your weapons," said Jack, sword in hand.

Aaron obeyed, saying nothing.

"So," said the captain, "this is now the second time that
thou hast attempted my life.   Man, if I had thee on board my
ship I would keel-haul thee, or maybe hang thee for mutiny.
Know, sirrah, that the mere conspiring to murder hath brought
many a poor rogue to the gallows.   Now I know not wherefore
thou didst resolve to make this second attempt.   Remember,
however, that the first score is not yet paid off.   Yet I heard
some talk of losses and the burning of boat-yards, whereby it
seems as if some greater Power had interfered to punish thee.
Go now.   Perhaps to-morrow I shall determine what further may
be done."

Aaron obeyed, walking away slowly and sullenly, the pistols
lying on the ground.

Then Jack turned to the girl who had saved his life.   "So,
Bess," he said, "you came out to murder me, did you?"

"Yes," she confessed.

"She stood before him, her arms out as if to stop the pistol bullet."

"I was in hopes that you had laid my words to heart, and had forgotten the past."

"I can never forget the past. Oh, Jack! 'tis too much to ask of any poor woman. 'Tis too much!" She burst into weeping. "Oh! I am an unhappy wretch, who would even murder the man I love better than all the world."

"Nay," said Jack, "there is no harm done, because, d'ye see, I am unhurt, and you changed your intention in time. If I did not know thee better, Bess, I might think this was a trick of thine. But Aaron hates me of old; and you—since I came home."

"I have never hated you, Jack. God knows I wish I was dead, and out of your way."

"My poor girl, you are already out of my way, if you would only think so. For the sake of a few love-passages, three years ago, why waste and spoil your life?"

"I cannot take back what I have given. To-night they told me that you are to marry Miss Castilla. That made me mad. But I am not mad any longer. Go to your new mistress, Jack. I will give you no more trouble—no more trouble. Make love to her as you did to me. Tear her heart out of her as you tore mine. I will give you no trouble at all—no trouble at all. I will not try to stand between her and you."

"Foolish girl! Forget me, Bess, and find another lover."

"I have tried to curse thee, Jack, but I cannot. Oh, I cannot! I have tried a dozen times. My lips will not form the words, nor would my heart mean them if I could say those words. I have tried this night to kill thee. But I could not. Therefore it is certain that I am not to do thee any harm. This is better, because, whatever happens, thy heart will not be thereby the more hardened against me."

Jack made no reply. Perhaps he was touched by what she said.

"Go, Jack. Go to thy mistress." This she said, not rudely or scornfully, but quietly. "Jack, I know now what has been lying in my mind. It is that I have a message for thee. It is that God HIMSELF will punish thee, and that in the way that will touch thee the deepest. I know not how that will be, and for myself I desire no harm for thee. I will henceforth neither speak nor think hard things of thee. But remember: no other

man shall ever kiss me, because I am thine, Jack—I belong to
thee.   Oh, Jack, my sweetheart, my love, God HIMSELF will
punish thee, unhappy boy, and that in the way that will most
touch thee."

Jack laughed lightly—yes, he laughed—and went his way.

This is what happened between the time when the penman
left his daughter and the time when he returned.   Said I not
that the Jaws of Death and the Gates of Hell were opened on
this night?

CHAPTER XXXVII.

HOW BESS RECOVERED HER SENSES.

WOMAN is a variable and a changeable creature.   Many poets
and philosophers have insisted upon this maxim.   Mr. Westmoreland, as well as Socrates, had good reason to feel the truth of
it, and could testify to it from his own experience, under the rule
of wife first, and of daughter afterwards; though the capricious
nature of the latter empress was a kind of heaven compared
with the clapper-clawings, rubs, and buffets which marked the
reign of the former.   The next morning the penman came down-
stairs meekly resigned to do the daily necessary housework,
which his daughter should have done—namely, to lay his desk
in order for the day's work, find something for breakfast, and,
towards the hour of noon, interrupt his calculations in order to
prepare dinner of some kind; which had been his lot for the
last two months; in fact, though he had not the wit to connect
the two events, ever since the return of the lieutenant on board
the French prize.   He was therefore truly astonished when he
saw that the room was already swept clean and tidy, a coal fire
lit, for the autumn morning was cold, and his breakfast set out
upon the table, just as he loved to have his food, ready to his
hand, without any thought or trouble about it, both plenty as
regards quantity, and pleasing as regards quality.   More than
this, his daughter Bess was busy with a duster among his papers—no one but Bess knew how to take up a sheet of paper, dust
the desk about and under it, and lay it down again in its place.

She wore a white apron, her sleeves were turned up above her elbows, and she was going about her work steadily and quietly, as if nothing at all had happened. More, again, when she saw her father, she smiled and saluted him. Now she had not smiled or said a single gracious thing to him for two months and more.

"Come, father," she said, "take your breakfast while the beer is fresh and hath still a head. The cask is well-nigh out, and I must have another brew. The knuckle of pork has got some good cuts left yet; as for the bread, it is dry, because it is baker's bread, and last week's baking. But to-morrow you shall have some new homemade."

This was a very strange and remarkable change. Nothing at all had happened to make her happier. On the contrary, her lover was certainly going to marry Castilla, and he was going away: her affairs were as hopeless as they could well be. Yet now her soul was calm! It may be that one cannot go on for-ever at a white heat of wrath; but some have been known to brood over their wrongs all the days of their lives. Her soul was calm. That was the change which had fallen upon her. Her eyes were no longer fierce, and her cheek was no more alternately flaming red and deathly white. Nor did her lips move continually as if she were vehemently reproaching some one. She told me afterwards, speaking humbly and meekly, that when she had tried to curse her unfaithful lover, her lips re-fused; and when she had tried to murder him—her heart failing her at the last—the words that she said to him, namely, that she would seek no more to harm him, and would think no more of him with bitterness, feeling assured that God would bring the thing home to him in such a way as would touch him most surely, these words seemed as if they were whispered in her ears or put into her mouth; and then suddenly, as she uttered them, all the rage and madness which had torn her for two months left her, and peace fell upon her heart. Those who please may put upon this confession any other meaning; for my own part, I can see but one. What that interpretation is I leave to the reader.

Mr. Westmoreland, however, when he observed this change, fell to shaking and shivering, betraying in his looks the most vivid apprehensions. The reason of this phenomenon was that in the old days before his wife ran away from him—Bess during the last two months had in other respects greatly resembled her mother as to temper—whenever a domestic storm of greater fury than usual was brewing, it was always preceded by a period of unusual activity in the house, with a strange and unnatural zeal for cleanliness and tidiness. The memory of this fact, and of the terrible storms which afterwards used to break over the poor penman's head, caused this awakening of terror. Was Bess in this respect also going to take after her mother?

"Child," he stammered, "what—what—what in Heaven's name hath happened to thee? Have I wronged thee in any way? Tell me, Bess, only tell me, what have I done to thee?"

"Why, father, nothing. I have been ill lately. Now I am better. Sit down and take your breakfast. For dinner you shall have something better than cold knuckle of pork."

He obeyed wondering and distrustful.

"I've been ill of late, father," she repeated; "and you've been neglected and uncomfortable. It's my fault that the room was this morning up to my ankles in dust and dirt. But I've been very ill, and couldn't do anything but think of the pains in my head."

"Well, Bess," he replied, rallying a little, "to be sure you've been a bit—so to speak—haughty for the last two months. It came on, I remember, about the time when the lieutenant came home."

"It was about that time, father. Two months ago I first began to have these dreadful pains in the head."

"If it was toothache, you should have gone to Mr. Brinjes and had it out. If it was tic, there's nothing to help it but a charm. But why not ask Mr. Brinjes to charm it away?"

"It was not the toothache. I dare say it was tic. But now it has almost gone."

"Was it, Bess—was it"—he dropped his voice—"was it anything to do with Aaron Fletcher? Sometimes I've thought there might have been a love disappointment. Was it Aaron Fletcher?"

"Aaron Fletcher is nothing to me, and never will be."

"Well, I'm glad to hear that, Bess, because Aaron is a bad man—a man of violence; a crafty man, my dear; a headstrong man; a man without virtue or religion; and an unforgiving man as well. I've watched Aaron, man and boy, since he was born. Aaron will end badly. Of late he has been drinking, and his business is broken up. Aaron will come to a bad end."

"Well, that's enough said about me, father. Go on with the cold knuckle."

"And now shall I hear thee singing about thy work again, Bess? and laughing again, just as before? It does my old heart good to hear thee sing and laugh. Nay, that doth never put me out, though I be struggling with the sine and tangent, and even with the versed sine. 'Tis when I hear thee weep and groan, and when to all my questions I get no answer, and when thine eyes are red and thy cheek pale, and when all day long I see thee sitting neglectful and careless—'tis then, my dear, that the figures swim before my eyes and the result comes all wrong. 'Tis then that if I try to write, my flourishes are shaky, and the finials lack firmness."

"Nay, father," she replied, "I fear I shall not laugh and sing again all my life. The kind of tic which I have had takes away the power of laughing and the desire for singing. But I hope never again to be so troubled."

"Alas!" said her father, "I would I were a preacher, so that I could exhort women to good temper. Sometimes when the learned and pious vicar is expounding the wisdom of the Chaldees —which is, no doubt, a most useful subject for the Church to consider—I venture to think that a word might be spared on the sins of temper and on the hasty tongue and the striking hand. Truly, for my own part, in all things but one have I been singularly blessed, yea, above my fellow-creatures. For I have a house convenient and weather-tight; I belong to the one true Church, being neither a Papist nor a Schismatic; I am assured of my salvation, through no merits of mine own; I am not of lofty station, but obscure, yet not of the vilest herd; I live sufficiently, and, when my daughter pleases to exercise her skill of housewifery, with toothsomeness; no man envies me, and I have no enemies; 'tis true my shoulders are round and I am weak of arm; but what of that? To crown all, I have been endowed by beneficent Providence with the love of divine mathematics and the gift of fine penmanship, so that in my work, whether I copy, or engross, or write letters, or work out logarithms, or consider the theses, lemmas, corollaries, problems, and curious questions advanced by ingenious professors of the exact sciences, I live all day long in continual happiness. I would not change my lot for any other, save and except for one thing. I am filled with pride, which I hope is not sinful, because it is in gratitude for the gifts of Heaven. But there is one thing, my child. I have wanted no blessing in this life, which to many of my fellow-creatures is, for no seeming fault of theirs, a vale of misery and tears. But, alas! I still found my comfort spoiled by the temper of thy mother while she remained with me. And I feared, Bess—I say that I feared lest thou might also take after her, and so the scoldings, the peevishness, the discontent, and the violence might begin again. I am not so young as I was then, and I doubt whether I could endure that misery again."

"Fear nothing, father. Why, whenever did I ask or do aught to make you think that I should upbraid you? As for my temper, I will try to govern myself. Fear nothing, father. To-day you shall have as good a dinner as you can desire, to make up for the past shortcomings. What will you have?" She spoke so gently and softly that her father was quite re-assured, and plucked up his courage.

"Well, child, since thou art in so happy a disposition—Lord grant that it continue!—I would choose, if I may, a hodge-podge, with an onion-pie. They are the two things, as thou knowest well, which most I love. With hodgepodge, onion-pie, and a merry heart, a man may make continual feast."

It was not a merry heart that returned to poor Bess, but it was the outward seeming or show of cheerfulness which not only returned, but remained with her, so that she now listened to her father's garrulous prattle with apparent interest, and gratified his love of good feeding by toothsome dishes, of which there was no more notable compounder than herself. This day especially she regaled him with a most excellent hodgepodge, in itself a dish fit for a king, and also with an onion-pie—a thing counted dainty by those of a strong digestion, though to some who have a delicate stomach it may be thought of too coarse a flavor, being composed of potatoes, onions, apples, and eggs, disposed in layers in a deep pie-dish, and covered over with a light crust of flour and suet.

While Bess was engaged in the preparation of this banquet

THE WORLD WENT VERY WELL THEN.

the barber came running across the road, as was his wont when
the morning business was completed, and he had any news of
importance to communicate. For the spread of news at Deptford is in this way: first it is whispered at the barber's shop;
then it is whispered by the barber to his customers and his
cronies; and next it is carried by them in all directions around
the town.

"Have you heard the news, friend Westmoreland?" he
asked, with the air of one who is the possessor of an important
secret.

"Why," Mr. Westmoreland replied, "since I have not seen
you before this morning, gossip, how should I hear any news?"

"You will be astonished," said the barber. "Those who
hold their heads the highest fall the soonest. One whom you
know well, friend, and have known long, is broke. Ay, you
may well look surprised and ask who it is. He is broke who
but a short time ago was master of a thriving business, and
seemed as if he would save money."

"Who is it, then?"

"I have myself suspected a great while what would happen.
For, thank Heaven! I can see as far as most men, and can put
two and two together, and am no babbler of secrets, but keep
them to myself, or talk of them with my friends over a pipe of
tobacco and a glass, being a discreet person. Wherefore, when
I heard of certain accidents, and saw in what a spirit they were
received, I made up my mind what would happen."

"Who is it?" asked Mr. Westmoreland, when this garrulous
person had partly talked himself out of breath.

"It is a man whom you know well; and Bess here knows
him very well too."

"If, Mr. Skipworth," said Bess, "you would tell my father
your news, we could then talk about it afterwards."

"Why, then, Aaron Fletcher is broke. That is the first
news. Since the burning of his yard he hath done no work.
not even to putting up some shed and carrying on the business. What were we to think of that? When he went privateering he made but little prize-money, but had quickly to
come home again. Therefore he hath been living on his stock,
and hath now come to an end, and is broke. This morning he
was to have been arrested. The writs are out for him, and the

officers came to seek him, with intent to take him to the Marshalsea, where his case would have been tried at the Palace
Court.''

"Would have been tried?" asked the penman. "Is it not
to be tried, then?"

"I said *would*, because for one thing which his creditors
thought not of—he hath escaped them. Otherwise he would
have languished in jail until his death."

Here the barber wanted to be asked further what was that
happy incident which enabled Aaron to scape prison; for one
who is a retailer of news loves not to expend it all at a breath,
but must still keep some back.

"His father," he continued, "was a substantial man, and
saved money, which the son has spent. He inherited, besides
the building yard, a good business, and a fast smack, the *Willing Mind*, for his trade across the Channel. Now the smack is
lost, the yard is burned, the business is ruined, and the money
is spent."

"An idle fellow," said Mr. Westmoreland; "a fellow who
loved not work. But how hath he escaped his creditors?"

"He will not go to prison; for in the night, we now learn
from certain authority, he walked over to Woolwich, where he
hath enlisted in the marines, and so is beyond the reach of his
creditors, who cannot now arrest him. So he escapes the prison, and exchanges the Marshalsea for a man-o'-war. Maybe
'tis better to be killed by a cannon-shot than to be starved in a
debtor's jail."

So, after more reflections on the folly of young men, and the
certain end of laziness and extravagance—which have been put
more concisely by King Solomon the Wise—the barber returned to his shop; and before noon every one in Deptford
had heard the surprising news of Aaron's fall.

This intelligence made Bess tremble, thinking on the madness of the last night, when this young man was so desperate,
being now assured that he was bankrupt, that he was ready to
commit a murder, caring little whether he was found out and
hanged or no; and she herself was so desperate in her wrath
and jealousy that she was ready to commit murder in order to
prevent another woman's happiness. Why, what would be the
condition of that guilty pair now were Jack lying dead? Since,

however, Aaron was bankrupt, it was now certain that he had already resolved to go away and enlist in the marines when he came to her and proposed the crime; and that he intended to leave the dreadful secret of the murder, had it been committed, to herself alone—a burden greater than she could bear.

For Aaron, 'twas the only way of escape, to 'list in one of his majesty's regiments. Naturally he chose the marines as the branch belonging to the sea. To carry a musket on board a king's ship, after being a lieutenant in a privateer, not to speak of commanding the *Willing Mind*, is to come down in the world, indeed. Yet that he cared for little, considering the alternative of a debtor's prison, terrible to all, but most terrible to a man who, like Aaron, had spent all his life in the open air; and most certainly it is better for the country that a stout and active fellow should be fighting her battles than that he should be laid by the heels in a prison doing nothing. Mark, however, what followed. Aaron walked to Woolwich that night; where there is a depot for marines, which in that war represented twenty-five companies. He enlisted in the morning. When they began to teach him his drill it was found that he already knew as much as was expected of any recruit when he is passed for service. Therefore he was, with others, marched to Chatham ready for embarkation. There are many remarkable coincidences in this history, but there is none more remarkable than the fact that Aaron should have been shipped as a marine on board the very ship, the *Calypso*, of which the man he had tried to murder was commander. This circumstance, with the consequences which followed, I can regard as nothing but providentially ordered.

When Aaron discovered who was the captain of the ship, he fell at first into despair, and was ready to throw himself overboard, looking for floggings continually and on the merest pretext, with keelhaulings and every kind of tyranny, oppression, and punishment. But he presently found that the captain took no kind of notice of him, even when he was on sentry duty on the quarter-deck, and seemed not even to know that he was on board.

CHAPTER XXXVIII.

HOW PHILADELPHY REFUSED A BRIBE.

WHEN Bess had given her father his hodgepodge and onion-pie, which he received as some compensation due to him for all past privations and recent neglect, she left him, and repaired to the apothecary's.

Mr. Brinjes was already wide-awake, and in earnest conversation with Philadelphy. On the table between them lay the famous skull-stick, object of the deepest veneration and awe to the negro woman.

"What will you do for me," he was saying, "if I give you this stick? I am old now, and I have no enemies to punish, nor many friends to protect, and I want nothing for myself except that which not even an Obeah man can procure for himself—his lost youth. What will you do for me, Philadelphy, if I give it to you?"

"Massa Brinjes"—she clutched at the stick, and held it in her arms, kissing the skull—horrid thing!—which grinned at Bess as if it were alive, "I will do everything. Ask me—tell me—I will do everything."

"We shall see. Those who possess this stick—it must be given, not stolen, or the virtue vanishes—can do whatever they please. Why, if it were your own, there would be no woman in the country so powerful as you. If you have enemies, you could put Obi on them, and go sit in the sun and watch them slowly dying. Ha! I have seen the wise women on the west coast sitting thus, and watching outside the hut wherein their enemy lay wasting away. And if you have friends, think of the good-fortune you could bring them. Why, Miss Castilla you could marry to a lord; not a beggarly ship captain, but a rich lord."

"No, no," said Philadelphy; "she shall marry Mas' Jack. No one like him."

"You could make her as rich as you could desire. If she wants children, you could send them to her. No need, then, to consult the cards or to watch the birds, because you could have everything your own way to command, once you got the skull-stick. As for wind and rain, you could call for them when you pleased. See "—he rose and looked up at the sky, which was covered with driving clouds, the wind being fresh— "see, you would like rain! 'Twould be good for madam's garden, would it not? I call for rain."

Strange! As he spoke, the drops pattered against the windows. Though 'twas a light and passing shower, yet it seemed to fall in reply to his call. He might have seen it on the point of falling, and prophesied after the event was decided. Truly Mr. Brinjes was crafty and subtle above all other men. But Philadelphy jumped and kissed the stick again. "You see, Philadelphy," he went on, "what you could do with this stick. It is wasted on me, because I am too old to want anything. I am past ninety, and you, I should think, are not much over seventy. If I die before I give the stick away, it is lost—its virtue is gone. But there is still time. What will you do for me if I give you the stick?" He paused and considered a little before he went on again. "Perhaps you think it will only compel rain, and is of no use as regards persons. Well, here is Bess to testify that I put Obi on Aaron Fletcher. He was formerly a thriving man until he offended me. What hath happened to him since? First, he was tortured with toothache; next, his smack was taken by French privateers; then he went privateering himself, and did no good; then his boat-building sheds were burned, with all his tools and timber; lastly, he went bankrupt, and hath now, I hear, enlisted in the marines to escape a prison. I have removed the Obi, and now leave him to his fate. What will you do for me if I give you the stick?"

Again the old woman clutched it and kissed it, with the unholy light of witchcraft in her eyes.

I wonder if the Sorceress of Endor had a skull-stick?

"Stop a moment, Philadelphy. What will you do for me?"

"Everything, Massa Brinjes. Nothing in the world that I will not do for you."

"There is only one thing that I cannot make my stick do for

me. Everything else in the world I can do. But this thing I cannot do, and you can."

Still clinging to the stick, the old woman implored him only to let her know what that was, in order that she might instantly go away and do it.

"Bess hath a sweetheart, and he hath proved a rover, as many sailors do. Bring him back to her arms and keep him constant, and I will bestow the stick upon thee."

"Nay," Bess cried, quickly. "Since my sweetheart loves me no longer, I will have no charms to make him. I have promised, besides, that I will trouble him no more."

"Tell me his name," cried the old woman, regardless of Bess. "Only tell me his name, and I will do it for her."

"Can you bewitch a man at sea?"

"I can, I can," she cried. "I will make his heart soft for her, so that he will forget every other woman, and want none but Bess. Why," she said, "every negro woman knows a love charm." This with some wonder that a wizard of Mr. Brinjes's power, and possessed of an Obeah stick, should not be able to do so simple a thing. "I can make him love her all the same as he loved her at first. I can make him love her so as he shall never love another woman. If that is all, Massa Brinjes, let me carry away the stick."

"Softly, softly. The thing is not done yet. If I give thee this stick I shall never get it back again. Wherefore let us have it paid for first."

"Tell me his name, then"—Philadelphy turned eagerly to Bess—"only tell me his name, girl, and I will make the charm to-day."

"Nay," Bess repeated, "I want no charm to bring him back."

"Be not so proud, Bess," said Mr. Brinjes; "you shall have what your friends can get you. As for you, Philadelphy, be not too ready. What? You think I would give such a stick for a trifle? You think Bess's lover is some common sea-swab, I dare say—a master's mate, at best, or a gunner, or perhaps a ship-wright. No, no; her lover is another guess kind, I promise you."

"If he was an admiral, he should come back to her. Tell me his name."

"Even if he were promised to marry your young mistress, Miss Castilla?"

A negro woman cannot turn pale, particularly one so black as Philadelphy, nor can her color come and go like that of a white woman; yet she changes color when she is moved. Philadelphy not only changed color, but she gasped, and looked upon Mr. Brinjes as one astonished and dismayed.

"To marry Miss Castilla?" she repeated.

"What if Bess's lover had deserted her for her young mistress?"

"Don't say that—oh, Massa Brinjes! I cooden do it—no —no—I could do anything else, but I cooden do it even for the stick."

"I say, Philadelphy, what if his name was Jack Easterbrook? Why, it is Jack. It is the captain who was Bess's lover. Where were your eyes not to discover that? You, a witch? Where were your eyes, I say?"

"I cooden do it—no—I cooden do it."

"Look at the stick again, old woman. Think of the joy of having the stick your own. Think of what you could do, with the stick to help you. What is the captain to you, compared with the possession of the stick?"

She looked at it with yearning eyes. Suppose that the thing which all your life you have been taught to regard as the symbol and proof of power was to be offered you at a price? This was the old negro woman's case; she could have the Obeah stick in return for—what?

"At the worst," said Mr. Brinjes, "it would make her unhappy for a week."

"No, no; Miss Castilla she set her heart upon the captain."

"Well," the tempter continued, "with the help of the stick you cannot only find a rich and noble lover for her, one who will make her happy, but you can also give her a charm, and make her forget the captain."

"No, no," said the old woman; "Miss Castilla will never forget the captain."

"Then, when his fancy returns to his old love, which it will do before long, your young mistress will be made unhappy. Come, Philadelphy, think of this stick; think of having it your own—the great Obeah stick."

"Who are you," she turned fiercely upon Bess, "to take away a young gentleman officer? Stay with your own people, and let the captain stay with his. Massa Brinjes, if I give you the secret to keep alive—ten, fifty, a hundred years if you like —will you give me the stick?"

"If you have that secret, old woman," said Mr. Brinjes, "I will tear it out of you if I have to rack every joint in your body with rheumatism. If you know that secret, it is as good as mine already. No, Philadelphy, it is the captain or nothing. Look at the stick again, Philadelphy. Take it in your hands."

"Oh, I will get the girl—what a fuss about a girl! as if she was a lady!—I will get her any other man in Deptford. Plenty handsome men in Deptford."

"I want none of her charms, Mr. Brinjes, for Jack or any one else," Bess said again. "Let her have the stick, if you like, and let her go."

"There!" Philadelphy cried, triumphantly. "You see? She wants none of my charms. Why, there, take the secret instead, and let me have the stick, and you shall live for a hundred years more."

Here one cannot but admire the way in which these two magicians believed each in the other's powers, but were uncertain about their own. For, first, if Mr. Brinjes by means of his skull-stick could draw down rain from the sky, why could he not move the captain's heart? And, next, if Philadelphy could turn a faithless lover back to his fidelity, why could she not so order Castilla's heart that she should resign the captain without a pang? But this she could not do. Yet the wizard believed in the witch, and the witch in the wizard.

"It must be Jack," said Mr. Brinjes, "or nothing."

"Then," she replied, sorrowfully, "it is nothing. Put away the stick, Mr. Brinjes, lest I die of longin', and let me go."

He replaced the stick in the corner. The skull grinned at the old woman as if in contempt because she had missed so magnificent an opportunity.

"Very well, Philadelphy," said Mr. Brinjes, returning to his pillows. "I do not believe you know any charm at all. You know nothing. You are only an ignorant old negro woman. In Jamaica they would laugh at you. You are not a wise woman. You only pretend to make charms. Why, anybody could make as good a charm as you."

She shook her head, but made no reply, still gazing at the stick.

"All your tricks are only pretence. You cannot, in reality, do anything. As for your cards, you cannot even tell a fortune properly. If you can, tell Bess hers."

Philadelphy drew from her pocket a pack of cards, greasy and well worn, and began to shuffle them and to lay them out according to her so-called science. Bess, who would have no charms, could not resist the sight of the cards, and looked on anxiously while the old woman laid out her cards and muttered her conclusions.

"The dark woman is Bess," she said—"the fair woman is Miss Castilla—the King of Hearts is the captain. Oh! the dark woman wins!" She dashed the cards aside, and would go on no further, but with every sign of alarm and anxiety rose up, and, tightening her red turban, she hurried away.

"Always," said Bess, "she has told me the same fortune. Always the same. Yet I know not."

"These divinations by cards," said Mr. Brinjes, "are known by many women even in this country, where there is so little wisdom. I wonder if Philadelphy lied when she offered to sell me that secret. If I thought she had such a secret—but I doubt, else why doth she continue so old and grow so infirm? No, she hath not that knowledge, which I must seek on the African coast. Bess, take courage. We will sail to that coast —you, Jack, and I; we will be all carried away together; and, first, I will find that secret, and, next, we will go forth to the Southern Seas, and there dig up the treasure of the great galleon."

She shook her head.

"As for me," she said, "there will be no sailing away, Jack, nor any happiness at all; and as for you, daddy, when you are carried away it will be with feet first."

"Perhaps! Yet I doubt! For I do continually dream of those seas, and clearly discern the ship, with myself upon the poop, and the island not far off, where at the foot of the palm-tree there lie the boxes. All shall be thine, Bess—to dispose of as thou wilt."

"Why," said Bess, simply, "what should I do with it but give it all to Jack?"

15

CHAPTER XXXIX.

HOW BAD NEWS CAME HOME.

NOTHING at all was heard of the *Calypso* for three or four months. It was not even known whither she had sailed, except that she was with Sir Edward Hawke's fleet. But it was known that M. Thurot had got out of Dunquerque with five frigates, on board of which were a large number of troops, with intent to make a descent upon Ireland, and we conjectured that perhaps the *Calypso* might have been ordered to join the squadron in chase of that gallant Frenchman. But that proved not to be the case.

It was in January—namely, on the evening of the 15th of January, in the year 1760—that the news arrived which filled the hearts of all with shame and confusion. 'Twas a wild and tempestuous night, fitting the nature of the intelligence which then arrived. The wind blew up the river in great gusts, and the rain drove slanting into the faces of those who were out. I remembered, afterwards, that I had met Philadelphy in the morning. The old woman was always full of omens and prognostications. Sometimes she had seen a ghost in the night— surely there was never a greater ghost-seer than this old negress—and sometimes she had been warned by one of the many signs which terrify the superstitious. "Hi! Massa Luke," she said, in her negro way, which it is unnecessary to imitate, "there's bad news coming, for sure. Last night the cock crowed twice at midnight, and an owl screeched round the chimney; there was a dog barking all night long, and I saw a ghost. There's bad news coming!" I asked her what the ghost was like, but she refused to tell me. Well, it is true that on many other occasions she foretold disaster (because to this kind of witch there are never any signs of good luck), and her prophecies proved naught. But on this day, alas! she proved a true prophetess of evil.

At the Sir John Falstaff some of the company, including Mr. Brinjes, who was never late, had already arrived, and were hanging up their hats, the candles being lit, a great coal fire burning, pipes laid on the table, and the chairs set.

"There hath arrived bad news," said Captain Petherick, the commissioner of the yard. "I heard talk of it at the navy house this morning. It is said that we have lost a frigate. They say also that we have lost her cowardly, a thing which one is not ready to believe. But I have not heard the particulars, and I know not the name of the craft. 'Tis pity, but 'tis true, that there should be found in every war cowardly commanders, in British as well as in French bottoms. Those of us who have memories can remember the last war, gentlemen. Well, we must quickly build or capture another ship, and find a better captain. We will give the command to Jack Easterbrook."

So saying, he sat down, and began to fill his pipe leisurely. Just as he had finished these words, and before Mr. Brinjes had time to do more than open his mouth, there came running into the room the landlord, having in his hand the *London Post* of the evening, brought down the river from town by some boatman. His face was pale, and his eyes full of terror.

"Oh! gentlemen," he cried, "gentlemen! Here is such news! I cannot trust my eyes. For God's sake, read the newspaper! But who shall tell the admiral?"

"Is it news from the fleet?" asked Captain Petherick.

"It is, your honor." The man looked as if he were afraid to tell his news. "Oh! gentlemen," he repeated, "who shall tell the admiral?"

"Is it bad news?" asked Mr. Brinjes.

"It is the worst news possible. Gentlemen—it is—it is—" He looked about him to see if the admiral was, perhaps, present, hitherto unseen. "It is news of—of—of Captain Easterbrook, gentlemen. Of no other, indeed."

"What!" cried the apothecary; "bad news? The worst news? Then is our boy dead." He sat down in a chair, and looked from face to face. "Jack is dead."

"It is the worst news possible," repeated the landlord.

"Jack is dead," said all together, looking at one another in dismay.

"Jack is dead," repeated Mr. Brinjes. "There hath been an action, and Jack hath fallen. Poor Bess! Yet, now he will never marry the other." The company knew not what he meant. "Well, every man must take his chance. I looked for other things—but— Jack is dead! Some die young, and some die old. To those who die old it seems as if their years have been but a dream. What matters, therefore, when a man dies? Wherefore—devil take all black negro witches with their lying prophecies!" Again the company asked themselves what Mr. Brinjes might mean.

The landlord shook his head.

"No, sir. No, gentlemen. Oh! you will not understand. Read the *Post*. Captain Easterbrook hath lost his ship."

"If," said Mr. Brinjes, "he lost his ship, of course he first lost his life or else his limbs. He would not be taken below while there was yet life enough left to fight his ship."

"Gentlemen," cried the landlord again, "your honors will not listen. It is in the *London Post*."

He held out his newspaper, but no one offered to take it. Every one knew now that something had happened worse than death. Then they heard the admiral's step as he entered the house and stumped along the passage with his escort of negroes.

"Gentlemen," said the landlord again, "who shall tell him?" Again he held out the paper. They looked at one another and held back. No one offered to take the paper; they were afraid. It is one kind of courage to walk up to a cannon's mouth, and another to become a messenger of bad tidings.

Then the admiral came in, followed by his two negroes. He saluted the company cheerfully, and gave his hat and cloak to his servants. This done, he took his seat in his usual place. But the other gentlemen standing about the fire did not, as was customary, follow his example. They hesitated, looked first at the admiral, and then at the landlord.

"Gentlemen, be seated," said the admiral.

"Sir"—it was Mr. Brinjes who spoke; "it appears that bad news hath arrived."

"What news?"

"It is news of Captain Easterbrook."

"Is the boy—is the boy dead?" asked the admiral.

"Sir, we cannot but suppose so. For he hath lost his ship. But as yet we have not seen the *Post*."

"No, no," the landlord again interposed, holding out the *Post*, which no one would take. "Gentlemen, stand by me, I beseech you. Sir, the captain is not dead."

"Then, poor lad," said the admiral, "he is grievously wounded, and like to die. Our boy, gentlemen, is grievously wounded, and like to—" Here his voice failed him.

"No, sir, he is not wounded."

"Then he is shipwrecked and drowned. Why is the man staring like a stuck pig? Alas! gentlemen, our boy is drowned." But the admiral looked uncertain, because the company, now understanding that something out of the common had happened, looked at one another and at the landlord, and spoke not.

"Sirs"—the landlord again offered the newspaper to one after the other, but no one took it—"the news is here printed. Otherwise, God forbid that I should dare to say such a thing. Your honor, it is here stated that the captain struck his colors in the very beginning of the action."

"Struck his colors!" The admiral caught the arms of his chair, raised himself as quickly as a one-legged man may. "Struck his colors! Jack struck his colors! Ye lie, ye drunken swab! Ye lie!" With that he delivered him so shrewd a blow with his gold-headed stick that, had not the landlord dodged, he would have been enabled instantly to carry the news into the next world. "Ye lie, I say!" Here his voice failed him, and his face became purple, and he reeled and would have fallen but that Mr. Shelvocke and Captain Petherick caught him and sat him in a chair, where he gasped and panted, and looked as if he were about to have a fit of some kind. As for the landlord, he stood in a corner, pale and trembling.

"Give me the paper," said Mr. Brinjes, when the admiral had somewhat mastered his passion. "Let us at least read what is here stated." He read it silently. "Gentlemen," he said, "this is a strange business. I understand it not. Here is more than meets the eye. It is a thing hard to understand. I will read it aloud. Courage, admiral, the story is impossible as it stands.

"'Despatches have been received from Sir Edward Hawke.

He reports an affair which, unless later intelligence contradict
it, is more discreditable to British honor than anything which
has been done since the cowardly flight of Benbow's captains.
The frigate *Calypso*, Captain John Easterbrook, with her consort the *Resolute*, Captain Samuel Boys, fell in at daybreak
with a squadron of the enemy, consisting of three frigates, one
of them being the *Malicieuse*. The names of the other two
are not given. The Frenchman bore away on discovery of the
Union-Jack, and the British ships gave chase. After some
hours the *Calypso* came up with the *Malicieuse*, the hindmost
of the three, the *Resolute* being then a quarter of a mile or so
astern, though crowding all sail. It is reported by Captain
Boys, he being then on his quarter-deck and glass in hand,
that the engagement was commenced by the *Malicieuse* firing
a shot from her stern-chaser which struck the *Calypso;* that
then he saw Captain Easterbrook strike his colors with his own
hand; that his officers ran about him, and he cut one down;
that the Frenchman immediately lowered a boat and boarded
the prize, driving the crew below; and that the other two
French frigates backed their sails, whereupon he withdrew from
the chase, thinking it useless to engage three vessels at once;
that he was not pursued; and that he knows no reason at all
why the ship was surrendered without firing a shot. 'Tis
thought that the *Calypso* hath been conveyed to Brest. This
account is the more extraordinary by reason of the character
for gallantry possessed by Captain Easterbrook, who was one of
Captain Lockhart's lieutenants on board the fighting *Tartar.*' "

"This is a very strange story," said Captain Petherick.
"By your leave, Mr. Brinjes, I will not believe it."

"Thank ye, old friend," said the admiral, hoarsely. "My
boy surrender? Never, sir—never. Damme, Mr. Apothecary,
wilt thou try to persuade us that such a thing is possible?"

"Nay, admiral, nay; I do but read what is printed. Lord
forbid that I should doubt the boy. What is this? Ay, they
have begun already their pestilent verses. 'Twill be just as it
was with Admiral Byng, when the journals were full of squibs.
Listen now. Oh! they care nothing about truth so long as
they can turn a verse and raise a laugh. Listen.

" ' The following lines have been picked up at the Rainbow.
'Tis thought they come from the Temple:

> " ' The Frenchman crowds all sail in fright ;
> The Briton crowds all sail to fight ;
> The brave *Calypso's* gallant tyke
> Claps on all sail in haste to strike."

And these have been recited at Dick's—

> " ' The captain brave his ship would save,
> And so this great commander
> Cries, "Heroes, I will scorn to fly,
> While I can still surrender.
> Stay, Frenchman, stay: your shot may play
> Too rough among my hearties ;
> I fear no foe : but yet, I know,
> To strike the better part is." ' "

"Oh! 'tis a lie—'tis a lie," the admiral groaned. "Gentlemen, my boy Jack! Gentlemen, I say—"

"We cannot believe it, admiral," said Captain Petherick. "Yet it is in the despatches."

"There is something that we are not told," said Mr. Brinjes. "But, without doubt, the *Calypso* is taken prisoner, and some one on board struck the colors."

The admiral stared about him with amazement and confusion in his eyes. Then he rose slowly. "I shall go home, gentlemen. I wish you good-night. Some one shall swing for this lie—some one shall swing." He moved towards the door, forgetting his hat and cloak, which one of the gentlemen reached for him. "Some one, I say, shall swing for this—this diabolical lie about my boy Jack. We shall see—damme, I say, we shall see! What, sirrah, the lantern not lit?" Indeed, it was not the duty of the negro to keep the candle burning through the evening ; but the admiral belabored him so lustily that the fellow roared, and the company trembled lest he should be killed. But a negro's head is hard. Then the admiral walked away. This was his last night with the club ; he came no more to the Sir John Falstaff.

The gentlemen, without his presence, sat awhile speechless. But the landlord brought in the punch, and they presently filled and lit their pipes, and began to whisper.

"Do you think, sir," asked Mr. Brasil of the apothecary— "do you think that the story may be in any point of it true ?"

"Why," said Mr. Brinjes, "as for truth, I suppose that is never got at, and this nut is hard to crack. How such a man

as Jack Easterbrook could haul down his flag before the action
began passes understanding. But then how men like Captain
Boys and his officers should be deceived, when only a quarter
of a mile distant or thereabouts, one cannot understand either.
And that the ship is taken one cannot doubt."

"If he comes home he will be tried by court-martial, and for
cowardice," said Mr. Shelvocke.

"That is most certain," said Captain Petherick; "and if he
surrendered cowardly, he will be shot. Gentlemen, this is an
event which affects our own honor. For though the boy is no
blood-relation of any here, he hath been our pupil, so to speak.
We have taught him. He is our son, in whom we hoped, and
in whom we believed. It is not the admiral alone who is struck.
It is this company of honorable gentlemen who would have
maintained to their dying day that Jack Easterbrook could
never turn out a coward. Why, a more gallant lad never trod
the deck, as witness Captain Lockhart, of the *Tartar*, where he
served. I say, gentlemen, this affects us all. We are brought
to shame by this untoward and unexpected event."

"Perhaps," said one of the company, "the captain was shot
at the outset, and it was the first lieutenant who hauled down
the flag."

But that seemed impossible, because no one could fail to
discern Captain Easterbrook at so short a distance, if only on
account of his great stature. Besides, Captain Samuel Boys
was known for a sober and honest man, who would certainly
not invent so grievous a charge against a brother officer.

"Perhaps," said another, "the ship was foundering."

Then they read the statement again, trying to extract from it,
if possible, some gleam of hope or doubt. But they found none.

"Gentlemen," said the apothecary, "I hope I shall not be
thought to be a man over-ready to believe this monstrous thing
if I submit that it may be true, and that the act was made
possible by one of those sudden madnesses which the people
believe to be the possession of the devil. We read of poor
women, in such fits, murdering their own tender children; and
of husbands beating to death their wives, without a cause; and
of learned scholars who have gone forth from their books to
hang themselves without any reason for despair. No man is at
all times master of his own actions; and doubtless there are in

the brain, as in the body, weak places, so that just as one man
falleth into an asthma, or a rheumatism, or the gout, by reason
of bodily imperfections, so may a man by mental disorder commit acts of false judgment, foolish conclusions, and mad acts
for which there is no accounting. Nor can we anticipate or
prevent such attacks. I once knew as brave a fellow as ever
stepped to snivel and cry for an hour together; and why?
Only because he was sentenced to be hanged. Yet he walked
manfully to the gallows in the end. And another, who fell on
his knees and wept aloud, because he was to have a tooth out,
which he dreaded more than he did the three dozen he had received a month before."

"Then you think, sir," said Captain Petherick, "that the
boy may have been mad?"

"I know not what to think. I tell the company what I have
seen. Some acts, I declare, are not consistent with what we
know of the man's previous life. What should we think did
the reverend Vicar of St. Paul's suddenly fall to singing a roaring tavern song of Poll and Nan? Yet that would be no whit
the worse than for Jack to become suddenly coward. There
are some who say that men are thus afflicted by divine visitation. That may be. A congestion of the liver and the mounting of vapors to the head may likewise produce such effects.
Yet we do not call a liver disease a divine visitation. I remember once, being then on the coast of Yucatan, a very singular
thing. Landlord, the bowl is out. I say, gentlemen, that I
once witnessed a very singular thing. There was a young fellow with us of five or six and twenty; a dare-devil dog who
had faced death so often that he feared him no longer, and was
looked to lead the way. The enemy showed fight, and we
came to close quarters, when the word was given to board.
What happened? He leaped upon the enemy's deck with the
greatest resolution, and then, to our surprise, he turned tail and
fled like a cur, dropping his arms and crying out for fear. We
tried that man, gentlemen, when we landed, and we shot him
for cowardice, just as Jack Easterbrook will be tried and shot,
if he be fool enough to come home. 'Twas a pity, too, for
after he was dead we found out the reason of this strange behavior. He was bewitched by an old woman to revenge her
granddaughter, his sweetheart, who was mad with him on ac-

15*

count of his many infidelities. The girl came out and laughed in his face while he was led forth to execution. Afterwards she confessed the crime to some of the girls; and when they began to talk of it, she took to the woods, where, no doubt, she presently perished. The old woman we punished. The night before she was executed, I went privily to her and offered her poison if she would give me her secrets, and especially the secret by which she knew how to prolong life as much as she pleased. But she refused, being an obstinate old woman; and next day the men gave her a bad time, being mad with her. Gentlemen, we are not on the Spanish Main; and there is no witch among us, except Philadelphy, the admiral's negro woman, who would not, if she could, put Obi on Jack. Yet if this story be true, then I doubt not that our boy was clean off his head, and no longer master of himself, when he struck his flag."

CHAPTER XL.

HOW THE NEWS WAS RECEIVED.

The next despatches brought confirmation of the news. There could now be no doubt at all that the *Calypso* had been surrendered by the captain, and that without striking a blow. The consternation and shame which fell upon us cannot be described; nay, not upon us only, but upon the whole town of Deptford, to whom Jack was nothing short of a hero.

"There is nothing," said my father, in the next Sunday's sermon—"there is nothing, my brethren, upon this earth which is stable. Our riches make themselves wings and fly away; disease falls upon the stoutest and strongest of us; old age palsies our limbs; death snatches away the youngest and brightest. Even in the very spring and heyday of life, when promise is strongest and hope most assured, the qualities of which we are so proud may fail us suddenly and without warning, so that the brave man may lose his courage, the loyal man become a traitor, and the strong man fall into the weakness of a girl. Remember this, my brethren, and in the day of your strength be humble." Those who listened applied the words to the disgraced captain and hung their heads.

But the admiral and his household were not in church. They sat at home, the flag half-mast high, madam and Castilla, by the admiral's orders, in black, as if in mourning for one who is lately dead.

"He is dead, Luke," said the brave old man. "My gallant boy, the son of my old friend, my son-in-law who was to be, is truly dead. How he died, and where, I know not. But he is dead, and his body is occupied by an evil spirit. What! shall we be ashamed because this cowardly devil hath struck the colors? 'Tis not our boy. He is dead. Castilla weeps for him; but as for me, I always looked that he might die early, as so many others do—being killed in action, or cast away. As yet we know not how he died, or how the devil was permitted to walk about in his body. Perhaps we shall never learn." But here he broke off and choked. "What an ending!—what an ending is here!—truly, what an ending! Why, if one had foreseen it, 'twould have been a Christian act to put a knife into the boy's heart when he came here sixteen years ago; and a joyful thing, had one only known beforehand what would happen, to be hanged for it afterwards."

I said that I hoped he would be able to write us some words of consolation.

"Consolation! Why, the captain struck his flag without firing a shot! Consolation? There are some things, my lad, which can never be forgiven or forgotten. Cowardly to surrender is the chief of these. Cowardly! Oh, that it should seem possible to use that word of our boy!"

Then I said that it would be best for him to stay abroad, and never to return to England.

"Ay," said the admiral, "unless he should resolve to come back and be shot. The women say he is bewitched. But who should bewitch him? No; our boy is dead, and some evil spirit is in his body."

This was the only consolation that the poor old admiral permitted himself. Yet it did not console. He stayed at home, being so covered with shame that he durst not venture forth, lest the boys should point at him. He told me so; and it went to my heart thus to see this brave old man wounded and bleeding, yet to know no single word of consolation.

"Luke," said Castilla, "do not, if you please, mention his

name to me. We must resign ourselves to the heavenly will.
No doubt this affliction hath been designed for some wise end."

This must always be the Christian's view; yet in my ignorance I have sometimes questioned the course of events which
thus afflicted and presently destroyed a brave man in his old
age, undeserving of this disgrace.

I know not who first started the rumor—perhaps it was Mr.
Brinjes himself—but it was presently spread over all the town
that the captain was bewitched. And so great was the popular
indignation, that had the people known what had passed with
Bess Westmoreland, I make no doubt they would have murdered her. Fortunately, there was no suspicion at all. No one
had seen them together, or knew that there had been any love
passages between them, or any jealousy. Most certainly they
would have murdered her, the women especially being full of
wrath against the unknown author of this misfortune.

But I was uneasy—listening to the talk of these termagants,
as they gathered in the streets, and cried out what should be
done to the witch—lest some one should turn suspicion upon
Bess. As for Philadelphy, who would have been suspected, it
was known that the captain was to marry her young mistress,
and therefore she could not be the witch. Now, of wise wom-
en, who know the properties of simples, and can read the signs
of good and bad luck, and tell fortunes by cards, there are always plenty; but of witches there was in Deptford only one,
and of wizards only one, and both of them known to be friends
of the captain.

"It is true, Luke," said Bess Westmoreland, when I found
her in the usual place. "Do not talk as if it were not true,
because I am assured that the news is true. Why, I knew that
something terrible was going to fall upon him. Mr. Brinjes
says there may be some mistake in the evidence of Captain
Boys; but I know better. It is quite true. What will happen
next, I know not. But I shall have my lover back again, whatever happens. The fortune always ended in the same way,
with love at last."

"Whatever happens, Bess? Why, he is now a prisoner of
war, and, unless exchanged, will remain a prisoner till the war
is ended. And if he ever return he will be tried and shot."

"Then he will stay where he is, and send for me," she replied, as if the recovery of her lover, should that be brought about, would be cheaply purchased at the cost of his honor. But women know little of man's regard for honor. "He will send for me; and if it were to the ends of the earth, I would go to him."

"Bess," I whispered, "it is rumored abroad in the town that he was bewitched. Is there any one who knows what passed between him and you when last you saw him?"

"No one knows except you, Luke. Aaron knows, but he is away."

"Then speak to no one about it. Let it not be suspected that you predicted this disaster, or the people, I verily believe, would burn you for a witch, Bess."

"Why, are they such fools as to think that I would suffer a hair of his head to be touched if I could help it? For Jack loved me once—how he loved me once!—three years ago! And I—oh! I love him always. What do I care what he has done? Let him but hold up his finger to me and I will go to him. I will be his slave. Oh! Luke, I would suffer gladly that he kicked and flogged me daily, so that he loved me. What do I care about his disgrace? That touches not me. My Jack will always be the same to me, whatever people may say of him."

"My poor Bess," I said. "Indeed, he hath a constant mistress. But, my dear, do not look to see him more. I fear we shall never be able to set eyes on his face again, for he cannot show his face among his fellows. The common fellow pays for his sins with a flogging, and when his back is healed he thinks no more of the matter. But the captain—look you, Bess—it is a most dreadful thing. For, whatever happens, he can never more sit among honorable men."

"He shall sit with me, then," said Bess. "As for what I told him, the words were put into my head—I know not how. They were a message. I was made to tell him. They were not my words; wherefore I knew that they would come true."

Thus, while the rest of us were overwhelmed with shame, she who loved him best (because now I clearly understood that Castilla had never loved him so well, else she could not have been so quickly and so easily resigned to her loss) thought little of the deed and much of the man. Thus it is that a woman may love a man so that whatever he does, whether he succeed or fail, even if he does disgraceful and shameful things, she will love him steadfastly. In Bess's simple words, he is always the same man for her.

"As for me," said Mr. Brinjes, "I am very sure that the lad was bewitched. I know not by whom, because Philadelphy would work all the charms she knows for his help, for Miss Castilla's sake. But bewitched he was. Wherefore, Luke, my lad, I shall wait until we learn where he is at present bestowed, and then I shall send him a letter. He must not look for a return to England at any time, unless he join himself with the Pretender, and hopes to return with him. But no: he must never return at all. And as for that young man, he is now near forty, and will never come to England again, I take it. But though Jack cannot come back here, I see no reason why we should not go to him; and so we might together set sail for the Southern Seas, and there dig up my treasure, and equip and man a stout squadron for the harassing of the Spanish fleets."

"Why, Mr. Brinjes," I told him, "you are now an old man —ninety years and more, as you have told us often. Is it for a man of ninety years to brave the hardships of the sea once more?"

"Hardships! Little you know of peaceful sailing among the sunny waters of the islands. There are no hardships and no discomforts. Why, 'twould make me twenty years younger to be back again in the Pacific Ocean and in those latitudes. I should be little more than seventy. What is seventy? A man is still green at seventy: he is in the full vigor of his manhood; there is nothing that I could not do at seventy, ay, and as well as the youngest of them all, save that my limbs were a trifle stiff, and I no longer cared to run and jump. But that stiffness sometimes falls on a man at six-and-thirty, wherefore I could not complain. Seventy! Ah! To be seventy again, with thirty years more to live! And then, if one were so lucky as to fall upon the great secret, another thirty, and another thirty after that, and so on as long as one chose to live. And that, my lad, I promise you, would be until I understood clearly what was on the other side." Thus he went on chattering, having almost forgotten how we began to talk: to forget the things

of the present day is ever a sign or proof of great age. "Ah!"
he sighed, heavily, " would to God that I could find myself once
more aboard a tight vessel on the Pacific Seas, with plenty of
men and lemons, and some music for the lads in the evenings,
and for amusement, taking a ship now and then, and making
the Spaniard walk the plank ! Jack should be our captain, and
Bess should go with us—I could not go away from Deptford
without Bess, and her heart is always set on Jack. Yet I do
not remember any women among the Rovers except Mary Read
and Ann Bonny, and they dressed like men, and pretended to
be men. They sailed under Captain Rackam, and a brave pair
of wenches they were. I dreamed last night that we were all
three on the poop of as fine a schooner as one could wish, bound
for the South Seas, by way of the Indian Ocean."

So we lost our hero. At least, so we thought we had lost
him. He was taken to a French prison. He would never be
so mad as to return to England, where certain death awaited
him. We should never see him again. And, as Captain Petherick truly said, we were all shamed by an act as truly cowardly
as ever British sailor committed. The newspapers continued
to speak of it; the evidence of Captain Boys was printed in
full, and there were more epigrams. And then other things
happened; and the loss of the *Calypso* would have been speedily forgotten but for a surprising and unexpected turn, which
was, so to speak, a second act in this tragedy of Jack Easterbrook's end.

Truly surprising and unexpected it was, and the intelligence
of it threw us all into an agitation worse, if possible, than the
first. For we were assured that the worst was over. The first
blow fell upon us like a thunderbolt from a clear sky, and now
we were rising to our feet again (except the admiral), stunned
and confused, yet in a fair way of recovery, as happens in every
earthly calamity, else 'twould be impossible to live. The child
we love—nay, the woman we love—dies, yet behold the sun
rises and sets, and presently the daily life goes on as before,
and the loss is partly forgotten. Suppose, however, the woman
were not dead, but came to life again, only to die with more
cruel suffering and with shame !

What happened, in a word, was this.

The crew of the prize had orders to take the *Calypso* to Brest, which was the nearest French port. They ordered their prisoners below to the quarters always designed for men in that unhappy position, namely, the forward portion of the cockpit, where they have to sit in gloom, lit only by one great ship's lantern all day and all night, save for such times as they are allowed on deck for fresh air in gangs and small companies. When the Englishmen were driven below, and the prize crew appointed, the *Malicieuse* parted company, and the *Calypso* was left to make her own way to Brest.

"On the second day," we read in the *London Post*, "the prisoners rose, and became again masters of the ship, which was brought into Spithead under the first lieutenant, the captain being kept a prisoner in his cabin. This extraordinary reversal of fortune, and other circumstances attending the case, have excited the greatest interest. The lords commissioners have ordered the ship to be brought to Deptford, where the court-martial on Captain Easterbrook will be held."

As is usual in news published by authority in the *Gazette*, and copied by other newspapers, there were no particulars of the manner in which the ship was recovered, except that she was navigated by the first lieutenant. Had the crew, then, mutinied against their captain, and confined him to his cabin? If not, how was he a prisoner?

It was impossible for me, who knew the whole circumstances of the case, not to feel that in this surprising reversal of fortune, and in the ordering of the court-martial, there was a direct interposition of the hand of Providence, such as may well make the guilty tremble. To lose life, and honor as well, which is dearer than life, as a penalty for broken vows, seems a terrible punishment, and out of proportion to the offence. But it is not every inconstant lover who hath expressly called down upon his own head, as Jack did, the wrath of God in case of his inconstancy. Man cannot with impunity call upon the name of the Lord. There is a story of one who learned how to draw the lightnings out of heaven, but he drew them upon himself, and so perished. Was not this the fate of Jack Easterbrook?

Alas! we were now wholly without hope. For needs must that he be tried; and he was condemned already, and as good as shot. While he was prisoner with the French, his life at least was safe; and if he chose never to return, he could certainly never be tried; and so his case would be in the course of time forgotten. But now he must be tried, and he must be condemned.

"But," said Mr. Brinjes, "he shall call me as a witness; and I will prove from books and from mine own experience that there have happened many cases of sudden madness, and that in such an access or seizure a man is not master of himself. And those who have travelled much in countries where the sun is hot, and especially those who have wandered, as the boy did, among savages, with insufficient food, and perhaps no covering for the head, are more than others liable to such fits—instances of which I can produce. It will also be set forth that the captain, not long before he sailed, received so heavy a blow upon the head that he was carried senseless through the town and across the river. Such a blow may of itself produce the effect of sudden madness. Men who have proved themselves brave sailors and fond of fight do not, unless from this cause, suddenly become cowardly. Why, he crowded all sail to get within range of the enemy."

"Yet he struck his flag," I said. "Is every man who runs away, after marching resolutely to meet the enemy, to plead that he was smitten with a sudden madness?"

As for the value of such evidence, I know not what it would have availed, but I think it would have availed nothing in the eyes of the officers who formed the court. But, as you will presently see, it never was produced. Perhaps the knowledge of what he could testify gave the apothecary an inward assurance which comforted him. For he showed no alarm, and maintained stoutly that his own evidence, with the prisoner's previous good conduct, would get Jack acquitted, if it did not get him reinstated in command.

But courts, whether martial or civil, do not thus examine into motives and causes. If a judge were to hear why a pocket came to be picked, or by what train of circumstances an honest man has been turned into a rogue, there would be no punishment at all, but rather general commiseration for sin, and forgiveness of all sinners, on the score of human weakness and the strength of temptation.

As for Bess, when she heard that the captain was a prisoner

and on his way to meet his trial, she said nothing, except that whatever happened the end was certain; and she waited. Her wrath and fierceness were all gone; she was now gentle and calm, though her cheek was pale, and round her eyes a black ring, by which I knew that she slept little and thought of Jack continually.

CHAPTER XLI.

HOW THE "CALYPSO" CAME HOME AGAIN.

Lo! when we awoke in the morning, the *Calypso* herself was lying in the river, moored nearly opposite to the mouth of the dock.

I made haste to the King's Yard, in order to hear the news, and there, as I expected, I found a little knot of gentlemen, in cluding Captain Petherick, the chief officer of the yard, and a few who, like myself, were brought thither by anxiety and curiosity. They were earnestly conversing with the first lieutenant of the ship. He was a man whose hair was now grown completely gray (wherefore he no longer used powder), being some fifty-five years of age, but for want of interest never having got any higher. By birth he was a Scotchman; he had, like many of his countrymen, a hard and strongly marked face, and his manner of speech was hard and slow, so that though he had such a tale to tell as surely never was heard before, his manner of telling it never varied even in the most astonishing parts of his narrative, except that now and then he broke off to express his own opinion on the matter. We presently, however, discovered that he felt great commiseration for the unhappy fate of his captain, young enough to be his son, and that he held much the same view as the towns-people, namely, that there must be witchcraft at the bottom of the affair. We learned also that the recapture of the ship would now present a very different complexion, being due, not as had been supposed, to a general rising of the crew, but to the most astonishing courage of the captain himself, and the display of reckless daring in a single-handed attack upon the prize crew such as one had never read of or heard of before.

As regards the striking of the colors, there was nothing new in what we learned. The captain with his own hand did certainly haul down the flag without firing a shot. Against that damning and capital fact nothing could be said. But as for what followed, you shall hear the first lieutenant's story.

"When the captain struck his colors, which he did with his own hand, the men looking on in sheer amazement, I myself ran to him, crying, 'For God's sake, captain! for God's sake, sir, consider what you do!' But the captain drew his hanger and slashed at me, so that, though the flat of the sword only struck me, I fell senseless. Then, as I have since been told, those officers whose place was on deck stood back, terrified by the wild looks and furious gestures of the captain. So great was the authority which he possessed that not a man among them all dared so much as to murmur. Then the Frenchman boarded us, and all except the captain, who was suffered to remain on deck, and myself because I was senseless, were bundled below, and the hatches clapped down. When I presently recovered, I too was allowed to remain above. Now for two nights and two days the captain sat on the quarter-deck, upon the trunnion of a carronade, his hat off, his hands upon his knees, his eyes blood-red, his face pale. Gentlemen," cried the first lieutenant, breaking off suddenly at this point, "'twould have moved a heart of stone only to look upon the captain in this misery of shame. Despair was in his eyes as he turned them from the sea to the ship, and from the ship to the sea. As for what the men think, there is but one opinion: that it was the work of the devil. He was bewitched or possessed. I know not if we have the right to try a man for an act done under demoniac possession, which we know to be sometimes permitted. But the madness had now left him, and he was in his right mind again."

There was not one of those present who heard this with a dry eye. But more moving things still were to follow.

"It was on the third day after the surrender," the first lieutenant told us, "and in the forenoon, the usual guard being set, the French officers and sailors all armed, and their commander on the quarter-deck. In the waist was gathered together a small party of prisoners taking their spell of fresh air; they were lolling in the sun, or looking over the bulwarks in the hope of discovering an English flag. Nothing was further from their thoughts than an attempt to recapture the *Calypso*. On that point there could be no doubt. They talked with each other in low voices, being very much dejected at the position of their affairs, and the prospect of a French prison, and they looked at their captain, who sat bareheaded on the quarter-deck. He, too, like themselves, was unarmed, and he sat without moving or making any sign of life.

"Suddenly he sprang to his feet, and caught the French officer, a much smaller man than himself, by the throat, tore his sword from him, and cut him down. The two sentinels rushed upon him with their bayonets, but he lightly leaped aside, and cut them down too. Then, armed with the sword, he sprang into the waist, and crying, 'Men of the *Calypso*, to the rescue of your ship!' he attacked the Frenchmen, cutting them down and driving all before him like a madman.

"There is a tall, stout fellow aboard, one of our marines. He was on deck at the time, and was the first who recovered presence of mind (the rest being clean taken aback by the suddenness of the thing). He seized a rammer, and sprang to the side of the captain, fighting with him and protecting him. Mark you, if it had not been for that brave fellow the captain would have been killed a dozen times over, as I doubt not he wished to be, seeing the reckless way in which he attacked the enemy. Nay, I wonder that in spite of this help he was not killed, seeing that they fired their pistols in his very face, and thrust at him with bayonets, and cut at him with swords; but all in vain. A fine sight it was, and such as will never be witnessed again by any of us, to see this hero fighting the whole of the prize crew single-handed save for the marine, who seemed to have no other thought than to protect his captain, and laid about him with his rammer as if it had been a quarter-staff.

"Well, gentlemen, you may be very sure that it was not very long before the rest of the English sailors on deck joined in with a true British cheer, fighting with whatever weapons they could pick up—namely, one with a marling-spike, one with a hammer, one with his fist, one with a dead Frenchman's bayonet, and so on—until in a few minutes we had the satisfaction of driving our conquerors under hatches, calling up our crew, and running up the union-jack. The captain it was who

*" Then the captain struck his colors, which he did with his own hand,
the men looking on in sheer amazement."*

hauled it up with his own hand. His face was black with powder, and streaked with blood, though he had not received a
scratch ; his hands were red with blood, and his sword streaming ; on the deck lay a dozen dead and wounded, though some
of them only stunned with the marine's rammer. When the
flag was up, the captain saluted it, and called on his men to
give three cheers, which they did with a will. After that he
ordered a double ration of rum, and every man to his duty.

" Then he turned to me. ' Mr. Macdonald,' he said, ' I would
to God your captain was lying dead among those poor wretches,'
pointing to the slain. I told him to take courage, because it
was by his act, and his alone, that the vessel was recaptured.
Then he hesitated awhile, and fetched a sigh as if his heart
was breaking.

" ' Whose hand hauled down the flag ?' he asked.

" I waited to hear what more he had to say.

" ' Where is the man,' he asked, ' who fought beside me
just now. I mean the man who interposed to save my life ?'

" I called the man, who stepped forward and saluted.

" ' So,' said the captain, ' 'tis my old friend. Sirrah, twice
hast thou endeavored to take my life, out of revenge. Once
hast thou saved it. Thou hast thy revenge at last, and in full
measure. Return to duty.'

" I know not, gentlemen," continued the first lieutenant,
" what the captain meant by those words, for the man saluted
and stepped back to his place, making no reply, either by look
or speech. Then the captain gave me his last orders. ' You
will take the command of this ship, sir,' he said. ' You will
enter in the captain's log a full account of the circumstances
connected with the surrender and the recapture of the *Calypso*.
Disguise nothing, sir. Nothing must be omitted. Write that
the captain hauled down the flag. Write that the captain cut
down the first lieutenant, who would have remonstrated. Write
that there was not a single shot fired, and the enemy carried
less weight of metal and a smaller crew.'

" ' With respect, sir,' I told him, ' I shall also write that the
captain retook the vessel single-handed.'

" ' Write, further, that the captain gave over the command
to you, with instructions to take the ship to Spithead, the
whereabouts of the admiral not being known, there to report

on what has happened, and to await the instructions of my lords the commissioners.'

"'Gentlemen,' the first lieutenant concluded, 'I obeyed orders. I sailed to Spithead, and reported the circumstances of the case. The commissioners have ordered me to bring the ship round to Deptford, the captain aboard her, prisoner, waiting his court-martial. We hope that though he certainly struck the colors, his subsequent conduct may save his life. For most certainly he was mad when he did it, or bewitched, or possessed of a devil. But he is mad no longer. I forgot to say, gentlemen, that although for two days he refused to take anything, and I verily believe he intended to starve himself to death, he has since eaten and drunk heartily."

This was the story as the first lieutenant told it.

Now when we heard it we were in a doubt what to do. For to neglect the unhappy prisoner altogether would seem heartless, whereas to try and see him, unless he manifested a desire to see us, would seem like intrusion. He sat in his cabin, we heard, all day, and at night, when it was dark, walked upon the quarter-deck. He spoke with no one save the first lieutenant, and made no reference to the approaching trial, the day for which they expected would be fixed very shortly.

First, however, my father wrote to him, and asked if he would wish to see him; but received a letter, thanking him, indeed, and putting off his visit until, the writer said, he should be forced to contemplate the near approach of death. Next, Mr. Brinjes sent a message that he wished to see him as his physician (a title which he assumed when he pleased); but the captain returned word that he had never been in better health.

As for myself, I waited for some days, not venturing to intrude upon his suffering, yet desirous of seeing him. At last I wrote a letter, begging him to tell me if I could do anything for him. To which he replied that he would take it kindly if I would come aboard and see him in his cabin. I obeyed with a sinking heart, for, indeed, what consolation could I administer, or with what countenance could I greet him, or could I pretend that he was not overwhelmed with shame?

When I went on board I was astonished to find, acting as sentry at the top of the companion, no other than Aaron

Fletcher. I knew not that he was on board the *Calypso*. Strange, indeed, that he should now be mounting guard as marine over the man whom he had many times fought, and twice tried to murder. He made no sign of recognition as I passed him.

Jack was in his cabin, sitting at his window, leaning his head upon his hand and gazing upon the river, with the crowd of craft upon it. He turned his head when I opened the door, and rose to meet me.

"Luke," he said, "canst take the hand of a coward wretch who hath surrendered his ship without a blow? Nay, nay, lad; tears will not help, and I am not worth a tear, or anything now but to be shot like a cur, and rolled up in a bit of sacking, and so tossed into the water and forgotten."

I asked after his health, but he put me off.

"Health?" he cried. "What matters my health? If you can pick up a small-pox, or a galloping consumption, or a fever, and send it to me, the worse the complaint the better I shall like it; or if Mr. Brinjes, who can cause all diseases, will send me one that will suddenly tear out my heart or stop my breath, it would be very much to the point at the present juncture. My health? Why, as the devil will have it, it was never better." He laughed. "Go tell Mr. Brinjes, or his swivel-eyed assistant, to make me up a disease or two in that saucepan of his that is always on the hob. 'Tis a crafty old man, and first cousin, I verily believe, to the devil."

He paused awhile, thinking what next to tell me.

"Tell the admiral— No, not yet; after my death thou shalt tell him all the truth, which I will tell thee directly. I cannot write to that good old man; yet, Luke, I must send him some message. Therefore— But no, there are no words that I can send him. I cannot ask his forgiveness, because he can never forgive me. I cannot thank him for all his kindness, because I am not worthy now so much as to send a word of gratitude. Let be—let be. When I am dead thou shalt tell him the truth. As for Castilla, she must forget me. Tell her that, Luke. I am certain that she will soon console herself. She never loved me as poor Bess used to love me. There is Mr. Brinjes; tell him—why, tell him that he must look for another sailor to steer his ship among the islands of the southern seas."

"Jack," I said, "it is terrible."

"Yes, it is terrible. It is very terrible, lad. But it must be endured. Trust me that I shall not stand snivelling before the file of marines at the end. That is, unless there be another—" Here he paused, and in his eyes there was apparent a look of such terror as I have never since seen in any man's eyes, while his cheeks turned white, and drops stood upon his brow. "Unless," he said again, "there comes another—" Here he broke off again. "Luke," he said, "if at the end I die craven, know of a surety that I die unforgiven, and that my soul is lost. But it cannot be that death will not atone." So he paced his cabin once or twice, and then, becoming more calm, he sat down again. "Luke, dear lad, I wished to see thee, but only thee, for the present. I have much to say. And first— of Bess. Do you know the words she said to me before I sailed ?"

"I know them. Bess told me herself."

"Does any other person know them ?"

"No one, I believe."

"Let her hold her tongue, then, lest they take her for a witch. Why, I know full well that she is no witch; and as for those words, they were spoken by her, but yet were not her own. I laughed when I heard them. The second time I heard them I laughed no longer. And now I will tell thee the whole truth, Luke; but keep it to thyself until I am dead, when I wish thee—nay, I charge thee—to tell the admiral and thy father. I crowded all sail in pursuit of the enemy; I pre- pared for action with as light a heart as a man can have who has a stout ship and a lusty crew. My guns they were loaded, and my men were at quarters, every man stripped to the skin, a good ration of rum served round, and as hearty a spirit as ever animated a British crew. I was as certain of making a prize of the *Malicieuse* as I am now certain of being tried and sentenced to death. Suddenly, we being by this time well within range, and our men prepared to give the enemy a broad- side, a shot from the Frenchman struck our bow, and sent the splinters flying. Then there came upon me a kind of dizzi- ness, and a voice shouted—yea, shouted in my ears—though none but me heard it, 'Thou shalt be struck where thou shalt feel the blow most deeply.' I tell thee the truth, Luke. But

tell no one, lest they seize poor Bess for a witch. Something
(I know not what) caught my hand, and dragged me, whether
I would or no—yea, compelled me—to the mainmast, and
placed the lines in my hand, and forced me to haul down the
flag. I know not very well what happened afterwards. My
men, I believe, were all smitten with stupid amazement, and
made no resistance: how should they, when the flag was
struck? They tell me that I cut down the first lieutenant.
Thank God I did no more than stun him! And presently,
when I came to myself, I was sitting on a carronade, and
the ship was a prize, and the French commander was on the
quarter-deck."

"But you recaptured the ship?"

"Why, 'twas a desperate attempt. I thought first that I
would starve myself to death. But a man does not like to
kill himself. And then, seeing the Frenchmen on the deck,
and some of my lads for'ard under the sentries, I thought to
make them kill me. Alas! they were not suffered to kill me.
Some of my men were wounded, and a good many of the
Frenchmen knocked o' the head; but I came out of the fight
without a scratch, and the ship was ours again. That is my
story, lad, in its truth."

What could a man say in consolation to a man thus afflicted?
Was there ever a worse case? My father, for his part, found
the case of Job worse, "because," he said, "not only did the
patriarch lose wife and children, and substance and health,
but he also lost that which made the patriarchal life more desirable than any which hath followed it, namely, the daily walk
with God, compared with which a man's reputation among his
fellows is naught indeed."

"Tell Bess," Jack went on, "what hath happened. Let her
know that she is revenged, and I am punished. She did not
desire my punishment. It will grieve the poor, tender creature,
who always loved me better than I deserved. Yet it is the
punishment—nay, I know it now—it is the punishment of
God himself."

He then told me, what indeed I knew already, the history of
his passion for Bess, which was as brief as it was violent, spar-
ing himself not at all.

"Never," he swore, "was a man more madly in love with
16

any woman than I with Bess, and never, I am sure, did woman
love man better than she loved me.   I confess, lad, that I made
her a thousand promises, the most sacred I knew, even upon
the Holy Bible, that I would never forget her, but would
marry her when I returned.   The man Brinjes was witness a
dozen times to these protestations.   As for him, he is, I think,
a devil.   For he egged her on to meet me as often as I wished
in his own house; and he laughed when I swore constancy,
telling me, when she was not present, that I knew the lesson as
well as if I were five-and-thirty instead of four-and-twenty, and
that every sailor was the same, but I the most fortunate of all,
because I had so beautiful a girl.   I meant not, however, Luke,
to deceive her.   I intended, when I sailed away, to keep my
word.   I was full of love to her.   Yet, which is strange, when
we had been at sea for two or three months, I thought of her
no longer.   When I came home with the prize I declare that I
had clean forgotten her; and when I saw her, I looked upon
her no longer with love, and wondered how I could ever have
loved her."

"Poor Bess!"

"It is strange, Luke, since I took the ship again, the image
of the girl hath returned to my heart.   I have thought upon
her daily, and I remember once more all the things that passed
between us while I was waiting for my appointment to the
Tartar.   Poor Bess!   She deserved a better lover.   How
could I ever forget her brave black eyes?   See, Luke!"   He
drew up his sleeve and showed his left arm—he had forgotten
when last he exhibited that tattoo.   "See, lad, her name is ever
before me.   Yes, a better lover she deserved."

"She desires no better lover, Jack."

"What?" he asked.   "Doth she not curse my very name?"

"Nay; she hath never cursed thee, Jack.   She loves thee
still: she hath always loved thee."

"A woman cannot love a man who is disgraced."

"Why?   She loves the man: it is not his honor or his reputation she loves.   That I have heard, but I have never understood it, concerning women, before; but now I perceive it very
plainly.   It is strange to us, because a man cannot love a
woman without thinking of her beauty; and so we believe that
a woman cannot love a man without thinking of his honor and

reputation, his strength and his name; Jack, will you see this poor girl? Will you let her come to you, and tell her kindly, in your old way, that you love again, as in the past time, and so heal her bleeding heart?"

"See her? Truly, I never thought," said Jack, "that she would any more come to me. I thought that she must be like Aaron Fletcher—only anxious to see me swing. Why, if the poor child can find any comfort or happiness in coming here, let her come, in God's name. As for me, dear lad, there is a load upon my heart which I thought would be with me till my death. But if she will forgive me, I think that load will be removed, and I can die with easier mind. Poor Bess! she will but get her lover in time to see him die. My heart bleeds for her. Go quick—bring her to me. Let me at least ask her forgiveness."

You may be sure that I lost no time in taking this fond message to Bess.

I looked that she would burst into weeping and sobbing. But she did not.

"I knew," she said, "that I should get my lover back. Now care I for nothing more. For if he must die, so must I die also. Death itself shall not have power—no, death shall have no power to separate us. On the day that he dies shall I die too. He loves me again. Why, do you think I care what may happen to either of us, since he loves me still?"

I led her on board, and took her to the captain's cabin, but at the door I turned away, and so left them alone.

Oh! behind that closed door what prayers and vows were uttered, what tears were shed, what tender embraces were exchanged, when, in the presence of shame and death, those hapless lovers met again!

CHAPTER XLII.

OF THE COURT-MARTIAL.

NEARLY all that follows is matter of history, and may be read in the gazettes and papers of the day. Yet, for the sake of completing the history, it shall be set forth in order.

The court-martial was appointed to be held on board the *Calypso*, on the forenoon of Monday, February the 2d.

On that day it was accordingly held, the Hon. John Cheveril, Rear-Admiral of the White, and Admiral of the Port, being the President. The court consisted of Captains Richard Orde, Frederick Drake, Saltren Willett, Peter Denis, and Joshua Rowley. Captain Petherick should also have sat, but he begged to be excused, on the ground of personal friendship with the defendant. He was present, however, and sat at the back of the court, with as sad a countenance as ever I beheld. (As for our admiral, he was in his bedroom with an attack of gout, which even Mr. Brinjes could not cure.) The court was thrown open to all. Few of the friends of the accused officer were present, but there was a great throng of people, not only from Deptford Town, but also from London. Truly, a court-martial on whose decision rests the honor, if not the life, of a man, is a species of judicial investigation which strikes awe upon the beholder, even more than the aspect of the judge, jury, and counsel in a civil court, the solemnity of the occasion being heightened and set off by the uniforms of the judges and the naked weapons of the sentries and guards.

The court was opened by the deputy judge-advocate. He was only an attorney of Deptford, by name Richard Pendlebury, but he wore a black gown over his coat, and being provided with a full wig, which might have been proper even to a sergeant-at-law, and wearing much lace to his bosom and his sleeves, and being a big burly gentleman with a full round voice, he looked as full of authority as a king's counsel. He began the proceedings by reading the warrant of the right honorable the lords commissioners of the Admiralty, empowering the admiral to assemble courts-martial. This done, the president ordered that Captain Easterbrook should be brought before the court. My heart beat fast and my throat choked when he appeared, bearing himself proudly, but with pale cheek, dressed, if one may say so, like a bride for her wedding, wearing his best uniform, his richest lace, and white leather gloves. Never, surely, did officer of the king's navy bear himself more gallantly. Once only I saw his cheek flush scarlet. 'Twas when, in the old familiar way, he clapped his hand to his side for the adjustment of his sword. Alas! he had no sword. That had been taken from him, and was now lying on the table before the president, the hilt towards the prisoner. Then he bowed to his judges and stood upright, and to outward show calm and collected, though a tempest of shame and despair was raging within.

Then the deputy judge-advocate administered the oath to the members of the court and took it himself in the form prescribed, after which he read the charge against the defendant, as follows:

"Gentlemen,— The charge against Captain John Easterbrook, Commander of the *Calypso*, here present before your honorable court, is that on the fourth day of December, 1759, he did cowardly and treacherously surrender and yield up his ship to the enemy, and he is here to answer this charge accordingly."

He then read the fifteenth of the Articles of War, as follows:

"Every person in or belonging to the fleet who shall desert to the enemy, pirate, or rebel, or shall run away with any of his majesty's ships or vessels of war, or any ordnance, ammunition, stores, or provision belonging thereto, to the weakening of the service, or shall yield up the same, cowardly or treacherously, to the enemy, pirate, or rebel, being convicted of any such offence by the sentence of the court-martial, shall suffer death."

These preliminaries being completed, the deputy judge-advocate proceeded to call his witnesses, and to each in turn administered an oath, which is more awful than that used in the civil courts, because it lays upon the witness an obligation to reveal everything that he knows concerning the case. The form is this:

"I, A. B., do most solemnly swear that in the evidence I shall give before the court respecting the present trial I will, whether demanded of me by question or not, and whether favorable or unfavorable to the prisoner, declare the truth, the whole truth, and nothing but the truth. So help me, God!"

The deposition of the officers had already been taken at Portsmouth for the information of the Lords Commissioners, and in every case these were first read aloud, and then confirmed by the witness, who added what he chose, and answered such questions as were put to him. And in the putting of

these questions it seemed to me as if the deputy judge-advocate was desirous of pressing and dwelling upon every fact
which might make the crime appear blacker, and of concealing
or passing over every fact which made in favor of the accused.

The first witness called was Lieutenant Colin Macdonald,
first lieutenant of the *Calypso*.

His deposition was short, and was as follows:

" At daybreak on the morning of December the 4th, being
then in company with the frigate *Resolute*, Captain Boys, we
sighted three ships, which we presently made out to be a squadron of three French frigates, apparently of about the same
armament as ourselves. They bore away at sight of us, as
not wishing to fight. Captain Easterbrook gave the word to
crowd all sail and up hammocks, the wind being then fresh
and nearly aft, and the sea lively, but the ship sailing free and
not lying down, so that all her ports could be opened and all
her guns fired. We presently found that we gained upon the
Frenchmen, and about noon we were nearly come up with the
Malicieuse, the slowest of the three, the *Resolute* being then
half a mile or so astern, and the other two French ships about
as much ahead of us. We were by this time cleared for action,
the men at their quarters, and everything reported in readiness,
looking for nothing but a close engagement, and a pretty hot
one, with the three ships. The captain's plan, he told me,
was to range alongside of the enemy, pour in his broadside,
grapple, and board, thinking that the *Resolute* would do the
like, and so we might capture the squadron. And this we
could have done, having faster vessels than the enemy, and
Captain Easterbrook being, as I take it, the smartest handler of
a ship in the service, though so young a man. But the Frenchman was not disposed to allow of this if he could help it.
Therefore he began to let fly with the stern-chasers, being, like
most of his nation, amply provided with these helps to running
away. His first shot knocked away part of our figure-head,
the splinters flying about the deck; but no one harmed. Just
then, to our utmost consternation, the captain turned pale, and
ran to the mainmast, where, with his own hands, he began to
lower the colors. I ran to him, crying, ' Captain, for God's
sake, consider what you are doing!' Whereupon he drew his
sword, and cut me down over the head, but fortunately with

the flat of the weapon only, else I had been a dead man. And I knew no more until the business was ended and we were all prisoners."

Being asked by the deputy judge-advocate what preparations had been made for an engagement, he replied that nothing was omitted that is customary on such an occasion; that they had ample time during the chase, and that no ship ever went into action better prepared. Immediately on sighting the enemy the bo's'n and his mates piped to stow hammocks; the carpenter and his mates were ready with their mauls and plugs; the gunner and his quarter-gunners examined and reported on all the cannon. When the ship was within a mile of the enemy the drums beat to arms, and the bo's'n and his mates piped " all hands to quarters " at every hatchway. Then every man stripped to the waist, and repaired to his proper place; a ration of rum was served out; the hatches were laid; the marines were drawn up on the quarter-deck and fo'k'sle; lastly, the lashings of the great guns were let loose, the tompions withdrawn, and the guns run out at all the ports. In one word, there was no point omitted that a commander who knows his business would neglect, and everything in such order as the most resolute captain could desire.

Being asked, further, if the enemy's consorts showed an intention of taking part in the fight, the lieutenant replied that he was not prepared to state positively, but he believed that one of them backed her sails, while the other appeared to be hauling her wind; but he repeated that it was the captain's design to neglect these vessels while he took the *Malicieuse* by boarding, and afterwards to engage her consorts with the help of the *Resolute*.

Being further pressed upon the distance of the *Calypso* from the *Malicieuse* when the captain surrendered, he replied that, to the best of his knowledge and belief, the *Calypso* was no more than a hundred and fifty yards astern of the *Malicieuse*, and gaining rapidly. Being asked what was the posture of the enemy so far as could be discerned, he replied the men were at quarters, and ready for action, but that all sail was crowded, and the Frenchman, it was quite certain, had no stomach for the fight, and would gladly have got clear off.

At this point of the evidence Captain Easterbrook was asked

if he had any questions to put to the witness. He replied that he had none, and that to the best of his knowledge the evidence given by Lieutenant Macdonald was true in every particular—a statement which made the court look serious, and troubled the mind of the deputy judge-advocate, because there is nothing which these gentlemen desire more than to fight a stubborn case; whereas, if an officer pleads guilty, and throws himself upon the mercy of the court, he has no chance to show his cleverness.

"With permission of the court," said the first lieutenant, "I will now give evidence as to the recapture of the ship."

"I submit to the court," said the deputy judge-advocate, "that the recapture of the ship has nothing to do with the charge against Captain Easterbrook, namely, that he did cowardly and treacherously yield up his vessel."

"Gentlemen," said the lieutenant, "with respect. If the ship had not been recaptured, the court could not have been held. And if it had not been for the captain, the ship would never have been recaptured. For he did a thing which, I venture to maintain, no other man in the service would have done, when he engaged, single-handed, the whole of the crew in charge of the prize."

So the court conferred together, whispering, and the president ordered the witness to proceed. Whereupon the deputy judge-advocate sat down and put his hands in his pockets, and gazed upward, as if this part of the evidence did not concern him.

The account which the lieutenant gave of the retaking of the ship was exactly the same which he had already given to the commissioner of the yard, Captain Petherick. It need not therefore be repeated here. Suffice it to say that at the recital there was not a face in court which was not suffused with emotion, and as for myself, I thought that surely after so gallant an exploit his sword would be returned to him.

"Gentlemen," concluded the first lieutenant, "'twas the most gallant act I have ever witnessed. Only by a miracle, and by his own valor, did the captain escape death. There were on deck thirty Frenchmen, all armed, and he with nothing but the sword which he tore from the French commander. And to back him only a dozed unarmed men, who, to tell the truth, for I was among them, were taken by surprise, and would never have plucked up heart save for the example of the captain. The first man to join him was a marine named Aaron Fletcher, who seized a rammer, and, armed with this weapon alone, stood by the captain, playing a man's part indeed; but for him, the captain would have been cut down a dozen times. But, gentlemen, that the ship was recaptured is due to nobody but to the desperate valor of the captain himself."

The court asked Captain Easterbrook whether he had any questions to put on this head, but he had none. Wherefore Lieutenant Macdonald stepped aside, and made way for the next witness.

Then the second lieutenant of the ship was called, and he gave evidence that he was at his station on the main-deck when the action began, and testified to the disgust of the men when they learned that the ship was surrendered. This was the more astonishing to them, as their captain had the reputation of uncommon courage. At first the men refused to believe that the vessel was surrendered, and called upon each other to fight it out.

The third lieutenant gave similar evidence, adding that, had not the men been fully convinced of the captain's bravery and judgment, there would have been a mutiny on board; and that they thought the ship must be sinking at least, or dangerously on fire, or that it was some stratagem, counterfeit, or design by which the captain thought to fool the enemy, and that they looked at each other and laughed aloud, waiting for the word to lay the guns, and fire. Further, that the enemy did not believe it possible that a British ship should thus cowardly be yielded up, and continued to fire upon the *Calypso*, the shot passing through the rigging and the sails, but doing no further mischief. Nor did the men believe that the ship was surrendered until the French boat came alongside, and the captain gave the word to back the sails and lay down arms, which they all did with a very bad grace, yet still persuaded that something fatal had happened to the ship, and that the colors were struck to save their lives.

The lieutenant of marines deposed that his men were drawn up in readiness on the quarter-deck and fo'k'sle, and stated plainly that he had no doubt of the issue, because the Frenchman had only one thought—namely, to get away; and, in his opinion, it had been the captain's intention to attack and take all three ships, with the help of the *Resolute;* and that nothing in the world had ever surprised him more than the strange behavior of the captain, from whom so much had been expected.

Captain Easterbrook declined to ask any questions of these witnesses. Was he, then, going to make no attempt at a defence?

They called the purser, who put in the captain's log-book, which is always done on these trials, I am told, but I do not know why. And then I thought we should surely proceed to the defence, because there could be no doubt of the main fact —namely, that the captain had certainly struck the colors.

But they delayed the case in order to call the master, who confirmed the first lieutenant's evidence as to the preparations for engaging the enemy; and the gunner, who also confirmed the evidence; and the bo's'n and the carpenter, who added little to the evidence already before the court, except the fact that when the men were under hatches and knew what had been done, the swearing and cursing of the crew were strong enough to lift the decks.

"Gentlemen," said the deputy judge-advocate, "there is no other evidence before the court."

"Stay," said the president, "call the marine of whose conduct in the recapture of the ship Lieutenant Macdonald hath spoken."

So they called Aaron Fletcher.

When this witness stepped forward, looking, it must be confessed, a much smarter and finer man in his scarlet coat than he ever looked as a landsman, Jack's face flushed. It was his fate never to be out of reach of this man's animosity. Twice had Aaron tried to take his life, when that was most worth having. Once he had saved his life when he himself had most ardently desired to lose it. Now he was present to give evidence in the hour of his open humiliation.

"I thought," he told me afterwards, "that I had drained the whole cup. But the bitterest drop was when that man stood before me, as if Bess, poor girl! had not yet forgiven me, and had sent her old lover to gloat over my discomfiture. She hath forgiven me, however; therefore I need not have been troubled."

The court ordered the man to be sworn, and bade him relate all that he knew concerning the affair, and particularly as to the retaking of the ship from the French.

"I was on the fo'k'sle," said Aaron, speaking boldly, and no whit abashed at the solemnity of the court and the rank of the judges—"I was on the fo'k'sle with the rest of the company, drawn up and armed, the muskets being loaded and inspected, waiting for the word to fire, which would have been in a few minutes, as we expected. Then a shot from the enemy struck our bows, and the wood went flying, but no one that I could see was hurt. And then I saw the captain strike the flag and cut down the first lieutenant. 'Mates,' I whispered, presently, 'either the ship is sinking or the captain has lost his stomach for the fight. If she sinks, we go to Davy's Locker; if he's played the coward, he will swing.'" As he said these words he turned his face to Jack with a look of triumph in his eyes. "We were all sent down below," he continued, "when the Frenchmen came aboard, and there we stayed with no arms and short rations. Two days afterwards I was on deck, taking my spell of fresh air with the others—about a dozen men in all. We were leaning against the bulwarks, wishing the job were over, and cursing the captain, who was sitting on the quarter-deck on the trunnions of a carronade, his hands on his knees, staring straight before him as if he saw the rope dangling before his eyes, already noosed for him. Suddenly I saw him spring from his place and catch the French officer, who was walking the deck, by the throat, and shake him like a dog. Then he threw him on the deck, where the Frenchman lay stunned and half dead, and he tore his sword from him; then he rushed upon one of the sentries and cut him down, and attacked the other. Some of the Frenchmen, seeing what was done, cried out in their own lingo and ran aft, some firing pistols and some drawing cutlasses; whereupon I called out to my mates and seized a rammer—which was the best thing for a weapon I could come at—and ran after them, and so to the captain's side, for I plainly saw that his design was to kill as many of the Frenchmen as he could, and to be killed himself, which I resolved to prevent if I could. And then the other Englishmen joined me, and in a very few minutes we had half of the prize crew killed or wounded, and the other half crying for quarter; but the captain was so furious that for some time he would give none, throwing himself upon all such as had weapons and would fight. Hard work I had to save him, but I did. When 'twas all over there wasn't a scratch upon him. I saved him, your honors. With a rammer I saved his life."

"Your courage," said the president, "does you credit. I shall take care that it is duly represented to the colonel of your regiment, and if your conduct is reported as equal to your gallantry, you will not go without your reward. The captain, you think, sought for death?"

"No one," said Aaron, "who did not want to be killed could have behaved as he did. Before the enemy called for quarter we had driven them together in the waist, where they were shouting and threatening to charge us with pikes and bayonets, but we had weapons by this time, and were ready to receive them. But they did not charge, because the captain leaped into the middle of them with nothing but his sword in his hand, laying about him like a madman. He was sober and in his senses when he cowardly hauled down the flag, but he was now, when he attacked the prize crew, gone stark mad. If he hadn't been mad, and not known what he was about, we should never have taken the ship."

"And you leaped after him?" asked one of the court.

"I had my rammer, which was almost as good as a quarter-staff; and I'd rather have a quarter-staff than a sword any day, or a pike either, if there's room for play."

"And this you did out of devotion or loyalty to your captain?" asked the president, astonished at the man's coolness, and the deliberation with which he gave his evidence.

"Nay, nay," he replied, grinning again; "I saved his life because I should have been sorry to see him die like a brave man. All I wanted was to see him swing, your honors, for striking his colors."

These words produced a sensation in the court, and all eyes were turned upon this witness who, though but a simple marine, carried devotion to his country's honor unto so great a height. But the officers of the *Calypso* whispered together, and I heard such words passed from one to the other as "rascal," "six dozen," "the first chance," "not good enough for him," and so forth, from which I conjectured that Aaron would find a warm welcome if he went to sea again on board this vessel. I think he must have heard the whispers, but he cared nothing for them; he was now enjoying a revenge sweeter far than any he had ever dreamed of or hoped for. This was, indeed, far better than to have murdered the captain with his own hand.

Therefore he turned his ugly face to the prisoner, and grinned with the satisfaction of his ignoble triumph. The court, however, seemed to take the words for an outburst of honest and patriotic feeling which did credit to this rough and simple fellow.

Captain Easterbrook refused to ask any questions of this witness either. It was now between three and four o'clock in the afternoon, when the president asked the prisoner if he designed to call any witnesses for the defence, and proposed to adjourn the court until the following day.

" Sir," said Jack, " I have no witnesses to call."

" Then," said the president, " you would doubtless wish for time to prepare your defence. It is now late; we will adjourn the court until to-morrow."

" Sir," said Jack, " I thank you. But with permission of the court I will make my defence without further delay. I will not trouble the court to adjourn."

The court conferred, and presently said that they would hear the prisoner at once, if he chose.

" Gentlemen," Jack began, " I have but few words to say; and as for defence, I have none. I have been at sea since my thirteenth year, and am now four-and-twenty. During this time I have been present in many actions, and I have never received aught but commendation from my superior officers. I served first under Captain Holmes, of the *Lenox*, and next on board the *Countess of Dorset*, when I was cast away on the coast of Patagonia, and, after wandering among the Indians, I was prisoner first to the Spaniards, and afterwards to the French. But I broke prison, and was appointed third lieutenant to Captain Lockhart, of the *Tartar*. I submit that my character for courage was never impugned on board any of these vessels, and Captain Lockhart hath thought fit to bear testimony in his despatches to my conduct in the many en-

gagements fought by his ship. You have also heard how I
was enabled, by the help of those of my crew then on deck,
to take the ship again."

He paused here, as if he were unwilling to say what was in
his mind.

"I submit to the court," said the deputy judge-advocate,
"that these facts, which I think the court will not dispute, do
not constitute any defence."

"They are no defence," Jack replied. "I state them because they form my only consolation in this hour. I have no
defence. The charge is true. My officers and crew would
have taken not only the *Malicieuse*, but the two other ships as
well. Their evidence is true in every particular. I wish to
testify that no commander ever had better officers, a handier
vessel, or a heartier crew. I threw all away. I struck the
colors. I cowardly and treacherously surrendered my ship
without firing a shot. I have but one prayer to make to the
court. It is that this act, which was wholly my own, may not
in the least degree prejudice the future of my brave lieutenants. It was this shameful hand, and none other, which
hauled down the flag of the *Calypso*."

When he concluded there was silence for a space, because
the court and everybody present were taken by surprise, and
because the contemplation of this tall and handsome lad (he
seemed no more) thus avowing, not proudly, but shamefully,
and yet honestly and fully, his own dishonor, overwhelmed us
with sadness. From his officers, standing together, there were
whispers, which could be heard all over the court: "He was
mad. A madman is not answerable for his doings. No one
but a madman would have done it;" and so forth. And I
verily believe, and have been assured, that there was not one
among them all who would not gladly have put out to sea
again under Captain Easterbrook, in full confidence that he
would fight the ship as long as a man was left alive to stand
beside him.

As for me, I had looked to see him call some witnesses. He
could not, it is true, call Bess Westmoreland; nor could he
tell the whole truth, else he would have stood before the court
and said, "Gentlemen, this is none other than the hand of God
which hath struck me for my sins, and because I broke my

solemn oath, passed to a woman. The hand hath struck me
in that way which most deeply and most bitterly I should feel.
For I never feared to die, nor to be wounded, but always and
before all things have I loved and prized honor and been jealous for my good name, and longed to distinguish myself and
to rise in the service. Wherefore, now have I been deprived
of the thing which most of all I prized, and stand before you
all, bereft of honor, a *cowardly* commander, so that there remains for me nothing but death; and whether I am hanged
or shot I care not, so that I may die soon. For there is no
place where I could live whither my shame would not also
follow me and be quickly blazoned forth to all the folk. Sentence me, therefore, quickly, and let me go."

This, I say, he felt, and knew to be the truth. Yet he would
not say it. But he might have called Mr. Brinjes, who would
have testified, which is the truth, though it did not perhaps
touch the case, that men who have been in places where the
sun is hot, especially such as have wandered about without
any covering for their heads, are often subject to sudden fits
of madness, during which they know not what they do; and
that perhaps this was the case with Captain Easterbrook. Nay,
I have heard learned physicians, disputing on such points, argue that sudden fits of madness are often produced by exposure to the hot sun; so that a man who hath once received a
sunstroke, as they call it, may, in such an access, commit murder, or any other crime, and not know afterwards what he
hath done.

The case being then concluded, and the whole evidence completed, with such defence as the defendant had thought fit to
set up, order was given to clear the court. Which was done,
the guard of marines taking the captain back to his cabin, and
the judges being left alone.

"He will die," said Captain Petherick; "I see in his eyes
that there is nothing left for him to desire but death. The
day of his execution will be welcome to him. Yet I hope that
they will not hang him like a cur, but will shoot him like a
brave man."

"He was certainly mad," said Mr. Shelvocke. "I remember once, being then off the Ladrone Islands—"

"Ay," said Mr. Brinjes, interrupting—I had not seen him

in court; yet he was there, dressed as if for the club—"Ay. The boy was mad. What? Would a coward have resolved upon so desperate an enterprise as to attack the prize crew single-handed? Death was before him—death if he failed; death if he succeeded; for to succeed was but to throw himself into a court-martial. Whereas, if he had suffered the ship to sail into Brest Harbor, he might have lived in France all his life in safety, and no one to know what had happened. Now, what can they do but sentence him to be hanged or shot? Luke, my lad, if I had Aaron ashore, I would make every one of his teeth like a lump of red-hot iron; rheumatic pains should grind his joints and twist his nerves; gout should tear and rend his stomach; tic should stick sharp teeth into his face. Well—patience! something will happen unto Aaron yet. If, now, the poor boy had been suffered to have his wish, he would have died in the moment of victory, when he had reconquered the ship. As for witchcraft"—here he whispered—"but that I know the poor wretch loves him still, and would rather die than suffer him to come to any harm, I should believe that Bess was at the bottom of the mischief. I say not that she is a witch; but no one knows what a revengeful woman can do when once she dabbles in the forbidden art."

Bess was, indeed, at the bottom of the mischief, but in a way which Mr. Brinjes could not understand; for he had not, so far as I could discover, the fear of the Lord before his eyes, and was, indeed, little better than a pagan.

"There is again," he said, "the old black woman. But then Jack was to marry her mistress, and therefore she would not harm him. Yet there must be a girl in it, and she must have put Obi upon him by the help of some, though I knew not that there were any other Obeah men in this country besides myself. If I were younger, I would go to Portsmouth and find that woman, and then Luke, my lad, she should be made to feel as if it had been better for her never to have been born."

"Bess, at least, is no witch," I said, for the fire of his one eye was so bright that I feared he might have fallen upon her, or, at least, compelled her to tell him the truth.

"This woman, whoever she may be, hath robbed the king's service of the most gallant officer. She hath deprived a lovely woman of her sweetheart; she hath covered us all with shame and confusion. Wherefore, may her flesh fall rotten from her bones! May—"

"Nay, Mr. Brinjes," I said, "when you find her you can curse her. Let not your curses loose upon an unknown woman."

He stopped, but it was because at this moment the court was thrown open and the prisoner was taken back to hear his sentence. We learned afterwards that there was a difference of opinion among the judges, some inclining to mercy on the ground of the captain's conduct in recapturing the ship. But in the end the sterner counsels prevailed; and, indeed, the commander of a ship can on no grounds be pardoned for surrendering to the enemy save in extremity. Suppose a man commits a forgery, is it any defence that before and after this act of wickedness he led a good and virtuous life? Suppose a boy picks a pocket, is it any defence that he is sorry, and would fain give back the purse and the money that was in it?

We went back to the court. Alas! the prisoner's sword was now reversed, and lay upon the table, the point towards the prisoner, which meant death.

"Guilty," whispered Mr. Brinjes, not looking at the sword. "Death is written in their faces." It was. And yet the brave officers who had already passed and signed the sentence of death, showed compassion in their faces.

As for me, I cannot even now, after nearly forty years have passed, think of that moment without the tears rising to my eyes. The court was crowded with fine ladies, who had come from London to see the trial. They thought, perhaps, to enjoy the spectacle of a gallant man brought to shame, but they could not without tears and sobbing look upon this poor fellow, tall and manly, brought forth to hear a sentence of death.

The deputy judge-advocate arose, and read the sentence in his hand, signed by every member of the court.

"Captain John Easterbrook, the court-martial duly held upon you for the loss of his majesty's ship the *Calypso*, find that you did cowardly surrender your ship. The sentence of the court is, that on a day to be presently appointed according to the will of his gracious majesty the king, you be placed upon the quarter-deck of the *Calypso* and be there shot to death. God save the king!"

"Gentlemen," said Jack, in a clear, firm voice, "I thank the court for their patient hearing of the case. I looked for no other verdict, and I desire no other. I acknowledge the justice of the sentence. God save the king !''

CHAPTER XLIII.

AFTER THE COURT-MARTIAL.

THUS ended the court-martial ; thus was made grievous shipwreck of a gallant youth's ambition, his honor, and his life ; yet, as to his honor, 'twas stoutly and steadfastly maintained by all sailors, and especially by the officers and men of the *Calypso*, that the captain's surrender (being done in a moment of madness or by power of witchcraft) was fully atoned for by his surprising recapture of the ship. That, too, has always been the opinion of his friends, though, for my own part, as the only one left who knows the whole truth, I cannot but acknowledge that the madness was sent by Heaven, just as much as that madness which the ancients feigned to have been inflicted on the Greek hero who slew cattle and sheep, thinking they were his enemies. Therefore, no atonement for his deed was necessary, seeing that it was itself a punishment inflicted by the hand of a justly-offended Creator.

I know not who told the truth to the admiral, but perhaps it was Mr. Brinjes, who went daily to see him on account of an attack of gout, brought on partly by his distress of mind and the shame of this untoward event, and partly by the fault of the poor old gentleman himself, who tried to drown care with port wine and punch. This attack obstinately resisted the apothecary's remedies. Indeed, though for the time he presently recovered, yet he came no more to the Sir John Falstaff, and never held up his head again, going in great heaviness, and, I fear, still taking more drink than is good for any man, until the disease mounted to his stomach, where, Mr. Brinjes being no longer at hand to assuage the pain, it speedily made an end of him.

On the evening of the court-martial the gentlemen of the club met as usual, though without their president. The conversation was enlivened, if one may say so, by the extraordinary and tragical incidents of the day. They drank not less, but rather more, in order to sustain their spirits; they took their liquor with whispers and lowered voice, as is done in a house where one lies dead; and they naturally talked much on subjects akin to what was in their thoughts, as if seeking consolation in recalling examples resembling the case which so much touched their hearts. Thus King Richard the Second is represented by Shakespeare as loving, when in captivity, to talk of the violent deaths of princes.

"I was present," said Captain Petherick, "at the execution of Admiral Byng, two years and a half ago. If family influence could have availed, he would have been spared. Yet he was shot, and went to his death with a smiling countenance."

"I remember," said Mr. Shelvocke—but I know not whether this was true—"the death of Captain Kirby and Captain Wade for cowardly deserting Admiral Benbow, and that was fifty-seven years ago."

Another recalled the well-known case of Lieutenant Baker Philips, shot in 1745, for surrendering the *Anglesea* to the *Apollon*, after the captain and first lieutenant were both killed. No mercy was shown to him, though it was proved that he had but two hundred men and forty guns (and of his crew fifty killed and wounded), against the French crew of five hundred men with fifty guns. Yet they shot him at Spithead, on board the *Princèss Royal*. As for other courts-martial, Captain Fox, of the *Kent*, was dismissed his ship for neglect of duty in 1747. In 1744, Admiral Mathers and four captains were cashiered for neglect of duty. In the same year the master of the *Northumberland*, the captain being mortally wounded, surrendered the ship before the lieutenant could get on deck. Wherefore, he was sentenced to be confined in the Marshalsea for the remainder of his life. "And there, gentlemen," said Mr. Underhill, "he lies to this day, and but last Monday se'nnight I saw him, and conversed with him—a poor, broken man, who vainly prays for death."

In short, the talk ran wholly upon trials and executions; the unhappy young man now lying under sentence of death was, so to speak, executed beforehand and in imagination by his friends, who stood (for him) upon the quarter-deck, eyes bandaged, arms folded, before the file of marines, and hoped (for him) nothing more than a happy shot through heart or head, which should put an instant stop to life. Then the conversation turned upon the various methods of violent deaths, all of which seem to be accompanied by great, and some by prolonged, agonies—such as breaking on the wheel, the punishment of the knout, or burning alive—and there was much discussion as to which method of violent death seemed the most preferable.

It was remarkable that Mr. Brinjes, generally one who talked more than any, for the most part sat apart during this gloomy talk, taking his pipe of tobacco without much share in the conversation, whether from excess of grief or from the callous disposition of old age, to which most things seem to matter little. But he muttered to himself, as old people use, without heed to those who are about them, and I overheard him.

"Ay, ay," he said, "the boy must be shot, I suppose, and then Bess will not live. She will certainly live no longer when he is gone. So I have lost both. She will go drown herself as soon as the shots are fired. But he is not dead yet; while there is life there is hope; who knows what may happen? 'Twill be three, and perhaps six weeks before the day of execution. Much may be done in six weeks. The lad is not shot yet, nor is Bess drowned. And as for Aaron, but he saved the captain's life. Wherefore, though he did it with an ill design, I harm him not." Presently he recovered his spirits, and looked about him, and began to talk in a more cheerful strain, though how he could put on a show of cheerfulness with the prospect before him of Jack's certain execution and Bess's self-murder passes understanding. "The lad is not shot yet!" he said. Why, what could be done for him? Nothing. A reprieve was past praying for. Yet it must be acknowledged that the popular indignation which had at first run high against the captain who thus cowardly surrendered, quickly subsided and changed into compassion when the circumstances of the recapture became known, so that perhaps a reprieve might not have been so impossible had there been any in high place to ask for it.

As regards the condemned man, whom I saw many times after the sentence, I declare that I have never known any man more cheerful and resigned to his fate than was this most unfortunate captain during the three weeks which passed between his sentence and the day of his execution. Of hope he had none; nor did he desire to live.

" If I were reprieved," he said, " whither should I go? how live? I am but twenty-four years of age, and I might live for fifty years to come, even into the next century, if the world endure so long, with the accursed remembrance of one day always in my mind, and among people who would never tire of pointing at the captain who surrendered his ship without striking a blow—one single blow—the most cowardly surrender in the history of the British navy. Why, 'twould be every day a thousand times worse than the pains of death. My worst enemy could devise no more cruel punishment than to send me forth free to walk the streets of an English town. Nay, Bess "—for she was with him—" 'tis idle to talk. I know what thou would'st say, dear girl. For a mad act—we know, my dear, why that madness was sent, and for what cause permitted—no man should be held responsible. Why, my first lieutenant was here yesterday, and said as much. But even he does not know, and the world can never know, the whole truth."

In those last days Bess was with him always. She came at eight in the morning, and she left him at eight in the evening. Everybody knew by this time that she was the captain's sweetheart; no one found it strange or wonderful, because Bess was the finest woman in Deptford, and the captain was the comeliest man; and people only sometimes remembered that he had been reported as promised to the daughter of the admiral. It astonished me, perhaps because I daily expected and feared it, that no one so much as hinted at the possibility of Bess being engaged in witchcraft, though all were agreed that by foul practices the captain had been deprived for the moment of his courage. It is no longer the custom to burn witches; yet I am sure that if any woman had been discovered, or even suspected, by the good people of Deptford to have been concerned in this wickedness, she would have suffered every torture they could have devised. Burning, mere burning, would have seemed too mild a punishment for a woman who could thus by her villainous sorceries turn a brave man into a coward. Again, if things had gone well with this poor girl, if Jack had returned home triumphant and victorious, and had then openly

sought his humble sweetheart, there were plenty of women who
would have said hard and cruel things concerning her, as is
their way with each other.   But now, when her lover lay under sentence of death, they refrained their tongues ; nay, they
even said good things of her, reckoning it to her credit that,
for the sake of the captain, she would receive the addresses of
no other man, and that she sent Aaron Fletcher about his business, and consorted with none of her former friends (who were
beneath the notice of a captain's lady), and sought in the society of Mr. Brinjes to acquire the manners and the bearing
of a gentlewoman.   When she went down to the Stairs in the
morning, those women whom she passed on her way stood aside
for her in silence, and looked after her with compassion in their
eyes, and even with tears ; and those, perhaps, the rudest women
of the place, fit companions for the rudest sailors, abandoned
in morals, soddened with drink, foul of tongue, and ever ready
to strike and to swear.   So that pity may find a home in the
most savage breast.

She sat with Jack, therefore, all day long in the cabin, which
was his condemned cell.   For the first day or two she wept
continually.   Then she ceased her crying altogether, and sat
with dry eyes.   She said nothing, but she looked upon her
sweetheart always, as if hungering after the sight of his dear
face.   But from time to time she rose and flung out her arms,
as if she could not bear herself.   This was natural when a
woman regains her lover only to lose him by a violent death.
One evening I walked home with her through the town, and
she told me, poor girl, what was in her mind.   "I shall not
live after him," she said—" of that I am resolved.   Why, if it
be as he says, that Heaven hath punished him for his inconstancy, was it not through my mouth that the punishment was
pronounced ?   Where he goes, I shall go.   When he dies, I shall
die.   In that same hour when the bullets tear his dear heart
shall I die too ; and so my soul shall join his.   I know not," she
said, wildly, " oh ! I know not whither we shall be sent in the
next world ; and I care nothing—no, nothing—so only that we
go there together.   I am quite sure that he is forgiven all his
sins, if ever he committed any, though I know not that they
can be worth considering.   And he dies for them.   What can
a man do more ?   As for me, I am not afraid, because I have

always gone to church every Sunday morning. Oh! I doubt
not we shall go to heaven together, and sit hand-in-hand, and
side by side; and perhaps we shall forget the past, somehow,
and then the old brave look will come back to my boy's eyes.
What would heaven be to him if I were not with him—and
what to me if my Jack were not beside me? And oh! Luke,
he loves me now more tenderly than ever he loved me before.
And I am happy, though I know that we have but a day or two
more to live. They tell me that to be shot gives no pain; else
I could not bear it, and must die first."

I pointed out to her the wickedness of self-destruction; but
she would not listen, crying wildly that she cared for no wickedness—not she—so that she could join in death, as well as in life,
the man she loved. Surely there never was woman who loved
man with so violent a passion; and now in these last days,
when it was all too late, there never was girl more truly loved.

" 'Tis the fondest heart, Luke!" said Jack, the tears in his
eyes. " Why, for thy sake, sweet Bess, I would be almost contented to live, and to forget the past. If we could go somewhere
together, where no man knew or could find out my dishonor—
if we could go and live on one of the islands in the Southern
Seas— But this is idle talk."

Then the time drew near when the sentence must be carried
out. We expected from day to day to hear that the time was
fixed.

About a fortnight after the sentence a sudden and most surprising change came over Bess. She left off crying altogether;
sometimes, even, she laughed; she seemed not to know, or even
to care, what she said or did. She would throw herself into
Jack's arms, and kiss him passionately; at the next moment
she would tear herself free, and stand gasping and panting,
and with wild eyes, as if with impatience, so that I feared lest
she should lose her reason altogether. I have heard that persons condemned to the flames by the accursed Inquisition
(which they dare to call holy) have been known to go mad
with the terror of looking forward to that awful torture. Sure
I am that no flames of the stake could be more dreadful to
Bess than the thought of the moment when her lover would
fall dead, pierced by a dozen bullets. Jack at such times
would try to calm her, but she shook him off, crying " No—no.

Let me be. Oh! I am choking. Oh! Jack—my dear—if you knew what is in my heart! Yes—Jack. I will be quiet. Oh! what a wretch am I that I should add to your trouble at such a time!" Then she threw herself at his feet, and caught his hands. "Jack," she cried, "you know that I am your servant and your slave. Oh! if I loved you when all the world spoke well of you, think how much more I love you now you have got no one—oh! no one but your poor fond girl!"

He raised her and kissed her. Nothing now could move him but the sight of her tears and suffering, which (I am not ashamed to write this down) brought tears to my own eyes.

"Let us pretend," she said—"let us talk like children—oh! we were once happy children, and we could pretend and believe what we pleased. Why—all this is only pretence. The cabin is our old summer-house; you are only twelve years of age, and I am a little girl; and we have been playing at courts-martial. No," she shuddered, "that is a dreadful game. We will play at something else. We are going away—you and I together, Jack—we shall take a ship and sail far away from England to the islands you have seen, and Mr. Brinjes talks about —we will live there—oh! no one will ever find us out. We have long to live. I will work for you, and you will forget all that has happened. Then we shall grow old. Do you think you would love an old woman, Jack, who had lost her beauty and gone gray and toothless? And then we would lie down and die together. Why—whatever happens, we will die together—we must die together. Jack—Jack— Oh! if we could go away; oh! if we could go away together—to leave it all behind, and to forget it!"

"Patience, dear heart," he said. "Patience, Bess; it tears me to see thee suffer."

I was with them; and—but who could see and listen to him without tears? I am not a stock or stone.

"Patience?" she replied. "Yes, yes! I will have patience! Jack, do you remember three years ago, the day we were in the summer-house, Luke being present, you solemnly made a great promise?"

"I remember, Bess. God knows I have reason to remember not only the promise, but how I kept it."

"Make me one more promise, Jack." She laid her hands

upon his arm. " Make me one more promise now. Luke is here again to witness for us."

" Why, child, what promise can I make thee now ? A dying man can neither make nor break a promise. Shall I promise to love thee in the next world ?"

" Nay, promise what I shall tell thee. Say, after me, I, Jack Easterbrook—"

" I, Jack Easterbrook," he repeated.

" Do swear solemnly, before God Almighty—"

He repeated these words.

" That I will grant to Bess Westmoreland one more request, whatever she may ask me, before I die."

He said after her, concluding with the words,

" Whatever she may ask me, before I die."

She fetched a great sigh, and kissed him again ; and, throwing her arms round his neck, laid her head upon his shoulder.

I could not, for the life of me, understand what she meant ; and still I thought that her brain must be wandering with her troubles.

CHAPTER XLIV.

HOW BESS WENT AWAY.

It was only three weeks after the sentence that the condemned man received a summons to prepare himself for his execution, which was fixed for Monday, February the 23d. This was a shorter space between sentence and execution than was awarded to the unhappy Admiral Byng, who had eight weeks in which to prepare himself for death. However, Jack complained not, and received the announcement in a becoming spirit, and presently sent a letter to my father, who lost no time in visiting him, and continued daily to visit him until the day of execution.

Now, here I have to write down a strange thing, and one which is hardly to be credited. From the day of his trial (when, as I have said, the court was crowded with ladies) to the day before the execution, the ship was visited by ladies curious to see, and, if possible, to converse with this young and unfort-

17

unate officer. But he would not receive any. Nay, every day
letters came to him full of tender messages and of prayers,
some of them entreating him to grant them an interview, some
openly declaring their passion for him, some humbly asking
for a lock of his hair, or a line in his handwriting, some begging him to observe secrecy in his replies, and some offering
their services in high quarters to procure him a pardon or a
reprieve. To none of these letters did Jack reply a word, but
tore all up and threw the fragments from his cabin window.
One day, however (it was after the day had been fixed for
carrying out the sentence), there came a lady on board who
would take no denial, but wrote down her name upon the back
of a playing-card and peremptorily ordered that it should be
taken to the prisoner. She was very finely dressed, and they
took her for a great lady, and obeyed her, taking the card to
the captain's cabin. She was so quick, however, that she followed the messenger, and so forced her way in.

"My handsome Jack!" she cried, but stopped short, because
she found another woman with him.

"Madam," said Jack, rising, "this is an unexpected honor."

"I came, captain," she said, "because we are old friends,
and because I would fain help thee if I can."

"No one can, madam."

"And because if I cannot, thou mayst still help me."

"You may command me, madam."

"Nay," she said, looking still at Bess, "why so formal, Jack?
'Tis terrible to think that in a few days—"

"Madam, my time is short; pray remember that, and be brief."

"Why, captain," she laughed, "'twas but a little thing; and
perhaps this lady will grant me five minutes alone—"

"It needs not," said Jack; "you can speak openly before her."

"In that case it will be needless. Yet I will try. Captain,
thou art condemned to die. 'Tis sad, indeed. Yet 'tis true.
Now consider my case. I am deeply in debt. I have quarrelled
with my lord. Marry me, and so take my debts off my back.
Nay, madam," for Bess sprang to her feet, "be pacified. 'Tis
but an empty form that I ask. He shall marry me, and I will
retire with the clergyman, and so he will free me at a stroke of
all my debts."

"Madam," said Jack, before Bess could find time to speak,

"you are unfortunately too late. It is impossible that I could gratify you in this request, because I am married already. This lady is my wife—my most unfortunate wife."

" Oh, madam !" said the actress, with a deep courtesy, " I beg humbly to be forgiven ! Believe me, I did not know. Well, captain," she heaved a sigh, " of all the men I have ever known thou hast gone nearest to make me think I have a heart. My poor Jack !" She seized his hand and kissed it. " Oh, madam," she turned to Bess, " I thought not of this. I thought I should find him over a bowl of punch, drinking away his care. Alas ! I remember you now. You loved him, and—I remember you— Poor child ! Who shall comfort thee ?"

So she stole away, weeping, and left them alone.

It was, indeed, true. The first service which Jack had asked of my father was to marry him to Bess Westmoreland. It was done secretly in the cabin, with no other witnesses than myself and the first lieutenant, Mr. Colin Macdonald. So Bess got her heart's desire, and the old witch's prophecy proved true—that in the midst of troubles she should marry the man she loved. But what a marriage ! After this my father, as I have said, visited him daily, and every morning asked the prayers of the congregation for one about to die.

Then, as day followed day, and there wanted but two or three more, Bess became still more strange in her manner, showing a restlessness and impatience, so that she could no longer remain quiet for five minutes together, but must needs be pacing backward and forward, not crying or lamenting, but with burning face and eyes afire.

The sentence was to be carried out on the Monday morning. On Sunday, with a heart as heavy as lead, I prepared to say farewell.

I went on board about ten o'clock, at the time of morning prayers. Bess was already in the cabin, seated at the window, which was open, though the morning was cold, her face pressed against the bars. Jack was at the table writing a letter for the admiral.

" It is nearly finished, dear lad," he said, looking up with a smile. " Courage ! The worst was over when the trial was done. To die would be nothing—but for leaving Bess. Be kind to her, Luke ; be kind to her."

I looked to see her burst into tears. But no—she listened without a tear or even a sob. "This night, after I have parted with her, will be long, I fear. Your father hath comforted me greatly in the matter of religion, wherefore I have now a sure and certain hope, if I may humbly say so, though hitherto I have thought little of these matters. It is a blessed thing for thoughtless sailors that we have a Church to rule our faith, and forms of prayer to save our souls. He will come to-morrow, for the last prayers, before seven. At eight, the boats of the ships in port will surround the ship, the death-signal will be displayed, a gun will be fired, the crew will be drawn up on the deck, and the prisoner will be brought out." Bess listened without changing her countenance. Was she, then, turned into stone by sorrow, like Niobe?

I cannot write down the words with which he bade me farewell, nor my own. Suffice it that we took leave of each other with, on my side, all that a bleeding heart could find to say, and on his, with a message which I made haste to deliver to the admiral, his patron and benefactor.

Then I left him alone with Bess.

It was arranged that they should part upon the hour when she must leave the ship and go ashore. He was peremptory that she must not try to see him in the morning, lest the sight of her might unman him. To stand upon the deck with eyes unbandaged, resolute, and firm, was the only duty left for him to perform. Therefore Bess must part with him on Sunday night. She acquiesced, still without a single tear. But when the hour drew near, instead of hanging round his neck and weeping, she took both his hands in hers and said,

"Jack—dear Jack—my own Jack!—you made me a promise the other day. The time hath come to keep it."

"A promise, dear heart? Why, what can I do for thee now?"

"You would grant any request that I should make. The time hath now come."

"'Tis granted beforehand, dear girl."

"My request, Jack, is that you will live, and not die."

"Bess?"

"That you will live, and not die. Listen! We have arranged everything for this evening. Mr. Brinjes hath managed all for us. See!"—she whispered him very earnestly.

He gazed at her in a sort of stupefaction.

"We shall not stay in the country. A Dutch boat waits us off Barking Creek; the master, a boy, and yourself will sail her across to Holland. If the wind is fair, we shall make a Dutch port in a day; oh! it is all arranged. We shall not stay in Holland, but take ship to the Dutch East Indies, and thence to the South Seas, where we will live—oh! my Jack—far, far away from the world; and I will work for thee. So we shall forget the past and Deptford, and—and—everything, and there will be a new life for us—oh! a new life, whether it be short or long, with no one to remind us of what hath happened. Oh! my poor tortured dear—it is through me—through me—that all this disgrace hath come upon thee; yes—and it shall be through me that thy life shall be saved!"

"Bess, I cannot! They would say that it was fitting that one who could cowardly strike the flag should also cowardly run away from punishment."

"What matter what they say? Shall we care what they say when we are sailing together among those islands? Will it touch our hearts any more to think of their praise or blame?"

"Bess, I cannot!—oh! my tender heart, I cannot!"

"Then, Jack, thou shalt. Thy promise is passed—a solemn promise before God. Wilt thou break that promise too, and go before Heaven, thy last act another broken pledge?"

Well, he fought awhile, and he yielded at length; and then she kissed him and went away; but she held her handkerchief to her eyes, so that those who saw her might not suspect.

At the head of the gangway, which, for the convenience of the court-martial, had been made into an accommodation-ladder, furnished with rails and entering-ropes, stood Aaron Fletcher on guard.

"Thou art satisfied at last, Aaron?" said Bess.

"Not yet, but I shall be to-morrow," he replied, whispering, because a sentry must not talk.

She said no more, but passed down the steps and into the boat.

In the afternoon, being in great distress of heart, I went to visit Mr. Brinjes. He was not sleeping, but was busied over a great number of small packages arranged in order upon the table.

"I have seen the last of him."

"Ay? Is Bess with him?" said he.

"I am troubled about Bess. I think she hath gone distracted; for she weeps no more, and once I saw her laugh. She catches her breath, too, and is impatient."

"For her distraction I will answer. I know a remedy for it, and that remedy she shall have. As for the catching of her breath, that too shall be cured: as for her impatience, I cannot help it, because it was impossible to complete the job before to-day."

I asked him what he meant.

"Hath not Bess told you, then? Why, she was to have told you this morning before she broke the thing to Jack. 'Tis a good girl who can keep a secret. It is not true, mind ye, that no woman can keep a secret. Where their lovers are concerned, they can keep fifty thousand basketfuls of secrets, and never spill so much as a single one."

He began to open the packets, and to count their contents. They contained guineas, about fifty in each packet, and there seemed to be no end to them.

"This," he said, "comes of twenty years' honest industry. If a man takes in his shop six half-crowns a day, and spends only one, in twenty years he shall be master, look you, of no less than four thousand pounds."

Heavens! could he really be the owner of so great a property? When he had counted the money he dropped it in three or four leathern bags, which he tied to a belt below his waistcoat. "Now," said he, "if we capsize, I shall go straight to Davy's Locker. Give me the skull-stick, my lad—so." He looked at the horrid thing with admiration. "I thought at first of giving it to Philadelphy, but now I will not, because she has lied to me about the great secret, which I find she doth not, after all, possess. So much I suspected. She shall not have the Obeah stick. Besides, Heaven knows whither we are going, or what powers we may want; therefore, I shall keep the stick." He wrapped a cloth about the skull, and tied it up so that no one should know what it was. Then he laid it upon the table.

I observed then that everything was ready as if for departure. The shelves were empty; the fire was out; there were ashes of burned paper in the grate; the famous charts were rolled up and lying on the table beside the skull-stick. What did it mean?

"Why," he said, "since Bess hath not told you, I will not either. But—I think we can trust thee, Luke—surely we can trust thee, if any one. Thou lovest Jack, I know, and Bess too, in thy mild and milky way. Why, a lad of spirit would have carried the girl off years ago, Jack or no Jack. However —that is enough. My lad, we want thy help. There is no other that we can trust. It is life or death—life or death— life or death. Say that to thyself, and *forget not to be here at nine of the clock this evening.*"

"What is to be done at nine?"

"It is life or death, I say. Life or death! Now go; I have much to do. It is life or death. Two lives or two deaths. Life or death. Therefore, fail not."

At nine o'clock I kept my appointment, wondering what would happen.

Bess was there, wrapped in a cloak and hood; in her hands she carried a small parcel. Mr. Brinjes was waiting, muffled and cloaked, his hat tied over his ears, and a roll—containing, I suppose, his charts and famous skull-stick—under his arm.

"Come, lad," he said, "thou shalt know soon what it is we have to do."

It was a dark and rainy night; the wind blew in gusts; the streets were deserted, save for some drunken fellow, who rolled along, bawling as he went. Mr. Brinjes led the way towards the river, and we were presently at the Stairs, where the boats lay fastened to the rings by their long painters.

"Take the outside boat of all," said the apothecary; "her oars are left in her on purpose. So, haul her to the stairs. Step in, Bess. She is but a little dingy, but she will serve. Luke you have to row. You may shut your eyes, and keep them shut, if you like, for I shall steer."

I began to suspect that something serious was to be attempted, but I obeyed without question or remonstrance.

'Twas then high tide, or a little on the ebb, so that at midnight the ebb would be at its strongest. I untied the painter and shoved off. Then I took my seat and the oars, and rowed while Mr. Brinjes steered.

The river was rough and dark, save for the lights displayed by the ships. The *Calypso* was moored very nearly off the mouth of the dock, but in mid-stream. Mr. Brinjes suffered me to row almost across the river, as if he were making for one of the stairs on the other side. Then he put her head up stream, and steered so that the boat approached the *Calypso*, whose lights he knew, not as if we were boarding her, but as if we were making our way across her bows to the Dog-and-Duck Stairs of Redriff. The precaution was not necessary, perhaps, seeing how dark it was; but the eyes of sailors are sharper than those of landsmen, and the watch must not allow a boat to approach a ship without a challenge. We crossed the bows, therefore, of the *Calypso*, I still rowing, and the boat apparently heading for the opposite shore.

But while we were still under the shadow, so to speak, of the great ship's bows, my cockswain whispered, " Easy rowing —ship oars."

I could not guess what he intended. 'Twas this.

The *Calypso* lay pretty high out of water. The tide was running strong. Mr. Brinjes turned the boat's head and ran her straight under the side of the ship. He then, being as quick and skilful in the handling of a boat as any man sixty years younger, stepped into the bows, and with hand and boat-hook worked the boat along the side of the vessel to the stern, where he hooked on, and whispered that we must now wait.

" We have more than two hours still to wait. I think the watch will have no suspicion, and 'tis better to wait here an hour or two than to hurry at the end, and so perhaps be seen and the whole plot spoiled. Here we lie snug."

We might be lying snug, but we lay more than commonly cold, and the wind and rain beat into one's face. Bess sat, however, with her hood thrown back, careless of cold or rain; and Mr. Brinjes lay muffled up in the bows. But in his hand he held the boat-hook.

The ship's bells and the town clocks and the Greenwich clocks made such a clashing in our ears, every quarter of an hour, as kept us aware of the time—never before did I understand how slowly he crawleth. Why, there seemed to me an hour between each quarter, and a whole night between each hour.

When the clocks began to strike midnight Bess looked up and the old man threw off his cloak. "Oars out," he whispered. "Gently. Don't splash. Here he is!"

We were immediately, though I knew it not, below the windows of Jack's cabin, which was the captain's stateroom. Below his window were those of the first and second lieutenants, and Mr. Brinjes had chosen the time of midnight because then the watches would be changing, and these officers would be on deck or else fast asleep. It was as he expected. The end of a rope fell into the water close beside the boat, and then, hand under hand, our prisoner came swiftly down. In a moment he was sitting in the stern. Then Mr. Brinjes let go, and the tide, hurrying down the river as fast as a mill-race, carried us noiselessly and swiftly away.

No one spoke, but Mr. Brinjes again took the ropes, and I began to row. We were very soon, keeping in mid-stream, past Greenwich and past Woolwich, I rowing as hard as I could, and the ebb-tide strong, so that we made very good way indeed.

Presently we came alongside a small vessel lying moored off Barking Creek, and Mr. Brinjes steered the boat alongside, and caught a rope.

"Now, Bess," he said, "quick; climb up."

She caught hold of the cleats, and ran up the rude gangway as nimbly as any sailor. Mr. Brinjes followed.

Then Jack seized my hand. "Farewell, dear lad," he said, "I thought not to see thee again. Farewell."

So he followed, and left me alone in the boat.

"Sheer off, Luke," said Mr. Brinjes, looking over the side, "sheer off, and take her back to the Stairs. Tell no one what hath been done. Farewell. We sail for the Southern Seas."

Then I saw that they were hoisting sail. She was a Dutch galiot, carrying a main and mizzen mast, with a large gaff mainsail. These, with a staysail, a flying topsail, and one or two bowsprit jibs, would, with this wind and tide, take her down to the North Foreland very quickly, after which, if the wind still continued fair, she might expect to make the port of Rotterdam in sixteen or perhaps twenty hours more.

When I had painfully pulled the boat up-stream and gotten her back in her place at the Stairs, and was at last in bed, I began to understand fully what had been done—namely, that a

17*

great crime had been committed in the rescue of a prisoner
sentenced to death, and that, with my two accomplices, I was
liable to be tried and—I fell asleep before I could remember
what the punishment would be.

CHAPTER XLV.

THE CONCLUSION.

THE next morning my father was astir by six; and I, hearing him, and remembering suddenly what had happened, could
sleep no more, but rose quickly and dressed. He was already
in wig and cassock; his clerk in readiness with Prayer-book,
Bible, and the materials wherewith to administer the Supper of
the Lord.

"My son," he said, "the ministration to a dying man is the
most awful part of a clergyman's holy duties; and yet it is that
which should most fill him with gratitude and joy. Terrible it
is at all times to watch the soul take its flight into the unknown
regions; most terrible of all when death comes violently upon
one still young and strong and in the prime of his day."

More he would have said; but here we were interrupted by
the arrival of the admiral himself, borne in an arm-chair by his
four negroes, his feet swathed in flannel, and himself wrapped
in warm cloaks, for 'twas dangerous for him to leave the warmth
of his own room.

"Doctor," he said, when the men had set him down, "you
are now about to comfort our boy in his last moments." Here
he paused awhile, the tears running down his cheeks. "His
last moments, poor lad," he repeated. "I could not lie still
and think that he should die without a word from me. Therefore, though I would not turn his thoughts away from religion,
I cannot let him die with never a word from his father's oldest
friend. 'Twere inhuman. Tell him, therefore, from me, that
I now plainly perceive that he was mad. Other men besides
himself have gone mad at sea. I know one who went mad and
jumped overboard, in a storm; and another who went mad and
ran amuck on the quarter-deck with a cutlass, wounding many
before he was disarmed; and another—but no matter. He

was mad. Tell him that for the act of God there is nothing but resignation. The thing might have happened to any. We are fools to feel any shame in it. As for all that went before and that came after his madness, tell him we are proud of him therefor, and we shall remain proud of him. But for his own sake, we are grieved that he was not killed in the recapture of the vessel. Bid him, therefore, meet his death with a calm heart—a brave heart, I know, will not fail him. Take him my last blessing, and my undiminished love. There is no question, tell him, of forgiveness. The act of God must not be questioned. But the pity of it—oh! doctor—the pity of it!" and with that he fell to weeping like a child.

And then the two old men wept together, but I, who knew what had happened and that there would be no execution that day, had no tears.

They carried back the admiral and put him to bed again, and I accompanied my father as far as the Stairs. As I returned slowly, my heart full of strange emotions, the bell of St. Paul's began to toll the passing knell. No need to ask for whom that bell was tolling. At the sound the women came to the doors and began to cry, and to talk together, full of pity, the kind-hearted creatures, shrews as they were, and slatterns, and drabs. The old men at the Trinity Hospital were gathered together in their quadrangle, talking of the boy they had known and loved. The barber and his four 'prentices were busy shaving, the shop full, everybody talking at the same time; and in his doorway stood Mr. Westmoreland, looking up and down the street, with troubled face.

"Where is she?" he asked. "Mr. Luke, where is my Bess?"

"Indeed, Mr. Westmoreland," I replied, "where should she be if not in her own bed?"

"She hath not been home all night. I have heard talk of her and Captain Easterbrook. But that poor young man is to be shot this morning. Where can she be? They tell me that she spends the days in his cabin. Sir, you know them both: I'faith, he hath played her false. Who would have daughters? Yet if she is all day long with him, needs must that she come ashore in the evening, Mr. Luke. Who, sir, I ask you, would have daughters to plague his old age? I thought she might have stayed at the apothecary's, and I have knocked, but I can make no one hear. Think you that Mr. Brinjes is dead? He is already of a very great old age. This is a terrible morning. That poor young gentleman must die; he must be cut off in the pride of his life and strength, the comeliest man I have ever seen, and he hath stolen my daughter's heart away. Why, what shall I do with her when he is dead? How shall I endure her despair and her grief; how find consolation to assuage her wrath when he is gone?"

I knew very well how that question would be answered. But I could not tell him what had happened.

"It is his passing-bell," the penman continued. "Lord have mercy upon his soul! He is young, and hath doubtless committed some of the sins of youth? the Lord forgive him! He hath often used profane language, and that in my hearing. The Lord forgive him! As for his striking his colors, that will not, I am sure, be laid to his charge. Besides, he hath atoned for this sin by his death. The Lord forgive him for an honest and brave lad! 'Twas once a joy to see him handle his logarithms. Will they bury him in St. Paul's churchyard? Poor lad! Poor lad! What shall I say to Bess to comfort her when she comes home?"

Thus he went on prattling; but I left him.

At the door of Mr. Brinjes's shop stood his assistant, knocking.

"Sir," he said, "I am afraid that something hath happened to my master, for I have knocked and cannot make him hear."

I advised him to wait half an hour or so, and then to knock again.

It was impossible to rest. I went again to the Stairs, where the watermen should be hanging about. There was not one man there, nor a single boat. Round the *Calypso* there was a great fleet of ships' boats, and Thames boats, all waiting for the execution. People had come down from London—even, they said, as far as from Chelsea—to see the sight. Why, they could see nothing from the river. True, they might have the satisfaction of hearing the roll of the muskets. There never was so great a concourse on the river, even on the day of Horn Fair.

At eight o'clock—the time of execution—everybody listened to hear the rattling of the guns. But there was silence. Pres-

ently, I know not how it began, there sprang up a rumor—only
a rumor at first—that the sentence would not be carried out
that morning ; then it became certain that there would be no
execution at all ; and it was spread abroad that, at the last moment, the captain had been respited. About eleven o'clock
the boats dispersed and returned again, the people disappointed. It was not until later that it was known—because at
first no one, not even my father and his clerk, were permitted
to leave the ship—that Captain Easterbrook could not be shot,
because he could not be found.

I found the apothecary's shop open—they had broken in
at the back—and the assistant was mixing medicines and pre-
scribing.

" Sir," he said, " my master is gone. He hath not slept in
his bed. He hath taken his money and his charts, but nothing
else."

" His money and his charts ? How do you know that he
hath taken his money ?"

" I know where he kept it, and I looked to see if it was gone.
Because, I said, if my master's money is still there, he will return. But it is gone ; therefore I know that he has gone."

" Whither hath he gone, sirrah ?"

" I know not, sir ; any more "—here he looked mighty cunning—" than I know whither Captain Easterbrook hath gone,
or Bess Westmoreland, or what you were doing with my master and Bess on the Stairs last night at nine o'clock."

Now, I have never learned if this man knew more than the
fact that we were upon the Stairs at that time. Certainly, he
could not know the whole truth.

" I think," I said, " that if I were you, I would continue to
carry on the business without asking any questions, until your
master returns."

" I will, sir," he replied ; and he did. His master did not
return, and this fortunate young man succeeded to a good stock
and a flourishing trade, and would doubtless have become rich
but for the accident of being killed by a drunken sailor.

When it became known that Mr. Brinjes, Bess, and the captain had all disappeared on the same evening, it was impossible
not to connect these three events ; and all the world believed
(what was perfectly true) that the girl had run away with the

captain, and that Mr. Brinjes had gone, too, out of pure affection for them.

The admiral presently recovered from his attack, but he went no more to the Sir John Falstaff, and entirely lost his former spirits; and, as I have already said, within a year or two was carried off by an attack of gout in the stomach. Shortly afterwards I was so happy as to win the affections of Castilla. She informed me that, although she was carried away by natural pride in so gallant a wooer as Jack, she had never felt for him such an assurance in his constancy as is necessary to secure happiness, and that when she heard of his infatuated passion for so common a creature as Bess Westmoreland, she was thankful for her release, though she deplored the sad cause of it. "We no longer," she often says, "burn women for witchcraft, but such a girl as Bess, who can so bewitch a gallant man as to make him invoke the curse of Heaven upon him if he prove inconstant, and thereby bring him to shame and disgrace, ought to be punished in some condign and exemplary manner." It is not my practice to argue with my wife, especially on points where we are not likely to agree; and as Bess will probably never return, and cannot, therefore, be punished, Castilla may say anything she pleases about her. For my own part, my heart has always been with that poor girl, who did not seek for or expect the honor of Jack's affections, and whose only witchery was in her beauty and her black eyes.

On the conclusion of peace, in 1762, Aaron Fletcher, with many other marines, was disbanded, but he was afraid to venture back into Deptford, where his creditors would have arrested him. I know not for a certainty what he did to bring the arm of the law upon him; but I know what became of him; for one day, being at Limehouse, I saw going along the road on the way to the Stairs, where were waiting several ships' boats, a dismal company of convicts, for embarkation to the plantations of Jamaica, or Barbadoes, or some other West Indian island. There were at least a hundred of them, walking two and two, handcuffed in pairs. Some of these were in rags, some shaking with prison-fever, some dejected, some angry and mutinous, some were singing—there are wretches so hardened that they will sing ribald songs on their way even to the gallows.

One there was of appearance and bearing superior to the rest,
by whose side there walked a young woman, his wife or mistress, bearing a baby, and crying bitterly; another, beside
whom walked a grave and sober citizen, the brother or cousin
of the convict, the tears in his eyes. But mostly there were
no friends or relations to mourn over this outcast crew. And
at the head marched a band of fifes and drums, playing
"Through the woods, laddie;" and a crowd of boys followed,
whooping and hallooing. When the procession was nearly
past, I was surprised to see among the men, handcuffed together, no other than Aaron Fletcher and Mr. Jonathan Rayment, the crimp. The latter was pale, and his fat cheeks
shook, and all his limbs trembled with fever. 'Twould have
been merciful to let him lie till death should carry him off.
But Aaron walked upright, looking about him with eyes full
of mutiny and murder. I know not if he saw me; but the
procession filed past, and the band went on playing at the head
of the Stairs while the wretches embarked on board the boats.
As for the crimes which Aaron and his companion had committed, I do not know what they were, but I suspect kidnapping formed part. I have never learned what became of Mr.
Rayment; but concerning Aaron there afterwards came intelligence that he could not brook the overseer's lash and the hot
sun, and fled, with intent to join the wild Maroons, but was
followed by bloodhounds, and pursued, and, being brought
back to his master, was, naturally, flogged. He then sickened
of a calenture and died. He was a bad man; but he was punished for his sins. Indeed, it is most true that the way of
transgressors is hard.

Lastly, to complete this narrative, I must tell you of a
message which came to me five or six years after the court-
martial. It was brought even from the Southern Seas. Heard
one ever of a message or letter from that remote and unknown
part?

There was a certain wild fellow, Deptford born, named Will
Acorn by name. This young man, for sins of his which need
not delay us, left his native town, where he had been brought
up as a shipwright, and went to sea. Nor did he come back
again for several years, when he reappeared, the old business
being now blown over and forgotten. And presently he came

to my house, I then living in St. Martin Street for convenience of business, and told me a strange story.

With some other privateers of Jamaica, where these fellows are mostly found, he must needs try his fortune in the South Seas. Accordingly, they got possession of a brig, or barco-longo, as they call this kind of ship in the West Indies, and they armed her with certain carronades and peteraroes, and, to the number of eighty or ninety stout men, all fully armed, put out to sea. In short they proposed to go a pirating among the Spanish settlements, as many have done before them.

It matters not here what was the success of their voyage—Will Acorn, at least, returned home in a very ragged and penniless condition. This, however, was the man's story:

" We sighted one morning at daybreak, being then not far from Masa Fuera, a large brigantine flying Spanish colors. She was much too big for us to tackle, therefore we hoisted the Spanish flag, too, and bore away, hoping that she would let us alone, and go on her own course. But that would not suit her, neither, and she fired a shot across our bows, as a signal to back sail. This we did, expecting nothing short of hanging, for she carried thirty guns at least, and we could see that she was well manned, and looked as if she was handled by a French captain, under whom even a Creolian Spanish crew will fight. Well, she spoke us when she was near enough, and ordered, in Spanish, that the captain was to come aboard. Now, as I was the only man who had any Spanish, our captain bade me to come with him. So I went, and we thought we were going to instant death, the Spaniards being born devils when they get an English crew in their power.

" Sir," this honest fellow continued, " think of our astonishment when, on climbing the vessel's side, they ran up the pirates' flag; to be sure, we were little else than pirates ourselves; but we knew not what countrymen these were. As for the crew, they were nearly all black negroes, and a devilish fighting lot they looked, being armed with pistols and cutlasses, while the decks were cleared for action, and every man to quarters, and the whole as neat and clean as aboard a British man-o'-war. And on the quarter-deck there stood, glass in hand, none other than Captain Easterbrook himself, the same as was tried by court-martial, sentenced, and escaped. He was dressed

very fine, in crimson silk, with a gold chain, and pistols in his
belt. I knew him directly ; but his face is changed, for now
it is the face of one who gives no quarter. A fiercer face I
never saw anywhere.

"But the strangest thing was that I saw lying in the sun,
propped up by pillows and cushions, the old Deptford apothecary, Mr. Brinjes. He looked no older, and no younger; his
one eye twinkling and winking, and his face covered with
wrinkles.

"'Will Acorn ahoy !' he sings out. 'Will Acorn, by the
Lord !'

"When he said this, there came out from the captain's cabin
a most splendid lady, dressed in all the satins and silks you can
think of, with gold chains round her neck, and jewels sparkling in her hair. Behind her came two black women, holding
a silken sunshade over her head. Why, sir, 'twas none other
than Bess Westmoreland, the penman's daughter, and more
beautiful than ever, though her cheek was pale, and eyes were
somewhat anxious.

"'Will Acorn ?' she cried. 'Is that Will Acorn, of Deptford Town ?'

"So with that the captain called us from the poop. 'Harkye,'
he said, 'you seem to be Englishmen. What ship is yours ?'

"So we told him who we were, and why we were cruising
in those seas. He listened—'tis a terrible fighting face—and
heard us out, and then bade us drink and go our way.

"'I war not with Englishmen,' he said ; 'but for French and
Spaniard I know no quarter.'

"He said no more, but his lady—Bess Westmoreland that
was—stepped out to us, and asked me many questions about
Deptford folk. And then she put into my hands this parcel,
which I faithfully promised to deliver into your hands, sir,
should I ever return home again. And I was to tell you that
they had found Mr. Brinjes's island, and she was as happy as
she could expect to be. And then Mr. Brinjes lifted his head
and said, in a piping voice, 'And tell him,' he said, with his
one eye like a burning coal, 'tell Luke Anguish, man, that we
committed the town of Guayaquil to the flames. 'Twould have
done his heart good to see the town on fire, and the Spaniards
roasting like so many heretics at the stake !'"

This was the message. The parcel contained a gold chain
and cross, set with precious stones, which I gave to Castilla,
hoping thereby to make her think less hardly of poor Bess.
But in vain ; though she wears the chain, which, she says—
though this is not the case—was sent to her by Captain Easterbrook, in token of his repentance, and his unhappiness with
the woman who bewitched him, and his continual sorrow for
the loss of her own hand.

It is now more than thirty years ago, and since then we have
heard nothing more. I conjecture that either they have long
since been swallowed up in a hurricane, Bess dying, as she
wished, at the same moment as Jack, or that they are still living somewhere in those warm and sunny islands of which the
apothecary was never wearied of discoursing.

THE END.

www.ingramcontent.com/pod-product-compliance
Lightning Source LLC
Chambersburg PA
CBHW020830030726
47496CB00001B/169

find the most compelling of all - Can we Humans, remedial students that we are, still learn from our own mistakes in time to finally evolve to the level of balance and connectedness that Mother Nature requires of us? I guess only time will provide the answer to that question. Meanwhile, I think there is something we can all learn from each other along the journey to exploring our own inner Wraeththu.

[1] Guilbert, John M. and Charles F. Park, 1986, *The Geology of Ore Deposits*, pp. 210-217, Freeman, ISBN 0-7167-1456-6

Klein, Cornelis and Cornelius Hurlbut, Jr. (1985) *Manual of Mineralogy*, Wiley, 20th ed., ISBN 0-471-80580-7

Paragenesis

Storm Constantine

Paragenesis

I have scars upon my left hand, but not upon my right. If I hold my hands up to the eternal sun, light shines through the flesh. But there is no flesh. I am idea, essence. I am the flash of sunlight off chrome; I am the seasons; I am the shadow beneath the eaves; I am a scrap of litter scratching across cracked asphalt. No, I am bones and blood. I am crude and heavy. I am what I am.

When I was sixteen, I ran away from my leaf-shrouded home in the enclave for the rich, about twelve miles from the city centre. Perhaps it began as a suicide bid. All I did was move my limbs, without conscious volition, toward the wilderness of stone and glass that circled the city itself like a plague. It was the hinterland of decay, spreading both outward and inward, threatening city core and enclave alike. People could lose themselves there, and I wanted to be lost.

I remember that day, she was standing at the kitchen sink with her back to me. She could always sense when I walked into the room. I'd see her spine tense beneath its dress of cotton, its caul of skin. How cruel had Mother Nature been to make her spawn a child she could only fear? Blessed was the day when she no longer had to touch me; when I could feed and bathe myself, tie my own laces, rub my own hurts. I could not despise her, for I shared her bewilderment, her bitterness. When I'd been born, no doubt she'd decided to make the best of it. I was a beautiful child, but for those hidden abnormalities. Later, she probably realised that even monsters could be beautiful. My father was a non-entity, consumed by work. We rarely saw him. Our home always seemed empty when she and I were in it together. The spaces between us were too great, and as I grew older, they became gulfs.

On that final day, I could not bear to see that stiffening spine any longer. She had birthed me and raised me; now her responsibility was over. I turned around and walked away; out of the shady house into the sunlight; past the bike lying on the tarmac, where a few red leaves had drifted down; past the rope that hung from the old willow, still swinging and where I never played. The street was devoid of children; empty. Empty. This had never been my home.

On the horizon, a grey green cloud hung above the city. It was a walk of about four hours to reach it along the main highway. Sometimes, a bus might come, rattling and armoured, but not very often. People with eyes like pebbles rode the bus; not coming from anywhere, going nowhere, just riding. Perhaps they thought time would stop for them in that way. I would not ride the buses, for I was afraid that if I did, I would be absorbed into that shadow community and never leave it. Another freak on the back seat.

It was mid-morning when I left the enclave, and already the sun was fierce in the late summer sky. At the high metal gates, the eyes of the guards were hidden behind black glass. They stood motionless, like automatons. I passed between them, showed my id card, and the gates slid open. A minute later, someone else might come by, and the guards would come alive. They'd touch their helmets, grin to show their white teeth and utter a pleasantry. But not for me. After I'd gone, one would say, 'That's the weird kid from Acacia', and the others would sneer.

I walked along the slip road that led to the highway. It seemed hotter beyond the enclave, and the air shimmered about me. Vigilantes had strung someone from a pole. I could see the body dangling on the other side of the road, surrounded by trees. A cloud of flies danced around it. Beneath it, someone had left some artificial flowers. Perhaps the enclave guards, high up on the gates and watchtowers, had seen it happen.

I cannot remember feeling anything then. I just walked, kicking up dust that smelled of metal and age, buffeted by the searing wind of passing vehicles. After an hour, a truck stopped to offer me a lift. The back was filled with people, crammed together like pigs on the way to a slaughterhouse. They were probably just crop-pickers, returning to the city. My feet were aching, so I hopped up into the back. Certain people always picked up on my strangeness, and this occasion was no different. My fellow travellers were like frightened animals: I saw furtive shuffling, and nervous eye movements. I didn't say anything. Eventually, one of the men offered me a cigarette and I smoked it, looking out through the truck canopy at the passing road. My mother will have missed me by now. Her relief will fill the silent house, washed by waves of shame. She will grip the edge of the sink and blink at the garden, where the sprinkler slowly turns on the lawn.

I did not resent being born different. The resentment came from other people's reactions. I was so ordinary in most respects. Dogs had never liked me; we could never keep one. Sometimes, things happened around me over which I had no control. It wasn't my fault. It was the look in her eyes. I made the saucepans fly once, but not toward her. She just screamed, her hands pressed to her face, staring at the mess on the floor. Other kids didn't like me very much, despite my parents efforts to find me friends. I didn't mind being alone. I'd tell my mother things she thought were her private thoughts, and then her mouth would compress into two white lines. Later, I'd hear her telling my father about it: 'He must *listen* to us, for God's sake! Do something!' I didn't listen. I just knew. It was like she told me things herself without words.

It was the doctors I hated the most. There was nothing wrong with me; I wasn't ill. But my mother kept taking me back to that neat office that smelled of nothing, and let the white coats prod at me. I said, 'just let me be', and they would smile tolerantly, spreading my legs on the table for another look. They must have taken a hundred photographs. 'It isn't Froehlich's syndrome,' I heard a doctor say to my mother, 'because apart from the genital abnormalities, there are no other physical deformities.'

Her reply: 'Then what is it? Can you operate?'

'That is a decision your son will have to make for himself later on. We have counsellors...'

She thought I should have been twins: a boy and a girl. But it wasn't that.

I got out of the truck on the outskirts of the city, in an area called the Longhills. Once, it would have been a thriving neighbourhood; now a ruin and an ideal place to hide, to think, to do whatever would come next. Tall buildings with broken crowns reached towards the veil of evil cloud that always hangs above the city. I think it is the city's aura, an expression of its soul, soiled and poisonous. The people who live in that place are barely human, but then I had been taught to think that neither was I. Perhaps this was the place where I belonged. I wanted to cast off the trappings of affluence and live close the edge of survival. Discomfort did not bother me.

I walked as best I could along the sidewalks, avoiding debris, bundles of cloth that may have been corpses and the smouldering remains of fires. What did people burn here? Sometimes, it seemed they burned their own possessions. I saw fragments of books, jewellery and crockery blackened among the embers. The smoke was toxic. Someone had burned a wasps' nest. A substance like syrup leaked from its collapsed mass. I saw few people. They kept out of the sun during the day. They slept then. Welfare trucks occasionally slid across an intersection ahead of me. They might contain bodies or miscreants or supplies. Perhaps all three at once.

At three o'clock in the afternoon, when the sun was at its most vehement, I stood in the centre of a street and looked up at the sky. Buildings loomed over me, derelict and rotting. I wondered what the point of it all was. Why do we continue to live? What drives us to survive in an environment so hostile to life, an environment we have made for ourselves? Civilisation was a Leviathan whose limbs were too weak to support it. Now it sank to its knees, bones cracking beneath its weight. And all who rode the Leviathan were tumbling down, their screams thin like that of insects. My difference was just one more symptom of this fall. Our purity was mangled and dysfunctional. In those moments, I saw myself as the avatar of the world's destruction, a cruel joke in the distorted form of the primal human. I could do as I pleased, for it did not matter what would happen to me.

Soon, I began to feel hungry, but willed the pangs away. I could see no way to feed myself. It was cleansing to be able to step aside from human needs. I felt excoriated, but also renewed. For a while, I sat inside a broken building, where the walls were black. I listened for sounds: the faraway throb of rotor blades, the occasional human cry, cut off short, and once the distant bark of a dog. I watched the sun slide down behind the splintered towers, and thought how in the enclave, the day would be drawing to a close. Men would be emerging from the units in the nearby industrial park. They would climb into their sleek transporters, hail a manly good-night to the guards on the wall, and drive the short distance up the tower-studded avenue to the gates of the enclave. Here, wives who sought to enact the rituals of a past Golden Age would be waiting in kitchens that were devoid of stain. The women wore aprons and smiled at their children, keeping back the pain, the fear, the utter chaos that massed on the horizon of their fantasy world. None of it was real, but then I had never really conspired in my parents' dream. My very existence cracked its fragile shell.

At dusk, a gang of girls stole in through the windows of my sanctuary. They saw me crouching in the rubble, which I quickly realised was *their* rubble, and began to snarl at me and utter strange ululating cries, their bodies dipping and rising like snakes. Their leader rushed at me a couple of times, brandishing a knife near my body, but I sat as still as I could, looking at her face. Presently, she came to a decision and gestured for her minions to get on with their business. They unfolded loot from tattered sacks, and set about dividing it amongst themselves. The leader flicked glances at me occasionally. I recognised something within her that later I identified as the indomitable human spirit. Society no longer existed for her, yet she continued to thrive, albeit in a debased fashion. The girls ate and laughed together, handing round a plastic bottle of murky liquid. After an hour or so, their leader offered it to me. It was a vile, base alcohol that left a trail of fire in my throat and tasted only of chemicals. The girls asked me nothing about myself, even though they must have made judgements about my cleanliness, my neat clothes. They were separatist females who hated men. They could have killed me, perhaps, but it seemed they recognised something within me with which they felt comfortable and could accept. I ran with them for a week or so, raking over the ruins, pillaging the debris. They seemed to repel rival male gangs by the strength of their voices alone, using a repertoire of chilling screams and cries. Boys would lope away from them like chastened dogs. Often, the leader would climb to the highest, most precarious point around and stand there with arms outflung, uttering a world-filling shriek of anger. They did not know about despair. I envied them.

In the asphalt wilderness of Longhills, there were few adults. Perhaps they had wisely moved away, or else been killed. Sometimes, choppers would drone over the streets and emit a stinging spray, which the girls told me was supposed to kill disease. Why would the city authorities bother? I didn't believe it. The spray probably just killed fertility.

I felt more at one with the desperadoes of the wilderness than any of the people who hid within the enclave. It was because these outsiders expected nothing and gave little in return. They did not make demands upon one another. Co-existence, and therefore a certain amount of co-operation, were the only remaining aspects of community. Pleasure was without contrivance: a good find among the rubbish; a chance meeting with a group who had something to barter; a basement found untouched, like an unopened tomb full of treasure; an abandoned welfare truck still laden with vitamin-enriched gruel. We were grave-robbers, really, for most of humanity had already died in that place. But I liked the simplicity and honesty of their lives, the fact they did not judge me.

One day, one of the gang was shot by a sniper and the leader told us we would have to move area. A sixth sense told her this was the beginning of something bad. So we gathered up what little we had and left Longhills behind, burrowing off through the darkness, and into another decayed sector called Coldwater Valley. It must have been an industrial complex at one time, and here the survivors were older and hostile to strangers. We prowled carefully between the arching metal structures that were now smothered with tendrils of quick-growing vines. Echoes were strangely muffled by the vegetation. Any human group we came across yelled and threw things to repel us; we were not welcome. Finally, one group, crazier than the rest, directed a fire cannon on us and killed all but five of us. Our leader was among the fallen; a blackened crisp in the road. How quickly life can be expunged. It seemed inconceivable that what was left of our companions had ever housed souls. We, the survivors, went back the way we had come, but it was the end of our group. We split up, and I went alone deeper into the madness of the ruined land that surrounded the desperate core of the shrinking metropolis. Its towers seemed to have huddled together, as if in fear.

There was much activity in the air nearer to the city core. Choppers roared through the skies, and once I saw one crash. People emerged from the jumbled ruins like cockroaches and swarmed all over the wreckage, picking it clean. I did not look like an enclave boy any longer. My head was thatched with lice-infested hair, my clothes were tatters, to which I was forever adding more layers, whatever I could find. I had learned to snarl in the way that meant, 'stay away if you value your health.' I also learned much about myself. Because the convenient utensils of life were no longer available, I was forced to live on my wits, and in this way discovered that the boundaries of my difference were much further than I had imagined. It began this way. I'd been going through the belongings of a dead man on the street, who had died of a sickness rather than murder. He had many treasures, which I was greedily transferring to my own pockets. Then a group of tearaways came slinking along the spiky walls around me, uttering low, hooting cries. Their message was for me to leave, to abandon my find. I do not think they would have attacked me if I'd simply obeyed this request. But there was too much for me to leave. I growled back. They must have thought I was mad; there were at least seven of them. Their leader dropped down from the wall and sauntered toward me, looking to either side all the time. I remained hunkered down beside the corpse, my hands dangling between my knees. I did not feel afraid at all. It was as if there was someone else inside me, far wiser than I knew; someone fierce and confident. An arrow of indignation flew out of me, and somehow touched the crumbling substance of the wall behind the gang leader. There was an explosion, a gust of dust and rocky debris, and then my would-be attacker was on his hands and knees before me, his head hanging down. He shook his hair and drops of bright blood flew out. At once, I jumped to my feet and snarled. My eyes felt full of sparks that I could shoot like bullets from a gun. The gang just melted away, dragging their fallen leader with them. After this incident, I felt so much stronger, safer.

Perhaps I overestimated my strength.

Some days later, I found a hole for myself deep beneath an old department store. It had been cleaned out thoroughly years before, but some people must have lived there for a while, because I found a few mattresses, some of which had not been burned. Rags had been hung from metal beams in what remained of the ceiling. It was a musty labyrinth full of silent ghosts. I imagined it had once been home to a whole community, who had either been smoked out or died from some contagious infection. There were no bones about as evidence, but the wilderness scavengers are very thorough, so that meant little. In this place, I made myself a nest. I did not think about the future, but took simple pleasure in surviving from moment to moment. The wilderness was the garbage heap of the world, yet I learned to see beauty in it: the different colours of the sky at various times of day and how they conjured sculptures from the rubble; shining through blown out windows; making a cathedral of light of the starkest structure. The passing of civilisation in itself was a wondrous thing. I would walk the cracked streets marvelling at the way stringy vegetation was slowly reclaiming the land. Mother Earth had learned the saying that revenge is a meal best eaten cold. She was implacable, eternal, and the green tidal wave of her reclamation was evidence of humanity's frailty and insignificance. The people had regressed, but in their barbarity possessed a startling innocence. The complex rituals of life had been pared away, and if the people were dying, at least they would do so with swift dignity, rather than being hooked up to machines in a long coma of slow decay. Those who lived in the cities, the enclaves, were deluding themselves. They should give themselves up to the inevitable. I thought I too would soon die, and these were my last days. Each one dawned fresh and vital. I wanted to experience life through my senses to the full, and because of this, learned how my touch was death.

He was older than me, yet seemed younger. We met when he strayed into my lair, and after a few warning shots of snarls and aggressive gestures, realised we were not enemies at all. He was like me: a runaway from the theatre of luxury. His mother had been a pill-head, who sometimes had not even recognised him, while his father, a scientist, had hardly ever been at home. I tingled with empathy as he described his former sterile environment: the ceaseless hum of domestic appliances, and the automata who kept the place running, while his mother lolled on the couch, living in some better world. He explained to me the phenomena of why people like us ran away. 'We know it is over. Society is dead, but some of us know we can still exist beyond it. It is like a sinking ship. We have to jump overboard with faith and hope, otherwise we'll just be dragged down with the wreck and drowned. This is the age of the individual; the age of the hive has passed. We are all floating in the sea, clinging to our bits of wreckage, but eventually we'll become sea creatures ourselves and learn how to breathe its element.'

How could I not love a person who spoke like that, with such passion and optimism? He did not know about my difference - especially the physical aspect. I did not want to tell him because he was my first real friend. If he knew, it would change things. He might be disgusted or, worse, full of pity.

Some girl he knew gave him a flask of alcohol. We flavoured it with the remains of a bag of sugar substitute we'd found in our basement, and one night sat across from one another and drank it. It felt shamanic, the rhythmic passing of the flask from one to the other. We both knew we wanted to be drunk, for there was business between us that the barriers of a sober mind inhibited. I was acutely aware that before the night was over he would know about me. I felt nauseous with nerves, eager for the intoxication that would free my tongue and allow me to speak the words that must be spoken.

He began to talk about the future again, rambling on about some faraway utopia that could be constructed from hopes and dreams.

Something about his vision made me uncomfortable, and I said, 'This is the end, not change. We are dying.'

He crawled over to me then and put an arm around me. 'No, no,

you are wrong. This is not death at all. You are living in the past. Look forward, not back. Don't let the past become your future.'

I wanted to believe, and partly did, unaware of how he spoke the most ultimate of truths. He put his head against my hair and said, 'I have to ask you something. Don't answer if you don't want to but... are you really a girl?'

I laughed a little, more out of embarrassment than amusement. What could I say? The answer was neither yes nor no. 'What makes you think that?' I asked.

I could tell he wished he'd never spoken. 'I don't know. The way you walk and talk. Just body language, I guess. I'm sorry. You must think this is just an excuse to...'

I touched his arm to silence him. 'I am what you say.'

He grinned in relief. 'I knew it. You want people to think you're a boy because people will leave you alone then.' He paused. 'I'm sorry. That sounded patronising.'

I shook my head. 'No, don't apologise. The thing is, I'm male too.'

He frowned. 'In your heart, your head?'

'No. In some ways, that would be simpler.'

'Then what *do* you mean?' The puzzlement had swept back; the tide of delight and anticipation had receded.

'It would be easier to show you,' I said and stood up.

The only light came in from outside, but then we of the wilderness rarely craved artificial light at night, other than a fire for protection. I peeled away all the layers of my tattered clothes, feeling as if each discarded item represented a year of my life. It was all being sloughed away. When finally I stood naked before him, he sat with his chin in his hands and said, 'You look male to me.'

I squatted before him and took one of his hands in mine, guiding him to the truth of the matter. He didn't say anything then, but kissed me. I felt his fingers digging into my shoulders like spikes. I could feel his heart racing. He'd wanted to do this for some time, and now felt he had been given sanction. I welcomed it too, but some part of me became annoyed that he looked upon me as a female and took it for granted that I must be dominated. Did women ever feel this way? It might sound like justification, but I feel that he was partly to blame for what happened to him. We should have come together as equals, but then I didn't know he was not equal to me. I was stronger than he was, and forced him into submission. It was only a game, I swear. I just wanted him to realise what we were, or could be.

It took him a day to die. I was helpless. I tried everything, but whatever mutant substance lived in me was poison to him. Not all the water in the world could wash away what I had done to him. My essence ate into him like acid, devoured his being. The only blessing was that he did not realise what was happening to him. With my hands, I was able to stroke away most of the pain. With my thoughts I willed his mind to a far place, that idyll he had spoken of, and there he died.

I set fire to our home and emerged from it into the night against a backdrop of flames. I had been right and he wrong. Humanity was dying and I was one of nature's weapons. I could never love, for to love me was to die. Could anything be crueller than that?

If only I had known the truth then. He could still be here now. The one who discovered that truth with me was but a pale spark to his radiant sun, but perhaps that was all part of it, the great lesson I had to learn.

For days, perhaps weeks, I roamed the wilderness, feeling more drunk than I had on that hideous night. I truly wanted to die, and even climbed the high, broken towers to think about throwing myself over, but even in my grief I was too afraid of being broken, dying slowly. I kept seeing his face, hearing his laughter, and then an image of his death would come to me, the terrible writhing, the whimpers. I was more of a monster than even my mother had imagined.

I came to an area that had been inexpertly flattened; a plain of rubble, from which rusting spikes rose like the bones of dinosaurs. Here, I collapsed and stared up at the sky, watching the colours change and the stars reveal themselves. I could move no further. Here, it would end. I felt strangely at peace, and numb. I could not feel my body.

When I saw the stooped shadow gliding towards me over the stones, I barely raised my head. Death had come for me. It loomed over me, breathing heavily, and dark greasy hair brushed my face. I saw a glint of metal and heard muttered words. 'Be still, my pretty. Do not fear. I shall come to you without pain.'

I did not know he meant to eat me. I just thought of sex and murder, but he opened a vein in my arm and began to drink, nibbling the flesh at the edge of the cut. He was a modern vampire, human and reeking, not at all the romantic vision I'd seen in old movies. As I lay there, feeling the pull as my blood pulsed into his diseased mouth, I was not sickened or afraid, but amused. It is not easy to find food in the wilderness, and some will do anything to live. If my death meant the life of a debased creature like this, then so be it. There was some justice in it, I thought.

But I did not die. I found myself awake with raw morning light falling down upon me. Beside me was a wretched creature who squirmed upon the ground, clutching his belly. His hair had come out in clumps and lay upon the stones. I felt weak, but also vital. As I looked at him, I laughed. Not only was my touch death, but it seemed I was also very difficult to kill. Part of my new role, I decided, was to stay with my victims until they found peace in death. I would do what I could to ease their agony.

Unlike my beloved, this one did not die after the first day. Sometimes, he was raving and hallucinating and became violent with a preterhuman strength. At other times, he wept and mumbled about his childhood, his fingers over his face. His body was hot and bloated. He must be strong. How long would it take him to die? After two days, it began to rain, and I dragged him into a ruined office block. The rain itself can be toxic. Here, I built a small fire, and then went foraging, killing four bedraggled pigeons. I came back with two birds, and some welfare rice I'd haggled for with a band of oldsters I'd come across. My attacker, my victim, could not eat, but I cooked the pigeons and watched him as I fed. There was no feeling within me, merely a faint sense of curiosity. His skin was peeling.

On the morning of the third day, I woke up and found myself alone. I thought my companion must have died in the night, and some scavenger had come in and taken the body. Then I heard the words, 'what am I?' and turned to see an angel in the doorway. As his skin had peeled, so had all the filth. He stood before me, holding out his arms, looking at his smooth flesh. I could not give him answers. There were none. I felt that I had made him into something more and above me. He shared my difference. I had birthed a daughter-son.

I had thought him the most degenerate of beings, yet I quickly learned that he blazed with vitality and intelligence. Perhaps this was just another aspect of the change he had undergone. He asked me questions constantly and experimented with the force of his being. Unlike me, he was curious about the way he could affect reality; make inanimate objects move, heal pain, hear the whisper of others' thoughts. He was proud of what he'd become, and did not hide it, but the shadow community to which he'd once belonged were now afraid of him. They did not want his healing power, his radiance.

They saw not an angel, but a freak.

Unperturbed, he became almost evangelistic about our condition. 'We must make more like us,' he said.

I was appalled and shook my head. 'No. You are a fluke. It is not meant to be this way.'

'How do you know?'

We were not easy companions, yet our similarities, and the fact that I had made him the way he was, kept us together. He had changed so much from the wretch he'd been. We lived in the office block where he'd undergone his transformation. One evening, he made me climb a nearby hydro-tower with him, where the rusting shell harboured clear water. He took off his clothes and dived in, summoning me to join him. 'We are not part of the filth now.' He sluiced my hair and rubbed the grime from my skin. 'I want the grief to run from your body with this water. You must be renewed, like I am.'

I think the transformation had affected his mind. He needed a religion to run.

'How did you do it?' he asked. 'Tell me. Tell me.'

'I don't know. It just happened. You were trying to devour me.'

The light in his eyes was like that of the stars; cold and distant. 'Yes,' he murmured. 'Yes.'

I should have known he'd act independently. One day, he took me to a building near our lair, and here revealed to me his twisting litter of children. I was horrified, yet also amazed. Twelve people, both male and female, shivered and whimpered at my feet; all of them infected with his blood. I had seen myself as an avatar of death, but remote and accidental. Here was someone who was an active instrument of it, only he did not realise the fact. He thought he was a god, with a god's powers. If I'd done something to end it then, what would the world have been like now?

Of the twelve, only four survived, and all of them male. We tried to soothe the agony of the others with the healing power in our hands, but the experience was harrowing. 'I think this process cannot be conducted with females,' my companion said, with scientific detachment. 'But we must try it with others.'

'No!' My protest went unheard.

I would not help him, other than to attend to his victims as they suffered. I didn't even think about killing him, or trying to stop it any other way. At the time, it just didn't enter my mind, but now I think it was because part of me knew that what was happening was preordained. My companion saw it as a cleansing ritual for the world. He loved the creatures he made, marvelling at their beauty. I saw them as perverted homunculi; as lovely as the angels of hell. Yet, despite this, they were also part of me and I was part of them.

I under-estimated the regard my companion had for me. He did not set himself up as a leader of our developing clan of beautiful monsters. That privilege he reserved for me, even though I shunned it. 'It is your responsibility,' he told me. 'You began this.'

'Only because you were hungry,' I reminded him.

'Can't you see the potential here?' he demanded. 'This is the beginning of something. It is what comes next.'

I could only look down at the corpses of those who had not survived. The cost of the selection process was too high. 'This is murder,' I said.

He nodded. 'You are right. We should give people the choice.' As an inducement, he now had seven successful transformations to parade before the eyes of the desperate.

I never became involved in his recruitment drives, and for many years no other human tasted my blood. I cannot say that I wasn't affected by my companion's enthusiasm, and grudgingly I had to accept the benefits of being part of a community, something I had never previously enjoyed, other than those few weeks of running with the girl-pack. This was different though. With the girls, I had been a tolerated outsider. Now, I was part of a group of individuals who all shared the same attributes. It was both scary and exciting.

Although we could not effect the change in women, a few of them, through persistent entreaty, still joined us. In many ways, we had more in common with them than with men. From our sisters, we learned about the wildest excesses of adorning our bodies. We became tribal and developed our own rituals connected with the inception of newcomers, or the simple celebration of our estate. Sex became sacred, yet less taboo. There was so much to explore, and so many delights concealed in the labyrinth of our dual gender.

One night, we undertook a rite to name ourselves, opening up our minds with the effects of narcotic fungi. My companion became Orien; a name he felt held power. As for me, I wandered the star-gleam avenues of my mind, until I came to a place where a white shrine glimmered against a backdrop of stars. It stood upon the primal mound of creation, guarded by two pillars, and surrounded by the waters of life. Here, I learned my true name, the person I was to become. I am Thiede. The first of all. And the name we took for ourselves as a group was Wraeththu; a word that held all the anger and mystery of the world. The visions told us the truth: we were no longer human and must forget all that we had been before.

We were close-knit, and did not merely co-operate with one another. Laughter was spontaneous, and in our wild nights of dancing, as new recruits struggled with the process of transformation, I learned about the fulfilment that close friendship brings. I was intrigued by the way the different personalities within the group interacted with one another; the partnerships that developed, the enmities. We weren't above petty squabbling, but if anything from outside threatened our group, the ranks would close and seal as tight as a steel door. We were not afraid to kill to protect ourselves, and sometimes that was necessary. Various human clans and groups heard about us, and some were afraid, and thought we should be eradicated. We were seen as vampires, as predators, who stole people away in the night. In fact, that was not true. We hadn't resorted to such measures since the first days of my companion's explorations. We had to keep on the move, but even so, humans would often sniff us out and come pouring over the ruins, holding flaming brands aloft, intent on burning us alive. Then we would rise up, howling, our wild hair flying, our faces striped with the colours of the night.

We never lost a single brother in our skirmishes. In our unity, we were immensely strong.

Everything that begins in the world starts small, be it a mighty tree from a seed, or a deluge from a single drop of rain. A cell becomes a child becomes a king or queen. The greatest concepts are based upon the most fleeting of ideas. Such it was with Wraeththu, the race that I spawned from my fear, my pain, my ignorance. I stand upon the pillars of the world, and look down to see the carnage perpetrated by the human race that had been its guardian. I am amazed that humanity, with all its cruel selfishness, ever rose to prominence, and that the world itself allowed the situation to continue for so long. We are the exterminators, who will rid the palaces of the earth of all its vermin. We have no choice in this role, it had been decided for us. We are the true messengers of the gods. The howls of slaughtered innocents rise from the ruins, the whimpers of the bereaved, the snufflings of the betrayed. I stand as a colossus above it all, looking down. There is a star in the sky that is the soul of my lost love, and my own soul has fragmented into a thousand parts, into each of my children. But I do not grow weak from it, only estranged. There is much to explore about myself, and for this I need a real wilderness, where all the devils of the earth and the angels of the air can come to tempt me and teach me. I cannot make the inward journey here in the city debris.

Last night, Orien came to me, worried that some of our brethren had split off to form a separate group. I tried to assuage his fears. 'This is the way it will go,' I said. 'We were the catalysts, nothing more. We must not interfere with the growth of our child.'

He thought I was mad, or damaged, and spoke softly. 'The time will come, soon, for us to move toward the city core.'

I nodded. 'I know,' I said. 'You will.'

He touched my shoulder. '*We* will. You cannot deny us, Thiede.'

And I smiled at him to reassure him, knowing that already I had left them.

The First

Wendy Darling

The First

Since the time of the Ascension, Wraeththu scholars have been hard at work studying the many documents uncovered within the Aghama's private library. Among the chief treasures are personal writings. The following short document was found tucked inside an antique guide to human sexual intercourse, a circumstance which documents not only the Aghama's sense of irony but also frames the subject quite appropriately.

Ai-cara 20

As progenitor of our race, I have had the privilege of witnessing many Wraeththu firsts. Included within that is the first Grissecon. This took place within the very early days, when Wraeththu consisted of a single wild band. Living amidst the ruins of the city in which I'd come of age, Orien and I led our group as we grew and, facing a hostile world, discovered the nature of our difference from humanity.

In Grissecon, we discovered a key to our own potential. The event was celebrated with a night of frenzied dancing and even more frenzied aruna. It was a momentous event. Still, I am writing today to say that this early time saw an event in my mind more important than what we later called the first Grissecon.

At the time there were only two of us, not a band, not a tribe, not a race. Still, two was more than I had ever expected. The one who later called himself Orien had come to me not as a companion but an attacker, feasting upon me like a vampire, and then succumbing not to death but to rebirth. Orien's transformation, only three days earlier, had been so spectacular that I was left humbled and, both then and for a long time afterward, completely bewildered.

He and I were still living in the ruined office block where he had been born from his filth and rags. Together we subsisted on what little food we could manage, haggling for rice and killing pigeons, the gray-winged neighbours doomed like us to the shuddering decrepitude of a city devouring itself. We had no direction in life, only hoping to survive and muddle through what seemed like the end of the world.

It was cold the night it happened. The sun had sunk behind the sagging shells of the surrounding office buildings, stone-clad steel hulks, their once-gleaming rows of windows dirty with smoke and grime. In the basement where we lived there was a fire, but winter was coming and, Wraeththu or not, we were cold that night.

Orien was tired, I could see that in the way his hands and jaw were faintly trembling as he spoke with me, the way he kept rubbing his head. He had a headache, he'd told me earlier. I'd tried to take away the pain but had been unable to work the trick. No matter to him, he told me, as overnight it would fade on its own. Whatever we were – we did not yet have a name for ourselves – we were quite resilient.

From the first Orien had been delighted with the results of inception, feeling pride and wonder in both his body and his abilities. He had far more curiosity than I had ever had and even in a scant three days, he had discovered much. All day long he had been taking it upon himself to teach me and now, trembling and tired with what I thought was pure exhaustion and perhaps a headache from lack of food, he began to share with me a new discovery.

As always, he prefaced his lesson with the acknowledgement that I was probably aware of these special powers, and would be either unsurprised or unimpressed. I took my abilities for granted, he said, whereas to him were something miraculous.

I told him there are no miracles.

As the sky turned a deeper shade of iodine red, Orien began to speak. Did I know, he asked me, that we needn't suffer the cold?

I laughed, telling him that of course we needn't suffer, at least so long as we could locate blankets or fuel supplies.

Orien scowled and scolded me for being "unimaginative." (Imagine that! I was once called "unimaginative!") It was then that he explained it to me: By directing our energies and our intentions, we could produce not only warmth but, he had a strong suspicion, fire. So far, on his own, he had only managed to produce heat, not fire. I told him that considering the outdoor temperature and coming winter, heat sounded like enough. I did, however, wonder how we could harbour the heat and use it to our benefit.

"Don't worry," he said, "just let me hold you."

Hold me? A shudder passed through my body as soon as the words had registered. I had never been held in my life – except once, the night I killed my beloved, burning and killing him with my essence. He had held me, stroked my hair. It had been a new thing to me, sweet and beautiful, that closeness, the lack of violence, the feeling of care. It had never happened again.

Orien picked up on my reaction. He did not even have to ask what the matter was. Using the faculties borne of the blood that had transformed him, he knew. At the time I didn't realize how well. I was startled when he said, "I was going to hold you and warm us both, but I see you don't want to be held. You have never been touched, have you? Never except with coldness and hate." Orien, for all our eventual differences, was very good at making inferences.

"No, that's not quite true," I told him. I followed with the story of my beloved. Until that moment I had kept this from Orien, alluding to it but never telling him the details. How could I bear it? It was too painful to relate. Every time I looked at Orien, I thought of my beloved, what might have been. Nevertheless, that night I shared my story.

When I was done, Orien looked sad but told me thank you. Then he took my right hand in his own, which was shaking, and gave it a squeeze. "You're cold," he said. "Let me make you warm."

He told me to lie down on the bed of cardboard boxes and newspapers where we slept. I did so, thinking he would be going off to bring me some secret stash of blankets or gather more firewood. But then, beginning with my shoes, Orien began to remove my clothing. When I asked him what he was doing – it was still cold – he assured me he would be making me warm. He knew the trick.

Drained from telling my story, I did not protest, remaining limp as Orien stripped me, tossing my clothes into a pile. I thought once I was naked he would begin, but then he announced that he would be joining me, exposing his own skin as much as mine. I thought he was mad but I often thought that, and so I closed my eyes as garments fell to the floor one by one.

"Now we will begin," he said to me.

"What will you do?" I murmured, feeling my skin prickle with goose pimples against the night air.

"Warm you," he answered.

My eyes were closed and so at first I did not know what he was doing. The cardboard shifted as Orien put his weight upon it, kneeling as he shared his newly discovered power. He was silent as he worked. At first I did not feel it, but then in my feet I felt a tingling. It could have been the cold. Soon, though, it grew stronger and then, I felt something else, like something stroking my bare feet, only without really touching it. My feet were getting warmer. Yes, just a bit warm, then a little warmer, then yet a little warmer.

"Do you feel it?" Orien asked me.

I opened my eyes and he was kneeling with his hands over my feet. I nodded yes, wondering, could he only do my feet? Orien worked over me then, moving from the feet to the calves to the knees and up my thighs. When he reached my mid-point, he asked what I would like warmed next. The look on his face was an odd one, strained and awkward. For a brief moment, I sensed he had something more to say, but then I realized I had better let him proceed. I was warm in my lower half but still cool in my upper – too cool. He swung his leg over me, spanning my middle as he spread his hands to soothe me with warmth.

He worked from my waist up to my chest, then from my shoulders down to my hands. I felt warm like a rock in the sun, even though the sun had set. It was only the weak light of our fire that flickered against our naked skins. Orien put his hands over my face, almost touching, and in an instant my cheeks grew warm. I smiled at him, appreciating this gift more than any other he had shown me. Orien smiled back, then bent down to kiss me.

It was the sharing of breath. I had not felt it before – that kiss that brings more than two sets of lips together, but two souls. I felt the need in Orien then. His body still cold, perhaps even colder than before, he wanted my warmth. I wanted to give it to him. My arms curled around his back and he hissed as slowly he lowered his body down onto mine. Our lips were locked together and thus, our souls. Hungry, yes he was, and wanting warmth.

Lying beneath him, I felt his Wraeththu organ pressed against mine. What a strange sensation, our petals touching. I felt suddenly that I had woken up, remembered something I'd forgotten. Since that fatal night, I had turned away from that part of myself, burying it not only in grief but in the myriad other matters to consider: food, shelter, Orien and then the special powers Orien so enthused about. Orien woke as well and soon, us kissing, tangled together on the cardboard, his ouana-lim came alive against me.

Something happened then, something I will never forget so long as I live. It is a moment most every har remembers. Pressed on my back enjoying (yes, enjoying!) Orien's attentions, I suddenly felt a shifting and then, to my surprise, I had become female, soume. Orien propped himself up on his arms immediately, even as I felt his ouana-lim grow yet more firm. He looked into my eyes with an ineffable look of wonder. "Can we?" he asked.

I felt so strange at that moment. I had always known I was different. Certainly the doctors had told me so often enough, My parents had held it against me. I was a girl and a boy, a hermaphrodite. I had a cavity like a female; it was the way I was built. Still, I had never felt my male parts disappear. I had never felt a hot burning not only between my legs but deep inside. It was a craving, as vicious as the hunger of the starved. I pulled Orien back down to meet my lips. "We can," I told him, speaking in a growl like a hungry she-cat.

Orien wasted no time, but slid into me easily, the feel of him an inner caress. Our parts were perfectly matched; they knew one another, completed one another, became one. That night we created a great heat, if not a fire. Souls and bodies merging, this for me was the real first Grissecon, no matter the later more public success with the group. On that cold dark night Orien and I discovered the knowledge of that great magic, aruna, and in so doing, took the first step in truly understanding the great magic that we are.

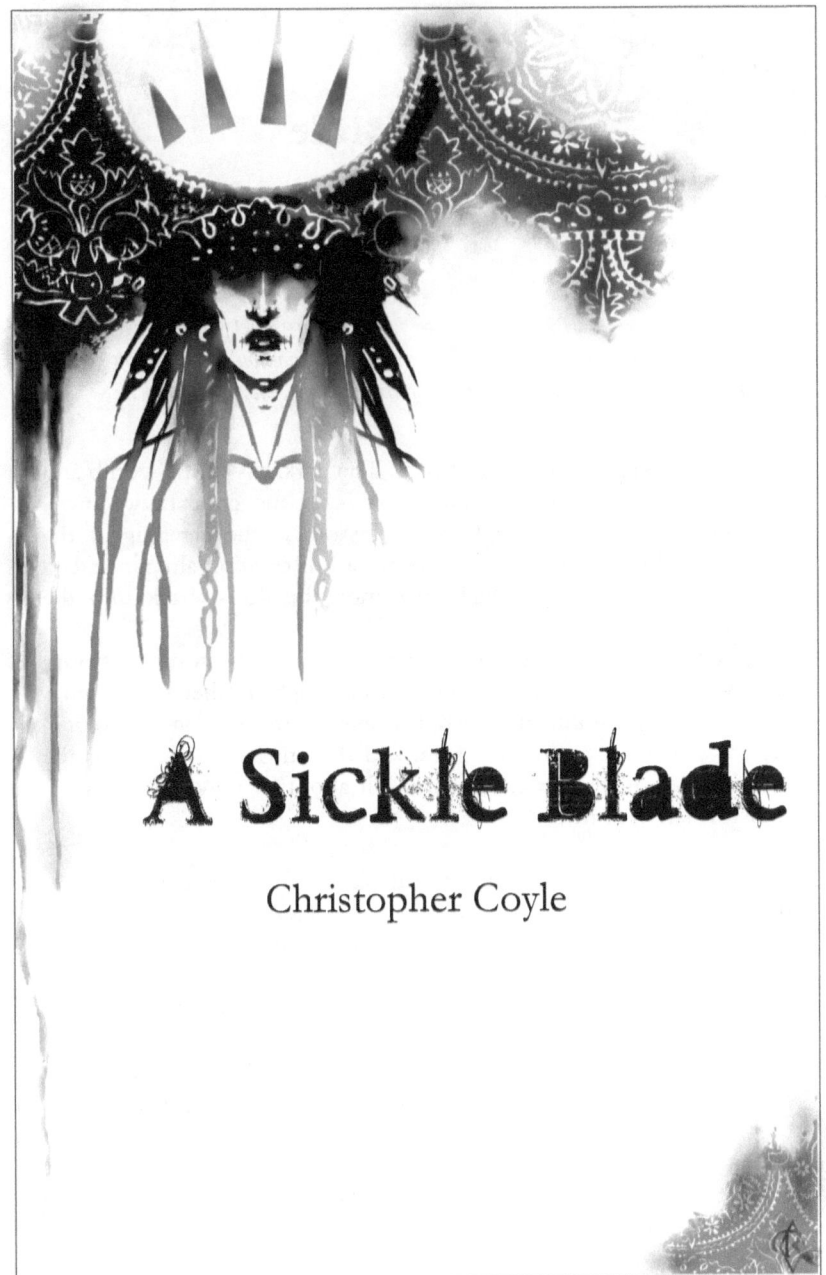

A Sickle Blade

Christopher Coyle

A Sickle Blade

Boline, a white-handled ritual knife, used in the tradition of witchcraft for the cutting of herbs and cords. Complement to the Athame, the ritual blade.

In the beginning, there was darkness. The darkness of the womb and the darkness of creation. I think there is a connection between the two: seeds sown in the night that blossom in the dawning of the light. I was brought forth from the gloom of creation almost sixteen years ago and tonight, I will once more be thrust back into the darkness, awaiting my rebirth.

I am naked and shivering, lying on a cold stone platform, somewhere deep beneath the city streets. Tight leather bands cross my chest; they dig into my flesh, prevent me from rising or moving. Shadows press in against my skin, and the only sound I hear is the breathing of at least twenty others, all about to undergo the same transformation as myself.

We had been locked together in a dank cell for three days; blind in the darkness, denied food or water. We had become weak from hunger and dehydration. The only way we'd known time had passed had been through the smallest fraction of light that had crossed the wall; sunlight that had somehow managed to find its way down below.

Then, after those three days of incarceration, the door burst open and they'd come in. Tall, beautiful, and terrifying, they called themselves the Uigenna. I had believed them to be the stuff of tabloid tales, stories told to frighten children into behaving, or characters taken from some book or movie. I was wrong, they were all-too-real, and I was to become one of them.

I'd been too weak to struggle as they'd dragged me down a hall into a large room filled with stone tables. I'd seen that other people, who must have been in that cell with me, were already being laid out on the tables; leather bonds strapped across their chests and legs, pinning them down. It was the first time I'd seen the others clearly, outside the darkness of our cell, but my mind didn't want to focus on anyone else's troubles but my own.

I'd been pulled towards one of the tables by two Uigenna, where they'd laid me out and tied me down securely. Other figures had come into the room, moving about the bodies on the tables and doing something that I couldn't quite see - at least not until one of them came up to me. In his hand, he'd held a wicked-looking knife. I hadn't been able to see his face, but when he'd suddenly slashed the blade across my wrist, it wasn't his face I looked at. I'd yelled in shock at the sudden pain, but my tormentor had not finished. He did the same thing to himself, slicing open his wrist without making any sound of pain. As the blood had flowed down his wrist, he'd reached down and pressed his open cut against me, mingling his blood with mine. Then he'd moved on, leaving me there alone.

A few moments later, they'd turned out the lights and left us in the dark. The wound on my arm started to itch, then it started to burn, spreading up my arm and through the rest of my body.

As I lie here on the cold stone, my mind wanders down the twisting corridors of memory, filling my head with a million thoughts and images dragged from the depths. The pain of my metamorphosis begins; fiery blades seem to carve away my flesh, and icy needles sliver their way through my insides. My psyche seizes upon the events that have brought me to this place, deep below the city.

The day began like any other: the same routine playing itself out in the same pattern. I woke up, got out of bed and hurried through my morning ritual of getting ready for school. Jumped into the shower, quickly cleaned myself, avoiding looking into the mirror for I knew and hated what would be staring back at me. I had not been an attractive child, and wasn't an attractive teenager either. My face had been attacked by acne for years now; my hair was stringy and unkempt; my body was flabby and fat. My mother said it was genetic, that I had glandular problems, but it was more psychological than anything else. When you hate yourself, it's easier to find comfort in food and the cycle becomes self-perpetuating - you make yourself even more unlovable. It even becomes something of a sick sort of twisted pride, a sign of how much you don't care about your body (even though you do).

After throwing on whatever clothes first came to hand, I grabbed up my backpack, stuffed my half-finished homework inside and ran to catch the bus. I hated going to school. Not because I hated learning. I was actually good at school; perhaps too good. Being fat, ugly and smart were three things almost guaranteed to ensure that you were amongst the least popular kids at school. This in turn meant you were ready prey for those higher up the social hierarchy than you. Needless to say, I was near the bottom of said hierarchy, quarry that even other prey could hunt without many feelings of remorse or pity.

For all prey, there is a certain safety in travelling in numbers; the protection of the herd. Of course, the slowest was often culled by the predators, while the others scurried for safety. He or she became a sacrifice to the rampant sadism of humanity. Unfortunately, over the last few months, my herd had been culled. One by one, they had either transferred to different schools, moved on to other herds, or had run away. Some kids had even killed themselves in despair over everything that had happened over the last few years. The world was changing around us, quicker than anyone could account for. Despite what they say about the resilience of youth, kids don't like change all that much. Too much change and we have little to ground ourselves. So, perhaps it was no wonder that kids were either killing themselves or disappearing at an alarming rate.

Adam, one of the latest to disappear from my herd, was the only one I had truly considered my friend. His disappearance struck me particularly hard. Adam had disappeared about a month before, apparently running away without leaving even a note or message to say why or where he had gone. There had been only a token effort made by the police to track him down, but in the last few months the reports of runaways and missing persons had drastically increased. If they were not found within 72 hours, the police just gave up, almost as if they knew what had happened to them, yet were afraid of admitting the reality of it. The usual explanation in the police reports was that it was most likely that the individuals had run off to join one of the strange new gangs that had been cropping up in the seedier parts of the city. Perhaps it was no coincidence that these gangs had been increasing in number and strength over the same period of time as the disappearances of kids and teenagers had escalated. These gangs had been spreading rapidly, yet although they seemed to be forming in large numbers, no one seemed able to find out anything about them. They disappeared at the first hint of danger, apparently possessing some instinct that warned them of journalists or cops.

I hoped that Adam had found a place among one of those gangs, and that he was safe, although a part of me resented him for getting away and leaving me to deal with everything here on my own. More than anything, I wished he had taken me with him. I was too cowardly to try running away alone and just as scared of the idea of committing suicide. As much as I may have hated myself and my life, I didn't want to die. So I remained where I was, living each day as I had the one before it. At home, I was safe and provided for. The only downside was the darkness, depressiveness and monotony of my life.

As usual, school seemed to last forever. I hurried from class to class, waiting until the last moment to dart through the throngs of students, to minimize the chance of running into any of my tormentors. Thankfully, that day, I managed to avoid any undue encounters and I thought I had made it safely through another week. I had grown to anticipate Fridays perhaps more than was normal for most kids, as it meant at least two days of relative safety and peace, where I could lock myself in my room and not see another living soul.

The bus let me off a few blocks away from my home, and I saw that my mother had yet to arrive. Usually, she picked me up at the bus stop after school as she passed by on her way home. She must have been running late at her office that day, but I dreaded she had been in a car accident, or some other calamity had struck. Normally, if she wasn't able to make it, she'd send one of the family's security guards to bring me home. Like most other well-to-do families in the area, with all the disappearances and gang related incidents increasing, my family had taken to hiring security guards whenever we went out. Of course, the security guards didn't seem to like me any more than the kids at school did, and probably for the same reasons. All I know is that I was standing out there, alone on the street, without any cover to hide from what might come. A sudden fear overtook me, a premonition that I was too vulnerable at that moment, and that it was all too likely I would be viewed as easy prey by any passing threat.

I am dragged from the comfort of my memories by an intense sensation that I cannot ignore. I think I'm screaming, although it's difficult to tell whether the heart-wrenching sound comes from my throat or from one of the others in the darkness around me. It *feels* as if I'm being burned alive, yet the next moment my insides are freezing cold. Wave after wave. The process repeats itself, dragging me through one world of agony after another. Each time I'm sure I'll die from the pain alone, but always something within me resists the temptation to surrender. The cold stone beneath me digs into my back. Each small grain of dirt feels like a blade. The fine grains of sand and gravel abrade my flesh like nails, tearing it away to reveal the bone beneath. My jaw is clenched tightly, my eyes are squeezed shut: quiet explosions of colour blossom before my mind's eye. From those explosions, more memories emerge. To escape the pain, my mind retreats once more into events that happened only a few days ago...yet seem more than a lifetime away.

Over time, through evolution, herd creatures develop a sort of sixth-sense about danger; an instinct that warns them of the approach of a predator. Whether it's catching a hint of musk on the air, hearing the rustle of the underbrush, or feeling an inexplicable urge to flee, this instinct has enabled herd animals to survive. Unfortunately, my own instincts and intuition were not quite as finely tuned as those possessed by other creatures. By the time I realized that I was vulnerable, standing alone in the open with no one else around, it was too late.

Just as the hairs on the back of my neck began to tingle, an explosion of sharp pain burst in the back of my skull. The shock of it nearly drove me to my knees. It sent my backpack skittering across the sidewalk and my glasses clattering to the road.

'Hey, Piggy, good to see ya!' A sickeningly cheerful voice came from behind me. A voice I recognized all-too-well. If I was near the bottom of the social hierarchy in school, then the voice belonged to a guy who stood near the top: Jamie Brown. You know the type: captain of the varsity football team, face and body of a Hollywood actor, personality of a barracuda. I'm sure that every school around the world has one of those types. One of those people who have been given everything on a silver platter, yet who decide for some reason that those less fortunate needed to be reminded of it constantly.

Jamie never went anywhere without his pack, all predators like himself, although he was clearly their Alpha-male. And I had the misfortune of being the prey they had cornered this day. There was no reason for them to be out where I lived, except for the corner store across the street from my bus stop where they were remarkably lax about carding people for cigarettes or alcohol. From the reek of beer and tobacco surrounding those guys, it wasn't too hard for me to figure out why they were around here. I just had the bad luck to be in the area at the wrong time.

Jamie and his pack were infamous amongst the herd students for the strange types of entertainment they enjoyed. No one who'd been forced to entertain them ever said a word about it, but there was a strange sense about these victims, as if their spirits had been totally broken. I had always believed that my friend Rick had committed suicide because of something Jamie's pack had done to him, and that was probably the same reason Adam had run away as well.

'What a great way to finish our Friday, eh guys?' Jamie crowed to his friends.

They crowded around me, jostling me from one body to the next until I was dizzy. The world around me was a blur of washed out colours, yet somehow Jamie's cruelly smiling face was crystal clear. 'A case of beer, some cigarettes, and now we have a little Piggy for some entertainment. Who could ask for a better way to start the weekend?'

Before I knew what was happening, before I could say anything in protest, I was manhandled into the back of Jamie's car, pressed between two of his friends. They had decided to take me someplace more private for their *entertainment*. The fear in my stomach churned acid that scalded its way up my throat, yet fear also kept my lips clamped shut. I was terrified of what would happen if I were sick. They were bigger, stronger, and meaner than I was. If I protested, or made any commotion, I would be beaten - and beaten bad. The further we got from my home, the sicker I felt. If there was any point in my life that I'd wished myself dead, this was the time.

Suddenly, I am awash with a coolness that spreads through every part of my body, soothing away the fire and ice, and the pain that has been my torment. Once more my wandering mind returns to my body. I gasp involuntarily at the unexpected release. Tears of relief fall down my face, even if this reprieve is only temporary. Around me, some of the others are weeping too, while still more moan and scream in the throes of agony. My body feels different somehow, as if it's too tight and too small to contain the energy that's building up inside me again. A thin blade of light cuts across my face, burning my sore eyes. I can hear myself groaning.

As I close my eyes against the light, a strange, dispassionate voice speaks over the cries. 'Three have already died and it looks like two more won't make it through the night. I want the bodies removed and tossed into the pit; we can burn them before dawn.'

I try to rise and open my eyes, to see who's talking and what he's talking about, but the straps hold me fiercely. The sweat-soaked leather is slimy against my skin, yet although I'm still bound, the straps feel a bit looser than before. Odd, considering leather tends to shrink when it's soaked, becoming tighter not looser. It almost makes me laugh: my mind attempting to rationalize the looseness of the leather straps instead of worrying about the talk of people dying and not making it through the night. Then my body once more explodes with pain. The fires within me flare hungrily back to life, feasting upon my insides with fangs that dig deep enough to scorch my soul. It's as though someone or something is trying to disembowel me from the inside out.

I don't know how long I was in the car, or to where exactly we were driving. Jamie seemed to be taking a convoluted route through the city and Carmine has never been the easiest of places to navigate. Within minutes, I was hopelessly lost and gave up trying to watch where we were going. I realized fairly quickly that trying to find my way back home would be hopeless. All I could hope for was that I would be able to get hold of my mother somehow, after the evening's *entertainment* was completed, because I knew already that this was a one-way trip as far as Jamie was concerned.

Finally, Jamie pulled his car into a narrow side alley in what looked to be one of the more rundown areas of the city. After stopping the car, Jamie and his friends quickly got out, ushering me in front of them through a small door into a dark room. The metal door closed behind them with a resonant clang that sent shivers through my body.

I could hear the heavy breathing of other guys in the darkness of the room; I could almost smell their anticipation. Apparently though, only Jamie really knew what was going to happen, because one of his goons suddenly asked, 'Are ya sure this is the right place?'

'Yes, now shut up!' Jamie barked back. He pressed a large hand against my back, propelling me further into the gloom and down a hallway.

The building stunk of old piss, of rotting meat, trash and other things that I didn't want to identify. The smell definitely did not ease the churning in my stomach.

'Down the stairs, Piggy.'

I felt like retching, but my body had begun to descend into a state of shock. I followed Jamie's directions, nervously climbing down the stairs. The other boys followed behind me, ensuring that I couldn't make a break for it.

The stairs emerged into a large basement, dimly lit except for small patches of sunlight streaming through grimy windows. Then, as soon as all of us had stepped into the room, a light array flickered on overhead, the bright fluorescent bulbs humming loudly. They revealed that we were not alone.

A tall figure stood illuminated in the harsh fluorescent radiance. Spiky hair dyed indigo, fashioned into a Mohawk that spilled down his back, contrasted with the whiteness of his skin, as did the black fishnet shirt and black latex pants that seemed moulded to his incredibly lithe body. His face was...the only word I could think to describe it was sculpted. His features were fine, narrow and angular, yet with a fullness of lips and a certain lushness about him that was reminiscent of marble sculptures from Ancient Greece or Rome. The fishnet shirt revealed that the figure was in fact a guy, yet the way he held his body and the way he moved seemed off somehow. There was something distinctly inhuman about him.

As the stranger saw us, he gave an odd, almost feral smile. He peered at me from eyes shadowed by his hair. 'Good, you brought him,' he said, in a soft, almost whispering voice.

'Yeah,' Jamie replied smugly, 'Just as ya asked - the Pig...er...the kid, Mikey. You got the money? Same deal as always?'

The stranger stepped forward, moving towards us with a sinuous grace that made me uncomfortable. Not that I wasn't already scared enough to piss myself, but I was so caught by the grip of terror, at that moment even a loosening of my bowels seemed impossible.

When the stranger spoke next, it was in a sort of pleased hiss that reminded me uncannily of a cobra about to strike, 'Excellent, Jamie...you will most assuredly receive what you deserve.'

'Great, just what I wanted to hear,' Jamie smirked and nodded his head, glancing smugly towards his friends as he said, 'See, what'd I tell ya? These guys'll pay good money for these scumbags. Best part is, no one cares what happens to 'em, so it's easy money.'

Just as the last word left Jamie's lips, the stranger snapped his fingers. At once, the room was again thrust into darkness. Movement erupted around me. Jamie and his pack were shouting and flailing about, and there were others in the murky shadows, moving with absolute silence except for the whispering slither of vinyl and leather. Bodies crashed into me as I tried to make a break for it, sending me spinning, until I couldn't tell which way was out. I strained my eyes trying to pierce the gloom, but all I could see was the afterimage of the fluorescent light burned against the backs of my eyes. Finally, I thought I spotted a gleam of light, a possible way out, so I started running, pushing my way past whatever got in my way; then someone hit me from behind and sent me sprawling to the concrete floor. I tried to pick myself up, but a hard boot slammed against my head and sent me crashing into oblivion.

When I awoke, I found myself in a large room, without much light. I quickly realized I was naked, my skin crusted with sweat and filth. It didn't take me much longer to realize I was trapped with others, who were in a similar state to myself. At first, I tried talking to these anonymous figures, but the oppressiveness of the room and the starkness of our situation soon left each one of us alone with our own thoughts. Thoughts crowded into my head: I had been sold into slavery, or kidnapped by some strange cult, or even that I would be forced to take part in some sinister government experiment. In the end, when the Uigenna came to drag us away and strapped me down to the stone table, I had given up trying to figure out what had happened, but found in myself a strange determination to get out of it somehow, to get out and become something more than a statistic of another inexplicable disappearance.

I open my eyes and gaze up at the lights above me. My body feels strange, different somehow. Looking down at myself, I see the straps have gone. I'm lying on a cot instead of a cold stone table. I'm covered with a thin grey blanket, my body's shape visible beneath the fabric. At once, I sit upright, my head reeling. This can't be real. The rolls of fat have gone, as if they melted away in that terrible crucible of heat and pain. What's left behind is a body lithe and willowy. And I can see myself clearly, without the thick glasses I've needed all my life. Warily, I lift the corner of the blanket to see what lies beneath. Something has been done to me. Something beyond words. This body is not mine: it can't be. I'm not sure if it's even male any more.

I lie back in the silence, unable even to think. I lie still, very still. I stare at the cracked ceiling.

Then a shadow falls over me and a voice murmurs, 'So, our sleeping beauty awakens.' It is the stranger from the basement: the tall, slender figure in ebony, ivory and indigo. He smiles and something within me stirs. There's something oddly familiar about him. And beyond this recognition is another feeling. He approaches me slowly. 'Good morning, Mikey. I'd ask if you slept well, but I remember how painful the change is.'

I pull the sheet up to my neck, say nothing.

He smiles wistfully and shakes his head. 'What? Don't recognize me? No, guess not... I was a bit different the last time you saw me. Well, guess that means we need to be reintroduced. Down here, they call me Athame, but the name my parents gave me was Adam.'

I stare at him, and shake my head in denial of his words, yet as I look into his eyes, they are familiar to me, and part of me believes him. He kneels next to me, lifting a delicate yet powerful hand to cup my face. Alien thoughts spark inside me again. 'I know you don't understand any of this. I know that this must come as a huge shock to you. It was a shock to me as well. But let me tell you, it is better this way. I couldn't save Ricky from killing himself, but I could save you.'

'Wha...what about Jamie...and the others?' I swallow, trying to ease the scratchiness of my throat, a bit taken aback by how different my voice sounds now.

Adam - Athame - merely chuckles. 'Oh, we had them undergo the change as well. Only Jamie survived.' Athame laughs again, this time a sound of dark amusement. 'He will find that he's not the top predator anymore.'

'Adam, what the hell is going on? How has this happened to me? How long have I been here? Have you starved me? But my eyes...?'

Athame puts a finger to his lips to silence me. 'This is your beginning. All that you knew, that you were, you've left behind. All the old limitations of human form are meaningless now. You are Wraeththu. You are har.'

They are just words. I stare at him, this creature of dream with Adam's eyes. 'But how...?'

'We gave you our blood, our difference. This...' His hand sweeps across my body, and I swear I feel electric heat pouring from it. 'This is our gift to you. Humanity's time is done. It is our time now. As Homo sapiens replaced Cro-Magnon, it is time for us to replace humanity. Nature has made us stronger and faster than man, as well as giving us other gifts, including the ability to make man into our own image.'

'Then what am I?'

'As I said, you are har, no longer man, but one of us. Don't be afraid of the changes. From now on, Mikey is dead and gone. As of this morning, you shall be known as Boline, the light to my darkness and the darkness to my light.' He leans over me and exhales. The steam of his breath conjures pictures in my mind: new possibilities unfolding, of dark days filled with riots, rage and flames; of a glorious glowing city filled with others like ourselves; of a new world rising from the ashes unlike anything anyone could have ever imagined.

Something within me blossoms in the darkness of my soul as those images fill my mind, a glowing bloom of light that fills me with a new sense of purpose, a new reason for being. I am no longer Mikey, the frightened and ugly kid from the suburbs of Carmine. I am Boline, the blade who will help usher in a new world.

The Dawn of Hope

Suzanne Gabriel

The Dawn of Hope

Human death came in quick flashes from the muzzle of the gun. The echoes continued to reverberate around the old garage for longer than it took for the bodies to fall. Some gambles don't pay off, we should have known we were pushing our luck. We'd gambled and we'd lost.

Civilization had crumbled to the point of non-existence; it wasn't very civil anymore. The city was a burned out war zone; a shell. Those humans with means or influence had fled to safe, fortress-like gated communities and we, the lost and disenfranchised, found safety of sorts in gangs that fought for survival against other gangs of humans; and we all fought 'Them'. We all feared Them – they called themselves 'Wraeththu', but we had other names for them. They were strange, terrifying beings: faster, stronger, wild and unpredictable, and far more deadly. Sometimes they made their presence known, winning strategically impressive assaults against human strongholds and sometimes they appeared out of nowhere, silently dispatching their victims and then disappearing without a trace.

We'd lost this one. Our gang had been harrying a group of these strange creatures for a few months, but we'd fallen into a trap they'd set for us.

More shots rang out, and one by one more bodies fell. I felt nothing other than a hopeless sense of resignation. These were not my friends, these were my fellow gang members; humans thrown together, as there was strength in numbers. In this part of the city it was almost certain death to be on your own, so membership of a gang was essential. I feared my fellow gang members as much as we all feared these Wraeththu. I was the last one left standing, being held firmly by two of Them. I hadn't fought; it seemed pointless.

Their leader approached me, sneering. "Been watching? If you got anything to say – better say it now."

"Goodbye cruel world?" The insolence of my tone and words certainly didn't match what I was feeling.

The Wraeththu threw back his head and laughed. "You're a pretty thing. You'd make a good little plaything." He grabbed my hair and kissed me roughly.

I fought then. I knew – or thought I knew - what happened when they "played"; I'd rather be shot.

There were a lot of them, kicking and punching, and only one of me – I lost, fast. Balled into a foetal position, I prayed for a quick end.

The leader rolled me onto my back and placed his knee on my chest as he drew a knife from his belt. The knife was big, silver, and cruelly serrated. He drew the blade across the heel of his palm; blood spurted up immediately and he licked the wound.

"Sharp!" He laughed spitefully. "This'll do some damage."

I swallowed hard and closed my eyes, but it didn't do any good, I could still see the blade.

I held my breath and when I felt him shift his weight a bit I bucked hard and rolled.

My bid for freedom didn't get me far; I ended up face down on the garage floor; my face pushed into the oily reek of old car grease and gasoline. They had my arm twisted so far behind my back that I held my breath afraid that even the slightest movement would snap it. I could feel their leader's weight on me, pinning me to the floor.

"I like a fighter," he growled, his face near enough to my ear that I could feel the heat of his breath.

The knife sliced into my left shoulder. The leader grabbed the wound roughly, pressing hard into my shoulder, twisting the wound until I yelled.

He lowered his face again, so that his lips were touching my ear. "Now you are mine."

Then one of his group shouted, "They know we're here! Let's go! Fast! Move out! Go! Go! Go!"

The creatures reacted to the alarm immediately. I was dragged to my feet and shoved at a tall Wraeththu in a leather jacket.

"Don't lose him," barked their leader.

They moved quickly and silently. I was dragged, shoved, and hustled along with them; out into the night street.

There were some yells and a popping noise. Something whizzed past my face. I heard a grunt from the creature dragging me and when he fell I dove for cover, crawling through a small hole in a chain-linked fence.

Then I ran until the first dark doorway arch I encountered. Although it smelled of urine and decay, I pressed myself as flat as I could and waited. It seemed like forever before the shouts and the running feet faded. Still I waited.

Dawn found me beneath a rusty fire escape hidden behind some battered garbage cans. I'd been woken by the sound of squeaky wheels and shuffling feet. I waited silently until they passed; two old men pushing an old shopping cart loaded high with junk. They muttered to themselves as they passed.

I weighed my options. I couldn't go back to my old 'hood. I was alone now and I'd be marked for revenge by all those with grievances, real or imagined, against those I'd relied on. I also couldn't stay out alone. You didn't survive alone. I'd have to squirrel into another area and try and work my way into a new group.

I felt awful that morning: a heavy queasiness accompanied by the chills, and my shoulder really hurt to move. I was weak and shaky. Daylight in the city was safer than night, but I still moved cautiously through the streets; it never paid to draw attention to oneself.

As the morning wore on, I felt progressively worse; nauseous. My stomach cramped. By midday my head was swimming. I felt so sick and dizzy. I stopped to retch a few times.

The earth began to rumble and a mechanical throbbing filled the air, a warning that motivated me to find safety behind a burnt-out wreck of a car. I huddled there as several army patrol tanks and armoured cars rumbled slowly down the street.

I'd often toyed with the idea of flagging one of these patrols down and throwing myself at their mercy, but they worked for those humans who existed in the gated communities; there was no room in those safe havens for disenfranchised hard-luck stragglers.

By late afternoon I was fairly sure I was dying; whatever disease I'd picked up was progressing rapidly. By the time I crawled into a rusty, crumbling dumpster, I could barely walk. I huddled there scared and feeling beyond miserable.

"Eww. He's a mess."

"Don't look at me! I haven't done anyone in weeks…"

I could hear voices.

"Well get him out of there! We can't have him hollering like that out here. He'll attract too much attention."

I tried opening my eyes, but it was hard; they didn't open all the way and my face felt swollen. I could make out several figures. My stomach lurched; they were Wraeththu. I closed my eyes again and sank away from the pain.

The next time I opened my eyes all I felt was tired.

I blinked a few times and gingerly tested my limbs. I was lying naked under a sheet in a dingy room. From where I was lying on the floor I could see grey light filtering through filthy windows high along the walls.

"Wakey wakey newbie," a voice drawled.

I turned my head toward the voice. A slight figure in a dark hoodie sat slumped against the wall opposite hugging his knees.

"What's your name?" he asked as he shifted forward and peered at me.

"Nolan." My voice sounded slightly slurred.

"They call me Mouse," he said. "It isn't my name, but that's what they call me. How you feeling?"

I sat up cautiously, holding the sheet tightly around me and peered around the dingy room.

"I feel okay," I said.

"Consider yourself lucky. You survived. A lot don't make it through, you know."

"Survived? What the hell did I have?"

"Have?" His laugh was a short bark. "You had *inception*." Mouse shook his head at my puzzled look. "Dumbass! You were incepted. You mutated. You went through 'The Change'. You're a har now. You're Wraeththu. One of us. Get it?"

I stared at him for a moment as his words sunk in. "A har?" I asked, blankly.

Mouse nodded. "Har. It's what we call ourselves. It's what you are now. Har. Wraeththu."

"But how?" This was surreal.

"How should I know?" Mouse shrugged. "We found you in the dumpster. You must have got blood from a har somehow at some point. It's the only way I know of for inception to happen."

I didn't say anything, but in my minds' eye conjured up the scene in the garage; I could see the Wraeththu gang leader and his knife. That must have been how it had happened.

I looked down at myself. I was definitely different. What little chest hair I had developed was gone, as was the hair on my arms. My hand came up to touch my face. My chin was smooth, not a hint of beard stubble. I felt a little different too. I felt slightly 'wobbly', as if I'd suddenly come out of a doorway to find myself balancing precariously at the very edge of a skyscraper's roof. I felt a vastness and expanse that both thrilled me and terrified me.

I looked up at Mouse. He smiled slightly.

"Yeah, there are differences." He said in answer to a question I had not asked out loud. "Brace yourself before you look under the sheet."

I dropped my eyes again to where the sheet lay across my lap and swallowed hard as an uneasy feeling twisted my stomach.

"Wraeththu blood turns humans into Wraeththu?" I was still trying to wrap my head around this new wrinkle in reality.

We humans had known the Wraeththu were *different* and that they were enemies of humanity, but other than that I did not know much else about them. They were shrouded in mystery and suspicion. So many rumours and wild stories about them were told it was hard to know what to believe.

"Blood and three days of hell. Those are the facts of life, my friend," Mouse replied, nodding curtly.

"So I'm Wraeththu now?" I asked again slowly. This seemed very surreal

"Mostly. There is one more thing that needs to happen. To be completely har you've got to spend some time with Dawson." Mouse leered at me for a moment. "And maybe a few of the others too." He smiled an odd tight smile before looking away quickly. "I'd better go tell them you're ready." He scrambled to his feet.

"Ready for what?" I called after him, but I got no answer.

Mouse and I often scavenged together. We usually set out in the mornings and in the mid-afternoon had hauled our treasures back to our home in an abandoned warehouse by now unused train tracks. I was one of them now; I was Wraeththu. To me, there seemed not much difference between being human and being one of them. Life was still harsh and violent, and we still struggled for territory and dwindling resources. My life had settled down to a dreary routine of scavenging, helping to maintain our territory, sleeping, cleaning, and trying to attract as little attention to myself as possible. Dawson, our crew leader, wasn't terribly fond of me; I didn't fit in.

That day's scavenging had been successful; we'd found a bag of old clothes and we'd managed to steal a case of canned peas.

That afternoon was different from most. When Mouse and I returned to the warehouse, our clan weren't the only ones there; Dawson appeared to be entertaining.

"You're late," Dawson barked.

"Sorry," I replied. "We had to be careful – wanted to be sure we weren't followed."

"Tanks! Bunches of them!" Mouse supplied, nodding enthusiastically.

Dawson waved his hand autocratically. "Come over here and meet my guests."

Mouse moved forward grinning, while I followed more slowly.

"This is Mouse!" Dawson said beaming at Mouse proudly. "He's one of our best! He can sniff goods out anywhere, and he can liberate them like a pro."

Mouse nodded vigorously and grinned more.

"And this," Dawson said with considerably less enthusiasm, gesturing in my direction, "is Nolan." He paused a beat. "He's new".

I nodded to the newcomers. There were seven of them and they were like no one I had ever seen before. They were beautiful. They wore clean, colourful clothing, jewellery, and their hair was long and styled. There was something else too, but I couldn't put my finger on it. They not only looked different, I was sure they *were* different; they seemed to radiate something. Self-confidence? Power? Authority? Serenity?

By comparison we were loutish, grimy riffraff stuffed into layers of ill-fitting scavenged clothing.

"And I am Maelduin," said one of the newcomers, a tall, tanned har whose dark blond hair hung in a neat braid down his back. "These are Acorn, Aydenn, Osiris, Zekki, D'rik, and Inari." He flashed a disarmingly charming smile; Dawson was clearly bewitched.

Our guests were all easy on the eyes. I will admit to being fascinated by them as well. The one who piqued my interest the most was the dark-haired swarthy beauty with big dark eyes, and a slightly aquiline nose, who'd been introduced as Inari.

Someone had started a fire in an old metal crate, and our crew members sat around it while our guests listened to Dawson talk about us. Actually, he talked more about himself and how wonderful his plans were, and his gripes about the world, which constantly failed to recognize his genius. He was pathetically desperate to impress our guests, but to me he came off as even more of an unimpressive braggart than usual. Most of our crew egged him on, flattering him, and encouraging his antics, but I saw that Dawson was a garish caricature compared to our guests and their composed self-assurance. I gave total credit to our guests, who managed to remain flawlessly gracious, their smiles never wavering.

"Dawson, you are unbelievable! A genius to be reckoned with!" Maelduin chuckled affably.

From my vantage, on the outside edge of the circle gathered around the fire, I was pretty sure that several of our guests exchanged a faint smirk, but no one else appeared to notice.

"That story, my friend, deserves a toast," Maelduin went on. "Allow us to offer you and your hara some refreshment so that we can offer up a toast to your continued success."

The suggestion was met with whoops of approval by members of my crew. Our guests began producing green bottles and fanned out among the twenty or so of us in Dawson's crew. Inari passed a bottle along to the eager hands of one of my gang with a smile, but he stayed seated next to Maelduin. I observed him for a moment, he seemed withdrawn, resigned, tired. To me he was the most intriguing and beautiful of them. I kind of identified with him, or at least I projected my own feelings of discontent onto him.

I watched my crew squabble over the bottles, each grabbing one and taking a swig before it was snatched from them. When one bottle was emptied another appeared. If these strangers had as much booze as they seemed to, I really needed to make myself scarce; no good came from bullies like Dawson and his 'favourites' when they got drinking. My attempt to slip away would have been successful but for the visitor named Acorn.

"No! Don't go, tiahaar! You mustn't go!" He called out. "Stay! This is good stuff. I promise." He grinned at me as he grabbed my wrist and flicked his long brown curls over his shoulder.

I was caught and Dawson had noticed. He glared at me as he got to his feet. "Where were you sneaking off to, Nolan?" he demanded. "Being rude to my guests?"

"I was going to go see about starting dinner." It was the first thing that popped into my head; the wrong thing. I should have just said I was going for a pee.

Dawson froze for a moment and then his eyes narrowed. We had precious little food. The case of peas we'd found today would be barely a mouthful for our own gang – sharing would only mean less for everyone. Dawson wasn't generous. He wouldn't think twice about accepting the strangers' offer of alcohol, but he'd not voluntarily offer them food in return.

"You were, were you? How… thoughtful." His voice was low and dangerous; he took a few steps towards me.

Acorn reacted; smooth and lightening fast. He dropped my wrist and slid his arms around my waist, and in a dancer-smooth move had swung me out of the way, inserting himself between me and Dawson. With his arm still firmly around my waist, Acorn fairly oozed 'sensuous soume' at Dawson, placing his hand lightly on our leader's chest.

"Dawson, you treasure!" Acorn purred. "How generous to offer us dinner! I might have known you'd try to do such a sweet thing. Hospitality like yours is a rare treat these days. You are to be commended! But we can't let you! No! No! No!" He shook his head emphatically.

Dawson looked confused for a moment but then swaggered smugly at the flattery.

"Of course not!" the har called Osiris laughed. "It would have been rather rude and pushy for such a large number of us just to descend on you unannounced and expect to be fed. We're trying to make a good impression on you, so we brought you and your hara dinner."

A murmur rippled through our crew and attention shifted away from us as the clan anticipated dinner. As I met his eyes, Acorn gave my waist a slight squeeze. I mouthed, "Thank you", and he responded with a slight nod and a ghost of a smile.

Dinner was not fancy; there were no table-cloths or cutlery, no plates or crystal, but it was divine. These hara had brought sandwiches – yes, huge chunks of juicy tender chicken, thick slices of plump tomatoes, crisp lettuce, in enormous crusty bread rolls. I was in bliss. When Osiris passed around enormous chocolate chip cookies for dessert I wanted to kiss him, but I didn't.

Later, much later, I was still sitting by the fire; full, content, and after several drinks, feeling mellow and sleepy. I was staring into the dying flames trying hard not to think of how long it had been since I'd eaten food like that and trying even harder to think about how long it might be until we ate that well again.

The box of books landed with a loud bang startling me out of my reverie. Mouse took a couple of paperbacks and tossed them into the fire.

I love reading. I love books. I had been taught to respect books, long ago in that other life I'd once had. Burning them just seemed so wrong but I had given up trying to teach my fellow crew members a love of books. I sat mutely watching the cover of one of the cheesy romance novels begin to bubble and then darken as the flames took hold: a picture of a buxom woman in a pale mauve gown swooning into the arms of a shirtless muscular man, a castle visible in the distant background.

"Don't let Nolan see you burning those books," Dawson sneered. "He'll cry."

The crew guffawed loudly; I did my best not to react.

"Do you like books, Nolan?" Acorn asked brightly.

"Yeah…" I mumbled self-consciously. "Love 'em."

"And burning them bothers you?" Maelduin asked, an eyebrow arched.

The dark one called Inari was suddenly alert, roused and now focused on the conversation.

"Well," I said carefully, "I understand why we have to burn them, fuel being as scarce as it is, but…. I dunno, it just seems wrong… and sad. It's such a waste."

"A waste?" Maelduin cocked his head to one side.

"There is so much art in them, so much information, and so much to learn from them. They represent most of the knowledge and ideas that the world has ever had. If we burn them, that information and those ideas are gone."

"Who cares?" said Mouse as he threw a few more books into the flames. "It's just human knowledge. Humans are finished. We're Wraeththu – we're a million times better."

"But, we *were* human," I couldn't help responding. "All of us. We can't forget that. How are we going to know we're better unless we can prove we've gone farther than humans did?" I pointed to one of the books he'd tossed into the pyre, *Basic Math and Pre-Algebra* "Basic Math isn't going to change just because we're now Wraeththu, nor will other basic facts…"

"Humans are stupid fucks," Mouse pronounced darkly.

"They weren't always," I insisted. This was a subject I felt strongly about. "Humans were around for thousands of years. They invented all sorts of brilliant things; they put people on the moon, created great works of art, and built strong civilizations… Humans weren't always like they are now. I know there were always wars and conflict, empires rose and fell, but there were always groups, and individuals that were trying to make things right… until something happened and all of society fell apart. Civilisation failed completely and Wraeththu emerged.

"If we don't preserve the written human record, we may never know who we are and why we are the way we are. If we want to understand today, we have to understand yesterday! Learning about all of humanity will help us know what things we must do and what things we need to avoid. We're moving out of human history into our own history…"

I suddenly realised how much I had said and how enthusiastically. Shame and fear silenced me then, but I was over the moon when I saw Inari's swarthy face break out into a wide grin; he appeared more engaged at this moment than he'd been all afternoon. He leaned over and grabbed one of the paperbacks. He held it up for me to see – it was another romance novel – one whose cover depicted a muscular man with a cowboy hat staring stoically off into the sunset as a woman with long hair clung to him.

"And what, pray tell," Inari asked with a mischievous grin and a twinkle in his eye, "will be learned from this… literature?"

I grinned back, thoroughly delighted. "Perhaps, some day in the future, a Wraeththu scholar will want to compare…"

"SHUT UP!" Dawson roared.

I shut up immediately – damn the booze for having sent my inhibitions and instincts for self-preservation packing!

"SHUT UP!" His voice was a shrill shriek, his face was red and his limbs flailed like those of a child before a tantrum. "No one gives a fuck what you think … you're just a fucking piece of shit … SHUT THE FUCK UP!!"

I ducked and rolled backwards out of the circle. The empty bottle Dawson had hurled at me glanced off my shoulder and skittered across the floor.

Dawson's abuse continued as I retreated behind the rows of stacked pallets. Howls of derisive laughter followed me as I stepped out into the freshness of cool evening air. Gangs are 'substitute families', my ass.

I swung myself up onto the broken bit of fire escape that still clung to the warehouse wall and climbed to the expansive flat roof. I heaved myself up onto one of the vent outlets that peppered the roof. I came up here often; to think, to escape, to cry, to dream. This evening it was to escape.

I hugged my knees and rested my chin on them. *I hate my life. I hate Dawson. What purpose does any of this serve?*

"It was the best of times, it was the worst of times, it was the age of wisdom, it was the age of foolishness, it was the epoch of belief, it was the epoch of incredulity, it was the season of Light, it was the season of Darkness, it was the spring of hope, it was the winter of despair."

It was an quote from an ancient book called *The Tale of Two Cities* by Charles Dickens and it played on an endless loop in my head. Its author wrote of revolution; peasants rebelling against aristocratic cruel oppression. While the storyline is full of chaos, violence, and repression, there is also a belief in the possibility of transformation, both personal and societal. The author had supported his revolutionaries' 'cause', but he had also pointed out the evil of fighting cruelty with cruelty. It is a slippery slope from being the oppressed to being the oppressor. Perhaps we were now facing this same plight; humans had treated Wraeththu cruelly, and now that humanity was failing, were we in danger of merely becoming the new oppressors? Same shit, different day? Maybe we stood at that point where foolishness became wisdom? When despair became hope? Or, I sighed with resignation, maybe I'm just a fucking piece of shit that spends too much time thinking and trying to make sense of things that just 'were'.

I sat on the roof brooding for some time, long enough for the sun to sink below the horizon on the other side of the river. The sky above me was now a dark indigo. Across the river, lights had begun to appear, twinkling in the darkness. A few moments later the flood-lights in the tall armed-guard towers burst to life and began their ceaseless roaming vigil, guarding the human occupants of the gated community from threats, from Wraeththu, from me. Ironically I felt like I was the most helpless creature on the planet. On our side of the river, there was darkness; the army had cut the power ages ago in a vain attempt to subdue both human and Wraeththu insurgents.

The crunch of gravel drew my attention. Inari crossed the roof casually and hopped up onto the vent box next to me. He didn't say anything as he stared out across the river at the prowling searchlights. I noticed his dark hair had a slight and regular wave; it hung loosely over his shoulders.

"You shouldn't be here with these hara," Inari stated.

"Ha!" I sounded bitter. "You're right, I shouldn't, but all life's a crapshoot isn't it? My Grandmother shouldn't have gotten sick, but she did. She shouldn't have put me on that bus, but she did. There should have been someone to meet me at the bus terminal, but there wasn't. I shouldn't be here, but I am."

"Sounds grim," Inari agreed evenly, "How old were you then?"

"I dunno… fourteen, almost fifteen?"

"And how old are you now?"

"About twenty… almost twenty-one, I think."

Silence returned and we both stared out across the river.

"Was it your Grandmother who taught you to love books?"

"Yeah. She worked in a library. It was an enormous old fortress of a building with an old broken down fountain out front. As they closed down schools, colleges, and smaller libraries, they'd bring all the books there. I was too little to stay home alone, so she'd always take me to work. They were all old people at the library, and I was quiet, so they didn't mind having me around. I learned letters and numbers helping to sort books by call numbers. I could sit for hours with books. There weren't any other kids – just books. By the time I was old enough to go to school there weren't any left in our area. So I just kept getting reading tips from the others and discussing stuff I read with them. When I was ten I decided to read the whole library – I was going to work my way through every single book…"

I saw a flash of white teeth in the dark.

Inari asked me a lot of questions; at some points it felt a bit like an interview, but I didn't mind too much. I was ridiculously flattered and way too eager to answer, too eager to please; no one had ever expressed any interest in me or my story. Have you ever heard yourself saying way more than you intended to? That was sort of how it was. I did try to reciprocate with questions of my own about him and his friends, but he was quite skilful at deflecting them. I told him about my life from my times at library to being part of the human gang. After I'd described the events surrounding my inception the conversation fell into a lull.

"Was Dawson your first?" Inari asked.

"Yeah." I acknowledged finally after an awkward pause. "He's everyone's first." These were not good memories. "He's the first and then it's open season for anyone who wants a go."

"Not a good situation," Inari observed; his voice was carefully neutral.

"It's over." I shrugged. "They got tired of me pretty quick. I don't have to do it anymore."

"You don't like aruna?" Inari sounded bemused.

"Pain and humiliation? What's to like?" As soon as I'd said that I wondered if aruna was why he'd followed me up there. After all the food and the booze his group had offered us it would probably be rude to refuse him, if that's what he wanted.

"But," I added hurriedly, "that doesn't mean I won't. I mean... I will, if that's what you want..."

"No ... but thank you," he said, his voice solemn. "It's been a long day and I'm too exhausted to be any use to a partner."

I couldn't see his face clearly in the dark, but it sounded like he was smiling.

There followed a few minutes of silence that felt very awkward to me. I was racking my brain to try and figure out what to say when he broke the silence. "That's human territory across the river isn't it? So what are they guarding? It looks like quite the operation. Something rather valuable it would seem? Weapons perhaps?"

"Something even more valuable." I sighed. "Their loved ones. It's a family compound."

"Ah.... A truth that some humans never understood, until it was too late. So tell me Nolan, how far did you get when you tried to read the whole library?"

I found myself back in my grandmother's library, running through the stacks, desperately trying to find her before the tanks and soldiers did. Along the way, I was trying to grab and rescue as many valuable books as I could. I was panic-stricken because I kept dropping so many of them, but there wasn't time to stop. I burst through a door and into an old storage room. I was overjoyed to find the fountain that had stood derelict in front of the old library for as long as I'd been accompanying my grandmother, was there in the storage room fixed and functioning; but as I barricaded the door to stop the tanks, the fountain changed into an old dishevelled silver Christmas tree that disintegrated when I touched it.

Nolan!

My eyes flickered half-open and the dream faded. I saw nothing but blackness There was no sound; the warehouse was still.

Inari and I had talked about reading and books for quite awhile. We'd gone back inside together but we'd parted ways; he'd headed back to the fire-lit circle and I to my sleep spot along the wall farthest from the main area. I began to drift back to sleep.

Nolan!

I was suddenly wide awake. I'd heard my name but not with my ears. I'd heard it in my head.

Nolan!

I sat bolt upright. There was no mistaking it that time; someone had said my name in my head – but the whole warehouse remained still and silent. I sat there tense, alert; peering into the darkness. A pale blue light appeared around a corner of boxes and seemed to float towards me. My heart was pounding as Inari crouched down in front of me.

Nolan, we have to be leaving now. Come with us.

I was frozen. This had to be still part of a dream; his lips weren't moving, yet I could hear his voice in my head. As my eyes were drawn to the light in his hand, my blood ran cold. This didn't make sense to me; I could see no source for the light. There was just an orb of light floating just above the palm of his hand.

Nolan? I looked up at him. Even in that light the confusion and fear I was feeling must have showed on my face.

Don't be afraid, Nolan! The last thing I want to do is hurt you. This kind of communication is called mind touch and the light is a pretty simple trick. You're Wraeththu – and you will learn to do this too. We'll teach you how. There is so much more to being a har than what your life is here. We've been travelling into the cities trying to find hara like you. You believe there is a better way, don't you? So do we. We believe that we Wraeththu can be more than just 'bigger and badder' humans and we're working to make that a reality. We're building our future. Come with us, Nolan. Please.

I opened my mouth to say something but he put his fingers lightly on my lips.

Shhhh. Quietly! We don't want to wake anyhar. We want to be miles from here before Dawson and the others wake up. Do you have any belongings to collect?

I shook my head slowly.

He moved his fingers from my lips and I felt a feather-light caress of my cheek.

Let's go.

It had only taken me a second to decide to leave the warehouse with Inari and the others. I did not want to miss this opportunity for escape by over-thinking and over-analysing; opportunities only knock once, they say, and sometimes not even that often. I'd made the choice purely on gut-instinct. Leaving with them just felt like the right thing to do; time would tell if I'd jumped out of the frying pan only to land in the fire.

As we picked our way through the back alleys, my new friends answered my questions readily, but their answers tended to fill me with more questions. This made me slightly uneasy and I entertained certain second thoughts, but for better or worse I had put my lot in with these strangers and the farther from Dawson's warehouse I got the more committed to this path it seemed I was.

We travelled steadily but cautiously, and by the time the sun began to rise we were miles past the bridge that spanned the river marking the territory between Dawson's crew and the territory next door, which was controlled by a harish band of 'nightwalkers'.

There wasn't much conversation as the day wore on. Everyone was on high alert, but so far I'd seen no one. We were halfway along a block of boarded-up and burnt-out shops when Zekki stopped suddenly signalling the rest of us to halt.

"What's wrong?" I whispered.

Danger! Aydenn replied into my head. *Can you feel it? Try. Let your mind feel, let it go… trust what it tells you.*

I wasn't exactly sure what he meant but I took a good hard look at the intersection we were approaching. It was as unremarkable as any other, with cracked pavement, weeds, and more boarded-up storefronts. Then I'm not sure what happened, I suddenly felt something; I felt jumpy and panicky – there was something wrong.

Zekki advanced two steps, stopped, then suddenly spun on his heel, signalling madly.

D'rik grabbed me and hustled me into one of the sheltered store entries between the now non-existent showcase windows. The rest of them crowded in after us.

Don't move. Don't breathe.

All of us were motionless as a heavily-armed human patrol slowly came around the corner; alert – their guns at the ready.

Maelduin was in front of us all at the edge of the store front alcove, closest to the street. He stood tall and straight, his eyes closed, his arms hanging at his sides, palms facing out to the street. His body was relaxed and he seemed focused inward completely.

The soldiers moved slowly, still holding their guns ready. We were sitting ducks. There was no way they'd miss eight hara crushed into a tiny store entranceway. I closed my eyes and waited for the bullets but nothing happened. Nothing happened for what seemed like ages.

I opened my eyes. A soldier stood not ten feet from where we were. He was scanning the area slowly. He was so close that when he turned his head and his gaze travelled over where we huddled I could see that his eyes were blue. How could he not see us? How could none of the patrol members see us?

D'rik was directly in front of me. His body suddenly became relaxed and his breathing deepened. I noticed he was staring hard at the alleyway that cut between two derelict shop buildings across the street. Suddenly his body went rigid, his breathing stopped, his eyes closed and almost simultaneously all hell seemed to break loose down that alley; it sounded like metal trashcans were being bashed around.

Several yelled orders had the patrol moving briskly into the alleyway. We waited a few breaths after the last human had entered the alley and then we ran; we ran until I thought my lungs would burst.

"I don't understand how they didn't see us."

The sun was setting and we'd taken shelter in a small garage that stood behind a tiny old house that was stripped of its siding and whose roof had caved in.

Maelduin smiled "I created a kind of psychic veil... a metaphysical barrier... between them and us. It clouded their minds enough to keep us hidden. You know 'out of sight out of mind'? Well this is sort of an 'out of mind, out of sight' thing." He chuckled at his own little joke. "We hara have so much potential – you'll learn. We're all still learning."

I mulled over some of the 'potentials' I'd already been witness to that day.

"D'rik? Can I ask you a question?"

"Sure," he nodded. "As long as you ask in mind touch."

I frowned. "I can't."

"Try. Think it into my head."

I tried. I thought hard about my question but D'rik just sat there patiently. I closed my eyes and tried again; still nothing.

"Nolan." Acorn leaned forward. "You're just beginning, so start with your eyes open and look at D'rik. Picture your words going into his head." He reached out to place his index finger on my temple. "Visualize your words going from here to here." He traced an arch toward D'rik's temple. "Focus and try again."

I took a deep breath and focused on the question, I repeated it several times to myself and then looked at D'rik and thought it at the same time as visualizing the arc Acorn had drawn with his finger.

"Try again," Inari encouraged.

I did; this time I sort of 'shoved' the thought out of my mind towards D'rik.

"Yes! I did!" D'rik grinned. "I made that commotion in the alley this afternoon. More Wraeththu conjuring – I knocked some garbage cans off a fire escape."

"He did it?" Acorn exclaimed. "Wow, that's awesome, Nolan!"

"Yup, Nolan asked if it was me who caused that hullabaloo in the alley."

After almost three full days of walking we'd left the dismal ruin of the city behind. We were now following the crumbling network of highways and byways of the open countryside. The sunshine, open fields and the fresh air were uplifting. I had not seen this much nature in my entire life. The tensions of the city seemed to melt away, our group chatted and laughed as we trekked.

Inari and I had spent many hours talking about books and authors we liked, debating literature styles, and discussing the exciting possibility of books that could be written about Wraeththu, for Wraeththu, and by Wraeththu. When we'd left the city, we had started out on wide multi-lane highways that had once seen thousands of rumbling cars and trucks, but now were desolate empty spaces where the once smooth asphalt was riddled with potholes and cracks in which wild flowers and grasses had taken root.

We'd veered off the main highway to follow a variety of smaller routes, always skirting old towns "just in case". Late in the afternoon of the third day, Aydenn suddenly turned off the narrow winding country road we had been travelling along and began walking up a gravel drive that wound between the trees.

"Wow," I commented. "I didn't even see this driveway until you walked up here!"

"I know." Maelduin smirked. "Thank you." He laughed good-naturedly at the confused look I gave him. "It's another one of those magic veils – we leave it here at the entrance. That way, unless you know it's there and are looking for it, you don't see it. It cuts down on unwanted visitors and snoops!"

At the end of the long drive was a large flat-roofed, two-story building that, judging by the truck bays must have been some sort of business premises, with a warehouse on the ground floor and office space above. I could also see some smaller buildings further back. What was most surprising was that this place, hidden out in the woods, bustled with activity. There were hara loading a wagon, others digging in a ditch, and others bound for somewhere carrying tools or boxes.

My companions were greeted warmly with big smiles and waves and calls of 'welcome back'.

Maelduin turned to me. "Welcome to your first 'home', Nolan. Make yourself comfortable, pitch in, make friends, and I'll see you at dinner." He pointed at Aydenn and D'rik. "You two are off to find out about the next convoy." Then he pointed at Acorn and Osiris. "You two need to come with me. We've got to check in with our fearless leader." Finally, Maelduin pointed at Inari. "You go get Nolan checked in and then join us."

"You…" Maelduin pointed at Zekki.

"I," announced Zekki, "am going to have a bath, and nap until dinner." With a grin and wink he was off.

Inari guided me into one of the open truck bays where a harried-looking har with straw-coloured hair twisted up into a knot was sorting papers. He looked up as we approached. "Inari! You're back! Good to see you."

"Good to see you too, Buzz," Inari said with a grin. "I'm signing in a new addition."

Buzz's eyes flickered over to where I stood and he nodded quickly. "He's already har? OK, good. Name?"

"Nolan," I said.

Buzz wrote that down. "OK, OK…" He grabbed a large clipboard "… Ummmm… let's see." He began to chew on the pencil. "You see we're reallllllly crowded – the convoy that was supposed to leave yesterday didn't because the wagon wheel fell off… Oy! What a mess… I can find you a temporary spot… and I'll move you into a real spot when the convoy leaves…"

"He's bunking with me," Inari said.

Buzz stuck the pencil into his hair-knot and looked me over with a bit more interest than he had initially. "OK, then. Since you're probably expected to check in with the boss – I'll take care of Nolan."

Inari nodded. "See you at dinner," he said to me as he headed off.

"Right, then," Buzz said. "A bath, some new clothes, and we'll get you settled." Then he yelled over his shoulder: "Hiko!"

A lanky pale har with a shaved head and four gold earrings ambled out of one of the old office spaces.

"Hiko, this is Nolan. He's just arrived. Can you take him and get him set up?"

"Sure!"

The bath was divinely warm and soapy; I felt reborn. Hiko seemed determined to 'transform' me; he'd found me some fabulous clothes, new boots, and a flashy jacket, and he'd produced a citrusy liquid he'd applied to my hair which allowed him to brush out the tangles almost painlessly.

When triumphantly he stood me in front of a mirror, I didn't recognize myself. The last time I'd had a proper bath and clean clothes I'd been an adolescent in my grandmother's tiny apartment; a scrawny, pale, shy boy with short cropped hair – an awkward ugly duckling. Now a slender exotic creature with large brown eyes and brown wavy hair that hung down the middle of his back stared back at me. I ran my fingers through my hair. I was a swan. I smiled at my reflection and was instantly struck by the resemblance between my reflection and an old dog-eared photograph of my grandmother I'd once found in one of her old books. My grandmother lived on in me.

Just how complete a transformation Hiko had achieved was evident when we reported back to Buzz. The har glanced up in my direction in a quick distracted acknowledgment of my presence, and then did a startled double-take, knocking over a pile of carefully stacked papers. An eyebrow rose as he looked me over thoroughly. "Well... wow! That's quite the cleanup," he said.

Hiko laughed. "OK. Apparently you approve. I'm going to show Nolan the compound. See you at dinner."

There were storage areas, horses, and wagons. There was a blacksmith and an expansive cultivation area that grew vegetables. There were chickens and goats. There was a recycling and repurposing area and more. I was impressed – thoroughly.

"We try to be as self-sufficient as possible," Hiko said proudly.

As we walked back towards the main buildings, I caught site of two smaller buildings set well apart from the others.

"What's in there?" I asked.

"The smaller cottage is where we house any humans that come through," Hiko replied. "The refugees, we help on through. Those wanting to be incepted are coached and prepared for the process. That's where I spent about a week when I first got here. The other bigger building is where they hold the inception ritual and then care for newbies until the change is done. After that, they're brought to the main buildings and there is a welcoming ceremony before they get to go off for the fun bit..." He grinned at me and winked. "Inari was my first." He seemed to catch himself and shot me a rather self-conscious look, then cleared his throat. "That doesn't bother you, does it?" he continued rapidly. "'Cuz sometimes we still think of sex and aruna as the same and having the same rules, right? But they don't, right? I just don't want you to feel weird 'cuz ... shit! ... I shouldn't have said anything," he finished somewhat sheepishly.

"Oh... no...," I said hurriedly. "Inari and I have never... you know – done it. I ... don't..." I felt my cheeks flush.

"You don't?" Hiko looked at me as if I had two heads. "Why?"

"Inception wasn't my choice, and I spent most of my 'change' alone, in a dumpster. The next bit was pretty awful too, so...." My voice trailed off and I shrugged.

"Oh, wow... I'm sorry," he said awkwardly.

We walked a bit in silence.

"Nolan?" There was a long pause. "I know you're bunking with Inari... and I just want to say..." Hiko was struggling with the right wording. "You know.... If the opportunity comes up... you know ... for you and Inari to ... you know..." He fixed me with an intense look. "Trust him, okay?"

We stared at each other for a moment, and then a sly smile crept across his face. "Trust me," he said. "You will not regret it."

A loud cacophony of banging pots and pans and hollering announced dinner; Hiko and I headed back at a jog to join the mess hall line.

I found the table with my travel companions and endured (and thoroughly enjoyed) the compliments and teasing about my make-over. I blushed and beamed and noted with a startling degree of satisfaction that Inari kept stealing sidelong glances in my direction despite being in deep discussion with a beautiful blond har who wore a red leather jacket.

Three days of travel on foot with not much sleep, the newness of the place, my relief at having what felt like a real home, combined with a full belly was catching up with me; I was struggling to keep my eyes open.

Acorn and Aydenn escorted me up to the sleeping quarters as Inari and Maelduin headed off for more meetings.

The sleeping quarters were on the second floor of the building. Up there, the open plan room had been divided into smaller, more private spaces using an eclectic array of materials and methods. A few tents had been set up, and blankets and old curtains had been strung up between pillars. Inari's 'room' was at the far end of the room. The space was marked by the corner walls and an old office cubical wall; a curtain panel provided privacy. Most of the floor space was filled with a large mattress. A bed and privacy: to me that was luxury. I kicked off my boots and sat down on the edge of the mattress. For the first time in ages I felt like things were good; I dared to begin to hope.

I don't remember lying down, and I certainly don't remember falling asleep, but I must have.

Gentle shaking roused me. It was Inari.

"Nolan! Wake up. There's a welcoming ceremony this morning. Six new hara are being welcomed to the tribe. I want you to come. Maelduin and I are assisting the hienama this morning."

I sat up groggily as Inari rolled off the bed. He had slept naked. In the early morning darkness I could see his body, pale and ghost-like as he dressed. He was beautiful.

"C'mon sleepy head." Inari teased.

I yawned as I began to grope around on the floor for my boots and yanked them on.

"You're still tired? Did my snoring keep you awake?"

I shook my head and yawned again. "Do *I* snore?" I asked curiously as I pulled on my jacket.

"No, but you're really cuddly" he said and waggled his eyebrows up and down. "Come on. After the ceremony I want to introduce you to the hienama. You need to start your spiritual caste training - you know, learn how to throw garbage cans around and cloud human minds." Inari flashed me a grin and headed out of the cubicle through the privacy curtain.

I stared after him for a second or two before following. I was not too sure about the training, the tingly quiver that surged through my gut at being told that I was cuddly by the har who had slept next to me naked invoked feelings that felt more erotic and earthy than soulful and spiritual.

I stumbled after Inari into the freshness of the pre-dawn air, still yawning. We went to stand before a raised dais, upon which was a semi-circle of lit torches. Acorn linked his arm through mine and we watched as the hienama, assisted by Maelduin and Inari, prepared for the ceremony.

At a signal, a procession entered the space parading the new hara in to stand before the three officiates who stood waiting on the raised dais. I probably should have been watching the procession like everyone else, but I found my gaze drawn to Inari. He looked solemn and regal in his pale robe, his dark hair hanging loose about his shoulders. Beautiful.

"They're naked under those robes," Acorn whispered in my ear.

I felt my face flush and was thankful the sun was still below the horizon.

The six new hara looked excited but at the same time terrified. The hienama, a rather forbidding looking creature with his head shaved save for the long braid that fell from the back of his skull, raised his arms and called us to silence.

He offered words of thanks for the new hara's safe transformation, then he spoke of the great potentials they now had. He also told them that while they must put the past aside, they were not to forget it: instead they should bring the new understanding that is Wraeththu to their new path. The great potential of Wraeththu, he said, was a gift of great privilege, and with it came a great responsibility. He spoke at length about transformation; hope, belief, and the future. His words were moving and profound. I wish I could have paid more attention and remembered them all, but some of the things he said resonated deep inside of me, kindling thoughts, stirring my soul. I felt more than I heard.

After the hienama's speech, a chosen har from the tribe would go and stand on the dais and a new har would be called forward. The chosen har would speak to the new har for a time. We were too far away to hear what was said but the words always seemed to make the new har beam; part of me envied them. The new har was given his "harish" name by his chosen har, and then those gathered around would repeat the name solemnly; sealing it to the individual. Then the two would walk to the side of the dais and wait, sometimes holding hands, sometimes linking arms. It was very moving.

By the time all six new hara had been welcomed, the sky in the east had lightened considerably, and the gathering began to murmur restlessly, sensing that the ceremony was all but over. Breakfast smells were beginning to drift out.

The hienama raised his arms again and silence fell once more. He turned his head towards me and beckoned me. "Nolan."

I froze. Acorn had to give me a gentle shove to get me moving towards the dais. When I got there the hienama looked down at me solemnly.

"Nolan, your inception was marred by violence and brutality. It should not have been so, but becoming Wraeththu is not only a physical transformation. We are reborn by new thinking, new choices, and new beginnings. The past must be the past. Choose the future, begin again. It is time to rise like the phoenix, reborn."

He acknowledged me with a slight bow, stepped back and motioned Inari forward.

Inari smiled gently. I imagine I looked as nervous now as some of the new hara had earlier.

"I had spent quite a few months trying to rescue hara from the violence and chaos in the city," Inari said, "but we only found those who embraced violence and revelled in their ignorance. They lived like the humans. I admit to being pretty discouraged, but finding you restored my faith, gave me hope again to trust that there are still those out there who believe in our future. I have a dream, Nolan... Finding you in the city rekindled my hope, that I," he smiled, "or rather, *we* can achieve that dream."

He pointed to the eastern horizon where the sky was now a rapidly expanding band of pale blue light.

"You are my dawn of hope," he said solemnly. "Hope for my dream, hope for the future. Out of the ancient language of my ancestors I give you your new name, Amal Sahar, literally 'hope dawns'."

Behind me, there was a murmur of many voices repeating the name. I felt tears well up. It was an emotional moment. I truly felt different, like I was no longer Nolan-the-outsider- from-the-city. I was now one of them: I belonged.

Breakfast was delicious. Zekki had me in fits of giggles, inventing new nicknames and rhymes for me based on my new name. I was hugged and congratulated; my smile muscles hurt from grinning so much.

Now as Inari ushered me into our sleeping quarters I started to feel slightly nervous and bashful.

'Trust him.' Hiko's words echoed in my head.

Inari pulled me gently into his arms and pressed his lips against my temple.

"Look Amal, we don't have to share aruna if you'd rather not – you're not a new har. But I just thought that ..."

I didn't let him finish; I pressed my lips against his. He looked surprised – pleasantly so.

"I trust you," I said. "I want this to be the first time."

The rest of the morning, and much of that afternoon passed, without

Inari or I even noticing. We explored each other's bodies. We shared aruna. He taught me how to let go and truly surrender. He also coached me through my first attempt as ouana. We lay together and dozed, revelling in the closeness and intimacy, and then we did it all over again.

It was sometime in the mid-afternoon that I woke up alone on the bed. I looked around the tiny cubicle and observed Inari standing at the window staring out, one arm leaning on the sill and the other braced on the casing. I sat up.

"We're going to do it," he said in a dreamy voice.

"We've been doing it since we came up here," I chuckled.

Inari laughed. "I mean you and I are going to build a library. A Wraeththu library. The First Ones are already building a city. It's going to be a real city! A great Wraeththu city! They're organizing and mobilizing. They're putting together experts and a government. I've already mentioned that a capital city needs a library and the First Ones agreed. We will go and build the most beautiful library ever. It'll rival the Library of Alexandria – we'll archive everything! We'll have stone tablets, old children's books, government archives, technology books, poetry, reference books and … and … romance novels." He laughed. "And we'll document all of Wraeththu too, our poets and story-tellers, our philosophers and scientists, our thinkers and our dreamers – because we will have them!" He turned towards me. "Close your eyes! Can you see it?" he entreated.

I closed my eyes and conjured up the only library I knew. In my mind the grey forbidding building became massive, the barbed wire and the security fences disappeared and the once empty planters were filled with flowers. I could also see the old fountain.

"Yeah, I can see it," I said. "Can our library have a fountain out front?"

Inari laughed. "Absolutely! We'll put a beautiful fountain outside our library. Believe it!"

I closed my eyes again and in my mind's eye the fountain, which had fascinated me for as long as I can remember, came to life as clear sparkling water bubbled from it.

I sighed contentedly as I pulled my consciousness back into the room. The years had changed so much, and yet… not.

Inari still stood by the window staring out of it, one arm leaning on the sill and the other braced on the casing, but he was not naked now. Pity. Nor were we in a cubicle in a repurposed human warehouse.

The fine leather of a divan creaked beneath me as I rose and crossed to where Inari stood at the window. I slipped my arms around his waist and rested my chin on top of his shoulder.

From here at the window of my well-appointed office in the administrative wing of Immanion's great Central Library I had an impressive view of the city. The main library building looked nothing like I'd imagined it way back then. It was white and gleaming: it rose, tall and airy, from its surroundings, full of inviting spaces and light. Behind the library rose the rooftops of the Hegemony administrative buildings where the day-to-day running of most of Wraeththudom occurred.

Beyond those governmental edifices rose the crowning jewel of Immanion, of all of Wraeththudom in fact – Phaonica, home to not one, but two Tigrons and their beautiful Tigrina. From here I could also see the rooftops of the rest of Immanion spread out below; some with terra cotta tiled roofs and some whose flat roofs had been converted into shady garden oases.

"Did you ever think this was possible?" Inari asked softly.

"Yes."

"You did?" He sounded sceptical.

"Of course. You told me it was."

"And you believed me? I didn't believe me!"

"I trusted you, and look… the library! Exactly as you promised – I even got my fountain."

We stood together in comfortable silence. The view from my window was both inspiring and comforting; Immanion was an impressive achievement. We Wraeththu were no longer angry youths, fighting for survival and thinking that we held all the answers. We had ascended the throne of power and were aware of how little we actually knew; an age of wisdom had dawned. We had weathered political storms, war, and uncertainty and had come through more tempered and more mature. We had emerged from the season of darkness into one of light.

Inari sighed contentedly. "Life has been good to us, hasn't it? We're both blessed."

"It has and we are." I agreed.

"I would feel even more blessed if you were to take my place as the moderator for a tedious afternoon of Maudrah poetry readings." Inari looked at me imploringly. "Refreshments will be served" he added hopefully.

"No dice," I said flatly. "That sounds dreadful."

"No doubt it will be," he agreed readily. "I will heap the blessings of all dehara from every corner of the universe at your feet if you'd go in my place."

"Are you offering to go plead the case for this year's budget to the Hegemony committee in my place?" I inquired dryly.

"Ouch!" Inari winced. "Is that today? I'd forgotten. You win! Your meeting outdoes mine on the 'ghastly way to spend an afternoon' scale."

He sighed stoically. "I suppose Maudrah poetry does have a certain charm. It must. Somewhere. Oh well. Although I shall suffer, I shall endure!"

"No doubt." I grunted.

"And I have no doubt that you will positively shine in today's budget session!" Inari said as he grinned and patted me on the back bracingly. "And afterwards, as compensation for all your suffering, I will buy you dinner at The Vivid Lily. Their seafood paella is beyond phenomenal!"

"Sounds like an excellent plan" I said crossing to the door and holding it open for him.

"... and then" Inari continued with a wicked grin "if you're really lucky I might let you take me home with you "

I laughed. "Seafood paella and you? I am definitely living in the best of times."

The Burned Boy

Gwyn Harper

The Burned Boy

When I first encountered the mutant, I thought only of revenge. They who called themselves Wraeththu had ruined my life and made me what I was – a freak, good only as a source of amusement for the crowds of fools who wanted to feel better about their own insect lives. Then, none of us realized that we were on the eve of something new and terrible, something that would change the world irrevocably. The mutant was the harbinger of that storm. Until I met him, I had no clue that our most fervent desires and deepest fears, our belief in the inherent goodness of the self, and the evil in others, can all be turned around in a moment of blinding self-enlightenment. Here, then, is my story.

It was summer. The circus had just arrived in Wry, a nothing town of small souls plopped down on a flat, dusty plain with mountains rising stark and blue in the distance. We were madly setting up. Jake, the assistant manager, handed me a bucket of water and a rag and sent me to clean the grime off chairs in the newly-erected tent that served as the boss's headquarters. I went in and started working when I overheard our owner, ringmaster, and scary-ass boss, Dr. Quintillus Sligo, say something that cut right to the place where I dwell in darkness.

"This mutant freak is gonna save the circus," Dr. Sligo said. I looked up and saw him waving dramatically at the big-screen monitor mounted on the scaffold behind him. He took a puff on his hookah. "I'm telling you, Tom, people will pay big time to see this monster."

"Even if true, we're taking a big risk with this one," said Tom Houston, the business manager, mopping a glistening brow with a tissue. A large man, he sat in his chair like a sack of flour. "I mean freaks is freaks, but they's still people. This one isn't, you know, human. It creeps me out to even be in the same room with 'im. It's like, I don't know, like I can feel his charm buzzing around in my gut."

"It's called sex appeal. What? Are you afraid you'll succumb to his allure? Be tempted? Even though you know it'll fry your innards?" Sligo leered at Tom.

"Fuck you!" Tom spat in the cedar shavings at Sligo's feet.

It was hot under the canvas. The roustabouts hadn't set up the air conditioning units yet. I pushed my long dark hair away from my sweating face, or at least the half that could sweat, and peered through the smoky haze created by Dr. Sligo's hookah. I had an eerie feeling. Another premonition perhaps. I'm prone to those and have learned to pay attention, because often they signal something about to happen. I had one shortly before my foster parents kicked me out of the house; another when, after travelling for days in the back of a truck, I saw the striped tents of the circus in the distance.

Dr. Sligo and Tom were playing our latest commercial meant for the local channels and I watched it over their heads. It was a lurid animé image of a nearly-naked creature with a mass of spiky, white hair that writhed like snakes. One half of its body was that of an overly-muscled man and the other half appeared as a curvaceous woman with one large breast filling half of a bikini top. It wore an obscenely tight pair of spandex briefs, bulging with unknown horrors. Standing, it shook its chains and roared, the sound like that of a klaxon. The announcer intoned:

You've heard the rumours – that mutants walk among us, coming at night, raping our young men, converting them into beasts like themselves. Many have scoffed. Now see the hideous truth for yourself: the Herm, a bizarre, mutant creature, half-man, half-woman. One week only in Wry, Fayettesburg, Lynly, and Red Rock.

Words scrolled up in a dripping Halloween-style font:

Dr. Sligo's Phenomenal Phantasmagoria of Terrors and Delights

Shows at 8, 10, and midnight. Go to Sligocircus.com

My mouth dropped. Could it really be one of them? Right here? How had Sligo captured it? I could not remember what the mutants looked like and had imagined ugliness, but the artist had drawn a beautiful, androgynous face with huge dark eyes framed by perfectly arched brows, a stunning contrast to that mass of blond hair. Did the creature really look like that? Hard to think of that as the face of pure evil. My gut seized with the force of my desires, intrigued and enraged at the same time. I couldn't stop staring.

"You see that kid back there?" Sligo was saying. "That's our audience. Look at him, just drooling over this freak. Remind me to send our promo department a bottle of wine. The artist did a good rendering. You, boy, come here."

"Me?"

"No, your twin over there. Yeah you."

Reflexively, I pulled my hair over half my face and approached cautiously, as I always did when walking into a new situation. The way my face looks makes any encounter a source of emotional pain. Sligo took a drag from the hookah and blew a smoke ring that expanded before hitting me. *Pwaft.* I coughed and Sligo laughed. Slim and elegant, he was dressed in an old-fashioned tuxedo. His jet black hair was curled, and his face painted white, with eye shadow and rouge that exaggerated his elegant bone structure. He reminded me of a vampire in the old movies. Appropriate too, as Dr. Sligo was a bloodthirsty bastard.

"What do you think, kid?" Sligo asked. "Would you pay money to see this thing?"

"Yes sir," I said. It was no lie.

"Tell me why. Don't you know these beasts could kill you in a most deliciously hideous way?"

"Um, yeah, I do. But that's what makes it so twitchy, ya know." I pulled my hair closer about my face.

Dr. Sligo was looking at me, curiously. "I don't remember you. Who do you work with?"

He didn't remember me? The bastard. "With Stubs Wheaton in the side show. Sir, you hired me four months ago in Greeley. I'm Janus, the Burned Boy."

"Oh right." Sligo paused to indulge in a coughing fit, then continued in a wheezing voice. "I remember. We billed you as Janus, god of two faces. It's a completely brilliant idea. I haven't caught your act yet. Let's see your other side. Move your hair."

Dramatically I admit, I swept my hair away from the left side of my face. People's first response, well, it always gives me a certain grim satisfaction, while at the same time increasing my self-loathing. I am Grendel. I am Medusa. No one could take that away. Tom winced, the usual reaction. But Sligo, he kept his face straight. No emotion. "Nasty," he said. "I remember hiring you now. It was a wretched day. A windstorm blew down one of the tents and a lion escaped. How'd that happen to you?"

"When I was ten, some mutants came up from the gutters, attacked my family. They killed my parents, stole my older brother, and then threw me on some hot coals. Or that's what my foster parents told me, anyway. I don't remember it. Must have blocked it out." I let the hair fall back, covering my shame.

"You must come from a fair piece away," Tom said. "These folks hereabouts haven't actually seen any mutants. They's just rumours to 'em."

"Yeah, I come from Mid-land, Carmine City. I despise the mutants. I'd pay to see this one just so I could spit at it."

"Hear that, Tom? I rest my case," Sligo said. "There are plenty of rumours circulating about these creatures, but very little fact because so few people have seen them up close and lived to tell about it. When I bought him, I thought that would be the draw, like putting a ghost in a cage. Here he is folks, a supernatural legend, as elusive as the Yeti or the Loch Ness monster, real and in the flesh. But then I saw him yesterday and realized I had it all wrong. The mutant's got something special, a kind of glamour. He can turn that morbid curiosity, that shiver of fear, into another emotion entirely – lust. We'll make bank. We could charge extra for the lube to take home." He grinned as if he could count the money already.

"And I'm tellin' *you*, Quin, something ain't right with this monster you've bought. It stirs up emotions I don't want stirred up. Whether it's fear or lust, I think it's dangerous. Plus, I'm not happy dealing in human trafficking, which is, of course, illegal. He's going to need guards twenty-four, seven."

"You're such a paranoid, Tom. He isn't exactly human so, to my reading of it, the trafficking laws don't apply. It's either this or you can send yourself a last paycheck because this business is going down the shitter, along with the rest of this sorry world. You and I both know it." Sligo puffed thoughtfully on the pipe and then eyed me through the haze. "What's your name, boy?"

"Jareth Nine."

"Well, now, Jareth Nine, you look like a healthy young man with some muscle. Care to make a little more scratch?"

"How much?"

"Two bucks more per hour for the duration of the tour."

Ah, now we were talking. "What d'ya want me to do?"

"In between your shows, I want you to watch the freak. That face of yours should scare anyone off. Make sure no one harms him and that he doesn't harm himself."

I could feel my teeth grinding. I've no self-control sometimes. Already thoughts of knives, guns, poison leaped to mind. "What if *I* harm him?" I growled.

Dr. Sligo flashed me a yellow-toothed grin. "Somehow, I don't think you will."

The circus grounds seethed in an anthill of activity. Roustabouts raised tents; the concession owners set up trailers on the midway; horses whinnied; elephants trumpeted; lions roared. Pungent, familiar smells enveloped me: sawdust, gasoline, horse shit, frying grease, buttered popcorn, and human sweat. This was the circus. It was home now. My other home was gone. My foster family was done with me, having told me to get out. Partly my fault I supposed. I walked through the commotion with the self-contained calm of someone isolated from the rest of my fellows and therefore having no need to concern myself with them. Why had I accepted the job from Sligo considering my feelings about mutants? Well, first off, there were the increased wages to consider. I was saving to get out of this hellhole, to take myself off to some desert island where I could be alone, without staring eyes or stupid questions. That was my goal. Then, there was curiosity. I wanted to see this mutant for myself, wanted to know if I had the balls even to be in the same room with it, because the very idea knotted my guts. I'd heard the rumours, that they raped people and shot some kind of weird stuff up in 'em that corroded out their insides. That was the stuff of nightmares, enough to give anyone the willies, even though I wasn't sure I believed it. There was something else. A call perhaps. I didn't know, then.

Dr. Sligo had refused to say exactly where and how he'd picked up the creature, but he had admitted that it had cost him a bundle, an investment, he said, and that the truck had arrived last night with the cage. They'd backed it up to the tent that would be the mutant's new home. Apparently, it had required an electric cattle prod to get it to move from the cage in the truck to the one in the tent. I approved of the cattle prod. So far the creature's whereabouts were top secret and that put me in possession of a valuable bit of scratch in the circus community. Gossip.

I decided to stop by the trailer I shared with Esmeralda, the bearded lady, and tell her. We had a good arrangement, Ez and I. We were both single, needed a place to crash, and the rent on the trailer, being that it was a piece of shit, was cheap. Anyhow, neither of us needed much space. No one wanted me for the night, and so my preferences made no difference, and she often spent her nights catering to weird kinks in whatever town we were in. She was quite a sight, as big as she was, tooling off in the evenings on her huge black motorcycle, her rear sagging off either side of the seat.

It happened today that I found her in her room, seated in front of the mirror, boobs erupting from a push-up bra, carefully gluing on her beard.

"Oh there you are, Jareth honey," she said, her voice as deeply resonant as a man's. "Show tonight, you know. They sent over a new costume." She waved a meaty arm at an open box on her bed from which spilled something lacy and shiny green. "It's even worse than the last one. I'm gonna have to wear a corset to get into it. Could you be a luv, and get some whisky for me – with ice." She batted her lovely brown eyes at me.

I obliged.

"This stuff is expensive you know, Ez," I called down the hall as I pulled the bottle from the cupboard, opened the freezer and got some ice, which I tossed in a glass. I listened to the glug of the liquid as I poured. "Maybe you should lay off."

"Maybe you should lay off the pipe," Esmeralda hollered back.

"My smoking's medicinal," I retorted. Yeah, that's what all the dopers say. I padded down the hall with its ripped shag carpet, orange and red, even more hideous than my face, and walked into her room. "Helps with the pain."

"So does this." She took the glass, raised it, cubes clicking.

"I have some news." I straddled a chair backwards and rested my chin on my forearms. Oh, this was going to be good.

"What's that?" She was frowning at the mirror.

"There's a new freak. They just brought it in last night."

"It? What's an 'it,' honey? Is it some old department store mannequin?"

"Oh, it's real all right. I heard Sligo and Tom arguing about it. Tom says it gives him the creepy-weirdies."

She paused in her gluing attempts, the beard half hanging off her round black face. "Okay, Jareth, quit fooling. Spill. What is it?"

"A mutant."

"Huh? A what? One of those things that lives in the big-city ghettoes? Honey, I thought they was just stories to scare people with. Something to sell the tabloids."

"Not stories, Ez. Remember, the mutants are the ones that burned me. Or didn't you believe what I told you?"

Her eyes flinched away. She took a gulp of the whisky. "To tell you honest, honey, what I thought about that story you told was that your foster parents made up somethin'."

"Why would they do that?"

"A hundred reasons, young'un. All having to do with protectin' you from the truth. So, this thing is real? And Sligo has the nerve to bring it here? Uh huhn." She rolled her eyes.

"Yep and he gave me the job of guarding it, between shows. Got a raise to do it."

"Well now, that's pretty good. Won't it be dangerous though? From what I've heard, those mutants have some weird powers that can mess with your head. If the stories be true."

"It's in a cage, Ez."

"You sure they haven't jus' found some poor starvin' kid and put a costume on him, like they did last year with that girl that had the fake twin coming outta her side?" She chuckled.

"Maybe. Wanna find out? Let's go see it."

"Now?"

"Yeah."

She sighed, took another swallow, set down the empty glass, then pulled off the beard, wincing as it came free. "Ow! Damn thing. Guess we better check out the competition, huh honey? Gimme a minute or three to get dressed."

Yeah, who could resist a genuine freak? She was now as curious as I was.

We found the new tent set up in the sideshow row – Freak Alley we called it. For now, there were no glaring signs, nor was there a talker stirring up a crowd, all of which would surely be there later. The tent was a nondescript blue and white stripe, just like the others, but already a small crowd of the community had gathered outside, all buzzing like cicadas on a hot June day.

Pavel, one of the lion tamers, with his mop of curly blond hair, stood outside. He raised bare arms, exhibiting tufts of underarm hair like so much dandelion fluff and said, "All of you keep your fuckin' pants on. I know y'all wanna see it. Me too. But Dr. Sligo gave the orders and my ass is hamburger if they're not carried out. No one's to disturb it. Nobody. I think it's sick or something. Wait 'til the crowds get here tonight. If ya wanna see it, come back then."

"What and pay for the privilege? I don't think so," Renny the clown hooted. He was always a loud mouth. He was wearing pyjamas and had shaving cream on one side of his face, so he must've come at a run. "Ah come on, Pavel, just a peek."

Another clown named Sparks said, "Yeah, what'll it take? A bribe?" He held up a pipe, which immediately got my interest, but Pavel glowered at him.

Esmeralda spoke in my ear, "Shove up there, honey." She raised her voice. "Hey, coming through on Sligo's business." Esmeralda's girth made for a formidable plough and we managed to jostle ourselves through the twenty or so circus folks, who gave us sour looks.

"What do you want, kid?" Pavel said, bending down to look at me, then snapping his gaze away. Like usual.

I looked him in the eye. "Dr. Sligo said I'm supposed to watch the mutant between shows. He's paying me to do it. Didn't he tell ya?"

"Yeah, but if I let you in now, there'll be a riot. This ain't the time."

"But..."

"Later, like I said." Pavel stood up straight and folded his massive arms, looking like some genie from old vids that I remembered as a kid. "That goes for all of you," he roared.

Grumbling, the crowd dispersed. Esmeralda shrugged. "You heard him, sweetie. I'm sure in a few months we'll all be sick of looking at this thing, whatever it is." She went off with them.

Being stubborn, I wasn't going to let it go so easy. There was more than one way to turn a trick and I'd learned to be a master at not getting noticed. I headed down the line of tents until I was enough distance away from Pavel's beady eyes, then I slunk through a gap between tents and came around the back along the dry dirt tracks where the trucks drove. I found the rear of the mutant's tent and partially unzipped the service entrance. For a moment I rested my forehead against the rough fabric and thought I could feel something, like a humming in my ears, or white radio noise. I pushed the flap aside and entered.

It was hot in there, stifling, and stunk like canvas. I came up behind the platform they'd erected, one of those portable stages. On it sat a cage, about six by six feet. Black curtains hung from the ceiling ribs on either side. It looked like it was meant for an animal. That gave me a strange feeling. What was this thing? There were rows and rows of chairs set up on risers in a semi-circle around it. Clearly, they expected a big crowd. But if there were chairs, that meant an act of some kind. My show had a different set-up. I was stashed away in one of a series of booths, each with its own freak. People filed by in the semi-dark. No one stayed long enough to sit down. Some gawked for a few moments, but most took a look, shuddered, and went on. What was so damn fascinating about this thing that it could attract a sit-down audience? The humming sensation in my head increased.

Cautiously, I walked up the stairs onto the stage, peered through the bars, and found myself looking down into the eyes of a being of startling and ethereal beauty.

Yelping in surprise, I stumbled backwards, and sat down hard on the stage. Slowly, I summoned the nerve to look again. He hadn't moved. I stared at him and he stared back with brilliant, heavy-lidded eyes as deeply blue as the sky at twilight. He was sitting cross-legged on the floor of the cage with his hands resting on his knees, wearing nothing but a pair of black leather jeans. I thought he looked a little older than me, maybe in his early twenties. The artist had some details right: a heart-shaped face with a sharp chin and high cheekbones. His hair, cut short and spiky around his face, shone platinum blond, almost white. The back was plaited into five braids that hung down to the middle of his back. His body was slim and athletic: strong arms, belly muscled like a washboard, and broad, bony shoulders. Small brown nipples decorated his chest, no hint of breasts there. Torque tattoos like flames encircled his biceps. The one physical flaw that I could see was a long white scar nestled in the crook of his right arm.

To my eye anyway, there was no difference between this creature and some stunning, androgynous boy model from one of the fashion zines, the kind that I couldn't get enough of, the kind that I stared at for hours while locked in my room with my hand firmly in my pants. He didn't look exactly human though. Not completely, because he seemed to glow. I know that sounds strange, but it's true. Luminous, that's the word. It was how I imagined an angel would look. Not an angel like we think of in white robes, strumming a harp. No, he looked like a biker-gang angel. Fey and dangerous. I could only sit there stupidly, and stare.

And then he spoke.

"So, you've come," he said.

It was like he'd been expecting me. Like he'd been sitting there waiting all his life until I came along. I can't tell you how that threw me.

"Huh," I said even more stupidly.

He merely blinked, one slow blink. His eyes hadn't done the little flinch and dart away like most of the others did. It was as if he was looking past my face into some hidden part of my soul. That messed me up worse than any flinch had ever done. I dropped my head, shaking my hair over my face. "What are you?" I asked.

"I am Wraeththu."

That was the first time I heard that name but it gave me the shivers as if I'd heard that word before. Strange and not strange. His voice was extraordinary: soft, modulated, like singing, rather than speaking; the timbre neither male nor female, but some kind of fluted mix of both as if manipulated by a synthesizer. It was a bedroom kind of voice that people would pay to hear, hypnotizing and erotic.

"That's your name?" I asked.

"No, my race. You are human scum; I am Wraeththu, the chosen ones."

Now that pissed me off. "Hey, butt-hole, not an attitude you should cop, sitting there in a cage with a bunch of human *scum* all around, who'd just as soon use you for target practice as look at you."

He raised his chin. "They won't use me for target practice."

"Confident of that, huh?"

"No, just practical. If they'd wanted to kill me, they'd have done it already. I'm to be a spectacle. A freak. They'll come to gawk."

"What's to gawk at? You look just like us, no different from any kid down the block. Just uglier." Not true in any stretch of the imagination, but my mean streak was asserting itself. He merely smiled in a superior manner that made me want to punch out his pretty face. Sliding his hand down his belly, he stopped at his crotch, patted it. "You think we're the same, do you?"

I shivered with some kind of primal intuition, while at the same time I was wondering what the hell he was talking about. Half-man, half-woman, the ad had said. So I asked him, "What do you mean?"

He laughed, then stood in a fluid motion, body long and lean, walked over to the cage bars, and pressed his face against them. My heart was in my throat. He said, "Wouldn't you like to find out?"

"I don't want to find out anything," I said, standing to face him. "I came to spit at you."

"You came to see the freak, a real freak, not just some accident of nature. You pitiful beings don't even know that when you look at me you're looking at your death. But on some level you *do* know it.

That's why you're afraid, why you want to stare. Your kind isn't long for this world now. Change is coming."

Now I could feel anger surging through me. "They'll break you!" I hissed. "They'll spit on you and starve you and beat you until you wish you were dead. And I'll be there to laugh."

"Why all this hatred?"

"Because of this!" Roughly, I pulled my hair back and turned my face to the side so he could get the full effect. "Your kind did that. You destroyed my family and threw me into a fire. Left me to die."

He leaned forward to look, seemingly puzzled, rather than repulsed. "Impossible. We haven't moved this far out – yet."

"I'm from Carmine City," I said.

That caused him to start and look at me, even more intently. "It can't be," he said. "Although, you do look like him. My head hurts. You should come back later." Slowly he dropped back down to his cross-legged position, pressing fingers to his temples. His eyes fluttered shut and began jerking around under the lids as if he was dreaming. I could feel the humming inside my skin again. The tingling ache that I often felt in the burned side of my face increased. I waited, anger rising, but he appeared to have gone into a trance. Banging on the bars, I shouted, "Wraeththu, Wraeththu scum!" No response. I picked up a pipe lying on the stage and lobbed it at the bars. It bounced off with a heavy metallic clang.

Pavel stuck his head in the door flap on the other side of the tent and yelled, "What the hell are you doing in here? I told you to stay out!"

Next thing I knew, he'd given me the bum's rush out the door and I was laid out flat on my belly, spitting straw. Renny and Sparks, now in full make-up, pointed at me, miming laughter. I felt ashamed, and skulked back to the trailer to shroud my anger in smoke and poisonous dreams. For the next six hours, I hid in my room, indulging my demons.

My act was always the same. The talker, Stubs Wheaton, stood outside the tent and called to the crowds in his whiskey-smooth voice: "Ladies and gents, come in and see the strange and rare oddities of the human condition. Yes, here they are, and you can thank your lucky stars, they ain't you. Come in and see Esmeralda, the bearded woman, hairy as a werewolf. Flat Stanley, the thinnest man alive. Delilah, the contortionist. She can put her legs behind her head and kiss her own ass. Sorry folks, this ain't a family show. And

Janus, the boy with two faces. Beautiful as a god on one side, hideous as a devil on the other..." And so it went.

Getting high as a kite before the show made it almost bearable. I'd go to the dressing room in the back of the tent, pin up my hair on the burned side of my face, leaving it long and flowing over my shoulders on my good side, strip down to a spangled loincloth, then hide in my cubicle in the dark. When the spotlight came on, I'd step into it, presenting my right side. Then the light would go off and I'd turn to my left side that was burned from my hip all the way up my arm and part of my back to my face, which had gotten the worst of it. The light would come back on and I'd hear gasps and sometimes screams as people filed by. Usually there was a stony silence. In case anyone thinks this was a humiliating way to make a living, I might remind them that I didn't have much choice. And once I got over the shame, I guess it was easy money. Well, I'm lying. I didn't get over the shame. It festered into a rage that by the time I was done for the night, I had to go smoke myself silly to keep from hitting someone.

But tonight, things were different. People came by but they weren't paying attention to me. I could hear them talking. "Did you hear? They've got one of those mutant things. Yeah, right here in the circus. I couldn't get a ticket until ten o'clock." And so on. This didn't help my mood at all. I figured they were going to be severely disappointed when they went into that tent and saw, not a frightening hermaphroditic monster, but some boy in tight leather pants sitting in a cage. But by the end of the show my curiosity was getting the best of me and so I drew on the white mask I wore when I had to go out among rubes, put on some clothes, and pelted over to the tent.

Standing outside listening to people leaving, I could tell it hadn't gone well. The buzz sounded angry, puzzled.

"Just some loud-mouthed punk taunting us. I'm getting my money back."

"I don't know. I think there's something to that mutant stuff. Didn't you feel it? He gave me the shivers, like he was speaking in my head."

"...some kid, talking a lot about how he was going to take over the world. Didn't look like a mutant to me. This is a big hoax."

Two young women emerged giggling. One said, "Oh Stephanie, wasn't he gorgeous! I mean he could have been a movie star. It was worth the money just to ogle him. If that's what mutants look like, sign me up."

And so on, just as I'd figured. I wasn't so sure myself that he wasn't some pretty boy that Sligo had stuck in a cage, except that he engendered strange feelings, which apparently others could detect as well. I remembered the discussion between Tom and Sligo and the note of fear in Tom's voice.

I waited in the shadows until they'd all left, then crept into the tent, which was dark, except for a spotlight shining on the cage. I took off the mask in order to see better. The mutant was hunched in one corner facing Dr. Sligo, who stood outside the cage in his full Ringmaster's gear, complete with top hat. He was holding an electric cattle prod, the kind they used to control the big cats. The mutant stared at him with narrowed eyes. Dr. Sligo glared back and said, "A pitiful performance. Half the crowd wants their money back. No dinner until I see something better out of you. There's a costume! Put it on." He threw some sparkly red garments through the bars.

"I can go for days without eating," the mutant said.

Sligo stabbed the long wand of the cattle prod through the bars, hitting the mutant in the groin with its pincher-like tip. With a sharp cry, the mutant dropped to the floor hugging himself.

"Don't fuck with me," Sligo hissed, giving him another shot to the back of the neck before withdrawing the wand. The mutant convulsed and then dry retched on the floor, which caused me to wince even though I thought I was all for torturing him. I must be going soft.

"What do you want?" the mutant gasped.

"They want to see a half-human monster, so you better become one. Take off those pants and show them what you've got."

The mutant grimaced at him. "Come in here and try getting them off me. I'll rip you apart."

Sligo chuckled. "How stupid do you think I am? I'll just throw water on you and then hit you with this thing until you pass out."

"And risk injuring your investment?" the mutant sneered.

"You're worth nothing to me unless I can sell tickets. And I can't sell tickets to a performance of a mouthy kid sitting in a cage."

"You want a sex show, Sligo? I didn't know you were such a complete pervert," the mutant said. "You know there isn't much to see, unless I'm aroused, and I'd need another har to achieve that."

What the hell was he saying? My curiosity had become overwhelming.

"Use your hand, you freak," Sligo said. "It's no matter to me how you display yourself."

"I refuse to debase myself for you, human scum! You can kiss my hot little harish ass." The mutant lunged forward, reaching through the bars towards Sligo's throat.

Sligo thrust the prod at him. The mutant grabbed the end of it and then screamed. It was like something out of a Frankenstein movie. The air around him crackled with blue lightning and his white hair seemed to stand up with static, writhing almost as if alive. I smelled roasting flesh, and suddenly, I couldn't stand it. I stepped forward into the lights and yelled, "Stop! Stop it now!"

Sligo jerked the prod away and then threw it to the ground as if it had burned him too. The mutant boy staggered back, sank down to the floor, and stared at his reddened hands. Sligo was shaking and pale even under his white make-up. "Crazy sonovabitch," he muttered. Slowly, he bent, put a hand on the stage, sat for a moment as if collecting himself, then hopped down. He found a discarded cup full of ice and slid it across the stage so that it smacked up against the bars. "Put some of this on those hands," he said. The Wraeththu grabbed the cup, spilled some ice into his hand, and immediately popped it into his mouth. He crouched back onto his heels, and began slowly rocking, mumbling something.

Sligo glared at me. "What the fuck are you doing here?"

"My job, Dr. Sligo. You told me to watch him between shows."

"So I did. Earn your pay now. Run and get some burn ointment and bandages. Hurry up. We've got another show in an hour."

The Wraeththu looked up. "Bring some water too. Please. My tongue feels like a balloon."

On my way out, I noticed that there was already a crowd lined up outside the tent. Stubs the talker was really promoting the shit out of this mutant thing. I honestly didn't know what was going to happen. I went to the supply tent and got the first-aid, then stopped by concessions and picked up some water bottles, a cup of ice, and a hot dog, because I didn't know if he would be hungry. I slipped back in through the exit door.

Dr. Sligo and the mutant seemed to have reached some sort of truce. Sligo had left, taking the prod with him, and the Wraeththu had shed his leather pants and put on the costume Sligo had tossed at him, a sparkly red halter top that looked like it belonged to Sheena, one of the equestriennes who was very flat-chested, and a long sheer red scarf tied over the hips. Underneath the scarf, the mutant wore tight spandex briefs that revealed a masculine bulge between his legs. That at least seemed normal. Or was it? The shape didn't quite look right. But oh, what lovely, long legs he had! The costume definitely made him look more feminine and made me somewhat queasy. What was he? Or she? He was sitting cross-legged in the cage, leaning his elbows on his knees.

"Here." I crouched down and handed him the water and food.

Stone-faced, he unscrewed the top of the water bottle and chugged it down. Then he stuffed the hot dog in his mouth. It was gone in three bites.

"You must have been hungry," I said.

"Yeah."

"I'll get you some more, later."

"I'd be grateful," he said. "I haven't eaten in three days."

I couldn't help it; I was beginning to feel sorry for the bastard. "What the hell is going on? Sligo wouldn't even treat a dog this way."

"I'm worse than a dog," he replied, wiping his mouth. "I'm the next stage in human evolution and it scares the shit out of the likes of you, doesn't it?" The lights above his cage reflected in his eyes like melted stars.

"If you keep talking like that, this crowd is going to lynch you and I wouldn't stop 'em," I replied.

"Then why did you speak up for me, earlier?"

"I couldn't stand to see any creature get burned like that. Empathy, I s'pose. Even *you* could probably imagine why. Here hold out your hands."

Obligingly, he stuck his hands through the bars. They were fine hands, long, slender fingers. The palms looked red with some bubbled blisters and two little blackened spots on his right hand. It could have been worse. I cupped the back of his hand in my palm preparing to put some ointment on it and got a sudden tingle all through my body as if my flesh was singing. I jerked away from him. "What the fuck are you doing to me?"

He looked at me in surprise, then his expression grew thoughtful. "I wonder."

"What the hell are you?"

"I'm a mutant freak, just like you said."

"No, you're something else. You're like, I don't know, a witch."

His lips twisted. "You have no idea."

"What did you do to make that blue lightning stuff?"

"Channelled some power." He laughed.

I could tell I wasn't going to get any real answers out of him. "Okay, Witch, give me your hand again." I smeared the ointment on his palms, carefully wrapped gauze and tape around them, and covered up the bandages with red silk scarves.

"Thanks, human scum," he said, but the tone was warm, teasing. Then he smiled at me, a shiny bright smile. And, oh wow, my insides lit up like a firecracker. I swear, no one had ever smiled at me like that before. It was as if the sun had suddenly broken through a hole in the roof. If I'd thought him attractive before, it was nothing like the breath-taken feeling I had now. I started to smile back, then remembered that smiling didn't improve my appearance. Glamour, that was what Dr. Sligo had called it, that special quality that Wraeththu have. I thought I understood it then. I didn't understand anything.

I turned away, feeling anxious again. "So, I see you're nearly naked now, but probably not enough for Sligo. What are you going to do for your act?"

"You'll see."

"No, I won't. I've got my own act to do. I'm a spectacle, just like you."

"So, why do you hate me and not them? Aren't we of a kind, in the same boat, so to speak?"

I flinched. "We are nothing alike. I despise your kind."

"Perhaps in time you'll change your mind." He seemed to be mocking me. It made me angry again.

"I doubt it. I've hated the Wraeththu all my life, before I even knew what to call you. That hate is like breathing to me."

He nodded. "It can be like that for us too. Where I'm from, the humans curse us, hunt us down. There's going to be war soon. What's your name?"

"My name?"

"Not such a hard question, is it?" He laughed softly.

"Jareth Nine," I said. "My stage name is Janus."

"Ah, of course. Janus, the Roman god of gates, doorways, and beginnings. He who has two faces and can simultaneously see both the past and the future. How appropriate. Can you predict the future, Jareth Nine?"

He was looking at me intently again, as if he could see past my disfigurement. I had one of those moments that hit the pit of my stomach, like falling through the air. I saw myself standing at a door, looking out into a forest of towering ponderosa pines, knowing that something terrible had happened. God of doorways and beginnings.

"Sometimes it seems so," I said cautiously. "I mean sometimes I get premonitions, usually just feelings, and then something significant happens."

He picked a piece of glitter off his thigh. I noticed that he didn't seem to have hair on any part of his body except that luxuriant growth on his head. Certainly, there was no shadow of a beard on his face. He nodded. "Yes, it makes sense. You're special, Jareth. I knew from the moment I laid eyes on you."

"No, I'm not. I'm just a freak." Yes, a freak, destined to be reviled by everyone and to live out my days in loneliness.

"No, I don't think so." He rocked forward. Slowly as if reaching for a skittish horse, he put his hand through the bars and touched the burned side of my face, brushing it with his fingertips in a gesture as delicate as the twitch of a butterfly's wing. It ignited the tingling sensation, this time more profoundly than before. I jerked away from him, angry again.

"So much pain," he said. He sounded sad.

"I hate you!" I stood up to leave. "I've gotta go now."

"Jareth, would you come back and see my act? I would feel better knowing there was at least one friendly face in the crowd."

"Mine wouldn't be friendly."

"At least it would be familiar."

"I have my own act."

"Leave early." He paused. "Please, Jareth Nine."

"I'll see you later," I said. "I'll bring some dinner after your show. That's all I can promise." I started to walk away, then paused, looking back at him. "I told you my name, Mutant. What about yours? Do you have a name, or do I just call you Wraeththu Scum?"

He laughed as if I'd made a joke. "My name is Kithara. I am one of Thiede's elite. That means nothing to you yet, but it will. I feel change blowing through me as keenly as a northerly wind. Don't you?"

"No," I said. It was a lie. Like a bug, I scurried back to my dark booth.

As I stood in my booth, turning first one way, then the other, beauty, ugliness, light, dark, and listening to all the idiot gawkers, it seemed that Kithara's spell, for so it must have been, fell away from me. When I was near him, he had the power to make me forget what I was, and even imagine myself as normal. Once reality kicked back in, I was left with anger and bitterness and only wanted to go back to the trailer to drug myself into oblivion. I refused to leave early to see whatever new act Kithara had dreamed up in order to keep Dr. Sligo from frying him. Instead I did my job, returning to his tent when the show was done.

Wearing my mask, I stood by the exit door and listened to the people emerging. Something was different this time. "It's a man, I tell you," one woman was arguing.

Her male friend replied, "No, it's a woman. I'd never be that turned on by a man."

"Maybe you're just one of those latent homosexuals," the woman said with a laugh, which brought an angry splutter in reply.

"Whatever it is, it's weird," another man was saying.

"Downright sexy as hell," someone else said.

Others emerged silent, almost embarrassed to look at each other. But I noticed many of them went and stood in line to buy tickets for the midnight show. Oh Kithara, what are you doing?

Dr. Sligo showed up, beaming, and waved the last rubes out of the tent, since they were hanging around as if they didn't want to leave. "Well, that was much better," Sligo chortled. "Our boy in there has real potential." He rubbed his hands together. "We can make this into something spectacular in the future, but for tonight, we'll have to improvise. Jareth, get Ricky to come in here and work on the lighting and then you run to supplies and get some long chains. Get a pair of acrobats' leather wrist cuffs with a metal link to attach to the chains. Then, pick up ten pounds of dry ice in a cooler and ask Barry in concessions to boil about six gallons of water for us. Hurry up, we've only got an hour until the next show."

So, we were going to create some mood with fog and special lighting. Okay. But why did Sligo want chains? I rounded up the equipment, then came back lugging an ice chest full of dry ice. Some kid was balanced on a ladder fiddling with the lights in the framework at the top of the tent while Ricky worked a slider box adjusting the spots, changing colours, bringing them up and down. "How will I know the timing on all this?" he asked Dr. Sligo.

"You're going to have to improvise," Sligo said. "Just watch what he does and create some drama. Try turning up the music now, so I can hear what it sounds like."

Through all this Kithara was standing in the cage in his glittery red costume with one hip cocked, arms folded, shooting us all a look of scorn.

Sligo turned to him. "If you're a good boy tonight, you'll get a reward, an actual bed to sleep in. Maybe a shower."

"And if I'm not?" Kithara asked.

"Cattle prod. Up the ass this time," Sligo said. He leered.

"Do you know if I even have an asshole?" Kithara said. He raked his teeth across his bottom lip in a way that was just completely sexy.

"Shut up," Sligo said. "Jareth! Hey, quit staring and come up here." He beckoned. "I want you to put the cuffs on him." I climbed up on the stage, noticing that they'd locked the chains around some steel loops in the stage floor.

"What's this for?"

"Audience can't see him so well in there behind the bars. With this he can come out as far as the edge of the stage." He turned to Kithara. "Now then, boy, I'm standing here with the prod, so don't try anything."

"As if I could get far if I made a run for it," Kithara scoffed. He held out his wrists. "Go ahead, slap them on, Jareth. I'm finding this rather kinky."

Sligo unlocked the cage door and I went in with the cuffs, which I fastened around his wrists. Standing so close to him was actually causing me to feel feverish. "I'm sorry about this," I mumbled.

"It's not so bad, Jareth," Kithara said. "We do what we must to survive."

We worked like fiends to get set up. I was wondering the whole time what on earth Kithara was going to do. It looked like I was going to find out this time because Dr. Sligo told me to stay to create the fog, which meant I got out of my own little show. That suited me right down to the ground. I kept my mask on and hung out in the curtain at the side of the stage, ready with a bucket of boiling water, the chest of dry ice, and a blow dryer. It was twenty past midnight when we were finally ready. I could hear the crowd outside: buzzing, restless.

"Consider this a rehearsal," Sligo told us. "Bring down the lights, Ricky. Mood music on low. Let them in."

We had a full house. Dr. Sligo got up on the stage and made an impressive speech. He told about the rumours of strange mutant beings that had arisen in a city ghetto east of here and were now secretly spreading out across the country. I poured some of the hot water on the dry ice and blew the fog out across the stage as Sligo described a horrific scene of a boy lost in a back alley coming across a gang of mutants who attacked him, ripping off his clothes and raping him. He writhed in the way the boy might have done and described the smoking ruin of his body graphically enough to make me shudder. "Now, we have captured one of these creatures, a mutant hermaphroditic being. Soon you'll see the truth for yourselves. Here it is – a creature from your darkest, sexiest nightmares!"

The spot hit the cage. Music swelled, an exotic Eastern sound with softly pounding drums and clacking finger symbols. I conjured some more fog. Kithara moved in the cage, weaving back and forth for several beats. Then he pushed open the door, emerged onto the stage, and began to dance. When he moved, you had to watch, whether you wanted to or not. It was as if he had invented the word seductive. He had unbraided his hair, so that it flowed about his body like a rippling cloak. Arms swirling as if gathering air, he stalked towards us, red scarves trailing from his hands. Murmuring, the crowd recoiled. Kithara laughed, throwing his head back and whirling about. He bent backwards and walked over his hands. I had no idea he was that flexible. The chains dragged and clattered along behind him, but he incorporated them into the dance, pulling them around his body, beating them on the floor in syncopation with the drums and running them across his mouth.

He slowly pulled off his halter top and let it fall, so that he was bare-chested, the effect of that disrobing so much sexier than if he'd started out that way. He removed the sheer, glittery veil from around his hips and used it as a banner, swirling it about, holding it spread in front of himself and dancing behind it, then pulling it through his legs like the most wanton stripper. He came right to the edge of the stage, threw himself onto his belly, reaching out towards the audience, beckoning, playing to both men and women. It was almost as if he was calling out to us, touching our deepest desires. He invited a young couple up on stage with him, a guy wearing a baseball cap and a woman with long blonde hair, and danced around them, caressing them both with light teasing touches. He was mesmerizing. I was hard as a rock and had visions of grabbing him, bending him over, and ravishing him. Faces in the audience looked fascinated, shocked, desirous. All eyes were riveted on him and I realized we had a star on our hands.

Dr. Sligo came up next to me, chuckling with glee. "He's a natural. He just needed a little prod, that's all."

"No pun intended," I said dryly and he laughed some more.

When it was over and we'd chased out all the people, Kithara collapsed into a heap on stage.

"Where did you learn to dance like that?" I asked, like some mooning fan boy.

"Some time I'll tell you," he said. "Right now, I'm starving and exhausted. Sligo better make good on his promise."

Dr. Sligo practically oozed delight. He said, "You'll find that I reward good behaviour and punish bad. You have pleased me, Mutant."

"His name is Kithara," I said.

Sligo laughed. "I see you're working your magic on our burned boy. Watch out, Jareth, or you'll end up fried inside as well as out."

I glared at Sligo, but his attention was on Kithara. Narrowing his eyes in menace, Sligo said, "Well, then *Kithara*, I'll have Pavel escort you to a trailer where you can get something to eat, shower, and sleep in an actual bed. The place will be guarded by large men with even larger guns. Just so you know."

"You're such a humanitarian," Kithara said.

That night I tried to sleep in my stifling trailer, lying naked on my bed, tossing and turning. Feverish. Every time I closed my eyes, I could see him, dancing on that stage like he owned the world. Maybe he did. I took care of myself numerous times, but couldn't be sated. He replaced all the dream boys I carried in my head; the only lovers I had ever known or would know. Finally, I couldn't stand it any longer and got up, intending to smoke myself into a stupor. Took out the pipe, tamped a little black chunk of choi in the bowl and hit it. Lay back for the rush. The sweet, pungent smell drifted around me, taking away the pain.

Outside I heard the purr of Esmeralda's motorcycle, back from her nocturnal prowling. It stopped. The door creaked open. I put on some shorts, wandered into the kitchen area where she was fixing herself a drink.

"Oh hi, Jareth honey," she said. "What are you doing up?"

"Can't sleep," I mumbled. The curtains were undulating in a light breeze. Looked like dancing fire, prismatic colours, spiralling out of control.

"Well, I gotta tell you, the whole town's abuzz about your mutant friend," she said. With a sigh, she dropped down on the sagging couch and put her feet up on a stool. "Leastwise, folks in the bar were talkin' about him."

I sat down in an armchair across from her. The early morning air felt good because I was sweating like a pig. "What are they saying?"

The words came out of my mouth, elongated, my lips moving slowly, as if I was under water.

"They're saying that he or she or whatever it is, is hot. Very, very hot. There were lots of arguments about whether it's a man or a woman or if it's really a mutant, like Sligo says."

I laughed. "Who knows. He's a freak, like us. Freakin' fuckin' freak."

She pursed her lips, leaning forward to look at me. "Are you all right, honey?"

"Fine, fine, I'm just fine," I said.

"Well, there were some of 'em talking smack about him. Said he made them feel dirty, that he was a homosexual abomination. One woman claimed he was a devil, said the Lord was going to punish anyone who went to see him."

"I don't know what he is," I said dreamily. "Devil or angel, I want to hate him, I really do. But Ez, you should see him dance."

Lying back, I felt the room tilt gently, whirling. Carousel music. Wooden horses with red, screaming mouths and flying manes, moving up and down. The paint on their long faces crackled and peeled back. I slipped into blessed oblivion.

Several days later, they began to picket us. A bunch of locals stood along the roadway outside the fairgrounds holding big signs and shouting that we were going to hell and that the circus housed abominations. Yep, that's me, an abomination. The local news scrambled out there with mikes and cameras. They interviewed Sligo, who appeared without his make-up, wearing regular clothes. In that disguise, he looked just like a decent human being, talking about how he was a businessman with a right to make a living. No laws being broken. No lewd acts. No minors admitted to the show and so on. He refused to let them interview Kithara but allowed them to film a portion of his dance. "Free publicity," he said to me with a pleased chuckle. The lines to see Kithara grew longer.

Meanwhile, I walked around in some kind of poppy-coloured haze. Sligo took me off other duties, had me work on Kithara's show. He said Kithara had requested me, which made my insides flutter like a drunken butterfly. We improved the lighting, staging, costumes, make-up, and props, and Kithara continued to knock 'em dead. His hands had healed remarkably fast with no trace of the burn. I stood behind the curtains and drank in his every move. I wanted to be like him. No, I wanted to *be* him, beautiful as a god on both sides of my body, an object of lust and worship, a shining Wraeththu angel able to rise above my sordid existence.

Sligo had given Kithara his own trailer, which just showed how tickled he was but he never allowed Kithara to go anywhere without an armed guard, both for his protection and to prevent him from escaping. Sligo carried that cattle prod around with him like a cane and occasionally popped Kithara with it, just to show him who was boss.

More people came to see his show. Both men and women danced along with him in their seats, watched him in fascination, writhed in frustrated lust.

The picketers outside the circus grew more numerous.

Six days into this madness, Esmeralda came home early. "I don't like the way it feels in town," she said. "There's some local preacher man who's got people all riled up. He's been holding rallies, telling everyone that we're harbouring a demon here. He said our mutant influenced his son to commit sodomy. All kinds of people have testified that they can't get images of our freak out of their heads and it's making them do lewd things." She laughed. "As if people need an excuse for that. I guess I've missed out. Haven't seen his show yet. Is he really that good?"

"He's something else," I said. "It's more than how he acts or what he does, although his dancing is incredible. It's something he projects. Glamour, that's what Sligo called it. Maybe he's a witch."

"Uh huh, well, if you ask me, Jareth honey, I think Sligo's playing with fire here. I ain't too religious, but I do believe in the Devil, and your boy over there, could be he *is* a demon of some kind. Have you thought of that? I mean, where did these mutants come from?"

That stopped me. It was a good question. Why would they appear like that, out of nowhere? Was Kithara just a freak of nature, or was there something more to it? How many other Wraeththu were there? Were we really in danger from his kind, as he said? Then again, maybe it was all just a big story. Maybe he wasn't really a hermaphrodite, just an effeminate boy who was fooling us all and having big laugh behind our backs. I realized that I'd been avoiding the hard questions because I wanted to stay glamorised. Anger reasserted itself and crawled around in my belly. I vowed, if he was playing us, playing *me*, that I'd break his pretty neck.

That night after his show, I went up to him with clenched fists, told him I wanted to talk. He nodded, invited me to eat dinner with him in his trailer. I was foolish enough to be pleased.

Kithara cooked an omelette for me. I was surprised he could cook. When I ventured to tell him that, he laughed. "We're not monsters, Jareth, eating raw flesh or dead things out of garbage cans. Besides, I was human once and my mom taught me to cook." He took a spatula and cut the omelette in two, sliding each half onto a paper plate. Then he poured more Merlot into two plastic cups. We'd already consumed a bottle and I was feeling pretty good. It didn't seem to have affected him much. He was wearing his black leather pants and nothing else; his eyes were smudged with black liner from the show, which made them look even larger, bluer, and more exotic than normal. He sat down in a rickety chair, pulled the plate towards him, and dumped an impressive amount of hot sauce onto it. Covertly, I watched him, watched the muscles in his arms bunch and shift under those flaming tattoos. I couldn't help it. I wanted to eat him up.

"I don't think you're a monster," I said.

"Don't you? When we first met, you wanted to spit on me."

"Worse. I wanted to kill you. But now I'm confused. I don't know what you are. Maybe you're an angel or a demon or maybe you're just a human boy who's pulling one big scam on us all."

"Mmm," he said around a mouthful. "What do your senses tell you about me?"

"I told you, it's confusing." The omelette was good. I tapped a little of the hot sauce onto it.

"That's the trouble with you. You don't trust your gifts. And you are gifted, Jareth. I can tell."

He had a way of getting to me, worming past my defences. It made me wary. "You're just flattering me."

"Now why would I do that?"

"Maybe because you have designs on my body," I said jokingly and was immediately horrified that I'd said that.

He slanted an eye at me. "Is that such an absurd idea?"

I could feel the good side of my face flaming. "Why would you make love to a freak like me?" I snarled, which only made it worse.

He cocked his head. "I thought we were both freaks, each in our own way. I find you interesting, Jareth. I want to learn more about you."

"I told you all you needed to know when we first met."

"I know you think the burn defines you, but it does not. There is more to be learned, I'm thinking. You express yourself elegantly sometimes, you know, better than most of the people around here.

Where did you learn about Janus, the Roman god?"

"Oh, uh, after I got burned and the Ramseys adopted me, well, I didn't like trying to be with other kids so much. Too painful. Most of them ran away or taunted me. So I stayed inside by myself and watched movies and read books, everything I could get my hands on. I loved all the stories about the ancient Greek and Roman gods and heroes. I read a lot of those and fantasy and well, other stuff," I ended lamely.

"I did too," he said softly. "Maybe we aren't as dissimilar as it might appear."

Suddenly I had the bad feeling that he was just flattering me for some nefarious reason of his own. "What do you want, Kithara? What are you doing here, in this circus?"

He shrugged. "I thought it was obvious what I'm doing. Trying to survive."

"I know you hate it. Do you have a plan for getting out of here?"

"Do you?"

"Damn it!" I slammed a hand down on the table. "I don't have anywhere else to go. I presume you have, um, people, others you can go back to."

He took a sip of wine. "How do you know this isn't just part of the master plan?"

"Was getting zapped by a cattle prod part of the plan? Because if so, you're a lot kinkier than I thought."

He smiled and I felt my mouth relax into an answering smile, which I quickly suppressed.

"You have no idea what kinky is," he said. He raised his cup towards me.

"Are you going to talk to me or just say vague and irritating things while you sit there all beautiful and mysterious?" I growled.

"Okay, Jareth, what do you want to know?"

"Everything. Tell me how you got here. Tell me about the Wraeththu."

"You want *my* story, then? I thought you'd already made up your mind to hate me. Why would explanations make any difference?"

"I want to understand," I said. I didn't tell him that I didn't hate him anymore, couldn't hate him.

He leaned forward, his eyes glittering. "Understanding is a sword that cuts both ways. How far are you willing to go to understand? To be pushed out of your comfort zone into a wider reality?"

"What?"

103

"Because you might not be the same again, once you know some truths."

"I'll take the risk," I said.

"At some point, I'll remind you that you said that," he replied. "More wine?"

"You're just trying to get me drunk so you can take advantage of me," I said.

He chuckled. "As tempted as I am to, as you say, take advantage of you, I can't. You would not survive the experience."

Despite the danger he presented, I was absurdly pleased. "Then, is the story true that Sligo tells when he introduces your act?"

"It is."

"How does he know about it?"

He sighed and got up. "Are you done? I'll take your plate." He dumped the plates in the trash, picked up the bottle of wine and his cup and moved to the mattress that served as a bed, which, along with the table and two chairs, constituted the only furniture in the place. He patted the pillow beside him. "Persistence should be rewarded. Come sit and I'll tell you."

I kicked off my tennis shoes, picked up the pillow, put it behind my back, and leaned up against the wall, keeping my good side facing him and sweeping my hair forward to cover my burn. He was seated about a foot away, lolling back against a pillow. I felt a heightened awareness of where his body was in relation to mine. We were actually on a bed together. It was more intoxicating than the wine.

"So where to start?" Kithara mused. "Let's see. Well, my birth name before I was incepted was Ian. Like you, I grew up in the suburbs of Carmine City. I was an only child, much indulged, and I think somewhat spoiled as a result. I was interested in all kinds of things: literature, science, music, and dance. My mother sent me to ballet classes. Ballet is unusual for a boy, but I was good at it, and didn't much care what other kids thought. Besides," here he rubbed a finger along my thigh, "I think I fancied boys, even then, and I loved those male dancers in their sheer white tights."

At this, my heart conducted a little somersault in my chest.

"When I was sixteen, my parents got divorced," Kithara continued, "and my mother moved into an apartment in the city. I fell in with a rough crowd, rode a motorcycle, and danced naked in a club, causing my mother no end of grief." Here, he chewed on his lip. Did I detect regret in his voice? He sighed. "You talk about being a monster. I think I was, before I became Wraeththu. Do you have any cigarettes?"

"No, I don't smoke, um, tobacco."

"Shit." He took another swig of the wine and continued. "I heard things about a band of strange mutants that lived in a no-man's land in the inner city. Beings that attacked boys and somehow infected them so that they became mutants too. Some people dismissed it as urban myth. I didn't. Instead, it fascinated and horrified me. By then, I was writing for my high school blog, one of the few responsible things I did back then, and I thought it would be just so hot, you know, to actually track down someone who had seen one of these creatures. It became an obsession. I ventured further and further into their territory, and through talking to people, streetwalkers, bums, cops, I was slowly putting together a strange and contradictory story. Some said they were like vampires, attacking people at night and sucking their blood; others thought they were just another gang trying to scare people. I found an eye-witness who said they were beautiful to look at, but deadly to touch. Soon, I was to find out for myself.

"One day someone emailed me and gave me the address of a man who, they said, had eyewitness info. That address was deep in the ghetto, which made me pretty nervous. But I went anyway. I found the apartment, knocked on the door. Suddenly I had the most creeped out feeling and started to walk away. Then, the door opened, and a man came out. I say a man, but I knew from the get-go that it wasn't a man."

"How did you know?"

Kithara raked a hand through his hair, making it stand up on top. He frowned. "I just knew. For one thing, he didn't look like anyone you've ever seen before. He was stunningly beautiful, very tall, porcelain skin, brilliant violet eyes sparked with gold and bright red hair that was long, almost waist-length, braided into many little braids. He wore a long black leather coat with a fringed scarf tied over his shoulders and red high-heeled cowboy boots. An incongruous combination to say the least. He laid a hand on my arm and said, 'I hear you are looking for me.'

"'I don't think so,' I replied, because even as stupid and naïve as I was, I knew he was trouble.

"He said, 'Yes, you are. I've been monitoring you. I know you've been drawn to us for some time now. You have only to take the final step.' Then he smiled, revealing long, perfect teeth. I started to run. Next thing I knew, I was surrounded by what appeared to be a gang of beautiful Goth boys, all different, and yet all with the same knowing light in their eyes."

"Wow," I said. Unaccountably, I felt envious.

"Wow, indeed." He shifted, taking another sip of wine. "They dragged me to a cellar, tore off all my clothes, put a tourniquet on my arm to pop up the vein, and then Thiede – that was the red-haired guy – injected me with a syringe full of his blood." Kithara fingered the thick white scar on his arm. "They went through a freakin' weird ritual with drums and chants. I was scared out of my mind. I thought they were going to kill me. And then, for three days while I went through althaia – that is the change – I wished that they had."

He paused, rubbing his temples. "On the third evening I woke up as myself but altered. Better, stronger, more beautiful. A new being. They named me Kithara and I became fully Wraeththu. I am clever, little Jareth. Under Thiede's tutelage, I blossomed. Soon I was in charge of a gang of my own and became responsible for more of the terrible rumours that drifted like smoke around the city." He looked at me from under his lids. My skin prickled, but I couldn't figure out what it meant.

He pushed a strand of hair back behind his ears. "I worked hard and earned Thiede's trust. He made me one of his elite. He has grand schemes, Thiede does, and has yet to reveal the full extent of them. We follow blindly because we must. The future belongs to Wraeththu, Jareth."

"So you say." I was becoming very uncomfortable; my burned face itched and I had to resist clawing at it. "What happened to you, then, Kithara? If you were so powerful, how did Sligo get hold of you?"

"I grew arrogant and careless," Kithara said. "And the Aghama punishes hubris."

"The Aghama?"

"The first of us... our god, if you like, or the nearest we have to one." Kithara grimaced. "I had a huge fight with Thiede about a plan to take over a human gang's territory. We had arms and hara enough to do it. Thiede said it wouldn't work and it would be on my head if it went wrong. And it did. Half my gang was killed; the other half captured. Our enemies auctioned us off on the internet to the highest bidder. In my case, it was Sligo who bought me. They tied me up, threw me into a truck, and shipped me out here. I thought I'd die from thirst. We stopped several miles away from here and Sligo came to inspect the goods. He insisted on being shown exactly what it was that made me different. It was completely humiliating. I offered to give him some first-hand experience, but he was too savvy for that." Kithara's mouth twisted.

"What, um, what exactly is it that makes you different?" I said, feeling shy, fearful of the answer, but I had to know.

"Ah, curiosity killed the cat," Kithara said, with a smile. He reached over and gently laid a hand on my crotch. I jumped in surprise and a jolt of pleasure shot through me. His fingers flexed.

"Kithara...," I began, but I didn't really want him to stop. I was a virgin with tremendous yearnings and he was pushing all the right buttons.

"I won't hurt you," he said, and began massaging me through my jeans. When he had succeeded in fully arousing me, which didn't take much, he ran two fingers along either side of my throbbing flesh, outlining it through my jeans. "There, that's a human male. I remember having one of those. A very demanding little beast. I have an organ something like that, but altered, and just as capable of pleasure, more so in some ways. But beyond that, I have a female portal too. I am both male and female. Do you want to see?"

I was somewhat squeamish, slightly drunk, immensely curious, and totally turned on. I nodded.

He laughed, thumbed open his pants button, pulled down the zipper, then raised his hips, and wriggled out of his leather jeans. He turned to face me. I looked. The devil take me, I had to. Oh god! It was emerging from a nest of short, blond fur, unfurling like a fern, a bizarre kind of flower, petals pulsing with colour. This was it, his secret. It was beautiful and it freaked the shit out of me. Like something from a pipe dream. Only then did I truly understand how different Wraeththu were. Alien. I was both shocked and excited in a strangely, savage way.

He leaned forward, wetting his lips with his tongue. "Touch me."

I shook my head violently.

"You wanted knowledge, human scum," he said. "So learn." He took my unresisting hand and brought it down to fold around his organ, stiff as a rod, but warm, flexible, and alive, petals peeling back. Then he moved my hand down and pressed one of my fingers into a narrow, moist opening. I gasped, closing my eyes.

"I'm aching for aruna," he said. "Please, let me touch you."

I couldn't speak, couldn't move, couldn't look.

I heard him spit on his hand, felt him unzip my pants, take me out, and stroke me in a firm grip, thumb spreading moisture. So hot;

so compelling.

"No, I can't do this," I moaned.

"I won't hurt you, I promise. Doesn't it feel good?"

"Yes," I gasped, "oh, god, yes." He was unrelenting. I found myself moving my hips, back and forth, pushing into his hand, blood throbbing, skin tingling, until the need became too great, too overwhelming. I threw back my head, and with a loud groan, shuddered out a glorious climax, all over everything.

I opened my eyes in time to see Kithara's face wracked with the same ecstasy I'd felt. Could he feed on my sensations? He lowered his head, opened those diamond-shaped eyes and stared at me, eyes burning as if he could laser holes right through me. So beautiful. He was all that I'd ever wanted, all I'd dreamed of, but he was not mine, could never be. And I was ashamed that he, a shining angel, had done this thing for me, a burned wreck of a man.

"No more, please," I said, pushing his hand away. Tears welled in my eyes.

Kithara rubbed his hand on the mattress, then reached over and tenderly moved my hair away from the burned side of my face. "You try to hide yourself," he said in that soft, melodious voice. "But I see who you really are, Jareth Nine, and you are beautiful."

A tear scorched down my cheek. "Are you going to kill me now?" I asked, pitifully.

"Not at all." He sat back, laughing softly. "I believe you are already partially Wraeththu. Would you like to become complete?"

"What the hell do you mean, partially?" I said. "That's not possible."

He opened his mouth to say something, but at that moment, I had one of my visions, accompanied by the falling sensation in the pit of my stomach. I closed my eyes and saw a murderous throng of people marching past the circus gates, armed with guns.

"Kithara, get dressed, quickly," I cried. "They're coming for you. I know it!"

We heard shouting. Far off, an elephant bugled. Someone knocked loudly on the trailer door and then Pavel burst in, panting. "Kithara, some men are coming and they don't look too friendly. Sligo sent me. He says to hide."

"Where?" Kithara asked, looking pointedly around his bare dwelling.

"Not here. Sligo said to go hide in his trailer," Pavel said. "Craig, you need to come with me." He waved at the roustabout who had been standing outside guarding Kithara.

"I'll take him to my place, Pavel," I said. He nodded.

Kithara followed me out into the humid night. I took him on a short cut through the tents. We heard more shouting in the distance.

Just as we arrived, the door to my trailer opened, projecting a rectangle of warm, yellow light into the darkness. Esmeralda stood there like righteous anger, large and imposing in her pink nightgown that had feathers around the neck and sleeves. "What's goin' on?" she called.

"A lynch mob," I said, grimly. "Coming for Kithara."

Her eyes grew wide. "Well, get in here." She stepped back inside. Hastily, we took the step up into the trailer and slammed the door.

"Do you think they'll search the grounds?" I asked.

"Can't say," Esmeralda replied. "Shit, I was afraid of this after what I heard in town the other night." She raked an assessing glance over Kithara. "So you're the demon boy who's got everyone all riled up. You look pretty harmless to me."

"Looks are deceiving," Kithara said, with a smirk. "I'm actually quite wicked. Tell her, Jareth."

"Might want to shut that smart mouth for a spell, honey. Better go hide in the closet."

Kithara nodded and disappeared down the hall.

"I'm going to go out there, see what's happening," I said.

"Be careful, Jareth," Esmeralda said. Then, unexpectedly, she gave me a hug. Her breasts felt like doughy pillows against my chest. Comforting.

I put on my mask and went out into the night. A steady breeze was blowing, hot and dry. People were running every which direction, but it wasn't hard to find the source of the commotion. Near the entrance to the big top arena, a group of about one hundred men were gathered in a semi-circle around members of the circus community. The intruders held guns, flashlights, lanterns, and ominously, several of them were carrying torches. I thought that it looked like some kind of bad movie, the final scene in Frankenstein. But this was real and frightening. I worked my way up close and hid behind a concession trailer.

A tall man and a short one were arguing with Dr. Sligo. Behind Sligo stood Pavel, Tom Houston, Stubs Wheaton and about a dozen others, including Craig the guard holding the shotgun. Dr. Sligo said, "What the hell do you people think you're doing here!"

"Haven't you heard?" said the tall man. "There's been an uprising of these mutant things in Mid-land. They've killed a bunch of people. We have to get rid of this threat, stamp it out permanent. Better get out of the way or you'll be guilty of harbouring a criminal."

"This one hasn't done any harm to you," Sligo said. "And he's under guard all the time. He's no threat."

"That's not so," said the short man. "He's influenced people, perverted our young folks. Dr. Sligo, either you turn him over or we're going to torch your circus." The man next to him grinned and waved his flaming weapon.

The circus crowd gasped and then there were angry murmurs. Sligo leaned over and whispered something to Pavel, who whispered back.

"Now, truly, there's no need for all this lawlessness," Sligo said, raising his hands, palms out. "As soon as you bring me a written warrant for his arrest, I'll turn him over."

"This is our warrant," one of the men said and shot his gun in the air.

"Hey, none of that, none of that!" Sligo yelled. "Fine, you want him. I'll take you to him."

He led the group down the midway, taking the long route towards the trailer that had housed Kithara, probably figuring he would be gone by the time they reached it.

This was getting serious. What would they do when they discovered Kithara wasn't there? Could we hide him successfully all night from these creeps? Possibly, but what if they came back tomorrow? I had no faith that the local cops would protect us.

It had become clear that Kithara needed to escape from the circus altogether and that he should leave under cover of darkness. Like now. How to do it? My head was in a whirl. He'd need a car, water, food, cash. How much money had I stashed away in the jar under my bed? Maybe six hundred dollars? Not much. Then I paused for a moment. Why should I help him? What was he to me but one of the savages that had killed my family? I should be happy to get revenge. But no, I didn't feel that way anymore. Things had changed, just as he had said they would. I could still feel his touch on my face, his soft voice saying, *I see who you really are, Jareth Nine, and you are beautiful.* A moment of revelation, as if he'd applied a cooling balm to my scorched soul. No, I could not stand by while they shot him like a dog.

The intruders were fanning out over the grounds. Circus people melted away before them. Time to act.

Walking calmly so as not to attract attention, I headed in the other direction back to my trailer. I stopped at a concession stand, grabbed a cooler and filled it with bottled water, chips, apples, sodas. Found a dolly and wheeled it along, seeking the dark areas between tents. I stashed it behind my trailer, then cautiously knocked on the door. Esmeralda opened it and pulled me inside.

"So, what news?" she asked.

I slipped off my mask. "There's an armed mob that seems determined to find our mutant. Did I mention armed, as in, with guns? He's got to leave, Ez."

"Of course he does, honey. We've been working on it."

"What d'you think?" Kithara said, coming into the room. I looked up and burst out laughing. He was disguised, wearing one of Ez's leather jackets which looked huge on him, his bright hair pinned up and covered by a bandana, and for the final touch, he sported one of Esmeralda's fake beards.

"Oh, that's perfect," I choked. "No one will recognize you."

In the distance, we heard shouting. "No time to be fooling around," Esmeralda said. "You better get going."

"What can I use for transportation?" Kithara asked. "I won't get far on my feet."

"I've been thinking about that," I said. "We need to steal a car. But getting the keys will be a problem and I don't know how to hot wire one."

"Not a good idea, anyway," Esmeralda said. "They'll track you down fast if you steal a car. You should take my motorcycle."

"No, Ez, you need your bike."

"Now don't you argue with me. I'm not goin' t'stand by and watch anyone get lynched. Here's the key. There's a set of saddlebags on the side that can carry some stuff."

"I've got some water and a bit of food outside in a cooler," I said. "You guys load up. I need to get some stuff." I went back to my room, got my backpack, and threw in some clothes, a pocketknife, a comb, toothbrush and other things he'd need. My glance fell on my tube of choi and the pipe. Shit, I'd need to go hide in a hole and smoke myself silly after all this. I stuck them in a pocket on my jean's leg. Then I crawled under my bed and pulled out my money jar. Took out a roll of bills, my savings for that desert island I'd planned to go to. Well, it would take a little longer now. Besides, I should give Esmeralda something for that bike. I went into Esmeralda's room, peeled three hundred dollars off the roll and set it on her dresser, then stuck the rest of it in the pack. I went back outside. "Here," I thrust the backpack at Kithara. "There's some money in there. All I could spare."

"I won't forget your kindness to me," Kithara said. "Both of you. I guess all humans aren't scum, after all." He kissed Esmeralda's cheek, then hugged me. It felt so good to hold him like that, to press our bodies together. I wanted to stay that way for the rest of my life. Well, not possible. I started to pull away, but he held on. "Come with me, Jareth," he said.

"I can't."

"Why not? What's keeping you here?"

"A job, for one. Where else in this world is there a place for someone like me?"

Kithara put a hand to the burned side of my face. I could feel energy crackling out of him. "You could have a place with us. You could become Wraeththu, Jareth. Come with me."

I was torn, anguished. What was here for me but shame and degradation? But become Wraeththu? I wanted all my organs intact, thank you. I slipped away from his arms. "No, I can't."

"Okay." Kithara leaned over and kissed my forehead. He climbed on the bike, turned the key and revved it. It purred into life. "Which way should I go?"

"You need to head for the mountains, that way." Esmeralda pointed.

"Go along the track at the back of the tents there," I said, "so they'll be less likely to hear you. Good luck."

Then we heard a familiar voice. "Where do you think you're going?"

Long coat-tails fluttering in the breeze, a slender figure emerged from the shadows into the light cast from the open trailer door. Dr. Sligo. He aimed a long barrelled pistol right at Kithara; then he laughed.

"I think the beard suits you, Mutant," Sligo said. "You can take it off now, you're not going anywhere. I've misdirected the townies, so we should have a few minutes while they search trailers on the other side of the fairgrounds. I know a safe place for you to hide, but you've got to come now."

Kithara folded his arms. "I'm sure you'll understand when I say no, and not only no, but, fuck you."

Sligo raised the pistol and came closer. "Would you rather I turn you over to the lynch mob, or perhaps blow a hole in your pretty little head before they get here? Get off the bike."

Kithara raised his hands, turned off the engine, then slowly swung his leg off the bike, and stood up. "I don't think you'll kill the golden goose, Sligo."

"Perhaps not. I just need to stand back and let them do it," Sligo replied, jerking his head in the direction the mob had taken.

We heard shouting in the distance. Sligo gestured with the gun the opposite way. "Now, make the right decision here, boy, for all concerned. Make it quick, we don't have much time before this whole situation is out of my hands."

"You created the situation, Sligo, when you decided to exhibit me as a freak," Kithara snarled. "It's probably not a good idea for me to kill you and give them a reason for hunting me down, but then again I'm tempted. There *is* the matter of a cattle prod and a few late night visits between us."

"You are laughable," Sligo said. "How dare you threaten me? I'm the one with the gun here. I could kill you right now and that bunch of rubes would give me a medal."

"Dr. Sligo," I pleaded, "you've seen how dangerous it is to have him around. He's a liability to us. Please, just let him go."

Sligo rounded on me. "I see you and Esmeralda are helping him get away. Not too loyal of you. No, not loyal at all. I'm thinking that if I put you both out on the highway, it'll be two less paychecks to cut. There aren't many jobs out there for freaks." Sligo swung the pistol away from Kithara and pointed it at me. Esmeralda and I both gasped. All I could see was that long barrel, cold and clinical, ready to deal out my death. My heart began thumping madly.

In a sudden blur of motion, Kithara lunged forward, striking Sligo in the chest with a flattened palm. There was a white flash and the air seemed to reverberate with the force of the blow. Sligo flew over backwards and landed on his back. Unmoving, he stared up at the sky with glassy eyes. Esmeralda screamed.

"Oh my god, did you kill him?" I gasped.

"Possibly," Kithara replied. He reached down, picked up the pistol, and shoved it into a pocket in his leather jacket. "Time to go, Jareth. Are you with me?"

Closer now, down the midway, I heard more shouting. Dark figures were running towards us. In shock, I stared down at Dr. Sligo lying in the dirt. Hands shaking, I reached down, felt his neck for that tiny throb.

"He's got a pulse," I said to Esmeralda. "What do we do?"

"I'm calling an ambulance," she said. She jerked a thumb at Kithara. "You better get out of here. Now."

Kithara mounted the bike, turned the key, throttled up, and the engine roared. The red tail light blinked off. He started to pull away. Panic rushed through me. Oh god, I'd never see him again.

"Wait," I called, running alongside until he stopped. Breathlessly, I said, "I'm coming with you," and scrambled on behind him.

"Take the backpack," he said, wriggling it off and handing it to me. "Hold on."

"Bye, Ez," I waved, as I slung the pack on my back.

"Good luck, Jareth! Be good now," she called.

Then we were flying through the night, bumping along on the dirt track behind the tents. There was a steep embankment to our right and in the distance I could see the lights of the highway. I was pumped full of adrenaline, freaked at what just happened, and yet I knew I wasn't in control anymore, if indeed I ever had been. Destiny was pulling me in its wake and, for once, I did not want to fight.

At that moment, I heard a crack like distant thunder and a loud whine zipped past my head. I turned and saw the headlights of a truck. It had just rounded a corner and was closing in behind us. Another loud report.

"Shit, Kithara, they're shooting at us!"

"I know, hold on tight," he said. "We're going for a ride." He gave the bike full throttle and pulled away from the truck. Then he turned sharply to the right and we charged straight up the embankment. Dirt clots flew. The bike's rear end shimmied, and then slid. It threatened to stall. Kithara put down both feet, pushing it along, then gunned it. I heard another shot and some lighter sounds: *pop, pop, pop.*

Suddenly Kithara lurched forward. "Oh fuck!" he said.

"What's wrong?"

"Nothing. Damn. Let's go." We reached the top of the embankment. Kithara turned left and drove like hell along the narrow track on top of the berm. I could see the lights of three vehicles below us, but they were falling back. We heard several more faint shots ring out. Too far away to be a threat. Up ahead the highway appeared like a river of light. The embankment began to descend. We rode down it, crashed through a fence, and reached the pavement that led to the highway on-ramp. We took it heading west towards the mountains.

We'd escaped! Even though I knew it might not last, I felt silly with relief. I closed my eyes, feeling the wind rushing by my face. Hugging Kithara's lithe body against my chest, I rested the burned side of my face against his back. He wanted me with him. Me. Whatever came next, this was my time to savour.

The high didn't last long. My face began to tingle and then burn. I jerked away from Kithara, put my hand to my cheek, bringing away a slick moisture. What? Something warm and wet was seeping through Kithara's jacket.

"Jesus, you're bleeding!" I shouted against the wind.

"I think I was hit back there." He hissed through his teeth. "It's starting to hurt."

Oh god! The dark stain was slowly spreading across his shoulder. "We've got to stop!"

"We don't dare. It's a matter of time until they send the cops after us. I want to put miles between us before then."

"Sligo wasn't dead, Kithara. Maybe they won't follow us. You *must* go to a hospital!"

"No way in hell," Kithara snarled and increased his speed.

"Damn it, at least let me drive! You could pass out and kill us both!"

"I won't pass out," he asserted.

"Yeah, I forgot, you're superman," I muttered. Right. I pressed my hand to the wound to try to stop the bleeding. Kithara flinched and then swore. The bike swerved. Cars whooshed by indifferently while I wondered at what point this whole nightmare would come crashing to an end. No premonitions appeared to guide me. I closed my eyes and breathed deeply, trying not to panic. Meanwhile the back of Kithara's jacket grew more slippery under my palm.

In the distance, a police siren wailed, then another one picked up the cry. "Kithara!" I warned.

"I hear them," he said. "Jareth, I feel so tired, I'm seeing spots."

"Shit! We'd better get off the road and hide somewhere. There's a truck stop up ahead. Pull off there."

For once he did as I asked. We cruised into a big parking lot with several tractor trailer trucks parked outside a greasy spoon café that had strings of old Christmas lights blinking around the windows. Cautiously, we motored up outside. Came to a stop. I swung off the bike and Kithara fell over sideways into my arms. I eased him down to the pavement.

"Sit here while I try to find some bandages to pack around that bleeding. Maybe ice would slow it down some," I said. The bleeding was getting worse, spreading into a puddle underneath Kithara. I was trying to hold it together, but panic was setting in. My guts felt fluttery. I thought I might puke.

A man emerged from the café. He wore a baseball cap over scraggly yellow hair that hung down to his shoulders, a dirty t-shirt that said *Aliens are among us,* and was bopping to music coming from earphones. Kithara slumped forward, his head hitting the ground.

"Hey dude, are you all right?" the guy said. He pulled his earphones down around his neck.

"No, he's not," I said, ducking my head to throw my hair over my face. "He's been badly hurt. Do you have any towels or something?" I raised a hand, dark with blood.

"Oh shit! Yeah. Come over to the truck here."

I supported Kithara against my shoulder and we hobbled over to the guy's rig. He hopped up in the cab, fumbled around, and emerged with two towels. Kithara sank down on the curb with a gasp. I peeled off his jacket and the t-shirt underneath, which I noticed was one of mine. Christ, there was blood everywhere! More blood oozed from a little black hole in his shoulder that had a raised, discoloured welt all around it. I took the towel and pressed it to the wound. Kithara grunted.

"Wow. That looks nasty. I'd better call 911," the guy said, bending over, his face tight with concern. He pulled a cell from his pocket.

"No, don't do that," Kithara said, menacingly. He scowled. "I mean it."

"Dude," the guy said.

In the distance I could hear the sirens wailing and knew I had to take a risk and hope this guy wouldn't turn us in. "Hey man, we need your help," I said. "Hear those sirens? That's the cops. They shot my friend here and I'm afraid they'll kill him if they catch us? Savvy?"

"They won't kill you if you give up?" The guy hesitated.

"Sure they won't," Kithara said. "We tried that already. That's when they shot me. So we ran." He winced as he peeled off the beard, then looked up at the guy with that angel face of his, gave him one of his irresistible smiles, then his face contorted in pain. "Please help us," he said.

"Um, well, what do you want me to do?"

"Which way are you headed?" I asked.

"West."

"Let us hitch a ride in the back of your truck," I said. "If they pull you over and search, you can say you didn't know we'd crawled in there. What d'you say?" I shrugged off my backpack and felt around in the pouch, pulled out the roll of bills. "I'll make it worth your while."

"No need, dude. I've had a few run-ins with the cops myself. Just be quick. I see lights flashing up there on the highway." He opened the doors on the back of the truck.

"Help him up. I'll get the bike," I said.

I held Kithara in my arms while we rocked back and forth in the dark. We were sitting on some old blankets in the back of the truck, which was full of car parts. I didn't know what time it was, but it seemed as if more than two hours had passed. We hadn't been pulled over and I couldn't hear any sirens, so I guessed we were safe for the moment. At least safe from being taken into custody. I wondered if we should have let the cops find us so Kithara could get medical attention. That is, until they figured out what he was, then god only knew what would happen.

The driver, whose name was Ben, had given me some crushed ice in a baggie and I packed that against Kithara's wound, then taped the towels on top. It looked like it had helped. The bleeding seemed to have stopped because it wasn't soaking through the towels. At least I didn't think it was. But then, he felt clammy to the touch, and was moaning and twitching. I felt so helpless and inadequate. Why had I done this stupid thing? What future did I have now? And the worst question to contemplate: what the hell was I going to do if he died? At this point, as far as I could see, my whole life was fucked. I couldn't go back to the circus, so I had no way to make a living. I was damaged goods, a freak no one wanted, and god, I was so scared. My throat closed up hard, choking me. A sob forced its way out, and with that surrender, the dam burst. I found myself crying in great heaving shudders.

He moved in my arms. His hand touched my cheek. "Jareth. Don't worry. It will be okay," he said. "I'm trying to heal myself from within, sealing off arteries. It's taking all my concentration. Sorry, I can't be with you right now. Just hold me. Lend me your strength."

"I'm trying," I choked. But he was out again, involved in his own struggle. Nevertheless the sound of his voice lingered, soothing. He said it would be all right. I believed him. I was an idiot. The truck rocked us back and forth. The road droned underneath. Slowly, my eyes closed.

My own yell woke me up. At first I thought it was a dream in which someone had thrust a knife in my guts. Ow, shit, there it was again. Not a dream. I struggled out from under Kithara's body, turned my head away and was sick on the floor. My face was burning all over and my lips felt swollen. What was going on? Did I have the flu or something? Not good. Needed to get out of the truck right away. "Ben! Stop! Stop!" I yelled and banged on the walls. No response. I picked up what felt like a fender and heaved it against the back wall. That appeared effective since the truck slowed and then lumbered to a halt. The brakes hissed. The back doors were wrenched open, cool air flowed in, and I could see Ben's cap silhouetted against a starry sky. "Hey, what's going on?" he said.

"Sorry man," I said. "But I'm feeling sick as a dog and my friend, he's not doing too good. We need to get out."

"I can take you to a hospital," Ben offered. "I don't want this guy's death on my conscience."

"Don't worry, I'll take him," I said. "Just let us off here." I shook Kithara. "Can you hear me, Kithara? We've got to go now." He roused with a groan. Ben climbed into the back, pushed the bike onto the lift, and lowered himself. In the dark, I felt for my backpack. "Damn! I can't see a thing."

"Just a sec and I'll get a flashlight," Ben said. I heard him crunching towards the cab. I raised the lift back up, laboriously rolled Kithara onto it, and lowered us down next to the bike.

It was a quiet highway. Two lanes. The air felt cooler, especially after the closeness in the truck. We must be higher in altitude. There was a fork in the road that headed up towards some mountains, blacker than black against the sky. Somehow I knew that was the way we needed to go. I slapped his cheek. "Wake up Kithara. You have to ride with me now. Please, wake up. I can't stand it anymore." I was nearly in tears again and plenty nauseated to boot.

He moved and murmured, "Hey, I'm awake now. Where are we going?"

"Someplace not here," I said as I helped him stagger to his feet and climb onto the back of the bike.

Then I was wracked with nausea again and had to double over. Ben appeared with the flashlight, cutting a bright swath in the darkness.

"Here," he said. "See if this helps."

Raising my head, I looked at him and wasn't prepared at all for his reaction. He yelled and raised a hand as if to fend me off. "Jesus H. Christ!" he said, "What the hell happened to you?"

"I'm sorry. It's just a burn I got when I was a kid. A really bad one. It doesn't hurt."

"No," he said. "This isn't a burn. It's like something spreading out, dude, like you're diseased or something."

Kithara moaned and then his skin began to glow with a soft light, as if a lantern had switched on inside of him.

"Shit, look at that! What are you two? What are you?" Ben said in terror. He dropped the flashlight. "I'm sorry, dude. Too freaky. Gotta go." He slammed shut the back doors of his truck, ran and leaped into the cab, and steamed off as fast as he could shift gears.

I watched the truck leave, feeling increasingly putrid, and wondering what the fuck was going on. What was Kithara doing? I reached down, grabbed the flashlight, and dumped it in the pack, figuring it might prove useful. Now, I'd better get out of here before someone saw Kithara's new incarnation as a nightlight. I got on the bike, reached back, grasped Kithara's wrists, and pulled his arms about my waist. "You've got to hold on now," I said to him. "Can you hear me, shithead?"

I felt him nod against my back. Then I recalled the vision I'd had in the circus tent of looking through a door at a wall of pine trees. It was a real place. I knew it and I knew we had to get there.

I toed up the kickstand, turned the key, and throttled up. A car whooshed by as I started slowly along the shoulder. I needed to let go of my conscious will and allow my subconscious, or fate, chance, or whatever it was, guide me. A lightning fork of pain sizzled through my limbs again. What the hell was happening?

The road wound back and forth up the mountainside, becoming more and more provincial as we rode along. The air grew chilly, especially when we descended into a dip, and I was glad of Kithara's body heat against my back, even though it was a strange, tickling sort of heat that seemed to be transferring itself to me, as if my skin were soaking up his magic. His glow had faded, but shit, I didn't know if that was good or bad. I felt like a rabbit seeking a hole to hide in, with a ticking time bomb strapped to my back.

Higher and higher we climbed. The scrub around us grew taller and eventually transformed into immense ponderosa pines, ranks upon ranks of them, their naked trunks like marching soldiers. It seemed familiar to me. This was the right way to go. Whenever there was a fork in the road, I took the less travelled route, feeling my way to some place I'd never been to before. I was past even worrying why I knew.

Eventually, I began to feel drained. Not surprising, after all we'd been through. It was amazing I'd lasted this long. The road narrowed down to two dirt tracks and then I saw a gated driveway. Over it arched a wooden signpost painted with the name *Tranquility Base*. That seemed hopeful at least. I got off, unlatched the gate, then drove down the long lane, framed on either side by the dense blackness of the forest. The road was mirrored above my head by a narrow ribbon of navy blue sky spiked with stars. The air felt as cold and rarefied as if I was on another planet. It was very quiet. The only sound was the bike's rumble that vibrated throughout my body.

At the end of the lane, a large clearing opened up with a meadow of starry sky spread out above. Rising in the centre of the clearing was a rustic, two-story house built of wood with rows of windows. There were no lights and no cars parked outside. It seemed dead. I stopped the bike, put my foot down to steady it; Kithara slid off sideways and fell face forward in the dirt.

With a cry, I jumped down and rolled him over. His eyes were closed, his skin felt cold and clammy. I shook him, yelling, "Kithara, wake up!"

He moaned, which was a relief. Blood had worked its way through the towel I had taped around his back. Damn! What next? I'd better get him inside. "Stay here," I ordered, as if he was going anywhere. I walked up to the door, knocked loudly. No answer. I got out the flashlight and walked around the back calling, "Anyone home?"

All appeared quiet. An owl hooted somewhere nearby. Of course the doors were locked. I found a rock, broke a pane out of a window off the back deck, and crawled in. Panning the flashlight around, I found a well-appointed living room with a lofty two story ceiling. There was a large fireplace in the centre and beyond that a hallway, presumably leading to other rooms. A kitchen area appeared to my right with huge windows all around. That was promising, although I felt too nauseated to eat. I found a wall switch. The lights worked. I went out the front door, hauled Kithara into a sitting position, and with hands under his armpits, dragged him into the living room and laid him out like a corpse on a rug in front of the fireplace.

What did they say about blood loss? Shock could set in? I

wracked my memory to recall the symptoms and thought they included cold, clammy skin and loss of consciousness. Check, all of the above. I needed to keep him warm. A pile of wood and kindling was stacked near the fireplace. I remembered the lighter in the pocket on my jean's leg and pulled it out. The pipe and the choi were still in there too. Thank god! Suddenly, I felt an overwhelming desire to smoke and make this unpleasant situation go away. I uncapped the tube and inhaled the familiar sweet, earthy fragrance, then firmly recapped it, and stuck it back in my pocket. I needed to keep a hold on myself because if I checked out now, Kithara would surely die.

After numerous tries, I managed to get a fire going. The warmth and bright flames were cheery and made me feel better. We might actually get through this. I removed the taped towels and examined his wound. The bleeding had stopped. Had Kithara's weird glowing trick accomplished that? The area around the dark hole in his shoulder was bruised and had swollen tremendously. It didn't look good. I worried about whether or not I should try to cut out the bullet. But what if that just made it worse? Leaning down, I kissed his cheek. Unaccountably, my lips seemed numb as if I'd been to the dentist. When I felt them with my fingers, they seemed swollen.

Feeling a burning need to relieve myself, I figured I should look for a bathroom. There might be bandages and antibiotic ointment for Kithara's back and I could see what was happening to my mouth. I found a bathroom down the hall. Flipping on the light, I glanced at my reflection in the mirror, and reeled back, gasping in horror.

What the fuck had happened? My burned side was bloody and weeping as if freshly abraded and the good side had turned an ashy gray color with scaly ridges like a lizard. My eyes were bright red. Frantically, I ripped off my shirt and then my pants. Shit, it was all over my body! My stomach convulsed and I erupted like a volcano into the toilet. Oh god, oh god! This couldn't be happening. I crawled around on the floor, mewling in terror. I couldn't stand it. Had to check out of this nightmare right now. I picked up my jeans lying crumpled on the floor, fumbled in the pocket, pulled out the tube of choi, the pipe, and lighter. Hands shaking, I hit the pipe with flame and inhaled, then leaned back against the tub as the drug hit my system. Felt a little calmer now, although my stomach still clenched with nausea. I examined my hands which were covered in that same gray substance. It looked as if the top layer of skin had been burned into ashes. I rubbed at it and a sore opened up, weeping. It was like the plague or something! Could Kithara have caused this? If so, I was going to kill the bastard, that is, if he survived.

I sucked in more smoke, angrily musing that now my transformation to monster was complete. Maybe Sligo wouldn't recognize me and I could go back to the circus to live out my life as a freak. I hadn't realized how much I had needed my good side, the side that was still beautiful. Now, even that was lost to me. I couldn't even cry.

The pressure on my bladder forced me to get up and shuffle over to the toilet. I closed my eyes until I'd finished, then realized my dick felt numb and sort of slimy in my hand. I looked down and nearly shit with fright. The skin had developed a pink, nacreous sheen, as if several layers had peeled away. A yellow discharge oozed from the end and there were growths along the side, like little fingers of fungus. At that moment, I lost it completely. Full blown hysteria. I flailed about, hitting things, hearing them fall. Dragged myself screaming along the floor. Oh fuck! I retched again, but nothing came up. Raw throat. Aching body. I banged my head against the tub, and it occurred to me that I could end this by bludgeoning myself to death. I banged it again.

A voice called to me. Cool and soothing. Kithara's voice. The sound reverberated in blue waves like balm to my fevered brain. I couldn't tell whether he was really calling or if it came from inside my head. *Jareth, you idiot, calm down. The illness is temporary. It will pass. Trust me.* Well, that sounded like him. No real answers, just more mysteries. Yet, it seemed to work. I leaned back, breathed deeply, and the pain retreated, like blowing out a match. The voice came again. *Jareth, I need you.*

He was sitting up, leaning against the couch and his eyes were open, regarding me hazily. Relief overwhelmed me, if from nothing more than having a friend to share my fears with. Cringing like a whipped dog, I knelt beside him and he stroked gentle fingers through my hair.

"What's happening to me?" I whimpered.

"Althaia," he said. "You're becoming har."

"It hurts."

"I know."

"You went through this? Why didn't you warn me? How long?" I bit my lip to keep from crying.

"Hush," he said. "It takes about three days. I won't lie to you, it'll be rough. But you'll make it. You're strong, Jareth. And when it's all over, you'll be like a butterfly emerging from a chrysalis, beautiful as you were meant to be. I promise."

That calmed me down, some. Three days. It wasn't permanent, then. I could endure for three days. But now, as the fear receded, a tide of anger washed over me.

"How did this happen? You didn't cut me and force your blood into my veins. Isn't that what they did to you?"

"You must have absorbed my blood through your burned face," he said. "Apparently it didn't take much to restart the process."

"What the hell are you talking about?"

He sighed. "I don't know how much longer I'll be conscious. I've lost a lot of blood, Jareth, and I need to go back into a trance soon. Can you get me some water?"

I pulled a bottle from the saddlebags and handed it to him. He drank greedily.

"What do you mean, restart the process?"

Kithara wiped the back of his mouth. "I believe that you went through a partial althaia when you were younger. That's what caused your face to look burned."

"What! I wasn't really burned? What are you talking about?" I turned and flopped down in exhaustion next to him. There's nothing like having a truth that has defined you; that you've lived with every day for much of your life, revealed as a lie. But I was too drained to feel as angry as I should. "Hold on. I need some medication before I listen to what you creeps did to me." I got my pipe out again, sucked in a hit.

With a little smile, he reached out a hand. "I could use some of that. My back feels like someone smacked it with a sledgehammer." I handed him the pipe. He took a hit and blue smoke issued from his lips. He closed his eyes. Long moments passed. "Much better," he said dreamily.

"Don't you go away, shithead. Not until you explain what happened to me."

"Not now, Jareth. I can feel myself slipping away and I have something more important to tell you. I need you to remove the bullet because I can't finish the healing process with the metal lodged in my flesh, disrupting the fields. You'll need something to clamp off the arteries so I don't bleed to death."

"Oh god, Kithara, I can't..."

"Yes," he gripped my arm. "You can." He shook me. "Stop

freaking out and pay attention. If I don't make it, you'll have to go back to Carmine City on your own, seek out Thiede, and take aruna with one of our hara. If you don't do it, the change won't be fixed. You won't be whole and your body will start to degenerate."

"Oh crap. What's aruna?"

"It's harish sex." He gave me a wan smile.

That didn't sound so bad except that the transformation was kicking in again. My whole body began itching, as if insects were crawling under my skin. Frantically, I scratched at my bare legs.

He grabbed my hand, curled his fingers around it. "You mustn't do that. It could leave permanent marks. Give me some more of your poppy. Let me sleep."

I gave him the pipe again. "Kithara, I'm scared. I can't do any of this. Not by myself."

He didn't respond, instead he took a hit, slumped back against the couch. His eyes closed. I watched him relax and the pipe dropped from his hand onto the rug, scattering chunky ashes. "No, you bastard, you can't leave me again!" I yelled, shaking his arm.

I heard his voice in my head. *Remove the bullet, Jareth. I'm counting on you.* Then his consciousness winged away, like a sparrow. I was truly alone now.

Jesus. Okay, remove the bullet. What did I need? Boiling water? They always boiled water in the movies. I guess it was to disinfectant the instruments. I had a pocket knife to cut him with but I'd need to find something to clamp the artery so it didn't bleed and I'd need bandages, lots of them, and a needle and thread. They must have those things around here somewhere.

I started to get up, but the pain hit me again, shrieking through my body like a whirlwind of locusts. I curled up into a ball, moaning, clutching my stomach, and then entered a realm of demons that seared my eyes with hot pokers, pulled out my intestines in long, snaky tubes, and gnawed off my testicles.

Awake, panting, drenched in sweat. The pale light of dawn vented in through the windows, giving the house a light, airy feeling as if we were outdoors. The fire had burned down to embers. I felt almost normal. Apparently, it was a respite in my transformation. With a start, I sat up, and looked over at Kithara. He lay at an angle, his face turned towards me, a braid of his bright hair escaping from the red bandana. Such an exquisite face. I stroked a finger down his long, narrow nose and across a high cheekbone. I wondered if he'd always been this beautiful or if becoming har had enhanced his natural appearance? His skin appeared waxen. Was he dead? I put my fingers to his neck, and after long agonizing minutes, felt a faint pulse. Hysterical laughter bubbled up from my gut. I didn't know if I could bear another night like the last one, spent literally in hell. I only hoped I could get the bullet out of him before the pain hit me again.

Stiffly, I rose to my feet and tried to walk. Had to hobble Quasimodo-like, one leg dragging along. I found the saddle bags that I'd pulled off the bike the night before. Ravenous, I devoured one of the apples I'd packed while at the circus, which seemed like an eternity ago, and chugged down an entire bottle of water. Now it was time. I couldn't put off the surgery anymore.

I went into the bathroom, studiously avoiding looking at myself in the mirror, and ripped the shower curtain off its rod. Searching through the drawers and medicine chest, I found some bandages, a bottle of alcohol, tweezers, and an eyelash curler, which I thought might work to clamp off the artery. I came back and dumped these things next to the sink. Rummaging around in the kitchen, I found a large pot into which I poured the alcohol, then added my pocket knife and the other instruments. They landed with loud metal clunks. A thorough search of drawers in a back bedroom finally yielded a packet of needles and a spool of white thread. They would have to do.

Spreading the shower curtain out on the floor by the fire, I rolled him onto it, threw some logs on the fire and poked it up 'til it crackled, warming the air. I brought a lamp over so I could see, plugged it in, angled it so the light shone on his back, then went to the kitchen sink and thoroughly washed my hands. I carried the pot of implements over, setting it next to him, then used my lighter to sterilize the needle and the edge of the knife, which I set on a clean paper towel, along with the eyelash curler and the tweezers.

The area around the bullet wound was puffy and bruised; red streaks radiated from the blackened hole. This didn't look good at all. I wondered how deep it went. Okay, Jareth, breathe, I told myself. I made an incision across the hole, extending the cut on either side. The skin was surprisingly tough and I had to lean on my hand to put enough pressure on the blade to cut through. Dark blood ran from the wound in small rivulets. I forced the incision open with my fingers and then had to stop and clench my stomach muscles to keep from puking.

More blood began to spurt from the incision. I found the little artery and clamped it with the eyelash curler, a feat that was not easy as the artery was like a piece of spaghetti. I pinched shut the other side of the artery, knotted the end of the thread around, and tied it off. It seemed to hold. Then, I sucked in a breath, stuck my finger in the hole, and probed about. Shit, I couldn't find it. Needed to go deeper. The hole was filling with blood and I could hardly see. I ran to the kitchen and frantically dumped out drawers until I found a turkey baster. Ah, that might work. I sterilized it and used it to suck out the blood. Once that was done, I cut further down into the muscle.

A warning streak of pain shot through my abdomen. Praying to whoever would listen, I murmured, "Please, don't let it start now. Just give me a little longer." Probing further with my finger, I finally felt a small oblong object. At that moment, Kithara flinched and hissed through his teeth. "Hang in there buddy," I said. At least he was alive.

Holding the wound apart with my fingers, I grabbed the bullet with the tweezers, wrenched it free, and held the bloody thing up to the light. It really didn't seem big enough to have caused all this trouble, but it looked wicked, its nose flattened by the impact. Great gouts of blood were pumping out of the wound and I realized the knot on the artery must have come loose. Fighting both my nausea and more searing bursts of pain, I sucked the wound clear with the baster, found the artery again, and tied off both ends. Then, I pulled the lips of the wound together and sewed up the hole, even though every time I shoved the needle through the skin, it caused me to grind my teeth in disgust. I never imagined sewing living flesh like a pair of ripped jeans. Here I was, Dr. Frankenstein, patching together dead bodies. I taped bandages over the wound, then sat back, feeling dizzy. The shower curtain underneath us looked like I had slaughtered a pig on it. There was a bright, metallic smell. I ran to the front door, opened it to reveal the broadening light of a fair morning, and puked up apple slush on the doorstep.

Kithara lay on the couch under a blanket, his body haloed by golden light. That, at least, seemed a good sign to me. I didn't think he could do that if he was dead. As for me, I was back in my own private hell, rolling about in pain on the bloody shower curtain, alternately boiling then freezing. My skin peeled off in great gray sheets stuck with bits of flesh. I thanked whatever deities might be in attendance that the owners of the house hadn't returned because I could imagine their reaction to the horror being played out on their living room floor. Kithara had promised it would be over soon and I clung to that idea like a rat on a raft. I need only endure.

My memory fluttered off to an earlier time of pain when I had awakened in the hospital with my face and body burned. On the television screen in the room, I saw a time-lapse vid of a caterpillar transforming into a butterfly. Fascinated, I watched the creature twitch and writhe in a strange dance within its thin-skinned chrysalis. I had imagined that the caterpillar was dreaming of its rebirth as a beautiful creature, and thought how fantastic it would be if I could do that, climb into a shell of skin and emerge new and unburned, spreading my gorgeous wings in triumph. Now, wracked with pain, I wondered if the caterpillar had been writhing, not in joy, but in agony. What a cruel joke of nature if that miraculous transformation was actually a time of caterpillar hell. I cursed the Wraeththu for inflicting this horror on me, and vowed that if I survived, I'd make them pay for it.

Night came and another day after it. I clawed and bled and cursed and prayed, while my caterpillar parts rearranged themselves.

It was night again. The serene light of a waxing moon shone in the windows transforming the room to ghostly silver. I sat up, weak, shaking, as if I'd been through a long illness. Kithara's face looked cold and pale in the moonlight, his hands folded like wings upon his chest, like one of those marble sculptures atop a tomb. I shivered. Was he dead? Rising, I stumbled over to where he lay, felt his neck, cold and dense under my fingers. No pulse.

Oh god, no, it couldn't be! Had I killed him? I pulled him to my chest, sobbing. Please no. Don't leave me. Not after all this. In terror, my mind walked away on dark paths.

I found myself standing at the door of the house looking out into the stoic ranks of trees, the towering, primeval forest, and feeling a terrible pain in my heart. This was the moment I had foreseen and now I understood its meaning. I had reached the low point of my life. I loved him. How tragic to discover it at the moment that he was lost to me. Everything I'd known or thought I'd known had been a lie. I was broken. My whole body ached and I was tired beyond imagining. What should I do now? Bury him? Then, try to find the mythical Thiede? Was the transformation complete? Dare I look at myself to see? Or should I just get out Sligo's pistol and end it?

There! I saw a faint shimmer among the trees. Rapidly, it approached and I could discern a being of light. An angel? A god? Was I dead too, then? It came closer, gossamer robes floating about a tall, slender body with a face of stunning beauty, surrounded by braided ropes of hair, gray in the moonlight. He or she? I couldn't tell. It stopped about twenty feet away from me, cocked its head to one side.

"Hello there Janus, god of beginnings," it said in a surprisingly silky voice with echoing undertones. "How fitting that you stand in a doorway, examining both your past and your future."

"Who are you?" I asked, amazed.

"Can't you guess? I am Thiede."

I stood there gawping like a rube until he said, "I imagine you have questions. Aren't you going to ask me in?"

I made a sweeping, sardonic gesture with my arm towards the door. He seemed to float up the steps, which made me doubt my sanity. At this point my hold on it was tenuous at best.

"Thiede, you're too late. Kithara is dead." My voice caught in my throat.

He walked up to the couch, bent down, and touched Kithara's face. A golden glow issued from his hand, passed into Kithara's skin. In the firelight, Thiede's hair was indeed a glorious, coppery red. He raised his eyes. "No, the spark of life is still within him. You gave up too easily, Janus. You must blow on the embers and bring him back to life."

"Well, how the fuck should I do that? I must say Thiede, now that you're here, I have a notion to give you a piece of my mind."

He laughed. "Another time perhaps. Have you heard the story of Snow White?"

"Yeah, and her seven dwarves. What of it?"

"How did the Prince bring her brought back to life after she bit the poisoned apple?"

"With a kiss?"

"Just so."

"All I have to do is kiss him?"

"I would be quick about it if I were you. The candle of his spirit is nearly burned out."

Warily, I approached. Thiede moved away and I knelt next to Kithara, looked into that marble face with the delicate lashes lying so still against his cheek. With my finger I traced the perfect arch of his brows, then down along his nose with the slight bump in the centre, to those curving lips, so soft. He was beauty incarnate. To kiss him seemed like a sacred act. I touched my own lips, which still felt swollen. I knew I looked like a monster. This was surely a case of Beauty and the Beast rather than Snow White and Prince Charming. I sighed, bent over him and lightly touched our mouths together. It was like kissing a corpse.

"Don't give up," Thiede said. "You are stronger than you know, Janus. Give him your breath. You are har now. You must think like one. Think magically."

I forced Kithara's mouth open with mine and huffed a long, slow breath into him, along with a fervent prayer for life. Somewhere I heard a clock ticking. I breathed into him again. *Come on, Kithara.* Suddenly, his back arched and he gasped in a lungful of air. I gave him my breath again and he returned it, the sensation like inhaling choi smoke. Now my senses seemed all mixed up. I was tasting colours and smells and sounds: fuchsia and emerald, the fragrance of orange blossoms, a meadowlark's song. He opened his eyes and looked at me, dazed.

"You're alive!" I cried. "Oh my god! Oh my god!" I hugged him to my chest, half dragging him off the couch.

"Ow! Fuck Jareth, you'll crush me to death," Kithara gasped.

"You deserve it. You scared me to pieces. How is your back?"

"It hurts. Mmmmph," he said when I kissed him again. Our breath seemed to pour together, mixing in the cauldron of our lungs into some kind of crazy flavour that just got tastier and better. I felt ecstatic.

"What is that sensation?" I asked. "Am I still drugged?"

"No," Thiede replied, amusement colouring his voice. "That was your first harish kiss. It's called sharing breath. Not too bad, huh?"

"Har? I'm Wraeththu now?" I cried. "Is that althaia thing over? Oh, thank god!"

Thiede chuckled. "Yes, you have nearly finished the transformation, although the effect would be significantly improved by a bath. Now, before I send you kids off to complete Janus' change, I have some things to tell you."

Painfully, Kithara wrenched himself upright. He looked daggers at Thiede. "So you decided to show up at the eleventh hour. I could have used your help weeks ago, when they first captured me. I've been through hell, Thiede. No thanks to you."

"It took me a while to find out where you were," Thiede said mildly. "View this as a learning experience, Kithara, something to humble that massive ego, or if you prefer, a vision quest to obtain the higher caste you now have. And you've accomplished something else of importance. You found Janus and now you'll bring him back to join us."

"Did you know all this ahead of time?"

"No, but I know it now," Thiede said. "Is there any wine around here?" With a rustle of garments, he composed himself in a leather chair near the fire.

"Wine? Yes, I saw some earlier in the pantry," I said, feeling dazed. What was Thiede? Clearly, he was more than Wraeththu. Was he a god? As I looked at a rack of wine bottles, I could hear the buzz of Kithara's voice, still angry. "*I* have a massive ego!" he was saying. "You shithead! You just don't like competition."

I had to smile. Was this how we talked to our gods? If so, I approved. I selected a bottle and then went hunting for a corkscrew.

Thiede's words weren't audible but they sounded soothing. The exchange went on for a while until Kithara's angry tone quieted. Then Thiede called, "Janus, is there anything to eat in there? Kithara is hungry."

My stomach woke up and snarled. I realized that I was starving too. It had been days since I'd kept anything down. Fortunately, the larder seemed well stocked. I opened up two cans of soup that I set simmering on the stove.

When I returned with wine and three glasses, I found Thiede sitting on the couch with Kithara lying stretched out, his head resting in Thiede's lap. Kithara's eyes were closed and he looked quietly content while Thiede fondly stroked his hair as if he was a cat. I felt a flare of jealousy. Thiede's elite, indeed. Were they lovers? Sounds buzzed in my head, as if they were speaking to each other on a channel that I couldn't hear.

Feeling like an intruder, I set down the wine. "Excuse me. I think I'll clean up this mess." I pulled the disgusting shower curtain along the floor, out the back door, and dumped it in the yard, figuring that would be enough for now, I'd clean it in the morning. I couldn't think ahead any further than that. I looked at the forest in the spectral light, feeling a strange sense of well-being as if I was pulling energy from the earth up into my body. With considerable trepidation, I looked down at myself, nearly naked, wearing only my grimy, stained briefs. My arms and legs appeared normal to me, pale in the moonlight. No sign of the ravages of althaia. I looked at my left arm. The burn was gone. Gone! I felt my face. Both sides felt normal. I couldn't detect the rough ridges of the burn, although that side seemed a little tender. I flew into the house and ran to the bathroom. With eyes as big as boiled eggs, I stared at myself in the mirror.

It was a fucking miracle!

My face was whole again! More than whole. It was exquisite! This couldn't possibly be me! I was so used to seeing the hideous burn that I hardly noticed my good side. Now it was as if some ideal version of that unburned side had taken over my whole face so that even though I looked like myself, I was a stranger to my own eyes. I had become one of those boys I used to pine after in the zines - a mix of masculine angularity and wide-eyed, full-lipped feminine softness. My skin glowed as if I'd been out in the wind, especially on the burned side. When I turned my face to the left, the only remnant of the burn was a thick, silvery scar slashed across my cheek where the bone used to be visible. It gave me a dashing look as if I'd been in a swordfight. My eyes were the same elongated almond shape with their fringe of dark lashes, but now the colour had intensified from hazel to a brilliant emerald green. This couldn't be me, could it? Was I dreaming?

Thiede was right. I seriously needed a shower. I was covered in dirt and blood and my dark hair was greasy with whatever nasty stuff my body had exuded. That alone convinced me this wasn't a hallucination. I grabbed soap and a washcloth and cleaned up the worst of it. All the while, I kept turning this way and that, probing the burned side with my fingers and marvelling at how supple and smooth it felt compared to the rigid, pitted mess it had been. If only I had known, I would have sought out the Wraeththu long ago.

Then I heard Thiede's voice speaking in my head. *You can admire yourself all you want later, Janus. I have something to tell you before I depart. I can't maintain this too much longer.*

Maintain this? Now what was he talking about? I came out into the living room to see Thiede seated in the leather chair opposite Kithara.

"Enter a new har!" Thiede said flinging his arms out in a grand gesture. He winked at Kithara. "Now tell me, Kithara, that you regret this little adventure."

Kithara was staring at me, open-mouthed. "Wow," he said. "Shit, Jareth, you're, well, 'stunning' doesn't do it justice."

A tingling wave of pleasure surged through me, settling in my loins. I hadn't had the nerve to look down there yet. Wasn't sure I wanted to.

"Come have some soup, Janus," Thiede said. "Both of you need to take it easy for a while. I want you to eat and gain strength."

"Yes, mother," Kithara said.

I sat down on the couch next to Kithara, who handed me a steaming bowl of soup. Thiede cradled a wine glass in one hand, looking at us much as a sculptor might admire his latest creation. "I always enjoy watching the birth of a new har," he said. "It gets me right here." He thumped his chest with the side of his fist. A log shifted, throwing sparks.

"Tell him," Kithara said.

I looked at both their faces. Kithara's eyes flicked away guiltily. Thiede crossed his legs and settled himself. "Well, Janus, as you know, we are a new race and do not yet understand the extent and limits of our powers. We've learned a great deal, but there is so much more to know. A good strategist must know his capabilities. We must go cautiously and test, experiment. It is unfortunate but inevitable that some may get hurt in the course of this self-discovery."

"What has this got to do with me?" I asked. This sounded suspiciously like some kind of justification for atrocity. I sipped a spoonful of the soup, vegetable beef. It was the most delicious thing I'd eaten in forever. Not standing on ceremony, I tipped up the bowl and drank it down. I could feel strength flowing into my body.

Thiede tapped lacquered nails on the arm of the chair. "This is about your parents and your disfigurement, Janus. I feel that you should know the truth, even if you hate us for it. Only then can you complete the healing process. So here it is. Initially through accident and then by experimentation, we discovered that our blood could transform young men into Wraeththu. We found that it didn't work on women or older men. That knowledge came painfully. We didn't know how young we could incept a boy. We didn't know much at all. We still don't. My acolytes spent much time searching for those with potential to improve our stock. One day in a park, I saw you and your brother and sensed that you both were special with the potential to develop occult powers, so we came in the night to take you."

"My brother, Jordan? Is he alive?"

"Yes. His name is Arahal now," Thiede said. "If Kithara is my left hand, Arahal is my right." Kithara nodded at that.

I sat up suddenly. This was extraordinary news. "Can I see him?"

Thiede smiled. "If you come back to Carmine City, most

assuredly."

"And what of my parents?" I asked.

"I'm sorry, Janus. They perished in the fire."

"So, there *was* a fire?"

"Yes, not intentional on our part and it wasn't what affected you. We succeeded in capturing you along with your brother, but there was a gun battle with the police and I was hit in the arm causing blood to spray on you." He pulled up a sleeve revealing some thick white scars on his upper arm. "My blood has, shall we say, rather unusual properties. You lost consciousness. In the confusion, we thought you were dead. My error, Janus. We were outnumbered and had to run. It was only years later that I learned you had lived. Apparently, your body had begun althaia, but your system didn't absorb enough blood to complete the transformation. Instead the althaia was arrested at a preliminary stage, making it appear as if you had been burned. An interesting result and not something I would have anticipated."

"Shit," I said, stunned. Memory began to return, in terrifying bits. A tall figure pulling me along as we ran. The cracking reverberation of gunfire. A sudden splatter of liquid scorching my body. Screaming. Shadows filled with flames. Waking to hear a solemn white-coated doctor explaining that my parents were dead and that I would carry burn scars for life. I ground my teeth. "You left me for dead? But then once you found out what happened, why didn't you come and finish the process?"

Thiede shrugged. "Other priorities intervened, and in any case it would have been a risky venture. I figured we'd bide our time. Perhaps it was a good thing in the long run, although it may not appear that way to you. Like a sword, you've been tempered in the fire of adversity. You do not yet know your own strength, Janus, but I've been following your flight from the circus. You've done well. You will make a fine addition to our tribe, if you choose to join us."

"Do I have a choice?" I growled. "And why are you calling me by my stage name?"

Thiede smiled. "Our souls progress in power by choosing a path through life's thorns. Whether or not the choice is real or illusory is a philosophical issue. Does the butterfly's wingbeat change the future? For myself, I prefer to think of it as playing chess with the universe. As for your name, when we complete the transition to Wraeththu, we usually take on new names as a symbol of rebirth. In your case, the name Janus is appropriate. The reason why is something you must work out for yourself. Welcome to your new life, Janus. I expect great things from you. Now, if you'll excuse me, I've got to run. Come and share breath with me before I go."

I was in shock and couldn't think of a reason to refuse. We both stood. He took me in his arms and kissed me. His body felt like malleable iron. His breath flowed like fog into my lungs, spreading throughout my body, finishing with a crack of lightning. He shredded me.

Then, he did the same with Kithara, taking a long time about it, somewhat to my consternation. Thiede was the consummate seducer. When he was done, Kithara looked as dazed as I felt, but colour had returned to his face.

Thiede stepped away from us and said, "Now, I leave you with another question. Was I really here?" He smiled, sly as a cat. And then he winked out. It was as if his body suddenly attenuated into a thin line and then disappeared through some kind of dimensional doorway.

"Close your mouth, Janus." Kithara laughed.

"What the hell was that?"

"I've given up trying to figure out Thiede. He's a law unto himself," Kithara replied.

"He's a bastard! Tell me I'm supposed to be happy about discovering that he's responsible for my parents' death, my brother's abduction, and my horrid deformity. Healing me now is small return for all that he's put me through!"

"Yes, that's true," Kithara said unexpectedly. "I'm not too thrilled about him abandoning me to a maniac with a cattle prod and a kink for hermaphrodites either. You have to understand, he's not playing in the same sandbox as the rest of us. It's not that he doesn't care. He does, but he's... well, it's hard to explain. I love him and I hate him, but it makes no difference. He's beyond my reach. So, here's what I think. You can focus on your hatred and pain or you can move on and revel in your new body."

It made a certain amount of sense. Kithara usually did. Besides, a terrible, aching need was building inside me. I moved into his embrace, feeling him mould against me. His blood thundered in my veins. We shared breath.

"Mmmm, that's lovely," Kithara sighed. "Remember what I said about needing aruna to make permanent the changes inside you?"

Aruna. The very name seemed to call me, beckoning with cool fingers. My insides were jangling, like cats climbing over each other in anticipation of dinner. "Harish sex. Yes, of course, how could I forget that?"

"Come." He took my hand. "I'll introduce you to the gift of the Wraeththu. This will make up for all that agony. I promise."

Steaming hot water felt desperately good against my skin. The bathtub in the master bedroom was huge and fit both of us perfectly. I rested in Kithara's arms as he washed my hair. He kept leaning over, sharing breath with me. It sent shivers throughout my being, as intoxicating as a hit of choi. I wanted him to keep doing that forever, but I was nervous. A virgin in every sense.

"Don't be nervous, Janus. Here, look." His soapy hand descended, wrapped about what used to be my cock. Tiny sparks darted upward from my groin. I looked away and he laughed. "You've seen one before. That night in my trailer. God, you made me horny then. Did you know?"

"I saw yours, not mine. It's a little different. I'm rather attached to my dick the way it was. Pun intended."

He chuckled. "This is even better. Look how beautiful you are!"

I cracked an eye and stared through the wavering water at what he had captured in his hand. It was strange and wonderful, long and lean, a feathered shaft, pulsing with colours, opalescent scarlet and gold.

"Oh," I said softly.

"Yes, indeed. I want that deep inside me." He climbed into my lap and gave me that dazzling smile that had first won my heart, although I'd been too stupid to realize it at the time. Then he bent forward, taking my mouth with his. My insides writhed and purred. We rubbed against each other, sloshing water all over the floor.

"I really hope the owners of the house don't show up. This could be very awkward," I said with a laugh.

"Silly," Kithara replied between kisses. "Thiede owns this house."

"Really? I'm not even surprised. I think my wonder-circuit has blown a fuse."

"Mmm, yeah. He's been buying places around the country. Safe houses for hara to gather. It's a movement, Janus, and you're part of it now."

"What if I don't want to be part of it? What if I just want to lie here and make love to you?"

"For now, I'll accept that," he said. "You're so goddamned beautiful. I want to lick you all over." And he proceeded to do just

135

that.

"Mmm, you're making me all tingly."

"I'm going to do much more than make you tingly. Did you ever get so stoned that when you came, you thought your head would explode?"

"You are the biggest fucking tease. Please, Kithara, I..."

"Good. That's the way I want you. Nice and desperate." He stood with a rush of water, and climbed out of the tub. When I followed, he captured me in a towel, gently drying me, stopping to bite my neck, to kiss my chest. I clung to him, laughing.

"I don't know what I'm doing," I said.

"Don't worry, I do." He winked. "First some vocabulary. See that? I'm ouana right now. Strangely, so are you. You need to think differently from a human now, Janus. Embrace your female side, your soume side." He pressed his hand against me, sliding a finger deep within, and hitting something that sent a pulse of pleasure through my loins. I shivered. Slowly he pumped the finger in and out, sparking more delights, while we shared breath, drinking each other's souls, until I was shaking in anticipation. Then, he took me by the hand, led me to the bed and laid me down upon it. He climbed on top, hovering over me. "This is what it means to be Wraeththu," he whispered, and pierced me with a sudden gentle violence that wracked my whole being in a shriek of joy.

"How does that feel?" He laughed.

"God!" was all I could manage.

"That's about right," he said. "It's divine fire." He began to move, each thrust triggering a higher level of pleasure. I began to gasp. He said, "I'm going to open you up like this for a while, until you're sore and delirious, then we share breath, like this." He bent down and exhaled into my mouth. His breath danced into me, turning into a whirlwind of scarlet and ivory blossoms. I returned the patter of a rainstorm, the beauty of a panther's leap. He kept an unerring rhythm that slowly became more and more intense until I was screaming, writhing, and clawing at him. "This is what I wanted to do to you that night in my trailer," he said.

"Oh god, please Kithara, it's so, it's so..." I moaned. He paused and I thought I would lose my mind. "If you stop, I'll kill you."

He laughed softly. "Now that we've scaled the heights, we dive off the cliff."

"I'm on the brink," I panted.

"Hold on, I've got you. We'll take the plunge together."

Deep within, I felt his lion-tamer's whip snap at a nerve that sparked and exploded, the pieces flying outward like stars of sizzling crimson and gold. "Oh fuck, fuck," I cried, overwhelmed, tumbling over and over in waves of pleasure. He continued moving, playing me out. The sparks drifted to earth, sinking with soft hisses into a vast lake.

For a long time I lay stunned, floating in that lake while the air filled with sparkling crystals, thrumming in my ears like tiny gongs. It was better than any choi-induced hallucination and I wondered: had I really died last night lying on a bloody shower curtain and was I now in heaven, healed and whole, with the lover of my dreams? What price must I pay for this? His thoughts were mine, his warmth pervading the air all around me. *Indeed your old self has died*, he hummed, *that is the price. You are reborn now, better, stronger. You are Wraeththu.*

I am Wraeththu.

Kithara rolled off me, pressing against my side, purring like a cat. I finally found my voice. "I can't imagine that sex as a human would have been anything close to that."

"Trust me, it's not," Kithara said. He kissed my shoulder. "That was sizzling hot. You're a natural talent. The first time is like going to the fair and taking a really scary wild ride. Nothing quite beats it, but I've found every time is unique and just as wonderful. Something to look forward to, huh?" He sat up, punched a pillow, and stuck it behind his head. "My shoulder still hurts and I really want a fuckin' cigarette right now."

"Are you unusually good at that? Aruna, I mean? Because it was just... wow."

He grinned at me. "Yeah, I am. Lucky you."

"What was Thiede saying about a massive ego?"

He hit me with the pillow. We laughed and wrestled for a while until I had him pinned and was staring into those electric blue eyes. He relaxed, unresisting, inviting, and began flexing his hips against mine. Looking at his just-tumbled beauty, lips kiss-swollen, a ruddy glow painting his cheeks, wild, platinum-coloured hair cascading about his shoulders, I wanted to pull him inside me and never let go. "Kithara, I need to ask you something."

"I'm not stopping you."

"Did you mean it back in your trailer when you said you thought I was beautiful, even though I was burned? Or was that just part of Thiede's master plan to turn me har?"

He reached up, stroked a finger along the scar on my cheek, the reminder of my past. "Yes and yes. When I first saw you, it was like seeing a glorious rose hit by an untimely blight. I could see your pain and your beauty; both called to me. I had the distinct feeling that we were destined to become lovers."

"And you didn't tell me?"

"Do you think you would have received the news well, at the time?" He chuckled. His finger drifted across my mouth.

I laughed. "Probably not, but when I met you, I also sensed that the cosmic dice were rolling."

"I told you that you are gifted. Thiede knew it long ago," he said.

"Now what, Kithara? Do we go back to Carmine City? I don't know if I want to join a gang of mutants wrecking havoc everywhere."

His hand moved down my arm, caressing. "Don't think about it now. Give the transformation time. All we need to do right now is make love to each other. Speaking of which," he slapped my rear playfully, "your turn to be ouana."

"Ouana? So, how do I make it...?"

"That's easy. Relax and it'll happen." He continued rocking his hips under me creating a gentle friction until the throbbing between my legs unfurled into a crimson sword.

"Payback time," I said, and he laughed.

Fumbling at first, I found what I sought and thrust. He yelped, arching his back, eyes rolling upward. I paused a moment, wondering if I'd hurt him. Our eyes met and he chewed his lower lip, panting gently. "Take me," he said.

Oh god! I took him hard, feeling a crackling storm of sensation throughout my being, like nothing I'd ever felt before. A purging fire. We breathed in each other's light, entangling our souls, which glowed and expanded to fill the universe.

In the end, he thoroughly converted me. If we are what we hate, we are what we love even more. In the shelter of his passion, I arose like a phoenix from the ashes of my former self and became beautiful and terrifying. I am Janus, god of doorways and beginnings, standing at the threshold of history, eying a painful past and a stormy future. Whatever comes, I am content, knowing that I had this perfect time with him in my arms. A week we stayed at *Tranquility Base*, drunk on aruna, until Thiede summoned us, and like good soldiers, we came.

Now, dressed in black leather, I ride, pressed behind Kithara on our bike, my arms wrapped about his waist, our hair mingling black and white in the wind of our speed – burning into the future.

Building Immanion

Martina Luise Pachali

 # Building
Immanion

Things are bright now, mostly, and we look hopefully into the future. Stories have happy endings, and the lost come home at last. But my home is lost forever now, and I can never go back there. Never. Because it's called Immanion these days.

You didn't think they put Immanion on top of some rundown human tourist resort, did you? Or on an empty promontory with no meaning? No, they built it on the site of one of humanity's old holy places, where one religion had replaced the other for millennia. The very rocks were steeped in aeons of belief.

And I'm one of the last humans ever to live and pray there, one of the very few yet young enough to be incepted into Wraeththu when they came and took over. I'm Yannis, which is the name my mother called me by. I had so many mystical and meaningful names given to me at the mystical and meaningful changes imposed on me throughout my life, I didn't really know who I was any more at some stage, so that's why I went back to my oldest, shortest and least holy name. I've had it with holiness.

My people were farmers and fishermen on the coast of what now is Almagabra, and I grew up with my siblings and cousins in the wild surf, helping with the boats and the harvest when called upon, but otherwise left to our own devices, as the children of our family had been since time out of mind. You see, my mother and her sisters were among the few women still fertile after all the evil things that had been done to the sea and the earth by humanity. They fairly revelled in pregnancies: the world must be peopled, and if necessary, by them alone, so it seemed.

But when one more of the endless tidal waves of war and catastrophe swept towards us, my mother and her sisters decided to send her youngest sons to safety to live with our uncles and cousins who were monks on the holy mountain.

You know, my family had always been very fertile, and in addition to our farms and fishing boats, we had always had that little monastery in the holy place where the younger sons that were a bit bookish and didn't stand to inherit much were encouraged to go. Seven of us, brothers and cousins, were sent there when the new wave of aeroplanes came and took pot-shots at our boats. I was nine at the time.

It was a long, arduous trek through a war-torn, maddened country that finally brought us there, under the guidance of my third-eldest brother who'd have been old enough to fight, but whose eyesight was so poor he'd be a danger to his own side in any fight without his bottle-bottom glasses. When we came to the holy place, there weren't many holy men left, either. In old monasteries built for hundreds, a few dozen old men were rattling about. In glorious churches decked with gold the falling leaves of every year were piling up, nobody being left to clear them away, or even to care.

Our uncles and cousins, however, were busier than ever before, being forced to provide for themselves entirely now no more pilgrims came. Even the much-disputed logging expeditions into the virgin forests of the holy wilderness were a thing of the past now, as nobody was left in the outside world to buy the wood. So, we were welcomed, we were made novices, given new names and put to work.

I didn't mind, really. I didn't mind baking and fetching and sweeping, getting up early and praying for hours, mixing the paint for those of my uncles who still painted holy pictures although they would be bought by no-one. This was safety, my mother had said. This was the holy place. No evil could touch us here. This place belonged to our god and his saints since time out of mind, and our god and his saints would protect us. No evil did come, but never would we have thought that we'd be swept away by the good, the holy of another flavour than ours had been.

You see, there had been rumours of a new and dangerous cult, utterly heathen, that took the young men in the lands to the west of the ocean and made them into less or more than men – depending on where you stood. And then there had been panicked whispers that the cult was coming over into our own lands, to the old places that had thought themselves immune to such folly as was spawned over there from time to time – really, at first Wraeththu was to us just one more of the many idiocies from over the sea. But of course, we, being firm in the practice of our faith, wouldn't succumb to such silly new beliefs.

While I grew up, news of the outside world grew scarcer and scarcer. We went through the year as always, we suffered through each Lent and celebrated each Easter, while outside humans were dying, and we didn't know. We were looking out at a sea that was always the same. And then, after a few years, my uncles and cousins thought I was old enough to be made a full monk, and the one who was a priest did a ceremony for me, and I was given yet another new name, and everyone started using it right away, only I wasn't sure who I was any more.

You know, I was in a difficult age anyway, and what with sex being utterly forbidden on account of us being monks, and all I ever got to see being scruffy uncles and cousins and brothers anyway, and a general application of lots of very cold spring water, I was very much at a loss about what to do with myself at that time. It was spring, shortly after Easter, and we were all nervous in the spring each year in any case, and now being called by another name didn't help at all. The cold water didn't help either, and I was very dissatisfied with myself and the world around me. The familiarity of the place and the unchanging sameness of the rituals we did and the pictures we painted (I was allowed to paint now as well, but I was never very good at it) were the only things that helped.

Then one day, a fellow monk arrived from a neighbouring monastery to exchange olives for our bread. He said that the wall had been torn down and some very strange strangers had come and were doing things to places. They'd made themselves at home in one of the largest and most abandoned holy settlements, and there they practised the most heathen and utterly unholy rites. There were even women among them, the monk whispered, although with them you could never tell if they were men or women. By the Holy Mother, our visitor concluded, you couldn't even tell if they had souls at all. We were well off here on our coast, what with them being far away and certainly not interested in this rocky wilderness.

Three days later, they came.

There was a large group of them, improbably on horseback, sauntering along paths that even our mules refused to negotiate. They were unarmed, and in a brisk, working mood. They came with notepads and pencils and measuring tape and pendulums and looked at our monastery as if they would buy it.

You really couldn't tell whether they were men, women, or human at all, as the old monk had said. They were clad in shiny metal and gleaming leathers, their long hair was mostly bleached to shimmering paleness, even if some of their faces were dark, and they had no beards at all. Their horses where lithe and more beautiful than anything I'd ever seen.

They stopped in front of our home, and we huddled inside, just me and one of my cousins peering out through the windows. Their ranks opened, and some of them fanned out with their measuring implements, ordered by those in the centre. As they spread out, these leaders came to view: deathly beautiful both of them, one of them with an abundance of tawny hair, the other one with a flaming red mane. They were discussing the lay of the land with those around them. I heard one of them calling: "See if you can get a clear view from the boathouse to the peak, Vadriel!" And I realised by the clear voice that shouted that this must be a woman.

I was enraged. Before I could even think, I threw open our door and pelted down the path towards them. My uncles and cousins and brothers called for me to stop but I didn't react – in my anger, I didn't recognise the name they shouted as my own, new monastic name. It didn't touch me the way your own name always does.

"Women are strictly forbidden!", I shrieked at them, slithering to a halt before their mighty horses on the loose, dry earth.

The red-headed one smiled at me with condescension. "Exactly what I'm always saying, little monklet", he drawled at me.

"Remember him, Orien", he said to his companion. "That one is young enough to incept. Now, what if we build the stairs to the right of that boulder, and have a ramp coming down the middle instead?"

I stood there, forgotten, my fate decided for me once more, although I didn't have the slightest idea at the time.

They went away eventually, and I was severely scolded. And then, nothing happened for quite some time, apart from some monkish neighbours coming by and telling us how the Gelaming had started building all over the place. These strangers, it seemed, called themselves Wraeththu and Hara and Gelaming, and we didn't really comprehend what all those names were supposed to mean. But then, among us names were variable and manifold, so we didn't really bother with what those strangers were calling themselves from one day to the other. We prayed at night, we worked all day. We were content and safe – yet.

At the height of the summer, on a day that was so unbearable that we were all hiding inside, wearing as little as possible (within the monkishly decent, of course), one of the strangers came back. It was the one called Vadriel, the one who had been down at the boathouse the last time. I recognised him by the pale blue streaks he'd dyed into his silvery hair. His hair was living moonlight, and I felt very ugly, scruffy and doltish when I went out to greet him with a tray of coffee, water, and sweets. You see, the general consensus among us remaining monks by now was to treat the strangers as neighbours or pilgrims and hope they'd leave us in peace.

Vadriel jumped off his horse, politely took my offerings, not even flinching at the dubious sweets, and then told me his name. I hesitated a moment before I told him mine as I wasn't sure which one would be right for him – in the end, it didn't matter.

"Well, Makari," he said, "would you introduce me to your fellow monks here? I've got something to tell you."

I asked him inside then, and all my uncles and cousins and brothers came out from their cells, having made themselves decent with black robes hastily thrown over sweating, t-shirt-clad bodies. My great-uncle Chrysostom who was considered leader of our little groups had even bothered to put on a high ceremonial hat.

Vadriel wasn't impressed; of course, he'd seen so much ceremony and power among his fellow Gelaming, a few hardly dignified monks from a dying, outdated religion didn't impress him at all. He looked all over us and then told us, quite matter-of-factly, that we'd have to leave. The Gelaming were going to construct the most splendid harbour here.

"Of course, we're not throwing anybody out. We're not that kind of hara. In fact, we've made the old place you call St. Johns habitable for you. It's the perfect size for all you remaining monks to live together and end your days in peace, quiet and contemplation. We do not wish to harm you. Although you're very much a thing of the past, we will protect you and provide for you, enjoy the diversity of your old-fashioned faith and respect you as a link to the powerful past of this holy place, which is now sacred to Wraeththukind as well."

My great-uncle made to protest.

"I am called Father Chrysostom, young man, and I can tell you that it's impossible…"

"I am not a man", Vadriel interrupted coldly. "We have put the age of men behind us."

My, but he was a sanctimonious little Gelaming limshit, don't you think? However, I was very much taken by him at the time. Vadriel the architect, Vadriel the planner, Vadriel who made everything new. Oh, my.

"Our way of life is different from that of our brethren in the next monastery, and theirs..." Chrysostom began again.

"You'll find a way, I don't doubt that. You'll work it all out; after all, you're all men of God", Vadriel cut him short. "You have until your feast of Christmas, which we call the solstice festival, to leave here and get to St. John's. Harvest everything, take down everything and take it with you, there's enough room at St. John's for you to put up your own place of worship and all. But after Festival, we'll need to start building here, so you really have to sort everything out until then; there'll be no going back afterwards."

With that, he grabbed another sweet off the tray, scattering loose sugar all down the front of his black leathers, winked at me, and was gone.

All our neighbours, we soon learned, had got the same summons, and when winter approached and all our harvesting was done, we moved to St. John's – what else could we do? However, losing our home wasn't the most important problem to Great-Uncle Chrysostom and the other uncles, but losing our independence, our way of doing things after our own methods, that would doubtlessly come into question when we'd be forced to live communally with all the other monks, hermits and holy men left at the sacred place.

It was not to be my problem, though. We brought our last mule-load of holy paintings to St. John's a week before Christmas, and Vadriel, who was responsible for building the harbour as we'd learned by now, came by to make sure we were settled in and had everything we needed. He wouldn't mar his great work with the grief and curses of the former inhabitants, of course. So he brought us whatever we wanted to make us comfortable, and one day when Chrysostom was arguing with the other elders at St. John's (and there were very many elders at St. John's, and each of them had a slightly different opinion on how things should be done), Vadriel actually interfered and told everyone he and his masters weren't going to stand for even one voice in the diversity of our holy practices to be silenced, and he personally would see to it that the Chrysostom people got to live according to their own rules. And then he said he was going to take the seventeen youngest members of the community with him for them to be incepted into Wraeththu as to provide a bridge, a living link between the old and the new inhabitants of this very, very holy place.

Of these seventeen, four came from the small place of Chrysostom's people. And of these four, I was one. My uncles lamented the decision, and Chrysostom himself went to the church to pray, refusing even to say goodbye to us. But most of us followed willingly. We were good little monks, and did what we were told.

We were ordered to get our stuff together at once and go with Vadriel; we went with him over the wintry mountain to the old place that was now the Gelaming's provisional headquarters, all the ghosts driven out, and music and strange scents drifting through the old, bare hallways.

We were given cells, we were sent to the baths and had our hair cut to a uniform length, and we were issued new clothes – all very monastic, really. Some of the Gelaming did some ceremony to welcome us, all very heathen but still strangely familiar, and we got to meet the boss of the whole endeavour, the har called Orien whom we'd seen that first day at our monastery. He gave us a speech about how important we would be, and how he hoped we'd learn quickly and fully understand the privilege and opportunity we were granted by the wisdom of the Gelaming.

We were given herbal teas to drink, we were given thorough lectures about what it would mean for us to become hara (with the physical part not very well fleshed out, though; there was an overawing sense of mystery that remained throughout the lessons), we were made to fast and sent to bed early for a week. We were monks, so none of this felt very strange to us. In fact, it was almost as if the Gelaming were just another mystic order that had taken over the old holy places.

With one immense difference. Well, never mind the music and the alcohol, the scents and the vanity among these refined and stylish beings; in their heart of hearts they were an order charged with a holy mission. But as I discovered the third night I was there, the place was awash with sex when we didn't look.

We were kept apart in an annex that had bare and clean cells, and the Gelaming had sprawled to live and work everywhere else, but on that night curiosity got the better of me, and I went to investigate, and I found them at it everywhere, even in the church, where three of them were doing something that involved a stream of clear light that looked holy beyond doubt. I was extremely repulsed and incredibly aroused at the same time, and I settled down to do some thorough peeping, my hand between my legs, when Vadriel grabbed me from behind and turned me around.

"This is not yet for you, little monklet Makari," he said, using the silly moniker his boss had coined for me that first day.

"You wait just a few more nights, and then it shall all be yours. You just wait."

His eyes that I knew to be as pale blue as the streaks in his hair by day bored into mine, now shining silver in the eerie light from the ceremony. He took me by my chin, and then he kissed me, deeply, on the mouth.

I had never been kissed before, but it seemed to me that beyond the kiss I could taste something more, something holy, Gelaming-style. Vadriel was cool and clear, his taste inexplicably sweet – I wanted to sink into his arms there and then. I collapsed against him, and delicious, unknown shudders wracked my whole body.

I regained my senses, burrowed against Vadriel's hard chest, and felt thoroughly ashamed of myself – I knew what I'd just done, although only by hearsay. Vadriel seemed amused. He kissed me again, sweetly, and showed me a pale amber light that had, inexplicably, formed into a perfect little ball on the palm of his hand. Tenderly, he blew it away to join the gigantic stream of light those three hara in the church were raising. All the holy pictures, I could see now, were gone, and all the walls and vaulted ceilings were painted a brilliant silver.

At the end of this week, we were incepted. Orien did it, the boss, who seemed to be their top priest as well, some sort of a harish bishop or metropolitan. Everyone was gathered in the former church; it was midnight, and there were seventeen of us, purged and scrubbed, in white robes. We were made to kneel down, we were given some holy substance to drink. Hara came and shaved off our hair at the sides of our heads. Hara sang and shouted ecstatically, and then Orien came forth from nowhere. He went to the first of us, my youngest brother; he had a knife suddenly, and he cut his own arm, and then my brother's arm. He pressed them together, the blood mingling, and then my brother collapsed into the arms of the hara hovering around him, and was carried away over the heads of the assembly, with the utmost reverence, like a holy object. So Orien went down the line of us.

I was last, and I was growing nervous as one after the other of my companions was carried away to his new destiny. I looked around the church for Vadriel, but he was nowhere to be found among those throngs of ecstatically chanting Gelaming. Then it was finally my turn, and I knew no more.

Of the seventeen of us, four didn't make it. They'd all been physically young enough, Orien explained to us survivors later, but they'd probably been too set in their monkish ways already for their minds to submit to the change. All four from my family made it, though.

I don't want to bore you with another Althaia-and-Feybraiha-story; you all know what happened to me in those nights. And you probably guessed that it was Vadriel who came for me after the pains had stopped, and how he took me all the way now, and how he was sweet beyond words.

We were taught many things, and some of them even by Orien himself, and some of them we'd already learned as monks, but we listened politely. The thing about the sex, which they called aruna, of course, was utterly different; we were encouraged to participate in anything that took our fancy. The only thing that took my fancy was Vadriel, but he gently discouraged me. The way of the Wraeththu, he told me sweetly when I came back for more on the second night, was not the way of humankind; we weren't clinging or possessive, and I was to get as much experience as I could. Did I tell you he was sanctimonious? So I turned away from him, disappointed but determined to acquit myself as was expected of me, and I went after anyone who wasn't on the trees by the count of three, so I could return to Vadriel and brag about it, and he'd take me back into his bed after I'd assured him what a worldly har I'd become. It worked every time, and there were many, many times during that winter.

And of course we were given new names; this was the fourth one in my young life, and I can hardly remember it nowadays. It was something long and convoluted, ending on "–iel", of course, Arconiel or Arcadiel, I honestly don't remember which. I was shortened to Arc soon enough, and Vadriel secretly still called me Makari in bed, and I didn't have the heart to tell him that even that hadn't been my name for long.

In the spring, all thirteen of us had our caste raised to Neoma, and we were put to work. We were to return to St. John's and tell our former brethren there of what the hara really were, and get them to tell us as much about the land around the holy places, of rocks and waters and groves, as they possibly knew; their traditions, Vadriel told me, would be invaluable for building the new city of the Gelaming, but they probably wouldn't tell outsiders, hence us with a foot in both worlds.

When I came to St. John's, I learned that Chrysostom had died during the winter, and the others from my family monastery had been absorbed into the communal life. Only my extremely myopic brother was still painting icons full-time, and he did it with incredible diligence and love, tiny icons with the most precise details he couldn't possibly see, but incredibly did.

Our uncles and cousins and brothers took us back, only marvelling in passing what had become of us; we were of the Chrysostom people first and foremost, and then we were hara, which to them was just another passing state. We lived on our own at the fringes of the community, falling in with our relatives when we had questions to ask or new knowledge to contribute, but for most of the others, things weren't so easy. Mind you, nobody ever asked for the four that were lost; monkish lives had been ephemeral and fleeting since time out of mind. But these nine ex-monks had become something alien and slightly repulsive to their former brethren; the Gelaming were just heathens, but these were renegades, and as time told on them, they were told nothing more, and one after the other drifted back to Phaonica, as the headquarters were known by now. Only the four of us were still wandering back and forth, singing and praying with the monks, and taking aruna with the Gelaming, as we wended our way between the two worlds.

But we were only hara, after all, and one night my myopic brother caught Vadriel and me making love.

We were really making love by then, all experience-gathering pretext almost forgotten, tenderly, trustingly, with deep feeling. We never dared call it love aloud, but it was.

My brother knew I'd changed beyond his imagination, but the moonlight concealed nothing, and he did wear his glasses, the poor silly thing, and he was honestly disgusted. He couldn't believe that I'd changed so much with just a little prodding from a drop of Orien's powerful blood, he believed the Gelaming had cut and sliced me and added bits, and he was sick on the spot, and wouldn't talk to any of us afterwards.

All thirteen of us were given new things to do now, and we'd mostly become Gelaming fair and square now.

Not I, and the reason for that was as follows.

Vadriel was building a harbour, right? At the site of our former monastery, remember? And I was at it with him, witnessing the destruction of my own home day to day, and it hurt me, but I kept quiet for Vadriel's sake. And he needed me for his work, too, relying on my knowledge of the place that was extensive, young as I was. I knew where the rock was brittle and where it was stable; I knew my way around and I could tell when the shortest way wasn't the fastest. So we built into the living rocks of my former home the beautiful harbour of Immanion, as those of you who have been there know it today.

Well, almost.

When the summer was over and autumn came, Orien came to inspect our work, and he brought with him the red-headed har who'd been there that first day, and that august individual was not content. He was sketching into the air with his long fingers, showing Orien and Vadriel how he wanted things straighter, more sweeping, less clinging to the land, more leading to the sky. I couldn't hear them; I hung back with all the others who'd worked at the project, looking worriedly at the hara sitting on their horses in the centre. He criticised for the better part of an hour, and then, while Orien and he passed on to inspect the next project, we builders sat dejectedly at the trestle tables we'd set up for the feast, unable to take even a single bite.

And then we went away to the former monk farm where we'd made our temporary home while we were working at the harbour, and there we slouched about, and got drunk, and fell into bed at some stage with nobody in particular.

So I missed my last night with Vadriel.

Because, the next morning when we returned to our building site to try and find out how we could rectify the faults our masters had found with our work, it was all done. Overnight, the rock had hardened in places where there'd only ever been shale, and stairs that had been curved and humble had become sweeping and grand, and quays that had been sturdy and natural had become straight and jutting. There was nothing left for us to do. Nothing at all, it was all finished and over with.

Vadriel, far from taking exception at this, was humbled. Those mighty Nahir-Nuri had done in a night what he couldn't accomplish in a summer, and they'd showed him how small his faith had been and how far he'd strayed from the path of the Gelaming – he stealthily looked at me when he said that. And then he rode off, without even kissing me goodbye, to go and beg those masters to permit him to learn at their feet.

I did tell you he had a streak of extreme sanctimony to him, didn't I?

He later built temples and towers for the Gelaming all over the world, but I never saw him again.

For the first time in my life, I was totally at loose ends, with nobody to tell me what to do, and nobody needing me for anything. The monks lived their secluded lives at St. Johns, and they actually do so still for all that I hear: a few confused elders and some sturdy middle-aged brothers, in a secret and forbidden park somewhere in shining Immanion, hidden from all eyes, hidden from a world that has changed beyond their recognition. I have never been back.

And the Gelaming were no longer interested in me; I was totally welcome to work and play with them, take aruna with whoever and contribute my share, build myself a home and perhaps find a partner, raise my caste and have some pearls as the years went by. I could have trained for the military, if I had wanted to; I could have trained in the new disciplines of Grissecon or made beautiful things by hand. But I was just a builder, hanging on to see the former wilderness of my home transform to shining Immanion as we know it today, and feeling thoroughly cheated.

I had sacrificed all that had been asked of me, like the good little monk I still was at heart. I had sacrificed myself first and foremost, then my home, destroying it with my own hands to build something new and infinitely more splendid, but that had been found lacking and summarily corrected. I had first sacrificed my family to be with my chesnari, and then I had to give him up so he was able to grow to his full potential (as he saw it, the sanctimonious little sod), and I was sacrificing myself every day to the new city, and every night my body to the ideals of the Gelaming community; every night my body was a holy vessel for the power of Wraeththukind, but my heart was empty and ashes, and shortly before the shimmering city was completed, the night before the inauguration of the building called Hegalion, when everyone was celebrating and taking aruna all over the place, I slunk away, a tiny blot of unhappiness removing himself from its brilliant face.

Specimen 16

Andy Bigwood

Specimen 16

*I looked at the blood pooling in my left hand and the ornate knife that I held in
my right, beautiful blood, ruby red, full of promise and chaos. My gift...*
   'Sixteen....' said an eager voice.

I gasped in pain as the inevitable migraine took hold; instinctively
cradling my hand against my chest so that they couldn't see.

"You ok back there, kid?" asked Joe, the paramedic in the
passenger seat, peering through the glass partition that separated us.

"I'm fine" I lied, waiting until the paramedic had turned back
around before checking my left hand.

The thin cut-shaped rash was already fading away, as I'd
expected. I'd had that particular dream before, and the imaginary
wound never lasted long.

I'd gone to the doctor a few days ago to get aspirin for the
headaches. I'd been careful *not* to tell him about hearing voices or
dreaming about knives and self-harm. I hadn't expected an
ambulance and a trip to a medical research centre

*Running through the trees, barefoot amongst the pine-needles, young branches
whipping at my legs and arms. Nothing could catch us, nothing.*

I tasted blood; I'd bitten the edge of my tongue this time. A
second dream so quickly after the last one was unusual; normally I'd
go for at least a couple of weeks without anything.

The Sign at the hospital said:

The Calcutt Institute -
Dwelling on the Beach of Eternity's Shore

I had no idea what the second line meant. It sounded like pretentious
twaddle to me.

By contrast to decrepit Pittsburgh, the Institute was clearly designed for the executive elite; it was way beyond even my Dad's pay-grade. It looked as if it had been transplanted stone by stone from Europe. As I clambered out of the ambulance, I wondered what the fuck I'd gotten myself into.

"James Conway?" asked a beautiful voice behind me.

I turned to see that the voice's owner was at least as attractive as her voice had been. Judging by the business dress, my guess was that I was looking at some high-up's Personal Assistant.

"Uh, yes, that's me, Miss...?"

"*Ms.* Jenson" she replied, emphasis on the '*mzz*', "If you'll follow me please, Doctor Calcutt is expecting you."

The doctor sat behind a large desk, a predator with steel grey hair, studying a folder full of hardcopy. After what seemed like hours, he closed the folder and examined me with piercing blue eyes.

"It says here that you have headaches..." He paused, waiting for a reply. "...I'm not interested in headaches" he continued, dumping one of the folders in his waste bin. "What I need are employees who fulfil certain very specific criteria. He paused, looking up my name. "James..."

A job offer? I hadn't even graduated yet and I 'knew' I wouldn't be winning any academic awards. That said, I had the distinct feeling that saying 'I don't want this job' might easily be interpreted as 'I don't want *any* job *ever*'.

"Uh, thank you doctor, uh sir. Um, what's involved exactly?"

"I'm afraid I can't go into specifics until you've signed the contract; intellectual rights you understand" Calcutt explained, pulling a sheaf of papers from a drawer and sliding them across the desk along with an uncapped fountain pen. His expression was unreadable, rather like a poker player who's just flopped a pair of kings.

I picked up the contract, fully intending to read it closely, looking for the inevitable loophole.

Employee: Mr./Mrs./Ms. __of __ (heretofore referred to as Medical Specimen:16) shall act as....

Sixteen... Sixteen... Sixteen

The number echoed in my head and something seemed to go 'thunk' in there, sort of an archetypal version of déjà vu.

Looking down, I found that I'd already signed, without

consciously doing so... and I hadn't even finished reading page one yet.

I passed the contract back, trying my best to look competent.

And that was that, I was doomed.

My apartment (Room No. 16) wasn't exactly large, but for someone who'd lived at home for all seventeen years of his life, it looked magnificent. The wardrobe contained several sets of gym clothes, each with my number in large red letters. I expected to have another of my 'dreams' that night, something about semi-clad primitives drawing intricate pentagrams, and calling upon deep powers, but instead, I slept like a babe and awoke feeling ready for anything.

The rest of the numbered specimens were waiting for me at breakfast.

"Finally woke up, huh, Sixteen?" said the nearest guy, arms folded across his muscular chest. "I'm Eleven. These here are Twelve, Fifteen, Fourteen and lucky Miss Thirteen there on the end."

"Go screw yourself, Paul" snapped the girl. "He's Paul, that's Calvin, Jeaki, he's Korean, and Salil from Saudi"

"I'm Sixteen." I replied. "I mean uh James... I'm James"

Slipping into my seat, I took my first swig of orange juice and set about finding out what exactly I was supposed to do for my pay. It turned out that none of us knew exactly what we were here for. The others had all arrived in the last few days, but hadn't been given any duties as such.

Just as I was finishing my food, a man in a doctor's coat walked in briskly, looking overly tall and a bit too thin. Introducing himself as Dr Blake, he instructed us to follow him. I instinctively took a dislike to Blake; something about him set me on edge.

Blake guided us to a sub-basement level that, if anything, seemed even bigger than the mansion above. We were taken to a room that was like a gym, but with loads of extra monitoring stuff. Three further doctors were waiting for us.

"Good morning" said a fat one. "I am Dr Gupta; this is Dr Hart, and on the end Dr Clarke. I am certain that you are wondering why you have been selected." We all nodded, or made noises of agreement. "You have noticed all, I am sure," continued Gupta, "that the number of lethal diseases has been escalating exponentially over the last decade or so... what the media call terrorist 'bio-weapons'" His speech was formal, as if he was briefing a CEO.

Suddenly this was serious and I'm sure I wasn't the only one wondering how deep in the shit I'd just fallen. I wish I'd read that contract.

"The truth is that there are no bioweapons," Gupta said. "They don't exist. What is happening is that the human genome itself is changing. Immune response failure is the most obvious symptom. More importantly, fertility levels have dropped off a cliff. Babies are still being born, true, but almost all are severely premature and need incubator care. Looked at from an evolutionary viewpoint, we are already technically extinct.

We all shifted uncomfortably in our seats.

Gupta smiled. "Fortunately, there's still hope. Every teenager in our Education Program was tested for genetic markers and certain other telltales. You six, I am happy to say, are all significantly healthier than the average and not suffering from any infertility issues that we can detect. We propose to test you in detail, both physically and mentally. Our intention is to identify the specific gene sequence that makes you special. Once we have that, we can create an aggressive gene therapy and tackle B.I.I.D.S. head on."

"Bids?" I asked

"Bigger Infertility and Immune Deficiency Syndrome - B.I.I.D.S."

I glanced at the other 'volunteers' and then back at Dr Gupta. "Given the stakes, I guess the only question is 'when do we start?"

For the next five days we were physically tested, mostly under Dr Clarke's supervision.

On the sixth day (a Sunday), Dr Blake stuck bio-monitor pads all over us and cheerfully announced that we were free for the rest of the day. The other specimens headed out like school kids released early, apart from Sarah who hung back waiting for me.

"Now that we're alone," she said, "I need to ask you something."

"Sure, what's bugging you?"

Sarah paused and looked me directly in the eye "What are you hiding, Sixteen? Why do you fear the researchers?"

I looked back at her, trying to gauge how much to say, whether I should laugh it off, say nothing, or tell all.

"I dream, Sarah," I replied, kind of surprising myself that I was opening up to her, "and sometimes those dreams are utterly alien, like I'm still 'me' but my reactions to the things I see are, like, way wrong. I'm worried that they'll think I'm unstable and kick me out."

"I did some poking around the other day," Sarah confessed,

changing topic abruptly. "Our medical records make interesting reading; particularly the section on paranormal ability. Each of us has an entry. Paul for instance is listed as a 'short range clairvoyant', and I'm listed with a talent for 'truth divination'."

"Weird. Do you really have superpowers?"

"I just know when people are lying to me. I'd call that a curse not a talent, trust me. Want to know what yours said?"

"Me?" I asked

"It said 'subconscious precognition' I figure they must think those dreams of yours are significant."

"Holy crap! What about the others?"

"Just 'further evaluation required'."

"I see. Have you asked Paul about this clairvoyant business?"

"No. I wanted to talk to you first. Paul's a bit…" her voice trailed off

I nodded despite myself. Paul tended to be a jerk. My mind was still spinning. If Calcutt and Gupta already knew…?

"Do you think they're right about your dreams?" asked Sarah

I shrugged "I don't see how they can be. It's more like seeing glimpses of life on a different planet… one with magic and all the people are like these weird elves, but without the pointy ears. You might just be good at spotting lies, and my dreams are probably just intensely weird dreams. Let's go ask the others and see what they think."

"….and that's basically what the med-records say" I concluded, "So fess up, any of you got talent?"

Telepathy said a very faint whisper in my head.

We all looked at Jeaki, whose face appeared to have drained of colour.

"It takes considerable effort" he replied, leaning against the wire fence for support. "My sensei believed that this ability drains my 'chi', my soul energy. He recommended that I should not use this gift frequently."

"Is the fertility thing just bullshit?" asked Salil suspiciously

"No," Sarah replied firmly "I was focusing on Gupta; he was telling the truth."

"So what do we do 'bout this, then?" asked Calvin

"Nothing" I said. "We're getting paid and fed. That's all that counts these days."

I figure they had us bugged. The next day there was no more physical testing. Instead, we were asked to perform the sort of psionic testing you see on bad science fiction shows. Dr Blake explained that it was almost like a new stage of evolution; good fertility, health and odd mental abilities seemed linked. Paul made a bad joke about X-Men. No one laughed.

"Blake's not telling the whole story." Sarah told us later

"His mind is not on us" added Jeaki "He is anticipating something."

Upon entering the cafeteria I was surprised to see it crowded, instead of the usual near-empty. Five of the tables were filled with tough-looking men wearing the black uniform of Citadel Garde Securitae, the CGS. These were the guys you called in when you expected terrorists for dinner, or had one in a cell that you didn't want to get loose. My vision seemed to tunnel in on the muscular CGS man on the far table, I'd seen him before.

Dead sightless eyes looking up at me. I kicked the corpse anyway. Scum.

Feeling deeply sick, I ran from the room and proceeded to throw up in the restroom sink. It wasn't that I'd just seen a dead man walking, it was the lethal hatred the dream-me had had for the *alien* on the floor.

Heading back to the psionics lab, I was about to turn the corner when I heard two familiar voices arguing.

"It's not ethical!" hissed Clarke

I slowed my pace, and then stopped entirely. I'm a sucker for good gossip.

"We're becoming extinct, David. We don't have time to pussyfoot around anymore." replied Hart "The fastest way to get the data we need is to use Six and go straight to live tests; that's what I've recommended to Calcutt."

"Calcutt? Jesus Christ, Jon. What if you get it wrong?"

"I'm not wrong. Besides, it won't be that fast-acting; we can flush it with a full blood replacement."

"It's bad science and I won't be a part of it. You don't know the dosage; you don't even have a defined outcome. As a friend, Jon..."

"Nonsense; if a bunch of streetscum can synthesise it, it's hardly rocket science. Besides, once we know how the Wraeththu's designer drug transcribes, we will have the perfect delivery system for Gupta's DIIPS Antidote."

Back down the corridor, the elevator door dinged and a CGS

trooper emerged. Hastily I resumed my walk to the lab. As I came into sight, the two doctors glanced at me and clammed up, clearly waiting for me to pass.

I wish I'd paid closer attention to the science stuff, but right then mention of a 'Six', presumably a Specimen Six, was all that interested me.

"So, who's this Specimen Six guy, then? Can we meet him?" I asked as soon as I got to the lab

"Who told you about Six?" snapped Dr Blake

"Dr Clarke and Dr Hart were arguing about him in the Corridor." I shrugged

"How come we ain't met this guy, then?" asked Calvin

"It was felt that he'd be a disruptive influence. We thought that it would be better if you settled in before you met him." explained Blake.

"Disruptive? I don't understand"

"Let's just leave it at that for now. You guys take a break. I have to speak to Dr Calcutt about this."

As soon as Black had left, I turned to the others, who looked as bemused as I did.

Sarah shook her head before I could ask.

In fact it was closer to an hour and a half before Dr Blake returned; looking stony faced. "Director Calcutt wishes to observe your interaction with Six over the security monitor," he said. "Follow me. I'll take you down now."

Blake ushered us down a level past several CGS checkpoints and into a room, where three walls were made of metal and the fourth what appeared to be one-way glass. The only furniture in there was a single chair.

Beyond the glass, we could see another room, where a teenager sat cross-legged in a meditative pose, his beautiful face serene. He'd clearly been given a uniform identical to the one I was wearing. The difference was that he'd ripped the garment to shreds, creating a sort of loincloth and long thin strips of fabric that he'd tied around his wrists and biceps, with shorter lengths tied into long rat-tails of hair that started near his ears and dangled down as far as his navel.

The prisoner (or patient) had managed to cut himself and had used his own blood as ink to draw arcane designs over every surface of his room; it looked like something straight from a film, one with cannibals or warlocks.

One of the squiggles of blood spelled the word *Aghama* and it felt almost like a drug-high to think that word. I kept my mouth shut.

"This is Six. He was a member of a Wraeththu gang," explained Dr Blake in a near whisper "We were lucky to acquire him – they are slippery customers – but this one slipped up. He's useful to us, not least because he's also a fully bipolar hermaphrodite. Genetically that makes him even rarer than you lot."

"I assume he's psionic as well?" asked Paul

"Oh yes. In fact if it weren't for Six's indeterminate gender, he'd rate as near perfect in all our tests. His immune system is extraordinary, but outweighed by his infertility as far as the main project goes."

With almost liquid grace, Six got to his feet and walked to the glass wall, taking his (her?) time inspecting each of us in turn. The one-way glass might as well have been transparent.

"Still giving out numbers so that you don't have to think of your victims as people, Doctor Roger Philip Blake?" he asked.

Blake looked away, clearly reluctant to meet Six's gaze.

Six turned his attention back to us and seemed to be looking me in the eye as he spoke. His gaze was steady and full of compassion.

"My name is Ashlem. I am Wraeththu, a har of the tribe Unneah. I wish we were meeting under better circumstances, but here we are, and I am unable to provide proper hospitality in this place." He gestured with both hands, and then grinned widely

It was odd, really odd. He was Wraeththu, streetscum of the lowest order. Murder, theft, drugs and wild partying were supposed to be all they cared about, everyone knew it; and yet Ashlem appeared to be more than that, honourable and blindingly charismatic.

I felt the glass under my fingertips and blinked, I'd stepped closer without realising I'd done so.

Ashlem stepped close placing his own fingers against the glass, his fingertips positioned so that they would have touched my own had the mirrored glass not separated us.

"I can't stop them, not yet. I will help if I can, when the time comes." he whispered

Something like static electricity stung my fingertips and I snatched my hand away.

I wriggled my fingers still feeling an odd tingling in the tips. Dr Blake didn't seem to have noticed anything odd and I definitely didn't feel like mentioning it.

"Now that you've met Number Six" said Dr Blake "We will start the tests. Focus on Six psionically and report anything you detect."

"Roger Philip Blake, you idiot!" snapped Ashlem, hitting the glass with his palm "They're untrained, they don't have the first idea how to do what you're asking."

Dr Blake smiled in a predatory way. "You've had training? Interesting."

Ashlem glared at Blake, clearly angry that he'd revealed something that he'd wanted to keep hidden.

"This won't end well, Roger Philip Blake."

Ashlem was right of course, we were complete novices with no clue what to do. Seeing no point in it, I just leant back against the wall and let my mind wander. Ironically that was probably the best tactic I could possibly have chosen.

I stood in the old graveyard. It was the perfect place, symbolic, We'd told them we only gave the new drug to blood brothers, or were they cowards unwilling to cut their own flesh? Silly Hafsexis, so macho, so predictable. Above, the full moon breaks clear of the clouds, bathing the four RedJakkers in his light as they lie upon the tombs, waiting for a gift far greater than the squalid addiction that they'd been promised.

To the left, someone cried a warning, too late; two pin-pricks pierced my thigh. Pain. Every muscle clenching inward. 'Taser' I thought... as everything faded

I blinked and pushed myself away from the wall. For a second time, nobody had noticed anything out of the ordinary had occurred.

As I'd half expected, Ashlem had been looking directly at me, but as soon as he was aware that I was actively looking back at him he switched his gaze to someone else. What I'd felt, hadn't been one of my dreams, I was certain. Although it had been superficially similar, this was more like remembering something, like someone's home video, but with an emotions track as well as sound. Then it clicked into place: I'd just 'seen' Ashlem's capture. He'd been trying to help those desperate addicted boys.

Suddenly Salil let out a piercing scream and clutched at his head.

Dr Blake took one glance at Salil and then at the Wraeththu before hitting the alarm button next to the door.

"It's a trap" announced Jeaki a few seconds later, his voice sounding pained. "Six wants the guards sent in. He figures that the more he can disable now, the less he'll face when he escapes."

By that point, three CGS had already entered the cell. The first one was already down, clutching his shattered knee. If it had been me, I'd have picked up the fallen nightstick, but Ashlem never gave it a glance, turning his momentum into a spinning kick that left the second guard's arm hanging at a sickening angle.

I'd never seen fighting like this; it wasn't a proper martial art, more like a cat in a sack. Ashlem was so fast and agile that the CGS seemed to move in slow motion. When he struck, bones broke. I'm sure the other Specimens just saw him going murderously berserk, what I saw was a display of non-lethal maiming.

The fifth CGS to enter the room didn't bother with tactics and simply spread himself wide and charged. In the relatively confined space, Ashlem had no way of dodging; once he was down it was pretty much all over.

I kept grimly silent. There was no point in telling the others that Ashlem was innocent, not now.

Sixteen Someone whispered deep in my brain.

I was awake instantly. If the words in my head were not enough, there was an almost painful heat in my fingertips. Pulling the sheets back with my left hand, I could see that the fingers on my right hand had reddened as if scalded. Ashlem. It had to be.

No. This isn't a dream murmured the voice in my head, in a patient motherly way. *Try to picture a word in your mind*

Obediently I pictured a word, forming it carefully one letter at a time, like a three year old with a crayon.

H.O.W.?

You recall all the static when you were touching the glass? The Nayati discharged a small amount of agmara through a focusing majhahn.

? I sent the question mark imagining it to be 6ft tall.

You don't have the words. Call it magic if you must; it isn't really, I'll explain later. replied Ashlem. *Basically I've made it so we can talk undetected.*

Why... We... Talk...? I thought carefully

Because you know I'm not evil. You know that they are wrong to detain me and... I need you to trust me.

If this had been a normal conversation, I'd have said 'yeah right. Trust a murdering Wraeththu? You're kidding', but this conversation was different, mind to mind. I could feel the intrinsic honesty and nobleness that I'd glimpsed in his memories.

Trust... maybe I formed cautiously

That's good, because I know what they plan to do to you next. he continued, with an undercurrent of urgency that practically grabbed me by my throat. *Dr Hart thinks that he knows my secret, he thinks he knows why we are stronger and faster and smarter; a drug that performs a simple trick with the DNA, something that he can copy. Hart is a fool, he sees the tip of the iceberg and assumes that there is nothing more They will inject you with my blood to see what it will do. It will do more than they think; it will alter the very fabric of who you are, make you better in ways you can't even conceive of, but it's not safe. All I can do is to ensure you are prepared.*

Why... You... Warn...?

We Wraeththu protect our own. They will make us blood brothers of a sort, and as it is my blood, it is also my duty to act as your hienama, your guide.

I radiated an unfocused feeling of alarm and confusion, which he ignored.

I can't sustain this link much longer. Just remember this, you mustn't eat anything tomorrow. You should tell the others not to eat either. Your body will react like food is a lethal poison. Also, and this is vital...understand, vital ... you must meditate, think about who you are, the core of what makes you You. You mustn't lose your sense of self.

My mouth went dry. Telepathy isn't like speech. I could tell Ashlem believed what he said was a certainty.

Remember to meditate. Ashlem's words drifted away, the tingling in my fingertips fading as well.

I think he was wise not to go into detail; had he done so, I wouldn't have been nearly so calm. I lay awake looking at the ceiling wondering what it all meant. It must have been earlier than I thought, because I was soon asleep again, dreaming of deep magics and profound rituals.

When I awoke, all doubt had fled, I was absolutely certain that I had to warn the others not to eat anything. Oddly I didn't think about avoiding the experiment. I guess it was another point where I could have said 'stop' and walked away. But I didn't. It didn't even occur to me as an option. I wonder now if my dreams had reached back in time and ensured that I took the course I did, or perhaps Ashlem's influence went deeper than he let on.

I tried to convince them at breakfast and failed miserably. Only Jeaki and Sarah took me seriously, the other three choosing to consume our uneaten portions.

Paul looked up from his cereal "Six is a seriously sick puppy; you can't rely on anything he's telling you."

"Have you asked Dr Blake about any of this?" asked Jeaki

"We can't tell Blake" I hissed urgently

"Can't tell Dr Blake what?" asked Dr Gupta, who I hadn't noticed, seated behind us

"Six telepathically warned Sixteen not to eat anything today,' replied Jeaki. "Something about a drug you're planning to test on us."

Dr Gupta looked surprised. "You say Six told you this telepathically?"

"Yes," I admitted reluctantly

"And where were you when he told you this?"

"My room"

"Goodness gracious; that is a range of nearly a hundred feet. How extraordinary."

"What about the drug test?" asked Sarah. "Was he lying to Sixteen?"

"It is true that Dr Hart has booked you for a drug trial," replied Gupta enthusiastically. "I can tell you that I have reviewed his work, and it is a breakthrough. I would even suggest that it is a work of genius, a gene therapy that doesn't actually alter the genes at all; a thing of beauty."

"But is it safe?" Sarah persisted.

"Of course, of course... Here, I'll show you." Gupta grabbed several sets of condiments and arranged them on the table. "Here, normal DNA: four proteins CTG and A in a double helix spiral. But what if we insert a third strand, making a triple helix? This way we keep your original DNA undamaged and use the third strand to add additional cell functions. We know it can be done. Six's DNA is already like this. It is a truly elegant solution, and also totally reversible."

"And will our fasting before the drug trial be a problem?"

"No, it should not have any bearing on the test." replied Gupta "It is your choice of course, but it really is quite safe."

My next clear memory is of (I guess) the next morning, walking nervously into a lab on the lowest level of the Institute. It was a lab I'd not seen before. The main feature of the room was six medical beds, each with a whole wall of medical monitors behind them.

I walked over to one of the bed and hopped up onto it, almost immediately my fingertips tingled.

Sixteen?

Yes

Did you meditate? Do you know who you are?

Yes I replied, thinking it odd that Ashlem believed that some stupid meditation was more important than the not eating thing.

I have generated as much luck as I can Sixteen, it's up to you now. His voice faded, leaving me wondering how one went about 'generating' luck? In fact the comment caused me to doubt everything Ashlem had said.

I returned my attention to the room, noting that the others had each chosen a bed and were standing next to them looking grim and tense. They might not have believed Ashlem's warning, but just now they were having second thoughts.

"Lady and Gentleman," announced Dr Hart. "Dr Gupta tells me that he's given you his *unscientific* explanation of what we are here to do." The emphasis on the word 'unscientific' seemed to be more about his opinion of Gupta's ability than our lack of knowledge.

"Ashlem thinks you've missed something." I said, bluntly

"Six? What could a streetscum kid like him possibly know about genetics?" asked Hart dismissively

I frowned. The man just radiated arrogance. He didn't just 'think' he was right; he 'knew' that he was, with a certainty that had no room for doubt.

"The genetic splice we will inject is based upon the performance enhancing drug used by Wraeththu gangs," Hart explained. "You needn't worry about addiction. The original designer apparently intended it to impart a permanent enhancement without any side effects. If we are successful, we will have taken a giant leap toward a solution to the fertility problem. We will be able to replace the damaged genes with a single vaccination. I predict we'll all get awards for pioneering this research. Oh...." He paused impatiently. "I am legally obliged to ask if any of you wish to back out."

We all looked nervous.

"You should know that if you exercise your right to refuse treatment, your contract will be terminated, without prejudice" Hart continued.

I assumed that 'without prejudice' meant if anyone did back out, they'd be blacklisted and doomed to a life of poverty in the gang-infested slums. Not exactly a great choice, that.

"Please sign these release papers and we'll get started," added one of Hart's assistants.

Lacking much else to do, I focused my attention on the dark

liquid in the syringes; it seemed that each of us was being injected with a progressively larger dose. Paul would receive the smallest infusion, whilst I was going to get the largest. Finally, it was my turn. The syringe was inserted into my arm and the entire vial of blood was pushed into me.

At last, I allowed myself to be scared. No, scared isn't a strong enough word: 'terrified'... I was fucking terrified. The stuff was in me now and I had to hope that Ashlem was right

It's started?

Yes

Then it's time for you to know the rest. In an ideal world this would have been explained. But I couldn't risk 'Them' knowing. There is no easy way to say this, they're giving you my whole DNA, not just parts they think they've isolated.

?

You're not going to be male anymore

WHAT?!

You'll be like me, a hermaphrodite.

No!

Calmly Sixteen, this is the ultimate gift, absolutely not a handicap

Once again the advantage of telepathic honesty came to Ashlem's aid. His last statement was wrapped in that emotion of utter certainty. The being called Ashlem har Unneah was utterly certain that what I was about to become was better than male, by several orders of magnitude.

Even so, the fact remained that I was in the process of being turned into a genderless mule, unable to....do things.

Ashlem's mental laughter, as gentle as a caress cut through my panic. *We Wraeththu look after our own Sixteen, you will never be outcast. And you aren't losing your gender, you're gaining a superior one*

I started to hyperventilate and sweat. It might have been the genetic splice kicking in, but if I'm honest, it was probably just good old-fashioned fear... No matter how Ashlem dressed it up, I was fucked.

"Feeling ok?" asked Paul

"Yeah, I'm just scared" I replied, irrationally unwilling to discuss what I'd just learned.

"See, it was just Six messing with your head, like we said," added Salil

"You think?" Sarah said. "Look at your arm."

Salil's arm looked like someone had taken a paintbrush and

painted fake blood vessels in a dark bruised red. I looked at my own right arm; the veins were already inflamed, bulging so that they looked like ivy wrapped around a tree trunk. So fast! My heart hammered in my chest.

"Clever, clever, clever," muttered the Dr. Hart. "The adrenalin levels are way up. The first generation of converted cells is creating it, telling Specimen 16's heart to beat faster ensuring that the serum reaches every part of the body quickly."

"Oh... great!" I gasped sarcastically. "Are you... going to... do a... fucking... running commentary?"

"Specimen 16 is exhibiting mild levels of distress, accompanied by adrenaline-induced aggression." said Dr. Hart, speaking into a recorder.

"Screw you too!" I snarled

Across the room, I could see the others watching me and looking fearful. Jeaki, Salil and Sarah had all begun to sweat; the other two seemed to still be ok.

"Specimens 13 through 16 also show signs of heightened adrenal activity," Hart continued. "No reaction from 11 and 12. Presumably the serum dosage was too low to initiate cellular integration."

"You... don't even... know... the correct dosage... do you?" hissed Jeaki

"Dosage is one of the test parameters," replied Hart as if it were obvious.

For the next few hours things went on about the same. With the exception of Paul and Calvin, we were all feeling pretty uncomfortable; but if I was honest, it was not really any worse than any of the fevers I'd had as a child. We kept each other's spirits up with bad jokes and anecdotes.

And then Sarah died.

It happened suddenly, one minute she was like the rest of us, panting and sweating, heart racing, the next she clutched at her head, and a single gout of blood spurted from her nose. To be fair, Hart's team were on her in seconds, one shining a light in her eyes, one keeping her upright so that the blood didn't choke her, and another checking the EEG sensor readouts.

"No good, she's gone," said one of the assistants. "No brain activity, no pulse."

For the first time that I'd known him, Hart had the decency to look worried. Although I suspected that it was worry about losing the

International Awards that he'd promised himself, rather than Sarah's condition.

We Specimens just sat there in shock, not moving, not speaking, trying not to think.

The next thing I recall is hearing the doctors arguing. Clarke was saying that he'd warned Hart, Gupta was showing concern for our safety, while Hart argued that Sarah must have had an undetected physiological condition that Clarke had missed.

Finally Director Calcutt walked into our room and took a look at us for himself.

"Flush the serum. Full blood replacement. Stat. You've obviously missed something." He ordered "Gupta, take charge here. Hart... my office."

Someone cheered weakly; it might even have been me.

Immediately there was a bustle of activity as intravenous feeds were wheeled in and hooked up, along with a second line fed to an empty plastic blood-bag.

My energy levels dropped about then, and I lay limply on my bed not really caring about anything that was going on. At some point the curtains had been drawn, leaving me feeling that I was floating in a sickly green limbo.

"Sixteen? Can you hear me?" asked Dr Gupta

"Yes" I replied, somewhat irritated.

"How are you feeling? Have your symptoms eased at all since the blood transfusion?"

"You've finished?" I asked in a wavering voice.

Gupta frowned and turned to one of the nursing assistants. "Have someone run a DNA marker check on the last bag of drained blood from each of them. I want to know the percentage of hybridized blood cells remaining."

"What....killed... Ssr..uh?" I asked

"Specimen 13 had a stroke. Her blood pressure spontaneously doubled; we've never seen anything like it. Thankfully she didn't suffer."

I closed my eyes again. Basically her brain had exploded.

Biohazard Level: One   Height: 6'3   Client: Citadel Securities Plc
Flight Risk: 70%   Weight: 11   Office: Calcutt Institute
Security Clearance: Low   Blood Group: O W   Project: Universal Vaccine (military)

Specimen 16

The sound of the curtains drawing back roused me again, this time all of the doctors were present. I glanced around at the others, they were all lying flat out, although Paul and Calvin were propped up and seemed slightly more energetic.

Gupta sighed before he addressed us. "I'm sorry to tell you that the blood replacement failed to flush out the hybrid DNA. The replacement blood was being hybridised almost as soon as it entered your bodies. I have reviewed Dr Hart's notes and I am ashamed to say that his research has not been as rigorous as I had been led to believe. Bluntly, we do not know what outcome to expect."

"Ashlem does... Get him up here." I replied

Gupta glanced at Calcutt, who shook his head firmly.

"At least ask him! You don't have to let him out." snapped Jeaki from the next bed.

Calcutt nodded once, his face grim.

With the 'big announcement' done, our curtains were drawn again and I was back in the light green limbo. Some time later a message came to me from Ashlem.

Sixteen, Jeaki

Yes? I sent, finding that I was getting more adept at this form of communication.

I've had a visit from those ghouls. I've told them nothing. If you've done as I told you and know your inner 'self' you should come through intact.

How. Much. Longer? I sent

As little as two days, as many as ten

Fuck! I sent.

I'm here for all of you, never forget that; it will be ok

"Am I still human?" I gasped, half jokingly.

"Actually no," replied Hart. "Every cell in the last tissue sample was hybridised. You'll be pleased to know that your adrenaline levels are reverting to normal. In fact your cells are now beginning to generate the RNA analogue I had predicted at the outset. I'd say your body is getting ready enter a phase of rapid cell division."

"Like... Sarah?" I gasped

"We know what to look for now," interrupted Gupta. "We can regulate that if it becomes a problem."

My growth spurt started about fifteen minutes later. I started to swell up like someone who's allergic to bee stings... what's the word? annapha-something shock.. My fingers became so thick that I couldn't form a fist. I wanted to scream, but my throat was constricted, swollen shut.

For the first and only time Dr. Hart was useful. Forcing my mouth open, he shoved a breathing tube down my throat and strapped it in place. After that I lost interest in everything beyond the sensations running through the cocoon that was my inflamed and apparently rotting carcass.

The shards of memory become tiny crystal daggers at that point, just a series of disturbing doctor-speak punctuating the excruciating pain.

"Body mass at 189%...."

"Second generation white blood cells appear to be attacking the hybridised human cells. Get me a readout on this tumour's DNA."

"We're losing another one! Damn it, his major intestine is perforating. Where's that DNA analysis?"

"Rapid onset, acne and eczema, vomiting and continued incontinence of both types, including haemorrhagic traces. Speculation: the specimen's body is rejecting and expelling any remaining unaltered cells."

"The new DNA hasn't stayed in the third strand; I'm seeing V and W proteins blended into all three spirals, exactly like Specimen Six's original DNA."

"I want a complete autopsy on Twelve. Check his brain, Stat!"

"Specimen 16 appears to be progressing faster than the others, probably due to the higher initial dose. Get him to CT, I want to know what to expect in the other two."

And finally

"What the fuck! What is that growing in his abdomen? That's no tumour, it has a differentiated structure!"

I don't remember hearing anything after that. I do remember a knife-like pain ripping my crotch apart like I'm being unzipped with a chainsaw. Any hope that Ashlem had lied fled in that terrible instant.

Remember your Self

I dreamed that I was falling through space toward a lake covered in a flock of birds.

I felt as if I were under scrutiny, I wasn't expected, I hadn't been announced. He reached out His hand anyway, and everything that had felt strange now felt 'right'. I was euphoric, it would be so easy just to stay that way, infinitely happy for infinity, but Ashlem's words leapt back at me. This, I thought, was why I'd been warned to hold onto my 'self', this was what Hart and the others would never understand... this was a trap.

You didn't have to just survive the pain; you had to survive its seductive absence as well!

When I awoke I found that I was curled up on my own bed, in the apartment. My cheeks were wet, I'd been crying in my sleep I guess. I didn't hurt anymore, not at all. The first thing I noticed was that the sound of the air conditioning had changed. Along with the steady hum that I'd become used to, was an annoying ultra-high pitched whine. Enhanced senses! A long, long, time ago someone had boasted that their super-serum would enhance the senses.

I opened my eyes; it was a revelation. I hadn't realized that there was anything wrong with my eyesight before that moment. Things in the distance had always been slightly blurry. Today I could see the speck of rust on the screw-head of the door hinge from the other side of the room.

Hair flopped into my eyes. I swept it out of the way. It felt softer, silky and more voluminous, definitely not the stringy mess I'd grown up with.

My heart froze, recalling Ashlem's affliction and his prediction about my fate. With a surge of energy, I rolled off the bed and stood up, feeling wonderfully normal. I didn't yet perceive the other changes, the ones I didn't want to think about. I allowed myself to believe, just for a moment that Ash really had been wrong and that fuck-wit Hart had somehow detected and removed that part of the gene splice.

As I got to my feet, my robe fell open. Everything down below had felt perfectly natural and normal; as a result I nearly died of shock when I looked down at my...at my what? The old friend I'd kept between my legs was gone, replaced with something more complex, sort of like fleshy petals that spiralled together to form an approximation of what had been.

I tried to be disgusted, but clearly 'it' came with a full set of instinctive software, all I could think was how beautiful the new organ looked. Tentatively I touched it with a finger...it was very pleasurable and almost painfully sensitive. I snatched my finger away. The rush of conflicting emotions was too great.

I slumped back on the bed and let the tears roll down my cheeks, until finally I got irritated with myself for being such a baby. I tried one of the meditation techniques I'd been taught, trying to dampen the emotion; it worked better than I'd expected, I felt a wave of calmness and passivity flow through me, and suddenly my beautiful/hideous new rod revealed the reason for its complexity, unravelling and retracting into an alternate configuration.

I sat up and looked down at myself; it was not unlike a woman's …parts. The real strangeness was that all of this, this, flexibility of function felt natural. I tried thinking about 'before', and found that I couldn't remember how it had felt. In the end I closed my eyes, folded my arms and tried thinking about something non-sexual (and failed).

Finished playing with yourself yet? asked Ashlem, his sending coloured with tender amusement and a hint of worry that tasted of peaches and cream.

Yes I replied instinctively, no longer needing to form pictures of my words

Good

Hey! I'm able to talk direct!

You are Wraeththu now. Our minds are on the same frequency, I don't have to boost my sendings to punch through all that human sludge you were using for a mind

A nasty embarrassing thought occurred to me. *Was I broadcasting?*

Just a bit

Suddenly something clicked into place, *Hang on, so all the Wraeththu are….?*

We're an entire new species, Sixteen, and that's the secret we have to hide. If humanity realises it's no longer top of the food chain, it will go badly for us all.

I was immediately flooded with more new desires, thinking of people… of beings, like myself. Along with it came distaste for human things.

This is so weird. I don't even think like me I sent.

It's understandable. You also have new instincts, which you aren't used to yet. At this stage you're a bit like a newborn, your mind doesn't have any inhibitions on the soume side of your character

Soume? What's that?

The female role you haven't tried yet.

Is that why I feel like a dog in heat? I asked.

*Don't worry. The state you are in is temporary. It's partly instinct driven; your body knows that it hasn't finished changing yet *

There's more? I sent, fearful of being ripped apart a second time.

Our blood can create new Wraeththu, but the change doesn't stabilize until the new one has... (Here I felt his sending glow with compassion) …umm 'used' that new equipment of his.

I like to think I was pretty quick on the uptake, despite being a wild hormonal soup right then. *So basically you have to rape me pretty fucking soon or I revert to being the old me?* I let the rage I'd been holding back roar outwards.

No. There is no 'old you'. Failure will mean death.

Well that one certainly dumped cold water on my feelings of vengeance and hope of a recovery.

Great. Just fucking great. How long have I got?

Plenty of time. But you need to be ready. If they put any two of us in the same room you are going to have to get it on fast. Hardly the romantic ideal unfortunately...

Any two? So the others survived? I remembered that shard of memory about an autopsy.

The others haven't completed their transformation yet, at least as far as I can tell. Jeaki is out of range and I never had a contact link with the others. If they did as I told them, they'll be with us eventually.

And if they all die? I'm pretty sure two of them died

If they don't make it, then I'll have to demonstrate yet more of those superpowers I don't have to get to you. Sixteen, I know you don't think much of me right now, but I promise you, I'll do all I can to get you through this.

I firmly folded my arms and tried to focus something else... not what....what... I now was. I was me; I was still me, wasn't I?

There is a limit to how long a person can just lie in bed feeling sorry for himself; particularly when, actually, they feel healthier than they have done in years. In the end it was hunger that motivated me.

I guess my mental state was even more fragile than I'd thought, being faced by a cafeteria full of humans made me want to puke and run. They stank!

Conversation stopped as I entered the room. None of them wanted to talk to me about it, but it was plain that the disastrous test was the only topic on any of their minds; at least as far as my paranoid mind was concerned. It was hard seeing our usual table empty. It didn't help that the food was off. The cereal had a tinny metallic taste and the milk smelled bad. In the end, I settled for raiding the entire supply of fruit and munching my way through a dozen oranges and six bananas, (including the skins).

"The serum must have screwed up my tastebuds" I explained to no one in particular. "The oranges are the only things that taste normal."

Everyone who'd been pretending not to watch quickly became

engrossed in their meals. Annoyed, I grabbed the other fruit bowl and headed for my room, finishing off another three oranges as I waited for the damn elevator.

As if telepathic herself, Ms Jenson appeared at my side to inform me the Director would see me in 30 minutes. Something about the way she spoke seemed 'off'.

"What's wrong?" I asked, chewing a delicious banana skin

"You don't remember?"

There was a feeling of vertigo; an abyss was at my feet. There'd been deaths, more than one for certain. "Not much, just fragments, I think I remember Sarah died."

"I'm so sorry James. It's just you left... and ...they think Jeaki might make it."

My fist slammed into the metal door putting a dent in it. "Sixteen. My name is Sixteen."

The door closed between us. All of them dead? The darkness howled around my mind trying to make me think about inevitable death. There was also a profound sadness, they would never get to experience how it felt being Wraeththu, they would have loved it. If only I'd persuaded them not to eat... or if... or if...

Talk to me Ashlem I thought, trying to distract myself.

Sixteen Came the instant reply, as if he'd been waiting for me.*What do you want to know?*

Plumbing first, do I stand or sit? I said, focusing on the practicalities.

His laughter bubbled through me, forcing me to see the humour, even then during my darkest moment. His compassionate emotions could probably heal the deepest wounds, given time.

Of all the questions, I'd expected... sent Ashlem *ok, ok, sorry... you needn't worry. It's your choice, and I'm sure you'll get the hang of it... with practice.*

I sent him an emotional dagger-glare but couldn't sustain it. It felt like a huge relief to talk to someone who truly understood what I was going through. I hadn't forgiven him, he'd clearly had his own agenda, but any plans I might have had of actually murdering him, were getting less likely with every passing minute.

I fired off a few more questions, trying to understand what I was now. For example the problem with the taste of the food was because it was processed. Apparently, my new tastebuds were picking up traces of engine oil and detergent. Nice.

Enough.... Ashlem sent, finally. *I can only sustain this link for short periods. Have you heard anything about the others?*

Jeaki's still changing. The others, they're all dead I replied grimly, trying not to think about the howling void their deaths left in my mind and heart.

I see. I got the sense that he regretted the deaths of my friends but was treating it like he'd expected it. *Do they still trust you?*

I'm invited to see the Director. They wouldn't let me near him if they thought I was a risk.

Use that; insist on seeing us, me or Jeaki, or both. Remember, you aren't stable yet, you have to meet one of us. As he spoke, the strength of his telepathy faded.

I sat still for a few seconds more. It would be quite logical for me to be concerned about Jeaki, I reasoned. It didn't all have to be about the other thing. I still didn't want to think about that.

Some minutes later, I was standing outside Calcutt's office, looking at that not-dead guard.

His name badge said Stanislav. He took one look at me and clearly decided that I was the enemy. I could smell the hatred oozing from his pores. I no longer fitted into the CGS man's comfort zone and I could almost feel him willing me to give him an excuse.

It really was annoying, this 'attack anything you don't understand' thing that the CGS had going on.

The last time I'd been in Calcutt's office, I'd feared the Director and what his opinion of me might be, but this time I took the chair and slouched, legs crossed at the ankle. Gupta was in there too.

"How do you feel today, Mr Conway?" he asked.

I didn't answer for a few seconds, partly because I wanted to figure out the answer for myself, and partly because I'd realised that I had no intention of helping Calcutt ever again. "Better" I said finally.

"Please be more specific," Gupta urged.

"You wouldn't understand"

"Try," snapped Calcutt.

"Better in every way imaginable, except that obvious one" I said.

"You aren't upset that we've done this to you?" Gupta asked.

I thought hard about that one as well. "Most of my friends are dead. I haven't had time to get my head around that yet. As for what you've done to my body, I'm getting used to it... gradually. If you want any more data then we need to cut a new deal. You seem to have me under armed guard." I flicked a meaningful glare in

Stanislav's direction. "That isn't anywhere in my contract, particularly given what just happened."

"Sub-section 6 paragraph 3." replied Director Calcutt. "Should the specimen become mentally ill, the Institute shall provide suitable long term accommodation and care."

"You think I'm insane?" I asked frostily

"Honestly, probably not. But the scans we've taken don't match anything remotely close to those we took from you last week. We need to understand what that means. There may be... implications."

This was so tedious and unsubtle; I couldn't believe that he was trying to intimidate me like that. "So, let's see, what works best, you threatening me with a padded cell, or a civilised renegotiation and my full co-operation?"

Calcutt paused. He'd assumed that I was still the easily manipulated door-mat that I'd been when we'd first met. I wasn't.

"Here's what I want," I continued "First, lose the security guard. Second, I want unrestricted access to Jeaki and Ashlem, and third, you are going to pay the compensation I'm owed, at the rate set out in the original contract. Agree to that, and I'll cooperate."

To my surprise he actually went for it. In fact he agreed so fast I began to worry that I'd missed something... which of course I had.

An hour later Stanislav and some CGS Guards came for me. There were six of them, all armed. They stank of fear and rage. I told him I didn't need an escort, but Stanislav simply shrugged and said, 'orders'.

My skin tingled as I entered the observation room, something about the place felt different and sort of not real. It was disorientating and I hated it. *What did you do here, Ashlem?* I wondered to myself.

"Welcome back, Sixteen" said a voice from behind the mirrored wall. Even if I hadn't recognised the voice, I found that I could see Dr Hart quite well. The mirroring was no more effective than sunglasses.

"Dr Hart? I thought they'd fired you."

"Fortunately, the fertility crisis is too large to let a few minor setbacks derail the entire project."

"Minor?"

"Yes, minor. Look at the big picture, Sixteen, the entire human race is at risk. The loss of a few volunteers was always anticipated."

I expected to feel the beginnings of a berserk rage, but all I could manage was a sense of pity. Pity, that he had so little compassion in his soul.

I sighed. "How did they die, Hart? At least tell me that."

"In Specimens Eleven and Twelve, the hybrid cells didn't spread out sufficiently," he explained in a clinical emotionless tone. "They suffered localized tumours that disrupted the surrounding organs as they expanded. Thirteen you know about. Fourteen mutated fully, but fell into a coma and died, we haven't figured out why. Fifteen will be joining us shortly. Now it's your turn. Tell me something."

I thought about it for a moment. Wondering what it was safe to reveal. "The mirrored glass doesn't work on me now, but I figure you already know that." I replied

A minute later Jeaki was pushed (almost thrown) into the room on the other side of the transparent barrier. He'd obviously been struggling with his guards and flew at the door snarling and denting the metal with his fists as he tried to reach them.

He was raw, dominant and wild; I felt an instinctive attraction to that. Even with his back to me I could tell he'd changed more than I had. His skin had darkened to a coffee colour but also mottled, like marble shot through with stripes.

At some level, I thought he was beautiful… attractive.

Finally he stopped hammering the door and turned, sensing my presence. His eyes widened as his gaze met mine and then he looked down openly checking out my body. To my surprise he turned away, preferring to face the wall than look at me. I concluded that he hated the sight of me.

The imagined rejection cleared my head somewhat. I wondered if Ashlem had spoken in Jeaki's mind as he had mine. If not, Jeaki had to be told.

Jeaki? I sent.

The room sort of tingled and I imagined that my thoughts were flowing along Ashlem's blood-inscribed graffiti, amplifying the telepathy so that it felt as if I'd screamed the thought at the top of my lungs.

----- replied Jeaki, sending his wordless emotional turmoil echoing around the room magnified a hundredfold.

"Damn," I whispered sadly. In that instant of contact, I'd absorbed enough to know that the telepath was reacting badly to his altered gender, certainly way worse than I was. Where I had (so far) managed to cope, Jeaki was in denial. Big time. It was driving him insane and his mental self-discipline was making things worse instead of better. Gone was the obedient corporate boy; the new Jeaki feared and loathed the female/soume side of his personality and had retreated into what seemed to be a primal male state, full of murderous, unreasoning rage. He hated and feared me for the temptation that I represented and hated the doctors for doing this to him. Hate was easy, as long as he felt that he wouldn't have to feel any of the new emotions.

I took an involuntary step back, shocked by the detail I'd picked up from his unfocused sending.

"Jeaki!" I yelled.

Getting no response, I tried sending to Ashlem instead. There was no reply. I began to fear that he had been removed and that I was left with no one who understood what I was going through.

I'm here came a faint sleepy reply *Wait... Are you in the Nayati? In the room, where we first met?*

Yes.

Be careful. I set up that room to have some odd properties. Keep things simple, and don't put too much effort into your sendings. he instructed. *Now, what's up?*

Jeaki's deranged. He's trying to think male thoughts only. I replied, concentrating as gently as I could on each word.

You will have to be more ouana... more male... than he is, If you are dominant, his soume instincts might respond

I'll try

Recalling that Hart was watching I turned to face the glass wall."You need to get Ashlem in here with him; he'd know what to say." I said.

"You think a streetscum like Six can cure Fifteen by just talking to him? The problem is physiological, not psychological."

Hart was so obvious, hoping to goad me into revealing things. Unfortunately my concern for Jeaki overrode my common sense.

"You'll just have to take my word for it. As you say, Jeaki's mind and his brain don't quite match up right now and its possib...."

Jeaki slammed against the plastic barrier, the sound loud enough to startle me. The impact had sent white fault-lines radiating across the transparent wall, another slam like that and Jeaki would break something. I couldn't block out the insane mix of hate and lust generated by his mind. He headbutted the reinforced glass screen again, and again. He was... I closed my eyes unable to watch, but there was no relief. I could feel his mind; he'd chosen death rather than embrace his new emotions. The next thump was also a squelch, abruptly the emotional storm faded from my mind.

I sagged to my knees and touched the glass watching, with insane fascination as parts of my dead friend's brain slithered down the wall. A hand touched my shoulder; I pushed Hart away surging back to my feet.

"Stay away from me! Monster! You let that happen. We're done. Finished. "

They led me back to my room, I found myself back in a soume mood-swing, crying my eyes out with compassion for poor mind-damaged Jeaki. The depth of my feelings shocked me. I began wondering if I wasn't swinging off the female end almost as badly as Jeaki had been off the male.

You're fine. Your mind is just playing in its new garden. reassured Ashlem, his mental sending sharp and clear *Now, show me what happened*

His demand for a tactical update seemed to call to my ouana-side, and I found my body and mind reverting to the more familiar thought pattern as easily as blinking.

I pictured the scene in my head and sent the whole memory to Ash as if it were a movie.

I'm so sorry you had to witness that Sixteen. he sent, his mind full of compassion edged with ruthlessness *Jeaki rejected the gift, its better he didn't linger*

It's ok, I think I understand. At the end, that wasn't the real Jeaki, it was like a fragment pretending it was whole

Exactly. I'm impressed, that you're 'getting it' so soon. Some hara take months to get that perceptive.

Was I really as self-obsessed as they are? I asked, more of myself than Ashlem.

I have no idea. I have after all only met you the once.

Ash... (It felt natural now to use a short-form of his name.) *I've just realised. They have no intention of putting us in the same room.*

Don't worry, I've always assumed that they wouldn't want us together; I'm far too dangerous in their eyes. All I've been waiting for is for you to be ready to take the final step. You have to be willing, or it's a perversion, a rape. I'm no rapist.

I shifted my weight uncomfortably, at the reminder of what that 'final step' involved.

Everything was moving so fast and I wished like hell that I had more time. Despite Ash's assurance that he didn't want to force the issue, there was an undercurrent of urgency to his sendings that made it clear that I was going to have to get over my squeamishness soon, damn soon.

Alright, damn it, I'll do it I sent

Your words are saying yes but your emotions are still saying 'no, no, no'. Let me know when you change your mind. he replied, his sending glowing with humour

Ok, assuming that I do work up the courage, what next? They aren't going to let you out, and they're going to be even less happy if you let yourself out. I can't see how you're going to pull this off.

Relax; I've had over a week to prepare. They have no idea how outclassed they are. I could have built the magaric equivalent of a battleship and they wouldn't know it.

Sorry, 'magaric' What's that?

Let's just say the graffiti isn't for decoration

I recalled the weird tingling, otherness and how the sendings had been boosted. I felt another of those 'thunk' moments as another massive chunk of my dreams stopped being meaningless fantasy and became solid precognition. I had seen the future, seen myself twisting reality, calling upon deities and defending my tribe. It meant I must have survived more than a few days; which meant sooner or later I'd be saying 'yes' and meaning it.

Sixteen? What's wrong?

Did I tell you I get precognitions?

A seer, really? But that's marvellous! he replied, full of genuine awe.

It is for you, it means I'm going to have to make that decision. Leave me alone now, I need to work up some courage, ok?

Ok

I stripped, made a mess in the vicinity of the toilet determined that I would master certain things without ever, ever, asking Ash's advice. After that, I stood in front of the shaving mirror, gripping the basin, looking at myself, really looking. The big changes had overshadowed the smaller, more subtle ones and I hadn't wanted to look in mirrors earlier. I couldn't help wondering how the cosmetics industry would react if they found out that there was an instant cure for ugliness, stubble and acne. Who could resist my newfound beauty?

After that I tried pacing up and down and then procrastinated by tidying the room. I ended up on my bed, watching a fly moving randomly near the ceiling.

Ash? I sent *I'm ready*

A second later the fly I'd been watching dropped like a stone, bouncing off my cheek and onto the pillow.

I brushed the fly away, disgusted.

Get down here as fast as you can. This is going to be tight.

Glory! Was he dominant when he wanted to be!

I started out walking slowly, trying to look like I was on normal business. That lasted until I saw the first CGS guard slumped against the wall snoring loudly. Seeing the body, I accelerated my pace to a sprint, hammering down the stairs, past Ms Jenson, slumped over the front desk.

It had to be Ash's work, but I had no idea how. I was used to things working in a regular sort of everyday way, and the only explanation that seemed plausible was that everyone had been gassed. But if that was the case, why was I ok? And how could Ash have gotten hold of the stuff and released it into the air conditioning? That seemed to indicate he had accomplices, but if he did, why did he need me?

I was completely wrong of course.

The elevator ride seemed to take forever, and I began to wonder if the mechanism had become damaged in some mysterious way. Finally the bell 'dinged' and I was racing through the Institute's lowest levels.

Where are you? I sent.

Third door past the Nayati Ash replied, clearly expending vast effort.

I slid to a stop in front of the door, only then noticing that I was barefoot.

"I'm here!" I said out loud, slapping my hand against the metal

"Good," Ashlem replied clearly. It seemed almost strange now for us to be talking aloud. "You remember I 'touched' your hand a few days ago? Place that hand over the lock"

Shrugging, I placed my hand over the swipe card slot.

"Ow!" I yelled as a bolt of static leapt from my fingertips and released the lock.

"What the hell was that?" I demanded rubbing my hand.

"Agmara, the energy of the soul," Ash explained. "I put a bit of my life-force in you as part of a linking majhahn, It's how I was able to send to you over such a long range."

The door swung open and Ash emerged. "Right, now we go to

the Nayati" he said, and hugged me briefly, which left me feeling better than it had a right to.

"I don't understand" I said following him into the room with its blood encrusted walls, the place we'd first met.

"When I was first captured they kept me in this room," Ash said. "I figured that they'd keep me here permanently so this was where I started building my Nayati... There's no word for it in English. It's a focusing point, a place to meditate and a place to do impossible things. By shedding blood to draw the design, I gradually built up a small store of agmara here. I then... oh, pelk it, the jargon can wait! Basically, I set it so that it would steal ten minutes of sleep every night from everyone in the building. When you signalled that you were ready, I reversed it and it gave them back their displaced nap time. Because reality doesn't like to be cheated, it's giving them their dreams in one solid burst."

"Really?"

"Yes, Really."

"So why are we still here and not legging it for the hills?"

"Two reasons. Firstly, this is, for the want of a better phrase, sacred ground, or at least as close as we're going to get. If we were doing this properly, we'd be within the tribal Nayati, The Great Harhunai Yasat Unneah. It'd be a big ceremony, singing, flowers, well-wishers, powerful protective majhahns, the whole nine yards. We don't have that, so it's safest to finish the inception here."

"And the second reason?" I asked, feeling overwhelmed despite Ash's attempt not to use 'jargon'.

"I'll explain later" he replied, his face turning serious, but not quite sombre.

It was time, I could feel it.

Are you ready?

Yes I sent, and this time I knew that my emotions truly matched my thoughts.

"Sending is better than talking," Ash said. "We can't lie that way. But we Wraeththu have a third method of communication that surpasses both, when two of us are... close. It's called sharing breath."

Leaning close he gently exhaled. His breath swirled across my lips like the gentlest of breezes. What happened between us wasn't only on the physical level, it was in my mind as well, full of colour, and smell, and sensations, and sounds, mixing into me, like water with brightly-coloured oil; intertwining and mingling, but never merging.

I sighed blissfully, inadvertently sending something of myself back at Ash. Our lips and minds touched. It was like waves lapping gently against the shore. First his mind would surge onto the beach of mine, and then I would be the wave lapping against his. I thought that it should go on forever, but at last it ended, and I was back in the Nayati. Strands of my mind gradually slithered back into place like the fronds of anemone retreating from the low tide.

"Nice symbolism," said Ash, smiling.

Our hands had clearly been as busy as our minds; both Ash's rags and my robe had been discarded as we shared ourselves. I looked down at myself, willing away any pretence of masculinity that my body might have. My body obeyed my desires, adapting.

Gently, Ashlem har Unneah pulled me unresisting toward that ultimate embrace.

Some things shouldn't be described; some things are beyond that and devalued by the attempt to describe. What we did next is one such thing. It is called aruna in the language of our race, the act of selflessness that can create life or pleasure, or power unlimited. It is as different from human sex as the sun's fusion is from a candle flame.

I rested, panting, my body slick with sweat, wrapped in Ash's enfolding arms.

I wasn't human anymore, not even slightly. I fully understood and embraced that fact now. The thin red line between 'us' and 'them' was now a yawning chasm into which the entire human race could fall, as far as I was concerned.

This then was the secret of Wraeththu. To explain all of it to a human would not only be wrong, it would be impossible; they are physically incapable of understanding. No human spy will ever infiltrate us, for the act of infiltration would also be a rebirth.

Ash rolled off me. I could see the Nayati was glowing. I shut my eyes and I could still see that radiance. I experimented, blinking. The patterns Ash had drawn seemed to fill the room now, not just drawn on the walls but drifting in the air around us.

"Your eyes aren't seeing that, your mind is," Ash said. "I told you about agmara; well sacrifices of blood such as I did are relatively weak. *Aruna*, what we just did... now that is a serious energy source."

"We... recharged it?"

"More of a supercharge than a recharge. All that pleasure you were radiating is now energy at our disposal."

"Awesome, so... the humans can sleep on and we'll escape? Brilliant!"

"Not quite that simple. I only stole a finite amount of sleep from them. Now, you'd better get your robe back on, you're going to have to sprint, we'll need every spare second." He offered me his hand to pull me upright. "I need you to find Jeaki's body and bring it here. We never leave our dead for humans to find."

"What about you?" I asked, whilst pulling on the bathrobe and fiddling with a half threaded belt.

"I'm going to try and buy us some more time."

It took a search through four labs before I found Jeaki's corpse strapped down in the operating theatre. Judging by the pen marks and yellow disinfected area on his smoothly tanned abdomen, the doctors had been about to remove some organs. I went cold, realising at last exactly how contemptuous my 'employers' had been. We specimens had always been fully expendable.

Any last sympathy I'd had evaporated like morning mist. If the humans wanted to cut each other to bits, I didn't much care; but Jeaki had been one of us, and they had no right.

We're coming I sent to Ash, pushing Jeaki's gurney out into the corridor

Just as I reached the Nayati, I heard someone shout, and a second later an alarm was sounding. I could hear running feet and the click-clack of guns being primed.

"Ash?" I asked, realising with a sinking heart that retrieving Jeaki had taken me too long, and that the borrowed time had already run out.

Ash grinned again; only this time I sensed the ruthlessness that had made our species so feared. I was reminded yet again that I knew next to nothing about him, other than those few brief glimpses of his soul. Ashlem har Unneah wasn't some pampered corporate son like me. He'd probably been fighting for his life, long before someone incepted him.

"Put him in that circle," he said pointing at a space surrounded by invisible symbols.

As I finished offloading Jeaki I heard a sound and turned. Stanislav lunged through the door. Instinctively, I took a swing at him. His head whipped around with a sickening crunch. I'd just killed my first human. What shocked me was that I felt no more empathy than I would if I'd stepped on a cockroach.

Ash closed his eyes and raised his arms. A moment later the blinding mind-light of the Nayati's patterns exploded outward. Thunder crashed around us as if a thousand lightning bolts had hit. On the floor, Jeaki's body spontaneously combusted, filling the room with the smell of roast meat.

"What just happened?"

"I let all the electricity in this building escape," Ash replied. "It's in its nature; it always wants to return to the Earth Spirit." He looked exhausted. "Every piece of electrical hardware in the building just fried itself. Anyone within six feet of a computer, a phone or a light fitting is seriously crispy around the edges."

I must have looked grey; this magical elimination of life felt deeply wrong, even if they were humans. It bothered me in a way that snapping the guard's neck hadn't.

"Don't give me that look," snapped Ash. "The police already

shoot us for being streetscum. If the authorities understood what they're really dealing with, we'd be facing genocide. This lot were getting far too close."

"But the research, the fertility problem…"

"If they're not breeding, that's a bonus," replied Ash coldly. "I know this is harsh, but it really is us or them. That means we can't leave the slightest clue that they ever created a Wraeththu here."

I had to concede he had a point.

An hour later I stood on the front steps of the Calcutt Institute, watching the flames beginning to take hold. The evidence was burning, all the files and disks thrown to the hungry flames.

I pulled on one of the backpacks that we'd looted from the CGS barracks. It wasn't going to be easy on foot, but I felt relief to be getting away; away from the all-pervading medical stench of the Institute, away from the dead with their accusing eyes, away from my human past.

I couldn't help thinking that there would be consequences, despite the removal of the Nayati. The deaths had been too easy and something in me said that there should be more to it, like karma or something.

"If they know we're alive they'll expect us to head for Unneah territory in Chicago," Ash said. "But I think it's time we spread out to the smaller towns. We need to start tribes everywhere we can reach."

I nodded in agreement.

Another dream flowed into my mind, far sharper and more precise now that I was fully Wraeththu.

Running through the trees, pine needles tickling the soles of my feet, twenty of my best hara running with me…

"We should head south," I said with absolute certainty. "My dreams never made sense to the old me. That's all changed now; I totally get it. I've dreamed all my life, wonderful dreams, Wraeththu dreams. My future is filled with mountains and the scent of pine. Starting from here that means we go that way." I pointed.

"South it is, then." Ash replied "A wise har always pays attention to his dreams."

You Can Never Go Back

Go Back

Christopher Coyle

You Can Never
Go Back

I fled. I had no choice. My skin felt too tight for my body, a fire burned in my stomach and my head pounded with a violence threatening to send me spiralling into oblivion at any moment. I turned from the terrible tableau unfolding before me and pushed my way through the teeming mass of bodies, uncaring of who saw my face or who I had to push aside. The stench of their enjoyment mingled with the sickly-sweet scent of viscera and squeezed its way past my clenched fingers to fill my nostrils with its cloying perfume.

The heavy door to the room was only a temporary impediment. A jerk of my wrist, the application of my shoulder against the door, and I was outside. The cold, moist air hit me like a fist, but it was a welcome relief from the oppressive heat in the examination room. I inhaled deeply, my hand falling from my face so that I could breathe in the night air. But, even outside, I could not escape what I had seen. Even as the door slammed shut behind me, I could still hear them talking excitedly about the body they were examining.

The stranger had stumbled into our village shortly after midday. He mumbled something before he collapsed, but his words quickly suffered as all such does from the wagging tongues. He lay there, untouched, for almost an hour after he fell, for my people were too afraid of approaching, mistrusting that the demon had truly fallen. Then they descended upon him like vultures, swiftly carrying his body to my father's house. Besides being the village's leader, my father also tended to the physical woes of the villagers. That was when I first caught sight of the demon, when they carried his limp, unresisting body through the door and laid him down upon the table.

My curiosity drew me over after the others had left to find my father. At first glance, the stranger looked dead, except for the occasional, shallow rise and fall of his bare chest. Only a pair of tattered, ripped pants covered his lower body, showing a map of

192

burns and bruises crisscrossing his torso. It looked like he had been struck repeatedly with a burning brand.

It seemed impossible to me that a demon could be burned, much less be as badly wounded as the stranger had been. Once, he must have been truly beautiful, for behind the bruises and scorched flesh of his face, you could still see the ghost of his former grandeur. His hair had escaped the plaits it had been braided in, tangled with twigs and leaves and hanging wildly about his injured features. Immediately, it was apparent that he was one of them. One of the demons from the south.

Hesitantly, I reached out a trembling hand to touch him, to see if he was flesh and blood. Before I could touch him, however, the door burst open and my father stood there.

"Get away from him, Jarren," he barked in a tone that brooked no disobedience. Pulling my hand back so quickly caused me to stumble backwards, leaving room for my father and the men who had carried the stranger to crowd in around the table.

My back against the wall, I watched with morbid fascination as my father began to work upon the stranger. The stranger's pants had to be soaked in water before they could be cut off of him, for they become crusted with blood and ichor from wounds that had not been apparent before. The moment that my father had removed the stranger's pants completely, it became immediately apparent to them that the stranger was truly different when my father stumbled back with a startled exclamation and one of the others yelled out in disgust. Apparently, I had realized far more swiftly what the stranger was before they had.

The demons are built differently than people. Their bodies are different, somehow combining aspects of male and female anatomy to create a set of genitalia that was fascinating, at least to my gaze. It was obvious the others in the room did not share my fascination, except my father.

He took the other three men off to the side, gathering them together as he whispered something urgently in a low voice. I probably could have listened in, and looking back, I wish that I had, but I could not tear my attention away from the fallen demon before me. No, he wasn't a demon. If anything, I thought of him as an angel who had been through hell.

"Jarren, stay here," my father's voice broke the glamour I had been caught in. As I looked over at him, his face was serious, but there burned a strange, curious light in his eyes.

"Watch the demon until we get back," my father continued as he and the others left, leaving me alone once again.

Bemused by my father's rather abrupt disappearance, I stood there against the wall, unsure of what to do. I probably would have stayed there until my father returned if the demon hadn't groaned out loud, his eyes fluttering open as he looked around in confusion.

"Where am I?" he mumbled softly as his pale, pale eyes finally settled upon me. I felt trapped by those eyes. They were a translucent jade and surprisingly sharp for someone who had been unconscious moments before.

"You...you're in Kreslow," I stuttered, unable to look away from the stranger's eyes.

His brow furrowed in confusion, but the stress upon the burns on his face caused him to grimace in pain instead. He tried to push himself up, but even before he raised his torso, he groaned in pain and slumped back against the hard wood of the table he was laying on.

I reached forward, pressing my hands lightly against his chest, trying not to cause any more pain than he must already be in. "Please, rest. My father will be back soon. He can help you."

The stranger shook his head, "No, he cannot..." Suddenly, the stranger's voice broke off as he was caught by a fit of choking. The blood flecking his whitened lips frightened me, but I tried to smile reassuringly as I brushed his hair out of his face.

"You'll be fine," I tried to reassure him, but I don't think that he heard me before he slipped back into unconsciousness.

I tried to make the demon, the angel, more comfortable, using a cool cloth to cleanse some of the crusted gore from his flesh. Before too long, my father returned. I heard him at the door and I dropped the cloth guiltily, backing away from the table as he came through the door. Whatever I was about to say, the excuses that were ready to spill from my mouth, was silenced by the crowd following my father. On all of their faces, I could see a grim determination fixing their faces into rictus masks.

They ignored me as they pushed into the room, my father leading the way to the body upon the table. He was dressed in all black, the clothing that he wore only when he was about to use his knives to bleed someone of the sickness within their body. My suspicions were confirmed when he pulled out the black leather bag that was his most valued possession. The black bag that held his knives, his needles, and the other tools he used for physicking.

What happened next will haunt me for the rest of my life, a nightmare I shall never be able to free myself from. Using an extract from a rare weed that rendered those who breathed its fumes in a sleep that bordered upon death, my father ensured his "patient" would not awaken. Rolling up his sleeves, he opened his black bag and pulled out one of his knives and began his grisly examination upon the demon.

The rational part of my mind realized that my father and the people of the village were terrified of the demons that had been increasing in numbers over the last decade. Where we lived, far in the north, we only heard occasional rumours from the southern cities and the news was frightening. My father and the other village leaders must have determined that this was the best way to find out about the demons, to learn what makes their bodies work and perhaps to find a way to fight them. To them, the stranger on the table was a monster that had to be studied and analyzed. To me, it was something surreal, a scene that one would expect to see only in Hell.

I had witnessed my father work before. I had even assisted him on occasion, but this time, I could not detach myself from what was happening. This time, something was different. It bordered on sacrilege and my heart cried out at the injustice unfolding around me. I looked around, desperate to see if there was anyone else there who I could turn to for help, who might understand. In each face, I saw something that scared me almost as much as the sight of my father elbow-deep in viscera and blood. Eagerness, anticipation, and an almost sadistic satisfaction at seeing a demon brought low gleamed from every face. That was when I knew that I had to escape. I had to get out of there. Let them believe that I was a coward, that the sight of so much blood had sickened me.

After I left the room, I wandered aimlessly along the street, not truly caring where I was going, just eager to put as much distance between myself and the others as possible. I had always felt like an outsider in the village, but no more so than at that moment. Right then, I just wanted to get away from everything and everyone.

I don't know how long I walked. I know I had left the boundaries of the village some time ago and I hadn't bothered grabbing my coat. The chill night air was sharp, even with the moisture of the coming snows, but the fire still burning within me was still hot enough that I did not feel the cold, at least not consciously. I wrapped my arms over my chest not so much as to try and ward off the cold as to try and keep my heart from bursting from my breast.

I suddenly felt a harsh hand upon my shoulder, my already pounding heart leapt to my throat as I was spun around to face two alien figures. They were tall, taller than anyone in the village, but possessed of a slenderness that bordered on gauntness. Yet, there was a certain lushness about them, a sensuality that transcended human definitions of masculinity or beauty. It did not take me but a few moments to realize that they were demons, like the one in town.

The taller of the two, whose hair was intricately plaited with ivory tubes and beads, leaned down until his face was close to mine. In a low voice that sent a shiver along my spine, he growled out, "Where is har? Where is Mendal?"

I knew he meant the other demon, the one currently lying helpless on my father's table, beneath my father's blade. When he shook me, I shattered. It must have shocked him to suddenly find the young boy in his grasp shaking like a leaf as he sobbed everything out. The demon's dark eyes, so different yet so alike those of the jade-eyed demon back in the village, were wide in disbelief as the words spilled from my throat in a relentless torrent that unburdened everything knotted up inside of me.

"Stay here with the boy," the demon holding me demanded of the other silent shadow before he released me and faded into the darkness. I was suddenly enfolded in a surprisingly strong pair of arms and wrapped in a heavy cloak of dark leather as I was pulled back against the demon's chest. I felt his breath warming the cusp of my ear as he suddenly chuckled, "Do not be afraid, little one. We are not demons, not all the time. We just take care of our own."

I didn't understand what he meant then. I almost wish that I didn't understand when he meant now. But at that moment, I felt warm and safe. When the other demon returned a few minutes later, his face was grim, but he offered me a slight smile before he looked at his companion, "Come, it is time for us to go. We must return to the others and tell them that Mandal has passed to the next life."

I felt the demon holding me begin to shake, as I had shook earlier, but it passed quickly. My chin was grabbed in a hand and I was forced to look up into the piercing, dark eyes of the demon. "First, child, as Kalen told you, we are not demons. We are Wraeththu. Second, you are coming with us. We have lost Mendal tonight, but I believe we have found a new spirit to join us. Third, I am Halcoln and we've a long journey ahead of us. We must go. Now."

I didn't question Halcoln's words as he and Kalen led me away from the village. My mind was muddied, my senses confused. I never saw the plumes of smoke twisting up into the night behind us, as I never looked back. It was many years before I found out what Halcoln had done while he was in the village. He told me that the remains of Mendal's body had to be purified by fire for his spirit to be freed. When I eventually returned to Kreslow, all I found was the ruined remains of a village that had been burned to the ground decades ago.

It's true what they say. You can never go back.

The Conservation of Momentum

Fiona Lane

The Conservation of Momentum

"… Some vows are made when you are very young,
personal vows that might never be spoken. I cannot
go back on promises that I've made to myself,
whatever others might think of my beliefs."

– The Bewitchments of Love and Hate

Winter came early that year, sweeping down from the high
mountains like an empty-bellied predator, bringing first the metallic
tang of snow in the air, and then a heavy blanket of white and silence
to the wide plains of Megalithica. Generations unborn would number
this year Ai-Cara-Less-40, but for the ragged army of hara shivering
as they rode, marched, trudged and stumbled across the bleak
landscape, it was a year only of cold and of death.

Terzian reined his horse to a halt, waiting for the stragglers to
catch up. They numbered upward of a thousand now; several small
tribes, his own included, had banded together, realizing that their
chances of survival were increased along with their numbers. Still, it
was an uneasy alliance as yet. They were strangers to each other, too
used to owing loyalty to none but their own small circle. Eventually,
Terzian knew, they would bond, their common danger and common
kinship uniting them against the dual threat of the elements and of
humankind, but for now it was a period of transition as they
realigned their hierarchies and reassessed their loyalties.

The same could be said of Terzian. Until ten days ago, he had
been an autocrat. True, his sovereignty had been modest – scarcely
three hundred hara had looked to him as leader – but it had been
absolute. Now, compromise was the order of the day. His own tribe
and another from nearby had joined forces with that of Ponclast,

another tribe leader from the north. Ponclast's band was by far the largest, numbering some five hundred or more hara, and perhaps in Ponclast's mind that gave him an edge of superiority, but he never said so aloud. His talk was all of alliances and councils and co-operation.

Terzian did not believe this talk for one minute. Ponclast was not a har who compromised. Terzian could see that in him – he carried his authority with him like a visible aura. Ponclast was a natural leader, a trait that Terzian could recognize well enough from his own personal acquaintance with it, and therein lay a potential source of conflict, with two rival generals vying for the top position. A long time ago, they had met briefly in the madness of the earliest days of Wraeththu. They had both changed a lot. Terzian had not known Ponclast then – even his name had been different – and did not know him now. Proximity might bring acquaintance, but not real knowing.

Terzian looked at the rag-tag band of pathetic creatures stamping and shuffling in front of him and snorted in disgust. Delusions of grandeur! This was no army, and there was no status or prestige to be gained by leading them. Merely surviving the winter would be an achievement for this lot. There was nothing to fight over. That aside, Terzian was intelligent enough to realise that with the rise of Wraeththu, the age-old power struggles of humankind were rendered if not exactly irrelevant, then at least somewhat obsolete. There were other, less destructive ways of engaging with potential rivals.

He watched the other har surreptitiously. Ponclast was mounted on a large black horse which he was riding at a smart trot along the untidy ranks of exhausted hara, encouraging them to pick up the pace. Terzian noticed that his high, leather riding boots had metal spurs at the heels, and these Ponclast used quite enthusiastically to keep his mount motivated. The bright metal of the spurs was reddened with blood from the animal's flanks.

Ponclast was a tall har, physically imposing, yet not heavy-set or muscular. His body was slender and attenuated, with long, graceful limbs and an almost regal bearing. He was dressed elegantly in what appeared to be military uniform, although not the utilitarian garments of the modern soldier; his garb seemed to belong to an earlier, more formal era. He wore a long black coat, high-necked and fastened with polished metal buttons, which flared out at the waist and draped over the haunches of his mount.

His black hair was very short, cropped close to his head. It looked brutal, authoritarian and intimidating, which Terzian suspected was the intention, but there was also a suggestion of military efficiency, a quality noticeably absent from the other hara.

Terzian watched those long legs flex around the horse's body again, driving the spurs into its side. Not for the first time, he let his imagination stray, conjuring images of those legs wrapped around his own body — unclothed. The marble-hard thigh muscles taut and defined, a product of all those hours in the saddle, the hardness between those legs which owed nothing to the riding of animals...

Against the saddle of his mount, between his own legs, Terzian felt a slow, rhythmic pulse accompanied by a flush of warmth. The horse danced a little under him, its movement only serving to increase his arousal. At that moment, Ponclast turned his head to stare long and hard at Terzian, as if he had been able to feel the other har's gaze upon him. Terzian suspected that he could do so; there was a mystery to Ponclast that Terzian did not fully understand. He silently hoped that the other har had not been able to sense any of his private fantasies. Their eyes locked for a moment, and Terzian knew with certainty that he had.

Ponclast spurred his mount and rode over, a black silhouette in stark relief against the white snow; a carrion crow of a har. He sat upright in the saddle, back straight, no sign of fatigue, although the group had been travelling for several days non-stop.

Terzian found himself offering up a brief salute as Ponclast arrived; it seemed the natural thing to do. Ponclast acknowledged the gesture with a curt nod of his head.

"They're too slow," he remarked, almost accusingly, as if he expected Terzian to personally increase the speed of each and every lagging har.

"They're tired. Exhausted. What do you expect?"

"I expect they will perish."

Terzian's face registered his dismay at this gloomy prognosis. Ponclast eyed him carefully, hawk-like in his intensity, and Terzian realized this was some sort of test. Of what, he wasn't entirely sure, but it sent a small stab of irritation through him.

"Well then we'll have to do something to prevent that, won't we?" he snapped.

Ponclast maintained his scrutiny for a few more seconds, as if coming to a decision, then his expression changed into what Terzian eventually realised — with shock — was a smile. It was not a reassuring look.

"Yes," he said, "Yes, we will. You and I." The smile-that-was-not-a-smile widened, displaying white, even teeth which in other circumstances might have been considered attractive, but in Terzian's mind only conjured images of sharks and tigers and other nameless nightmare beasts.

Ponclast edged his horse up against Terzian's, positioning himself close enough so that he could stretch out a comradely hand and lay it on Terzian's shoulder. The hand was sheathed in a black leather glove. In spite of himself, Terzian felt a small flicker of electricity run through his flesh at that touch.

"Look at them," Ponclast said, indicating with a desultory nod of his head the mass of hara milling and stamping on the frozen ground. "They're sheep. Every one of them. Lost without someone to guide them. To lead them."

Terzian gritted his teeth. "And that would be you, I suppose?"

Ponclast slapped his shoulder with his gloved hand. "You and me. Together. I can't do this alone – I need someone to share the responsibility. To share the burden"

"Don't patronize me," Terzian growled. "I don't think you're the sort of har who needs anyone to hold your hand."

Ponclast roared with laughter.

"You're quite right, Terzian. I don't need any forelock-tugging, awe-struck acolytes. I need a har with the ability to lead and to take decisions and to think for himself, and that, as you have just so ably demonstrated, is you, Terzian."

Terzian was somewhat mollified, although he still considered that Ponclast was attempting to manipulate him through flattery.

"We don't have the luxury of being fragile little flowers who need reassurance about their own importance," Ponclast continued, making Terzian wonder if the other har really could overhear his thoughts. He resolved to be more circumspect in his internal opinions around this har, if such a thing were even possible.

"You and me, Terzian. We're going to have to lead this tribe. We're going to have to run things. Because there is no one else."

Terzian knew that Ponclast was right. In this world, there were leaders, and there were followers, and Terzian had an innate sense of which category he belonged to.

"We can't stay here," Ponclast went on, obviously assuming Terzian's complete agreement on the matter just discussed. "There's little in the way of shelter, and the weather is only going to get worse. We're running out of food, too."

"What do you suggest?" Terzian asked

Ponclast displayed his white teeth again.

"There's a town about an hour's ride from here."

"I know that," said Terzian. "It's occupied. By humans."

"I think we should make it... *unoccupied.*"

"Really?" Terzian scrutinized Ponclast's face, trying to determine if he was serious. "And how do you intend to do that? Are you just going to ask them to leave?"

Ponclast affected sincerity. "Do you think that would work?"

"Don't be ridiculous."

"You're quite right. "I think we're going to have to go down the traditional route of mindless violence and the excessive use of force."

"That's your plan? I can't say it fills me with confidence."

"Oh, Terzian, have a little faith. They're only humans, after all."

"I think you'll find they're armed humans. With an irrational dislike of Wraeththu-kind. They can be pretty dangerous, as I recall."

Ponclast made a cutting gesture with the side of his hand. "And we are armed hara, but that is of little consequence one way or another."

"Try telling that to all the dead hara we've left behind."

"Too many, I agree. It is time for us to fight back, Terzian. Time to bring the fight to the enemy. On our terms, not his."

"What do you mean?"

Ponclast gave Terzian's mount a slap on the rear with his hand. The beast snorted, laid back its ears and edged forward a few paces nervously. Terzian snatched at the reins to control the animal.

"Come on," Ponclast urged. "It'll be dark in an hour. We need to get camp set up. Come to my tent and we will dine together. We can talk more then. In the meantime, let's get these useless, lazy hara moving."

With a kick of his spurs, Ponclast set off into the gathering gloom, shouting a mixture of curses and encouragement at the assembled hara. Terzian watched him go, his face an unreadable mask. Then he set off at a brisk canter to join the sudden flurry of activity.

Ponclast's tent was luxurious compared with the accommodation afforded to most of the rest of the tribe, but that was scant comfort. The reality was a mouldering collection of rugs, fabric, and ancient, rank animal skins stretched over an unsteady frame. The icy wind found its way easily through the many gaps in the structure, and the smell was something that Terzian found did not easily dissipate from a har's hair or body even once he had left the source behind.

Nevertheless, as the snow started to fall again, and the last of the daylight died, it was still a better place to be than outside.

The interior was lit – dimly – by a couple of small and improvised oil lamps. Their greasy flames added a smoky undertone to the complex perfume of damp and decay enveloping the place.

Terzian's nose wrinkled involuntarily, but he did not complain. His own dwelling, if it could be dignified with such a term, was no more than a few sheets of some tough, synthetic material he had salvaged from a rubbish pile. In comparison, Ponclast's lair was positively magnificent in its opulence.

"Please, do come in." Ponclast said, holding the tent flap open for him in a welcoming manner. As Terzian entered, Ponclast grasped his hand and shook it firmly, a gesture that Terzian found slightly bizarre both in its unexpectedness and its conventionality. Harish tribes had been quick to cast off human customs and invent their own rituals and greetings. He felt Ponclast's other hand, still gloved, investigate further up his arm, and realized that the gesture had been reclaimed for its original, more practical purpose. Ponclast was checking if he was armed.

Naturally the knife was removed from him.

"I hope you don't mind," said Ponclast smoothly, in a tone which informed him that it made no difference whether he did or not, "But I've learned to be cautious."

"Of course, "Terzian said, "As have we all."

"Please, do take a seat." Ponclast indicated a lumpy pile of fabric set some distance above the ground.

"Thank you." Terzian settled himself carefully on the rags. Ponclast's polite, mannered formality unnerved him a little. In times of apocalyptic upheaval and the general breakdown of society, etiquette tended to be one of the first things abandoned. The scattered, half-feral Wraeththu tribes who wandered these desolate plains were not known for their social graces. Terzian found that he appreciated Ponclast's attempt to maintain certain standards of civilized behaviour, even in the most uncivilized of circumstances.

Ponclast slid his gloved hand into one of the large pockets inside his long, black coat. He produced a metal implement with a wicked looking pointed claw at one end. Terzian felt his muscles tense involuntarily, but Ponclast merely reached down and removed a round metal container from a pile of similar objects sitting on the floor. He plunged the pointed claw into the cylinder and ripped a jagged hole in the top. With a polite smile, he handed it to Terzian.

In the dim light, Terzian had no idea what was actually in the can, but he hadn't eaten all day, and the intriguing smell of its contents overcame even the sour background miasma, so he thrust his fingers into it, taking care to avoid the jagged metal edges, and began to excavate the contents.

Ponclast repeated the performance with another can, then once again delved in his pocket and produced a tiny spoon with which he delicately scooped small morsels of food from the can and ate them as fastidiously as a cat. For no reason he could think of, Terzian felt vaguely embarrassed by his own method.

"Have a drink." Ponclast pointed to a bottle of clear liquid sitting next to the pile of cans. Terzian picked it up, sniffed and slugged a mouthful. The raw alcohol burned his mouth and traced its warm fingers down into the pit of his empty stomach.

"This is… very nice," he said, with all the sincerity he could muster.

Ponclast put down his spoon and gave him a piercing stare with his hawk-eyes

"No," he said carefully "No, it is not. It is quite vile. As is this abominable tent, the execrable weather, and all the tedious indignities of our pathetic circumstances. This is not living; this is merely a squalid, meaningless existence which not even animals should be forced to suffer."

Terzian did not even bother to disagree.

"We cannot survive like this," Ponclast continued. "Which is why we must take action to improve our lot – and sooner rather than later."

"They will have supplies at the town," Terzian mused, finishing off the contents of his can. "We could wait till after moon-down and mount a raid."

Ponclast sighed. "My dear Terzian, a few stolen scraps will not keep us for long, nor do anything to mitigate our wretchedness in the long term. We need more than that. We need the entire town."

"Are you seriously intending to mount an all-out attack?"

"I am."

"That's crazy!" Terzian set down the can, which he found he'd been clenching tightly in his hand "The population of that town must be – what, approaching five or six thousand? Maybe more. And the majority will be adult men and women equipped with firearms and ready and willing to use them."

"You forget one thing, Terzian. They are merely humans. We, on the other hand, are Wraeththu."

Terzian laughed out loud. "Very nice propaganda speech, Ponclast, but ideology is no match for guns."

"Actually," said Ponclast smoothly, "that is where you are wrong, Terzian." He reached yet again into his voluminous pockets, whose depths appeared home to an almost endless supply of artefacts, and to the other har's alarm produced a pistol, which he raised and pointed steadily at Terzian's head.

"What are you doing? Put that away, put it down, there's no need... No!"

Terzian watched in horror as Ponclast's leather-encased finger squeezed firmly on the trigger, pulling it back to its furthest reach. There was a faint click, and nothing happened.

"What the...? Fuck!"

"Now, Terzian, we don't use that word anymore."

"I'll use any fucking word I want! What the fuck do you think you're playing at?"

Ponclast regarded the gun lovingly and ran his hand down its barrel seductively.

"Technology, Terzian. Human technology. Have you ever thought about it? How it works? What has to happen to make it work? This gun, for example... Do you know how much effort went into making it? Metal was mined and smelted, machines were constructed to manufacture the parts, the parts were assembled, in the correct way. It's a simple machine in many ways, a gun, yet complex enough that just one failing part can render it useless."

"We are not humans, Terzian," There was a tiny light of something resembling fanaticism in his eyes which Terzian found vaguely disturbing. "We do not need the crutch of crude technology, because we have a different way of addressing the universe. We can see beyond the mundane façade of what humans think of as the real world. We can touch the divine – be one with the energy that binds everything together."

"You're completely mad, aren't you?"

It was Ponclast's turn to laugh.

"Perhaps a little, but there is truth in what I say, Terzian. A speck of gold buried in the mud and grit that threatens to obscure it, waiting to be washed free by the careful prospector. Let me be a little more prosaic, since I can see that you are not a har given to fancy.

Wraeththu are different from humans in more than just the obvious way which we all know and enjoy to its fullest. We have psychic abilities, too. Telepathy, telekinesis, the ability to use and manipulate energies inherent in the very fabric of matter and space.

"Oh, most of the lumpen herd of common hara will never develop these abilities to any noticeable extent, but a few of us are gifted beyond the average, and with dedication and study, we can expand these latent talents beyond our wildest imaginations.

"Look at me, Terzian, and tell me that you do not believe. You cannot, because you know it is true. Deep within yourself, you *know*."

Terzian was on the verge of dismissing Ponclast's assertions as the rantings of a lunatic, and yet some part of him wanted – *needed* – to believe that it could be true. If it were not, he could see no future for himself and his kind but more of this grim, meaningless journey through a life of hardship and danger. Ponclast offered something more – not a better life in itself, perhaps, but the hope that such a thing could be possible, and hope was always better than despair.

"And if it is true," he said cautiously, "exactly how does that help us in our current situation."

"It helps us, Terzian, because that which can be done to one gun can be done to many. The humans will defend their town with their idiot, fallible technology in which they have so much faith, and I will cause it to fail, as I caused this gun to fail. An atom can alter an entire universe, if moved in a particular way. Without their guns, the humans are nothing."

"And once they are disarmed, you intend to kill them?"

Ponclast rolled his eyes melodramatically. "No, I thought we would simply give them a good talking-to!"

Terzian flushed slightly, in spite of himself.

"There is no room for sentimentality and squeamishness." Ponclast continued, with some agitation. "This is war, Terzian. A war to the death, them or us, and it's going to be us, make no mistake about that. If you do not believe that with every fibre of your being, then you may as well pull the trigger on that gun right now, and I will not intervene in any way this time."

"I have killed humans when the need arose, and I can do so again," Terzian stated flatly. "However, the adolescent boys can be incepted, and the women make good servants. No point in wasting resources."

Ponclast appeared delighted. "I underestimated you, Terzian. You have a strategist's brain. That will prove useful to us in time. Do you have any other suggestions?"

"Wait another three days. The moon is full at the moment, and rises early. In three days time, it will be behind the hills after midnight, giving us the cover of darkness when the townspeople are at their most vulnerable."

"The element of surprise," Ponclast agreed. "It has much to recommend it. We have sufficient supplies to last us three days, and it will give us time to prepare before we strike, swiftly, from out of the dark. I shall use the time to build up my energies. You can assist me with that, Terzian. If you are willing." He paused meaningfully. "Are you willing, Terzian?"

Terzian stared at Ponclast. In the dim light, the other har seemed different. A change had come upon him, like a lizard which slowly alters its colouration to suit its background. His skin had taken on a soft radiance. The close-cropped hair no longer seemed so harsh and masculine, but looked like plush velvet, inviting touch. The sharp angles of his face now revealed a refined and sculpted bone structure beneath, and the dark eyes were large and liquid.

Terzian felt a dizzying rush of lust. He realized, with something like surprise, that it had been many weeks since he had taken aruna. Circumstances had been difficult, and his energy had been focused elsewhere. Besides, if he were to be honest, there were few – if any – hara within his group whom he considered attractive. Certainly none who had been able to ignite such a rush of desire quite so effortlessly as Ponclast had done.

There were undoubtedly hara who were more beautiful than Ponclast, but Ponclast had something different about him, something more. Terzian could feel it, sense it – smell it, even, despite the all-pervading stench of the tent. It was the scent of power, and it was dangerously aphrodisiac.

Ponclast reached out with one gloved hand and stroked Terzian's cheek. There was nothing intimate or tender about the gesture – he might have been checking the condition of a piece of livestock – but Terzian found himself trembling, and only partially from fear. He felt the soft grain of the leather brush across his face, then move downward, coming to rest at the nape of his neck. Terzian could feel his own pulse throbbing there, strong and rapid, and he knew that Ponclast could feel it too.

He knew that if he was going to make any attempt to take control of this situation, it would have to be now, or not at all. Part of him wanted to do battle with Ponclast, to pit his own will and determination against the other har's strength. Another part of him wanted nothing more than to be overwhelmed by Ponclast's power, to be taken, and used; forced to submit, forced to give up his autonomy, given no choice…

The light within the tent grew dim, then bright, then dim again and Terzian could not tell if it was the guttering of the oil lamps or his own vision. He was unused to this feeling of helplessness, and yet there was a familiarity about it, as if it was something he had known, or would know. The air shimmered and wavered, and Terzian closed his eyes, taking refuge in the darkness of his own mind.

His surrender was acknowledged with a triumphant, wordless blast of thought from Ponclast. Terzian felt himself pushed to the ground, onto the damp, mildewed carpet laid over the bare earth. He felt gloved hands pulling his clothing away roughly, then running up his thighs, firmly prising them apart. They did not have to try very hard.

A leather-encased finger entered him, investigating and probing. Terzian wondered briefly if he should ask, or demand, that Ponclast remove his gloves. It seemed somehow wrong to have the skin of a dead animal between him and his seducer, a barrier where there should be none, but Ponclast showed no inclination to shed his borrowed skin, and seemed adept enough at finding the right places within Terzian's body despite his handicap. Perhaps he never took the gloves off and was by now so used to their presence that they felt like his own skin.

The fingers withdrew, leaving Terzian filled with nothing but frustration. Not for long. With a sudden, savage thrust Ponclast drove into him long and deep. No leather this time, for which Terzian was grateful, just the smooth, silken hardness of Ponclast's ouana-lim. Skin against skin, flesh against flesh, har inside har.

There were sounds inside Terzian's head; roaring or drumming, he couldn't tell which, nor did he particularly care at this instant. Ponclast thrust angrily into him again and again, making no particular effort to pleasure the other har, but, strangely, doing so nonetheless. Terzian realized that this was going to be a very brief experience. He found himself almost wishing for the slow ecstasy of a more measured encounter, but that was obviously not Ponclast's plan, and he knew there was no point in attempting to persuade the har otherwise.

The noise grew louder; a wailing, keening sound adding its discordant harmony to the base notes of Ponclast's ragged breathing and Terzian's own thundering heartbeat. As the sound reached its eerie climax, Terzian tensed and shuddered, and was suddenly filled with a hot rush of liquid. The essence of Ponclast's body mixed with his own secretions, and seemed to spark a chain reaction inside him, spreading through his body and out to his extremities.

The howling did not stop. If anything, it became louder. Terzian lay on the floor, panting and trembling a little, and realized that it was not in his head at all, but all around them.

Without ceremony, Ponclast withdrew himself from Terzian and rose to his feet gracefully.

"Timber wolves," he said, and suddenly the noise lost its supernatural quality, and Terzian could hear it for what it really was.

"They come out from the forests at night, searching for prey," Ponclast informed him.

His ouana-lim was still hard and erect, thrusting out at an aggressive angle from his body like a weapon, and glistening wet in the low light. A few drops of the combined essences of their bodies dripped from it onto the dirty rug on the floor. Terzian would not have been surprised to see the liquid eat a hole in the stained fabric, like acid, but nothing of the sort happened. There was only the addition of another stain to the ancient carpet, joining the many already there.

Ponclast ran one hand along the length of his engorged organ, either in an attempt to remove the sticky, residue, or simply because he enjoyed it. At some point, his gloves must have come off, because his hands were now bare. Obviously his own flesh demanded something finer than mere animal hide. Terzian looked closely. He had been expecting some disfigurement, or scarring perhaps, which would account for Ponclast's reluctance to remove the gloves, but the hands were perfectly normal.

The howling stopped abruptly, leaving a jarring silence broken only by the lesser wailing of the wind finding its way between the gaps in the wall of Ponclast's tent.

"The pack will go hungry tonight unless they travel further afield," Ponclast said. He grinned fiercely, wolfishly. "We are not the prey, Terzian, we are the predators!"

When Terzian left Ponclast's tent, he did not return directly to the unwelcoming embrace of his own shelter. Instead, he made his way down towards the river which ran through the shallow valley in which the group of hara were camped.

The stink of Ponclast's tent was in his hair, in his clothes, in his nostrils. It seemed to have ground itself into his skin, through his pores, into the very fabric of his being. Even the clean outside air would not rid him of it.

The night was intensely cold and utterly still. The layer of snow underfoot had frozen crisp and iron-hard, and it crunched noisily with every step that Terzian took. Above him, the cold silver disc of the moon was haloed by a wide circle of light. Looking up at it, Terzian felt the first freezing flakes of snow touch his face. Their icy sharp bites lasted for only a moment before they immolated themselves upon his burning skin.

He reached the edge of the river, which lay like a dark scar on the paleness of the landscape. The moon was reflected on the smooth surface of the water, leaving a long trail of light which might easily have been a path which could be taken to reach the other side. Terzian stopped at the river's edge – the banks were not steep here – and began removing his clothing.

Strangely, he did not feel cold. There was not the slightest movement to the air; no wind to rob his body of its living warmth. He felt alive and invigorated in a way that he had not in the stultifying confines of Ponclast's tent.

He removed his boots last and tentatively set his naked feet to the ground. The frozen snow burned, but only for a moment; then an enveloping numbness took the discomfort away. He walked the short distance to the water's edge and continued without hesitation into its freezing embrace.

In the dark, with the moonlight reflecting on its surface, it was impossible to tell what lay under the water. There might have been rocks, weeds, potholes, open jaws, unseen hands waiting to grasp at his ankles and pull him under – anything. Terzian's mind was focused on other things, however, as he waded further out into the deeper part of the river. The physical shock of the cold water was almost unbearable; it took the breath from him, forcing to concentrate on inhaling and exhaling in short, staccato gasps.

Above him, the moon looked down dispassionately. If he tilted his head backwards, Terzian could see clearly all the contours and marks upon its surface, the legacy of a thousand impacts, yet despite these imperfections, it was still a thing of beauty, a sister planet for the Earth, a companion in the emptiness of space. Knowing it was there somehow mitigated the loneliness of existence. Terzian took one last, deep breath, held on to it, and plunged swiftly under the freezing water.

Instantly he erupted upwards again, shedding a spray of water droplets glittering like multi-faceted jewels in the cold light. He gasped for air, as if he had been under the water for hours, not mere split seconds. Water streamed from his naked body, down his chest and arms, into his eyes and ears and mouth. His long, fair hair was drenched and sodden. Pulled down by the weight of the water, the ends of it trailed in the river, bait for any passing fish or malign water spirit who might wish to seize it.

His sudden explosive exit from the water had shattered the stillness of the night. The moon's calm reflection was utterly destroyed, broken into a thousand pieces of light, flickering like fireflies. Terzian wiped his face with his hands, clearing his eyes so that he could see again. Water had potency that air did not, the power both to chill the body and to cleanse it. To his relief, he could no longer smell Ponclast or his tent.

He waded back to the shore, shivering violently now. When he reached his discarded pile of clothes, he hesitated for a moment. Part of him wanted to abandon them there, but he knew he could not afford to lose them, the boots in particular. Instead, he scooped up the pile and doused them in the river. When he retrieved them, they were heavy and wet, but he gathered them up nevertheless.

As he stood up and turned to make his way back to the encampment, he was overcome by the sudden conviction that he was being watched. He stood very still. For a moment he thought he saw something shining in the dark. Something yellow and gleaming, like the eyes of a beast. He stared hard into the blackness, but if eyes had been upon him, they had not cared to stay and observe further.

Clutching his bundle of wet clothing, he set off across the frozen ground back to the encampment, ice crystals already forming on his cold, naked skin.

Three nights later, when the moon was hidden and veiled behind the surrounding hills, a ragged regiment of hara made their stealthy approach to the human-occupied town. Although it was late, and many of the old and young were asleep in their beds, the town was still alert and defended by a not inconsiderable force of the able-bodied.

The human race had fallen on hard times. No longer could they rely on their technology, their society and their sheer numbers to ensure their absolute dominion over all else. Nowadays, it was every town, village and settlement for itself. Wild creatures roamed the hills and forests around the town, preying upon the weak and unsuspecting. Some took the shape of human beings, but were not. The townspeople knew that no help would be forthcoming from others of their own kind should an attack come, and so they kept guard, their back to the walls, their guns trained outwards.

Ponclast was unconcerned.

"We knew they'd be armed. I predicted it, did I not? Hold your nerve, Terzian, I am prepared."

Ponclast had a strange expression on his face; distant, and somewhat vacant, his eyes glassy and heavy-lidded. He appeared almost drugged, and, in fact, Terzian had seen him slipping some small, greenish kernels into his mouth at regular intervals. He decided he didn't want to know what these were.

"I am prepared too."

Ponclast smiled vaguely. "Prepare for the worst, hope for the best." He said gnomically.

This did not fill Terzian with confidence, but he held his peace. There was no point in unnerving the rest of the tribe. He looked round at the ranks of hara. Ranks was too formal a word for them, he thought. Disorganised rabble would be more accurate. These hara were used to fighting, but they were a wild and chaotic bunch. Some training and discipline would not have gone amiss, the better to forge them into a true combat force, but it was too late for that now. They would simply have to make the best of things.

He turned his attention to their target. The town had been turned into a sort of crude fortress by the expedient of blocking off all but one road into it and barricading obvious weak points with whatever had come to hand – old vehicles, furniture and broken masonry. It wasn't completely secured by any means, but neither could anyone expect simply to stroll in without the permission of the inhabitants. Permission which was obviously not going to be forthcoming on this occasion.

Terzian had keen eyesight, and he could see the occasional glint of something metallic, the odd shadowy movement, which told him that the humans were there, their guns at the ready. If they, in turn, were aware of the exotic barbarians at their gate, then they showed no sign.

There was a palpable aura of impatience emanating from the assembled hara. Many of them were hungry, they were all cold, and the town lay like a fattened and docile animal before them. Just beyond those flimsy barricades was food and warmth and shelter from the encroaching weather. The hara shuffled and stamped. A few muffled curses reached Terzian's ears, and then an unearthly howl, like one of the hidden timber wolves saluting the rising moon. But this sound was not made by any wolf – it came from the throat of a har; primal and protean, full of savage energy.

Terzian felt the hairs rise on the back of his neck, even as he turned to glare and silence the restless throng with a short hand-gesture.

"Our time is upon us!" Ponclast announced to all.

He lifted both his hands, which Terzian noticed were ungloved, and a strange light danced between them, iridescent and rainbow-hued. It followed the movements of Ponclast's hands, wavering tremulously in the air. He seemed to be caressing and stroking it like a lover, without actually touching it.

"Go forth and claim your birthright. Inherit the Earth, Wraeththu children. A new day dawns for us all, and when the sun rises tomorrow, it will be upon a landscape of the mind such as has never been seen before."

Mad, though Terzian. *Quite, quite mad.*

If the rest of the tribe shared his assessment of Ponclast's mental state, they did not show it. From the shadows, from behind the cover of trees and decaying buildings, they surged forward eagerly, an unstoppable wave of bodies, eerily silent now in order to maintain the element of surprise for as long as possible.

At some point, an alarm must have been raised by the human lookouts. There was a series of shouts from behind the barricades, then the impression of movement and urgent activity.

Terzian watched Ponclast closely. The other har's eyes were closed. He appeared to be in a state of intense concentration, and the flickering light seemed to be all around him now, licking over his body like cold flames, rippling and changing colour. Static electricity crackled the air.

Terzian wondered if he should stay with Ponclast or join the attack on the town. The harish forces had reached the barricades now, and were tearing furiously at the piles of timber and rubble and barbed wire. The shouts from the human defenders had taken on a note of panic. Terzian recognized the sound of fear; he knew it all too well. Obviously their armaments were malfunctioning in some way, because the only sounds to be heard were the smashing and splintering of the inadequate defences, the noises of alarm from within the town, and the triumphant battle cries from the invaders.

Fire flared suddenly, an orange gout of flame lighting up the dark. Faced with the impossible uselessness of their weapons, the humans had resorted to less technological tactics: a bottle of petrol, a lit rag, and the crude new weapon hurled at the seething mass of night-creatures swarming towards them. The bottle smashed and vomited its fiery contents all over the crumbling barricade, spreading its flames like a contagious disease, infecting everything combustible, but the wave of hara parted like the sea around it and continued their inexorable progress towards the buildings beyond.

At that moment, a single, shocking report rang out, as loud as thunder to Terzian's ears. Sound and movement ceased abruptly, just for a brief moment. The barricades burned in silence. The human defenders looked on nervously. The onrushing hara froze, their momentum dissipated. Then another shot, and a scream, and murmur that became a roar, and the riotous cacophony began again, but this time chaotic and directionless. More shots peppered the night, and hara began to run for cover, lithe bodies illuminated by the flickering orange light, half-concealed by the smoke; some running, some falling.

Terzian spun round to look at Ponclast. The strange light around him had dimmed considerably, and his extended hands were empty. His face was now damp with sheen of perspiration, his mouth open and gasping, and his eyes wide and staring, although as Terzian grabbed his arm roughly he realised that whatever Ponclast was seeing, it was not the scene in front of him. Spitting a curse, he dropped the arm as if the flesh was poison, and ran off in the direction of the burning barricade.

It was a rout. Hara were fleeing in all directions, any form of discipline or teamwork they might have had now lost in the mad scramble to save themselves. Terzian started shouting and waving vigorously with his arms, indicating the direction of safety. He realised that he was making a very visible target of himself by doing so, but tried to put any possible consequences of his actions out of his mind.

Hara began running towards him, the relief in their eyes visible even in the smoky, flickering darkness. They needed someone to take charge, to tell them what to do, and they were drawn to Terzian like moths to the moon.

Emboldened by the sudden reversal in their fortunes, the human defenders now went on to the attack, small groups making sorties from the buildings, zigzagging in the shadows, trying to outflank the retreating hara and cut off their escape routes. Terzian realised with a sick feeling in his stomach that they were far more disciplined and practiced in the art of guerrilla warfare than his own tribe.

That will have to change, he thought grimly, seizing hold of a young har who was blindly running in the wrong direction, back towards the flaming remains of the barricade.

The har struggled furiously in his grasp.

"We have to go back!" he cried desperately.

"No, we have to retreat," Terzian spoke in an even tone, trying not to panic the har even more, but he held onto him firmly.

The har refused to accept this and struggled harder.

"We must! We have to go back. Moth is there!"

Terzian looked at the har closely. He looked very young, probably only a year or so past inception, if that. He had been one of Terzian's original band – a name, Lirren, attached itself to the face – and Terzian remembered vaguely that he seemed always to be in the company of another har, brown of hair and skin. Moth; as soft and silent as his namesake. The two were inseparable, and apparently did not take aruna with any other hara, if the rumours were to be believed. While Terzian did not actively discourage this behaviour, he considered it slightly abnormal nevertheless. Now, looking down at the distraught young har's wet, tear-streaked face, he realised that he should have put a stop to it much earlier. Too late to do anything about it now.

"If Moth is back there, then he is dead," he said, surprising even himself with the blunt cruelty of that statement. This was not the time for softening blows.

The har wailed piteously in denial, struggling furiously, but unable to free himself from Terzian's iron grip.

"Let me go!" he cried desperately, "I have to find him. Just let me go! Please!"

Terzian hesitated. The har looked at him with pleading eyes, large and grey. Terzian made his decision, and with a snarl of disapproval released him. Without a backward glance Lirren ran off toward the flames and smoke and welcoming gunfire. Terzian shrugged and turned his back on the vanishing har, resuming his efforts to guide the other hara to safety. *If that idiot wants to kill himself, then let him do it. There are others who want to live.*

Ponclast was eventually discovered back at the encampment, in his own tent. Terzian didn't even try to conceal his anger.

"There are at least a hundred dead hara back there!" he snapped, jabbing his forefinger furiously in the direction of the town, where a dull orange glow could still be seen illuminating the horizon.

"I am aware of that."

"Are you now? And what do you intend to do about it? Wave your magic wand or your pretty lights and bring them back to life?"

"Don't be facetious, Terzian, it's not your style at all. This is a setback, true, but the concept is sound. We simply need more power."

"I'm glad you think it's that simple."

"But it is, Terzian! I admit, I am inexperienced in these matters, and at present lack the required abilities to defeat an entire town. However, in time I shall increase my strength, and then we will be unstoppable."

"We don't have time," Terzian said bleakly.

Ponclast laced his gloved fingers together thoughtfully and frowned.

"You're right," he said "The road to enlightenment and knowledge is a long and weary one. We do not have the luxury of setting our feet upon that trail, narrow and difficult as it is. But there is another path we might take, a different direction..."

Terzian sighed heavily. He had little time for Ponclast's more fanciful notions; he wanted straight answers and certainties.

"We need more power, Terzian," Ponclast insisted, "and if it is not available to us by legitimate means, then we shall have to acquire by... other means."

"Get to the point."

Ponclast beckoned with his finger. "Come, sit here beside me Terzian. Now, tell me, what do you know of gods?"

Terzian laughed derisively. "There are no gods! Gods are the invention of humans – pathetic creatures too scared to face the world without their comforters."

"Is that so? And what of the Aghama?"

"What of him?"

"Does he exist? Or is he an invention too?"

Terzian shrugged. "How should I know?"

"If he does not exist, then where did we come from?"

"I have no idea."

"Come now, Terzian, you must have thought about it. It is quite evident that we did not spring from nowhere. There must have been a first."

"I suppose so," Terzian agreed somewhat grudgingly

"And this first Wraeththu has taken on a great significance among his diaspora; we have accorded him the status of deity, and named him Aghama. Some hara worship him."

Terzian grunted in disgust. "I don't!"

"It doesn't matter whether you do or not, Terzian," Ponclast continued calmly. "Neither does it matter if this first Wraeththu still lives and walks among us, as some believe, or whether, as is more likely, he died some ignominious death at the hands of humans. He is an ideal, an archetype, an external expression of a particular part of the Wraeththu psyche. A method by which hara might, with diligence, discover their own inner deity."

"And what does this have to do with capturing the town?"

Ponclast smiled grimly. "There are other areas of the Wraeththu psyche, Terzian. Darker areas, areas with fewer rules or self-imposed restrictions. And there is power to be had by accessing these areas. More power, in fact, than is available by the…"

"…legitimate..?"

"…methods. Quite so. I see we understand each other, Terzian."

"Perhaps. Do you really think this is something we should be considering?"

"And what else would you have me do?" Ponclast's irritation manifested itself. "How else would you have me protect our kind? I am all too aware of the implications of what I am proposing, Terzian, never think otherwise, but we have little choice. Would you prefer that I just fold my arms, thank the Aghama for this bounteous lesson in life, and quietly allow us all to perish? I will not do that, Terzian – I will use whatever methods are necessary to ensure our survival, whatever tools are at our disposal.

"And you, Terzian. Are you willing to sacrifice more Wraeththu lives on the altar of your principals?" Ponclast gave him a hard stare "You, who were so nobly incensed by the needless deaths of our comrades such a short while ago? If you want to save the rest of our tribe, you will have to sacrifice something in return. The energy of the universe must balance. Its momentum must be conserved. One does not get something for nothing."

Terzian found that he had no answer. Ponclast was right – they could not afford to be overly fastidious about how they chose to wage this war they were engaged in. What mattered was victory, not how it was achieved.

He remembered the events of three nights ago, in this very tent. This felt like the same thing; a surrender, a giving-up of some part of himself. It was the price he had to pay for his own survival.

Ponclast must have sensed his acquiescence, because he leaned over and laid his hand on Terzian's arm, patting it reassuringly.

"You know I'm right." he said "You know this is the only way. We cannot shy away from the realities of life simply because we find some of them distasteful. When fate summons us, we must be ready to meet the challenge. We must be a match for it. We must not fail in our moment of truth. We must dare to do what must be done." He rubbed his gloved hands together. "Now, come – button your coat, it's cold out. And it's time to get down to business."

Terzian paused for a moment, then stood up, carefully fastened his worn overcoat and followed Ponclast through the loose flap in the tent that served as a door.

Outside, a blizzard had descended upon the camp. Hard, frozen pellets of snow were being driven almost sideways by the wind, which howled as if it were a cousin to the timber wolves. Terzian hunched his shoulders and lowered his head into the oncoming blast, feeling its harsh and gritty fury scouring his skin.

A har could wish for more weatherproof clothing on such a night as this, he thought. In fact, a har could wish for many things – a warm bed, clean sheets, a full belly and a safe haven from both the storm and the naked aggression of the human race, none of which would come to him unless he were prepared to fight for them and take them – by whatever means necessary.

Ponclast headed away from the main encampment, towards a small stand of trees some distance away, with Terzian following behind, clutching his inadequate coat as tightly around his body as he could. The moon must surely have risen by now, but its cold light was hidden behind the cloud; it was pitch black, so black even the snow underfoot was as dark as bare earth.

Fortunately for them, the thicket of trees was quite dense and provided some shelter from both the wind and the driving snow. Ponclast fought his way through the tangle of bushes and long grass under and around the trees, tearing at the vegetation with his hands, until they came to a small clearing in the middle of the wooded area.

It was an open area, roughly circular in shape, measuring approximately twelve of Terzian's longest strides in diameter. The snowfall of the past few days lay undisturbed here, white and even..

Terzian and Ponclast stopped at the edge of the clearing, both breathing heavily from their exertions.

"Why are we here?" asked Terzian. It seemed a little too convenient, this magic circle in the middle of nowhere, as if Ponclast had planned all this in advance.

"You'll see." Ponclast rummaged in his endless pockets and produced a small leather pouch. He fastidiously removed a glove, pulling each leather finger in turn, then undid the cord holding the neck of the pouch closed and thrust his bare hand inside. When he pulled it out his clenched fist was full of some substance Terzian could not see.

"Stay there," he said.

He walked halfway into the centre of the clearing and began carefully sprinkling a dark powdery substance into the snow in a thin line. He walked around the clearing, marking a circle in the snow. Outside the circle, his footprints left a trail all the way around, but inside the snow remained virgin and untouched. As Ponclast walked, Terzian could hear him chanting strange words, the shapes and sounds of which were like no language Terzian had ever encountered before. They seemed louder in his ears than they should have been, echoing metallically inside his head, driving out his own thoughts.

Ponclast finished his circuit and rejoined Terzian. He took the last of the dark powder from his bag, and, dropping it in a thin stream, completed the circle. Immediately the sounds inside Terzian's head stopped, as did all the external noise; the wind, the dry rattle of the snow, the thrashing branches of the trees. An unearthly silence descended, and with it came an oppressive sense of anticipation.

Within the circle, the air appeared to glow slightly, flickering like a guttering candle flame. In its centre, Terzian thought he could make out some strange shapes twisting and writhing, forming and reforming. As he watched he thought he caught a glimpse of something familiar, but every time he tried to focus on the images, they dissolved and regenerated into something else.

"What's going on?" he demanded. "What's happening?"

Ponclast was staring into the writhing mass, a curious, wide-eyed look of horror upon his face that might almost have been comical under other circumstances.

"We are summoning demons, Terzian. Or gods. It's all the same thing."

It was quite apparent now to Terzian that Ponclast had planned this all some time in advance. He wondered if Ponclast had ever believed that his attempt to disable the townspeople's guns would succeed. Obviously he was the type of har who liked to have a backup plan.

"What's happening?" Terzian repeated, somewhat resentful that Ponclast had not chosen to divulge his plans to him, and also, if he were to admit it to himself, rather curious about what would happen next.

"We must enter the circle. We must confront our demons in order to become our own gods."

Terzian wondered if Ponclast had finally misplaced what remained of his sanity. The light within the circle was steadier now, losing its inchoate formlessness and becoming a steady beacon, drawing the onlookers inwards. It looked to Terzian like the moon had fallen from the heavens and now rested earthbound on the snow, glowing silver in the blackness.

Within the clearing, the wind began to stir again, gently at first, then with increasing strength, blowing loose strands of Terzian's hair across his face, blinding him momentarily, and setting up a dismal, grief-laden moan all around them. It seemed as if the air was rushing headlong into the circle of light, creating a vacuum into which everything else around might also be drawn.

Terzian pushed the whipping tendrils of hair away from his eyes and mouth. The wind was pushing him —or perhaps pulling him— toward the circle. He had no idea what would happen if he were to step into that light. Nor, he suspected, did Ponclast.

He turned to look at his companion. Ponclast's eyes were closed, and he was making small, protective signs with his hands, tracing unknown symbols and sigils in the air, only to have them torn away by the buffeting blast of the wind.

"Are you going in?" Terzian found that he had to shout to make his voice heard above the din of the howling gale; he could barely hear himself. He wondered if Ponclast had heard him at all. The other har showed no signs of acknowledging his query; his eyes remained shut and his hands continued their nervous flutterings.

Suppressing his irritation, Terzian leaned over towards Ponclast and shouted in his ear.

"ARE. YOU. GOING. IN?"

Ponclast's eyes fluttered open, and Terzian could see the fear in them.

"I cannot," he said, his voice cracked and barely audible above the roar of the wind. He winced, as if in pain. "I dare not."

Terzian could contain his annoyance no longer. He had not come out here on this filthy night with a har he considered to be half-mad merely to watch an entertaining light show.

"This was your idea!" he bellowed. The wind tore the words from him, despite the force behind them. "You're supposed to know what to do. You can't just back out now."

It was plain from the look on Ponclast's face that he could, and would.

Terzian snorted in disgust, and without hesitation, walked forward and into the circle of light.

He stepped over the carefully-drawn circumference of the circle and into an unexpected oasis of calm; the wind ceased to buffet his body and torment his ears, the cold retreated from his extremities, and the blackness of the night was replaced by a cool, ambient glow all around him. It took him a few moments to adjust to the sudden change; he felt disorientated by the jarring transition from storm to calm, from night to apparent day, and from forest glade to... *somewhere else.*

He looked around for Ponclast, but could see no sign of the other har, which did not surprise him. There was no snow underfoot, no trees and no sky visible above. He had no idea if he was still in the clearing or not. He wondered if he should announce his presence, but that seemed foolish. He had no idea what he had let himself in for, or what his fate would be now that he had entered this strange place. Better simply to let whatever was to happen take its own course.

He waited expectantly, alert for any sign of danger. Every nerve in his body was taut and stretched. At any moment, he expected to be consumed by fire, or cast down into a bottomless pit, or have any number of nameless horrors visited upon him. What he did not expect was the low, musical voice which spoke into his ear.

"Why is it you are here, Terzian?"

The voice came from behind him. He spun round, half expecting to see nothing at all, but was startled to find himself in the presence of a tall creature, more than twice his own height, whom he was sure had not been there when he entered the circle.

Terzian tried to reply, but his mouth was dry with fear. The thing in front of him was neither har nor human, of that he was sure, yet Terzian felt reluctant to accord it the status of either demon or god that Ponclast had spoken of. For all its strangeness, there was a familiarity about it. It was like himself, he could see that – its

223

hermaphrodite nature announced very clearly by the wet, pulsating orifice between its legs, petalled mouth pouting and dripping an iridescent fluid, surmounted by the enormous erect phallus which the creature gripped tightly with one hand, apparently to support its unusual length.

Terzian did not know whether to be repulsed or aroused by this unusual sight. He tried to look away, but found he could not; his fascination was too great.

"Who are you?" he asked, his heart sinking at the utter banality of the question.

The creature laughed. It was a pleasant sound, the voice pitched neither high nor low.

"You know the answer to that, Terzian," it said. "Or at least you will. In time."

Terzian shook his head. "I don't know who or what you are, or where you have come from, or what you want."

Again the creature laughed, or produced the sound which Terzian had taken to be a laugh before. On second hearing, he was not quite so sure. Like every other aspect of the creature, its laughter was at the same time both disturbingly familiar and utterly alien. Its face appeared harish in configuration, beautiful and alluring, with large dark eyes, but upon closer inspection Terzian could see that the eyes had no whites; they were simply black ovals set in the creature's face, reflecting neither light from outside nor emotion from within.

"It is not *I* who wants, Terzian. The wanting is *yours*. The desire. The unmet need. Tell me what it is that you want, Terzian."

"I don't..." he began, but the lie died before it could even be spoken. He remembered the events of earlier that evening, the battle, the humans, the wish for them to be gone, and for all they possessed to be his. A warm bed, clean sheets, a full stomach. It seemed petty in its mundaneness now.

"Not at all," the creature reassured him. "You want to live. To grow, to be strong; to continue your line. It is what all living things want; it is nothing to be ashamed of."

"I am not ashamed of wanting these things."

"Good. Because I will give them to you."

"Just like that?"

"Of course not."

"Oh."

"You must give me something in return."

"I thought you said you didn't want anything."

"I don't, but you must still give me something in return. The equation must balance."

"I have nothing to give you."

"Of course you do, Terzian. You must give me what is of most value to you."

"I don't think you have much use for a rusty knife."

The creature produced its noise again, and this time Terzian was convinced it had nothing in common with laughter.

"Quite right. I want your soul, Terzian."

"Fine, take it."

The look of perplexity on the creature's face gave Terzian a moment's gratification.

"You're not supposed to give in so easily, Terzian. You're supposed to argue, and convince me of how much you value your soul."

"I don't."

"Yes, I can see that. Well it's no use to me then."

"In that case, I don't have anything else to offer."

The creature studied him carefully, pursing its pseudo-lips, and running its hand along its erect phallus. Terzian recalled Ponclast in his tent, three nights ago, in a similar pose.

"I see it." The creature said.

"See what?"

"The thing you value. The thing you must give to me."

"Which is?"

"Your love."

"My what?"

"Your love. Your softness, your compassion, your tenderness, your surrender. You want to give it to someone, Terzian, but there is no one worthy, and perhaps there never will be. Give it to me. You're not using it, after all."

Terzian decided that this conversation had taken a very surreal turn. He had no idea what this creature wanted from him, or how he was supposed to give it. *Give me your love*. What did it mean by that?

He had no experience of love, either of giving it or receiving it. He thought about Lirren and Moth; the soft, secret looks he had seen them exchange; the brief contact that excluded everyone else in the world. He thought about how Lirren had struggled in his grasp, like an animal caught in a trap, and run back into the fire and the bullets, into his own certain death, because he could not bear to live in a world that did not have Moth in it. Was that love? If it was, it was a weakness, a sickness and something that Terzian had no use for.

Perhaps in another time and another place, there would be a space for such things, but not here and now, at the edge of existence and the edge of extinction. Only strength could help them survive; all else would merely drag them down. He would give up his weakness gladly; cut it away from himself like a gangrenous limb, leaving only the stronger part of him. And in return he would gain power and control. It was a good bargain.

"Take it," he said, "I have no use for it."

"Are you sure?" The creature looked at him slyly.

"Quite sure."

"You promise that you will give it to me, and to me only?"

"I do."

"Then know this, Terzian. This promise is a vow. It may not be broken without consequences. What is given can be taken away again, what is gained may be lost. You must be faithful to this vow, Terzian. You must be faithful to me and only me. No other may have your love once you have surrendered it to me. Are you sure that you can keep this promise?"

"Yes, I'm sure."

The creature reached out one long arm and touched Terzian gently on the cheek. Its fingers felt cool and soft.

"My beautiful Terzian," it sighed. "So strong, so confident, so sure of your own heart. One day it may betray you."

"I'll deal with that when it happens."

"Of course you will. I offer you one last chance, Terzian. You may withdraw from this agreement now if you so wish, and all will remain as before."

"I do not wish. What I wish is for you to give me victory over the humans. Give me the town. Give me a life."

The creature nodded gravely. "Very well. We have an agreement then. I will take your offering. Give me your knife."

Terzian hesitated for a second, then withdrew his knife from its sheath and handed it to the creature, who took it, smiled politely and sidled around the back of him. Terzian felt the hairs on the back of his neck rise.

"Don't look round." The creature warned, and it was all Terzian could do to comply with its instructions.

He felt a tug on his hair, which was bound with a leather cord behind his head in a long tail reaching to his waist. Then another tug, sharper and more painful, and another, and then the tugging ceased and his head felt strangely lighter.

The creature reappeared in front of him holding something rope-like in its hands, corn-coloured and gleaming. Terzian recognized it. It was his own hair.

"This represents your sacrifice," the creature told him. It took the length of hair and dropped it into a flat silver dish in the centre of the circle. It lay there like a dead thing. Lifeless. It seemed impossible to Terzian that it had ever been a part of him.

The creature cast a handful of powder into the dish. There was a sudden bright flash of vermilion flame and the hair burned fiercely for a few seconds. When the flames died, there was no trace of it remaining, no sign that it had ever existed.

"Is that it?" asked Terzian cautiously.

"No, of course not. Lie down now."

Unaccountably, Terzian found that he was naked and soume. He could not remember removing his clothing, and he could not remember experiencing any feelings of desire for this creature, but now he felt the unmistakeable butterfly flexions between his legs, and the beginnings of wetness, an ocean tide, a river awaiting release.

He stared in fascination at the creature's phallus. It was several times the size of an ordinary har's ouana-lim, both in length and girth, and it pulsed and throbbed as if imbued with a separate life of its own. Petals furled and unfurled at its tip, as if in anticipation, and enclosed within the blossoming velvet, one long tendril could be seen flicking outwards, like the tongue of a snake.

Terzian remembered a dream he had once had, of a nameless, faceless har, hot between his legs, sliding endlessly into him, again and again, reaching into somewhere so deep inside him he could not put a name to it. He lay down on his back and drew his legs up, grasping his own ankles, resisting the urge to slip his own fingers into himself and feel the wetness there, to touch the hardened and prominent swellings inside him, within easy reach of his searching fingertips. He wanted more than that. Much more.

The creature – Demon or God, or whatever it was – knelt down between his opened legs and guided its massive ouana-lim to the entrance to his body. It teased him with a few gentle strokes, causing his soume-lam to grasp and claw futilely at empty air, before bearing down mercilessly into him

Terzian gasped aloud. A searing pain seemed to run the full length of his body, from his crotch to his breastbone. He experienced a moment of fear, wondering if the creature's size would damage him and tear his flesh, but the pain was followed almost instantly by an ecstasy so intense he found that he could not breath. Motes of light danced in front of his eyes, tiny explosions of colour and movement.

After a while, he found he could no longer tell if what he was experiencing was pain or pleasure; it was merely a sensation so overwhelming that he could do nothing but ride it to its inevitable conclusion. Every time the creature moved inside him, he could feel it pulling and stretching him, tugging at his flesh, and at something else, deep within him, something vital and living. It felt as if his entire viscera were being slowly pulled from him, one agonizing piece at a time.

Something warm and wet ran down his face, and he managed to raise one hand to wipe it away. He thought it must be blood. That, and the hot liquid escaping between his legs. It must be his lifeblood, leaking from him, slowly and inexorably, leaving him empty and dying. More liquid spilled down his face, from his eyes, clear liquid, and he realised it was not blood, but he could not remember what it was, could not remember ever experiencing this before.

He could no longer hold on to himself. His body split itself asunder, erupting with liquid fire. Deep within, he felt the tongue lash out and strike him in his rawest nerve, and hold and grasp that nerve, and then he felt the GodDemonCreature begin its long, agonizing withdrawal, and with it went something of himself, something soft, something vulnerable, pulled and pulled from him, until he thought it would never cease, stretching to the breaking point, tearing free. Leaving. Leaving him. Leaving him empty.

Leaving him with nothing but the wet liquid on his face which he found to his surprise, as he raised his trembling hands to his face, was only tears.

Extract from Terzian's diary, found amount his private papers after his death.

The next morning, when we returned to the town, we found it deserted. All the humans had fled, and we made our way past the burnt-out barricades and broken glass of the previous evening and into the narrow streets in an eerie silence, cautious and expecting a trap or an ambush at any moment. It never came.

Eventually we found one inhabitant, cowering in a cellar and raving to himself. He spoke of demons and fire and death, and the look in his eyes was of such terror that I cannot even begin to describe, however there is no sign of any damage to the houses, either by fire or other means. I think it is all in his mind, or what there is left of it. Ponclast thinks he is of an age to be incepted, but I do no not want the taint of madness among our tribe. I will decide his fate within the next few days.

We gathered up the bodies of our fallen comrades and burned them. Among the dead I recognized Lirren and his companion, Moth. As their bodies were found some distance from each other, I consider it unlikely that they died together.

We have named the town Galhea. There is food in abundance here and fuel for the winter. The houses are simply furnished, but in good repair. Already our hara have started making them their own. It is good to see the improvement in morale that has resulted from this turn of events.

Defence must now be our first priority – we have a substantial prize in our grasp and it is not beyond the bounds of possibility that others may attempt to take it from us.

We need to become more organized, less self-indulgent. I am instigating a number of measures which will improve our efficiency by allocating jobs on the basis of ability; those who are strongest and best able to fight will be our front line. Those who cannot will be given other more domestic tasks. It is only logical, given our current precarious circumstances.

In a somewhat surprising twist, many of the fighting hara have cut their hair short, after my own recent fashion. They think that our victory was in some way due to this. Or perhaps they are trying to gain my favour through flattery. Either way, I think this is a welcome development. It provides them with a badge of solidarity and comradeship, and is quite practical for those engaged in active lifestyles, although it does not matter so much for the domestic hara.

Yesterday morning, I inspected the troops. They are a rough bunch, still, but I can see an improvement already in their discipline and team spirit. As they stood there, lined up in their ranks, standing to attention, I felt a surge of pride in them, and as I gazed along those newly formed regiments, I felt what I can only describe as an intense connection to ages passed. Perhaps this is a strange thing to say, given that we have turned our backs so firmly on the past, locking and bolting and barricading that door with the cut of the inception knife, but in those proud soldiers-in-the-making I could see the ghost of every army that had ever trodden the earth. The empires of old, forged with the blood and sinew of their fighting troops.

We will be the new empire; our feet will shake the world as loudly as any that came before us, and more. This is our beginning. We are the Varrs – that is the name we have taken for ourselves. We are the future; it is ours for the taking.

As for myself, I have taken possession of a large house at the far end of the town. It has some history to it, that much is obvious. The furnishings are elegant – it promises a lifestyle of some luxury, and while I do most certainly appreciate that after the way I have lived these past few years, I must be careful not to allow myself to be seduced by the easy comforts it offers. It will require staff to run the place efficiently – there is a har called Ithiel whom I think would make a good steward; I shall inform him of his new position later today.

I am hopeful that some of the human women may still be found and given positions of domestic service. Also, if there are any young males of sound mind and body, we should have them incepted. There are too few of us. We number barely a thousand, and this town once had a population of several times that. We need to increase our numbers.

Ponclast claims to have another solution to this problem, and as is often the case with Ponclast, this is of the more esoteric variety. He is of the opinion that we should breed.

I must confess that this is not something I had given much thought to. It seems obvious that this is possible – we are true hermaphrodites, dissection of cadavers has proven the existence of internal reproductive organs – but we are sorely lacking in any knowledge of how this might be brought about. It is abundantly clear that merely taking aruna does not cause conception, or our population problem would be solved instantly.

Ponclast insists we must experiment. Having had experience of

Ponclast's "experiments," I am in little hurry to discover what he has in mind this time.

I have spoken to no one of the events of three nights ago, nor shall I ever. I am still not sure I understand exactly what occurred within that circle. Ponclast saw everything that happened, but he is the only one who knows, and I intend for it stay that way. He will not be living at the house with me – he intends to move further afield so that he might continue his experiments in private. I think this is probably for the best. We are bound to each other now, in some strange way. We know each other's most intimate secrets. We have seen each other's demons.

I do not think this is necessarily a good thing, but it is a fact, and we must live with it as best we may.

Whether what I have done is for good for ill, there is no point in worrying over it. It is done, and cannot be undone. It is over. And yet – it still haunts my thoughts if I allow it the space to do so, and a sense of dread comes over me, although of what, I cannot say.

Last night I was standing in the hallway of the Great House, with its dark, polished wood, and long staircase leading to the upper rooms. There was little in the way of lighting – we are conserving oil and candles as much as possible until we can begin producing our own – and the shadows seemed oppressive.

Just for a moment, at the top of the stairs, I thought I saw a har. He should not have been there, for I am the house's only occupant at the moment, so I called out to him, but he did not reply. I looked again, peering into the darkness, and he was gone.

In the light of morning, I could laugh at myself for being so fanciful were it not for the memory of the har's face. The vision is fading, but in my mind I can see him still, faintly, through the gloom, a strange, ethereal figure at the top of the stairs, familiar with the place, as if this was his home. He had yellow-gold hair and violet eyes. When I think of him, a sense of foreboding comes over me that I cannot explain and cannot run from. The darkness approaches.

May the Aghama have mercy upon my soul.

Song of the Sulh

Maria J. Leel

 # Song of the Suth

Raven sat in a tree high on a wooded hillside. A young Mountain People tribesman just shy of his twentieth birthday, gawky adolescence had long given way to lean, powerful assurance. The Place of Blue Smoke was the ancient name his people had given these rugged, convoluted mountains. Water vapour and oily residues from the forests combined, draping the peaks and valleys with smoky tendrils of hazy-blue fog.

What light filtered down through the forest reflected from Raven's burnished, red-gold skin only to be swallowed whole by the skein of long, dark hair that hung like a cloak about his shoulders. No glimmer or reflection betrayed him as he sat still and silent watching those below him. There had been no flicker of movement from him in over two hours. Nothing to suggest he was there. Inside he seethed and thrummed with barely contained hatred.

Wraeththu.

The Incomers.

The Interlopers.

Raven's tribe, the Mountain People, had lived with the impact of such interlopers for generations. For years his people had lived peaceably within the natural laws of their homeland. They followed the rhythm of the seasons and lived as subjects – not conquerors – of the land that supported them.

Then the first interlopers had come. Humans like themselves. They brought with them new technologies, new attitudes and above all the desire for mastery – not of themselves, as was the Mountain People's way, but of the land and her people.

Raven's people had been driven off their lands, their beliefs and way of life pushed to the rawest edges of bare survival.

Then the world began to change. Society began to break down. Wars erupted all over the globe and, sensing her chance, the land began to fight back too; hurricanes, volcanoes, floods, fires and pestilence. The Interlopers and their ways looked doomed to ancient memory. The Mountain People rejoiced. Hope flared in their hearts. It would be their time again, time for them to reclaim their gentle relationship with the land.

But it was not to be. The hope was short lived. The creeping madness affecting the Interlopers did not discriminate. It took Mountain People along with their oppressors. Raven's own father succumbed, as did many of the older male tribesmen. Only the women and the young men appeared to escape it. But then the women stopped being able to have babies and the number of tribe's children dwindled.

Then along came the new Interlopers.

Wraeththu.

For years there had been rumours of gangs in the cities. Whispers on the breeze of wild boys involved in crazy cults; stealing boys away from their families, changing them somehow, making them inhuman, making them hate humans.

That they had sex among themselves was neither shocking nor unnatural to the Mountain People. They had long understood the androgynous nature of the soul and regarded homosexuals as "two-spirited" individuals to be revered. Raven himself had experienced sexual encounters with both males and females.

What did seem unnatural and shocking to Raven's people was that there appeared no place for women as this brave new world was forged. To them men and women were part of the circle of life, no one part more important than the other and no one part able to exist without the other. As Wraeththu increased in number, the tribe mourned the loss of women as much as they mourned the loss of the Mountain People and their ways.

Raven had another reason to hate Wraeththu. His mother had been killed by marauding Uigenna intent on sport. Raven had been only twelve. He had gone out looking for her when she failed to return from foraging for healing herbs. From behind a tree he'd heard the Uigenna depart, laughing and boasting of their triumph. Fearing the worst, he'd ventured into the clearing. Not much remained, but what did left him in no doubt that it was his mother. He gathered what was left and returned to his people so that she could be honoured and given the burial rituals that were her due.

High in his tree the memories smouldered and flared inside him. Even through his mist of hatred, Raven had to admit this Wraeththu tribe were not like the Uigenna and Kheops raiders he had, so far, encountered.

For ten days he had watched them. Raven had seen that these Wraeththu, although clearly not of this land, had a great affinity for it and were closely in tune with the turn of the seasons. Their clothing, surprisingly practical and highly adaptable, reflected this closeness in the earthy greens, browns and dark oranges they favoured. Like the Mountain People they chose to wear their hair long and loose.

A few days previously they had celebrated the Summer Solstice with feasting and dances. And when a vicious thunderstorm had suddenly blown up, they had known of its coming and had secured their camp.

Hate them though he did, these Wraeththu intrigued Raven.

But time was passing and his people were expecting him. It was time to cut short his musing. He slipped silently out of the tree and melted into the forest. During the hour hike back to his home on the edge of the old reservation, he caught a couple of cottontail rabbits and gathered some yellow dock leaves.

At the edge of the old reservation stood an old log cabin, Raven's home since his parents died. The cabin belonged to the Elder Two Comet. Outside a smoking fire pit was tended by Pale Fawn, another orphan adopted by Two Comet. Close to Raven in age, she was his dearest friend. She looked up as he approached, her dark hair falling back from her face as she smiled in greeting.

As was their custom, they set to work preparing the evening meal together, singing the ancient songs of their people as they worked. Raven skinned and gutted the rabbits, throwing the entrails to the half-wild dogs that hung about on the edge of the reservation. Pale Fawn put a pot of water on to simmer and prepared the vegetables.

Later, once the meal was prepared, Two Comet joined them, responding to Pale Fawn's call. A proud elderly man with gentle and wise eyes, his hair now grey and much of his physical strength gone, he retained an equal measure of dignity and humility.

They sat, cross-legged, on rugs surrounding the fire pit and shared stories of their day. Two Comet had officiated at a ceremony to bring good fortune to a couple trying desperately for a child, while Pale Fawn had spent much of her day gathering healing herbs and visiting the sick. At length Two Comet turned to Raven.

"Well now, my son, and have you spent your day observing your new friends?"

Raven gave a derisive snort. "Friends!" he spat.

Two Comet shook his head with amusement. "Raven, my son, you seem to spend so much time watching them, I can only assume you wish to befriend them."

"Wraeththu!" Raven uttered the word as if it left a sour taste in his mouth. "Killed my mother... stole my friends... stealing our world... robbing us of..."

"I am well aware of your feelings, my son." Two Comet's gentle but firm tone cut right across Raven's habitual rant. It was an old argument, often repeated. Pale Fawn rolled her eyes.

"Tell me what you have seen." Two Comet continued. "Be honest and leave out nothing."

Unwillingly, as if the details were wrung out of him, Raven spoke of what he had seen. This group of Wraeththu *was* different. Not like the Uigenna or Kheops. They had their own ceremonies and celebrated their own sacred times. They had an affinity for the land, although clearly they were not from this land. Raven admitted, grudgingly, that these hara intrigued him.

Two Comet listened intently. At the end of Raven's story he lowered his eyes, pursed his lips and inhaled deeply. Raising his eyes to look directly at Raven he said, "My son, I think you should join these Wraeththu. I think you should willingly become one of them."

Raven was on his feet in an instant, screaming at Two Comet. He would never become Wraeththu, never. He was a Mountain People Tribesman – a member of the Wolf Clan – a warrior and protector of the people. He would die before betraying his heritage. Pale Fawn placed her hands over her ears and closed her eyes tightly.

"Noble as that sentiment is, my son," said Two Comet to Raven's departing back, "there is little point being a warrior and protector of the people when soon there will be no people to protect."

As Raven's angry footsteps disappeared into the forest, Pale Fawn removed her hands and opened her eyes. She regarded Two Comet gently.

"Don't worry," she smiled, "His temper is hot but it's always short lived."

Two Comet gave an exasperated snort. "A fire cracker that one – always wasting his energies on the unimportant!" He shifted his rug and made himself more comfortable.

"But now, my daughter, let's take tea together. I have much to discuss with you."

Raven marched unheeding through the forest as dusk gave way to darkness. A red-mist shrouded his eyes and black thunderclouds boiled in his heart. As usual in these circumstances, his feet led him to the place where his mother's bones were laid to rest. It was one place where he always found peace. He sat beneath the tree that honoured her and exhaled slowly. Gently her essence seeped into him, calming him and slowing his racing thoughts. She stayed with him throughout the night as a battle raged within him. She crooned and soothed and gave wisdom.

As dawn crept along the eastern horizon like a golden skein, Raven made his decision. The dawn brought clarity and his remaining doubts fled with the departing night.

Raven sat beneath his tree a while longer. He watched the sun erupt from the horizon and illuminate the forests he knew so well. A new life was unfolding before him, one he had never even allowed himself to dream of. But the desire had been there, he had to admit that to himself now. Sunlight shone through the mists in numerous gauzy hues, the occasional pointed crown of a pine tree standing stark against the illuminated cloudscape. The entire landscape crackled with energy and power; Raven drank it in greedily.

He returned to the reservation just as Pale Fawn was serving breakfast. A place had been set for him in his usual spot by the fire pit. Pale Fawn handed him a couple of boiled eggs and some freshly baked corn bread. Raven nodded his thanks and turned to Two Comet, who eyed him impassively through the smoke of his pipe.

"I agree," said Raven, simply. He didn't need to say anything else.

Two Comet's face broke into a thousand wrinkles as he smiled. "This is good, my son. For though you are Wolf Clan and warrior and protector of you people, you are also warrior and protector of tradition. We live in strange times – and we must find strange solutions to the problems that trouble us."

Two Comet closed his eyes, "You know I have the gift of foresight – for I am Wild Cat Clan – seer and protector of the earth. There is no future for the Mountain People, save the one we create for ourselves. You must carry your tradition to a new tribe who will accept and value it. To the new tribe of Wraeththu who have come to our forests."

He inhaled deeply and looked directly at Raven, "But before you do this – there is one more task you have to perform for the Mountain People. There will only be one more child born to this tribe. It will be carried by Pale Fawn and you will be its father. I will carry out the ceremony to ensure a successful conception."

"But Two Comet," interrupted Raven, "what chance of success do we have? Only yesterday you carried out the same ceremony for Red Bear and Nuna – and they've been trying for months."

"And it is hopeless," sighed Two Comet. "But who am I to rob them of their hope? They will come to acceptance in time. For you and Pale Fawn it is different – I know this."

"How can you know?" asked Raven.

Two Comet looked heavenwards in exasperation, "Raven, my son, you set too much store in magic. Pale Fawn has lived with me since she was a young girl. I know her cycles. This is her time."

"How do you feel about this?" Raven asked Pale Fawn.

"I have my own path to walk." Pale Fawn replied. "For I am of the Clan of the Wind – like you a keeper of tradition but also a teacher. I should very much like to walk my path with your child."

Raven chewed on his corn bread, "Seems it's all decided then," he shrugged.

"You better believe it," Pale Fawn chuckled.

For the rest of the day Raven and Pale Fawn sat on a rug by the fire pit close but not touching. Two Comet burned herbs around them, sprinkled them with blessed water, hummed and chanted incantations. They joined in the chanting at times that seem appropriate. By the evening they were both light-headed and deep in a meditative state.

Two Comet kissed them both on the brow. "I shall spend the night close to your mother's bones," he said. "We were good friends and I've neglected her company for far too long. Make good use of my cabin." With that he walked off into the gathering dusk.

The two young people both rose to their feet. Pale Fawn smiled uncertainly. Raven returned the smile, took her hand and led her into the log cabin. Inside they lit oil lamps, softening the light by draping coloured rags. They laid animal hides on the floor and surrounded them with cushions.

Raven removed his clothing and did a twirl. "Well, you might as well see what you're getting!" He laughed.

Pale Fawn smiled and placed his hands on the lacings at the front of her dress. "You do it," she said.

Raven became more serious. It wasn't his first time but it was, he knew, hers. She deserved better than flippancy. Gently he undid the lacings and eased the dress to her shoulders. She shrugged and the dress fell to the floor. Underneath she was naked and she was beautiful. He had not noticed before.

Raven felt the breath catch in his throat. He ran his hand the length of her arm and interlaced his fingers with hers. He raised her hand and kissed her palm. She led him to the pile of animal hides and he lay down beside her.

For a while they caressed, stroked and became familiar with each other in a completely new way. When the time seemed right, Raven moved over her and found his way inside. She gasped slightly, her eyes widening, then she relaxed against him and they rocked gently together. Together they found a climax, and afterward together they lay spent on the floor.

Several times that night they made that journey. In the early hours of the morning they lay in each other's arms, covered in a blanket to keep out the night's chill. Pale Fawn slept with her head on Raven's shoulder. Raven, wide-eyed and awake, stared into the darkness.

It was always like this.

The intensity of his encounter with Pale Fawn was made all the more poignant by the knowledge of their imminent separation. He loved her dearly. She was the closest thing to family he had; they had been friends longer than he could remember. But it wasn't just their separation that bothered him; it was the feeling of incompleteness. Whether with men or with women he always felt deep down that sexual encounters could be so much more than they were. The union could be on so many more levels. So much magical energy was created only to dissipate unused. If only it could be harnessed, channelled. He knew all this instinctively but had no idea how to bring these things to fruition.

Pale Fawn stirred in her sleep. Raven stroked her hair, kissed the top of her head, soothing her to stillness once more. He revelled in being this close to her, the night scent of her hair, the bliss of her skin against his. He was going to miss her more than he dared think about. He closed his eyes and held her a little closer. Eventually sleep claimed him, too.

It was well after dawn when they woke. A few more kisses, a few more caresses, then by unspoken agreement they returned to a state of companionable friendship. The cushions and animal skins were cleared away, the coloured rags removed from the lamps. To all intents and purposes it was just another day.

Raven stoked the fire, Pale Fawn set about making the breakfast, and somewhat later than expected Two Comet returned from the forest.

"I'd forgotten what a talker your mother was," was all he would say.

They shared their usual companionable breakfast and then Raven went away quietly to pack. A few things only, cast into a striped canvas haversack. He chose his best boots to wear, brushed leather trousers and the fringed shirt of russet and green that Pale Fawn had made him in the spring. He left his hair loose but plaited in the coloured feathers that signified his tribe and clan.

He rejoined his companions at the fire pit. Two Comet, sitting comfortably on his rug, looked up at him.

"You look well, my son."

"A fine Mountain People tribesman," agreed Pale Fawn. "Any tribe would be proud to count you in their ranks."

Raven took her hands in his, kissed her fingers and pulled her into a fierce hug.

"You take care of yourself," he said and slid a hand over her belly, gripping slightly, "and of this one too."

Pale Fawn nodded. She did not speak. She was a warrior's daughter and would not weep.

Two Comet stood up, placing his hands on Raven's shoulders.

"Go well, my son. You have much to teach these Wraeththu and much to be proud of. But remember, they also have much to teach you – so take to them an open mind and the ways of an apprentice."

The embrace was long. Raven finally pulled away, smiled his farewell to them both and walked away without looking back. He was the son of a warrior; he wasn't going to weep either.

A thousand thoughts raced through Raven's mind as he left his home. How should he address these people? What form of greeting should he use? He strode purposefully through the forest trying not to think about what he'd left behind. He passed the tree in which he's spent so many hours watching them, closer now than he'd ever been to these Wraeththu – this tribe he had, until a few hours before hated with a passion. Now that he had resolved to join them, he walked swiftly in case his courage failed him.

Raven reached the edge of the clearing and marched directly into the camp. He stopped by the central fireplace and cast down his bag by way of a challenge. All around him Wraeththu looked up from their work. Each tribesmember engaged in various crafts, some weaving with tiny beads, brightly coloured wool and feathers, some fashioning leather goods, others butchering, others preserving meat in the smoke from the fire.

Raven stood in the clearing, momentarily at a loss for words as the Wraeththu continued to gaze at him. Their gazes held nothing but a gentle amusement; Raven could detect no flicker of hostility. Still struggling for words, he felt his resolve slither away.

The drapery at the mouth of a nearby tent was drawn back. A gentle-eyed har with waist-long dark blond hair emerged.

"We wondered when you would come to talk with us," he began, his voice low and melodic. "We sensed you the first time you climbed that tree —and we sensed the hostility you felt towards us. But now I sense that feeling has left you. Will you take tea with me?"

Around him the gentle amusement had given way to smiles of welcome. Raven felt somewhat overwhelmed by the strength of this welcome, particularly given his recent animosity, and was glad to escape to the privacy of the tent. He sat down upon a richly decorated rug opposite the blond har.

"Firstly, introductions," said the blond har, handing him a steaming bowl of tea. "I am Curlew, the leader of this tribe. Our tribe are the Sulh, and this," he indicated, "is Mist, our Shaman."

To his left sat another har, like Curlew dressed in natural shades of brown, green and orange, his hair a cloud of shimmering grey-blue, his eyes fathomless pools of inky black.

Mists graciously bowed his greeting and asked, "And are we to know your name and tribe?"

Raven felt on safer ground here. Story telling was an important skill among his people and his heritage a matter of pride.

"My name is Raven," he began, "I am a tribesman of the Mountain People who have lived in the Place of the Blue Smoke for over a thousand years. I would like to tell you the story of my people."

Curlew and Mist listened intently and did not interrupt his flow, recognising the time for questions was later.

As Raven's tale drew to an end, Curlew and Mist thanked him.

Mist replenished his tea, "You and your people have much to be proud of, Raven. Yours is a great culture. I am curious, though. What has brought you to us now?"

The killer question.

Raven steeled himself. "My people are dying, our numbers dwindle, and as my people die our culture dies with them. The only chance is to join a tribe who will accept our culture into theirs. The only chance...." he faltered. "So far the only Wraeththu tribes I've seen are Uigenna and Kheops – and from what I've seen they have no concept of culture – none!"

"I understand you reservation regarding the Uigenna and Kheops," said Curlew, nodding. "We too have had dealing with them – and difficulties. You chose wisely in coming to us for we are scholars and greatly prize the ancient knowledge. Am I to understand then that you wish to join us? To become Wraeththu?"

Raven nodded. Mist and Curlew exchanged a glance.

"The thing is, Raven," Mist began. "Before you become Wraeththu, there is much you need to understand about us. Why don't you start by telling us what you already know, or think you know, and we'll fill you in on the rest?"

Discussions lasted all through the morning. Curlew and Mist quizzed Raven on his perceptions of Wraeththu, his attachment to his humanity, his fears of pain and change. They had a lengthy conversation regarding his sexual orientation and experience. Raven noticed that both Mist and Curlew became alert, fascinated when he openly admitted that he'd found his sexual encounters unsatisfying, incomplete somehow, as if there was more to be attained but he'd no idea how to reach it. For what reason Raven would never be able to say, he held back information about the child he believed he had so recently conceived with Pale Fawn.

Discussions were disturbed briefly by a har bringing lunch, a thick, spiced soup with hunks of corn bread. Pragmatically Curlew stated that conversation never went well on an empty stomach.

After lunch they were joined by Batalha. Unlike the rest of the Sulh, he was dressed in a simple white robe. Everything about Batalha was pale and insubstantial – his hair, his eyes, his skin – as if he were a wraith that could vanish in a heartbeat. Curlew introduced him as scribe and history keeper.

"That's a bit of a fancy name for it," Batalha quipped. "Really I'm just a field researcher."

Through poetry and song Batalha held Raven fascinated telling the creation myths of Wraeththu and the Sulh tribe. As he sang he played complex rhythms on his small, many stringed harp. By early evening Raven's head was reeling.

Finally they joined the rest of the tribe for supper around the fire. The blissful evening air soothed his pounding head as he ate the simple meal.

Abruptly his attention was caught by a har on the far side of the fireplace. Not overly tall but built solidly, the har was dark haired but pale skinned, his hair shaved completely on one side of his skull and tumbling down in thick curls on the other. A complex blue woad tattoo curled and coiled over the shaven skull, intricately defining the eye socket and the climactic point of the cheekbone. The tattoo wound down around his throat and appeared to continue down the left hand side of his body.

Raven, surprised by the strength of his interest, had to ask Mist who the har was.

"Fen," came the reply. "From the waterlands of Alba Sulh. One of our warrior phyle, fearsome and loyal." Looking around the camp Raven could see a few hara that were clearly also of warrior phyle – although none of them as physically arresting as Fen.

After supper Raven wandered a little way away from the camp. He sat down on a fallen branch with his head in his hands. There was so much to take in, so much that was new. Curlew had deeply shocked him when he'd told him that on inception changes would take place within his body that would render him both male and female. Batalha had shocked him further when he'd stated that although there was no record of it happening as yet, he believed that Wraeththu would one day go on to procreate. However, Raven's reservations about the lack of place for women in this new world of Wraeththu were somewhat appeased. Batalha told him, sincerely, that he felt women too had a new path to walk – their time was not yet done. Raven found he believed him.

These thoughts chased each other around his head as he sat on the fallen branch. Familiar forest sounds echoed around him, soothing scents floated by on a cooling breeze – and then something else.

Raven sat bolt upright. "I know when I'm being watched," he told the night.

A patch of darkness detached itself from the shadows and moved into view. Fen.

"Scared I'd run off?" asked Raven, hiding his surprise that it was the har he'd been staring at earlier.

Fen nodded. "You know too much."

"And you'd what? Kill me?"

Fen nodded again, slipping a narrow-bladed knife from his boot. "I'd have slid this gently down the side of your neck into your shoulder, severing the subclavian vein. You'd have died in seconds – silently."

For a moment Raven glared at him. "Then it's as well I've decided to stay," he hissed, pushing past Fen as he returned to camp.

The following morning Raven informed Mist and Curlew of his decision to stay. They greeted this news with evident relief and pleasure. He did not mention his encounter with Fen the night before.

Whilst the tribe tucked into their breakfast eggs, Raven drank only an herbal tea prepared for him by Mist. His pre-inception purification had begun.

Raven withdrew from the rest of the tribe spending long hours in meditation with Mist, who described every detail of the inception process: the fasting, the ceremony, the althaia and the aruna to follow. Raven suggested a few native herbs that might assist each process.

Late that afternoon Raven, Mist and Batalha went foraging in the forest. They collected humming bird blossoms to stimulate kidney function and detoxification and dug up the small roots of greenbriar to purify the blood. Mist pressed Raven for every detail of the plants, their habitats, their range, and their properties. Batalha listened intently, all the while humming to himself.

"Batalha takes in everything," Mist told Raven, "He has a phenomenal memory and 'records' everything – as a song."

The group wandered further into the forest gathering leaves, roots and bark. All the while Raven was aware of a dark shadow – Fen? – behind them; clearly he was still not entirely trusted.

At last they returned to camp. Raven drank more of the herbal tea, which appeased his growling stomach not at all. Then followed more chanting and meditation and finally sleep.

The next day followed a similar pattern, although a further cleansing ritual was required. At Mist's request a small hut had been constructed from scented boughs and leaves. Raven joined Mist, Curlew and Batalha inside as heated stones were brought in. Cedar, sage and sweet grass were cast upon the stones as the heat and humidity soared. The sweat lodge had been an important part of Mountain People lifestyle and Raven felt quite at home there.

Batalha's serious songs of cleansing and reverence soon gave way to a bawdy many-versed ballad about the joys of aruna.

Still humming the chorus, they emerged hot and sweaty. Raven was glad of the herbal tea, although he was getting heartily sick of the flavour. That night following meditation, Mist looked intently at him.

"You are ready," he said. "Tomorrow we will perform your inception."

The ceremony was performed at a simple forest alter. The entire tribe assembled. Mist performed the rituals, while Curlew provided the blood. When it was over, Raven was helped back to the quiet confines of Mist's tent as the changing processes began.

Althaia.

The transformational force that rips, sears and burns through the body, driving men to the edge of insanity and beyond. Mist and Raven had prepared well. They had gathered mullion. Its roots and leaves smouldered; the smoke a mild sedative that soothed inflammation. To control his fever, Raven sipped a tea made from the leaves and dried berries. As Raven's skin began to blister and erupt in sores, Mist applied the salve they'd prepared from mint and greenbriar. Raven remained lucid by chanting the ancient healing words from the mantras of his people. Where he felt it appropriate, Mist chanted with him.

Althaia would never be easy but Raven's passage into Wraeththudom was far gentler than most, Mist told him – Mist was impressed. And already, at this early stage, the point of rebirth, their two cultures, Sulh and Mountain People, had begun to blend.

In the late afternoon of the third day, Raven and Mist lay sleeping. Althaia was done, the changes made. The doorway drapes were thrown wide open so a refreshing breeze could blow through and remove the tattered vestiges of stale energy and discomfort. The bedding had been changed and Raven lay upon it, gleaming and perfect.

He stirred and awoke to find Mist gazing sleepily at him.

"You are wondrous" Mist told him. "You made your transformation well. How do you feel?"

Raven stretched and yawned, enjoying his new body. "The strongest and fittest I've ever felt," he said. "And the most alive."

"We must seal the changes with aruna," Mist reminded him.

"Sure, but close the drapes would you? I don't want the rest of the tribe in on this."

Mist graciously nodded and complied.

Raven sat up, pulling off his shirt. "So where do we start?"

"Well, sharing of breath is customary."

"A kiss, you mean?"

"A kiss, yes, but it's more than that, a kiss of mutual visualisation. We share our thoughts, feelings, memories."

"Show me."

"What would you like to see?"

"How did you get your name?"

Mist smiled. "A happy memory," he said stroking Raven's cheek, drawing him closer. As their lips met, Raven was hit by a blast of power that made him gasp.

Undaunted, he plunged his hands into Mist's copious blue-grey hair and found himself soaring over a rolling green landscape of hills, fields, hedges and woodland.

"Alba Sulh," said Mist from deep somewhere in Raven's own head, "our homeland, the western borders to be precise – my home." The time of this vision, Raven could sense, was shortly after Mist's own inception. He had gone out to discover his new name and, as was often the custom, he'd decided to take inspiration from nature. When human he'd enjoyed climbing a hill near his village, a large rocky outcrop set on a wide plain. From the top you felt as though you could see forever.

There was a freshening breeze as he'd started to climb. As he climbed higher the wind blew stronger. On reaching the top it had become a howling gale and the view he'd hoped to see was obscured by low cloud and wisps of fog. He sat down with his back to a rock watching the cloud and fog swirl past him. Shapes and colours billowed around, patterns and stories, visions of new paths and new journeys. A mist vision – gifted only to shamans.

The new har had returned to his tribe knowing his name and his purpose. His tribesmates came to greet him with wonder for he was greatly changed. Gone was the short-spiked tawny hair, replaced by a mist-coloured cloud and his eyes, once blue, had become all-seeing obsidian.

Mist pulled away gently. "Your first breath-vision," he smiled. "Now you try."

Clumsily, erratically, Raven showed Mist the story of his own name. He showed how as a child his mother had taken him on her lap and told him the story of his naming. Shortly after his birth, as soon as she was able, she had taken herself and her precious bundle up into the forest. She'd sat beneath her favourite tree, the one beneath which she was now buried, and awaited inspiration. A black, glossy bird swooped down and stood before her feet. He bowed low, offering her a gift of fruit. As she accepted, the bird began a capering dance, stretching his wings and drumming his feet.

"Raven," she'd said. The bird bowed once again and flew away.

She had been both pleased and disturbed by this experience. Raven was a proud name associated with warriors but she had also been raised on stories of the Raven-Mockers. These were witches of indeterminate sex who the tribe believed robbed the dying of life, feasting on their hearts to add length to their own lives. In time she had begun to think of Wraeththu as the Raven-Mockers and grew fearful for her son.

Mist drew away. "We do not eat hearts," he said, sadly.

"Nor do you steal lives to add length to your own. You add to the lives of others," Raven told him. "Now finish what you've started and seal my changes with aruna — for I am Raven and will not be mocked!"

Mist laughed uproariously, flinging Raven onto his back.

"As you wish," he said. "I hope in aruna you find what you seek." He breathed a single breath down the length of Raven's chest and belly, following it with the lightest of touches with his fingers, igniting every nerve cell along its path.

Raven gave him a look that said, "If you don't do something now, I'm going to explode."

Mist laughed again, piercing him, and Raven's spirit was catapulted high into the sky, looking down on the camp and over the mountains. He was momentarily disorientated.

Beside him Mist said, "Come and fly with me."

Over the treetops, above the resinous mists, away from the forests towards grassy plains and the sea and then beyond, Raven and Mist's essences coiled around each other. On, across the lapping waves to a necklace of islands, long drawn out ribbons of sand where long ago the forests had found their way and made their home. Through the trees, across the sands, past crazy wooden houses that reached up to the sky and tumbling in the surf, free of the shackles of flesh Raven and Mist became lost in each other and the landscape around them.

Then climax and a return to flesh.

Mist pushed his own sweat-soaked hair away from his face and turned to Raven.

"Better than before?"

Raven nodded.

"That place, the islands. They're important to you."

Raven shook his head, "I've never been there."

"Then they will be important to you sometime in the future."

"Can aruna do that? Show you the future?"

"It can. It can take you out of time, all times become one, all places become one."

"Amazing!" Raven grinned. "That's going to take some thinking about. But right now... can we do it again?"

Mist laughed. "Give me a moment would you?"

Raven settled down quickly into his new life. The band of Sulh he had joined were information gatherers, herbalists, anthropologists, and historians. Batalha was the group's memory.

They foraged for food, kept a few hens in a portable run, made craft goods to sell and trade, living as lightly on the land as they could. It was a way of life that resonated strongly with Raven's own.

Many days were spent with Batalha roaming the forests, observing how the land and that which lived upon it worked together. Raven told him the myths of his people, the herbs they used for healing, the magical rites they practiced to ensure success and longevity. All the while Batalha hummed and sang softly to himself.

"Back in Alba Sulh they're creating a library" Batalha told him "The Great Library of Kyme. The Mountain People and all they knew will not be forgotten."

Other times Raven worked with the artisans making jewellery and leather goods. In this way the artwork of the Mountain People became absorbed into that of the Sulh.

Always Raven was aware of the presence of the warrior phyle there to protect the tribe, each of them with their curling woad tattoo. Fen particularly held his attention. Raven watched him now, out of the corner of his eye, sharing a joke with another tattooed warrior, Fen's mouth split wide as he barked with laughter. Although he no longer felt watched or mistrusted Raven was constantly aware of the Waterlander's presence.

He asked Mist about it one day.

"Waterlanders are like that," said Mist. "Strong soul energy. They suck you in."

"I can't imagine a land made of water."

"Ask Fen about it."

"I couldn't"

"Don't be a coward!" Mist laughed, "You fancy him! Do something about it."

"I don't!" Raven spluttered in protest. Mist cocked an eyebrow at him.

"I do," sighed Raven, "Dammit!"

Later Raven found Fen sitting on the same fallen branch by the lakeside the he himself had sat on, a long time ago it seemed, the night he first came to the tribe. Fen was smoking a cigarette and blowing smoke rings in the air. He acknowledged Raven's arrival with a nod of his head but said nothing.

Raven sat down beside him. "Mist and Batalha have been instructing me," he began.

Fen nodded again but didn't look at him.

"About Alba Sulh and The Waterlands to the east."

Fen cocked his head and looked sideways at him.

"I've lived in the mountains all my life. I can't imagine what waterland looks like."

"It's wet," said Fen. "There's a lot of water."

Raven began to babble, "Only I... Er... Mist said I should talk to you..."

Fen's face split into the broadest grin Raven had ever seen.

"That's the clumsiest request for a snog I've ever heard in my life!" he hooted. "Come here, I'll show you."

Raven had become used to the higher vibrational energy of the Sulh, his encounters with Mist had prepared him somewhat, but now he realised that Mist must have been holding back. Either that or he'd underestimated the strength of the soul energy possessed by The Waterlanders.

Fen's kiss nearly knocked him off the branch. On a blast of power he was transported to an alien land, wholly flat. Reed-fringed strips of land barely encroaching on the vast expanses of water that stretched away before him. He was, he realised, inside Fen's head, sharing an oft-visited memory. The Waterlander stood upright in a coracle, kept in balance and moved along solely by Fen's will.

It was sunset. Streaks of purple, orange and crimson smeared the sky and reflecting in the water beneath. It was impossible to tell where sky ended and water began and all the while the haunting call of a curlew urged him onwards.

"Home," said Fen, deep inside Raven's head. "And the call of the curlew, I've been following that for years. I followed it to Curlew himself, then to Megalithica, then here to this mountain and now to you."

"How could you leave a place like this? It's magical."

"There's magic everywhere you just have to look – you know that. There's magic here in these mountains of yours."

Later, lying spent in Fen's bed, the tendrils of aruna still caressing them, Fen told Raven the legend of Avalona, the first city of Alba Sulh.

"No-one really knows how it came to be there. It lies southwest of The Waterlands. Some say it fell, fully formed from another realm through a rift in the fabric of reality. Others say that a great red-haired king and his red-haired sister battled with magic over the swamp lands and created the rift. It's supposed to be an amazing place full of twisting towers and flying creatures..."

"You've never been there?" Raven asked, tracing the undulating tattoo down Fen's chest.

"No, the only one of us ever to visit was Curlew and he was weird for days after."

"Weird? Sounds intriguing. Can we go there?"

"What, you getting tired of your precious mountains, Mountain Boy?"

Raven punched his arm.

High on a cliff edge Mist smiled at the scene below. The two of them stripped to the waist, red gold skin and a skin so pale as to be almost blue, the bluish tinge heightened by the coiling tattoo. Mist was amused; clearly a competition was underway; Mountain people methods verses the Waterlander's way. Raven lay on the stony bank of the gushing river, arm plunged deep in the water, Fen a little way off, perfectly still, spear poised in hand, a growing pile of fish between the two of them. Whatever the outcome Mist recognised a chesna bond in the making and acknowledged that the tribe would eat well that night.

Raven lay on a mossy rock with his hands behind his head, Fen by his side, both watching as Batalha trudged along the ridge line above them. Batalha had appeared pale and insubstantial when Raven first came to the Sulh, and as the weeks passed he seemed to become increasingly transparent, ghostlike even.

"Is Batalha ill?"

"Not exactly," Fen sighed, chewing on a stalk of grass.

"It's what Sulh scribes do."

"I don't understand," said Raven.

Fen sighed again. "They're a strange lot. They seem to flit between this reality and others. I'm not sure if they truly exist here. They gather and absorb information, storing it, making songs and stories of it. Ask him anything and you'll get the most complete answer you could wish for. But holding it all takes its toll. He's near to bursting. He needs to take aruna with another scribe so that they can send all they've discovered back to Kyme."

"Kyme? Oh, yes – the Library. So why don't we have a second scribe? So that they can, I don't know, ship home, more often?"

"Smart boy! We did have. He was killed in a raid by the Uigenna."

"When?"

"Several months ago, before we came here." Fen stretched. "Batalha needs contact with another scribe and soon. Otherwise he'll die."

"So we've got to find him another scribe."

"Yeah."

It came as no surprise to Raven when a day or two later Curlew announced that the tribe would be moving on. Mist had been meditating for days and had picked up another roving band of Sulh further north up the coast.

"Looks like you'll get to travel after all, Mountain Boy," Fen teased.

Efficient in everything they did, the tribe was ready to travel in a matter of hours. The caravan, an assortment of hara on foot, pack horses and carts stood ready to leave. Fen headed a group of warrior phyle at the front, while a similar group brought up the rear. Batalha, now too weak to walk any great distance, was carried on a litter. Mist walked alongside Raven.

"We have plenty of food prepared." he said, "and many items to trade. That should buy us safe passage through Colurastes territory."

"Colurastes?"

"Another Wraeththu tribe. Relax!" said Mist, catching Raven's expression. "They're far more peaceable that the Uigenna."

Day in, day out the routine was the same. Travel by day, rest by night. They kept to the woodlands fringing the coast, occasionally travelling inland to avoid the rotting remains of a human settlement. For food, they ate dried fish and meat supplemented by what they could forage along the path and what could be caught fresh.

Raven began to miss the warmth and resinous scents of his erstwhile home but was fascinated by the altering landscape. The leaves took on hues of burnished copper and gold before falling as the long summer gave way to autumn. As they travelled north, the winds became increasingly bitter. They wrapped Batalha in animal skins and fed him dried fruit.

"What will happen if we don't find another scribe in time?" Raven asked Fen one night as they shared a cigarette.

"Not sure. He'll die is all I know. Personally if I was carrying all that knowledge around I think my head would explode."

Mist's predictions proved correct; they had little contact with the Colurastes, the so-called "Snake People." Curlew parleyed with tribal leaders, offering goods for safe passage and seeking information. Raven found the Colurastes odd, vain creatures; their snake-like moving hair disturbed him.

"Freaks," said Fen, but quietly.

"Yes," said a Colurastes leader one day. "We have seen a group similar to yours, camped inland on the banks of a river, about two days away." Curlew paid him with the sinuous beaded snake charm he'd taken a fancy to and, in appreciation, the Colurastes chief made them a gift of persimmons and dried peaches.

The phyle found the other Sulh exactly where the Colurastes had directed them, in a clearing by a great river: a collection of painted tents and covered wagons. Wrapped in animal skins the tribe came to meet them.

Raven saw the two scribes immediately. Like Batalha they dressed in simple white robes, kept out the cooling air with woven jackets and had an otherworldliness about them. One obvious difference: they appeared infinitely more substantial. The pair hurried over to the litter and made arrangements for Batalha to be carried into their tent to rest.

"He needs building up a little after your journey before we can begin The Singing," said one, but did not explain further.

The resident Sulh leader spoke, "I am Kaldar, and we welcome you. We sensed your coming and have prepared a meal. Please, join us in the pavilion; we can sort out sleeping arrangements later."

A larger tent stood apart from the others, circular with a high arching roof, intricate animal designs decorated the canvas in shades of black and ochre. Inside a woven wooden lattice supported the walls and the ceiling poles that reached high towards an opening in the roof. The floor, spread with animal skins, was liberally scattered with woven cushions. On one side of the tent stood a low bench covered with platters and trays piled high with freshly steamed fish, vegetable stews, corn bread, fragrant meat dishes and pots of strong coffee.

Curlew thanked Kaldar and his phyle, and then Mist offered up a blessing. It had been a long time since the group had feasted so well and it was a long time before anyone spoke again.

The last dregs of coffee had been squeezed from the pot and the final scraps of cornbread had been used to mop up gravy. Curlew and Kaldar were now deep in conversation.

"Kaldar recommends we make our camp in the lee of the woods behind the pavilion," Curlew announced. "He also invites us to a celebration tonight, which I've accepted. It's too long since the Sulh came together and shared stories of their homeland."

"The legend of the red haired king and his sister could stand another telling," laughed Kaldar.

In the shelter of an oak tree Raven and Fen erected their tent and made it as homely as they could. Then, finding themselves with time on their hands, they went to inquire after Batalha.

"He's just awoken," said Ranian, one of the other scribes. "You can see him, but keep it brief."

They found him lying on a low bed in the corner of one of the tents. The walls had sheep's wool woven into the supporting lattice, and with a small wood-burning stove glowing by the far wall, it was surprisingly snug.

"Trust you to bag the best quarters," said Fen, as he plonked himself inelegantly on the end of the bed. Showing more consideration Raven sat down cross-legged on the rug.

Batalha grinned, "Trust you to complain about it!"

"So what happens now?" asked Raven.

"I need a little time to gather my strength and then Ranian, Ashnan and I will peform The Singing."

Raven looked confused.

"We take aruna to heighten the senses, to enhance the power of mind touch," continued Batalha, "and at the moment of connection the knowledge we have gathered will stream back to Alba Sulh, to Kyme, as a series of musical tones. The library has adepts ready and waiting around the clock to receive the knowledge sent to them from all over the globe. After The Singing I will be purged and can begin to learn again."

"When will this happen?"

"A day or two – when the other scribes think I'm ready."

It was closer to two weeks. Autumn plunged quickly into winter in these parts and a dusting of snow already covered the ground. All over the camp braziers burned, the air scented with sage to heighten awareness and dissipate negative energy.

When the day arrived, the pavilion had been draped inside with cloths of purple and blue, the scribes were ensconced within. Outside the rest of the tribe gathered to chant incantations to speed the success of The Singing.

At Mist's signal, the tribe began, first whispering words of power, a low, sibilant hiss darting to and fro around the circle. Then coloured mists seeped from the entrance of the pavilion, through the seams and the opening at the apex; magenta, gold, cyan. A note, pure, high, clear split the air. It was joined by another, and another, the harmony ricocheting off branches and tents. The chanting of the tribe grew as the notes intensified, and then, moved to add rhythm, they stamped their feet and beat together sticks.

The sound wave grew ever stronger, undulating around the camp, making the air shake, the ground judder; on and on until Raven was forced to cover his ears. Then, a wave of pure energy, tinged with white and gold, exploded from the pavilion, out across the land, high into the sky, scattering all in its path, each member of the tribe knocked clean off their feet.

And then, a shattering silence.

"Let's see what the little buggers at Kyme make of that lot," said Fen, flat on his back.

For several days after The Singing, at Mist's insistence, the entire tribe rested. Batalha, confined to his bed once more, fretted, wanting to be out in the world again discovering more. To Raven's eyes he appeared far more solid and substantial than he'd ever seen him, but the pale hair and skin and the almost transparent blue of his eyes still gave him an ethereal quality.

Raven sat stitching animal hide together to form a winter jacket whilst Fen sat in the corner attempting to pick out a tune on Batalha's harp.

"For God's sake put the damned thing down" snapped Batalha. "Either that or let me teach you how to do it properly".

Fen grinned his widest grin. "Sure, teach me. It'll give me something to do during the long winter months. Don't be surprised, boys, but I reckon Curlew and Kaldar are planning to combine resources and over-winter right here."

"What for? It'd be much warmer back down south."

"They reckon they've got a reason to stay. I think we won't be going back down south again until spring. So, that gives you plenty of time to teach me to play this thing."

"Wonderful," said Batalha.

Fen was right. Both groups would be overwintering by the river. Days passed and new routines formed; parties went out foraging for food and firewood, hunting for meat and, whilst the river remained unfrozen, replenishing dwindling fish stocks. Batalha and the other scribes had meetings with members of the Colurastes tribe, cultural exchanges, always accompanied by Fen and other members of the warrior phyle. Raven declined to attend these meetings; the Colurastes gave him the creeps. Mist shook his head but let it go.

Mid winter's eve arrived and Raven was glad to see it; the days would now begin to lengthen. The pavilion was garlanded with greenery and a mighty feast was prepared. The entire tribe would attend, as would representatives of the local Colurastes.

"Behave," Mist warned Raven.

"Of course," answered Raven and he did, but he wasn't fooling Fen.

"Don't worry," Fen said, cornering Raven by the drinks table. "It won't be long now. You'll see your mountains again." As it turned out it was sooner than either of them had anticipated.

Raven sat up with a start. It was pitch black, the middle of the night, and a cry had awoken him. The camp was silent and Raven knew the cry had not come to him from without but from within.

He'd also recognised the voice. It was Pale Fawn.

By his side Fen sat up and lit an oil lamp.

"What is it?" he asked.

"Someone I care about is in trouble, they need me."

Fen leaned back on an elbow. "Tell me."

Raven sighed. "You're probably not going to like this but here goes. I have a friend, a close friend, almost a sister, who's still alive. She's carrying my child."

Fen glanced away, a faraway look in his eyes. "I had a sister. I lost her. You remember the story of Avalona falling, fully formed, through the rift?"

Raven nodded.

"Well, I don't know how true that is but rifts do form all over Alba Sulh, particularly in The Waterlands. Dykes were blown, sluices flooded, the land practically turned itself inside out to return to its natural state. Serena fell through one of the rifts – snatched away in front of me. As Wraeththu we're supposed to sever all family ties, but I think that's bullshit. If you have family, you should hang on to them."

"So you think I should go to her?"

"Yeah, I do. We'll talk to Curlew and Mist in the morning... but I'm making one condition."

"Being?"

"I'm coming with you, Mountain Boy."

Curlew and Mist were supportive. Kaldar initially was more hesitant.

"An advance party would be useful," Mist persuaded him, "to ready our old camp and prepare for our return in the spring."

Kaldar, seeing the sense in Mist's argument, agreed and supplied two horses to speed their journey, plus enough dried food to see them through. Batalha came to see them off. By mid-morning they were on their way.

The two of them, travelling light, made swift progress, unencumbered as they were by the rest of the tribe, the wagons, tents, food stores that accompany a tribe on the move. Raven tried to reach Pale Fawn by mind touch to let her know they were on their way, but heard and felt nothing in return. He hoped she knew.

They followed the same coastal paths they had travelled the previous autumn but now the trees, devoid of their leaves stood stark, black skeletons against a translucently pale sky. The paths took them south into warmer weather. It felt to Raven as if they were chasing the spring. Each day the light lasted a little longer, the wind bit a little less cruelly and buds and green shoots shook the land from its winter dormancy.

The journey that had taken them weeks in the autumn took a few short days on their return.

It was early morning when they reached the reservation; they had been riding since dawn. Shafts of light played between bands of mist as they travelled through the achingly familiar terrain of Raven's childhood.

They found Pale Fawn sitting on the steps of Two Comet's cabin, waiting for them.

"I knew you'd come," she smiled. "I heard you calling me."

Raven kissed her head and introduced Fen. She stood, a little unsteadily, to shake his hand, her swollen abdomen making her a little ungainly.

"Where is everyone?" Raven asked her.

"Gone," she replied. "All gone. Dead or flown, but all gone."

Raven was almost too scared to ask. "Two Comet?"

She shook her head, indicating a cairn of stones that stood on the far side of the clearing.

"He died on mid-winters eve. Raven, I have to leave, too. There's nothing left for me here."

"Come back with us," offered Fen. "We can make a place for you with the Sulh."

Pale Fawn shook her head again. "No," she said, "my place is not with you."

Raven made to protest, but she held up her hand and looked him square in the eye.

"You found your new tribe and your place in it. Now I have to find mine." She gestured east. "There's a voice calling me. I have to follow it, find them, but I need your help to do it."

Raven looked uncertain.

"This lady knows her mind," said Fen, "You want to pick your battles, Raven, and this isn't one of them."

Pale Fawn smiled at him.

Pale Fawn had little to take with her, just one bag, as they left the camp, Fen riding one horse and Raven, with Pale Fawn before him, riding the other.

They left their forests and mountains behind, again travelling towards the coast – this time, not north but east, away from the familiar trees, and the place that for so long had been their home. Their journey took them across grassy planes where the wind created waves and ripples among the new growth towards the shore and a sandy beach.

Pale Fawn pointed east again. "I have to go further," she said "It's not far, but hidden. They have to stay safe and I'll be safe with them. Please," she beseeched, "I have to go".

"Suppose it's just ocean," said Fen.

Raven shook his head. "No, there are islands," he said. "I saw them in a breath vision with Mist."

They found a small boat, sound and sea worthy but with its sail missing. Fen and Raven dragged it to the water's edge and helped Pale Fawn on board. Once afloat Fen stood on the gunwale and balanced himself against the mast.

"This worked on the meres back in the Waterlands," he said. "I don't see why it shouldn't work here."

He closed his eyes, connecting his thoughts with the timbers of the boat and the water beneath, willing one to slide over the other. Slowly the boat began to move, gliding out to sea.

"It's the same process," said Fen with a grin, "just bouncier water."

It was late afternoon when they made landfall on a sandy shore with a backdrop of thick trees close to an abandoned settlement. The sun was setting behind them and Pale Fawn began to shiver. Raven held her close to warm her as Fen beached the boat.

"They're on the other side of the island," she said. "They're calling me, telling me to hurry."

"Tell them to wait," said Fen. "You're exhausted and have travelled enough for today. You need food and shelter. Tell them we'll set out again in the morning."

Pale Fawn screwed up her face and concentrated hard. "Yes," she said. "It's alright, they'll wait."

"Let's get you indoors," said Raven and half carried her to the nearest house.

These were the crazy houses of his aruna vision; wooden,

unstable-looking, top-heavy with arms and platforms that reached to the heavens.

"Architectural style 'early maniac,'" muttered Fen, "What were they? Sun worshippers?"

They found a sound room downstairs and a wood-burning stove with a hot plate. They settled Pale Fawn into a battered easy chair and wrapped her up in rugs. Raven scouted around for firewood and got a fire going. Fen went through their rations.

"I reckon we can do better than dried fruit and fish," he said and disappeared outside.

He returned a short while later. "Abandoned restaurant," he said holding up a cooking pot full of tinned vegetables and bottled water. "Chairs and tables strewn everywhere and covered with blown sand but a very well stocked larder." He'd even found tea and most importantly a tin opener.

"He's a hunter, this new lover of yours," said Pale Fawn. Raven gave her a look. "It's alright," she said with a slight smile, "I know." Raven left it at that.

First they made tea and then a thick soup from the vegetables. They had to rouse Pale Fawn to get her to eat and then left her to sleep again, stoking up the fire to make it burn all night and made themselves as comfortable as possible, wrapped up in rugs on the wooden floor.

At dawn Fen made another raid on the restaurant and brought back breakfast. Then they set out again, this time on foot, towards the other side of the island. A sandy track led them away from the settlement and eastwards once more.

Oleander fringed the edge of the dense woodland; in spring there would be a profusion of pink and white blossoms. In the forest itself, vast stands of evergreen pines stabilised the shifting sand and interspersed between the dark pines, leafless oaks were draped thick with Spanish moss, the bearded lichen hanging from the high tree branches and reaching to the forest floor.

It seemed to Raven as if the island were shrouding a secret, keeping it safe from prying eyes.

An hour's walk brought them to the western shore and a tall, auburn-haired woman standing on the beach. Behind her was a small harbour and moored there, a sailing ship.

"You are welcome," she said. "We've been waiting."

"You're the voice that's been calling me?" asked Pale Fawn.

"I am," affirmed the woman. "We sensed you on the ethers, you and the child you carry. The child is special, and she and you need protection. Now is not the time for such singular individuals to be abroad. It is not safe. The world of Wraeththu is young and far from stable. You must be hidden for now. That is what we offer you."

The woman turned to Raven, "You are the child's father?" he nodded. "And you are now Sulh? You chose wisely; they are one of the more enlightened tribes. I am sorry you will be unable to join Pale Fawn at this time. It is imperative that who we are and our homelands remain a secret."

"Don't worry," she said as Raven began to protest, "Pale Fawn will be well cared for. And the fears you have, about the future of women in this brave new world of ours? Women shall have a place, but this young culture is not ready to face that yet."

"I trust her," Pale Fawn said, turning to Raven, "and I want to go with her. Will you trust me?"

Raven put an arm around her and kissed her forehead. He did not trust himself to speak.

Throughout this interchange Fen had been silent but he had been watching the woman intently.

"Have you ever travelled to Alba Sulh?" he asked, "And are we to know your name?"

The woman gave a wry smile. "In my work I have travelled widely and for now you may call me 'Morgana,' although in time you will come to know me by a different name."

Fen snorted slightly. The woman ignored him.

"We must embark," she said. "The seas are treacherous at this time of year, so we only have a short window of opportunity to sail., That's is why we had to get you here quickly." They walked with her to the small harbour and paused by the gangplank.

The woman turned to Raven. "Worry not. One day you will see Pale Fawn again and visit our homeland, but for now your path lies with the Sulh."

Raven took Pale Fawn in his arms and held her tight.

"I'll be fine," she said. "Come and visit. One day. And you," she said turning to kiss Fen on the cheek, "take care of my Raven for me."

Fen kissed her back. "Of course."

She went on board with the woman and stood at the bow as the ship slipped away. For a while she stood there watching them and

Raven stood, Fen's hand on his shoulder, watching his past and future sail away. Then Pale Fawn moved from the stern to the bows, setting her face towards her future.

Fen turned Raven around and walked him back to the forest path.

"Come on, Mountain Boy, time to go home."

"Where's home?" The first words Raven had been able to utter for a while and he nearly choked on them.

"Home's where your people are," Fen replied, giving him a squeeze, "and right now my home's with you."

Raven turned back to watch the ship slipping over the horizon. "We still have a long way to go," he said.

Fen tugged on his hand, "Yeah... 'the woods are lovely, dark, and deep, but we have promises to keep, and miles to go before we sleep'[1] – Come on Raven," he smiled, "this is just the beginning."

And Raven smiled and allowed himself to be led away.

[1] Quote from 'Stopping by Woods on a Snowy Evening' by Robert Frost

The Rune-Throwing

Kristi Lee

The Rune-Throwing

Hroth focused on his breathing: deep inhalations through the nose and exhalations through barely parted lips. The frigid air burned as it drew up his nostrils. Steam from his breath blended into the fog that rolled and shifted. The beach was eerily quiet, muffled, except for the soft lapping of the water on the rocks of the nearby shore. The fog was so dense and soupy, Hroth couldn't even see the bay, though he was only sitting a stone's throw from the water. While he didn't expect to hear anything else aside from the occasional cry of a seagull, his ears were beginning to play tricks on him. Had he just heard something? Was someone there? It was his third day of fasting in solitude as part of a communal meditation, and the line between reality and imagination had become as insubstantial as the folding mist around him.

The rasping croak of a raven, unmistakably real, made Hroth look up reflexively, but he couldn't see anything through the blanketed white that surrounded him. Seconds later the distinctive black bird swooped in, landed off to his right and immediately began preening its wing. Hroth watched it impassively, knowing it to be his familiar. Roc was a friend who had been with him since his earliest days as a har. He gazed at the bird steadily, acknowledging their shared past, before he closed his eyes, waiting to hear what Roc had to say.

"The wise ones are pleased with your journey," Roc croaked. "You shall tell your story to one you have not yet met."

Hroth's eyes flew open. "Soon?"

"It is not for me to say when. But when you do, you should take him under your wing, as I have you."

"Under my *wing*, indeed," Hroth said ruefully.

Hroth himself was no seer, though his friend Hansggedir fancied he read his scrying cards with accuracy. Only when the raven spoke to him about the spirits and their will did he believe he was given a true glimpse into the future. Roc made the raven version of a clucking sound, hopped over to Hroth's closed bag and began pecking at it.

"I've been fasting, so I don't have any treats for you," Hroth apologized. "If I'd known you would visit during my meditation, I'd have brought you something."

"No matter," Roc rasped in his gravelly avian voice. "The time for the new ones is come. Go and prepare yourself as you always do."

Hroth nodded toward the raven, which cawed and flew off. He closed his eyes and counted down, thirty-two precisely deep inhalations and exhalations, before he again opened his eyes and yawned. With as fluid a movement as he could muster, he stood and stretched, then bowed at the waist toward the sea. He murmured his thanks to the Aghama for the time of quiet and peace, and cast a few thoughts toward the sea spirits, as though skipping rocks across a lake. After gathering his few belongings from his vigil, he slowly walked up the rocky beach to the path that would take him to Freygard and his kinshar.

He realized he was gritting his teeth and forced himself to relax. It wasn't so bad to feel like a freakish pariah, or so he tried to convince himself. Hansggedir, faithful, loyal friend that he was, ensured that he became neither a dry leaf due to lack of aruna nor fell into despair. Rune-throwings were hard on Hroth. Already he was leery of being with the other Freyhellans even in their modest number, of hearing whispers and looks of fearful respect. For once he wanted to blend in, to be chosen. Just once he wanted his rune stone to be selected, to complete the rite of inception with a new har. Damn Roc for getting his hopes up. The last thing he wanted to do was revisit that nightmarish day, much less have to share it with a jelly-legged har barely recovered from his althaia, all senses screaming for aruna. He sighed.

Back in his modest home, Hroth built a fire, tending it until it crackled merrily in the hearth. After heating water for a hot bath, he thoroughly washed his hair. His thick tresses were his one vanity, though the golden colour was the same as nearly every other har in Freyhella. One of the humans he'd seen whose althaia must be complete had dark russet hair, the sides shorn, as was their custom before inception. Hroth had gone on his vigil to be with them in spirit, and he was anxious to see them in their transformed state, especially given his familiar's instructions.

Once clothed in a woollen dressing gown, he sent a message via mind touch to Hansggedir. *Are you up?*

Yes! Hansggedir replied at once. *I'm not a slug. You obviously have me confused with Sveinn.* Hroth could hear the laughter in his friend's mind voice. *I'm glad you're back. The rune-throwing will be at dusk.*

So I assumed. Will you come braid my hair for the occasion?

Of course. I'll be there shortly.

Smiling at the thought of seeing him, Hroth padded around his small house, hanging a kettle above the flames to make a pot of tea. To salve his pride, he wore a ceremonial cape made of silver fox to each ritual at the Hall of Voices. While it was on his mind, he retrieved it, draping it over a chair in his bedroom. He'd just finished some smoked fish and tea-soaked bread when Hansggedir knocked on the door.

"It's open!" Hroth called out. A wave of cold air rushed in, ebbing once the door closed again. Hansggedir's tall form appeared in the kitchen, his eyes sparkling.

"You can call on me for more than my plaiting skills, you know," he said by way of greeting.

"I know, and I do, so don't pretend otherwise." Hroth smiled and lifted his face to receive his friend's kisses on each cheek. "Not today. There's always a chance that I'll be chosen for one of the newest hara."

"The odds are stacked against you," Hansggedir observed, plucking a piece of sweetbread off of Hroth's plate.

"It's not odds, it's the choice of the spirits. But thanks for reminding me that I've never been deemed worthy."

Hansggedir looked abashed. "That's not what I meant!" he insisted. "It's that there aren't many inceptees. I know you and your self-abasements only too well. I'd never insinuate that it's anything about you as a har that's kept you from being selected. Honestly," he grumbled, hitting Hroth a bit roughly on the back of the head before leaning over to kiss the same spot. "Quit taking yourself so damn seriously, no matter what that raven tells you. Where's your brush?"

Hroth pointed at the other end of the table. After popping the bread in his mouth, Hansggedir picked up the brush and came to stand behind him, brushing through the waist-length hair.

"And your ties?"

"Oh. My bedroom."

As Hansggedir loped off, Hroth called after him, "There are a few raven feathers. Bring those, too."

Nearly half an hour passed as they chatted. Hansggedir created several circlets of braids, intertwining leather strips and at the end, placing the raven feathers over Hroth's left ear.

"Exquisite," Hansggedir sighed appreciatively at his work.

Hroth let out a low laugh. "Thank you. I'm almost glad I can't do it myself." He stood up. "Let's go to the rune-throwing, even though it makes me uncomfortable being around so many hara."

Hansggedir made a noise of discontent.

"Aghama help any of them if you get chosen. Where's your cape?"

"On the chair in my room."

Hroth went into his bathroom to evaluate Hansggedir's work in his modest looking-glass. It was indeed intricate and to be admired, though hara always did so from a distance.

"You look stunning, as always. Come away from that mirror!" Hansggedir joked, and Hroth found it in himself to smile as he left the room.

"I'm afraid my vanity didn't go away when I became har," he admitted, allowing Hansggedir to help him put on the fox cape. "Though I don't see myself as the catch I once was. Nohar else does, either."

"We all have our flaws. Yours is just more difficult to hide."

"Try impossible."

"Oh, Hroth." Hansggedir shook his head. "Of all days, today the focus won't be on you. You're revered and beautiful. What you're missing cannot possibly detract from that. Come on, don't brood over it."

"Oh! The fire." Hroth gestured at his fireplace.

"I'll get it."

Once Hansggedir had tossed water on the logs, the two friends went out into the crisp air of late afternoon and down the road to the Hall of Voices, greeting other hara along the way. These rituals were becoming few and far between since the human population had been morbidly decimated by plague and disease. Everyhar in Freygard took great joy in welcoming the few humans who could still be incepted into Wraeththu.

They walked up to the tall wooden doors, held open with golden hooks to welcome those attending the occasion. Two stone pillars, each topped with a wide granite bowl, flanked the doorway. The bowls held stones, each carved with a different rune. Each har in Freygard had chosen a symbol after his inception and made a pilgrimage to the sea to find the two stones that would represent him in future group settings. They were marked with the har's symbol and deposited in bowls for the rune-throwing.

Hroth reached up to a bowl and pulled out an oval, flat stone, dark mossy in colour. Its rune was an ash tree. He wasn't sure whose rune it was, but for that day's ritual, it didn't matter.

"Let's sit up front," Hansggedir suggested.

"Let's not!" Hroth argued. "I don't like being stared at, and I make hara uncomfortable."

"Only those who are ignorant. And who cares about them? Come on. I want every damn Freyhellan to see my masterpiece of handiwork."

Hroth growled under his breath. "Fine."

Golden-haired hara with strong features filled benches three deep. Despite his disquiet, Hroth felt a warmth of pride at seeing his kinshar assembled together. He'd been among the first to offer himself to the exotic creatures who had arrived, an amalgam of the sexes, fey and beautiful. He chatted with a friend he'd not seen in quite some time, until finally Trygve, their hienama, beat his staff against the floor four times. At that, silence claimed the room.

"Tiahaara," Trygve intoned, "today we welcome three new hara into our midst. It is the rune-throwing, a time for the spirits to guide these newly through their althaia to the hara with whom they will take their first aruna. Each new har will pick in turn, and that har will come to stand by his side. May the Aghama watch over us and may our new hara grow in light."

There was a thrum of excitement as the three newly incepted hara walked forward, each clad in ceremonial garb of leather and fur. The table used for inception three days earlier now stood gleaming on a dais, holding a bowl with the stones of all present.

One by one the new hara went up and selected a rune. Two had fair hair, and the third one a waterfall of burnished mahogany. Hroth felt his stone heat in his hand as the third har approached the deep bowl and reached in. The Hienama read the three runes: twilight, blood, and ash tree.

Hroth nudged Hansggedir, spreading open his palm to show that indeed, he had been chosen.

"I guess I won't be seeing you for a couple of days," Hansggedir murmured under his breath.

"I'll be busy," Hroth whispered without thinking. He was stunned and out of sorts; Roc's prediction had been too direct a portend. "But— why now?"

"Why not?"

Hroth shook his head, then stood and walked up to the new hara with the two others chosen until they all stood side by side.

"Journey well, tiahaara," Trygve said. The hienama placed a daub of scented oil at the throat of each of new har, symbolizing their sacred seal to Wraeththu. "With your first aruna you will shed completely your human self. Let the celebrations begin!"

The new har at Hroth's side gave him a hesitant smile, glanced down at Hroth's left arm, and then his alarmed gaze flew back up to Hroth's face.

"I'll explain later," Hroth said.

He steered the har toward the adjoining room where tables groaned under the weight of food and drink. "What's your name?"

"My new one?"

"That's the only one now," Hroth said gently.

The har flushed, which only added to his refined beauty. "Ottar."

"Ottar," Hroth echoed. "I'm Hroth. Don't worry, you're in good hands. Well, hand," he said with a wry smile. "Are you from Freygard?"

Ottar heaped his plate with smoked fish and poured himself a large chalice of mead. "No. I fled from the upcountry. I'd rather not speak of it — I'm ready to leave that behind."

He spoke fervently and Hroth felt new gratitude to the spirits who presided over the rune-throwing — and to Roc for having spoken to him on the beach.

"And so you should." Hroth had taken a chalice of mead but was sipping it, mindful of his recent fast. He didn't want to be out of sorts with Ottar; that would dishonour the har's first aruna.

Ottar seemed nervous as he chewed some tart berries. He was obviously trying to keep his eyes trained on Hroth's face and was failing miserably as his gaze returned to Hroth's stump, again and again.

Take him under my wing? he thought sourly. *He may flee my bed as soon as the act is over.*

"Not to be rude, tiahaar," Ottar said at last, watching avidly as Hroth licked some marinade off of his fingers, "but—" He gestured at Hroth's left arm. "Did that happen before or after you became har?"

"After. I'll tell you what happened, but it's not a pleasant story, so I don't want to elaborate now."

Ottar chewed thoughtfully, his gaze sliding over Hroth like quicksilver. Hroth knew he could be considered a short straw to draw, as it were, especially by somehar who didn't know that he'd been one of the first Wraeththu in Freyhella — and that he was tender-hearted to a fault. A rising tide of dignity rose in him.

"I assure you that your first aruna will be a memorable one, and not just because you picked the rune held by the only one-handed har in Freygard," Hroth said a bit defensively.

"Yes, light an extra candle to the Aghama, dark one!" Hansggedir boomed from behind Hroth. His eyes sparkled with mirth and drink. "You're fortunate— Hroth is quite skilled."

"Flatterer."

"It's only the truth!" Hansggedir grinned at Hroth and took a deep quaff of mead. "Journey well."

"I will, tiahaar."

Ottar's mobile face belied his conflicting feelings: desire, trepidation, excitement. Confused agitation poured off of him in waves. No doubt the senses in his new harish body were going haywire.

"What's your name, seal-eyes?" Hansggedir prompted.

"Ottar."

Hansggedir gave Hroth a look of disbelief. "Has there ever been a more apt name?"

"It's indeed fitting," Hroth agreed. "Go on — you're making him even more uncomfortable. Find Sveinn and drape yourself on him. He's used to your blunt speech."

"Hroth, I'm fine," Ottar stammered, a flush creeping up his long neck. "I just — I just didn't expect..." His voice trailed off helplessly.

"You're the luckiest har in this room," Hansggedir stated emphatically. "And don't listen to any troglodyte who tells you otherwise."

Hroth began to shove him away with his shoulder.

"I'm leaving! Loki's stones," Hansggedir swore, grinning as he swaggered off.

Ottar seemed more relaxed after this banter, to Hroth's relief. He glanced at the new har's plate and saw much of the food was untouched. "Do you mind if I have a piece of your fish?"

"Not at all!"

Hroth put his cup down on a nearby table, but Ottar, with a heated smile, fed it to him instead.

"Mmmmm. Salty," Hroth murmured.

He picked up a piece of candied ginger and placed it in Ottar's awaiting mouth. Ottar kept his eyes trained on Hroth's as he chewed, and then said, "Sweet. And spicy."

"Much as I suspect you'll taste," Hroth said in a low voice, gratified when a flush again crept up Ottar's neck.

"You'll be the first to know," he said. "It better be soon. I feel like I'm on fire!"

"I won't make you linger," Hroth promised, tracing Ottar's fine jaw with his fingers and giving him a reassuring smile.

They stayed for another hour or so, Hroth meeting the other new inceptees and introducing Ottar to a few of the other founders. When Hroth discovered that they'd circled around to Hansggedir and Sveinn, he gratefully knew they could leave. What had Hansggedir said about other hara's perception of him? Beautiful and revered? Respected and preferred at his usual distance was more like it. *Better to go ahead and enjoy the novelty of a new har and then let him get on with his life*, he thought resignedly to himself.

"Go on!" Hansggedir said at last. Ottar gave the older har a grateful look.

"Come and get your blessing from the hienama," Hroth suggested as they made their way toward the doors. He stood behind Ottar as Trygve made a symbol of power over the new har, then drew him into a firm embrace.

"Welcome, beloved," he said, and Hroth was surprised to feel tears prick at his eyes. The hienama caught his gaze and gave him a sympathetic look before releasing Ottar.

"My house isn't far away," Hroth said as they left the Hall of Voices, accepting well wishes along the way. The other hara would celebrate and make merry until the early hours of morning, but Hroth had no reason to begrudge them their fun. Once they were outside, Ottar threaded his arm in Hroth's and Hroth turned to smile at him.

"You're really tall!" he noted.

Ottar laughed. "Guilty."

"Not guilty, just tall."

At first they walked in silence, but then Ottar asked Hroth about his cape.

"It's one of the only things I kept from my human past," he said, glancing down at it. "It belonged to my grandfather. He was quite the hunter, and it took him several years to track and kill the foxes whose skins now keep me so warm. Seems a bit barbaric to me now, but when I was a young boy it seemed that he was a giant among men."

"I can imagine!"

Hroth watched his own breath, each exhalation creating a huff of white into the cold air. He felt more comfortable now that he was away from dozens of pitying eyes, but grew increasingly discomfited as they approached his house. It was quite rustic, and Hroth almost never had guests, besides Hansggedir and Sveinn.

"I live just up here."

He turned up a cobbled street, which at first glance appeared abandoned. Many houses were in disrepair, abandoned by their human owners and the few neighbours Hroth did have were all at the celebration.

Once inside his house, Hroth took off his cape, watching as Ottar took in his surroundings.

"I prefer to live simply," he explained. "Would you like some tea?"

He ran his fingers through Ottar's dark hair. It was as silky to the touch as it looked, and Ottar gave him a bold smile.

"No, but thank you. I'd like…"

"Yes, of course. Let me get a fire going in my bedroom so the room's not so cold."

"I can help," Ottar said quickly, looking at Hroth's left arm.

"It's okay. Do me a favour, first." He looked beguilingly at the new har. "Share breath with me."

"With pleasure."

Ottar turned and cupped Hroth's face in his hands, pressing his lips firmly to Hroth's. With a soft moan, Hroth opened his mouth to Ottar's questing tongue, the kiss quickly turning to a tangle of tongues as it evolved into a sharing of breath. Ottar's breath was lapping waves and sunrise, fresh with a taste of clear sapphire. Hroth let himself be carried away by his desire, eventually pulling away with a throaty laugh.

"You burn hotter than any fire, but I want us to be able to lie on top of my blankets. Let's go to the bedroom."

Ottar clung to him, stealing kisses as they stumbled down the short hallway. Hroth made quick work of getting the fire started, then waved his hand toward two pillared candles, which burst into life.

Ottar's eyes grew wide. "How did you do that?"

"It's a skill that comes with caste ascension," Hroth explained. "Not hard. You'll get there as you study with one of the Pyralisits. All in time. For now, though, it's time for you to discover some of the bountiful delights of being har."

Hroth pressed his lips to Ottar's, kissing him before it became a sharing of breath. Ottar rubbed Hroth's back while with his one hand, Hroth let his fingers slide under Ottar's tunic to press against his warm skin.

"Will you undress?" he husked, nibbling on Ottar's earlobe. "And undress me? I can't wait to taste every part of you."

"Yes, please," Ottar groaned, his arousal evident and pressing against Hroth's hip. Soon they were gloriously naked. Almost shyly, Ottar held Hroth's left arm and brought the stump at his wrist to his mouth to kiss it.

"Does it hurt?" he asked in a low voice.

"No, but in times like this, I do especially miss it," Hroth admitted with a rueful smile. "Lie back. I'm going to play your body like the beautiful instrument it is."

Ottar was reduced to monosyllables and moans of pleasure as Hroth did as promised, lying down between his legs, kissing and licking his tangy flesh. He found the nub of his outermost sikra, and as he rubbed it, Ottar bucked and cried out. Once he'd awakened three of the sikras and Ottar was thrashing on the bed, Hroth decided it was time to take pity on him. With a swift thrust and growl of possession, he joined Ottar's body, pushing deep into tight heat. Again and again he took him, riding the waves of pleasure as Ottar instinctively clenched his new organ around him.

The butterfly tongue in his ouana-lim lashed out to connect to the burning star in Ottar's body. Ottar arched off the bed with a wild cry, spontaneously bursting into tears even as he laughed aloud.

"No har told me it would be like *that*," Ottar murmured once his breathing slowed.

"It isn't like that all the time," Hroth said gently, kissing his eyelids. "But there's something truly magical the first time your harish body is brought to life."

After a while Hroth got up and gave Ottar a glass of water, which he drank gratefully.

"Will you tell me about your injury?" he asked afterward. "I hate to keep asking, especially after what we just experienced but... I really want to know."

"Of course," soothed Hroth. "I understand. It's been a couple of years since I've told someone new. Let's get comfortable."

Hroth took Ottar's lead, which meant that Ottar suggested that they sit in front of the fire on one of Hroth's woven rugs.

"I'd like it if you'd let me lay my head in your lap," Ottar said as he sat up, pulling Hroth's hand to splay on his chest. "Maybe it's this aruna thing, or just you, but I don't mind being a bit, well, needy."

"Now that we Wraeththu are a bit more civilized, one's first aruna should be a ceremony of joy and rapture," Hroth said, opening his arms. "Be as needy as you wish. Back in the very first days, it was a bit more brutal. Are you certain you want to hear my story now?"

"Yes, unless it makes you uncomfortable."

"No. It doesn't."

They situated themselves in front of the blazing fire, Hroth able to play with Ottar's hair, the chestnut colour taking on a coppery glow from the fire.

"There weren't many of us back then," he began, "and the human population was seized by terror, certain that the world was ending. Theirs was, but not in the way they expected. We first Wraeththu were choosy, selecting those who could seek and find us out, who wanted to reach beyond their human selves. I prowled the cities, sending out a siren call to those who could hear it. But it became too much with all of the disease and despair. I left my fledgling tribe for a time to go to the countryside, now nearly abandoned, to meditate and draw energy I knew I would find out in nature. I had to get away from the decaying centres of human civilization."

Hroth's fingers slid through silky hair to even softer skin, and smiled as Ottar made a contented, purring sound. Despite the violence Ottar must know was coming in his tale, Hroth knew the new har's blood throbbed hot in his veins. Once he'd finished his story and maybe after a bit of wine, it would be time for Ottar to experience the role of ouana.

"I went to an abandoned farm in one of the valleys, beautiful in its disrepair. I retreated far within myself, and was in such a deep state that I was able to be ambushed. It was a group of three humans, one ill and two distressingly strong. I'd been caught so unawares that they were able to restrain me. They thought if they made a sacrifice of me to one of the old gods, he would take pity on them, and make the plague go away. Probably they were hoping both for health and also for creatures like me to vanish as well."

Ottar had moved to lie on his side and was staring intently at him.

Seeing the anguish that filled his expression, Hroth gave him a soft smile.

"This happened a few years ago, dear Ottar. I'll get through the story, but please don't be troubled on my behalf. This night should be one of memorable joy, not melancholy."

"I won't obsess about it, I promise," Ottar said, placing a hand on Hroth's knee. "Already it doesn't startle me like it did at first. Thank you for trusting me enough to tell me."

"It's not exactly a secret I can hide!" Hroth said ruefully, shaking his head. "Here. Let me share breath with you and show you that way."

Ottar seemed a bit perplexed, but gamely he climbed into Hroth's lap, straddling him and wrapping his arms around Hroth's strong shoulders. The older har let his hand and arm smooth down to the swell above Ottar's buttocks, hot skin warmed by its proximity to the fire. Hroth didn't want to overwhelm him since it had been a gruesome experience.

"If it's too much, break the connection," he said.

"I will. I've seen a lot of terrible things myself," Ottar noted, his fingers rubbing Hroth's neck under his braids.

"Of course."

Ottar leaned in to press their lips together. Hroth let the kiss remain just that for a time, enjoying the warm sensuality of the purely physical connection of lips and searching tongues. He guided it to a sharing of breath, bringing a smattering of images to send on the current of their breathing.

There were his terrified tormentors who'd bound him to a table as he snarled, struggling against the ropes that burned against his chafing flesh. They'd prayed to the ancient god, offering Hroth to be like him, the dirty cleaver held high as Hroth roared in comprehension. Roc had appeared, cawing and attacking the humans, but there were too many of them.

After that came the sickening sound and then pain exploded up his arm as though his veins carried burning acid. Hroth had gone berserk. Wild energy erupted all around him as he screamed and screamed, both aloud and in his mind. The world went redblack, a pulsing, wild agony at the wrist where his hand had been. Everything in him focused on that, miraculously knitting together gashed arteries so he didn't bleed to death.

Some time later he was rescued by hara from his tribe; Roc had flown to them and led them to the house, now silent except for

Hroth's sobs and groans. His maelstrom of chaotic power had stopped the hearts of his human captors.

Back in the here and now, Hroth sensed Ottar's distress and changed what images he sent to soothing things. Ottar drew away, gasping for air and looking at Hroth with both pity and awe.

"I... I..." he fumbled.

Hroth was about to reassure him once again when there was a cawing sound and flapping of wings. Ottar blinked in surprise at the raven that perched on a wooden chair, eyeing them with its beady gaze.

"That's my familiar," Hroth explained. "He came to me during my own althaia. I thought it was part of my hallucinations at first, but he's remained with me ever since, appearing from time to time."

"This is the one," Roc croaked. "You shall train and guide him. He is destined to bring tremendous change."

Hroth bowed his head in acknowledgment, deciding to keep that information to himself until more time had passed.

"You can—" Ottar began before chewing on his bottom lip. "Can you understand it?"

"Yes, seal-eyes. For reasons I still don't fully understand, the spirits chose me to be able to communicate with Roc after that day."

"Tend to him," Roc cawed. "I will visit again at the solstice festival. Be careful in the mind realms you visit. I cannot follow you there."

The raven tilted its head, glancing at them and then to the bed before cawing again, a messageless cry. It hopped and half-flew back out of the room.

"Let's go back to the bed," Hroth suggested, and Ottar eased off of his lap to stand, holding out his hands to help him up from the floor. Once standing, he pulled Hroth into an embrace.

"I'm so glad were picked for me," he said fiercely.

"So am I. I'm glad you're glad. I had more than my share of doubts. Not of my ability, but it's wearing on me, knowing I make hara uncomfortable."

"Well," said Ottar, some shame reaching his eyes, "if I'd known you were missing a hand and that you can talk to birds—"

"Only Roc," Hroth interrupted.

"One bird. Still, it would have been a lot that's so different."

"Speaking of different, you should have a go at being ouana," Hroth murmured before sucking hard on Ottar's neck to distract him.

"What's that? *Oh*."

With a low chuckle, Hroth led Ottar down another path of harish arunic delights.

Later in the night, shivering violently, Hroth came to himself. He thought somehar had been calling him. He looked around, dazed, his arms wrapped tightly around his chest. His skin felt like slick marble, and his jaw was clenched against the cold. Startled, he stopped walking, uncertain whether or not he was in an exceptionally vivid dream. If not, all evidence seemed to indicate that he'd walked to the sea and gone in— all while asleep.

Hansggedir? he called via mindtouch. The evening's events poured back to him, gushing like a geyser. *Ottar?!*

Hroth! Thank the gods! Where are you? Ottar's frantic voice sounded in his head, warming his frigid body if only for a moment.

I'm just outside of Freygard. I'm... naked. And freezing. I seem to have gone swimming while sleepwalking.

I'll get a horse. I'm coming to get you.

Yes, please!

Hroth began to jog toward the town, grateful when he saw Ottar approach him. He was on Hansggedir's horse, his face a mask of worry and relief. He pulled up and jumped down, enfolding Hroth in his arms.

"You scared the shit out of me!" he said, bathing Hroth's face with kisses before wrapping a blanket around him. "I was so worn out I didn't hear you leave. Tell me this didn't have anything to do with our taking aruna."

"No, I promise." Hroth's teeth were chattering so much he could barely get the words out.

"Here. Have some sheh." Ottar held a flask to his lips, and Hroth gratefully drank some of the liquor. "And then let's get you back to your house. Hold on to me, okay?"

"I don't think I could do anything else," Hroth admitted as a chill wracked his body.

"This has certainly been a memorable day," Ottar said ruefully, situating Hroth behind him. "And this has never happened to you before?"

"Never. I've been deep into meditations before, but not like that."

All at once he had a flash of memory, a fireworks display of images, dazzling half-remembrances of a spirit thundering with arunic power. And a young har— or had it been a vision of what Ottar might have looked like when he was young?

"A little bit is coming back to me," Hroth said once they were at his house. Hansggedir met him outside the door, where he told them he'd heated water for a bath.

"That must have been some kind of aruna," Hansggedir said as he took the reins from Ottar, tying up his horse before they went inside. His tone was light, but his expression was anxious. "Nothing against you, Ottar, but I'd recommend not doing anything along those lines the rest of the night."

"That's really the last thing on my mind," he said, shaking his head.

"There's something about you," Hroth said wonderingly to Ottar. "Nothing frightening, although waking up out by the ocean, naked, is bizarre. I think you have a message for me."

"I think you're full of shit," Hansggedir grumbled. "Take your bath and get some sleep. Maybe I should stay with you."

"No, I want Ottar to stay." He turned to the new har. "You didn't cause whatever this was, but I think it's significant that I had such a vivid dream when you were here."

Ottar looked rather dubious, but then Hroth said, "Please stay. I don't know why it's important, but even Roc said that you will be important to my life."

"I don't know who died and made you hienama, but—"

"Let it go!" Hroth exclaimed, interrupting Hansggedir. "I'm a bit different, and you know it. I'm sorry I scared you. Both of you. Not to mention that I find it pretty unsettling. Now I'm going to get that bath."

"Good idea," Ottar said hurriedly. It was obvious he'd been quite shaken by the events of the evening, and Hroth was glad he'd agreed to stay. Hansggedir took his leave, muttering about tying Hroth to his bed.

"Please don't worry about me," Hroth said once he'd soaked and felt like himself again. Ottar was wrapped around him, holding him tightly.

"I just don't want to be known as the har that might have caused you to sleepwalk or sleepswim to your death!"

"Well, I can't promise that, but I do hope that I've not scared you so much that you'll never want to visit me again."

Ottar shook his head. "I still have a lot to learn about being har, and you seem like an excellent teacher. Just don't go sleepwalking again if you can help it! Maybe the spirit was a harmful one and Trygve should have an exorcism."

"That might be a bit extreme!" Hroth laughed. "But now that you mention it…"

"Do you think you can sleep? Is there anything I can do to relax you?"

"Well, I do love having my hair played with, and it's rather a mess. And tell me about your hopes and expectations of being har. You're definitely no longer human!"

Eventually Ottar teased out the tangles, and with a healthy quantity of wine, they both fell asleep once more. Hroth dreamed, but wasn't called away from his bed. He saw the impossible, a young har child, with Ottar's large eyes. When or how he could arrive, the dream gave no hint. But when Hroth awoke, all he could remember was the name the portend must have:

Tyr.

Something's Coming

Wendy Darling

Something's Coming

Like a Hot Glowing Coal
Heart

It seems so long ago, that first time I laid eyes on Sphinx – before he got his name.

The world was so different then. Myself as well. And, oh, was *he* different!

Yet it was only a few years ago. Lately, it seems time does not fly. It races at the speed of light.

That afternoon I was not aware of time at all. I had spent most of the daylight hours on round-up duty, rushing about town collecting new recruits. There were plenty to be had in that town. It was mainly residential, with lots of plump families with frustrated teenage boys just dying to break away. And what could have been more seductive, more sinful, than breaking away with us? The Wraeththu. The destroyers. The defilers. The debased. Even those who struggled wanted it. I think so, anyway.

But back to that afternoon. I'd taken twenty boys that day. I hadn't delivered them back to headquarters myself, but had captured them all personally – by various means – before handing them to those further down the line, who piled them into the Jeeps like frightened cows to the slaughter. They wanted us, yes, but they were also afraid.

Sphinx was special that way. Very. Let me recall the moment.

I was coming down a side street towards a row of houses all on fire. I smelled burning flesh, and from the bodies cooling on the lawns, I knew some of our tribe had been at work. They had obviously left the area, however, and it was just the burning houses and myself, alone.

Except for Sphinx.

He stood near the corner of the block, at the end of a driveway. Next to him was a white mailbox, perfectly white, no marks, no soot, and on it a street number, printed silver on black: 21. Which was, I judged later, a sign I had to take him; he was, after all, the twenty-first boy of the day.

He was sixteen or thereabouts, I judged, not quite fully grown, with dark brown hair in loose curls that rested on his head like a crown. His face, dark with large deep brown eyes, would have been handsome had not his expression been so... *blank*.

It wasn't only his expression either. It was *him*. There was a row of houses on fire. He appeared neither frightened nor shocked. He didn't seem angry either. Not a flicker of emotion on his face or in the psychic ambient. Normally I could feel fear. He had none.

This didn't change even when I approached him. He didn't even look at me!

He was staring at the fire. I would have said he was bewitched or filled with wonder, but as far as I could tell, he wasn't filled with anything. He was just looking.

Maybe it's shock, I thought to myself.

When I was right up beside him and he still hadn't looked at me, I adopted his posture: arms crossed, eyes up to the blaze. Maybe I'd see something amidst the flames and understand what had the boy so transfixed.

I don't think Sphinx and I saw or felt the same things. I saw the peeling vinyl siding – smelled it too. When part of a nearby house crumpled, I saw the grim remains of a girl's bedroom, soot pouring out while the walls still stood out pink with painted white clouds. Was that a body I saw on the remains of the bed, or did I only imagine it?

I watched these things without a sense of guilt but instead, a sense of inevitability. I was like most of us, to a large extent happy that change had come at last. The old ways had come to an end. We were the new thing, and so even if there were old things we liked, we had to destroy them. Most of them anyway. Destroying a suburb and taking the boys? It was only just.

Sphinx didn't budge a bit in a whole five minutes, I don't think. I'm not even sure he blinked in those days. He wasn't normal.

I stopped looking at the fire and studied him. *Not normal.* But... *what?*

Some, I suppose, would think it peculiar I spent any time at all studying this lone boy. "Either you grab 'em or you kill 'em – you don't just stare at 'em!" Well, I say, these people weren't there, facing a boy they just couldn't decide about. Should I take him or...?

Finally, to break the deadlock, I reached out and took hold of his hand.

The shock of it ran up my arm. I didn't see feeling in his face and I hadn't, before touching him, been able to sense anything from him either. But holding his hand, I felt a power in him, a kind of strength made potent because it was so self-contained, like a hot glowing coal on a sheet of ice in the dark.

He finally looked at me. And he was still not afraid. I tugged him away from the mailbox, into the street. I ran. Holding my hand, he ran with me.

Running, Running, Real Hand
Sphinx

Burning. Running. Legs burning. Muscles though, not like houses. Lungs burning. More houses burning. Black dirty air. Everything burning and hot.

My legs were going. Going! Everything was rushing up to me. Burning house far away, then burning house closer, then burning house gone. The blur of the road went on and on, endless. Look at the road, look at the road!

With the houses on both sides, and the road going on and on, it was like a tube and we were inside it. Running down the tube. Tube full of smoke. Left, right, up a hill. Sometimes we stopped.

We? Oh, yes. We...

His hand around my hand was a real thing. A *real* thing. Real hand. Real boy. I was running, but he was there with me and didn't go away. Real as my own breathing. Hot sweaty hand. Running, running, real hand.

Running was that moment. Hand was that moment. But earlier, other moments. I remember now. Brain makes loops around moments like yarn and I pull them back. Moments...

Wasn't running that morning. Opposite. Lying in bed. Nobody there, just me.

The sun was there though. Shining white, didn't look hot, although it was hot on the bed. The glass on the window was hot.

Burning sparkles in the glass and white glowing hot sheets. White walls. White sun, burning against the clouds. Burning... smell?

The nurse ran in. *Something, something, something,* she said. She shook me. *Something, something, something,* she screamed. I heard her. Go? Run? Wraeththu?

She left and I saw. Sun not so white. Gray smoke. Noises in the hall. Sun still there. Still hot. No nurse. Sun lower. *Something, something, something...*

Oh. Now I knew: *Run away, I'm setting you free, run from the Wraeththu!*

Just What We Need
Heart

I had fun running with Sphinx. It reminded me of when I'd been younger, out with my dog, running through the streets together in another city, what seemed like years ago. With all the other boys, I'd got them into a Jeep and had them taken off, but with him, we ran until we were gasping, stopping to breathe, then starting up again.

It was during these breaks that I began to get an inkling of just what was going on with Sphinx. He hadn't said a word to me since I'd seen him, although I'd spoken to him. I didn't think he was deaf, though. He wasn't shocked or scared either. He just didn't react to things, at least not the normal way. When we'd stop to rest, he would usually just stare at stuff. Sometimes I'd follow the path of his eyes and find it'd be a fence or a stray dog. But sometimes I just couldn't figure out what he was seeing; he was looking out into open space or an empty field or just the road, even though it was empty.

Maybe he's just crazy, I decided. *Great, just what we need, more crazies. Manifest will be so thrilled.* By the time I was thinking these thoughts, however, we were almost back at headquarters. I didn't have it in me to turn back. Or abandon my new find, even if he *was* a crazy.

Our headquarters was a beauty, an old high school. The thing was built like a fortress, with only small narrow windows and what was really funny, you had to cross a kind of concrete drawbridge to get in the main doors. Inside the walls were all painted cinderblock, the floors gray linoleum. Very institutional. Very prison-like. Very much the refuse of Humanity. Revelling in the juxtaposition, we found it perfect for our needs.

I walked in with Sphinx beside me, pretty much like a trusting dog. It was kind of dim in the lobby because it was afternoon and too soon to turn on the emergency power we'd rigged up. Not that I needed the light; I knew my way around.

I nodded to the three guards on duty. "Last one for today?" asked one of them, Mica.

I nodded.

"Good. Manifest wants to see you."

I studied the har's face, to see if I could read anything from it, but he simply looked to be conveying an order. "I'll see him after I take care of this one," I said, indicating Sphinx.

As I started down the stairs, Mica took off to relay the message up to the "principal's office."

To get Sphinx where he needed to go, we had to go through the cafeteria. This had been left pretty much as is, since it was just as accommodating to us as it had been to high school kids (which a lot of us had recently been, come to think of it). There were lots of hara in there as we passed through. Most of them were done eating and were basically just kicking back, playing cards, some playing music. A few came up to me and said stuff, just heys and whatnot, a couple asking about Sphinx, trying to talk to him. He didn't act like he heard any of it though; he was just blank-facedly looking at stuff. I think that's when I first started getting an idea of his name.

Anyway, once we passed through there, it was up some stairs and through this sort of bridge over to the gym. This was the area we took care of two of the harshest aspects of our life as Wraeththu: all the inceptions and a lot of battle training. It was the ideal place really, with a couple of weight rooms, big storage rooms formerly used for equipment, some offices, a big gym area and of course, locker rooms that were just as a good as a jail.

Originally the locker rooms had been divided into girls and boys, both underneath the gym, on opposite sites. We'd made some modifications to this; now there was one set of rooms for human boys (the "waiting room") and another for boys actually getting incepted (the "changing room"). Sphinx followed me down to the waiting room, docile as a lamb.

Down there, the electric lights had been given some power, and in the dim light I saw a good fifty boys piled into the changing area, sitting on benches and on the concrete floor. All of them were naked. There were only about ten hara guarding them because all but the passive ones had been drugged up a bit, or mesmerized, into staying quiet. It is true, however, that if any of the boys were to step out of line, those hara would've taught them a quick lesson, probably fatal.

After I'd located the boys I found that day and determined they were all OK and apparently no worse off than when I'd found them, I had a word with one of the guards. "This is my last one for today," I said, indicating Sphinx. "He won't give you any trouble, I promise."

The guard nodded and stepped away.

I have no idea what exactly I said to Sphinx, but when I went to go, he suddenly reached out and grabbed my hand.

Again, there was the connection. He was a hot glowing coal, he really was. And up my arm I felt his message, without words but still clear: *You are real, real, real...*

Pulled Me, Pushed Me
Sphinx

I had his hand but then I didn't have it anymore and I was alone. Alone with lots of people. They were everywhere, spread out on the floor, sitting up, leaning against the wall. Too many people. I had been alone so long. I liked to be alone!

Something touched me on the shoulder. Person touching me. *Something, something, something,* he said, jerking his head. Pulling on me. Over there, down, down...

I didn't want to go. It was a pile of people almost. I didn't want to go down there. But he pulled me, pushed me, pulled me, pushed me. I didn't fight, but I didn't want to be moved. *Something, something, something,* he shouted. More pushing. People moved away on the floor, I felt it.

Finally I crashed down. Pain. My head hit something hard. Bleeding. Pain around my eyes, somebody turned me over. Somebody grabbing my shoulders, hard, shaking me. *Angry at me,* I realized. The power of touch. I wiped the blood away from my eyes and closed them. If I closed my eyes, he wouldn't see me, and couldn't be angry with me.

The Principal's Office
Heart

After that I went up to the principal's office. Ha ha, what a joke we had going on there. Actually being called up there *was* similar to actual high school because it either meant you were in trouble or that you had done something really good and were going to get commended. I had been doing pretty well lately in my meetings with Manifest – he seemed to have taken an interest in me – and walking back through the labyrinth of hallways towards the school's administrative offices, I felt confident the meeting would be quick and to the point. That is, unless Manifest had something up his sleeve.

Manifest was an interesting character, which of course he'd have to be, to keep control over *our* lot. We were certainly a lot worse behaved than any high schoolers. To him, however, we weren't any trouble. At first glance you might not have thought it, because of his pretty hair and refined manners – product of the privileged class, I always surmised – but Manifest was a tough customer, who could go pretty much from shaking your hand to hacking it off, if you pissed him off. We all tried not to piss him off, but my efforts had actually been working, and as I just said, we'd been getting on lately, my position moving up in the tribal hierarchy.

As I approached the main door to the office suite, one of Manifest's guards, Thorn, spotted me and cocked his head meaningfully towards the interior.

"What's up?" I whispered, once I'd reached the door.

"I don't know, but he's impatient about something," Thorn told me. "All day long he's been nervous. I can feel it and it's like ants crawling all over me."

"You don't know what it is?" I asked.

"No, and when Luster had to nerve to ask," he said, referring to Manifest's second-in-command, "all he said was that something important was going to happen today. So far as I know, though, nothing has."

I nodded and patted Thorn on the shoulder. "Thanks." Being the sort of har that people felt comfortable confiding in was definitely proving to be helpful.

Inside the suite, I found Luster at his desk pushing about papers, as usual. "He's been waiting," he announced, his tone rather patronizing. If Manifest was disarming in his unpredictability, Luster was annoying in his *pre*dictability. As far as I was concerned, he was nothing more than an elevated pencil pusher with a lot of authority. I'd seen him kill out in the field, but more often his weapon was a searingly arrogant, cruel attitude. Although he had his uses, most hara in the tribe despised him.

I strode past Luster and knocked on the principal's door, using my own unique knock pattern, although with Manifest, you could be sure he always knew who was on the other side of the door, whether you knocked or not. "I'm waiting," I heard him call, and in the same moment, my hands were on the doorknob letting myself in. Thorn was right; he certainly *was* impatient about something.

Manifest was standing in the corner, hands clasped behind his back, looking like he'd just that moment stopped himself from pacing. Around him the room held its usual look – half war-room, with maps and notes strewn on every surface, half private study, with bookcases holding Manifest's personal library and choice artwork, all seized, mounted on the walls.

I greeted him and was waved into a chair. He gave me a summary of that day's progress in the town and what they expected for the next day. Within the week, the town would be completely under our control. That afternoon they had secured the last of the gas stations. Meanwhile tribal business was going smoothly as well. In the locker room I hadn't visited, fifteen inceptions were in progress. So far only two of the boys had died.

Considering Manifest was our phylarch and I at that point only a minion, even if a rising one, it was a lot of information I was being given, almost as if I were his equal, maybe even his superior. "So what else is up, that you called me here?" I asked, wanting to bring the dynamic back to what seemed more usual while also displaying the directness I knew Manifest valued in me.

"Well, to be honest, I wanted to hear about *your* day," he said. "I hear you've done very well today in your recruiting."

I smiled at the compliment. "Yeah, pretty well. Do you want a report?"

Manifest thought for a moment, then shook his head slightly. "No, not detailed, just how many?"

"Twenty-one," I replied. "All strong and healthy."

Manifest, who hadn't taken a seat even during his lengthy report to me, now drifted towards the padded leather chair and sat down facing me, lacing his hands together on the desk. "Twenty-one? Well done." He stared down at his hands, then looked up. "Anything special about any of them?"

This was a usual question of his, any time we'd go over recruitment numbers. Often I would pick up on interesting character traits that other hara would miss in our new recruits, simply because I'd either observe them or get to know them before they were brought in to headquarters. Once they were brought into the waiting room and realized where they were and what was going on, their fear often warped any true reading of their character.

An answer popped into my head almost before I could think. "Yes, the last one," I said. "Found him last thing before I was coming back."

"Where was he?" Manifest asked.

"He was staring at a fire actually, this row of houses burning down" I said. "It was the weirdest thing... He was just staring at it, not angry, not scared, not anything."

Manifest pushed back from the desk suddenly. "Staring at a fire?" When I nodded, he gazed at the floor, considering. "This is most... remarkable. Please go on. You say this boy is unusual?"

I was starting to get nervous. It seemed like there was some relationship between Manifest's agitation and my recruitment work. I hoped I'd be able to soothe him rather than piss him off. As I mentioned early, not pissing him off was a specialty of mine.

So I told him about Sphinx. He didn't have a name then, of course, but I described in some more detail him watching the fire and then about the tingling up my arm. Manifest leaned forward during this part of the story and asked me some questions about what kind of power I'd felt. "Just something really strong," I said. He nodded and had me go on. I told him about the running, although left out the part about me thinking Sphinx was perhaps either crazy or an imbecile.

Manifest figured out my game before I had even got to the part in the locker room, however. "He doesn't speak, does he?"

I did a double-take. "Um, no, he doesn't, or at least, he hasn't *yet*. How did you know?"

Manifest looked up at the ceiling, then back to me, smiling. "Well, among other things, you haven't said this boy's name once and I know you usually get at least that information. Plus it would further account for why you mentioned this boy in the first place. Is there anything else?"

A wave of relief washed over me. For some reason, I now felt I was on Manifest's good side. "Yes, actually. When I left him in the waiting room, he grabbed my hand and I swear, I could feel his thoughts go right into me. I'm not really trained for that yet, but I swear, it happened."

"Fascinating," Manifest said, rising from the desk. "This is a valuable find. I'd like you to bring him to dinner tonight."

For the second time that meeting, I did a double-take. "Excuse me?"

The unpredictable feistiness that was Manifest's trademark suddenly came to the fore. "You heard me – that's an order. Believe me, I know when I've got a good thing, unlike some hara. Off with you until eight o'clock, officers' dining room. Bring this boy with you. Luster will be there, but nobody else except a servant or guard. Got that?"

"Got it, tiahaar." Not that I had a clue what was going on, but I wasn't going to piss him off by asking. "Am I dismissed?"

Manifest was back in the corner, glancing at some notes. "Yes, yes, get out of here."

I had a feeling that in a sense, I had long since disappeared from the room. The only one Manifest cared about was Sphinx.

Screams Are a Sound
Sphinx

Screams echoing, all around a shiver, but nobody talking. Pressed in the corner, cold cement against my back, I heard. Scream again. Scream. Nobody talking.

Next to me, a fist so tight the knuckles are white. I stared at the hand, dirty, clenched. Clenched again with another scream. Then suddenly, the hand was gone, over a face. The boy's face I saw, red, crying.

The screams were far away, not there. Somewhere. Strange echoes of home. Screams are a sound. Something people do, but I don't understand why.

The boy saw me looking. *Something, something, something,* he said. Said it again. I listened, message flew into my head. His knuckles weren't white anymore, they were red. The boy turned away from me.

I don't remember what I did, but the screams didn't scare me.

A Human Body
Heart

I headed down to the waiting room just before seven o'clock. I wanted to get Sphinx ready for dinner and I thought some preparation time was advisable. Not that I'd ever prepared any unhar for dinner with my phylarch. Hell no! Sure, I'd scrubbed some up in order to present them for inspection – Manifest or Luster normally showed up personally to inspect the recruits – but I'd never had to make them presentable for a formal occasion, just make them something more than loathsome humans.

Coming across the connector hall to the gymnasium wing, I could already hear the screams. Fifteen boys undergoing althaia, Manifest had said, and they all, (all thirteen remaining), seemed to be screaming at once. Despite the number of times I'd heard it, I shuddered and felt myself squirming uncomfortably. Heading down the stairs to the waiting room, I reminded myself forcefully that not only was the pain they were going through a necessity, but it was a lot less than what I'd gone through. These boys had it good – unlike me. I'd been thrown in a kind of closet, in the dark, for several days. At one point that was our tribe's usual method. Now we were more civilized; boys were locked in the changing room.

Coming to the entrance of the waiting room, I was met by the guard, Rock. "Everything OK?" I asked.

He nodded. "Well, so so. They hate the..." He cocked his head in the direction of the changing room. "Some of them were freaking."

"That's normal," I said, suppressing a shudder as another set of screams permeated the air. I pushed it out of my mind and said, "I'm here pick up the last recruit I brought in. Need to get him ready for dinner with Manifest."

Rock was incredulous. "Dinner? With Manifest? Sure you don't mean dinner *for* Manifest?" he asked, chuckling.

"No," I replied, not joining in his apparent amusement. "He's invited me and this unhar upstairs." I stepped through the door and Rock followed me. "So do you still have all his clothes?"

"His clothes?" Rock furrowed his brow. "Um... what was he wearing again?"

I describe the outfit: thin gray pants and vee-necked short sleeve shirt, also in gray – some kind of hospital garb. As Rock walked off to retrieve the clothing from a storage locker, I gave the matter of clothing some thought. Why had this apparently healthy teenage boy been dressed in hospital garb?

Anyway, a half a minute later, Rock returned with a metal basket of Sphinx's clothes. I set it down on the desk near the entrance and pulled out the shirt. I was only seeing if it was clean, but then something caught my eye, a permanent ink stamp inside the collar:

PROPERTY WELLS PSYCHIATRIC INSTITUTION

"Oh shit," I said, dropping the shirt and grabbing the pants – marked with the same stamp.

How could I have been so stupid? I'd offered Manifest a mental patient as my most promising find of the day! Something told me Manifest wasn't going to be pleased, but dinner was still on, that was orders, and so I had to go through with it. Clutching the basket, I headed into the main room to fetch the ex-patient.

"Over there," Rock pointed, once I was inside.

Sphinx had found a dark corner to hide in. His face was in shadow, only his bare knees and lower legs catching the light. So pale, his skin. *No wonder, if he's been living in a mental ward*, I thought.

That whole fact explained a lot about him. Like the fact there most likely *was* something different going on in his head than in the other boys'. This probably wasn't a good thing, however. Suddenly I felt a stab of panic: What would we do with him if he couldn't be incepted? Would I have to take him back to town? Or would we just execute him?

Approaching him through the mess of bodies – Rock at my side, in case any of them stirred – I almost felt pity for him.

His eyes were closed when we reached him. "Wake up," I said. After waiting a moment, I grabbed his knee and shook it. "You, wake up!"

Rock shouldered me aside. "He's a stubborn one. See that cut on his forehead? Wouldn't let us move him when he came in, managed to smash it on a bench corner." He went behind around Sphinx and pulled him up by the armpits. "What surprised me was, he didn't cry at all. Didn't react almost. Just found a spot for himself and closed his eyes."

Rock took my hand, then the boy's, then joined them together. Sphinx's palm was hot and dry, and through it I got another message: *Away, away, away.*

"Thanks," I said. Gently I pulled on Sphinx's hand. Haltingly, but obviously willingly, he followed me towards the showers.

I had no experience as a nursemaid. I picked the stall furthest down the aisle. "This one," I said, coming to a halt and squeezing his hand. Glancing at the boy, I had no idea if he understood me or not. He might have, but the point was, he didn't look at me when I spoke.

I set the bundle of clothes on the bench in the dressing chamber. I parted the curtain for the shower, peered in, then looked back to Sphinx. Could he even wash himself? I turned on the water and adjusted it to something comfortable.

The procedure turned out to be easier than I'd expected. All I had to do was lead him to the entrance and Sphinx stepped right in. Maybe this was how they'd done it at the institution, one of their routines. Relieved, I headed back down the hall to grab some soap and a towel.

Rock noticed me rummaging in the supply box and came over. "Going to soap him up yourself?" he kidded.

I straightened up. "No, actually I think he can do it himself."

"Too bad, he's got a fine body."

Soap in one hand, a towel the other, I turned back down the aisle. "A *human* body, Rock. Lay off a bit."

I rushed up to the stall, intending to simply thrust the soap in Sphinx's direction. What I saw when I rounded the corner stopped me in my tracks.

The boy had sunk to the floor and was sitting cross-legged. Head bent forward, his hands were pressed together, fingertips to his forehead.

"Are you praying?" I asked, forgetting myself.

He didn't answer me. The hot water poured down over him, tangling his dark curls into his face. He looked like something I'd seen in church, some kind of holy statue.

I looked at the soap. Ironic, it seemed, to clean up someone who at that moment looked the epitome of purity, but I suspected the cleaning was necessary, so I pressed on with it. Stepping in, I took hold of those praying hands and slipped the soap between them.

The response was automatic; he gracefully rose to his feet and began to scrub himself.

I stepped back to observe. There was nothing unusual about his method. Then again, I thought to myself, probably monkeys could learn to wash themselves. It wasn't a difficult thing. Call me cold, but finding out where Sphinx had come from had drastically reduced my estimate of him. I hadn't brought back a choice inceptee – I'd brought back a sick lab animal.

All the same, even through that fog of misgivings, I couldn't help developing some positive impressions. As Rock had said, the boy had a fine body, with narrow hips and a broad, yet slender, chest, and a lovely neck dripping with his curls. His humanity kept me from wanting him in the true sense, but my systems were charged nonetheless. But would he ever be har?

Sphinx finished washing. He didn't look at me or say anything, but stood waiting. I took up the towel and leaned into the shower past him to turn off the water.

When I said "Here, let me," I wasn't even thinking. He didn't resist, but let me dry him off like a child. The feel of his shoulder muscles beneath my hands was enough to bring me fully ouana.

I stepped away and slowly exhaled. "You must stop this," I said to myself, out loud but quietly. Stretching my arm as far as it would go, I offered the towel to Sphinx, hoping he could finish off himself. Luckily for me, he did, and by the time he was through I'd managed to get myself in order.

By then the dinner hour was fast approaching. I held out the shirt and Sphinx came right up and put it on. It was the same for the rest of the clothes and in a couple of minutes we were through. *At least the boy isn't a complete imbecile,* I thought, a tiny bit relieved.

But time for dinner. I took his hand. "We're going to eat now," I announced. "Just follow along and soon we'll be having the grandest meal in town." I didn't know if he understood a word, but when I began to walk down the aisle, he followed right along.

Food on the Table
Sphinx

Growling stomach as the doors went by. So many doors. The doorknobs round and golden, like golden apples. I passed so many of them, quickly, as I went... went *somewhere*. It was upstairs, up several stairs, down halls, and then a big door, with another shiny golden apple doorknob.

The one with me knocked and the door opened. Some slim shadow person moved out of the way. Besides the shadow, only two people were at the table. It was a big table – with food on it. *Dinner.* My eyes understood what my ears had not. I followed along and sat down quickly, willingly.

It was the first food I'd seen all day. I tried to reach for some of the bread in the basket next to me but somebody grabbed my arm. No bread, had to wait. Waiting I knew – knew if I didn't, something would happen – something bad. So instead of taking the food, I *saw* the people.

A golden man looked at me, from across the table. He had golden eyes, hair, shirt, everything gold. In the sun he would have made shining warm light. In the light inside, his eyes were cold.

Next to him was the one who'd brought me. I had not looked at him much before. Golden hair, too, like the other one, but dark clothes. He was smiling as he said something to the last man.

The last man was right next to me. He wasn't so much a man as something else, like some kind of machine. People give off energy and he gave off a lot of it. And the way he was looking at me, I felt the energy come in my direction.

Something, something, something, he said, and took up a fork to eat. Waiting was over and for me, he was gone, or might as well have been. I grabbed a piece of bread. Meat. Something green. No more looking at people, just eating.

Then, just as I took my first bite of bread: *It's you.*

The Turning Point
Heart

That dinner had turned into a disaster. Or so it seemed at first, as the four of us sat at the table, three of us talking, Thorn to the side, serving, and Sphinx attacking his food like a hungry wolf.

I had half-expected Manifest to either shout or laugh me into the hallway as soon as he saw what Sphinx was like. But even though he hadn't done that, I was still tense, waiting for the inevitable attack on my judgment. I had made a poor decision and I was waiting to be called on it. There was *no way* Sphinx was any kind of choice recruit.

Manifest didn't seem ready to make any snap decisions, however – despite the fact Sphinx hadn't spoken a word, didn't appear to be listening to anything (said or said to him), and had absolutely horrendous table manners. Instead, Manifest calmly ate his dinner, passing idle conversation while staring at Sphinx intently.

"So this is the one," he said finally, pushing his plate away. "I mean, this is *the one*."

"Excuse me?" I straightened in my seat. "This is the one I told you about, if that's what you mean."

"That's not what I mean."

"He doesn't speak, Manifest. He's—"

"*Abnormal*," Luster sneered. "Jeez, Heart, how could you?"

I bowed my head, ready to accept my superiors' fury. "Yes. He is. I found out... *after* I brought him back here... that he used to live in a mental institution. There were stamps inside his clothes. I think he might be autistic or something."

Luster burst out laughing – the hard sinister, gloating laugh we all hated. "I don't believe it, Heart. You *idiot!* The 'best, the strongest, the wildest' – well, maybe this one *is* wild, but not how we meant – and you go picking up some freak who—"

"Shut up!" Manifest snapped, making Luster flinch. "Not another word, Luster. Now, tell me more, Heart. *All* of it."

And so I started over from the beginning, in detail. I began with the burning houses and worked up to the shower, omitting only my own arousal. I was still afraid Manifest would round on me sooner or later and I didn't want to look even more foolish.

As I told my story, I studied my companions' expressions, the tone of their questions. Luster alternately rolled his eyes and scowled, apparently ready to call me an idiot first chance he got. Manifest, though... He was getting even more agitated than he had the first time I'd told him. When I described Sphinx praying in the shower, he went completely rigid.

He didn't move a muscle until I was finished. Then he said: "It's him."

My face must have gone blank as pavement. I glanced over to Luster, who appeared similarly baffled.

He spoke first. "*Him*? It's him? It's him *what*?"

Manifest didn't respond. He was studying Sphinx again. By now the boy was long through with his dinner. For some minutes, he'd been playing with a shiny spoon.

"OK, you two," Manifest began. "I understand – you don't know, you don't feel it the way I do... so let me explain."

He folded his arms together, resting them on the table, and leaned forward, as if he was going to share a secret. Which he did.

"All day long I've been... anxious," he admitted. "You both know that. What you don't know is why." He paused and looked up at the ceiling. "It started right about the time we first arrived in town, before we had even launched our first attacks. This feeling of anticipation, as if something special, some *turning point*, was going to happen and everything was going to change."

"For our tribe?" Luster asked. "Because if you mean that, why of course—"

All Manifest had to do was glare and Luster shut up. "No. I mean… Well, you'll see what I mean. *If* you let me talk. Let's see… Yes, well, every day I'd go about my business and this feeling kept growing. It wasn't a bad feeling, like being scared, it was just this nagging feeling of 'Something's going to happen.' I had no idea what, except every time I went around to check things out – in town, in the changing rooms, just day-to-day stuff, I got this feeling that we were coming up to some kind of turning point. And I think we've reached it."

"What makes you think that?" I dared ask. "Obviously you've learned something specific, or you wouldn't be so obsessed with this boy here."

Manifest cracked a smile. "You're right. I have learned something. Came to me in a dream." He laughed, eyeing our no doubt surprised expressions. "I know, and you thought I was a completely practical, pragmatic har. I *am*, you know, but we're not men, are we? We are more than that, we've got magic and more besides, and last night I think I got a glimpse of what that can mean.

"I had trouble sleeping at first. That feeling of 'Something's coming' had grown so big I wasn't just thinking about it now and then, but I was turning it over and over in my head, all the time. What was coming? Could I do something to make it happen? Should I maybe be more scared of it? I must've finally conked out though, because next thing I knew it was at least a couple of hours later and my head was full of the most potent dreams I've ever had.

"I can't explain it except to say that, Heart, you've brought in the har – the boy, *now* – I dreamt about. The things you've told me – the fire, running, the praying – and the things you haven't told me, but I can *feel*… it's just like the dream. I won't say I saw a face, but when I look at that boy, I know it's *him*."

There was a silence, and then Luster cleared his throat. "You say 'the boy, *now*,' tiahaar. Can I take from this that you are considering incepting him? Surely you can't be—"

"I'm not going to tell you to shut up again, Luster." Manifest looked to me, apparently feeling I'd be more likely to agree with him. "That's the next step, Heart. We've got to incept him."

I chose my response carefully. "Do you really think that's, um, *wise*, Manifest? Or possible?"

"Possible? Well, of course it's possible! As for it being wise, yes, absolutely, I believe it is. You want to know why, Heart?"

I nodded, having no idea where he was leading.

He took my hand and squeezed. "Because at the end of the dream there was a vision, a certainty of feeling, that this *person* I was dreaming of had become *har*. A very special, powerful har. And I saw him taking aruna – *with you*."

A flash of adolescence came back to me and I blushed. "Um…" I said, searching for words. "That's very *interesting*, tiahaar."

Manifest still had my hand, and with it he pulled me to my feet. "You like the idea, admit it. Yes… I can sense that you do. It's all right, Heart, he's yours."

I felt a little faint. I rubbed my face with my other hand. "Thanks."

Luster, who'd shrunk up and stayed quiet since being snapped at, finally spoke up. "So this inception – when's it going to happen?"

Manifest let go of my hand and moved to stand behind Sphinx, who'd stopped playing with the spoon and was simply staring at the table. "We will have him wait all through tomorrow, with a full fast. Then tomorrow night, we incept him."

Luster was frowning. "We've got a round of boys who might not be done with their althaia by tomorrow. Shouldn't this boy wait for the next round?"

"Absolutely not!" Manifest snapped.

This time I jumped. "Um, what are your plans?" I asked, recovering my composure.

"Yes," Luster chimed in. "Did you get special plans from your *dream*?"

Manifest sighed (probably wanting to tell him to shut up again). "No, actually this is something I've been thinking for some time." He went back to his chair and rested his hands on the back of it. "This mass incepting we're doing in the changing room. It's working well, better than it used to, but I think we could do even better. The attendants – they're helping. The different medicines we've been experimenting with – I think those are making a difference, too. But doing that many at once, with only really a couple of helpers? And the way they all still suffer so badly? Surely we can do better."

"But what about the fact we want only the strong to survive?" Luster questioned. This was a major part of the philosophy of inception – if you didn't survive althaia, you weren't meant to be har.

"I think only the strong *will* survive," Manifest replied, "but I don't think it's necessary for everyone who gets incepted to come out the other side feeling like he's been through some kind of damn war or torture session!" At this he stepped back from the chair, surprised at his own outburst, I think. "Sorry, it's just something I've been thinking about. I guess it all fits in with this being a turning point. Things are going to change around here, and I think it starts with this boy.

"I wouldn't want him to go through the normal procedure. I'd guess that to be how he is, he's already had plenty of bad stuff happen to him, and living in a mental ward, *seen* a lot of bad stuff too. I think if anybody needs a special inception, with *special* care, it's him. And if he comes out the other side fully incepted and at least no different than he is now – which he won't, because I *know* he won't – then he'll have been our test subject for what we do in the future."

He picked up his wine glass and gestured for us to do the same. Thorn stepped over towards us with the wine bottle and poured. Manifest raised his glass in a toast. "To the turning point." We chinked our glasses, and glanced down at Sphinx. The boy had fallen asleep.

You Will Be, You Will Be
Sphinx

Darkness. Quiet. A strange place. Not my old room.

I'd been sleeping in a bed. A new starting point.

I sat up. Do I wait? Do I get up? Will someone come for me?

Suddenly there was a light, at first just a narrow line, but then opening up. Three lines of light; a door opening into the dark room. Quickly, the door closed. A bright light was thrust into my face.

So you're the one! a voice shouted at me, straight into my head, right then, right into my head. *So special! I don't think so. You're nothing!*

I squinted against the light, covered my ears from the sound that was not a sound. I couldn't see the body, but I saw the face, caught by the light, ugly in its rage.

A strong hand grabbed my wrist, jerked me onto the floor. *He thinks he can have you, but he can't. You're nothing! Nothing!* Pain and pain and pain as he kicked me, as the words seared into my brain like no other words had in a long time.

I didn't say anything. I didn't scream. In fact, I was even quieter than before. I shut my eyes. Why couldn't I shut my ears? Shut off my body?

You're going to die, whether Manifest wants you to or—

The kicks stopped. Somewhere in the room, just over me, in the darkness, there was a struggle. Hitting, kicking, cursing, growling. I kept my eyes shut.

The door slammed and it was quiet, except for a strange sound. Somebody took my wrist again – gently. The light came on, pointing towards not the golden one, not the *Nothing!* man, but towards the other one. The boy from the shower. His face was bleeding.

He took my other hand. "Are you OK?" he asked me.

I jumped back. His words had come too close. They were loud and big and I couldn't run away from them. I scrambled to the bed.

He scrambled after me and a moment later, took me in his arms and held me. *Of course you're not OK*, he said, this time in the less scary words, the *real* words. *But you will be. You will be.*

Be His Protector
Heart

His rescue came almost by accident. If I'd been passing down that corridor just a moment later, I might not have noticed the golden figure slipping quickly into Sphinx's Forale chamber. I had planned on stopping by but… as fate would have it, I was in the right place at the right time.

Luster and I fought like animals, clawing and kicking at one another in the near dark, while somewhere nearby Sphinx huddled in silence. I knew what Luster had been doing – I'd felt his malevolence and Sphinx's terror right through the door – and I was also aware at what had driven him to it. He was used to being Manifest's closest aide, his closest confidante. Manifest's obsessive fixation on the boy, and his decision to bring him to us through inception, threatened his position. I wonder now whether Luster had a thing for Manifest and it was lover's jealousy.

At the time, of course, I didn't care about such distinctions. All I wanted was Luster out of that room away from Sphinx. Although just a few hours earlier, I'd been resigned to having him rejected and probably killed out of hand, ever since Manifest had made his decision – and promised him to me – I had been filled with an overwhelming sense of protectiveness. Maybe I was fighting with a lover's jealousy, too, although I didn't know it at the time.

Finally I routed Luster out of the room, into the hall. Several guards and high-ranked hara were there waiting, including Manifest. I thrust Luster, bleeding from nose and mouth, into the arms of the nearest guard. "He just tried to kill that boy," I said.

Manifest stepped forward, rigid with anxiety. "What did he do? Is the boy hurt?"

"No, he's not hurt," I said. "Not seriously, anyway. Just a little roughed up. His mind, however..."

"Say no more," Manifest said softly. "I want you to go to him now. You must make him feel better, as much as you can." He walked with me the short paces back to the door. "Afterward, leave guards at the door and go back to sleep. Then during the day, watch the door yourself."

I nodded. "Be his protector."

"Yes. And one more thing. In the afternoon, I want you to go in and try to talk with him. Tell him about Wraeththu, about us. I don't care if he doesn't speak back, doesn't nod or blink. I think he will understand."

I reached for the doorknob. "I'll try," I said.

Manifest smiled. "I know you will. There will be a reward for you, Heart, of that I'm sure."

Dutifully, I sat with Sphinx for a half an hour at least, cradling his trembling body. I pulled a blanket of calm and safety around us, trying to soothe away the terrors Luster had wrought.

I knew Luster had been screaming at him through the powers of his mind, because I had sensed it, but I didn't know exactly what he'd said. The fact that Sphinx had picked up on them, however, gave me hope that perhaps he wasn't beyond my reach. And so I whispered to him words of comfort, assurances of protection, like a mother talking a young child after a nightmare.

Finally Sphinx was asleep and I left him curled up in bed like a sleeping dark-haired angel. I took the flashlight with me and flicked the switch high on the wall for the emergency light. I didn't want him waking up in darkness.

After a few hours sleep in my room in the barracks, I returned to the Forale chamber to stand guard and, in a sense, stand vigil. I didn't go in to see him. Nohar was to talk to a human during Forale, except during the time of explaining, if in fact there was one. It used to be that nohar ever explained, but simply took any boy they wanted. Understanding and consent were irrelevant. Nobody had asked me if I wanted to be incepted. I'd simply been locked in a closet, pulled out for the Harhune, and then thrown back into the closet.

By the time I was sitting outside Sphinx's room, however, our practices had changed and boys were often told in advance what would happen, to some degree at least. Of course none of them were ever given any real idea of what inception would entail, for it would make consent even more impossible. For most it was bad enough to have the vague details – of a coming time of suffering, of being (as they saw it) unmanned, of becoming something alien.

With Sphinx I left nothing out. As he lay staring at the ceiling, stomach growling, I first told him as much as I knew about the history of Wraeththu: how we began (or thought we did), the battles we had fought, who our leaders were. In the second half of my talk, I told him what Wraeththu are: our powers, our bodies, and inception, the trial we undergo to attain them.

I knew Sphinx wouldn't scream in fear or try to escape when I told him these things. I couldn't imagine that at all. He would endure it just as he'd endured everything else, in stoic silence.

It was close to midnight when a messenger came to tell me it was time. He waited while I fetched Sphinx, who followed me out as if he hadn't a care in the world. I followed the messenger, not actually knowing where we were going. Manifest had, I assumed, found an alternate location for this *alternate* inception. The regular changing room was still in use and as he'd said the night before, this inception was to be special.

To my surprise, the rooms we were taken to were only just around the corner from the main headquarters offices. As far as I knew, these rooms had never been used for anything, but simply kept vacant. Up until then, I hadn't really wondered why. After the messenger opened the main door, however, I understood. Manifest had been planning to use them all along.

These rooms had once been the nurse's offices. Like the administrative suite, there was a reception area with several rooms leading off it, in this case, exam rooms and offices. It would be, I immediately realized, an ideal environment to carry out a more controlled, medicalised inception.

Manifest stepped out of one of the exam rooms. "Good, you're just in time. Rock and I have everything ready."

"Rock?" I asked, moving forward with Sphinx beside me.

Manifest nodded and headed back into the room. "Of course. He carries out the inceptions downstairs, so I wanted him for this new procedure as well."

"Of course," I said, feeling dazed. The exam room certainly didn't look like the room I'd been incepted in or, for that matter, the changing room. In the centre of the room a low bed had been prepared with a set of clean, white sheets. Beside it was set up a chair and a tray with various medical implements, one of which was a large syringe. The entire room was clean and bright. A counter with a sink ran along the wall and to the left of that, a door led into a restroom with a shower. (How I wish I'd had one of those for use during my inception!)

"Welcome to the future," Manifest said finally, once I'd finished my appraisal. "Now let's get to work. First, tell me, you explained things to him?"

I nodded.

"Good, at least that's done with. Now let's just have him lie down…"

It was in the end nothing more than a medical procedure. Manifest began by having all Sphinx's clothes removed; the boy did not resist. Next Manifest gave Sphinx some water with drug tablets mixed into it. Some sort of strong sedative, he told us, something to last several hours. I had an intuition that Sphinx wouldn't need it – he seemed stoic beyond belief – but it was merciful all the same.

Finally Manifest asked me to kneel at the head of the bed and hold Sphinx's shoulders. "He may struggle," he warned me. Again, I didn't think he would, but of course I obeyed.

Rock volunteered to operate the syringe. "You know I used to use these… *before*… for a whole different sort of procedure, though nearly just as painful." I'd never known this about Rock, but it didn't surprise me.

I watched him find a vein in Manifest's arm and easily draw out a full portion of blood. Then swiftly and smoothly, he shot the blood into Sphinx's arm. Neither of them flinched. On Manifest's orders, Rock carried out the procedure two more times, just to be sure.

Manifest, holding his arm at the elbow to stem any bleeding, concluded with a speech. "You are unhar," he said. This was some slight ceremony. "Through this act, I bring you to a new body and a new way of life. I hope that in this new method, the transition is a smooth one. You deserve only the best."

Only Something Happening
Sphinx

Darkness. Eyes closed. Something was simmering, waiting inside me.

Then light – stars! Stars shot into my eyes, into my mouth, down my throat. Like fire it was, hot and filled with pain.

People put their hands on me, but I didn't care. I didn't scream, didn't struggle. Fire shot through me, down into my gut. My flesh was churning, changing, every part of me. I did not fight it. It was only something happening, something I couldn't fight.

I remembered, in the middle of it. Heart – I knew his name, I remembered it, too – had told me what was happening. It was like with the nurse warning me. I didn't know what she said until afterward. Like that... only different. This was clear. Heart had *told* me and I *remembered*. I was changing into Wraeththu. No matter what, I should not be afraid.

I was awake, I was asleep. I was terrified, I was calm. Sometimes I saw things in the air, sometimes it was just dark. Other times people were coming to me. My arms were stuck with needles. People spoke to me softly, and sometimes I would feel a bit better, go off to sleep.

At some point later, I woke up and it was Manifest with me. I remembered him and his name now, too. He would not touch me but he sat near to me and smiled, offered me comfort. My skin was burning and my gut was being cut by a hundred knives. It was easy for me to resist the pain, however.

"Would you like more of the drugs?" he asked me.

I squinted my eyes, staring at his mouth, and thought about the question. "No, I'm fine," I said slowly. "I don't need the drugs."

A jolt like electricity shot through me at the sensation of speaking to someone.

Manifest was just as shocked as I was. "You can speak!"

I nodded, weakly, and he said, "It won't be much longer."

I'm not sure, but I think it was two more days.

During those days, Manifest left me alone again. Hours went by. I lay still as cells generated, fluids balanced out. Gradually my skin began to clear. I felt my guts come together once again, solid and healthy, instead of the churning torture. There were other changes, too, but I was too tired to see.

Finally the change was complete. The people taking care of me smiled. They said kind words to me and I understood more than *something, something, something.* "You look incredible!" they said and "Won't they be surprised!"

They gave me a shower, standing close and soaping me up and down, when I was too tired still to do it myself. I thought about Heart and the other shower. I couldn't speak to him then, but now I could. And he had promised me, we would.

Things Are Different Now
Heart

I had been waiting nervously on the bed for about an hour when there was a rap on the door. "Come in," I said, and arranged the hair around my face.

The door opened a few inches and one of the two althaia attendants stuck his head in. "He's just finishing his shower. We'll dry him off and put him in a robe, then send him on to you. Are you ready?"

I didn't pick up any emotions coming off the har so I tried, and failed, to read the expression on his face. "Well, that depends," I said. "How's he turned out?"

The har smiled enigmatically. "Oh, you'll see."

This was as much as Manifest had told me that morning. I had no idea how things were going with the inception, not even at this late hour. All I knew was that it was over and whatever the result, it was going to come into the room soon and we would be sharing aruna.

Once the attendant went away, I leaned back and tried to calm myself down. Whatever I was about to face, I would be on my best behaviour. Nothing less would be acceptable, not when it was Manifest's orders.

There was another rap on the door, accompanied by a tendril of thought, an announcement: *It's him.*

I smiled, thinking immediately of Manifest's pronouncement.

The door opened slowly, creaking on its hinges, and there in the entrance stood one of the most entrancing hara I'd ever seen. His hair, which even as a boy had been as full and beautiful as a woman's, now shone with an irresistible gleam, begging to be touched. His body, tall and lean, tantalized me from beneath a robe of semi-transparent yellow silk. And his eyes, those deep brown eyes I'd first seen as they stared blankly at a fire, now looked at me deliberately, intelligently, longingly.

Come, I gestured, and he stepped forward into the room. The door closed behind him. When he stopped, half-way across the room, I gestured again. "Come sit," I said, thinking at this stage I might need to speak out loud.

He sat at the foot of the bed, gingerly, as if he was afraid he would break into pieces like a piece of old porcelain. A flicker of memory came back to me; I remembered feeling that way myself after my inception.

"I'm glad to see you made it through. So how are you?" I started off.

He focused on me as I spoke but did not reply, simply tilted his head and looked puzzled.

Oh, no, he's the same now, only more beautiful, I thought to myself.

But then, he spoke. "I can..." he began, "I can speak. I understand you... Heart."

"That's good." I was stunned. "So what do you say?"

Again there was a brief silence. His eyes locked with mine with a focus they had never had before. "I say... things are different now."

I nodded. "Yes, they are." The force that had drawn him to me even as a human boy tugged on me now that he was har. "Want me to show you just how different?"

I reached out for his hand. A jolt of power went up my arm. His brown eyes studied me, and he pursed his lips. "Show me," he said.

An hour or so later, as we lay tangled in the sheets, I was still showing him – and he was showing me. We couldn't seem to stop touching one another. It was mainly me doing the talking, but he told me things as well. Where he'd come from, what his inception had been like. Hearing him was like taking part in a miracle. And the power I felt even in the tips of his fingertips, never mind what I'd felt in aruna, was a miracle, too.

Looking at Sphinx, I couldn't help thinking his new harish body was animated by a different person. The human boy was gone, replaced by a har just as intense, but with the ability to truly share that intensity with the world. The vision of Manifest's dream was a true one.

It was during a pause in my talking that he reached out and pointed at my chest. "Heart," he said. "Your name."

I nodded. "Yes, and a horrible pun – *har-t*." When he didn't laugh, I wasn't surprised. He was changed, but nothing could make up for his past. Which reminded me...

"You know," I said, "I don't even know your name. What is it?"

"John," he said flatly.

I got up from the bed. "John? Well, that won't do as a harish name. You need a new name."

"A new name?" he asked. From his expression, I sensed I had confused him again.

"Yes," I said. "A new name, for your new life. A new difference."

I stepped back and thought about what I might name him. Manifest and I hadn't discussed it. I wondered if he had some particular name in mind, since he sometimes liked to give names to his hara, especially those he incepted personally. But as I looked at Sphinx, his high cheekbones and wide eyes, which until today had only stared blankly, incuriously, the name came to me.

"Sphinx," I said, half to myself, then louder: "Sphinx." I placed my hands on his head. "That's your new name."

"Sphinx," he repeated. "I like it."

Pro Lucror

Storm Constantine

Pro Lucror

The creature of darkness slunk out into the night and glared at the vague moon, which was faintly visible through the smog that hung over the city. He cursed quietly, shook his tousled hair, and stepped into the street. He walked along the centre of the road, where litter blew. There were bloodstains, sometimes, to step over. This was the place of ruins, best avoided. This was the place of demons. The creature walked away from it, towards the weakening, shrinking heart of the city, where humans tried to cling to a normal life. Armoured cars purred past, their ghostly lamp eyes gleaming dully.

He knew what he sought: a huge building without windows. There it was: the mausoleum of hope. The creature sighed, his hollow eyes fixed upon the immense stones. He leaned against a lamp post across the street from the building and waited; a trim tiger.

After maybe an hour, an automatic elevator in the building opposite slid to ground level and opened its metal doors, spewing forth uniformed workers from the vast interior. A soft, female yet metallic voice crooned: 'Home to bed everyone. Home now to bed. Wake up fresh tomorrow. Fresh. Work hard tomorrow.'

Exhausted figures began to stumble away.

The creature stirred restlessly. His hands were numb from cold. He scanned the figures, seeking the one he had come for, but they all looked the same. It was impossible to discern individual features. The creature sighed again and slunk away down the street. He must take a further risk.

The streetlights were already dimming and patrolling guards lurked in every darkest corner. The creature hurried: it screamed inwardly with frustration.

A voice echoed from the darkness: 'You're out a bit late aren't you... er...'

The creature turned slowly, and saw a guard whose face was

mostly hidden by a black glass visor. The creature did not speak, but smiled a little. It would be enough.

The guard cleared his throat, gestured with his black gun. 'Well... er... hurry along home. The streets are no place for young... for you to frequent after dark.'

The creature inclined its head and walked away. He heard the buzz of static, then a faint metallic voice issue from the communication device in the guard's helmet.

Jarad entered silently into his apartment. He walked softly into the kitchen, so as not to awaken his neighbours, for the walls were thin. He turned the light onto dim and downed a swig of his week's ration of milk. Unsatisfied, he turned on the water tap, but the supply had already been disconnected for the night. He shrugged resignedly and made his way into the plush living room. At the threshold he turned up the light a little.

The creature was curled up in a chair, waiting for him. He regarded Jarad stonily.

Jarad's entire body went hot, then cold. 'Why are you here?' His voice was harsh.

The creature's beautiful face adopted a smile. 'It's where you live,' he said.

Jarad wiped his mouth with the back of one hand. He could still taste milk, and it was sour. 'How did you get in?'

The creature smiled wistfully. 'I learned where you hide your spare key. Wasn't that difficult. Your mind print was all over it.'

'You must go,' said Jarad.

The creature shook his head slowly.

'You must,' Jarad urged. 'You can't stay here. You shouldn't be here. Go!'

'I can't. You must know that. If you want me out, you must use physical force. But I doubt you'd do that either.'

Jarad flared his nostrils. 'If you're found here...' He shook his head. 'You had no right to come, to invade my privacy.' He hesitated. 'What do you want?'

'Want?' The creature extended his legs, clad in soft leather, and rose from the chair. He advanced upon Jarad and touched him on the cheek with a long fingered hand. 'I think you know.'

Jarad flinched away. 'Get back to where you came from.'

The creature laughed. 'Remember, you came from there too, Jarad.'

'I escaped,' Jarad said. 'My choice. I won't live that life. If you're here to persuade me otherwise, you're wasting your time.'

'You are deluding yourself,' said the creature. 'You can't survive here. Not for long. You can't hide. Eventually, all this will be gone, and then what?'

'If that happens, I'll deal with it. I live from day to day.'

The creature slunk back to the chair and arranged himself gracefully. He crossed his legs and rested his elbows upon the chair arms, linking his long fingers beneath his chin.

Jarad felt as if the creature stared holes in him.

'It is just a sickness you have,' said the creature. 'This fear, this denial. It can be cured.'

'Not your way.'

'What happened was wrong,' the creature said. 'You are not the only one to think it. There are mistakes, because we are so young. It was a mistake. It can be undone.'

'It can't,' Jarad said. 'You are the mistake – all of you.'

'Jarad... some things *can't* be undone. You know that too. You are one of us.'

'No,' Jarad said. 'I wasn't given a choice about that either. Now I make it.'

'You can't ignore what you are.'

Jarad laughed coldly. 'I'm doing pretty well, thank you. Watch me. You can sit there as long as you like, say what you like. It won't change my mind.'

'Sleep on it,' said the creature. 'I'll give you that time.'

Jarad shook his head. 'It will make no difference.' With a final wordless sound, he loped to his bedroom and shut the door carefully behind him. As he undressed, he watched the door all the time and then lay in bed staring at it. He shouldn't sleep, but he was too tired to resist. He was always tired.

Jarad awoke when the radio in the wall chimed: 'Awake! Awake! To work! To work hard! A good breakfast and off you go!'

Jarad winced. There were prices to pay for living in the 'decent' area of the city over which the Society Government had tenuous ruling. Jarad stretched in his bed, and then froze. He saw that the creature lay asleep beside him. *Typical*, thought Jarad. *Only you could sleep through such an alarm.* But he couldn't help smiling. The creature was naked beneath the quilt, which covered him from the chest down. His tawny skin was as smooth as fur. Jarad's hands felt hot and dry. It took all his strength not to reach out and touch. All his strength to confine that heat to his hands.

'I hate you, most beautiful of creatures,' he said aloud.

The lovely eyes unveiled at once and blinked at him. 'You talk in your sleep,' the creature said. 'You never used to do that.'

'How would you know? We never slept together.'

Jarad got out of bed and dressed himself quickly in his plain uniform clothes. 'I'll have to get you out before the cleaners arrive,' he said. 'If you're seen…'

The creature laughed softly and pulled the quilt over his head.

'Get up!' Jarad snapped. 'If you're seen, security will be alerted.'

The creature sighed, and then threw back the quilt. Jarad stared for a moment, then averted his eyes.

The creature sat up. 'Come home, Jarad. We want you back with us.'

'Who sent you?' Jarad asked.

The creature pushed back his long honey-coloured hair that fell down over his chest, nearly to his waist. 'Not anyone in particular,' he said, 'although your name has been mentioned often. You are a lost child, Jarad. We care for you.'

Jarad laughed caustically. 'Care? Is that what it is?'

'Yes. Listen, I'll be honest with you. Manticker is planning an assault on City Heart. It will be destroyed – you along with it, most likely. Get out now, while you can. I know for sure that if you return to us, Wraxilan will discipline those who wronged you.'

'Why? Why should he care?'

'The Lion cares for his own. You are part of his phyle, part of Oomar.'

'Yet you say he did not send you, nor did he bother to look for me himself. You're lying. He doesn't give a shit.'

The creature raked his hands through his hair. 'He didn't know what happened. None of us did. We only found out once you'd gone. You lost yourself pretty well. I only found out where you were because we took someone who had heard of you. That was a big coincidence. It was meant to be. Come home. Wraxilan will give you a blade. You can cut throats with it, if that's what you want.'

'Why should I be so important?' Jarad asked. 'Aren't numbers the important thing? There is only one of me. You can always find more, incept more.'

'You are one of the best,' the creature said. 'We cannot let you slip away like this.'

'But look what I have here,' Jarad said, making a sweeping gesture with one arm. 'Would I have all this back there? Warmth, comfort, clean water?'

'You would have freedom,' the creature said softly, 'and me also, if you so desired.'

Jarad made an angry sound. 'Doesn't everyone have you?'

The creature shrugged. 'That didn't used to bother you. I know you wanted me, Jarad, and I'm sorry I played with you. It was just a game, and I didn't know you'd simply disappear. I'm sorry I wasn't there for you when you needed me.' He grinned mordantly. 'Do you see what you've done? I just apologised and I never do that!'

'You would give yourself to me, just to lure me back?' Jarad uttered a snort. 'There's more to this than you say. I don't flatter myself I'm that desirable.'

The creature stood up and dressed himself. 'You are. That was the point of the game.'

Jarad frowned. 'I can't be like you anymore. Don't you understand? They took that from me, all desire.'

The creature nodded. 'I understand... really. But it can be changed.'

Jarad put his hands over his face. The possibility was there, he knew that. He had run away to lick his wounds. Perhaps he had always wanted to be found.

'Did you never think of me?' the creature asked.

Jarad did not lower his hands. 'Of course, until I made myself stop.' He heard the creature draw nearer.

'We can heal you, you know that. The question is: Will you allow it?' He took hold of Jarad's hands and pulled them away from his face. The creature's scent filled his head; bittersweet musk. He exhaled over Jarad, his breath bringing brief visions of comfort and safety.

Jarad knew he should pull away. He must. 'Call me by name, Jarad.' The creature's arms were around his body, lips so close to his own.

'Lianvis,' he said. 'Don't do this.'

'Come home.'

Their lips touched and all physical sensation faded away. In the visions that followed, the city was dyed red in the light of a setting sun. There were no humans, no labour facilities, no cars, no pain. Birds wheeled among the broken towers and the green crept back over the land. Jarad was lost in that world, that beautiful lie. He saw himself with Lianvis, in a bower of roses that grew in the corner of a deserted parking lot. It was a dream he'd once had.

Lianvis pulled away, creature no more. 'Will you come with me?' Long fingers caressed Jarad's face.

'Yes,' Jarad said, weakly.

Jarad guessed that Lianvis had really expected him to put up more of a fight, and was therefore disorientated by his relatively easy victory. He took Jarad swiftly into the eastern forbidden zone of the city, where their own kind could gather in daylight. The human security patrols did not venture there. The SG believed that if the undesirable element was contained within its own sector, the populace of City Heart was safe. It was a short-sighted view that would eventually mean the end of human occupation in the city.

A café called 'Chains', supplied with produce by the black market, provided breakfast for anyone awake at that hour. The sausages frying so temptingly in the filthy kitchen were made of dog meat.

While Lianvis bartered at the counter for black coffee and burnt toast, Jarad went to sit at a table outside. There were no other patrons.

Lianvis returned with food. 'Here,' he said. 'Eat.'

Jarad grimaced. 'I don't think so. I think I should go home.'

'Too late for that,' Lianvis said. 'Let's just say I have musked your apartment. The next human who enters there will almost certainly report the matter to the authorities, since they know that token, and they will have bad dreams for three months.'

'You are disgusting!'

'A scent through the pores, that is all. What do you take me for?'

'What you are.' Jarad sipped the coffee.

Lianvis studied Jarad carefully. He wouldn't be able to see into his companion's mind. Whatever Jarad said about denying what he was, he still expertly shrouded his thoughts. Lianvis would know that Jarad had been attacked some months back, and that terrible things had been done to him, because the perpetrators would have bragged about it afterwards. They were hara, they were braggarts. It didn't take psychic ability to predict that. But none of them would have guessed Jarad would disappear for good.

'Wraxilan, questioned those responsible for the assault on you,' Lianvis said.

'Questioned...'

'They insisted it had only been "a bit of fun."' Lianvis grimaced.

'Really. And the Lion accepted that?'

'Fun gets out of control sometimes. He knows that.' Lianvis paused. 'I know it wasn't that, Jarad. You always kindled jealousy very easily. It caused resentment.'

'So much so, some trash tried to gut me. Yeah, that fun really got out of control.' Jarad spat at the ground by his feet, but he couldn't spit out the bile in his heart.

'I'll take you to Wraxilan tonight,' Lianvis said.

Jarad shrugged.

'Are you worried about facing those who attacked you?'

'No.'

'You should talk about it. We all know pelki happens, but not among our own kind.'

Jarad put his head to one side. 'It was rape, Viss. Don't dress it up with a tame word.'

'Pelki is not tame,' Lianvis said. 'That is why we use it.'

Jarad laughed coldly. 'I bled so much I thought I would heal up completely, that it would all just *go*. Perhaps it has. Perhaps I'm human again. Perhaps I'm male.'

'That's not possible. If you've been injured you should see a healer.'

'Sometimes, it aches.'

'Jarad...' Lianvis reached out and laid a hand over one of Jarad's, which was curled around his coffee mug.

Jarad did not pull away from the contact. 'They hated me. Why? I didn't ask to be made Wraeththu. I had no choice.'

'I know.'

'Did you... have a choice, I mean?'

Lianvis shook his head.

'It's wrong,' Jarad said and took a big mouthful of the scalding coffee, pulling away from Lianvis' touch. 'By staying with them, we condone it.'

'I'm not sorry about it,' Lianvis said. 'I'm happy with what I am. We don't have to be like the others.' He paused. 'There's someone I want you to meet. He's a thinker. He talks sense.'

'Really!'

'Yes. His name is Velisarius. He's also a healer. He'll help you.'

Jarad grimaced. 'I know of him. He's a freak. Seems to me he's into justifying his existence by getting into religion. That's no answer.'

'You're wrong. It's not religion.'

Again, Jarad laughed. 'There is no room for hippy mystics in Wraeththu, Viss. I'm surprised your friend is still alive.'

'It would do no harm to talk to him.'

'Whatever. I was stupid enough to fall for the breath-sharing, lost my wits, lost my life, so here I am! Do what you like. I don't care.'

'I don't believe you. I don't think you really liked that life you'd made for yourself. What the hell did you do in that squalid building?'

'Process data. It was mindless. I wanted that.'

'Wraeththu are here to stay,' Lianvis said. 'You had better get used to it. You are har.'

'I'm not sure I am anymore.'

Lianvis drained his coffee. 'Come on, I'll take you to Velisarius. Before anything, we should get you checked over.'

Velisarius lived, quite appropriately in Jarad's view, in an old church which was squeezed between high abandoned buildings. Jarad and Lianvis had to clamber over rubble to reach the main entrance. A group of very young hara were playing a game with bones in the litter-strewn entrance hall. They must have been incepted recently. Jarad immediately felt old, and yet his own inception had only been two years before.

At Lianvis' request, one of the hara took them into the presence of Velisarius. Jarad expected the har to be meditating or chanting, but when they were conducted into the small room at the rear of the building where Velisarius lived, the self-styled mystic was making a table. The air smelled of freshly cut wood. The symbolism of that was not lost on Jarad. He sneered inwardly.

Velisarius glanced up from his work. He looked younger than Jarad had expected. His long hair fell in a plait over one shoulder. 'This is a surprise,' he said to Lianvis. 'You're not usually about so early.'

'I've brought somehar to meet you,' Lianvis said. 'This is Jarad.'

'Ah,' said Velisarius, in a tone that indicated he knew who Jarad was.

'Will you look him over?' Lianvis asked. 'What happened to him… it caused injuries.'

Velisarius nodded. 'I'll take a look, if he wishes it.'

'You're not a doctor,' Jarad said, unable to keep the venom from his voice.

'No,' Velisarius agreed. 'I was a second year medical student.'

Jarad grimaced. 'Oh. Okay.'

Velisarius went to wash his hands at the sink at the back of the room. 'What were you before?' he asked.

'Still at school,' Jarad said. 'We were raided. Only five of us survived inception.'

'I was taken because I was stupid enough to walk around at night on my own,' Velisarius said. 'Still, it was what was meant to be. Will you undress and lie down on my bed? This won't take a moment. I can tell from looking at you that the damage was not too great.' He smiled. 'I mean, physically.'

'You didn't study psychiatry, then?' Jarad said, unzipping the front of his uniform.

'Sadly, no,' Velisarius said, 'although there are many hara who need it. Lianvis, go and find somehar who can make us tea.'

Lianvis, who still stood at the threshold, departed without a word.

Jarad lay down on the bed. 'I'm not sure about this, but I guess I want to know as well. Can you really tell from looking at me how bad it is?'

Velisarius nodded. 'I can tell a lot from a simple glance, yes. I read auras.'

'Of course you do.' Jarad raised his knees. He felt vulnerable, embarrassed.

Velisarius put a hand on Jarad's brow and a soothing cool wave of energy passed from his fingers. 'Relax,' Velisarius said. 'I'm a healer.'

'I can feel that,' Jarad said. He felt drowsy, as if the other har's energy was anaesthetic. Velisarius's gentle touch was also cool.

'Hmm,' Velisarius murmured.

'What?' Jarad raised his head to see Velisarius peering intently between his legs.

'This will require a minor operation. I can do it now, if you like.'

'What's wrong?'

'You've healed all wrong.'

'I knew it! I said to Viss I'd healed up.'

'Well, not quite that bad,' Velisarius said, 'but I'll need to make an incision.'

'Maybe you should just leave it.'

Velisarius glanced up. 'I'll pretend I didn't hear that.'

'I mean it.'

'I don't have to be a psychiatrist to tell you that a har denying half of his being is unhealthy,' Velisarius said. 'Don't move. I'll be right back.'

Jarad led his head flop back and closed his eyes. He wasn't afraid of pain. He was afraid of what he was, all the feelings he didn't understand, that woman inside him.

Jarad rested in Velisarius' room for most of the day, lulled by the sound of a saw through wood, the hammering of nails. Lianvis sat on the floor beside him and read a book. Jarad dozed, drifting in and out of consciousness. One time he woke up weeping; it was as if some other personality was living in his body. Velisarius had packed the wound, and now Jarad's lower body throbbed in pain, as sensitive nerves protested at the intrusion. Lianvis said nothing but put his hands on Jarad's belly. Healing warmth flowed from his fingers.

'You see,' Lianvis said softly. 'We *can* be different. You'll heal quickly.'

By evening, Jarad felt more or less normal. He ached slightly, but it wasn't too much to tolerate.

'Be thankful for your new physiology,' Velisarius told him. 'You'll be as good as new in a day or so.'

'Lianvis said we should talk,' Jarad said.

Velisarius smiled. 'I hope we will. Come back any time.'

He was not touting for converts, then.

Outside, night had come. The sky was clearer than it had been for a while. The moon was just past full. Lianvis and Jarad walked through the narrow backstreets, with high walls to either side. They went to the area known as City Zoo, where abandoned warehouses had been turned into nightclubs. Loud music boomed from every open doorway, and the light within those places was red, turquoise, livid green. They were in search of Wraxilan, and Lianvis knew his favoured haunts.

This was the territory of the Uigenna, the largest and most powerful Wraeththu tribe, into which Jarad had been incepted. Exotic hara, clad in their strangest costumes, lined the streets, eyeing up the competition and the talent. The wind carried litter and sighs. Huge, scrawny alley cats lithed along the sidewalk, glancing from left to right for adversaries. Jarad could see that Lianvis was smiling: clearly he savoured this environment. Jarad simply thought it shallow and crass. Whatever initial attractions the Uigenna way of life had had for him, he'd quickly grown to despise it. Most hara he'd met were stupid, posturing fools.

The smoke of dry ice billowed out from the clubs, pungent with the smell of sweat and incense. Lianvis turned into one of the open doorways, pausing only to make sure that Jarad was still following. Two tall hara, whose faces were tattooed with curling black patterns, stood aside to let them through, nodding a greeting to Lianvis as they did so.

The light inside was crimson and it was difficult to see much through the smoky atmosphere. A long bar that ran down the side of the main room served lethal hooch that was brewed in the cellars below. This noxious liquor was flavoured with various fruits and caramel, and coloured with livid food dyes, which tended to stain the teeth. Heavy industrial dub pulsed from the immense sound system, and the entire space was one enormous dance floor, filled with gyrating bodies.

Jarad looked back; the street seemed very far away. He had been here before. He'd met friends here often. Strange, he couldn't remember some of their faces now.

There was a mezzanine gallery above the dancers, and Lianvis led Jarad to the metal stairs that led to it. Up there, hara were lounging on cushions, smoking marijuana in tall pipes.

Tiny spotlights picked out various revellers and in the light of one of them sprawled Wraxilan, the Lion of Oomar, and leader of this phyle of the greater tribe of Uigenna. He was magnificent, like a dream of androgyny made flesh. His wild blond hair looked almost white. He lay on his nest of cushions, his head thrown back, eyes closed; a plume of smoke emanated from his pursed lips. His perfect arms were covered in tattooed serpents, some of which had the head of a lion. Wraxilan was neither shallow nor crass. He was, however, dangerous, brutal and merciless. He had the murderous impulses of a psychotic man and the cold vindictive zeal of a paranoid woman. Jarad had always avoided him, kept his head down. There were privileges to being in Wraxilan's inner cabal, obviously, but he was quick to take offence, and those who fell out of favour sometimes disappeared.

Jarad hung back while Lianvis approached the phylarch. A group of twenty of so hara sat around him, and they now appraised Jarad with cool or suspicious gazes.

After Lianvis had spoken, Wraxilan sat up and stared directly at Jarad, who made a gesture of respect by touching his brow. It was impossible to converse over the music, so Wraxilan got to his feet and gestured they should go through a door behind him. Jarad's heart was beating fast. His mouth was dry and his wound began to throb once more, making his belly feel hot.

Beyond the doorway was a narrow, dimly lit corridor. Wraxilan led his companions to another room. He opened a door to reveal three hara experimenting in dim light with some sort of drug: a pale green powder they were rubbing into each other's eyes.

'Out!' Wraxilan said and the room's occupants gathered up their equipment and hurried away.

There were cushions on the floor in here also, and Wraxilan sat down. He gestured for Lianvis and Jarad to do likewise. 'So,' he said, 'the wanderer returns.'

Jarad, lost for words, raised his hands briefly, then let them fall back into his lap.

'Drink?' Wraxilan asked. He pulled a flask from the pocket of his brushed leather shirt.

'Thanks.' Jarad took it, swigged a mouthful of sweet fiery liquor. He handed the flask to Lianvis.

'It's good that Viss found you,' Wraxilan said to Jarad. 'You shouldn't have left us. After what happened, you should have come straight to me.'

'At the time, I wasn't thinking straight,' Jarad said carefully. 'Also, you were out of the city and I was in fear for my life.'

Wraxilan nodded. 'Understandable. I was watching you, Jarad, sizing you up. It annoyed me when you left.'

'I had no idea.'

'No.' Wraxilan gestured emphatically. 'Well, I'll get to the point. I need hara like you. There are too many fools. They're no use to me. They're the sheep. I want wolves.'

'Hmm,' murmured Jarad.

'It all bores you, doesn't it?' Wraxilan said. 'I like that. The ones who attacked you didn't like it at all. They wanted to bring you down a bit, make you know your place. But you just walked away. I wasn't happy about that.'

'What do you want me to do for you?' Jarad asked.

'Help me do what has to be done,' Wraxilan replied. 'Organise our phyle. See to training, organise raids, that sort of thing. We can't hide in the ruins forever. We have to take this city, and every other city. Humanity's time is done.'

'Big plans,' Jarad said. 'Is this under Archon Manticker's direction?'

A flicker flashed across Wraxilan's eyes at the mention of the tribe leader. It was no secret Wraxilan coveted Manticker's power.

Such was the way of the ambitious *protégé*. Manticker had incepted Wraxilan, and once they had been close. 'We all do what is best for our tribe,' Wraxilan answered.

Jarad nodded. 'Of course. But what will your other hara think about my place in your scheme?'

Wraxilan gestured carelessly with one hand. 'Don't worry about what hara think of you. They won't dare to touch you again.'

'OK,' Jarad said. Here was another thing he really had no choice over. 'Whatever you want.'

Wraxilan laughed, rather uncertainly. 'You puzzle me. I expected you to haggle over terms.'

'No,' Jarad said. 'Your terms are clear. Your protection will be useful. No doubt I still have enemies.'

'I like you,' Wraxilan said. 'You talk straight. No bullshit. That's good.' He paused. 'What do you want me to do with your attackers now?'

Jarad paused for a moment. One thing he was sure of was that turning up again and causing trouble or drama amongst hara who most likely hated him was unwise. Best to keep a low profile. 'What's done is done,' he said eventually. 'If they try anything again, it might be a different matter.'

'I am prepared to punish them.'

'I know. Perhaps that is enough.'

'You know what I think?' Wraxilan said. 'This experience has sharpened you, made you strong. You're a changed har, my friend. Use it to your advantage. Work well for me, and you'll keep a good position.'

'I'll do my best,' Jarad said.

'I heard you visited Velisarius today,' Wraxilan said, in a tone that was just a shade too casual. 'I hope he fixed you.'

Jarad shrugged. 'Just about. I'll be healed in a day or so.'

'Good. I look forward to that.'

Jarad inclined his head. The meaning was clear.

Wraxilan stood up. 'Well, get Viss to find you a room around here somewhere. I'll see you later.'

'Happy now?' Jarad asked, once he and Lianvis were alone.

'What?' Lianvis appeared to have been lost in thought.

'I did what you wanted. I'm back with a vengeance.'

'Are you?'

Jarad stood up. 'So find me a room.'

Lianvis hesitated. 'Wraxilan's is not the only way, Jarad. It's good to be part of his troupe, but the heart doesn't have to go where the body goes.'

'I'll talk to your healer friend if it's what you want,' Jarad said. 'But now, I'm just tired.'

'Then let's go.'

They found a disused room, or rather an abandoned room, because there were some bits of furniture in it: a bed, a chest of drawers, lots of clothes and rubbish lying around. Someone had left this room one day intending to return, but had never done so. Jarad took off his uniform. He'd never wear it again. He'd wear the clothes a dead har had left behind.

Lianvis appeared anxious about something. Jarad didn't know what. 'I'm not going out into the club again tonight,' he said. 'Want to stay here with me?' He sat down on the bed, which was low to the floor, just two thin mattresses on top of one another, covered by a grimy quilt.

'Okay.' Lianvis sat down beside him. 'You seem really distant, Jarad.'

The balance of power had shifted. It had begun from the moment they'd set foot in the club.

'I'm here,' Jarad said.

'How do you feel?'

'Fine.' He put a hand on Lianvis' shoulder. 'You made me an offer, remember?'

'Perhaps you should wait.'

'What I'm planning won't hurt me.'

Lianvis smiled uncertainly. 'I see.'

'I want to fuck you,' Jarad said flatly. 'So deep it hurts.'

Lianvis moved away from him slightly. 'Don't call it that. It's not that.'

Jarad laughed coldly. 'Well, I don't know what you'll be doing, but I'll be fucking.'

Lianvis stood up, leaving Jarad to bite only at empty air where once Lianvis's neck had been. 'That's not it. You say you despise the others? Now you sound like them.'

Jarad leaned back on his elbows. His face was inscrutable.

'What we can do together transcends…' Lianvis's voice trailed off. He must see he didn't really have an audience.

'I know what it is,' Jarad said. 'I thought we had a deal.'

'We did.' Lianvis sat down again, raked his hands through his hair.

'What's the matter with you?' Jarad asked. 'I bet you've laid all of Wraxilan's phyle and half of every other one in Carmine. What's so different now?' He grinned slowly. 'No... don't tell me it's *that*!' He laughed aloud. 'Do you think you're kelos over me, Viss? Is that it?'

'If you're not careful,' Lianvis said, 'your bitterness will be your undoing, Jarad. A bad thing happened to you. But you are Wraeththu. Get over it.'

'You didn't answer my question.'

'No.' Lianvis paused. 'I'm not kelos over you, but I am learning new things. One of them is that sex isn't just for mindless gratification. For us, it can be different.'

'How so?'

'It can be like a drug, a natural high. It can give us power, real power. I've seen it. If you go into it with an open mind, you can go anywhere.' He laid a hand on one of Jarad's arms. 'Let me show you.'

Jarad's eyes were still cold, but he said, 'OK. Whatever you want.'

'Share breath with me.'

They lay down together, and in their sharing it was clear that Lianvis was trying to project what was precious and divine about their potential union. When Jarad reached to undo Lianvis's trousers, Lianvis stayed his hand. Jarad pulled away from him. 'Viss?'

'Wait,' Lianvis said. 'Share breath for longer.'

Drawing out the memories was like pulling shards of glass from Jarad's flesh, but Lianvis made him do it. He relived those harrowing hours when the Uigenna had abused and violated him. They had done terrible things, far worse than Lianvis would have imagined. It was more than simple resentment or envy that drove them, much more. It was self-hatred too, and terror of what they had become.

When they broke the kiss, Jarad was shuddering, his face pressed into Lianvis's hair.

'You had to face it,' Lianvis said. 'Understand that.'

Jarad raised his head. He felt very tired, weary of life itself. 'Your foreplay sucks,' he said.

A week later Jarad saw two of the hara who had changed his life to darkness. Given the close-knit nature of their community, he was surprised it hadn't happened sooner. The moment he saw them, he acknowledged this and realised he'd been waiting. They were with a third har he didn't know. They weren't slouching around looking menacing or slinking in a pack down some twilit alley; they were horsing about in the sunlight, unloading foodstuffs from a truck, throwing sacks to each other. *Laughing.*

A needle went through Jarad's heart. The carefree laughter pained him more than if they'd turned and recognised him, growled insults, spat in his face.

Lianvis was trying to educate him, Jarad knew. But Jarad was impatient with the carefully-worded sentiments about how hara could be great and good. All Jarad saw were monsters, made even more monstrous because they were beautiful. Talk of the world being gifted to a superior race was nonsense to him. Who were they kidding? Most of the time, the hara around him behaved like characters in a bad B-movie of a post holocaust world. Posturing, strutting, dressing up, learning how to sneer in the best possible way, and how to carry a weapon so that it looked cool. When Lianvis said things like, 'think of our ultimate potential,' Jarad wanted to say, 'Yeah, yeah, by the way, your hair looks good.' He felt that the sarcasm of that would be lost on this new earnest Lianvis. Perhaps it was like religion – clutching at straws when the hurricane was going to blow them all away anyway.

And Lianvis was worried about Jarad – Jarad could feel it. He knew that Lianvis could sense him slipping away into a hinterland, present in body but not in mind and spirit. Jarad didn't care. He simply didn't know how to. And as he stared from the shadow of the porch of an abandoned store, fixing his eyes on the hara who had ruined him, he felt Lianvis touch his mind. He was like a stalker, ever vigilant, and now he melted through the sunlight, the sun behind him, hair lifted in the breeze of his own movement, tall and stately. He was dressed in close-fitting rags of burnt orange and gold. His arms were scored with tattoos. He was radiant. Like an advertisement for a better life a long time ago.

Don't Lianvis said through mind-touch. *Come away.*

He is just flesh, Jarad thought, *or a lovely moving image. None of it is real.* He projected to Lianvis: *What are you afraid I'll do?*

Nothing. It's what you're thinking that scares me.

Then get out of my mind. It's not your garden.

I'm going to see Velisarius. Come with me.

Jarad sighed. *I wish you'd stop trying, Viss. It's starting to annoy me.*

You don't want me to give up on you. Not really.

Lianvis was before him now, his back to the sun so it was hard to see his face. Jarad noticed the hara at the truck had stopped what they were doing to look at Lianvis. They didn't even notice Jarad standing there. He was forgotten, although surely they must've heard the news he'd returned. Lianvis simply eclipsed him, he supposed.

Lianvis linked his arm through one of Jarad's and firmly dragged him away, back in the direction from which he'd come. 'Wraxilan wants your anger,' he said. 'Why do you give in so easily and let him have it?'

'There's nothing *else* to do,' Jarad said.

'You could try to stop feeling sorry for yourself,' Lianvis said. 'You want to hurt me by being like this. It doesn't hurt me, though.'

Jarad was impatient with these conversations. They didn't interest him. He wondered whether in fact he actually liked Lianvis, further than the fleeting pleasures his body could afford. And even that seemed tawdry now, another big pose. *Our sex is better than humanity's – big deal. Doesn't make us any smarter.* He decided the next time he wanted to fuck Lianvis, he'd try to step back from the sensations and see whether the whole thing was really quite boring.

'I'm not trying to hurt you,' Jarad said. 'I just wish you'd wake up to the fact the world is a crock of shit.'

Velisarius was surrounded by a troupe of adoring acolytes. He really fancied himself as some kind of harish messiah, Jarad thought. Yet another posturing idiot. He was no different from Wraxilan; he just read from a different script. The hara were preparing to meditate, hanging onto Velisarius' soft words as if they were scented apples thrown from the Tree of Life.

Jarad hoped that he wouldn't be asked directly to take part in what they were doing. The whole idea of it embarrassed him. Perhaps Velisarius and Lianvis picked up on this. Perhaps they conversed with each via mind touch to discuss how best to handle Jarad, make him malleable. Jarad stood at the back of the room, smoking a cigarette. The smoke made beautiful slow-moving patterns in a fan of sunlight falling through a narrow window. He forced himself not to look at them, refusing to see messages there.

When the group started to chant softly, Jarad went outside. He could still hear them, but once removed from the sight it didn't annoy him so much. He looked up at the sky. How empty it was. Not a chopper in sight. Things had changed in a short time. City Heart was a metallic glitter he could see across the river. From here, it was possible to believe life went on there just the same, as it always had. From here, in the sunlit afternoon, when most hara were asleep, it was possible to believe in some kind of future. The light was so mellow; it had always been this way. Certain sounds were archetypal and eternal. A dog barked in the distance, but there was no sound of children playing.

Wraxilan had given Jarad time to settle. The phylarch was not wrong in his assumptions. Already, Jarad was thinking that in two days' time when the moon turned towards darkness, he would present himself at Wraxilan's side and say 'I am here. What do you want of me now?' If it was raiding into the human-controlled zones, or subduing another harish phyle that Wraxilan considered might be problematical in the future, Jarad would do it. He made no distinction between human and har; neither species commanded his respect. In this, he knew, he would be very useful to Wraxilan, in the place of hara who might baulk at going against their own kind. Jarad looked down at his hands, which he held out in front of him palms down. The skin looked tired.

He did not hear Velisarius come up behind him and started when the har placed a hand on his shoulder. He didn't like being taken by surprise and even though he knew from the first instant who it was, he was tempted to snarl, wheel round and throw a punch, just to make a point.

Velisarius laughed. 'You would have found no target,' he said.

Jarad shrugged, dropped the end of his cigarette to the floor, ground out its fire with his foot. He saw four cigarette butts lying in the dirt and realised he'd stood there longer than he'd thought. 'Prayer meeting over?' he asked.

Velisarius stood beside him, gazing at the distant City Heart. 'You want to know what's going to happen to Wraxilan?' he said.

'I think we all know,' Jarad replied.

'He will meet his match,' Velisarius said. 'He will be broken in two, but not before he breaks our Archon in two. Wraxilan has his path, washed in blood, of course. He will be reviled and feared, and Manticker will be cast down and left for dead. He may well in fact die... in one way or another. But in the end, when history looks back, Wraxilan and Manticker will both be enshrined as hara of prominence.'

'Supposing Wraeththu survive that long,' Jarad said drily. 'Foraging vermin will soon die if there is nothing left to forage upon.'

Velisarius turned and gazed at Jarad with an unreadable expression.

'You must admit,' Jarad said, 'their chances are slim.'

'You still regard yourself as apart,' Velisarius said.

'Because I am.'

'Yet you're still here, after a week. You could have left easily. I don't see anyone following you, stopping you. Wraxilan must know you better than you know yourself.'

'I'm not interested in your talk,' Jarad said, 'or your prophecies. I'll do what Wraxilan wants for a while. When it all goes bad, maybe I'll travel.' He grinned without humour. 'See new lands, meet new people and kill them.'

'You're not a natural killer, Jarad. Why try to pretend that you are?'

Jarad grimaced. 'Is there a point to this conversation? If you have something to say, spit it out, I'll ignore it, then we can both get on with our day.'

Velisarius paused before answering. He pursed his lips, sighed through his nose. Jarad guessed the har was thinking it was probably a waste of breath to say whatever was coming next. He wouldn't be wrong.

'Don't think I disagree with you entirely,' Velisarius said. 'Most of what you believe is right, and what disgusts you, disgusts me also. Uigenna can't continue in this way; they are sleepwalking. Wraxilan is right too, in certain respects. But he understands only how to rule through fear and that is weak. It is an armour with chinks.'

'So you choose the path of the prophet instead. It is bloodless, but no less controlling. You will preach a different brand of fear.'

Velisarius laughed softly. 'You are wrong about me, Jarad. I'm not the sanctimonious, pious creature you believe me to be. I just can't walk in hot blood all the time. It makes me weary. Hot blood clouds the senses. You must know this.'

Jarad shrugged.

'There are other ways,' Velisarius continued, 'and only a fool would think they are without pain, trial, cruelty and terror. That is our legacy; we cannot avoid it. Our kind is fated to evolve from horror and we might all have to do terrible things to plant seeds of growth.'

'Do you know this off by heart? Do you have it written down?' Jarad snarled. 'It will make a great holy book some day.'

'I know it off by heart,' Velisarius replied drily. 'But only because it is a universal truth.' He paused again. 'OK, enough talk. I'll get to the point. Wraxilan wants your talents because he thinks they will help him. I want you for the same thing, but I think I can offer you more in return. Interested?'

Jarad laughed in a forced way. The question demanded that response. 'You mean you're planning to overthrow Wraxilan?'

'No, I am planning on taking the hara in whom he probably isn't interested anyway to create a new tribe. This will be a tribe who relearns the lessons we have lost in the debris of humanity's fall. We will learn new lessons also. It is time for us to reach towards our potential. It is not here, grubbing in filth and squabbling like rabid dogs amongst ourselves. As part of the way to accomplish this, I realise we will need hara like you, hara with that cold fire, but also with intelligence. I don't want mutton heads.'

'You mean like a body guard, or a militia?' Again Jarad laughed. 'You won't get away with it. Wraxilan might not be interested in the prayer-boys you have, but he won't look kindly on anyone hiving off. You know that. He'll pursue you, wipe you out. And, by the way, there is nothing you can offer me he can't.'

'Well, there is, but you won't see it just yet.'

'You're a fool to trust me. I'll go back and report all this. Wraxilan will be pleased with me. I'll earn points with him. Are you insane?'

'You won't tell him,' Velisarius said quietly. 'I'm not a fool. Give me a cigarette.'

Jarad did so. He had to admit that, in spite of himself, he was intrigued. But he didn't want to believe that what Velisarius suggested was possible, because it would spoil his cynical view of Wraeththu.

'We would have to go far from here,' Velisarius said, accepting the light Jarad offered him. 'We will have to go at the moment the young wolf goes for the throat of the old wolf. In that moment, we will be ready and our departure will not be noticed. The phyles will rise up and the power struggle for Uigenna will begin.'

'Manticker,' Jarad murmured. He felt a clutch about his heart; he had to admit Velisarius was right. 'Will it be soon?'

'You feel it,' Velisarius said.

'Are you ready?'

'Mostly.' Velisarius fixed Jarad with a stare. 'I don't say the things I do to try and impress you. It's simply information you might find useful. Be prepared and alert. While the plans are in motion, the outcome is not yet decided. There are always hidden variables.'

'I'm touched that you care.'

Velisarius laughed without humour. 'It's not care, Jarad. Like I said, you'd be useful to me too.'

Wraxilan did not live, as Jarad had expected, in some harsh industrial space where the light was like metal. He lived in a ruin, yes, a shopping mall that had been turned to legend by wisteria. It had once grown in the central plaza; now it grew everywhere, nourished perhaps by corpses beneath the green. In places there were carpets of a trailing vine with small leaves.

'So where do I start?' Jarad asked Wraxilan.

Wraxilan was like a great cat; when he wasn't stalking, he was sprawling. He liked heat. And like a cat, he had nests in various parts of the community; always soft cushions, curiously clean. Now he jabbed a finger in Jarad's direction. 'What I like about you is the fact you don't care, not about anything. Yet I know you will do as I ask.'

Jarad said nothing.

Wraxilan uncoiled from his cushions, began to pace. If he'd had a tail, it would be switching now. 'I know this because it is written all over you as if in black ink. It is the story of your life as it is now.'

'Well, I'm ready to do as you ask.'

Wraxilan studied him for a moment. Jarad knew what was on his mind, and didn't have to have psychic abilities to be aware of that. Now the phylarch's gaze became veiled. Perhaps untruths would follow. 'You must admit that everything we've been through has affected some more than others, and I mean in a bad way.'

'You could say that.'

'And perhaps you could also say that extreme measures might be needed to make Uigenna what it should be. By that I mean cutting away the dead wood.'

'There's no reason you can't break away,' Jarad answered. 'Most would follow you, and they would be the ones you want.'

'I'm not thinking of breaking away. I'm thinking of... remodelling.'

'I see. What do you want me to do?'

Wraxilan laughed. 'I can see you really would do anything. We're both thinking the same thing, I know it. I'm touched you would go that far for me, even though I'm aware you wouldn't do it because you care or because you're particularly loyal. It's just a job isn't it?'

Jarad said nothing.

'I can fight my own battles,' Wraxilan said. 'What I want you for is the aftermath.'

'There might be more than one battle,' Jarad said. 'Like I said, most would follow you, but not all.' He paused. 'Can we speak plainly?'

'Of course.'

'This is about removing Manticker, isn't it?'

Wraxilan stared at Jarad for long, uncomfortable seconds with his tiger eyes. He was weighing up how much he trusted this har before him. Manticker was still powerful. 'He's not who he was,' Wraxilan said at last. 'I'm not the only one who thinks that for the good of all hara he must stand down. He doesn't organise our phyles well; he just wants to go out crazily destroying everything in his path. He thinks he's invincible.'

'He's not called Manticker the Seventy for nothing,' Jarad said.

Wraxilan snickered. 'Oh, I know that, but his vision is not acute. He can't see that we must consolidate our forces, train them properly. We must not be like humes, but we must stop being scattered. Every time I, or others like me, try to call a meeting of the phylarchs to discuss strategies, he manages to disrupt or postpone it. He has his cronies, and they undermine me also. He's like a firecracker. Silent till he's lit. Then the fire comes upon him, and he summons all around him to go out on some crazy killing spree, often into territory where they do not have the advantage. Instead of planning and aiming for targets that are of strategic value, he mindlessly charges into... just anywhere. Hara die; it's a waste. Yes, he has been successful in this way for a couple of years, and that's why the more stupid among us follow him, but things are changing. I hope you agree with me on this.'

Jarad thought for a moment. He supposed he should try to have an opinion. 'Manticker won't go away quietly, but then we wouldn't be having this conversation if that was at all likely.'

Wraxilan nodded his head briefly. 'Yes, yes, but I need to know your exact thoughts on him. Do you agree with me?'

'I've already said I will do as you ask. Is that answer enough?'

'Not if you have any doubts.'

'I have no doubts.'

'Good. As you must know, there are others like you. For the time being, you will not meet them. But after tonight, you shall.'

'Tonight? That soon?' Now a shiver of discomfort coursed up Jarad's spine. Did he want to get involved? No, not really. But he'd said he would.

'You will be sent word,' Wraxilan said. 'Go to the Animal bar about 8.30. I'll send someone to you there. You won't need his name, nor he yours.'

'As you wish.'

'That is all for now. It's best you don't know anything further until you're needed. Stay close.'

It was a dismissal. Jarad inclined his head and walked away, scuffing through the tiny leaves; they released a stinging, green scent as he crushed them.

Jarad went directly to Velisarius; he wasn't sure himself why he did so. He had no intention of going with the har – or did he? Instinct guided his feet to the old church. He didn't question it.

Velisarius was, as usual, surrounded by other hara listening to him talk. He noticed Jarad in the doorway immediately and came to him, led him back to the porch. He did not appear agitated but Jarad sensed tension in him. 'When?' Velisarius asked.

'Tonight,' Jarad answered. 'I can tell you no more than that because that's all I know. But the plot is big. Wraxilan has planned it carefully I imagine.' He paused. 'You didn't think it would be this soon, did you? Are you ready?'

'I'm always ready,' Velisarius answered. 'I'm not sure you are, however.' He looked Jarad in the eye. 'Find me if you want to. You know the offer is there. I won't press you more than that. Just think about it carefully. Is Wraxilan's world the one you want to live in?'

Jarad glanced away. 'I doubt I'll be able to get further word to you. Wraxilan has asked me to stay close. I don't want to compromise you. As it stands, he might know I've come now. Fortunately, you've been treating me. I have good reason to visit.'

Velisarius twisted his mouth into a grim smile. 'If what you say is true, he no doubt knows you were here earlier too.'

'Come outside,' Jarad said.

They went into the street, where there might be harish eyes watching from the rooftops. 'There is always one good reason,' Jarad said. He took Velisarius's face in his hands and kissed him. 'That should be enough.'

Velisarius appeared dazed. He hadn't expected that. 'Be careful,' he said, and went back into the church.

The Animal bar was an area where Wraxilan's staff tended to congregate for relaxation, close to Wraxilan's residence. There was a yard out back with benches and tables, dominated and greened with ancient fig trees. Moss grew over the walls and the tiles underfoot. Tame doves roosted among the fig leaves, filling the air with their purring song. The tables were spattered with their droppings. Jarad sat here alone, as he always did when visiting the place. He smoked cigarettes and drank the strong beer brewed on the premises, but not too much. His senses needed to be clear. Around him, conversation and laughter sounded like the cackle of hyenas. But there was no corpse for them to bicker over yet. It was as if he were invisible. Nobody paid him any attention. Perhaps they considered him jinxed.

Jarad watched the sun sink below the walls of the beer garden. He felt nervous, disorientated. Surely Manticker's hara must have suspicions of what was planned? He had strong adepts among his crew. Wraxilan was insane. This could not go well. *What the fuck am I doing?* Jarad wondered. He didn't feel in control of himself.

A har came out from the bar and began to light lamps hanging from the trees. Shortly afterwards, a blond-haired har came into the garden and sauntered to where Jarad sat. He loomed over Jarad, helped himself to a cigarette from the packet that lay half empty on the table.

The har sat down. He looked younger than Jarad, smug with a false certainty he was splendid and superior. Jarad knew the aura well; he despised it.

'We'll leave here in five minutes,' the har said. 'In the meantime, look as if you are interested in my company.'

Jarad uttered a short, choked laugh. 'We are *not* in a movie,' he said.

'You sure about that?' The har flicked back his hair, took a draw on the cigarette.

'Not really, no.'

'Can I have some of that beer?'

Jarad pushed his glass across the table. 'Polite of you to ask,' he said.

The har took a swing. 'Five minutes: we go.'

The har offered no name and Jarad did not ask. As twilight came sifting through the streets and the harish quarter came alive, they walked in silence. They were lightly armed, carrying only knives. Before they left the bar, the unnamed har mentioned, in response to a query from Jarad, that heavier arms would not be needed. Jarad voiced no further questions. His feet would lead him to his destiny, whatever that would be, one way or another.

Manticker's hara could be heard before they were seen. These were not remotely human noises, nor even animal, but something deeper, wilder, more profane. Jarad's skin prickled. *How could they not know what was coming?*

His companion signalled for them to stop walking, then led them into the shadow of a wall. Ahead, about two hundred yards away, was a hill; any building that had once covered it had been razed. Here a fire was burning; the flames leapt high, playfully, like the tail of a phoenix. Even from this distance, shadowy forms could be discerned moving around the fire. Were they simply celebrating their latest slaughtering foray or was it some kind of ritual taking place up there? Jarad could not tell. He closed his eyes, attempted to extend his senses. As far as he could feel, there were no sentries or lookouts posted. Could Manticker really be so lax about security?

'When the Lion comes, it is safe for us to move closer,' Jarad's companion murmured.

Jarad opened his eyes, nodded. He wanted a cigarette badly, but any har with sharp senses might see the red spark in the darkness. He didn't want to take the risk and have that baying pack coming down to investigate.

'You can smoke,' said the har, clearly picking up on Jarad's desire. 'They're out of it, off their faces. They're not looking for trouble.'

'Don't underestimate your enemies,' Jarad replied, but he pulled his cigarettes from his jacket pocket, simply turning his back to light one.

'What's your name?' the har asked.

Jarad didn't want to say. He shrugged. 'What's yours?'

'Terzian.' The har suddenly became very still, his posture tense. 'Wait...'

Jarad ground out his cigarette quickly.

'They're coming. Wraxilan is coming.'

Jarad pulled on Terzian's arm. 'Down!' He peered ahead as they crouched beneath the wall, trying to penetrate the shadows cast by the light of the fire on the hill. 'What does he want of us? Did he tell you?'

Terzian shook his head. 'We wait. We'll know.'

'Fucking stupid strategy,' Jarad muttered. 'They're as bad as each other.'

'Maybe so,' Terzian replied. 'But one will win. Who is your money on?'

Jarad could see Wraxilan's hara approaching now. He had to admit they were more organised than he'd thought. They were part of the shadows; ghosts gliding through patches of darkness, slinking along the tops of broken walls like cats, looking almost like cats. Unless you knew they were there, you would not notice them.

'How many on the hill, you think?' Jarad asked.

Terzian drew in his breath. 'Manticker's elite comprise about fifty hara, but he loses some of them regularly. Between thirty-five and fifty, I'd say.'

'Do you sense any sentries?'

A pause. 'No.'

'It's too easy,' Jarad said.

'There are others like us, pairs of hara closing in,' Terzian said. 'We don't know anything, so Manticker can't pick up too much from us.'

'Our intention is enough,' Jarad said dryly.

The shadows he'd perceived around them were now close to the hill.

'Let's move forward a short way,' Jarad said.

Still crouching down, they edged along the wall, keeping close to it. As they drew nearer to the hill, Jarad could see a tall shape silhouetted against the flames, arms outspread. He paused, gestured for Terzian to do likewise. Sometime in the last few minutes, the power had shifted. Jarad was leader now.

A tingle went through him. He knew the tall figure was Manticker. What was going through that har's mind? He had survived countless battles, he had earned his epithet annihilating seventy armed humans in one raging spree, he had always won against desperate odds. Yet now he had let himself become vulnerable. Did he really believe he was so safe, in the heart of this merciless community he had created?

Jarad was overwhelmed with a feeling of futility. How was Manticker any worse than Wraxilan? None of it meant anything. He should turn now, leave, perhaps even seek out Velisarius and wait for the clamorous psychic cry that would mean either Wraxilan or Manticker was dead. Then he could make decisions.

But then there was a voice in his mind. *Oh, but you cannot go. Not you, Jarad.*

Jarad sucked in his breath; his body jerked.

'What?' Terzian hissed.

'Nothing.'

'That wasn't nothing. You whole body just kind of... rippled. What is it?'

Jarad turned, looked the har in the eye. 'Well, put it this way. *Someone* knows we're here. I got a message.'

'What did it say?'

'That we can't leave.'

'I wasn't thinking of doing that. Tell them.'

Jarad sighed, suppressed a spasm of irritation.

The hill was surrounded now by Wraxilan's hara, and on the summit ahead of them all had become quiet because Manticker's hara had become aware of the approach. Jarad moved forward again, more quickly.

He saw Wraxilan step onto the path of flattened dirt that led up the hill. It was flanked by torches. Wraxilan looked confident, commanding, a natural leader. In comparison, Manticker and his troupe stooped above him like addled witch doctors, bewitched by flame.

Jarad found himself halfway up the hill, Terzian close behind. It was as if they weren't actually there in body, but merely spirit witnesses.

Manticker was naked from the waist up, dressed only in some kind of shamanic garb; a kilt of rags, fur and feathers. His hair was a wild, matted tangle, dangling in ropes over his chest and down his back; his face was daubed with chalky lines of paint. The air smelled of blood around him.

They are the two selves of Wraeththu, Jarad thought. He wondered if some toxic fume from the fire ahead had affected his mind. Manticker was the wild primal feminine, the Dark Mother, crouched in shadows, goddess of entrails. Hers were the secrets of life and death, the essential secrets in the deepest part of every living thing. Wraxilan was the male principle of the sun; open, visible, radiant swaggering. There were no secrets there. If Velisarius were here, he would surely say that this moment was a nexus point and the only way forward was for these two forces to combine, to become bigger than the sum of their parts. But neither Manticker nor Wraxilan would see that. They did not know they were avatars of greater forces.

Manticker uttered a hiss through his teeth. 'What is it, cub?' he asked.

'Time for change,' Wraxilan said, in a reasonable voice.

'That is every moment of every day,' Manticker said. 'You took long enough to get to this moment.'

'Then you are prepared for it to be you and me?' Wraxilan gestured around him. 'Leave these hara out of it?'

Manticker nodded, just once. 'Why create waste?' He leapt into the air, spun around, and kicked Wraxilan in the face. Wraxilan fell backwards, but had scrambled away before Manticker could land another blow.

And so they fought their archetypal battle. Leaping shadows against the flames, a fatal dance. There were no weapons involved other than their own sinew and bone. The hara around them were silent, perhaps not even daring to breathe. First the advantage went one way, then another. It was as if time had stopped, placing them in an arena of no-time.

Neither can win, Jarad thought. *Don't they know that?*

No, they don't....

Jarad shuddered. Was this Velisarius in his mind, or Lianvis? Were they watching from somewhere close? The touch did not feel familiar to him, though. It was distant, cold, a star of thought from some lightless reach.

There was blood upon the combatants now, claw marks down Wraxilan's chest, visible where his shirt had been torn away. A cut above Manticker's eye rained ichor down his face, onto his chest: it had filled his mouth. Maybe they would carry on fighting until they had torn each other utterly to pieces, and then still the battle would continue, in motes of harried air, in leaves and dust and ashes.

Jarad realised his hand was resting upon the hilt of the knife tucked into his belt. This body wasn't his. Even this mind wasn't his. He was riding a vehicle of flesh, an observer.

Time stopped. Then sped up. Jarad reeled backwards against Terzian. He hadn't been aware of making any other movement, but heard Terzian breathe 'What the fuck?' Terzian's hands were upon his arms, holding him up, gripping hard. Above them, the fight had paused. Manticker was staring at his belly; a blade was sunk there nearly to the hilt. The pause didn't last long. Wraxilan roared a lion's victory cry. And pounced. Gripped the knife, turned it. Turned it and gouged flesh for what seemed an eternity. Then he kicked Manticker away from him.

For a moment, stillness. And then a cacophony of snarls, shouts, growls. Both troupes of hara bayed at one another, their bodies rising and falling from crouched to upright postures. They looked like apes standing off against each other, rival tribes thrown into confusion because one leader had fallen. Wraxilan stalked around the fire, his arms held high, his head thrown back. Manticker lay on the ground, trying to rise, panting, as his lifeblood pooled about him from the ruin of his guts.

Wraxilan pointed at Manticker's hara. 'Finish it!' he roared and his own hara leapt forward with whoops and cries. So much for keeping other hara out of it. Manticker's hara ran and were pursued. Only three remained by their leader, figures cloaked from head to foot, their faces almost invisible but for mouths painted black, and white chins.

The cries were dying away as Manticker's faithful scattered. Only now did Wraxilan lower his arm.

The three cloaked hara stooped down by Manticker, inspected him, but they must have known it was over. Jarad could feel Manticker fading away. The flames of his fire were not so fierce now; soon that too would die.

One of Wraxilan's aides had remained. Jarad did not know the har's name, because he was rarely around and somewhat secretive, but he was older than most; an advisor. Now he glanced to where Jarad and Terzian stood upon the path. He beckoned them with a jerk of his head. 'Did you see who threw that?' he demanded.

'No,' Terzian said. 'I did not see it.'

Jarad shook his head. Had he thrown the knife? He really didn't know. But there was no blade in his belt now. Wraxilan would not approve of this unasked-for assistance. He could fight his own battles. But Terzian must have seen. Why would he protect Jarad now? They did not know one another.

One of the hara crouching by Manticker stood up, threw back the hood to his robe. He looked to be soume-prevalent, very feminine. His hair was dark, hanging to his waist. He pointed at Wraxilan. 'You are cursed,' he said, matter-of-factly. 'You have my word for it.'

Wraxilan uttered a snort and gestured at Jarad and Terzian. 'Kill them,' he said. 'We don't want his witches left alive.'

Terzian moved forward at once, but Wraxilan's advisor said sharply, 'No.'

Wraxilan turned to him swiftly. 'No?'

The advisor nodded once. 'They are Sulh. Leave them be.' In his words was the unspoken message: *Don't mess with them.* The Sulh were a foreign tribe, their hara often found close to phyle leaders and others of high rank. They were not feared exactly, but they were respected. No one knew who their leaders were. The advisor addressed the Sulh now. 'Take these remains and be gone from this place. Our quarrel is not with you.'

The Sulh set about lifting Manticker between them. Parts of him, it seemed, had become detached. Jarad turned away. He felt disorientated. Something huge was finishing in his life, something new beginning. The Sulh were moving away, melting into the darkness. But, Jarad was sure, they would not forget this night. He would not want to be cursed by a Sulh.

Feeling attention upon him, Jarad turned around again. Wraxilan was staring at him, his expression guarded. 'Who threw the knife?' he asked. It was clear it had to be either Jarad or Terzian, since neither of them had joined the pursuit. That in itself was unusual behaviour.

Jarad simply stared back.

Wraxilan nodded, sucked in his cheeks. 'Perhaps,' he said, 'it was the Aghama.' Then he laughed, a little crazily.

'It saved time,' Terzian said, 'but the outcome would have been no different.'

'Wouldn't it, now?' Wraxilan said.

Terzian placed a bunched fist upon his own chest. 'You are Archon.' He bowed his head.

'Yes.' Wraxilan stared into the night, in the direction the hunt had taken, but nothing could be heard of it now. Embers popped in the fire, sounding like cracking bones. 'We must celebrate,' Wraxilan said. 'The Archon and his faithful elite.' He held out a hand and Terzian took it, kissed it. Jarad hung back.

Wraxilan looked past Terzian, directly at him. *And you?* His eyes seemed to say.

Jarad could barely function. He certainly couldn't speak. Everything had changed. These hara were no longer like mindless gang-boys playing at being hard and street-wise. They had become figures of history, and their words – every word – would be remembered. This night they had begun a new future, one that perhaps they might not have had before.

'It is as it is meant to be,' Jarad managed to say. But he could not bring himself to bow his head, or to kiss Wraxilan's hand. He had played his part.

'Come with me,' Wraxilan said quietly.

'I will be with you,' Jarad replied, 'but I need some time. I will come to you.'

'Squeamish, Jarad? Surely not.'

At the mention of his name, Jarad heard Terzian draw in his breath. That name was known.

'Not that,' Jarad said. 'This is... overwhelming. More significant than... I need some time.'

Wraxilan narrowed his eyes. 'Very well. But don't take too long.'

Velisarius and Lianvis were waiting in a doorway, in a narrow alley not far from the hill. Jarad wasn't looking for them, but of course they'd been looking for him. Lianvis uttered a sigh at the sight of him, embraced him. Jarad remained unyielding in his hold. He stared at Velisarius over Lianvis's shoulder. 'Did you speak to me?' he asked. 'In my mind?'

Velisarius shook his head. 'No, but I heard... something. Not words, not even an idea, but... something.'

'Who was it?'

Lianvis let go of Jarad, stepped back. His expression was bleak.

'Perhaps there is a wider interest in what happened tonight than we thought,' Velisarius replied. He drew in his breath. 'Our hara are ready to leave. Wraxilan's inner circle will be occupied this night. They will not notice us depart, and then we will simply vanish into the landscape. Listen...' He put a hand upon Jarad's shoulder. 'You hear that?'

There were sounds upon the night, not all of them audible with the physical ear. Songs of mourning, songs of victory, songs of yearning, the barking of dogs, the howl of cats, the clamour of metal breaking. 'They know,' Jarad said. 'They all know.'

'The writing of history,' Velisarius said dryly. 'It's interesting.' He paused. 'You won't come with us.' It wasn't a question.

'This isn't my world,' Jarad replied. 'There is one, but it isn't here, nor with you.'

Velisarius smiled. 'I know. We will remain allies, though, Jarad. Don't forget that. One day, hara close to you will question it, but don't forget.'

'Jarad,' Lianvis said, so many feelings in the simple sound of his name.

'Be safe,' Jarad said, reaching briefly to touch Lianvis's cheek.

'I will always know your name,' Lianvis said. 'Whatever it becomes.'

'Go south,' Velisarius said. '*If* you will take advice from me. There are hara waiting for you. They don't know it yet, but they are. Uigenna are not the only way, and neither is mine.'

Jarad laughed coldly. 'Hara waiting for me? What am I to do with them?'

'You will know,' Velisarius said. He addressed Lianvis. 'Come, Viss, we have work to do. We cannot linger.'

After Velisarius and Lianvis had gone, Jarad remained where he was, unable to move. What compunctions coursed through his flesh? He could barely tell. Something had touched him this night, *controlled* him... or had it simply been the actions of a part of himself that had become detached from his conscious being? He blinked up at the sky, so full of stars. The sky had come back to the earth as the lights of humanity winked out.

A sudden breeze came down the alley, scooping up litter and dust in its wake. Jarad would follow it, go where it led him. As he began to move, he felt as if the Jarad he'd been before was left standing behind him like a ghost. He'd stepped out of that shell. And the name came to him then: *You are Ponclast. You always have been. Own the name, and bring it to our history.*

The Future of Our Dark, Delirious Imaginings

Wendy Darling

I've been fascinated with the future, post-apocalyptic world of Wraeththu since the very first day I picked up *The Enchantments of Flesh and Spirit*. Humanity on its way out, decaying cities, electro-mechanical technology falling to the wayside, and of course goth-punk-industrial hermaphrodites with jaded attitudes and magical abilities – what's not to like? So, really, it's not surprising that I'd be among those tossing out the idea of a book specifically focusing on those early, after-the-fall days.

The idea for this book first came up around five years ago, back when Storm and several others were working on the Wraeththu role-playing game book (*Wraeththu: From Enchantment to Fulfilment*). I was involved as an editor and idea bouncer-offer ("Wendy, what do you think?") and as the game involved role-playing as hara in the early days of Wraeththu, there was a lot of discussion about those times. How did the first tribes come about? What kind of turf battles went on? What was it like for those first hara, for example those living in cities that were still majority human? And when and how did Wraeththu first start exploring their magical abilities? Eventually the RPG came to include a great deal of background information covering these questions, plus a short story ("A Sickle Blade," included in this anthology) illustrating and exploring the origin story of one particular har.

While the RPG book was still in production, talk began of soliciting some of the best writers in the *Wraeththu Mythos* world to write stories set in the first few years of Wraeththu's genesis. This went along with an idea we had about creating follow-ups to the main game book focusing on individual tribes. Each book was to include a story set amidst the world of a particular tribe, like the Colurastes, the Sulh, or the Gelaming. And so we began the process of asking around and did receive some entries which, as it turns out, we are now finally publishing in this volume, even though the RPG project itself, along with the original tribal stories project, fizzled out.

The present collection includes stories created both specifically for this project, works commissioned five years ago for the earlier project, plus a couple of stories which originally appeared online as fan fiction but which demanded the increased exposure and recognition of print. It also includes the short story ("The First") that appeared in the program book for the original Grissecon convention held in Stafford, England, back in 2003. There was a contest among fan fiction writers for whose story would appear in the program and my entry, written as a follow up to Storm's seminal story "Paragenesis" (first in this collection and the origin of its title), was selected as the winner.

But back to my attraction to those very early Wraeththu. Images from the first three novels, the *Wraeththu Chronicles*, gripped me and set my mind to wild imaginings: Seel with his multi-coloured, rag-adorned hair; Irraka squatting in an old town hall; Cal being called into Wraxilan's supermarket-turned-tribal-headquarters and asked to host a pearl. I could see it all so clearly, both the characters and their environments, and the images were very appealing.

In my mind's eye, I imagined early Wraeththu with the faces, clothes and attitudes of loads of figures out of early 1980s pop culture – Billy Idol, the gangs of *Mad Max*, musicians in New Wave and Punk bands. If you watch Depeche Mode's early videos, from their first ones to up to those of 1986 or so, you'll see Martin Gore gradually growing more and more androgynous. When I first read Swift's description of Gelaming dress ("skimpy but complicated"), I immediately thought of Gore's outfit in videos like "Master and Servant." The eye make-up, the teased, tortured hair, the shiny lips, leather straps and dog collars – to me, that was Wraeththu.

What's more, when I got to know Storm and learned more about where and how she'd been inspired, I found that she also had been looking to pop culture, especially the music world. While I got a lot of my impressions from music videos, Storm, back in the day, was working with actual bands, including actual proto-Wraeththu! So evidently I got the right idea of Wraeththu before I even really knew their true inspiration. And while it's true that later on, in the *Wraeththu Histories* and in some fan fiction, we see Wraeththu maturing, wearing "grown-up" clothes and such, I think I will always imagine hara, at least first-generation hara, as wild androgynous 1980s young men.

Just as the idea of the characters caught my imagination, so did Storm's description of their environment. In *The Shades of Time and Memory*, Moon's wanderings in the City of Ghosts (which I later learned was a post-apocalyptic Chicago) conjured up the sort of images featured in the television documentary series *The World Without Us*: disintegrating skyscrapers, covered in vines, inhabited by wild animals; alleys turned to streams; museum collections turning to dust. Other images came to mind as well: post-plague Philadelphia in *12 Monkeys*, post-nuclear ruins in *Threads*; the destroyed cities that make up *The Matrix*'s "real" world. There's even an H.P. Lovecraft short story I recall about a ruin of man, devoured by nature.

Post-apocalyptic environments have a lot of appeal to me, based largely, I speculate, on a gleeful sort of joy at seeing humanity getting what it deserves. Nearly all of us are in small or large part guilty of conspiring in the rapidly accelerating decline of this planet – land, sea, air, plants, animals, unique human cultural groups. And seeing images or reading descriptions of the potential consequences of this destruction – what the world would be like without us or with most everything destroyed – appeals to me, almost as a sort of self-flagellation in my head. We're doing this and this is what may happen: a message, a warning.

But if the near future is to be populated by wild, goth-punk androgynous boys with magic powers and eye makeup, born out of humanity's downfall, I shouldn't really be upset, should I?

Wendy Darling, Co-Editor
May 2010

Early Wraeththu Inspirations

Storm Constantine

I've written often about how the Goth scene of the 80s greatly influenced the development of Wraeththu, and this is true insofar as the novels drew upon that scene, but seeing as the concept has been with me since my early teens, its initial influences go much farther back.

I've recently been pondering what first spark set it all off and have been reinvestigating things I was into as a teenager and before – what I can remember. Music has always played a big part in my life and I often think how lucky I was to be young through the tail end of Hippydom, on to the Glam scene of the 70s, later Punk, New Romantics and then Goth. In comparison to what's around nowadays, which seems a bit dreary to me, that was a heady ride! But despite how those flamboyant scenes inspired and directed me, there was one perhaps more intrinsic influence that I have recently remembered. (Some delving into the hard drive of the mind was required!)

 I don't know exactly how young I was, but it was between 7 and 10 years old. Every weekend, my parents used to farm me out to grandparents so they could indulge in a hedonistic lifestyle, a propensity for which I inherited from them! My father's parents lived in a detached house with a big garden, and after my uncle left home, (he was a lot younger than my Dad), I used to sleep in his old bedroom, which was larger than the one I'd been allocated since a baby. I remember one summer day sitting on the floor in that room, poring through my uncle's book shelves, which contained all the books he'd been given

351

as a child. It was a sunny day, and that quiet time in the afternoon, when all you used to be able to hear was the sounds of kids playing in the distance and bird song. I pulled out a copy of The Second Jungle Book by Rudyard Kipling and began to leaf through it. It wasn't an illustrated volume as such, but had large chapter headings, which were like wood cuts. In a couple of these illustrations, the jungle boy Mowgli was depicted, but this was a far cry from how he was portrayed in the later Disney movie. He was shown as androgynously naked, with streaming hair. I just stared at these images in absolute fascination. They excited me, which I suppose was in some pre-sexual kind of sense, but as well as making me want to read the book, it inspired me to make up my own stories about this gorgeous being. So began my fantasies of the long-haired androgyne. I really think this must have been a defining moment in the creation of Wraeththu. All pictures here are by J Lockwood Kipling, from the original edition of The Second Jungle Book.

Thus, with my interest in the androgynous dramatically established, when the Glam Rock scene exploded in a maelstrom of glitter and

feather boas in the 70s I was naturally drawn to it. But my introduction to it as an ingenuous school girl was another image that brought me up short. It was either in the girl's magazine *Jackie* (how many UK 40-50 somethings remember *Jackie*?), or *Fab 208*, another required periodical of the fashionable teen. *Fab 208* was connected with Radio Luxembourg, the then cool pirate station to listen to at night. Anyway, to

that image. It was of the band, T Rex, one of their first promotional pictures following the success of their first and second singles in the charts. When I first saw it, I remember actually being surprised, because it so echoed the kind of fantasies I had. For a moment, I experienced a kind of territorial annoyance that other people were tapping into my private dreams. Marc Bolan and Mickey Finn were shown as white-faced and long-haired, with a dreamy expression in their eyes that spoke of mystical secrets. These were the creatures of my fantasies made flesh. I didn't have a name for them then; they just existed as shadowy entities in my head. But somehow, here they were, externalised and in print, and soon to be drooled and swooned over by a battalion of pubescent females. I can remember vividly the disgust I felt at seeing T Rex gig footage on TV, where thousands of sweaty, hysterical teenage girls were screaming at their idols. I was too repulsed even to consider being part of that. Even at that young age, I felt my interest was more aesthetic. I shunned the reaction of the masses, downright infuriated they misunderstood and belittled the allure of these on-stage personae. It can hardly be contested that T Rex was the first 'slashable' band, if you understand my meaning. Right from the start there were rumours about their sexuality and the whispered suggestion that Bolan and Finn might actually enjoy rather more than a musical relationship. How true these rumours were I have no idea, because it's feasible an outrageously bi-sexual slant might have been deliberately introduced to increase sales and provoke publicity. You only have to rewatch the movie Velvet Goldmine (an accurate portrayal of those times, I think), to see how everyone in the alternative scene of the day suddenly thought it was fashionable to be bi. But I knew nothing of any of that, because I was young, naïve, still at school and my social life revolved around friends who had ponies. (Yes, it's true, even though it changed rather swiftly after that.)

I began to write stories inspired by the fantastical public image of T Rex. Bolan and Finn, as the band, were as fictional no doubt as the  things I wrote, but I didn't care about that. What is most annoying is that I destroyed a lot of what I wrote, because I went through a phase of being terrified of my parents reading my writing. Even then, I wrote mild 'slash', and I often felt guilty about it. Why, I don't know, because now I don't think my parents would have minded one bit, if in fact they'd ever bothered to read my exercise books full of stories, but schoolgirls can have rather strange ideas about the older generation. What I feared most was that they would laugh. My stories were set in a fantasy world and I really regret now that they didn't survive. I still have a few of them, but so many were lost. In fact, these early stories were set in the world that eventually turned up in my novel 'Sign for the Sacred', so it's as 'old' as Wraeththu, which is quite bizarre to realise. I began a novel called 'Sun Incarnate', which I still have, even though I never finished it. Mickey Finn was the physical inspiration for the character Micythus, who was the original prototype for Resenence Jeopardy. When I finally got round to writing 'Sign for the Sacred' though, it was not with all those early influences in mind.

Of course, I can't leave David Bowie out of the equation either. In particular, his album 'Diamond Dogs' was a soundtrack for me to write to, and I think that album was also somewhat inspired by William Burroughs' work. Bowie came prominently onto the scene after T Rex and was another seminal artist of the Glam movement. It's hardly a secret that the film 'Velvet Goldmine' fictionalised (and

perhaps fantasised) his relationship with wild child of rock, Iggy Pop. Bowie's on stage antics with his guitarist, Mick Ronson, made headlines and naturally he became another of my muses. Looking at these two pictures here, of Bowie and Ronson, I think they demonstrate how I visualised the proto-versions of Thiede and Ashmael, even though those characters were created a decade or so after this particular era

of music. I see in Bowie's (then) on-stage personae the roots of Thiede: the trickster, the magician, the manipulator, a creature of many colours.

But long before Wraeththu came into being, I began a sequel to 'Sun Incarnate', called 'Child of the Morning', even though I'd never finished the first one. I just had a different story to tell, influenced by new inspirations, although set in the same world. Micythus was still in it, although this time as a secondary character to the main protagonist, Phrynis. 'Child of the Morning' was greatly influenced by such writers as Mary Renault and Jane Gaskell. It was the story of a beautiful boy taken into captivity and having to cope with life in a royal harem, beset by bitchery and betrayal. By this time, I'd read 'The Persian Boy' by Mary Renault, (but for the fact 'Child' had completely different characters, it was a kind of homage to 'The Persian Boy'), and my interests in beautiful, androgynous creatures had truly coalesced. Also, my musical and aesthetical inspirations had moved on. I'd left school and had gone to the local art college. Round about this time, The New York Dolls – the epitome of proto Punk/Glam sleaze – released their first album. The minute I saw photographs of them in the music press, I knew they were my kind of band. And when I bought the album, I wasn't disappointed. 'Personality Crisis' and 'Jet Boy' are still classics, and I don't think anyone can deny that The Dolls were a huge influence on alternative music, especially early Punk. They were like something out of a science fiction movie. They belonged in a post holocaust world of sexbots and ravaged cities. There were reports in the music press of guys making out at the back of venues at their shows. The Dolls were another influence on my writing and their weird, almost comic book decadence went into the pot to help create Wraeththu. Round about this time I also discovered William Burroughs' novel, 'The Wild Boys' (later to be immortalised by Duran Duran, though in rather censored form!). Blatantly homo-erotic, bizarrely magical, this book I think gave me the courage to write more honestly, and more confidently. Its narrative is hardly linear, and neither can you really engage with any of the characters, but the ideas, and some of the imagery, (especially the tribal stuff),

totally captivated me. Shortly after discovering The Dolls, it was time for The Ramones to make an appearance, and although this band were hardly beings of ambivalent sexuality and glam, the music was great. If anything, it was an extension of the Dolls' dementia. 'I Don't Wanna Go Down to the Basement' and 'Beat on the Brat', were two especial favourites of mine. I also developed a huge crush on Joey Ramone (sadly now dead), and he made it as physical inspiration into several of my stories in various guises.

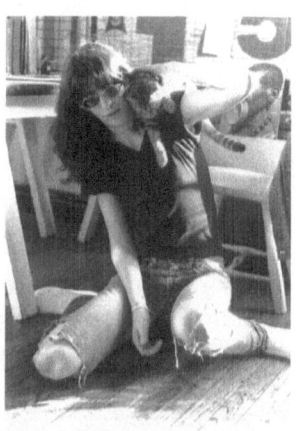

It was during these years, from the last year of school and the short time I spent at art college that I wrote the first Wraeththu stories and poems, but I didn't actually come up with the term 'Wraeththu' until a couple of years after that. This was when I had a dreary receptionist's job at a building company, situated out in the middle of nowhere, far from the edge of town on an early industrial estate. We didn't get many visitors. I used to spend my time, when my work for the day was done, writing stories and poems, drawing pictures and reading ancient dictionaries, full of antiquated words. I remember I used to draw pictures of my co-workers as cartoon animals, which for some reason were very popular, even if they weren't always very flattering! When the company finally went into liquidation, I wrote a fantasy tale about the whole sad demise – really should try and dig that out, it had its amusing moments – and gave it to all my colleagues as a keepsake. But during that time, I found the word Wraeththu in an etymological dictionary and for some odd reason fell in love with it. It meant 'wrath' but also 'rake' as in the gardening or farming implement. However, it wasn't the meaning of the word that snared me, just its shape and sound.

For a long while, I left the world of Wraeththu behind, as 'real life' concerns of a more demanding full time job, and a partner who actually resented me writing, came to the fore. But the siren call of that world was not to be denied. In the very early 80s I discovered my independence, ditched the controlling boyfriend and bought a house, several rooms of which I rented out to friends, including members of the band 'The

Closets of Emily Child' whose guitarist became my new partner. This band had a cameo part in 'The Enchantments of Flesh and Spirit', although none of the real people involved actually inspired any of the characters. They just wanted the band to be in the book! These were the days of early Goth, when New Romanticism metabolised into

something darker yet in many ways more camp. I began writing my Wraeththu stories again, determined now to finish a novel, egged on and encouraged by the manager of the The Closets, who was there to be Mr Pushy for me when I was too shy and embarrassed to let people see my work. And happily, there was a new generation of musician pretty boys to inspire me. Bands like Gene Loves Jezebel, Getting the Fear/Into a Circle and Christian Death all had members who physically inspired the characters of 'Enchantments' and its sequels. Jay and Mike Aston from Gene Loves Jezebel certainly helped shape the characters of Cobweb and Terzian respectively. And looking at these old pictures of them, it's easy to see why.

Pellaz's earliest physical inspiration was undoubtedly a strange meld of Mowgli of the Jungle Books and Johnny Thunders from the New York Dolls, but strangely, I never had a real life person who inspired the look of Cal. He was – and remains – an archetype, almost impossible to capture in a picture. The idea and shape of Vaysh came from Getting the Fear's vocalist, Bee (later that band became Into a Circle). If you can find any pictures online of the later band's EP covers, you will see why they were an influence for Wraeththu material. Seel was inspired partly by Christian Death's David Glass, who in his youth was positively unearthly in appearance.

It's interesting for me to wander back down the memories and recall how the ideas for my fictional characters came together. The living people whose public personae inspired many of the Wraeththu are now twenty or thirty years older, and the enigmatic beauty they once possessed has no doubt long gone. Most of the wild boys of those days have probably now

settled down to a humdrum life with wives and children, have become drug burnouts, or are - at worst – dead (quite a few are, come to think of it). Happily, I discovered while researching some of these people online that several, such as Bee, David Glass and the Aston Brothers are still working in the music industry and thriving. I hope others are also continuing to be creative and successful. But whatever those shining boys might be doing now, or not, they are immortalised as they once were within the pages of the Wraeththu novels.

The people mentioned here were only physical inspirations, and sometimes more than one of them contributed to the creation of a character's appearance. The personalities of the characters had nothing to do with real individuals; they were entirely made up. Perhaps the Jungle Boy Mowgli and the likes of Joey Ramone and Johnny Thunders are unlikely companions, but they were all part of the formula.

Storm Constantine
June 2010

Picture Credits: All of the photos were trawled off the internet and photo-manipped by Wendy Darling. No credit for photography was given on any of the sites I used. Apologies to any original photographers not credited.

About the Contributors

Storm Constantine

Storm is the creator of the Wraeththu Mythos, the first trilogy of which was published in the 1980s. However, the influences and inspirations for the Wraeththu world go much further back than that, and continue into the future as she plans more stories for it. Storm is the founder of Immanion Press, created initially to publish her out of print back catalogue, but which evolved into the thriving venture it is today. She has written over thirty books, including full length novels, novellas, short story collections and non-fiction titles. Her interests include magic and spirituality, Reiki, movies, music and MMOs. Among her many occupations, most of which are unpaid, she runs a Reiki school, the Lady of the Flame Iseum, which is a magical group affiliated to the Fellowship of Isis, and a guild called Equilibrium on the EU servers of World of Warcraft. She lives in the Midlands of the UK. Her website can be found at
http://www.stormconstantine.com

Wendy Darling

Based in Atlanta, Georgia, USA, Wendy Darling is co-author of *Breeding Discontent*, published by Immanion Press in 2003 as the first *Wraeththu Mythos* novel. She has been involved in Wraeththu in many different capacities, including editor of the revised *Wraeththu Chronicles*, webmaster of the *Inception* and *Forever Wraeththu* fan web sites, and staff at several Wraeththu conventions. Her full-time job is as a web projects manager at Emory University, but she engages in many side projects and hobbies, including photography and writing. She has also forged relationships with Wraeththu fans around the world and has been fortunate to meet several authors whose work is included in this collection. At home she is ruled by two cats, cats she did not have in her life until she met and visited with Storm, who as usual had a strong influence on her. Wendy enjoys international travel and tries to visit Storm and her husband Jim as often as she can.

Andy Bigwood

Andy is an author, artist, draughtsman, bookbinder, cartographer and illustrator from West Wiltshire, UK, where he lives alone, only venturing out for disastrous foreign holidays and the occasional convention. Trained in technical illustration, in Bath (shortly before the evolution of computer aided art), Andy has provided artwork, cartography and cover designs for a variety of Fantasy, Horror, and Science fiction novels winning the British Science Fiction Association Award for best artwork for the anthologies 'disLOCATIONS' and 'Subterfuge'. Specimen 16, is Andy's first published short story.

Brad Carpenter

Brad's introduction to the television industry began 15 years ago courtesy of Rob Tapert and Sam Raimi at Renaissance Pictures with their shows "Hercules: Legendary Journeys" and "Xena: Warrior Princess." His training in the world of scripted episodic continued over several seasons of HBO's much lauded, "Sex and the City," and broadened into the unscripted world with 67 episodes of Bravo's "Queer Eye for the Straight Guy."

After being fortunate enough to work on the first Emmy award-winning season of NBC's "30 Rock," Brad went on to Co-Produce "Life Is Wild," a family drama for The CW Network shot on location in South Africa. Over the past two years, Brad has been alternating between Producer duties for Showtime's "Nurse Jackie" starring

Edie Falco, and HBO's "Bored To Death" starring Jason Schwartzman, Ted Danson and Zach Galifianakas. Brad is currently developing a television series based on "The Wraeththu Chronicles."

Christopher Coyle

Born, died, and reborn again within moments of being first brought screaming into this world, Christopher grew up in a military family. With constantly moving and always being the new kid around, he chose to immerse himself in creating worlds within his mind. From even an early age, he knew he wanted to be a writer, to continue to share those worlds with others. From having worked as a designer and art editor for a game company founded by Margaret Weis, working on such projects as Dragonlance and Sovereign Stone, he jumped at the chance to work with another of his childhood idols when he decided to move to the United Kingdom once more, involving himself with the Wraeththu world. Now, years later, Christopher is ecstatic at once more being able to involve himself with the Wraeththu Mythos, while he is working once more on developing his own new worlds, and going back to college in order to finish his degree in Graphic Design. He likes to stay busy, that Christopher!

Suzanne Gabriel

Born in the USA to nomadic Canadian parents, Suzanne grew up in Canada, the UK, and USA. She is a wife and mother of three children (more if you count the 'fur kids'). She completed a Master of

Science degree in Food Science and Nutrition and spent several years working in the food industry doing quality control, new product development, and marketing/PR and sales. Suzanne currently works full-time at a University where her job includes managing her Faculty's social media endeavours, web site administration, and other duties as assigned. Suzanne is fascinated by old cookbooks, old etiquette books, and antiquities museums. Even when there isn't any music Suzanne is likely to be dancing and she will go out of her way to hug a tree. She adores animals, travel, history, archaeology, science, hiking, laughter, yoga, and photography. Recently she has become involved in the Society for Creative Anachronism – 'going mediaeval' on people has become a way of life! She has come to realize that she has way too many hobbies and interests but she wouldn't dream of giving any of them up. In fact she plans to add more to the list.

Gwyn Harper

Gwyn has always had one foot in the mundane world and another in the land of Faerie. She wrote her first novel at the tender age of ten, but when adults informed her that few people make a living writing fiction, she relegated her scribbling to the back-burner, and instead pursued an interest in ancient civilizations, which turned out to be almost as poorly compensated. She earned advanced degrees in anthropology and archaeology and has worked as an editor, researcher, educator, and exhibit designer. In recent years, Gwyn has returned to her love of word-smithery, pursuing academics by day and hunting muses with her elf friends at night. She writes in various genres including historical fiction, fantasy, and sci fi. Her avatar enjoys exploring the lively cyber realm of fanfiction and playing with gender-bending concepts. Gwyn lives in a mountainous desert where she is kept busy by her family, a slew of imaginary characters, and a sultan reincarnated in the form of a very demanding cat.

Danielle Lainton

Danni has always been in love with the arts in all forms but didn't start thinking seriously about it until she studied Visual and Performing Arts at college. Rather than going to University, as was hoped and expected, she worked in the music industry for a while before getting married and having children. Still yearning to be creative, she began work for a local wedding stationer. The products may not have been to her taste but as her experience grew she became more involved with the design work until she was the

principal designer for the company. Eventually, she decided to go it alone and started her own business, Uber Angel, which deals primarily with alternative weddings and commissioned artwork. She is also creative director of Switchblade Apparel Ltd, a company that customizes leather jackets. She also produces original artwork for Immanion Press and has recently started dabbling with website design. Even though she tended towards sculpture and photography as a student she now produces most of her work digitally, using a graphics tablet, but still in a traditional drawing style. Her inspirations are many and they come in whims; one day she's working on a pin-up girl and then the next she may feel like drawing zombies and vampires, or even a combination of them all!

Fiona Lane

Fiona born and brought up near Glasgow during the Time Of The Flared Trouser and Unfeasibly High Platform Shoes. By the time we all came to our senses, she had relocated to Aberdeen, and spent several years waiting for a number six bus, in a horrible collision involving the nature of time and the Aberdeen weather. During the eighties, while she was waiting for the Internet to be invented, she acquired a husband and a couple of replacement units, and they all now live in

a field full of sheep in Aberdeenshire, along with the odd cat or two and Fiona's posse of obsolete computers, many of which she has single-handedly restored to a completely non-functioning condition. She once kept chickens, but they were messy and she couldn't use them to buy vintage shoes from Ebay. The eggs were good though. She likes gin and hats, and dislikes the oppression of the proletariat. Her hobbies include cooking, gardening, and staring into the abyss.

Maria J. Leel

Originally from the fenlands of Peterborough, Maria J. Leel now lives in the infinitely hillier Shropshire and has thigh muscles that recognise the difference. She manages a half acre garden with the assistance of her husband, Malcolm, two cats and four chickens. Trained originally as an ecologist and teacher she made the logical career progression to First Aid trainer for St John Ambulance. She wrote her first play at the age of ten and has been writing dramatic pieces and short stories ever since. One of these days she really will have to sit down and write that first novel. Maria spent a year travelling the world volunteering on various environmental projects and lived for a while on a kibbutz in Israel. As a result she has an abiding interesting in alternative lifestyles and communal living. She is a member of the dark and mysterious world of Morris dancing, plays guitar and is a member of the local rowing club – so those thigh muscles are really getting a pasting.

Kristi Lee

An award-winning fanfiction author since 2003, Kristi is known throughout her various fan communities as Thevina. She's had an obsession with redheads and things of a Celtic nature since a very young age, which has only increased in adulthood. Her real life and fan life have crossed as she's an independent academic. She's been a professional singer, a prospect analyst, a graphic designer, an award-winning costumer, coordinated seating for an opera

company, nude modelled, and in 2009, had a total fangirl moment when she was able to meet in person her all-time favourite living composer, Phillip Glass. She was only introduced to Wraeththu in December of 2007, but says another lifetime highlight was meeting Storm in person in 2008. As of April, 2010, she's begun writing original fiction for the first time and is very excited by the prospect of having fans of her own who might wish to write fanfiction some day. Since Wraeththu hermaphrodites sadly don't exist out in the world for her to fawn over, instead she continues to feed a perhaps unhealthy fascination for men in kilts.

Martina Luise Pachali

Martina Luise Pachali was born in Germany in 1967 and has been inventing and telling stories all her life. She has studied Japanese and Medieval Latin in Munich, Germany, where she lives with the obligatory two cats. Wrangling databases for a living and reviewing books for additional pocket money, her interests as a writer mostly lie with collaborative storytelling, net literature, and the grassroots entertainment movement fuelled by the internet and the possibilities of cloud computing and user generated content.

Ruby

Ruby is the official artist for the Wraeththu Mythos, who creates all the covers for the Immanion Press editions. She started drawing from her imagination long before she could or indeed would talk. Still heavily influenced by the fairy tales and myths absorbed from her childhood Ruby has grown into a multimedia illustrator interested in exploring the darkly sensual, symbolic and surreal undercurrents of life. Ruby's illustrations blend perfectly the mythological, the classical and the future fantastic and are also evocative of Beardsley and Mucha. She is now a much sought-after cover artist and interior illustrator for books across many genres, and is the creator of the ongoing Wraeththu Tarot project.

Storm Constantine's Wraeththu Mythos

Also published by Immanion Press

By Storm Constantine

The Wraeththu Chronicles
The Enchantments of Flesh and Spirit
The Bewitchments of Love and Hate
The Fulfilments of Fate and Desire

The Wraeththu Histories
The Wraiths of Will and Pleasure
The Shades of Time and Memory
The Ghosts of Blood and Innocence

Wraeththu
(omnibus edition of the Wraeththu Chronicles)

The Hienema
Student of Kyme

Other Mythos Novels

Breeding Discontent by Wendy Darling and Bridgette Parker
Terzah's Sons by Victoria Copus

Visit http://www.immanion-press.com for details of these and other
Immanion Press publications

Storm Constantine's Wraeththu Mythos

Paragenesis
Stories of the Dawn of Wraeththu

Edited by Storm Constantine
and Wendy Darling

Stafford, England

Cover Art and Wraeththu Mythos Logo: Ruby
Interior Illustrations: Ruby (story frontispieces and headings, 22, 82, 248, 302, 337), Danielle Lainton, (76, 140) Andy Bigwood (172, 189)
Editors: Storm Constantine and Wendy Darling

Set in Garamond

IP0029
First edition by Immanion Press, 2010
An Immanion Press Edition
http://www.immanion-press.com
info@immanion-press.com

ISBN 978-1-904853-73-2

Contents

Introduction

Brad Carpenter

It was a dancer friend of mine who first turned me on to Storm
Constantine's "The Wraeththu Chronicles." One day he handed me a
chunky paperback copy of the original omnibus edition, and it soon
became my constant companion. Over the following weeks, I
voraciously consumed my way through all the fantastical adventures
contained within its pages until I had devoured the entire glorious
meal. Luckily for us all, there were several more courses yet to come.
Constantine had begun expanding her series with three more books
comprising, "The Wraeththu Histories."

If you're already a fan of the Wraeththu series, the collection of short
stories within "Paragenesis" will feel like a good long drink of water
in the desert, to be savoured to the last drop. The term "Paragenesis"
comes from the Greek for "born beside" and roughly translates to
"the effect of one upon the development of another." [1] The stories
of "Paragenesis" explore some of the early milestones along
Wraeththu's journey of self-discovery. As Wraeththu continue to
differentiate themselves from humans, they quickly begin creating a
new civilisation in their own image. Gangs will become tribes, and
tribes will mature into nations. Humanity, on the other hand, must
come to grips with the fact that they have been bumped off the top
of the evolutionary chain by a stronger, more durable species that is
also of combined gender.

Throughout the Wraeththu series, Storm Constantine reminds us
that evolution never takes a holiday. Mother Nature's work continues
on, shaping all creatures to be better at surviving and integrating into
the world around them. Creation begets more creation; and so it has
been within the rich literary world of Wraeththu as well. With a

growing legion of online fans inspired by her novels, Constantine has been able to carefully nurture an ever-expanding world of fan fiction. In addition to two stories penned by Constantine, "Paragenesis" contains work by brilliant authors who have sprung up from the prolific world of the "Wraeththu Mythos." In this way, the world Constantine has created continues to recreate itself. Creation progresses out of its own momentum: a theme throughout the Wraeththu series itself.

If you're new to the world of Wraeththu, then you're in for a provocative introduction that will likely seduce you into reading the whole series. In the post apocalyptic world imagined by Storm Constantine, human civilisation has all but completely broken down. Having polluted the environment to the point of crippling toxicity, humans have found themselves increasingly unable to reproduce. Urban conditions have deteriorated severely, wars in the Middle East over oil and religion have stretched the military precariously thin, and Global Warming has destabilized the weather patterns to the point where many of the continents have begun to be reshaped. Those with money, power, or highly prized workforce skills, have hunkered down within high-security gated enclaves. Those without such means have had to resort to living on the streets, surviving as best they can. Deep within the decrepit concrete jungle of the inner cities, where street gangs battle over territory, a new mysterious clan has emerged. They call themselves "Wraeththu." Stories of them are often so fantastical, that many scoff them off as pure fiction.

With all the various rumours surrounding these inexplicable youths, few have guessed their true nature. Wraeththu are a new advanced species that appear to be Mother Nature's cure for the ills that we have inflicted upon the planet. Their blood can heal us by transforming us into one of their kind. Some humans are abducted into the fold. Others hear the call and join willingly. Our civilization has become obsolete. If we are to survive at all, it will now have to be through them.

The ones who call themselves Wraeththu look at us as though we're something out of the Stone Age. They know they're genetically superior. Their firm, panther-like bodies are stronger and more resilient than ours. They have telepathic abilities, and can manipulate energy in ways that seem purely magical to us. When they combine

8

these traits in order to defend themselves, their combat skills are hard to beat, even against some of our best technology.

To Wraeththu, Humans seem oddly imbalanced and incomplete. They refer to us as "half-sexes." Being hermaphrodite allows Wraeththu to transcend any limitations of gender. To Humans, a Wraeththu's exotic combination of both masculine and feminine traits has the power to entice, or confound, or terrify.

Of all their prized survival skills, Wraeththu most treasure their power to seduce. Their dual gender nature allows them to express their own masculine and feminine energies as each circumstance dictates, giving them the advantages of both. When seducing humans, they can project whichever gender seems most useful at the time. In the presence of both men and women, they can easily project both energies, so as to be able to seduce both sexes at once.

When Wraeththu seduce each other, the attraction is much more complex. They recognize sex as more than merely a means to satisfy the need for procreation and pleasure. Their simplest sensual acts, such as the "sharing of breath," can reveal memories, emotions and untold secrets. Deeper coupling can be used to release healing energy, expand group consciousness, or to explore other planes of existence. In the emerging Wraeththu culture, sensuality and the combining of one another's "essence" becomes a fundamental spiritual practice.

But how did the first Wraeththu come to be? And is it really simply an "accident" when the first "mutant" discovers that his blood can transform a human into one of his kind? Or was this really divine intervention necessitated by an immediate need to evolve? And if so, where did this intervention come from? Just when Constantine's Wraeththu series answers some of these questions, the author skilfully provides additional mysteries tantalisingly out of reach in order to keep us asking for more.

Post-apocalyptic fiction has been around for as long as the written word. From Noah's Ark and the great flood in the book of Genesis, to Mad Max and the host of films that followed, we've long been fascinated by what could be waiting for us at the end of civilisation as we know it. Given the precarious state of our modern world, is it any surprise that we often find ourselves wondering what happens next? I'm far from what I would consider to be a survivalist, but as I watch our news devolving into scenarios that would have passed as science fiction back in the 80's when Constantine first published "The Wraeththu Chronicles," I start glancing nervously at the box of camping gear tucked away in the bedroom closet. At those doubtful moments, I'm wondering whether or not that meagre collection of survival tools might end up becoming our most treasured and useful possessions.

Happily, the Wraeththu series is apocalyptic literature at its most optimistic. Unlike other stories of the genre, the world that Constantine has created doesn't simply imagine our civilisation in ruin, only to leave us in a desolate landscape, regretting our short-sightedness and blind stupidity. Constantine's Wraeththu novels imagine another leg on evolution's journey. The author provides a world in which our extinction has been thwarted by a radically new game plan. The age of the division of the genders has passed. God has put the rib back into Adam, and his children have been made whole once again. This more evolved version of ourselves understands its place in the garden, and will now serve to tend and nurture it. Wraeththu are the promise fulfilled. The world as we know it has ended because we have emerged from the cocoon as something better, and a new age of wisdom and growth has become possible.

As Wraeththu quickly discover, however, their genetic superiority does not mean that they can abandon their heritage. They are born from Humanity, so like it or not, we will always be a part of them. The question posed as we watch Wraeththu struggle to develop is whether or not they will be able to learn from Humanity's mistakes in time to not repeat them. Wraeththu fiction resonates deeply because we are desperate for the solutions that this more advanced species provides. As I would imagine is the case with many fans of Wraeththu, I would love to somehow truly become one of their advanced species. But even if we can't physically transform into one of these glorious creatures (and I have to admit that I haven't completely accepted that fact), then maybe we can instead bring out their more evolved qualities from within ourselves. Wraeththu may seem magical to us, but perhaps that's only because we haven't yet learned how to reach our own full potential. And thus the theme I